Q is for Quarry & R is for Ricochet

Sue Grafton has become one of the most popular female writers, both in the UK and in the US. Born in Kentucky in 1940, she began her career as a TV scriptwriter before Kinsey Millhone and the 'alphabet' series took off. She plans to take Kinsey all the way through the alphabet to Z. Sue lives and writes in Montecito, California and Louisville, Kentucky.

Also by Sue Grafton

Sue Grafton

Q is for Quarry

&

R is for Ricochet

PAN BOOKS

Q is for Quarry first published 2002 by Penguin Putnam, Inc., New York, by G.P. Putnam's
Sons. First published in Great Britain 2002 by Macmillan.
First published in paperback 2003 by Pan Books.
R is for Ricochet first published 2004 by G.P. Putnam's Sons,
a member of Penguin Putnam Group (USA) Inc., New York.
First published in Great Britain 2004 by Macmillan.
First published in paperback 2005 by Pan Books.

This omnibus first published 2008 by Pan Books
an imprint of Pan Macmillan Ltd
Pan Macmillan, 20 New Wharf Road, London N1 9RR
Basingstoke and Oxford
Associated companies throughout the world
www.panmacmillan.com

ISBN 978-0-330-45787-3

1 3 5 7 9 8 6 4 2

A CIP catalogue record for this book is available from
the British Library.

Printed and bound in Great Britain by
Mackays of Chatham plc, Chatham, Kent

Q is for Quarry

THIS BOOK IS DEDICATED TO

Bill Turner and Deborah Linden

Bob and Nancy Failing

and

Susan and Gary Gulbransen.

Thanks you for making this one possible.

The author wishes to acknowledge the invaluable assistance of the following people: Steven Humphrey; Dr. Robert Failing; Retired Sergeant Detective Bill Turner and Retired Chief Deputy Bruce Correll, Criminal Investigations Division; Sergeant Bob Spinner, Forensics Science Unit, and Diana Stetson, Jail Administration and Custody Operations, Santa Barbara County Sheriff's Department; retired Coroner's Investigator Larry Gillespie, Santa Barbara County Coroner's Office; Betty Pat Gatliff, Forensic Sculptor; John Mackall, Attorney at Law; Lucy Thomas and Nadine Greenup, Reeves Medical Library, and Anna Bissell, R.N., O.C.N., Santa Barbara Cottage Hospital; Martin Walker, M.D.; Robert Sorg, Bob's Canvas Shop; Chuck Nation, Nation's Auto Upholstery; Linda Perkins, DeBrovy's Custom Canvas; Richard Madison; Anita Donohue, Julian Ranch; Lamar and Cheri Gable; Jay Schmidt; Maggie Harding, and Joe B. Jones.

Special thanks, also, to Joe Mandel, Gregory Spears, and Chris Kovach for the use of their names.

ONE

It was Wednesday, the second week in April, and Santa Teresa was making a wanton display of herself. The lush green of winter, with its surfeit of magenta and salmon bougainvillea, had erupted anew in a splashy show of crocuses, hyacinths, and flowering plum trees. The skies were a mild blue, the air balmy and fragrant. Violets dotted the grass. I was tired of spending my days closeted in the hall of records, searching out grant deeds and tax liens for clients who were, doubtless, happily pursuing tennis, golf, and other idle amusements.

I suppose I was suffering from a mutant, possibly incurable form of spring fever, which consisted of feeling bored, restless, and disconnected from humanity at large. My name is Kinsey Millhone. I'm a private detective in Santa Teresa, California, ninety-five miles north of Los Angeles. I'd be turning thirty-seven on May 5, which was coming up in four weeks, an event that was probably contributing to my general malaise. I lead a

SUE GRAFTON

stripped-down existence untroubled by bairn, pets, or living household plants.

On February 15, two months before, I'd moved into new offices, having separated myself from my association with the law firm of Kingman and Ives. Lonnie Kingman had purchased a building on lower State Street, and though he'd offered to take me with him, I felt it was time to be out on my own.

That was my first mistake.

My second was an unfortunate encounter with two landlords in a deal that went sour and left me out in the cold.

My third office-related error was the one I now faced. In desperation, I'd rented space in a nondescript cottage on Caballeria Lane, where a row of identical stucco bungalows were lined up at the curb like the Three Little Pigs. The block—short, narrow, and lined with cars— ran between Santa Teresa Street and Arbor, a block north of Via Madrina, in the heart of downtown. While the price was right and the location was excellent—in easy walking distance of the courthouse, the police station, and the public library—the office itself fell woefully short of ideal.

The interior consisted of two rooms. The larger I designated as my office proper; the smaller I was using as a combination library-and-reception area. In addition, there was a galley-style kitchen, where I kept a small refrigerator, my coffee pot, and my Sparkletts water dispenser. There was also a small fusty half-bath with a sorrowful-looking toilet and sink. The whole of it smelled like mildew, and I suspected at night wee creatures scuttled around the baseboards after all the lights were turned off. By way of compensation, the building's owner had offered unlimited cans of an off-brand paint, and I'd spent the better part of a week rolling coats of white latex over the former pulsating pink, a shade reminiscent of internal organs at work. He'd also agreed to have the rugs cleaned, not that anyone could tell. The beige high-low, wall-to-wall nylon carpeting was matted from long wear and seemed to be infused with despair. I'd arranged and rearranged my desk, my swivel chair, my file cabinets, sofa, and assorted artificial plants. Nothing dispelled the general air of weariness that infected the place. I had plenty of money in savings (twenty-five thousand bucks if it's anybody's business) so, in theory, I could have held out for much classier digs. On the other hand, at three fifty a month, the space was affordable and satisfied one of my basic principles in life, which is: Never, never, never, to live beyond my means. I don't want to be compelled to take on work to meet my overhead. The office is meant to serve me, not the other way around.

Since the bungalows on either side of mine were vacant, I was feeling isolated, which may account for a newfound ambivalence about my single status in a world of married folk. Except for two brief failed marriages, I'd been unattached for most of my natural life. This had never bothered me. More often than not, I rejoiced in my freedom, my mobility, and my solitude. Lately, circumstances had conspired to unsettle my habitual content.

Earlier that week, I'd encountered my friend Vera with her husband, (Dr.) Neil Hess. I was sneaking in a late-afternoon jog on the bike path at the beach when I'd spotted them sauntering along ahead of me. Vera was a former employee of California Fidelity Insurance, for which I'd also worked. She'd met Neil, decided he was too short for her, and tried passing him off on me. I knew at a glance they were smitten with each other, and despite protests to the contrary, I'd persuaded her that he was her perfect match, which had turned out to be true. The two of them were accompanied that afternoon by their eighteen-month-old son in his stroller and a grinning golden retriever pup, frolicking and prancing, tugging at his leash. Vera—massive, lumbering, milky, and serene—was clearly expecting again, apparently in mere days, judging by her swollen state. We paused to chat and I realized that in the three and a half years since I'd last seen her, my life hadn't changed a whit. Same apartment, same car, same work, same boyfriend in absentia in a relationship that was going no place. The revelation generated a prolonged pang of regret.

Meanwhile, Henry, my beloved landlord, was off cruising the Caribbean in the company of his siblings and his sister-in-law, Rosie, who owns the tavern half a block from my apartment. I'd been bringing in his mail, watering his houseplants once a week and his yard every couple of days. Rosie's restaurant would be closed for another five days, so until the three of them returned home, I couldn't even have supper in familiar surroundings. I know all of this sounds ever so faintly like whining, but I feel morally obliged to tell the truth.

That Wednesday morning, I'd decided my attitude would greatly improve if I quit feeling sorry for myself and got my office squared away. To that end, I'd gone to a thrift store and purchased two additional (used) file cabinets, an upright wooden cupboard with assorted pigeon holes, and a funky painted armoire to house my accumulation of office supplies. I was perched on a low stool surrounded by cartons I hadn't unpacked since I'd moved into Lonnie's office three and a half years before. This felt a little bit like Christmas in that I was discovering items I'd long forgotten I had.

I'd just reached the bottom of box number three (of a total of eight) when I heard a knock at the door. I yelled "I'm here!" When I turned, Lieutenant Dolan was standing on the threshold, his hands sunk in the pockets of his tan raincoat.

"Hey, what are you doing here? It's been months." I got up and dusted my hand on the seat of my jeans before extending it to him.

His grip was strong and warm, his smile almost sheepish, as pleased to see me as I was to see him. "I ran into Lonnie at the courthouse. He said you'd rented this place so I thought I'd pop in."

"That's great. I appreciate the visit."

"I see you're getting settled."

"About time. I moved in February fifteenth and haven't done a thing."

"I hear business is slow."

"It is—at least the kind of jobs I like."

I watched while Con Dolan made a circuit of the room. He seemed ill at ease and covered his discomfort by wading through a steady stream of small talk. He chatted idly about Lonnie, the weather, and miscellaneous matters while I made what I hoped were the appropriate responses. I couldn't imagine what he wanted, but I assumed he'd get down to his purpose in due course. He'd never been the type to drop in unannounced. I'd known him for ten years, the greater portion of which he'd headed up the homicide unit of the Santa Teresa Police Department. He was currently out on a medical disability, sidelined by a series of heart attacks. I'd heard he was eager to return to work full-time. According to the scuttlebutt, his chances ran somewhere between slim and none.

He paused to check out the inner office, glanced into the half-bath, and then circled back in my direction. "Lonnie said you weren't crazy about the place and I can see your point. It's grim."

"Isn't it? I can't figure it out. I know it needs something, but I can't think what."

"You need art."

"You think so?" I let my gaze trace the bare white walls.

"Sure. Get yourself some big travel posters and some double-sided tape. It'd perk the place right up. Failing that, you might at least wipe the dust off the artificial plants."

He was in his early sixties and his cardiac problems had left his complexion looking sour. The usual bags under his eyes had turned a dark smokey shade, making his whole face seem sunken in circulatory gloom. He was apparently marking the time away from the department by shaving every other day, and this wasn't the one. His face had tended to be pouchy in the best of times, but now his mouth was pulled down in a permanent expression of malcontent. Just my kind of guy.

I could tell he was still smoking because his raincoat, when he moved, smelled of nicotine. The last time I

SUE GRAFTON

remembered seeing him he was in a hospital bed. The visit had been awkward. Up to that point, I'd always been intimidated by the man, but then I'd never seen him in a cotton hospital nightie with his puckered butt on display through a slit down the back. I'd felt friendlier toward him since. I knew he liked me despite the fact his manner in the past had alternated between surly and abrupt.

I said, "So what's up? I can't believe you walked all the way over here to give me decorating tips."

"Actually, I'm on my way to lunch and thought you might join me—if you're free, that is."

I glanced at my watch. It was only 10:25. "Sure, I could do that. Let me get my bag and my jacket and I'll meet you out in front."

We took off on foot, walking to the corner, where we turned right and headed north on Santa Teresa Street. I thought we'd be going to the Del Mar or the Arcade, two restaurants where guys from the PD gravitated for lunch. Instead, we soldiered on for another three blocks and finally turned into a hole-in-the-wall known as "Sneaky Pete's," though the name on the entrance sign said something else. The place was largely empty: one couple at a table and a smattering of day drinkers sitting at the far end of the bar. Dolan took a seat at the near end and I settled myself on the stool to his left. The bartender laid her cigarette in an ashtray, reached for a bottle of Old Forrester, and poured him a drink before he opened his mouth. He paused to light a cigarette and then he caught my look. "What?"

"Well, gee, Lieutenant Dolan, I was just wondering if this was part of your cardiac rehabilitation."

He turned to the bartender. "She thinks I don't take very good care of myself."

She placed the glass in front of him. "Wonder where she got that?"

I pegged her in her forties. She had dark hair that she wore pulled away from her face and secured by tortoise-shell combs. I could see a few strands of gray. Not a lot of makeup, but she looked like someone you could trust in a bartenderly sort of way. "What can I do for you?"

"I'll have a Coke."

Dolan cocked his thumb at me. "Kinsey Millhone. She's a PI in town. We're having lunch."

"Tannie Ottweiler," she said, introducing herself. "Nice to meet you." We shook hands and then she reached down and came up with two sets of cutlery, encased in paper napkins, that she placed in front of us. "You sitting here?"

Dolan tilted his head. "We'll take that table by the window."

"I'll be there momentarily."

Dolan tucked his cigarette in his mouth, the smoke causing his right eye to squint as he picked up his whiskey and moved away from the bar. I followed, noting that he'd chosen a spot as far from the other drinkers as he could get. We sat down and I set my handbag on a nearby chair. "Is there a menu?"

He shed his raincoat and took a sip of whiskey. "The only thing worth ordering is the spicy salami on a kaiser roll with melted pepper jack. Damn thing'll knock your socks off. Tannie puts a fried egg on top."

"Sounds great."

Tannie appeared with my Coke. There was a brief time-out while Dolan ordered our sandwiches.

As we waited for lunch, I said, "So what's going on?"

He shifted in his seat, making a careful survey of the premises before his gaze returned to mine. "You remember Stacey Oliphant? He retired from the Sheriff's Department maybe eight years back. You must have met him."

"Don't think so. I know who he is—everybody talks about Stacey—but he'd left the department by the time I connected up with Shine and Byrd." Morley Shine had been a private investigator in partnership with another private eye named Benjamin Byrd. Both had been tight with the sheriff's office. They'd hired me in 1974 and trained me in the business while I acquired the hours I needed to apply for my license. "He must be in his eighties."

Dolan shook his head. "He's actually seventy-three. As it turns out, being idle drove him out of his mind. He couldn't handle the stress so he went back to the SO part-time, working cold cases for the criminal investigations division."

"Nice."

"That part, yes. What's not nice is he's been diagnosed with cancer—non-Hodgkin's lymphoma. This is the second time around for him. He was in remission for years, but the symptoms showed up again about seven months ago. By the time he found out, it'd progressed to stage four—five being death, just so you get the drift. His long-term prognosis stinks; twenty percent survival rate if the treatment works, which it might not. He did six rounds of chemo and a passel of experimental drugs. Guy's been sick as a dog."

"It sounds awful."

"It is. He was pulling out of it some and then recently he started feeling punk. They put him back in the hospital a couple of days ago. Blood tests showed severe anemia so they decided to transfuse him. Then they decided while he was in, they might as well run more tests so they can see where he stands. He's a pessimist, of course, but to my way of thinking, there's always hope."

11

"I'm sorry."

"Not as sorry as I am. I've known him close to forty years, longer than I knew my wife." Dolan took a drag of his cigarette, reaching for a tin ashtray on the table next to us. He tapped off a fraction of an inch of ash.

"How'd the two of you hook up? I thought he worked north county. You were PD down here."

"He was already with the SO when our paths first crossed. This was 1948. I was from a blue-collar background, nothing educated or intellectual. I'd come out of the army with an attitude. Cocky and brash. Two years I knocked around, not doing anything much. I finally got a job as a pump jockey at a gas station in Lompoc. Talk about a dead end.

"One night a guy came in and pulled a gun on the night manager. I was in the backroom cleaning up at the end of my shift when I figured out what was going on. I grabbed a wrench, ducked out the side door, and came around the front. Guy was so busy watching to make sure my boss didn't call the cops, he never saw me coming. I popped him a good one and knocked him on his ass. Stacey was the deputy who arrested him.

"He's only ten years older than me, but he's the closest thing to a mentor I ever had. He's the one talked me into law enforcement. I went to college on the G.I. Bill and then hired on with the PD as soon as a job opened up. He even introduced me to Grace, and I married her six months later."

"Sounds like he changed the course of your life."

"In more ways than one."

"Does he have family in the area?"

"No close relatives. The guy never married. A while back, he was dating someone—if that's what you want to call it at our advanced age. Nice gal, but somehow it didn't work out. Since Grace died, the two of us have spent a fair amount of time together. We go hunting and fishing any chance we get. Now that I'm out on medical, we've done a lot of that of late."

"How's he dealing with all of this?"

"Up and down. Too much time on his hands and not a lot to do except brood. I can't tell you how many times I heard that one: guy retires after thirty years and the next thing you know he gets sick and dies. Stacey doesn't say much about it, but I know how his mind works. He's depressed as hell."

"Is he religious?"

"Not him. He claims he's an atheist, but we'll see about that. Me, I always went to church, at least while Gracie was alive. I don't see how you face death without believing in *something*. Otherwise, it makes no sense."

Dolan glanced up just as Tannie appeared with two large plates loaded with freshly made sandwiches and

fries, plus two orders for the other table. Dolan interrupted his story to have a chat with her. I occupied
myself with banging on the ketchup bottle until a thick
drool of red covered the southeast corner of my fries. I
knew he was leading up to something, but he was taking
his sweet time. I lifted the top of the kaiser roll and
salted everything in sight. Biting in, I could feel the egg
yolk oozing into the bun. The combination of spicy
salami and snappy pepper-hot jack cheese turned out to
be the food equivalent of someone hollering *Hot Damn!*
on the surface of my tongue. I made one of my food
moans. Embarrassed, I looked up at them, but neither
seemed to notice.

When Tannie finally left, Dolan stubbed out his
cigarette and paused for an extended bout of coughing
so fierce it made his whole body shake. I pictured his
lungs like a set of black cartoon bellows, wheezing
away.

He shook his head. "Sorry about that. I had a bad
cold a month ago and it's been hard to shake." He took
a swallow of whiskey to soothe his irritated throat. He
picked up his sandwich and continued his story between
bites, taking up exactly where he'd left off. "While
Stacey's been laid up, I've been doing what I can to get
his apartment cleaned. Place is a mess. He should be out
of the hospital tomorrow and I didn't want him coming
home to the sight of all that crap."

He set his sandwich down to light another cigarette, rolling it over to the corner of his mouth while he pulled out a cylinder of papers he'd tucked into his breast coat pocket. "Yesterday, I went through a pile of papers on his kitchen table. I was hoping to come across the name of a friend I could contact—somebody to cheer him up. Stace could use a little something to look forward to. Anyway, there was nothing of that nature, but I did find this."

He placed the curling sheaf on the table in front of me. I finished my sandwich in one last bite and wiped my hands on a napkin before I reached for the papers. I knew at a glance it was a copy of a Sheriff's Department file. The cover page was marked 187 PC, indicating it was a homicide, with a case number following. The pages were held together with fasteners, sixty-five or seventy sheets in all, with a set of handwritten notes inserted at the back. I returned to the cover page.

Victim: Jane Doe
Found: Sunday, August 3, 1969
Location: Grayson Quarry, Highway 1, Lompoc

Under "Investigating Officers," there were four names listed, one of them Stacey Oliphant's.

Dolan leaned forward. "You can see he was one of the original investigating officers. Stace and me were the ones who found the body. We'd taken a Jeep up there and parked off the side of the road to go deer hunting that day. I guess there's a gate across the road now, but the property was open back then. The minute we got out, we picked up the smell. We both knew what it was—something dead for days. Didn't take us long to find out exactly what it was. She'd been flung down a short embankment like a sack of trash. This is the case he was working when he got sick. It's always bugged him they never figured out who she was, let alone who killed her."

I felt a dim stirring of memory. "I remember this. Wasn't she stabbed and then dumped?"

"Right."

"Seems odd they never managed to identify her."

"He thought so, too. It's one of those cases really stuck in his craw. He kept thinking there was something he'd overlooked. He'd go back to it when he could, but he never made much progress."

"And you're thinking what, to have another go at it?"

"If I can talk him into it. I think it'd make a world of difference in his attitude."

I leafed through the photocopies, watching the progression of dates and events. "Looks like just about everything."

"Including black-and-white prints of the crime scene

photographs. He had another couple of files but this is the one caught my eye." He paused to wipe his mouth and then pushed his plate aside. "It'd give him a lift to get back into this and see about developing some information. He can act as lead detective while we do the legwork."

I found myself staring. "You and me."

"Sure, why not? We can pay for your time. For now, all I'm suggesting is the three of us sit down and talk. If he likes the idea, we'll go ahead. If not, I guess I'll come up with something else."

I tapped the file. "Not to state the obvious, but this is eighteen years old."

"I know, but aside from Stacey's interest, there hasn't been a push on this since 1970 or so. What if we could crack it? Think what that'd do for him. It could make all the difference." It was the first time I'd seen any animation in his face.

I pretended to ponder but there wasn't much debate. I was sick of doing paperwork. Enough already with the file searches and the background checks. "Stacey still has access to the department?"

"Sure. A lot of folks out there think the world of him. We can probably get anything we need—within reason, of course."

"Let me take this home and read it."

Dolan sat back, trying not to look too pleased. "I'll be over at CC's from six until midnight. Show up by eight and we can swing over to St. Terry's and bring Stacey up to speed."

I found myself smiling in response.

TWO

I spent the early part of the afternoon in my new office digs, hammering away on my portable Smith-Corona. I typed up two overdue reports, did my filing, prepared invoices, and cleaned off my desk. I started in on the bills at 3:00 and by 3:35 I was writing out the final check, which I tore from my checkbook. I tucked it in the return envelope, then licked the flap so carelessly I nearly paper-cut my tongue. That done, I went into the outer office and moved all the unpacked boxes back into the closet. Nothing like a little motivation to get the lead out of your butt.

My supper that night consisted of a peanut-butter-and-pickle sandwich, accompanied by Diet Pepsi over ice. I ate in my minuscule living room, curled up on the sofa tucked into the window bay. In lieu of dinnerware, I used a fold of paper toweling that doubled as a dainty lip wipe when I'd finished my meal. With spring on the move, it was not quite dark out. The air was still chilly, especially once the sun went down. Through the partially opened window, I could hear a distant lawn mower and the occasional fragment of conversation as assorted people walked by. I live a block from the beach on a side street that provides overflow parking when Cabana Boulevard gets jammed.

I slid down comfortably on my spine, my sock feet on the coffee table, while I settled in to work. I went through the file quickly at first, just to get the lay of the land. A detective named Brad Crouse was lead investigator on the case. The other investigating officers, aside from Stacey Oliphant, were Detective Keith Baldwin, Sergeant Oscar Wallen, Sergeant Melvin Galloway, and Deputy Joe Mandel. A lot of manpower. Crouse had typed the bulk of the reports, using multiple carbons, which Stacey had apparently then photocopied from the old murder book. Judging from the number of strikeovers, I had to guess Detective Crouse had not been first in his class in secretarial school. I fancied if I put my ear to the page, I'd pick up the churlish echoes of his long-ago curses embedded in the lines of print.

It's odd going through an old file, like reading a mystery novel where you spoil the ending for yourself by peeking ahead to the very last page. The final document, a letter from a soils expert in San Pedro, California, was dated September 28, 1971, and indicated that the sample submitted by the Santa Teresa County Sheriff's Department would be impossible to distinguish from samples taken from similar deposits across the state. Sincerely. So sorry. End of the line for you, bub. I went back to the beginning and started reading again, this time taking notes.

According to the first officer at the scene, the girl's body had been rolled over the edge of an embankment, coming to rest about fifteen feet down, some fifty feet from the highway. Con Dolan and Stacey Oliphant had spotted her at approximately 5:00 P.M. on that Sunday— 1700 hours if you're talking military time, as this report did. She was lying on her left side on a crumpled canvas tarp, her hands bound in front of her with a length of white plastic-coated wire. She was wearing a dark blue Dacron blouse, white cotton pants with a print of dark blue daisies with a dot of red in each center. There was a leather sandal on her right foot; the matching sandal was found in the brush a short distance away. Marks in the dirt suggested she'd been dragged across the grass near the road. Even from the top of the slope, Dolan and Oliphant could see numerous stab wounds in her chest. It was also apparent her throat had been slashed.

Oliphant had made immediate CB contact with the Lompoc PD. Because the location was in the county, two on-duty sheriff's deputies were dispatched to the scene. Deputy Joe Mandel and Sergeant Melvin Galloway arrived twenty minutes after the initial call. Photographs were taken of the decedent and of the surrounding area. The body was then removed to a Lompoc mortuary, pending arrival of the coroner. Meanwhile, the deputies searched the vicinity, took soil samples, bagged the tarpaulin along with a nearby broken shrub and two pieces of shrub stem that appeared to be stained with blood.

On Tuesday, August 5, 1969, Mandel and Galloway returned to the crime scene to take measurements—the distance from the highway to the spot where the body had been found, the width of the blacktop, the location of the stray sandal. Sergeant Galloway took additional photos of the various areas, showing the embankment, damaged shrubs, and drag marks. There were no crime scene sketches, but perhaps they'd become separated from the rest of the file in the intervening years.

I took a minute to sort through the photographs, which were few in number and remarkably uninformative: eight black-and-white prints, including one of the roadway, one of an officer pointing at a broken shrub, one of the embankment where the body was found, and four of the body from a distance of fifteen feet. There were no close-ups of Jane Doe's face, no views of her wounds or the knotted wire with which her hands had been bound. The tarp was visible beneath her, but it was difficult to judge how much of the body, if any, had been covered. Times have changed. Current practice would have dictated fifty such photographs along with a video and a detailed crime scene sketch. In the same envelope, I found an additional five photographs in faded color showing the girl's sandals, pants, shirt, bra, and panties laid out on what looked like a sheet of white paper.

The autopsy had been performed on August 4, 1969, at 10:30 A.M. I squinted, inferred, surmised, and otherwise faked my way through the report, deciphering enough of the technical talk to figure out what was being said. Because her body was in a state of advanced decomposition, the measurements were estimates. The girl's height was calculated at 63 to 65 inches, her weight at 120 to 125 pounds. Her eyes were blue, her hair dyed a reddish blond that showed dark roots. In the left earlobe she wore a thin gold-wire circle with a horseshoe configuration. In her right earlobe she wore a similar gold-wire loop with a bent clip in its lower end. Her facial characteristics were indistinguishable due to skin slippage, gas crepitation, and decomposition. Examination of the body showed eight deep stab wounds in the middle of the back below the shoulder blade area: two stab wounds at the base of the neck on either side; five stab wounds between her breasts; and a large stab wound under the left breast, which had penetrated the heart. There was considerable maggot activity. Because of decomposition, the pathologist was unable to ascertain the presence of any scars or identifying marks. There were no skeletal fractures or deformities, no visible injuries to the external genitalia. Her fallopian tubes and ovaries were unremarkable and her uterine cavity was empty. Cause of death was listed as multiple stab wounds of the neck, chest, heart, and lungs.

At the conclusion of his exam, the pathologist removed Jane Doe's fingers, the nails of which she had painted with silver polish. These were tagged by an officer and turned over for shipping to the FBI Identification Division in Washington, D.C. Films taken of her upper and lower jaws showed multiple metallic restorations. She also suffered from what is commonly referred to as buckteeth, with one crooked eyetooth on the left side. A dentist, consulted later, suggested that the extensive dental work had probably been done in the two years before her death—that being 1967 through 1968. He judged her to be in her late teens to early twenties. A forensic odontist, examining the maxilla and mandible at a later date, narrowed the girl's age to fifteen years, plus or minus thirty-six months, noting that she probably died before she reached the legal age of eighteen.

On Wednesday, August 6, Sergeant Galloway submitted the following clothing and evidence to the deputy in charge of the property room:

1. One navy blue, full-length, puffed-sleeve blouse of Dacron-voile material—make unknown—blood-stained.
2. One pair home-sewn female white pants with blue flowers with red centers—size unknown.
3. One pair bikini panties, pink—size medium, Penney's label.
4. One black bra, size 38A, Lady Suzanne label.
5. One pair female brown leather sandals—buckle type, with four brass links on leather straps. Size 7½. With gold letters "MADE IN ITALY" on inner sole.
6. One soiled canvas tarpaulin with blood and miscellaneous stains.

The dead girl's earrings, a clipping of her hair, and the plastic-coated wire taken from her wrists were also booked into evidence.

The Sheriff's Department must have sent the essential information about the deceased to other law enforcement agencies, because a series of follow-up reports over the next several weeks covered all manner of missing persons believed to match the description of Jane Doe. Three stolen automobiles were recovered in the area, one containing assorted articles of women's clothing in the rear seat. This turned out to be unrelated, according to handwritten notes entered at a later date. The second vehicle, a 1966 red Mustang convertible with Arizona plates, reported stolen from an auto upholstery shop in Quorum, California, was subsequently returned to its rightful owner. The third stolen vehicle, a red 1967 Chevrolet, was tied to a homicide in Venice, California. The driver was subsequently arrested and later convicted of that crime.

A vagrant was picked up for questioning but released. There was also a report of a twenty-five-year-old employee who'd absconded with $46.35 in currency and change stolen from a service station owner outside the town of Seagate. The caretaker at a nearby state beach park was contacted and questioned about any persons he might have seen in the area. He reported nothing unusual. In three separate incidents, hitchhikers were picked up for questioning, but none of them were held. This was the summer of 1969 and there was a steady stream of hippies migrating north along this route. Hippies were generally regarded with suspicion, assumed to be high on drugs, which was probably the case.

At 10:30 A.M. on August 6, 1969, Detective Crouse interviewed a clerk named Roxanne Faught, who worked at a minimart on Highway 101. She'd contacted the Sheriff's Department after reading about the murder in the papers and reported that on Friday, August 1, she'd seen a young girl who matched the description of

Jane Doe. Miss Faught stated that the girl had helped herself to coffee and a doughnut, which she was unable to pay for. Faught paid for them herself, which is why the incident stuck in her mind. Earlier she'd noticed this same girl hitchhiking north, however she was gone when Faught left work at 3:00 P.M. The girl in the minimart carried no luggage and had no wallet or purse. Several other people contacted the department with leads, but none of these panned out.

As the days went on, calls came in reporting vehicles of various makes, models, and descriptions that had been seen near the quarry both before and after the body was discovered. As with any investigation, delving into the one crime seemed to bring a number of peripheral crimes into focus: loitering, trespassing, public drunkenness, petty theft—all of which turned out to be immaterial to the case. It was clear that many local citizens were busy remembering odd and freakish incidents that had occurred in the weeks prior to the homicide. For all anyone knew, one of these reports might hold a vital clue about the girl who'd been murdered or the person, or persons, who'd killed her.

Every phone call, every out-of-state inquiry, and every rumor was dutifully tracked down. At the end of each report, there was a list appended, giving the names, addresses, and phone numbers of those who'd been interviewed. The managers of the JCPenney stores in

Lompoc and Santa Teresa were contacted with regard to the article of clothing that bore the Penney's label, but it was learned that the item was available at any store in the chain. In the end, the girl remained unidentified, and as autumn rolled into winter, new leads diminished. The stained canvas tarp bore no identifying labels. The plastic-coated wire was submitted to the crime lab for analysis. The lab determined that wiring of that nature "would most probably be utilized in low-voltage-amperage conditions where little or no tension would be exerted on its length and where maximum protection from abrasion and moisture was required, perhaps an auto light system, or small low-voltage lighting equipment." By December of 1970, the intervals between reports had lengthened and new information had dwindled.

Stacey had worked the case at various times during the following years. He'd consolidated the list of witnesses, and it looked as though he'd arranged them in order of their importance, at least from his perspective. Many had been eliminated because the information they'd provided was too vague or their suggestions too far-fetched. In some cases, it was clear from later file entries that their questions and concerns were not relevant to the investigation. He'd followed up on every call in which a missing girl had been reported. In one instance, dental records were not a match for Jane

Doe's. In another, the police advised the Sheriff's Department that the girl in question was a chronic runaway and had returned home within days. In a third case, the mother of the subject called and informed investigating officers her daughter was alive and well. Stacey had even tried using telephone numbers listed in the reports in hopes of contacting persons whose information seemed pertinent, but many numbers were out of service or had been reassigned to other parties. Having reached the last of the reports, I went through again, consigning the pertinent dates to a stack of blank index cards, converting the facts from their narrative form to disconnected bits of information that I'd analyze later.

When I finally closed the file and looked at my watch, it was only 7:15—still early enough to catch up with Dolan at CC's. I pulled on my shoes, grabbed my jacket and shoulder bag, and headed out to my car.

The Caliente Café—or CC's, as it's known—is a neighborhood bar that offers an extensive menu of American dishes with Spanish surnames. The food was probably the management's attempt to keep the patrons sufficiently sober to drive home without incurring any DUI's. The surrounding property had undergone a transformation since my last visit two years before. The restaurant is housed in an abandoned service station. The gasoline pumps and below-ground storage tanks had been removed at the time of the conversion, but the contaminated soil had simply been blacktopped over and the resulting quarter acre of tarmac was used to provide patron parking. As time went on, the neighbors had begun to complain about the virulent seepage coming up from the ground—a chemical molasses fierce enough to darken the soles of your shoes. In the thick of summer heat, the asphalt became viscous and smelled like oolong tea—which is to say, smoldering tires. In winter, the surface seized up, buckling and cracking to reveal a mealy substance so caustic it generated nosebleeds. Stray cats were subject to wracking coughs on contact. Wandering dogs would suddenly stagger in circles as though in the grip of neurological dismay. Naturally, the owner of the property wasn't interested in paying the hundreds of thousands of dollars required to excavate this hellishly befouled soil, but the EPA had finally stepped in, and now the parking lot had been uprooted in an effort to remove all the contaminated dirt. In the process, numerous Chumash Indian artifacts had been uncovered, and the site was suddenly embroiled in a dispute among several parties: the tribe, the landowner, the city, and the archaeologists. So complex was this litigation that it was impossible to tell who was siding with whom.

It was a testimony to loyal patrons that for months they'd continued to tromp across this malodorous earth, endured delays and inconveniences, suffered picketers, public warnings, posted notices, fumes, muddy shoes, and the occasional pratfall just to get to their daily drinks. The parking lot was now fenced off and the path to the front door consisted of a narrow walkway of two-by-four planks laid out end to end. Approaching the establishment, I felt like a gymnast teetering on the balance beam before an ill-timed dismount.

The red neon sign that hung above the entrance still hissed and sizzled like a backyard bug light, and the air wafting out smelled of cigarette smoke and corn tortillas fried in last week's lard. A shrieking duet of blender motors was accompanied by castanets of clattering ice cubes being whirled together with tequila and Margarita mix. The Caliente Café opens at 6:00 every morning and doesn't shut down until 2:00 A.M. Its further virtue is that it's located just outside the city limits and thus provides an ever-present refuge for off-duty police officers who need to unwind at the end of a hard day—or after lunch, or after breakfast.

As I crossed the threshold, I confess I was hoping to run into a Santa Teresa vice cop named Cheney Phillips. Our long acquaintance had never progressed as far as romance—he had a girlfriend, for one thing—but one could always hope. Rumor had it the two of them had split up, so I figured it wouldn't hurt to put in an appearance.

Part of what sparked my interest was the fact I hadn't heard from Robert Dietz in months. He's a semiretired private eye who worked as my bodyguard in 1983 when a cut-rate hit man was hired to rub me out. Our connection since then has been intense and sporadic, with long, inexplicable intervals between visits. Only two weeks before, I'd called him in Carson City, Nevada, and left a message on his machine. So far, he hadn't bothered to call me back, which meant he was either out of the country or had moved on to someone new. Though I was crazy about Dietz, I'd never thought of him as my beau, my steady, my significant other, or my main squeeze (whatever the hell that is). Oh sure, Dietz and I had fooled around some over the past four years, but there was no commitment between us and no promises on either part. Naturally, I was irked at his neglect, even though I was equally at fault.

I caught sight of Dolan at the bar. He was wearing a worn brown leather bomber jacket. I paused for a moment to scope out the crowd and saw his gaze slide in my direction. Dolan's been a cop for too many years not to keep an eye on his surroundings, perpetually scanning faces in hopes of a match for one of the mug shots that had once crossed his desk. Off duty or on, no cop can resist the notion of a wholly unexpected felony arrest.

He raised a hand in greeting and I steered a course toward him, threading my way among parties waiting for tables. The stools on either side of him were occupied, but he gave the guys a look and one of them stood up to make room for me. I placed my shoulder bag at my feet and perched on the stool next to his. The ashtray in front of him was thick with butts, and it didn't take any of my highly developed detecting skills to note the number of cigarettes he'd smoked, including the one he was in the process of lighting from the still lit. He was drinking Old Forrester and he smelled like a Christmas fruitcake, minus the dried Maraschino cherries. He was also snacking on a plate of poppers: batter-fried jalapeño peppers filled with molten cheese. I thought I'd avoid pointing out the continuing error of his ways. There's nothing more obnoxious than someone calling attention to our obvious failings.

I said, "I thought I might run into Cheney Phillips. Have you seen him?"

"I think he's in Vegas on his honeymoon."

"His honeymoon? I thought the two of them broke up."

"This is someone new, a gal he met in here five or six weeks ago."

"You're kidding."

"Afraid not. Anyway, forget him. He's not your type anyway."

"I don't have a type. Of course, I don't have a boyfriend either, but that's beside the point."

"Have a popper."

"Thanks." I took one and bit into it, experiencing the spurt of melted cheese before the heat of the jalapeño set my tongue aflame. The jukebox came to life, and I peered over my shoulder as the strains of a country-western melody line-danced its way across the room. The Wurlitzer was ancient, a chunky, round-bodied contraption with a revolving rainbow of hues, bubbles licking up along its seams.

I turned my attention back to Dolan, trying to figure out how much he'd had to drink. He wasn't slurring his words, but I suspected he was so conditioned by his own alcoholic intake that he'd show no signs of drunkenness even if he fell off his stool. I wasn't sure if he'd been drinking continuously since lunchtime or had gone home for a nap between cocktails. A glance at the clock showed it was only 7:35, but he might have been sitting there since 4:00 P.M. I didn't look forward to working with the man if he was going to be pie-eyed from day to day. His constant smoking didn't appeal to me, either, but there was nothing I could do about it so the less said the better. "How's Stacey doing? Have you talked to him yet?"

"I called him at six and said we'd stop by to see him. Guy's sick of being poked and prodded, really wants out of there. I guess they'll release him tomorrow once the test results are back."

"Did you tell him your idea?"

"Briefly. I said we'd fill him in when we got there. What'd you think about the case?"

"I really love all that stuff. I usually don't have the chance to see police reports up close."

"Procedure hasn't changed that much the past twenty years. We're better at it now—more thorough and systematic, plus we got new technology on our side."

The bartender ambled our way. "What can I get for you?"

"I'm fine," I said.

Dolan lifted his whiskey glass, signaling for a refill.

"Aren't we on our way to see Stacey?"

"Right now?"

"Well, there's no point in getting into this if he's not going to agree."

I could see Dolan debate his desire for the next drink versus his concern for his friend. He pushed his glass back, reached for his wallet, and pulled out a handful of bills, which he tossed on the bar. "Catch you later."

I grabbed my bag and followed him as he headed for the door.

"We'll take my car," he said.

"What if you want to stay longer than I do? Then I'm stuck. Let's take both cars and I'll follow. That way, I can peel off any time it suits."

We wrangled a bit more but he finally agreed. I was parked half a block down, but he dutifully waited, pulling out just ahead of me as I came up on his left. His driving was surprisingly sedate as we cruised out the 101 in our minimotorcade. I knew if he got stopped and breathalyzed, he'd easily blow over the legal limit. I kept an eye out for cops, half-forgetting that Dolan was a cop himself.

Once close to St. Terry's, we found street parking within two cars of each other on the same block of Castle. It was now fully dark and the hospital was lit up like a lavish resort. We went in through the rear entrance and took the elevator to 6 Central, the oncology floor. The lights had been dimmed, and the wide, carpeted corridor muffled our footsteps. Three spare IV poles and two blood pressure monitors were clustered against the wall, along with a linen cart, a multitiered meal cart filled with trays from the dinner served earlier. I caught sight of a few visitors, but there was none of the lively interplay between patients and family members. Getting well takes work and no one wants to waste energy on superficial conversation. Passing the nurses' station, Dolan gave a nod to the clerk at the desk.

Stacey was in a private room, looking out on a darkened residential street. He seemed to be sleeping, his hospital bed elevated at a forty-five-degree angle. Poking out from under his red-knit watch cap were wisps of ginger-colored hair. Two get-well cards were propped upright along the wide windowsill, but there was nothing else of a personal nature. The television screen was blank. On his rolling bed table, there were a pile of magazines and a paper cup filled with melting ice.

Dolan paused in the doorway. Stacey's eyes came open. He waved and then pushed himself up on the bed. "I see you made it," he said, and then to me, "You must be Kinsey. Nice to meet you." I leaned forward and shook his hand. His grip was strong and hot, almost as though he were metabolizing at twice the normal rate.

While Dolan went about the business of rounding up chairs from opposite corners of the room, I said, "I believe you knew the guys who trained me—Morley Shine and Ben Byrd."

"I knew them well. Both good men. I was sorry to hear about Morley's murder. That was a hell of a thing. Have a seat."

"Thanks."

Dolan offered me one chair and settled in the other. While the two of them chatted, I studied Stacey. He had small mild blue eyes, pale brows, and a long deeply creased face. His color was good, though it looked as though he hadn't shaved for days. He seemed to be in good spirits and he spoke with all the vigor of an active man.

After some preliminary conversation, Dolan brought the subject around to the Jane Doe investigation. "I gave Kinsey the file to read. We thought we should talk about where we go from here. The doc still talking about letting you out tomorrow?"

"Looks that way."

The two of them chatted about the case while I kept my mouth shut. I don't know why I'd expected Stacey to resist Dolan's proposition, but he didn't seem at all opposed to our resurrecting the case. He said to Dolan, "Speaking of which, Frankie Miracle got out. His parole officer, Dench Smallwood, called me and said Frankie found a place in town. By now, he probably has legitimate employment."

"That'd be a first."

I said, "How does Frankie Miracle fit in? I remember his name from the file."

Dolan said, "He got picked up in Lompoc August 1, two days before Jane Doe's body was found. We always figured he was good for it, though he denied it."

Stacey spoke up. "He killed his girlfriend in Venice July 29 during a meth binge. He stabbed the woman umpteen times, then he helped himself to her car and all her credit cards and started driving north. She was found a couple days later when neighbors complained about the smell."

"Dumb-ass signed her name to the charge slips every time he stopped for gas," Dolan said. "You'd think someone would notice a 'Cathy Lee Pearse' with no boobs, a mustache, and a two-day growth of beard." He shifted in his chair and then rose to his feet. "You two go on and get acquainted. Time for me to step outside and grab a smoke."

Once Dolan left, I said, "You have a theory why Jane Doe was never identified?"

"No. We expected a quick match, someone who'd recognize her from the description in the papers. All I can think is she wasn't reported missing. Or maybe the missing-persons report got buried in the paperwork on some cop's desk. There's probably an explanation, but who knows what it is? By now, it's unlikely we'll ever find out who killed her, but there's a possibility we can get her ID'd and returned to her folks."

"What are the chances?"

"Not as bad as you might think. Once enough time passes, people are more willing to speak up. We might tweak someone's conscience and get a lead that way." He hesitated, taking a moment to smooth the edges of his sheet. "You know, Con's wife, Gracie, died a while back."

"He mentioned that."

"It hit him hard at the time, but he seemed to be pulling out of it. But ever since he got sidelined with this heart condition, the guy's been in a funk. As long as Gracie was alive, she seemed to keep him in check, but now his smoking and booze consumption are out of control. I've been trying to find a way to get him back on track, so the minute this came up, I jumped on it."

"You're talking about Jane Doe?"

"Right. I was happy you agreed to help. It'll give him a lift. He needs to work."

I smiled with caution, listening for any hint of irony in his tone. Apparently, he didn't realize Dolan had voiced the very same concerns about him.

When Dolan returned, he stood looking expectantly from me to Stacey. "So what's the game plan? You two have it all worked out?"

"We were just talking about that. Kinsey wants to see the crime scene before we do anything else."

I said, "Right."

Dolan said, "Great. I'll set that up for tomorrow."

THREE

Dolan picked me up at my place at 10:00 in his 1979 Chevrolet, Stacey in the backseat. He did an expert parallel parking job and got out of the car. He wore a dark blue sweatshirt and a pair of worn blue jeans. The exterior of the Chevy was a mess. By day, I could see that the once-dark brown paint had oxidized, taking on the milky patina of an old Hershey's bar. The back bumper was askew, the left rear fender was crumpled, and a long indentation on the passenger side rendered the door close to inoperable. I managed to open it by means of a wrenching maneuver that made the metal shriek in protest. Once seated, I hauled, trying to get it shut again. Dolan circled the car, shoved the door shut, and secured the lock by bumping it with his hip.

I said, "Thanks." Already, I was worried about his prowess at the wheel.

He leaned in the open window and held his hand out

to Stacey. "Give me your gun and I'll lock 'em in the trunk."

Stacey winced audibly as he torqued to one side, slipping his gun from his holster and passing it to Dolan. Dolan went around to the rear and tucked the guns in the trunk before he got in on his side.

The car's upholstery was a dingy beige fabric that made it difficult to slide across the seat. I remained where I was as though glued in place. I turned so I could look at Stacey, who was sitting in the backseat with a bed pillow wedged behind him. His red knit watch cap was pulled down almost to his brows. "Threw my back out," he said by way of explanation. "I was moving boxes last week. I guess I should have done like Mother taught me and lifted with my knees."

Dolan's hiking boots were muddy, and waffle-shaped droppings littered the floor mat on his side. He adjusted the rearview mirror to talk to Stacey's reflection. "You should have left those for me. I told you I'd take care of 'em."

"Quit acting like a mother hen. I'm not helpless. It's a muscle pull, that's all; my sciatica acting up. Even healthy people get hurt, you know. It's no big deal."

In the harsh light of day, I could see that, despite the transfusion, his skin had gray undertones, and the smudges beneath his pale brows made his eyes appear to recede. He was dressed for the outdoors, wearing brown cords, hiking boots, a red-plaid wool shirt, and a fisherman's vest.

"You want to sit up here?"

"I'm better off where I am. I'm never quite sure when I'm going to need to lie down."

"Well, just let me know if you want to switch places."

I tugged at my seat belt, which was hung up somewhere. I spent an inordinate amount of time trying to get the mechanism to release a sufficient length of belt so I could clip it into place. Meanwhile, Dolan put the car in gear. The engine coughed and died twice, but finally sputtered back to life, and we were under way. The interior smelled of nicotine and dog. I didn't picture Dolan as the doggy type, but I didn't want to ask. The floorboards were strewn with gas receipts, discarded cigarette packs, and assorted cellophane bags that had once contained potato chips, cheese-and-cracker sandwiches, and other heart-healthy snacks.

We gassed up at a service station adjacent to the freeway and then he eased the car out into the traffic, heading north on the 101. As soon as we were settled at a steady speed, Dolan punched in the car lighter and reached for the pack of Camels he had resting on the dash.

Stacey said, "Hey! Have mercy. You've got a cancer patient back here."

Dolan again angled the rearview mirror so he could see Stacey's face. "That doesn't seem to stop you from smoking that pipe of yours."

"The pipe's purely recreational. At the rate you smoke, you'll be dead before me."

Dolan said, "Nuts," but left the pack where it was.

Stacey tapped me on the shoulder. "See that? The guy looks after me. You'd never guess that about him."

Dolan's smile barely registered, but it softened his face.

After the town of Colgate, the railroad tracks and the highway ran parallel to the ocean. To the north, the Santa Ynez Mountains loomed dark and gray, dense with low-growing vegetation. There were scarcely any trees, and the contours of the foothills were a rolling green. Much of the topography was defined by massive landslides, sandstone and shale debris extending for miles. Dolan and Stacey conducted a conversation that consisted of fishing and hunting stories—endless accounts of all the creatures they'd shot, hooked, trapped, and snagged; gutted, skinned, and toted home. This, with men, passes for a load of fun.

We sped past the state beach park, where camping sites consisted of adjacent oblongs of asphalt that looked suspiciously like parking spaces. I'd seen campers and RV's lined up like piano keys while the occupants set out aluminum picnic tables and chairs, stoking up their portable barbecues in areas much smaller than the yards they had at home. The children would gorge on hot dogs and potato chips, frolic in the ocean, and then bed down in the car, hair sticky, their bodies infused with residual salt like little cod fillets. For Dolan and Stacey, the sight of the line of campers triggered a recollection of another unsolved homicide—two teens shot to death on an isolated stretch of beach. After that, they spent time pointing out the various locations where past homicide victims had been dumped. Santa Teresa County had provided a number of such spots.

A few miles beyond Gull Cove, Dolan took the turnoff and headed west on California 1. I found myself lulled by the passing countryside. Here the hills were undulating, dotted with shaggy masses of the dark green oaks that marched across the land. The skies were pale blue with only the faintest marbling of clouds. The air smelled of the hot, sun-dried pastures sprinkled with buttercups, where occasional cattle grazed.

The two-lane road wound west and north. From time to time, the route cut through irregular, high-arching rock beds. On one of these stretches, thirty-two years before, a mammoth boulder tumbled down the slope, shattering the windshield of my parents' car as we passed. I was sitting in the rear, playing with my paper doll, scowling because I'd just bent her left cardboard leg at the ankle. I felt a flash of uncontrollable five-year-old rage because her foot looked all crookedy and limp. I was just setting up a howl when one of my parents made a startled exclamation. Perhaps the falling rock was briefly visible on descent, bouncing in a jaunty shower of smaller rocks and dirt. There was no time to react. The force of the boulder smashed through the windshield, crushing my father's head and chest, killing him instantly. The vehicle veered right, careening out of control, and crashed against the rocky hill face.

The impact flung me forward, wedging me against the driver's seat. From this confining cage of crumpled metal, I kept my mother company in the last, long moments of her life. I understand now how it must have felt from her perspective. Her injuries were such that there was no way she could move without excruciating pain. She could hear me whimper, but she had no way to know how badly I was hurt. She could see her husband was dead and knew she was not far behind. She wept, keening with regret. After a while, she was quiet, and I remember thinking that was good, not knowing she'd left her body and floated off somewhere.

Dolan swerved to avoid a ground squirrel that had skittered across the pavement in front of us. Instinctively, I put a hand out to brace myself and then I focused on the road again, disconnecting my emotions with all the skill of a vivisectionist. It's a trick of mine that probably dates back to those early years. I tuned into the conversation, which I realized belatedly had been directed at me.

Dolan was saying, "You with us?"

"Sure. Sorry. I think I missed that."

"I said, this guy, Frankie Miracle, we talked about last night? He got picked up on a routine traffic stop outside Lompoc. The schmuck had a busted taillight, and when the officers ran the plate, the vehicle came up stolen and wanted by the Los Angeles County Sheriff's Department. Galloway reads him his rights and throws him in the hoosegow. Meanwhile, the car's towed to the impound lot. When Galloway sits down to write his report, he reads the APB, indicating the registered owner's the victim of a homicide. He goes back over to the jail and tells Frankie he's under arrest for murder and reads him his rights again. Two days after that, Stacey and I go deer hunting and come across the girl."

"Yeah, if it wasn't for the taillight, Frankie could've been in Oregon and we might not've tied him to the situation here."

"What about the weapon? I don't remember any mention of it."

"We never found the knife, but judging from the wounds, the coroner said the blade had to be at least five inches long. Rumor has it, Frankie carried something similar, though he didn't have it on him when we picked him up."

Stacey said, "He probably tossed it or buried it. Country up there is rugged. Search and Rescue came through and did a grid search but never turned up anything." He leaned forward and tapped Con on the shoulder, pointing to a side road going off on our right a hundred yards ahead. "That's it. Just beyond this bridge coming up."

"You think? I remember it was farther down, along a stretch of white three-board fence."

"Oh. Maybe so. You could be right about that."

Dolan had slowed from forty miles an hour to a cautious fifteen. The two peered over at a two-lane gravel road that cut back at an angle and disappeared from view. It must not have looked familiar because Stacey said, "Nuh-uhn. Try around the next bend. We could have passed it already." He turned and stared out the rear window.

In the end, Dolan made a U-turn and we circled back, making a second slow pass until they settled on the place. Dolan pulled onto a secondary lane, gravel over cracked asphalt, that followed the contours of a low-lying hill. Directly ahead of us, I could see where the road split to form a Y. A locked gate barred access to the property with its No Trespassing signs. On the near side of the gate and to the right, a Jeep was parked.

Where's Grayson Quarry?" I asked, referring to the crime scene as designated on the official police reports.

"Around the bend to the right about a quarter of a mile," Dolan said. As he edged over on the berm and set the handbrake, an elderly gentleman in jeans, cowboy boots, and a leather hat emerged from the Jeep. He was small and wide, with a full-sized Santa belly pushing at the buttons of his western-style shirt. He approached our car, walking with a decided limp. Dolan cut the engine and got out on his side.

Stacey murmured, "That's Arne Johanson, the ranch foreman. I called and he agreed to meet us to unlock the gate."

By the time Stacey eased out of the backseat, I'd emerged from the passenger side and shoved the car door with one hip. Now that Dolan was in the open air, he lit a cigarette.

Stacey moved toward the old man and shook his hand. I noticed he was making an effort to appear energetic. "Mr. Johanson. This is nice of you. I'm Stacey Oliphant with the County Sheriff's Department. You probably don't remember, but we met in August of '69 back when the body was found. This is Lieutenant Con Dolan from Santa Teresa PD. He's the fellow who was with me. Two of us were up here to hunt when we came across the girl."

"I thought you looked familiar. Good seeing you."

"Thanks. We appreciate your help."

The old man's gaze drifted in my direction. He

seemed puzzled at the sight of me. "Like to see some ID if it's all the same to you." This was directed at the guys though his eyes remained on me.

Stacey moved his jacket aside to expose the badge attached to his belt. His badge specified that he was retired, but Johanson didn't seem to notice and Stacey didn't feel compelled to call it to his attention. Dolan rolled his cigarette to one corner of his mouth and took out a leather bifold wallet with his badge, which he held up. While Johanson leaned forward and studied it, Dolan took out a business card and handed it to him. Johanson tucked the card in his shirt pocket and glanced at me slyly.

"She's with us," Dolan said.

I was perfectly willing to show him a copy of my license, but I liked Dolan's protectiveness and thought I'd leave well enough alone. This time, when the old man's eyes returned to mine, I looked away. I pegged him as a throwback, some old reprobate who believed women belonged in the kitchen, not out in the "real" world going toe to toe with men. He had to be in his eighties. His eyes were small, a watery blue. His face was sun-toughened, deeply creased, and bristling with whiskers that showed white against his leathery skin. He shifted his attention to Dolan's cigarette. "I'd watch that if I was you. It's fire country up here."

"I'll be careful."

Johanson took out a set of keys and the four of us walked over to the metal rail gate with its ancient padlock. His stride had a rocking motion that suggested an old injury. Maybe in his youth he'd worked the rodeo circuit. He selected a key, turned it in the padlock, and popped it off the hasp. He pushed the sagging gate aside, forcing it back to a point where it was anchored in the grass. The four of us passed through, Dolan and Stacey leading while I tagged behind them and Johanson brought up the rear.

"It was two cops who found her, coming here to hunt," he said, having either missed or forgotten the reference Stacey'd made to their prior meeting.

Dolan grunted a response, which didn't seem to discourage the old man's garrulousness. "We got wild boar on the property. Owner lets hunters come in now and then to cull the herd. Boars is aggressive. I've had 'em turn and charge right at me, gash a hole in my leg. Mean sons a bitches, I can tell you that. Peckers like razor blades is what I heard. Mating season, the female sets up a squeal brings the hair right up on the back of your neck."

"Actually, Lieutenant Dolan and I were the ones who found the body. We'd come up to hunt."

"You two. Is that right? Well, I'll be. I could've swore I knowed you from someplace."

"We're all a bit older."

51

"I can testify to that. I'm eighty-seven year old myself, born January 1, nineteen double ought. Broke a hip here a while back when my horse fell on me. It hadn't healed too good. Nowadays, they can take out the old joint and put another in its place. This gimpyness don't straighten out, I might get me a brand new one. Say, what's this all about now, anyway? I'm not entirely clear."

Stacey said, "Sheriff's Department is going over some old files, taking another look. We're reworking this case in hopes of resolving it."

"And you come up here why?"

"We wanted to see the crime scene so the reports would make more sense. Those old crime scene photographs don't tell how the area's laid out, relative distances, things of that sort." This again from Stacey. So far I hadn't said a word.

Johanson's eyes strayed to my face with the same thinly veiled curiosity. "I can understand that. I brung my son down here when they was hauling her body out of the ravine. He was fourteen and thought it was just fine and dandy hitchin' rides every time he had to go someplace. I wanted him to see where he could end up."

"You have a son that young?" I said, trying not to sound too surprised.

The old man grinned, showing blackened and

crooked teeth. "Got two," he said. "I been married five time, but I never had kids until this last go-round. Youngest boy's thirty-two yesterday. I got him workin' on the ranch. Other boy's a bum. I guess I have to think of it a fifty percent success instead of fifty percent failed."

Dolan dropped his cigarette to the ground and crushed the ember thoroughly with his heel. "You think that's what happened to her? Someone offered her a ride and ended up stabbing her to death?"

"That'd be my guess. You know they never did figure out who she was. Pitiful, you ask me. All these years, her mom and dad never knowed what happened to her. Prob'ly still think she's comin' home and there she was laid out with her throat cut ear to ear."

Stacey said, "Identifying the girl is part of what we hope to accomplish."

Dolan was already firing up his second cigarette. "We appreciate your time, Mr. Johanson. I'm sure you're busy and we don't want to keep you. Thanks for meeting us."

"Happy to oblige. You needn't bother about me. I'll just tag along 'til you're done and lock the gate again."

"We won't be long. We'll be happy to lock the gate after us when we leave."

"I don't mind the wait."

Stacey and Dolan exchanged a glance, but neither said another word as they trudged the remaining distance to the edge of the ravine.

Johanson trailed along after us. "Wadn't any gate here back then. I figure the feller must have cruised all up and down, looking for a place to dump her, and chosen this. He must not have knowed about the quarry. Lot of traffic on this road any time of day; fellers heading to the mine. Bad weather's different. Operation closes down if things get too bad."

"I'm surprised she wasn't found by one of the Grayson employees," Stacey remarked.

"Because she smelt?"

"That's right."

"Might've been for all I know. Lot of them boys are Mexican. Called 'em 'wetbacks' in those days. Made a point not to bring attention to theirself, especially where the law's concerned. Probably thought it was a dog if they caught wind of her at all. I'm sure the last thing occurred to them was some young girl been kilt."

Dolan's response was noncommittal, perhaps in hopes of squelching further conversation. Ignoring Johanson, he scrambled a few steps down the embankment. The ground seemed soft, though the surface was powdery with dust. He anchored himself with his right foot on the downside of the slope and stood with his hands in his jeans pockets studying the undergrowth.

"She was right about here. A lot more brush in the area back then."

"We cut that back on account of the fire department," Johanson said. "They come out usually twicet a year. Owner won't clear brush without a threat. Too cheap."

"With the fire danger up here, you can't ignore the brush," Stacey said, ever so polite.

"No, sir. That's what I say. You'll find a few more trees. Back when that girl was throwed down there, that 'un and this one wasn't here. Both black acacias. Grow like weeds. I'd cut 'em down myself, but owner won't hear of it. Now, oaks I don't touch. Couldn't pay me to fell one unless it's eat out by rot."

Dolan and I were both ignoring the man. I watched Dolan as he scrambled back out of the ravine and stood scanning the portion of Highway 1 that was visible from where we stood. "My guess is he backed in and opened the trunk of the car. He probably used the painter's tarp to drag the body the short distance from there to here. The tarp was heavily soiled on one side and you could see a path through the underbrush where it'd been flattened by the weight."

"Kids used to pull in here for petting parties," Johanson said. "Monday mornings, ground'd be littered with rubbers, limp as snake skins. That's why we put in the gate, to keep cars out."

I looked at Stacey. "Was she wrapped in the tarp?"

"Partially. We believe he killed her somewhere else. There were blood stains in the grass, but nothing to suggest the volume you'd've seen if she bled out. He probably used the tarp to keep the stains off the interior of the trunk."

Dolan said, "If we'd had some of this new high-tech equipment back then, I bet we'd have found plenty. Hair, fiber, maybe even prints. Nothing neat about this killing. He just happened to get lucky. Nobody saw the murder and nobody spotted him when he toppled her down the slope."

Johanson perked up. "Neighbor down the road—this is C. K. Vogel—I don't know if you remember this, but C. K. seen a light-colored VW van on the particular morning of July 28 up along that road over there. Painted all over with peace symbols and psychedelic hippie signs. Said it was still there eleven o'clock that night. Curtains on the winders. Dim light inside. It was gone the next morning, but he said it struck him as odd. I believe he phoned it in to the Sheriff's Department after the girl was found."

Dolan's skepticism was unmistakable, though he tried to be civil—not an easy task for him. "Probably unrelated, but we'll look into it."

"Said he seen a convertible as well. Killer could've drove that. Red, as I recollect, with an out-of-state license plate. If I was you, I'd make sure to have a talk with him."

I said, "Thanks for the information. I'll make a note."

Johanson looked at me with interest. Suddenly, he seemed to get it: I was a police secretary, accompanying the good detectives to spare them the tedium of all the clerical work.

The breeze shifted slightly, blowing Dolan's smoke in my face. I moved upwind.

"Something I forgot to mention about Miracle," Stacey said. "When we went back to the impound lot and searched Frankie's car, we found soil samples in the floor mats that matched the soil from the embankment. Unfortunately, the experts said it was impossible to distinguish this sample from samples in other quarries throughout the state. West Coast has the most extensive marine deposits in the world."

"I saw that report. Too bad," I said. "What'd Frankie say when you questioned him?"

"He gave us some long garbled tale of where he'd been. Claimed he'd been hiking in the area, but it was nothing we could confirm."

Dolan said, "He was higher than a kite the day they picked him up. Grass or coke. Arrest sheet doesn't say. He's a meth freak is what I heard."

"Everyone under thirty was higher than a kite back then," I said.

Mr. Johanson cleared his throat, having been excluded from the conversation too long to suit him. "Being's as you're here, you might want to see the rest of the property. This is the last ranch of its size. Won't be long before they tear down the old house. Probably build subdivisions as far as the eye can see."

My impulse was to decline, but Dolan seemed to spark to the idea. "I'm in no hurry. Fine with me," he said. He gave Stacey a look. Stacey shrugged his assent and then checked for my response.

I said, "Sure. I don't mind. Are we finished here?"

"For now. We can always come back."

Johanson turned toward his Jeep. "Best take the Jeep. Road's all tore up from heavy rains we had a while back. No point throwing up dust and gravel on that fancy car of yours."

I thought he was being snide. I checked for Dolan's reaction, but he was apparently in agreement with the old man's assessment.

We piled in the Jeep, Stacey in the front seat, Dolan and me climbing into the rear. The seats were cracked leather, and all the glassine windows had been removed. Johanson started the engine and released the emergency brake. The vehicle's shocks were gone. I reached up and grabbed the roll bar, clinging to it as we began to lurch and bang our way up the deeply rutted gravel road. Like me, Stacey was clinging to the Jeep frame for stability, wincing with pain from the jolts to his injured back.

The grass on either side of us was rough. A hillside rose on our left and then leveled out at the top, forming a mesa where numerous pieces of heavy equipment sat. Much of the remaining ground was stripped and terraced, broad fields of rubble unbroken by greenery. "That's the quarry," Johanson said, hollering over the rattle and whine of the moving vehicle.

I leaned forward, directing my comments toward the back of his head. "Really? That looks like a gravel pit. I pictured limestone cliffs."

"Different kind of quarry. These is open pit mines. Grayson Quarry goes after the DE. That's diatomaceous earth. Here, I've got a sample. Take a look at this." One eye on the road, he leaned down and removed a chunk of rock from the floor of the Jeep, then passed it across the seat to me. The rock was a rough chalky white, about the size of a crude round of bread with irregular gouges in the crust. I passed it on to Lieutenant Dolan, and he hefted it as I had, finding it surprisingly light.

I said, "What'd you say this was?"

"Diatomaceous earth. We call it DE."

I felt a tingle of uneasiness run down my spine as his explanation went on. "DE's a deposit made up mainly of siliceous shells of diatoms. This whole area was underwater oncet upon a time. The way they tolt me, marine life fed on diatoms, which is these colonies of algae. Now it's pulverized and used as an abrasive, sometimes as an absorbent."

Stacey raised his voice against the crunch of the tires over gravel. "I used to use it to filter beer when I was making it at home."

The road began to climb and the Jeep labored upward, finally rounding a bend. The old house came into view—massive, dilapidated, Victoriana under siege. Clearly, the structure had once been regal, but weeds and brush were creeping up on all sides, consuming the yard, obscuring the broken lines of wood fence. Years of neglect had undermined the outbuildings so that all that remained now were the rough stone foundations and occasional piles of collapsed and rotting lumber.

The house itself was a two-story white frame, flanked by a one-story wing on either side of the facade. There were four porches visible, providing shade and sheltered ventilation so that doors and windows could be left open to the elements. A porch wrapped around the house at the front, with a second porch stacked on top. A widow's walk encircled the roof. The numerous paired windows were narrow and dark, many of the panes sporting the sort of tattered holes that rock-throwers make when they score a hit.

Johanson waved at the house, scarcely slowing his

speed. "Been empty for years. I'm in the gardener's cottage on 'tother side of the barn," he yelled.

I found myself averting my gaze as we passed the house and headed for a compound of structures I spotted in a shady area ahead. Barn, toolshed, greenhouse. There were arbors of grapevines as gnarly as rope. Weathered wooden tables were arranged under the trellises. I had the sensation of cold blowing down on the back of my neck.

Johanson pulled up in front of a ramshackle frame cottage. Beyond, I could see a raw wood barn that listed to one side, and beyond that there were endless stretches of three-board wood fence.

I leaned forward again and laid a hand on Johanson's shoulder. "Excuse me, who'd you say owns this?"

He killed the engine before he turned. "Miz LeGrand. I guess I should say Miz Kinsey to be accurate. She's a widder woman, must be ninety-some by now. Married to Burton Kinsey, the fella who leased the quarry from her pappy. He made his fortune off the mine, though the whole of it was rightly hers oncet the old man died. . . ."

I'd ceased to listen and the silence in my head seemed as profound as temporary deafness. He was talking about my maternal grandmother, Cornelia Kinsey, born Cornelia Straith LeGrand.

FOUR

Friday morning, I arose at 5:59, switching off the alarm a moment before the clock radio was set to burst into song. I stared up at the skylight above my bed. No rain. Shit. I didn't feel like exercising, but I made a deal with myself: I'd do the jog and skip the gym. I leaned over and scooped up the sweats I'd left folded on the floor. I wriggled into pants and top. I sat up and tugged on a pair of crew socks, shoved my feet into my Sauconys, and had my key tied to the laces before I'd left my bed. It occurred to me that if I just made it my habit to sleep in my sweats and crew socks, it would be a lot more efficient. All I'd need were my running shoes and I'd be ready to go. I went into the bathroom and availed myself of the facilities, after which I brushed my teeth, splashed water on my face, and then used my wet hands to comb the sleep-generated peaks and valleys from my hair. I trotted down the spiral stairs, checked the thumblock on the front door and pulled it shut, then rounded the studio to the gate.

The neighborhood was quiet and the air felt damp. I walked half a block down and one block over, crossing Cabana Boulevard to the bike path that parallels the beach. I began to jog, feeling sluggish, aware of every footfall and every jolt to my frame. With me, jogging is seldom a subject for debate. I get up and do the run, unless it rains, of course, and then I burrow in my bed. Otherwise, five mornings a week, I shake off the sleep and hit the road before I lose my nerve, knowing that whatever I'm feeling at the outset of a run will be gone by the time I reach the end. The gym I can do without, though I'd been good about lifting weights for the past several months.

The sunrise had already presented itself in a dazzling light show that left the sky a broad and unblemished blue. The surf looked forbidding, a silt-churning cold, applauded only by the sea lions who waited offshore, barking their approval. I ran a mile and a half down to the Cabana Recreation Center, did a U-turn, and then ran the mile and a half back, finally slowing to a brisk walk as I headed for home.

I'd been resisting the urge to ponder events from the day before, but I could feel my thoughts stray. Dolan and Stacey had both caught the name "Kinsey" as soon as Johanson mentioned it, but my expression must have warned them to keep any observations to themselves. I had said little or nothing while the ranch foreman

SUE GRAFTON

showed us through the barn, the old orchards, and the greenhouse, which was largely abandoned. Most of its panes were intact. The air was humid and smelled of mulch, peat moss, compost, and loam. In that protected environment, alien vines and opportunistic saplings had flourished, creating a towering jungle that pushed against the glass on all sides, threatening to break through. The minute we walked into the space, I knew I'd been there before. Cousins I'd discovered in the course of a previous investigation had sworn I'd been at Grand's house when I was four years old. I had only the scantiest recollection of the occasion, but I knew my parents must have been there, too. The three of them— my father, my mother, and her sister Virginia—had been banished from the family after my parents eloped. My father was a mailman, thirty-five years old. My mother, Rita Cynthia Kinsey, was an eighteen-year-old debutante whose mother was convinced she was destined for someone better than Randy Millhone. Instead, my mother ran off with him, thumbing her nose at the entire Kinsey clan. Virginia sided with the newlyweds. Thereafter, all three were cast into the Kinsey family equivalent of the Outer Darkness.

Despite being exiled, my parents apparently made secret visits to the ranch whenever my grandparents were away. Rumor had it there were numerous contacts with the three remaining sisters, but I only knew of two

64

occasions. On the first, there was an incident in which I'd fallen off a porch and hurt my knee. I did remember the sight of the scrape with its alternating stripes of dirt and blood, which smelled like iron. I could also remember the searing pain when my mother dabbed at the abrasion with a cotton ball that seemed to hiss on my skin. She and I took turns blowing on the wound, huffing and puffing to dry the medication and thus ease its sting. On the only other drive to Lompoc I remembered, my parents were killed before we ever arrived. My grandmother had known of my existence since the day I was born. I was still smarting from the fact she'd never bothered to make contact.

Walking the property with Arne Johanson, I'd dreaded the idea of entering the house, and I'd been hoping to avoid it when I realized Stacey's breathing had become labored and much of the color had drained from his face. I laid a hand on his arm and called, "Con?"

Dolan turned and looked back. Stacey shook his head, making one of those gestures meant to assure us we needn't worry about him. Johanson had forged on ahead and he was still chattering about the ranch when Dolan caught up with him. "Mr. Johanson? Sorry to cut this short, but I've got a meeting coming up in town and we have to get back."

"This won't take long. You don't want to miss the house."

"Maybe another day. We'll take a rain check."

"Well. I guess that's that then. Whatever you say."

Within minutes, he'd delivered us to Dolan's car and we were back on the highway. The drive home had been low-key, with Stacey slumped on the backseat, the red knit cap pulled down to shield his eyes.

"Are you all right, Stace?" I asked.

"Walking wore me out. It's my damn back again. I'll be better in a bit." In the absence of animation, his face looked old.

Dolan readjusted the rearview mirror, keeping one eye on Stacey and one on the road. "I told you not to come."

"Did not. You said the fresh air'd be good. Said I ought to take advantage while I was up to it."

I said, "You warm enough?"

"Quit worrying."

I turned my attention to Lieutenant Dolan. "What's next?"

Stacey answered before he could. "We'll meet at my place tomorrow morning. Ten o'clock suit?"

"Fine with me," I said.

Dolan said, "Sounds good."

We dropped Stacey first. He lived close to downtown Santa Teresa, five blocks from my office, in a small pink stucco rental house perched above a pink cinder-block wall. Dolan had me wait in the car while he retrieved Stacey's gun from the trunk and then followed him up the six stairs to the walkway that skirted the place. I could see how tightly Stacey had to grip the railing in order to pull himself up. The two disappeared, moving toward the rear. Dolan was gone for ten minutes, and when he returned to the car, he seemed withdrawn. Neither of us said a word during the drive to my apartment. I spent the remainder of Thursday afternoon taking care of personal errands.

Having finished my jog, I walked the block between the beach and my place. When I reached my front door, I picked up the morning paper as I let myself in. I tossed the *Dispatch* on the kitchen counter and started a pot of coffee. As soon as it began to trickle through the filter, I went up the spiral stairs to take my shower and get dressed.

I was halfway through my bowl of Cheerios, sitting at the counter, when the telephone rang. I dislike interruptions at breakfast, and I was tempted to wait and let the answering machine pick up. Instead, I leaned over and grabbed the handset from the wall-mounted phone. "Hello?"

"Hello, Kinsey. This is Tasha, up in Lompoc. How're you?"

I felt my eyes close. This was one of my cousins,

SUE GRAFTON

Tasha Howard, the only member of the family I'd ever dealt with at any length. She's an estate attorney with offices in Lompoc and San Francisco.

I'd met her sister, Liza, a couple of years before, and during our one and only conversation discovered hitherto unplumbed depths of disaffection in my otherwise placid frame. My reaction was probably only a side effect of the fact that Liza was telling me things I didn't want to hear. For one thing, she told me, in the giddiest manner possible, that my mother was regarded as an idol among her living nieces and nephews. While this was meant as flattery, I felt it dehumanized the woman whom I'd never really known. I resented their prior claim, just as I resented the fact that my pet name for our aunt Virginia, that being "Aunt Gin," was a term already in wide use among these same family members. So, too, was the penchant for peanut-butter-and-pickle sandwiches, which I'd assumed was a secret link between my mother and me. Granted, my reaction was less than rational, but I was left feeling diminished by the idle tales Liza told.

Tasha was okay. She'd bailed me out of a jam once and on another occasion she'd hired me for a job. *That* hadn't turned out well, but the fault wasn't hers.

Belatedly, I said, "Fine. How are you?" We always have conversations that sound like they're punctuated by transatlantic delays.

68

"I'm good, thanks. Listen, it looks like Mother and I will be coming down your way to shop and we wondered if you were free. We can have lunch if you like, or maybe get together for drinks later in the afternoon."

"Today? Ah. Thanks for asking, but I just started work on a case and I'm completely tied up. Maybe another time." I hoped I didn't sound as insincere as I felt.

"Must be a busy time of year."

"Feast or famine," I said. "It's the nature of the beast." I was really trying my best not to be prickly with her. Even in the briefest of conversations, we often manage to butt heads on the subject of family relationships. She favors closer ties while I favor none.

"I suspect you'd refuse no matter what."

"Not at all." I let a silence fall.

We breathed in each other's ears until she said, "Well. Mother will be down again on Tuesday. I know she's anxious to talk to you. Are you still in the office on Capillo?"

"Actually, I'm not. I've rented a bungalow on Caballeria. I just moved in a couple of months ago."

"I'll tell her."

"Great. That's fine. Not a problem."

"I don't want you to take offense, but I hope you'll be polite."

"Gee, Tasha, I'll try to behave myself. It'll be a struggle, of course."

I could hear the smile in her voice. "You have to give me credit for persistence."

"Right. Duly noted. I have you down for that."

"You don't have to be sarcastic."

"That's my dry sense of humor."

"Why are you such a pain in the butt? Couldn't you try meeting me halfway?"

"I don't understand why you insist on pursuing me."

"For the same reason you insist on rebuffing me. Being pigheaded is a family trait."

"I'll give you that. It still pisses me off that Grand thinks she could treat my parents like shit and then waltz in years later and make it all evaporate."

"What's that got to do with us? Pam and Liza and I didn't do anything to your parents *or* Aunt Gin. Why should we be held accountable for Grand? Yes, she behaved badly. Yes, she's a bitch, but so what? Maybe your mother and Aunt Gin delivered tit-for-tat. At the time your parents died, we were only kids. We didn't know what was going on and neither did you. It seems ridiculous to nurse such bad feelings. To what end? We're family. You're stuck with us whether you like it or not."

"So far, I've done very well without 'family.' So why can't you drop the subject and get on with life?"

"Why can't you?" She paused, trying to gain control

of herself. "I'm sorry. Let's try again. I don't understand why every time I call we get into these *wrangles*."

"We don't get into wrangles *every* time."

"Yes, we do."

"No, we don't!"

"Name one conversation when we didn't come to blows."

"I can name three. You hired me for a job. We had lunch together that day and we got along fine. Since then, we've chatted on the phone two or three times without bickering."

"That's true," she said, reluctantly, "but I'm always aware of the anger percolating just under the surface."

"So what? Look, Tasha, maybe in time we'll find a way to settle our differences. Until then, we're not going to get anywhere arguing about whether or not we're arguing. I don't claim to be rational. I'm nuts. Why don't you let it go at that?"

"Okay. Enough said. We just wanted you to know we're still interested. We hoped yesterday's visit to the ranch would provide an opening."

"Ah, that. How'd you find out?"

"Arne Johanson called Pam. He said he saw someone who looked so much like your mother, it gave him goose bumps. I was surprised you'd even step a foot on the family ranch."

"I wouldn't have if I'd known."

"Oh, I'll bet."

"That aside, I do recognize what it costs you to keep in touch. I don't mean to be quite so belligerent."

"No apologies necessary."

"Uh, Tasha? That wasn't an apology."

"Skip it. I got that. My mistake," she said. "The point is, I'm a lawyer. I deal with belligerence on a daily basis."

"I thought you did estate planning. How could anyone get belligerent about that, it sounds so dull?"

"Shows what you know. Anytime you talk money, there's the potential for folks to get nasty. Nobody wants to talk about dying and nobody wants to give up control of the family purse. When it comes to the beneficiaries, there's usually an undercurrent of entitlement," she said, and then hesitated. "On a related topic, you probably heard there's talk of razing the Manse."

"The 'Manse'? Is that what it's called? I thought a manse had something to do with Presbyterians."

"It does. Our great-great-grandfather Straith was a Presbyterian minister. In those days, the Church didn't have the money to build a parsonage so he paid for it himself. I think he intended to deed it over to the Church when he died, but cooler heads prevailed. At any rate, the house is a mess. It'd be cheaper, at this point, to tear it down."

"I take it Grand doesn't want to spend the money to bring the old place back."

"Right. She's tried to enlist the support of a couple of historic-preservation groups, but no one's interested. The location's remote and the house itself is a hybrid. Turns out it's not even a good example of its kind."

"Why not leave it as it is? It's her land, isn't it?"

"It's hers for now, but she's ninety years old and she knows none of her heirs has the money or the passion for undertaking the job. Besides, she's got another house in town. She hardly needs two."

"That's right. I remember now. Liza told me most of the family live within blocks of her."

"We're a cozy bunch," she said, dryly. "Meanwhile, she's got all kinds of developers sniffing around. Mostly local vintners with an eye on the slopes. Turns out the soil's perfect. Plus, she gets a lot of coastal fog, which means a longer growing period."

"How much land does she have?"

"Twenty-three thousand acres."

There was a silence while I tried to compute what she'd just said. "You're kidding."

"I'm serious."

"I had no idea."

"Doesn't matter for now because she'll never sell. Great Granddaddy made her promise she'd keep it just as it is. The issue won't get sticky until she goes."

73

SUE GRAFTON

"Hasn't she put the estate in some kind of trust?"

"Nope. Most of those old trusts were established in the thirties—people in the east who'd had wealth in the family for generation after generation. Out here, all we had were ranchers, down-to-earth types much more likely to form limited family partnerships. At any rate, nothing's going to happen as long as she's alive," she said. "Meanwhile, if you change your mind about that drink just give me a call. You still have my number?"

"I better take it down again."

Once I hung up, I had to sit down and pat my chest. I'd actually ended up entertaining a few warm feelings about her. If I didn't watch myself, I was going to end up *liking* the woman and then where would I be?

On my way over to Stacey's, I popped by the office to make sure all was in order. I opened a window briefly to let in a little fresh air and checked my machine for messages. I took care of a few routine matters and then locked up again. I left my car where it was and walked the five blocks to his house, arriving in advance of Con Dolan. Stacey'd left his front door open and his screen unlatched. I knocked on the frame. "Hey, Stacey? It's me. Mind if I come in?"

He responded with a muffled "Make yourself at home."

I stepped inside and closed the screen door behind me. The floors were bare of carpeting, and the windows had no curtains or drapes, so my very presence seemed to set up an echo. I could smell coffee being brewed, but otherwise the place felt unoccupied. The room was stripped down, as though someone were moving in or out with the job only partially completed. The interior of the house couldn't have been more than eight hundred square feet, most of which was visible from where I stood. The space was divided into living room, kitchen, a bedroom, and a bath, though the door to that was closed. The floor was linoleum, printed in a pattern of interconnected squares and rectangles, blue on gray with a line of mauve woven in at intervals. The woodwork was stained dark; the walls covered with yellowing paper. In places I could see tears that revealed the wall coverings from three lifetimes down; a small floral print covered by a layer of pinstripes that, in turn, covered blowsy bouquets of faded cabbage roses.

Under the windows to my right, there was a mattress, neatly made up with blankets. A TV set rested on the bare floor nearby. To my left, there was an oak desk and a swivel chair. There was not much else. Six identical cardboard boxes had been stacked against the far wall. All were sealed with tape and each bore a hand-printed label that listed contents. A closet door stood open, and I could see that it had been emptied of everything except two hangers.

I tiptoed to the kitchen door and peered in at a small wooden table and four mismatched chairs. A Pyrex percolator sat on the stove, a low blue flame under it. The clear glass showed a brew as dark as bittersweet chocolate. The doors to all the kitchen cabinets stood open, and many shelves were bare. Stacey was obviously in the process of wrapping and packing glassware and dishes into assorted cardboard boxes. A heavy ream of plain newsprint lay on the counter, wide sheets that must have measured three feet by four. He was clearly dismantling his house, preparing his possessions for shipping to an unknown location.

"See anything you like, it's yours. I got no use for this stuff," Stacey said, suddenly behind me.

I turned. "How's your back?"

Stacey made a face. "So-so. I've been sucking down Tylenol and that helps."

"You've been busy. Are you moving?"

"Not exactly. Let's say, I may be going away and wanted to be prepared." Today his watch cap was navy blue. With his bleached brows and his long, weathered face, he looked like a farmer standing in a fallow field.

He wore soft, stone-washed jeans, a pale blue sweat-shirt, and tan sheepskin boots.

"You own this place?"

"Rent. I've been here for years."

"You're organized."

"I'm getting there. I don't want to leave a mess for someone else to clean up. Con's the one who'll come in." The unspoken phrase *after I'm dead* hung in the air between us.

"Con told me they were trying new drugs."

Stacey shrugged. "Clinical trials. An experimental cocktail designed for people with nothing left to lose. Percentages aren't good, but I figure, what the hell, it might help someone else. Some survive. That's what the bell curve's all about. I just think it's foolish to assume I'm one."

Con Dolan knocked at the front door and then let himself in, appearing half a second later in the kitchen doorway. He carried a brown paper grocery bag in one hand and a smaller white bag in the other. "What are you two up to?"

Stacey put his hands in his pockets and shrugged casually. "We're talking about running away together. She's arguing for San Francisco so we can cross the Golden Gate Bridge. I'm holding out for Vegas and topless dancing girls. We were just about to toss a coin when you came in." Stacey moved toward the stove, talking to me over his shoulder. "You want coffee? I'm out of milk."

"Black suits me fine."

"Con?"

Dolan held up a white sack spotted with grease. "Doughnuts."

"Good dang deal," Stacey said. "We'll retire to the parlor and figure out what's what."

Con took his two bags into the living room while Stacey produced a tower of nested Styrofoam cups and poured coffee in three. He returned to the counter and picked up the pile of newsprint and a marker pen. "Grab those paper towels, if you would. I'm out of napkins and the only kind I've seen are those economy packs. Four hundred at a crack. It's ridiculous. While you're at it, you can nab that sealing tape."

I picked up the roll of tape and my coffee cup, while Dolan returned to grab two of the kitchen chairs. Then he came back and picked up the two remaining cups of coffee, which he placed on the desktop in the living room. He reached into the larger of the two bags and hauled out three wide black three-hole binders. "I went over to the copy shop and made us each one. Murder books," he said, and passed them out. I flashed on my early days in elementary school. The only part of it I'd loved was buying school supplies: binder, lined paper, the pen-and-pencil sets.

Stacey taped two sheets of blank newsprint to the wall, then unfolded a map of California and taped it to the wall as well. There was something of the natural teacher in his manner. Both Dolan and I helped ourselves to doughnuts and then pulled up chairs. Stacey said, "I'll take the lead here unless someone objects."

Con said, "Quit being coy and get on with it."

"Okay then. Let's tally what we know. That'll show us where the gaps are. For now, you probably think we have a lot more gaps than we have facts in between, but let's see what we've got." He uncapped the black marker and wrote the name "Victim" at the top of one sheet and "Killer" at the top of the next. "We'll start with Jane Doe."

I pulled a fresh pack of index cards from my shoulder bag, tore off the cellophane, and started taking notes.

FIVE

He printed rapidly and neatly, condensing the information in the file as we talked our way through. "What do we have first?" He lifted his marker and looked at us. Like any good instructor, he was going to make sure we supplied most of the answers.

Dolan said, "She's white. Age somewhere between twelve and eighteen."

"Right. So that means a date of birth somewhere between 1951 and 1957." Stacey made the requisite note near the top of the paper.

"What about the estimated date of death?" I asked.

I thought Dolan would consult the autopsy report, but he seemed to know it by heart. "Dr. Weisenburgh says the body'd been there anywhere from one to five days, so that'd be sometime between July 29 and August 2. He's retired now, but I had him go back over this and he remembered the girl."

"All right." Stacey wrote the DOD on the paper

80

under Jane Doe's date of birth. He went on writing, this time dictating to himself. Rapidly, we went through the basics: height, weight, eyes, hair color.

Dolan said, "Report says blond, though it was probably a dye job. There was some suggestion of dark roots."

I said, "She had buckteeth and lots of fillings, but no orthodontic work."

Stacey's mouth pulled down. "Maybe we should stop and have a chat about that."

Dolan shook his head. "They didn't do braces much when I was growing up. My family was big—thirteen kids—and we all had crooked teeth. Look here. Bottoms buckled up, but these top guys are good." He turned to me. "You have braces as a kid?"

"Nope."

"Nor did I," Stacey said. "Well. I'm glad we got that out of the way. So what's that tell us, the buckteeth?"

"Well, I'd say most kids with a severe overbite have already seen an orthodontist by the time they're ten," Dolan said. "My niece has three kids, so I know they start early—sometimes do the work in two or three stages. If this gal was going to have braces, she should've been in 'em by the time she died."

"Maybe her family didn't have the money," I suggested.

"That could be. Anything else?"

SUE GRAFTON

"Cavities like that, you're talking poor diet, too. Candy. Soda pop. Junk food," Dolan said, with a quick look at me. And then to Stacey, "Not to sound like a snoot, but kids from your basic middle- to upper-class families usually don't have rotten teeth like that."

I said, "Think about the toothaches."

Stacey said, "She did get 'em fixed. Matter of fact, the forensic odontist thinks all the fillings went in about the same time, probably in the year or two before she died."

I said, "That must have cost a bundle."

"Think of all the novocaine shots," Dolan said. "You'd have to sit there for hours with that drill screaming in your head."

"Knock it off. You're making my palms sweat. I'm phobic about dentists in case you haven't heard. Look at this," I said, showing him my palms.

Stacey frowned. "They ever circulate a chart of her amalgam fillings?"

Dolan said, "Not that I know. I've got a copy in here. Might come in handy if we think we got a match. We do have the maxilla and mandible."

I looked over at him. "Her jaws? After eighteen years?"

"We have all ten fingers, too."

Stacey made a note on the paper. "Let's see if we can

82

get the coroner's office to run another set of prints. Maybe we'll get a hit through NCIC."

"I can't believe she'll show up, given her age at the time of death," Dolan said.

"Unless she got arrested for shoplifting or prostitution," I said, ever the optimist.

"Problem is, if she got arrested as a juvenile, her records would be sealed and probably purged by now," he said.

I raised a hand. "You were talking about why she was never recognized; suppose she was from out of state, some place back East? I get the impression the news story didn't get nationwide attention."

"Story probably didn't rate a mention beyond the county line," Dolan said.

"Let's move on to her clothes. Any ideas there?" Stacey asked.

I said, "I thought it was interesting her pants were homemade. If you add that to the issue of poor dental hygiene, it sounds like low income."

Stacey said, "Not necessarily. If her mom made her the clothes, it'd suggest a certain level of caring and concern."

"Well, yeah. There is that. Those flowered pants were distinct. Dark blue daisies with a red dot on a white background. Someone might remember the fabric."

Dolan said, "I'd like to go back and look at that statement the minimart clerk made about the hippie girl who came in. What's the woman's name, Roxanne Faught? We ought to track her down again and see if she has anything to add."

Stacey said, "I talked to her twice, but you're welcome to try. Is that store still open?"

"As far as I know. It was closed for a while, so it might have changed hands. You want me to take a drive up there?" Dolan asked.

"Let me do that. I can go this afternoon," I said.

"Good. Meanwhile, what else? What about sizes?"

We spent several minutes working through those details. This time Dolan flipped back through the pages, looking for the list of clothing booked into property. "Here we go. Shoe size—7½. Panty size—medium. Bra size was 38A."

I said, "That means she's got a fairly large torso, but a small cup size. Barrel-chested. Girls like that tend to look top-heavy, even if they're thin."

Dolan turned a page. "Says here her ears were pierced. 'Through the left earlobe is a gold-colored wire of a "horseshoe" configuration. Through the right earlobe a gold-colored wire with a bent clip in its lower end.' People might remember that, too."

Stacey added that to the list and then said, "Is that it?"

I raised my hand. "She wore nail polish. Silver."

"Got it. Anything else?"

"Not that I remember."

Dolan got to his feet. "In that case, if you'll excuse me. I gotta have me a smoke."

At lunchtime, I volunteered to make a trip to the nearest market and pick up the makings for sandwiches, but they'd apparently gotten wind of my peanut-butter-and-pickle fetish and voted to go out for Chinese. We took Con's car and made the crosstown trip to the Great Wall, with its pagoda facade and a gilded statue of the Buddha sitting over the front door. In the parking lot, I waited while Stacey and Con tucked their guns in the trunk of Con's car. The three of us went in.

The interior walls were painted the requisite Chinese red with red Naugahyde banquettes and round white paper lanterns strung like moons around the perimeter. Stacey didn't have much appetite, but Con seemed more than willing to make up for it. I was starving as usual. We ordered pot stickers and spring rolls, which we dunked in that pale Chinese mustard that cleans out your sinuses. We moved on to Moo Shu Pork, Kung Pao Chicken, and Beef with Orange Peel along with a dome of white rice. Con and I drank beer. Stacey had iced tea.

While we ate, the guys speculated about the killer, a matter in which I deferred to them: I have no formal training in homicide investigation, though I've encountered a few bodies in the course of my career. Given the nature of the murder, they theorized that the perpetrator was most likely male, in part because women tend to be repelled by close-contact blood-and-gore killings. In addition, the multiple stab wounds suggested a brutality more commonly associated with men.

"Hey, these days, women can be brutes," Con said.

"Yeah, but I can't see a woman hefting that body into the car trunk and hauling it out again. A hundred twenty-five pounds is a lot of dead weight."

"As it were," Dolan said. "You think this was planned?"

"If it was, you'd think he'd've worked out a plan for disposing of the body. This guy was in a hurry, at least enough of one that he didn't stop to dig a grave." He was making notes on a napkin and the pen made occasional rips in the paper while the ink tended to spread.

Con opened his packet of chopsticks and pried the two wooden sections apart, rubbing one on the other to smooth away any tiny wooden hairs. He doused both his chicken and his beef with enough soy sauce to form a shallow brown lake in which his rice grains swam like minnows. "I'm surprised he didn't pick a dump site more remote."

"That stretch of road looks isolated if you don't know any better. No houses in sight. He probably didn't have a clue about the quarry traffic running up and back."

"I'm with you on that. Forensics says the wire he used to bind her wrists was torn off something else so he must have grabbed whatever came to hand. Guy was making shit up as he went along." I watched as Dolan formed a pincer with his chopsticks and tried picking up a chunk of chicken, which he couldn't get as far as his mouth.

"Question is, did he target that girl in particular, or was he trolling for a victim and it was just her bad luck?"

Con said, "I think it was a fishing expedition. He might've tried five or six gals and finally one said yes." He shifted to a scooping technique, using his chopsticks like a little shelf onto which he pushed the bite of chicken. He got the hunk as far as his lower lip. Nope. I saw him shake his head. "I don't think we're dealing serial. This feels like a one-off." He tried again, this time lunging, his lips extended like an anteater's as he lifted his chopsticks. He captured a snippet of orange peel before the rest fell back onto his plate.

I grabbed a fork from the next table and handed it to him.

Stacey made a doodle on the napkin, which by now was completely tattered. "Hang on. Let's back up a second. Agewise, it seems to me like she's bound to be closer to the high end—sixteen, seventeen, eighteen, and up, instead of the twelve, thirteen end of the spread. Young girl like that, somebody's going to report she's gone, regardless of whether she leaves voluntarily or stomps out in a huff. You're a parent, you might shrug and not think too much about it, but when she doesn't come home, you're going to worry. You call around and find out her friends haven't seen her either and you're going to call the cops. If she's twenty and disappears, it might not raise any flags at all."

"Right. She could've had a history of taking off. This might have been one more in a long string of disappearances."

Dolan pushed his plate aside. "As long as we're making wild-ass guesses, here's another one. I don't think she's local. Killer didn't get into any facial mutilation so he must not've been worried someone would know who she was. He didn't know how long she'd be lying there. Suppose she's found the same day and they run a description of her in the paper? She's local, somebody's going to add two plus two and figure it out fast."

I said, "What if she's from another country altogether? England or Spain. There are probably plenty of places where dental care didn't rank that high in those days. It might also explain why she wasn't reported missing."

Dolan said, "A missing-persons report might've gone through Interpol and never reached us. It's worth checking. Maybe they have something on file."

"There's a note in there somewhere—woman claims she saw a hitchhiker who fit the girl's description outside of Colgate. This was a couple of hours before the clerk in the Gull Cove minimart saw that hippie girl on August 1. Could be she was working her way up the coast," Stacey said.

Dolan reached for his black binder with its incident reports already marked with torn scraps of paper. He turned a few pages and checked the marginal notes he'd written in a surprisingly wee hand. "You're thinking about Cloris Bargo. She says July 29, four-thirty in the afternoon, she saw a young white female, five foot two to five foot three, age sixteen to seventeen, navy blouse, flowered slacks, long blondish hair, leaning against the base of the Fair Isle overpass. Bargo saw a vehicle stop and pick her up, heading north on the 101."

"That's worth another look. If Jane Doe was thumbing rides, we might backtrack and see if we can figure out her point of origin, maybe rough out a timeline."

Stacey reached for his map of California and unfolded it, flapping and spreading the unwieldy sheet across the tabletop. "If she came from the south, she'd have traveled the 405 as far as the 101," he said. "The main arteries from Arizona into California are Highways 15 from Las Vegas, Nevada, the 40 from Kingman, Arizona, the 10 from Phoenix, and 8 coming up from Yuma. Starting from anywhere else, she'd have taken a different route."

Dolan pushed his plate away. "You're never going to pin that one down. She could have come from anywhere. On the other hand, you talk about July 29. That's the same day Frankie Miracle killed his girlfriend and hit the road. If Jane Doe was thumbing rides, he could've picked her up."

We left the subject at that point and moved on to other things.

After lunch, Con dropped me at the office, where I caught up with the notes on my index cards and then spent a few minutes doing digital research, which is to say, walking my fingers through the telephone book. My job was to verify reports about the young hippie girl, hitching rides in the period between July 29 and August 1. Con was going to hit the phones and track down the whereabouts of Frankie Miracle's former cellmates, while Stacey searched out his legal skirmishes in previous years. We agreed to meet that night at CC's to share what we'd learned.

I had a prior address for Roxanne Faught, but nothing for Cloris Bargo. As it turned out, luck was on my side and starting with the obvious paid off for once. A check of the white pages revealed one Bargo, not Cloris, but a sister who didn't even bother to quiz my purposes before she gave me the current phone number and the Colgate address. Shame on her. I could have been a stalker or a bill collector.

I checked my city map and drew a bead on my destination—a tract of middle-class homes just beyond the Fair Isle off-ramp, where Cloris Bargo had seen the girl. I locked the office, fired up the VW, and took Capillo Avenue as far as the 101.

The day was mild and hazy, the landscape muted, as though washed with skim milk. I rolled down my car windows and let the speed-generated wind blow my hair to a fare-thee-well. Traffic was light and the trip to Colgate took less than six minutes.

I took the off-ramp at Fair Isle and headed toward the mountains, counting the requisite number of streets before I turned left on York. The house I was looking for was halfway down on the left side of the street. This was a neighborhood of "starter" homes, but most had undergone major renovation since the sixties when the area had been developed. Garages had become family rooms; porches had been enclosed; second stories had been added; and the storage sheds in the rear had been enlarged and attached. The lawns were well established and the trees had matured to the point where the sidewalks buckled in places where the roots were breaking through. The children, mere toddlers when their parents had moved in, were grown and gone now, coming back to the neighborhood with children of their own.

I pulled up in front of a two-story white stucco house with a frame addition on the left and an elaborate new entrance affixed to the front that involved arches, a rustic wooden gate, climbing roses, and a profusion of hollyhocks, hydrangeas, and phlox. I let myself through the gate and climbed the porch steps. The front door stood open and the screen was on the latch. From the depths, I could smell something simmering; fruit and sugar. The radio in the kitchen was tuned to a call-in show, and I could hear the host berating someone in argumentative tones. I placed a hand on the screen, shading my eyes so I could see the interior. The front door was lined up exactly with the back door so my view extended all the way to the rear fence that separated two yards. I called, "Hullo?"

A woman hollered, "I'm out here! Come around back!"

I left the porch and trotted along the walkway that skirted the house on the right. As I passed the kitchen window, I glanced up and saw her standing at the open window. She must have been near the sink because she leaned forward and turned off the tap as she peered down at me. Through the screen, she looked thirty-five, a guess I upgraded by ten years once I saw her up close.

I paused. "Hi. Are you Cloris Bargo?"

"Was before I got married. Can I help you with something?" She turned on the water again and her gaze dropped to whatever dish or utensil she was scrubbing.

"I need some information. I shouldn't take more than five or ten minutes of your time." It was weird having a conversation with someone whose face was two feet higher. I could nearly see up her nose.

"I hope you're not selling anything door-to-door."

"Not at all. My name's Kinsey Millhone. I'm a private detective. Your name came up in connection with a case I'm working for the Sheriff's Department."

She focused on me fully, her gaze sharpening. "That's a first. I never heard of the Sheriff's Department hiring outside help."

"This guy's a retired north county detective reactivating an old murder case—that young girl stabbed to death back in 1969."

She put something in the dish rack, dried her hands on a towel, and then reached for the radio and turned it off. When she made no other comment, I said. "Mind if I come in?"

She didn't extend an invitation, but she made a gesture that I interpreted as consent. I continued down the walkway to the rear of the house, where the concrete drive widened, forming a parking pad. On the right, a clothesline had been strung between a wooden pole and a bolt secured to the side of the garage. White sheets flapped lazily in the breeze. The backyard was nicely landscaped; the flower beds bordered with prefabricated foot-high sections of white picket fence. Someone had recently put in flats of pansies and petunias, now drooping from the transplant process. A sprinkler head attached to a hose sent a fan of water back and forth across the grass. The outdoor furniture had seen better days. The hollow aluminum frames were pitted in places, and the woven green-and-white nylon webbing was faded and frayed. In the far corner, I could see a large expanse of tilled ground with several young tomato plants, a row of newly planted peppers, and five empty bean poles, like teepees, waiting for the emerging tendrils to take hold. I saw no sign of kids or pets.

I climbed six steps to the porch. She was waiting at the back door, holding it open for me. She stepped back and I entered. Her attitude had shifted in the brief time it'd taken me to circle the house. The set of her jaw now seemed stubborn or tense. There was something in her manner that made me think I'd best provide concrete proof of my identity. I handed her a business card.

She took it and placed it on the counter without reading it. She was trim and petite, in tan Bermuda shorts, a white T-shirt, no makeup, bare feet. Her dark hair was chin length and anchored behind her ears with bobby pins.

"Nice flowers," I said.

"My husband takes care of those. The vegetables are mine."

The heat in the kitchen felt like South Florida in June—not yet oppressive, but a temperature that made you think seriously about leaving the state. Two big stainless steel pressure cookers fitted with racks sat on burners over matching low blue flames. The lids were lined up on the counter nearby, their little pressure cooker caps resting on the windowsill. Freshly sterilized lids, seals, ladles, and tongs were laid out on white sackcloth towels like surgical instruments. A third kettle contained a dark red liquid, as viscous as glue. I picked up the rich, hot perfume of crushed strawberries. I counted twelve pint-capacity Mason jars lined up on the kitchen table in the middle of the room. "Sorry to interrupt."

"That's all right." She returned to the sink. Everything about her smacked of Midwestern farm values—

the canning, the sheets on the line, the truck garden, the unadorned face.

"You remember the case?"

"Vaguely."

I noticed she didn't ask to have her memory refreshed, so I volunteered the help. "A sheriff's deputy took a report from you. According to his notes, you spotted a girl hitchhiking near the Fair Isle off-ramp July 29, 1969."

"You mentioned the date before."

I ignored the minor reprimand. "You indicated seeing a vehicle stop and pick her up. Turns out she fit the description of the murder victim found in Lompoc a couple of days later."

Cloris Bargo's expression was modified by the appearance of two swatches of pink, like blusher applied by a department store cosmetologist. "You want iced tea? I can fix you some. It's already made."

"That'd be great."

She opened one of the kitchen cabinets and took down a burnished blue aluminum tumbler, which she filled with ice cubes. She poured the tea from a fat glass pitcher she kept in the refrigerator. I knew she was stalling, but I wanted to give her room to declare herself. Something was going on, but I wasn't sure what. She handed me the glass.

I murmured, "Thanks," and took a big healthy swallow before I realized it was heavily presweetened. I could feel my lips purse. This was equivalent to that noxious syrup you have to drink before blood draws designed to diagnose conditions you hope you don't have.

She leaned against the counter. "I made it up."

I set the tumbler aside. "Which part?"

"All of it. I never saw the girl."

"No hitchhiker at all?"

She shook her head. "I'd met the deputy—the one who wrote up the report. I was new in California. My family hadn't been here six months. I hardly knew a soul. There'd been a prowler in our neighborhood, and this deputy was sent out to talk to us. He'd gone house to house, asking if anyone had seen anything strange or unusual. I was off work. I'd just had an emergency appendectomy and I was still recovering. Otherwise, I wouldn't have been home. We ended up having a long talk. I thought he was cute." She stopped.

"Take your time," I said.

"A week later, the paper mentioned his name in reference to the murder investigation. I'd never told a lie in my life, but I picked up the phone and called the Sheriff's Department and asked for him. Once he got on the line, I said the first thing that came to mind."

"Your claim that you'd seen a girl whose description matched the victim's was completely false," I said, hoping I'd misunderstood.

"I just said that. A lot of people must have called in with information that didn't pan out. All I wanted was a chance to talk to him again."

I was silent for a moment, thinking, *Shit, shit, shit.* "Did it work?"

She shrugged. "I married him."

"Well, that part's good, at any rate."

Her eyes strayed to the window. I saw a car pass along the driveway, cruising toward the rear. I looked back at her.

She lowered her voice. "Do me a favor."

"Sure."

"Don't mention this to my husband. I never told him the truth."

"He doesn't *know*?"

She shook her head.

"Would it really matter to him after eighteen years?"

I heard the car door slam shut and her husband's hard-soled shoes *tap-tapping* across the pavement between the garage and the back porch. There was a pause while he checked his pansies and petunias. In my opinion, they needed watering. He apparently agreed. I heard the shriek and squawk of the faucet handle when he turned off the water, moved the sprinkler, and turned the water on again. He continued toward the back door while she went on rapidly. "Every time someone asks how we met he tells them the story of how I took the time to call in the report. He admired I was such a conscientious citizen. Says it's one of my best traits. He claims he fell in love with me on the phone. Then he said it seemed like fate since he'd seen me in person just the week before. He thinks I'm different. A cut above, he says."

"Tricky."

"You bet."

The back door opened. Her husband came in, pausing to wipe his feet on the mat before he entered. Nice-looking guy. He was in his fifties with steel gray hair and blue eyes, his lineage probably Dutch or Scandinavian. He was tall and lean in a well-knit frame, without an ounce of fat. He wore street clothes—tan dress pants, a dark blue dress shirt, and a tie with a pattern of blue and tan. He had his badge on his belt. I wondered what his job was after twenty years with the SO. He'd already removed his gun and his holster, which he'd probably locked in the trunk of his car. "What's tricky?"

"Getting the pectin just right," she said without batting an eye. Having lied to him once, she was apparently an old hand at this.

"I'm Kinsey."

"Joe Mandel. Don't let her fool you. She makes the best strawberry preserves you ever ate."

"I'll bet."

His face was creased, hair thinning as age began to take its toll. He looked athletic, and I assumed he was fast on his feet, still capable of tangling with the bad guys when circumstances required it. "Looks like a science lab in here. You two cooking up trouble?"

"More or less," I said.

He exhibited no particular curiosity about who I was or what I was doing in the kitchen with his wife. He leaned over, bussed her on the cheek, and patted her arm. "I'm going to change and do some yard work. We'll go to Sizzler tonight, get you out of this heat. You need help?"

"I'm fine, sweetie. Thanks."

"Nice meeting you," he said, with a quick smile at me.

I smiled and raised a hand in response. Cloris watched him depart, her expression fading from warmth to something more subdued.

"He seems nice."

"He *is* nice. That's why I married him. He's decent. It would never occur to him to lie to me."

"Why don't you tell him, then?"

"Why don't you mind your own business? I can handle this myself."

SIX

The drive from Santa Teresa to Lompoc takes an hour by car, but I stopped at Gull Cove, which marks the halfway point. In my heart of hearts, I knew why I'd volunteered for this part of the job. Aside from the fact I needed time alone, I was flirting with the notion of going back to Grand's old house. Like a newly reformed drunk, I'd sworn off with conviction just the day before and now found myself thinking maybe one more quick visit wouldn't do any harm.

I reached the Gull Cove minimart at 2:00 P.M. The business had been housed in an enormous shambling structure covered with cedar shingles, an appealing mix of modern and traditional, with a few Cape Cod elements thrown in for good measure. The building had also housed a twenty-four-hour diner, a curio shop, and a tiny two-station beauty salon. Even at a distance, it was clear the entire place had been closed down. I could see windows boarded over, and the asphalt parking lot was cracked and faded to a chalky gray. The surround-ing grass was a dull brown with assorted weeds and wildflowers growing to knee height. On the hillside behind the building, a lone tree had died and stood now like a scarecrow, its twisted branches raised toward the sky as though to beckon birds. The population of Gull Cove was pegged at 100, but I couldn't for the life of me spot so much as one.

I parked my car near the front steps and got out. The wide wooden deck creaked under my feet. A notice posted on the main door announced that the complex was closed for renovations. Someone had drawn a Happy Face in pencil with the mouth turned down. Someone else had written "WHO CARES?" in ballpoint pen. A third party, perhaps human, had taken a big dump near the padlocked door. I peered through the minimart's front window, which was dusty and streaked where winter rains had hammered at the plate glass. The interior was stripped; not one fixture, counter, or display case remained. It looked like the renovations would be going on for some time.

I turned and stared at the road. The Gull Cove complex was the only commercial structure for miles, a hundred feet from the highway and a natural stopping-off point for travelers who needed to take a break. It was easy to see why someone thumbing a ride might get dropped off in passing. Perhaps after doughnuts and coffee, our Jane Doe found a lift as far as Lompoc, which had turned out to be the end of the line for her.

I went back to the car and checked my notes, looking for Roxanne Faught's last known address: Q Street in Lompoc, thirty minutes to the north. Seemed like a long way for her to travel for a clerking job. I fired up the engine and hit the road again, heading north, the Pacific Ocean on my left. Today the swells were low and without chop, the color a darker reflection of the blue sky above. Idly, I thought about Grand's house. It was possible I'd catch a glimpse of the place if I happened to pass that way. Surely, it was visible from the highway if you knew where to look. I turned on the car radio to distract myself.

I reached the outskirts of Lompoc. The town is flat and compact, a one-story panorama of wide streets and small houses. A constant wind blows off the ocean, funneled by the rolling hills that cradle the town. Three miles to the north is Vandenberg Village and beyond that, Vandenberg Air Force Base. The entire valley is given over to horse farms and cattle ranches, much of the agricultural land planted to fields of commercial flowers, many of them grown for seeds. Though I had no idea what I was looking at, I could see stretches of bright yellow and vibrant pink. Beyond them were acres of what appeared to be baby's breath. Many farms were being sold to real estate developers; the sweet peas, poppies, and larkspurs being crowded out by crops of three-bedroom houses in neatly planted rows.

The town itself boasts the Lompoc Municipal Pool and a substantial civic center along with all the standard businesses: the Viva Thrift Shop, banks, attorneys' offices, automotive and plumbing supplies, retail stores and gas stations, coffee shops, pharmacies, and medical complexes. Lompoc is a base town with neighborhoods of temporary residents whose military careers will always move them from place to place like pieces on a game board. It was hard to see what people did for amusement. There wasn't a bowling alley, a concert hall, or a movie house in sight. Maybe local culture consisted of everyone renting videotapes of last year's money-losing movies.

Q Street wasn't hard to find, coming as it did between P and R. The address was on the left side of the street, and I slowed as I approached. The house, resting on cinderblocks, was an oblong wooden box covered with sheets of asphalt siding imprinted to look like dark red brick. A porch, stretched across the front, sagged in the middle. Two whitewashed tires served as makeshift planters from which pink geraniums spilled. An old white claw-foot tub had been upended and half-buried in the yard. A blue-robed plaster Madonna stood in the shelter of the porcelain rim. I pulled in at the curb and got out.

An old man in overalls was in the front yard bathing a dog. The man looked ninety, if a day, and was still staunchly constructed. He'd strung a garden hose through the half-opened kitchen window, and I assumed the other end was attached to the faucet. As I crossed the grass, he paused in his work, releasing the hose nozzle, shutting off the stream of water. He had a square, jowly face, a lumpy nose, and a straight, nearly lipless mouth. His hair was slicked back, plastered down with pomade, and even then, so thin I could see through to his scalp. His skin was mottled brown from sun damage, interspersed with patches of red. His blue eyes were vivid dots under pale, sparse brows. The air smelled like wet dog hair and a pungent flea soap. A medium-sized pooch of no determinate breed stood knee-deep in a galvanized tub. He looked skinny and frail with his coat plastered to his frame, thinned to transparency. Dead fleas, like pepper, seasoned the flesh underneath. The dog trembled, whining, and wouldn't quite meet my eyes. I kept my gaze averted so as not to embarrass him.

The old man said, "Help you?" His voice was surprisingly high-pitched for a man his size.

"I hope so. I'm looking for Roxanne Faught and this is the only address I have. Any idea where she is?"

"Ought to. I'm her dad," he said. "And who might you be?"

I showed him my card.

He squinted and then shook his head. "What's that say? Sorry, but I don't have my specs on me."

"I'm a private investigator from Santa Teresa."

"What do you want with Roxanne?"

"I need information on an old case. Apparently, a girl came into the Gull Cove minimart when Roxanne was working there in 1969. I'd like to ask her some questions about the incident."

He squeezed the hose nozzle and the spray of water showered like a light rain over the dog's back and haunches. "That the one got killed?"

"Yes, sir."

"Well. I guess that's all right then. I know a sheriff's deputy came by a couple times asking the very same thing."

"You're talking about Stacey Oliphant, the guy I'm working with. Is your daughter still in the area?"

"Close enough. How about this. I'll go give a call and see if she's willing to talk to you. Otherwise, there's no point."

"That'd be great."

He laid the hose aside, lifted the dog from the tub, and set him on the grass. The dog gave one of those profound total-body shakes, flinging water in all directions until his coat stood out in spikes. The old man picked up a heavy towel and gave the dog a vigorous rub, then swaddled him in the towel, and handed him to me. "This's Ralph."

Since I was hoping to curry favor, I took the dog without protest. I could feel warm doggie bathwater seeping from the towel through my shirt front. Ralph lay in my arms, a damp bundle of bones, as trusting as a baby, his eyes pinned on mine. His tongue flopped out the side of his mouth, and I could swear he smiled. I jiggled him a bit, which he seemed to enjoy. I really don't understand how animals persuade human beings to behave like this.

The old man reappeared, closing the door carefully. He made his way down the steps. He wasn't quick on his feet, but he seemed to get the job done. He had a scrap of paper in his hand. "She's home right now and said it's okay to give you this."

I handed the dog over and took the paper, glancing down at the phone number and address. "Thanks."

"It's a little house off the highway. You go down here about ten blocks until you hit North Street and then turn right. Once you get to Riverside you turn right again. She's about five blocks down."

Roxanne Faught had turned her front porch into an outdoor room, with pale sisal carpet, a dark green painted porch swing, two white wicker rockers, occasional tables, and a double-sided magazine rack, one half stuffed with issues of *People* and the other with copies of *Better Homes and Gardens*. Five terra-cotta pots of bright orange marigolds lined the edge of the porch. When I arrived, she was sitting on the swing with a bottle of beer and a freshly lit cigarette. The house itself was white frame and completely nondescript. There were windows and doors in all the proper places, but nothing that made the house distinct. Roxanne was in her sixties and attractive, though the creases in her face were exaggerated by all the makeup she wore. Her hair was, in the main, a coppery blond, showing gray at the roots where four inches of new growth formed a wide band. Her brows were plucked to thin arches and her dark eyes were lined in black. The smoking had darkened her teeth, but they were otherwise straight and uniform, suggesting caps. She wore a long-sleeve navy T-shirt with the sleeves pushed up, jeans, and tennis shoes without socks. She took a sip of beer and pointed at me with the bottle. "You have to be the one Pop just called about. Come on up and have a seat."

"Kinsey Millhone. I appreciate your seeing me on such short notice. I wasn't sure where you were living so I started with him."

"I've been in town all my life. I guess I don't have much sense of adventure. My great-aunt died and left me just enough money to get the house paid off. I can survive without working if I watch my step." She paused and picked up a strand of two-toned hair, which she studied critically. "You can see I quit going to the beauty shop. Cheaper to color it myself, when I get around to it. I can't give these up," she said, gesturing with her cigarette. "I smoked so long I'm probably doomed, anyway. Might as well enjoy." She coughed once, loosening something deep in her chest. "What can I help you with? Pop says you're here about that girl got killed, what was it, twenty years ago?"

"Just about. Eighteen in August."

"You know what's interesting about her? She's got a grip on folks. Here she is dead all that time and she still has people out there wondering who she is and how to get her back where she belongs."

"And who killed her," I added.

"Yeah, well good luck on that. You got your work cut out. Sit, sit, sit. Can I get you a beer?"

"I'm doing fine right now, thanks." I settled on one of the white wicker rockers, which creaked under my weight. "I can see where you'd want to spend the day out here, watching traffic go by. Nice."

"That's the thing about retirement. People keep asking me, don't you miss work? Well, no way, José. I could go the rest of my life and never leave this porch.

I'm so busy as it is I can't figure out how I ever had time for a job. Between housework and errands, there's half the day gone right there."

"What else do you do?"

"Read. I work in the yard, play bridge with some gals I've known for years. How about you? You like the work you do?"

"I'm not that crazy about being stuck indoors, but the field work's fun."

"So now. What can I tell you that you don't already know?"

"One thing I was curious about. Gull Cove is thirty miles south. Seems like a long way to drive for work you could have found in town."

Roxanne coughed again, clearing her throat. As with other smokers I've known, her coughing was habitual and didn't seem to warrant a remark. "That's easy. I was diddling the owner. That's how I got hired." She laughed. "Seemed like a good idea at the time. He moved on to someone else and I got fired. Big surprise. My fault entirely. It's like Pop used to say, 'Don't shit in your own Post Toasties, Roxanne.'"

"Live and learn."

"You got that right. Anyway, I was working seven to three. This was summer and hotter than blue blazes, even with the breeze coming in off the ocean. You know the place at all?"

"Actually, I stopped off there on the drive up."

"Then you've seen for yourself. Not a shade tree in sight; building stuck there on the side of the hill. By August the sun's hot enough to boil water. Anyway, this was a Friday morning. I remember because I got paid once a week and I had bills up to here. So I'm working away—it's just me by my lonesome. Business was never heavy and I could handle it myself. This gal comes in. She's checking the aisles, walking up and down like she has some shopping to do. Then I see her move to the rear where we had a coffee machine and a self-serve case of deli sandwiches and sweets. Customers would serve themselves, then come to the register to pay once they had everything they needed. We kept tables and chairs outside on the deck and most of 'em would take their purchases out there and watch the ocean while they ate. You had to look over the four lanes of traffic whizzing by on the road, but you could see it all the same. Different every day. I never got tired of the sight myself. Any rate, she helped herself to a cup of coffee and a doughnut and had both of them scarfed down by the time she got to the front. She'd tossed the cup somewhere in back, maybe thinking I wouldn't notice she'd just had her fill. Next thing I know, she's halfway out the door. I rang up the charges and then I caught up with her. That's when she told me she was broke. Well, hell, I thought. I've been broke in my day and I don't begrudge anyone some brew and a bite to eat, so I told her I'd take care of it. She said, 'Thanks. I mean that.' Those were her exact words. 'Thanks. I mean that.' And off she went. Couldn't have taken more than four minutes all told, and I'm talking from the time she came in."

"I'm surprised you remembered her at all."

"Somebody tries to run out without paying? You better believe I remembered. Especially when she turned up dead." She paused to stub out one cigarette and light another. "Pardon my manners. I hope this doesn't bother you. Do you smoke?"

"No, but we're outside and I'm upwind. What else do you recall? Anything in particular?" I wondered how anyone could remember so brief an encounter after so much time had passed.

"Like what? Ask me questions. It's easier that way."

"How old would you say?"

"Twenties."

"Not in her teens?"

"Could have been. She was a good-sized girl."

"You mean fat?"

"I wouldn't say *fat*, but she was big. Big wrist bones, big feet. Had what Pop would call good child-bearing hips."

"You remember her clothes?"

"Oh lord, I think I gave that sheriff's detective all this same information at the time. Why don't you ask him?"

"I thought I'd go back over and see if anything new comes to light," I said.

"Pants and a blousy shirt—you know, big sleeves."

"Belt?"

She feigned irritation, giving me a mock cross look. "You get right down to the nitty-gritty, don't you? Scars, moles, other identifying marks? What do you want? I only saw the girl up close once."

"Sorry. I take it she wasn't wearing a belt."

"Don't think so."

I could feel her withdraw and knew I needed to pull her back. "What about her shoes?"

"I'd say boots if I had to guess."

"It's not multiple choice. Just whatever comes to mind. Take the pants. Were they patterned or plain?"

She brightened. "Now, that I do know. It's what I told the cops back then. Daisies."

"You remember the color?"

She shrugged. "Daisy-colored. You know, yellow and white. Probably some green in there someplace. Is that important?"

"I'm just groping around. What about the shirt?"

"Plain. I hope you don't intend to ask me every little thing."

113

I smiled. "Really, I don't. Was the shirt dark or light?"

"Dark blue voile."

"Which is what? Sorry, but I don't know the term."

"I'm not sure myself, but I know that's right because I went back and looked it up."

"You kept notes?"

"I kept the clipping from the paper. It's in the other room."

I could hear a dim alarm bell ring. What I was getting was rehearsed. "Did you get the impression she was local or on the road?"

"Traveling, definitely. I saw her hitchhiking earlier when I was coming in to work. I'm sure she hadn't eaten in a while. She wolfed her food right down."

"She could have been stoned," I said.

"Oh. I hadn't thought about that. She probably was, come to think of it. That might explain where her money went. She spent it all on dope."

"Just a possibility. I wonder how far she managed to travel without funds. Or do you think she had the money and just didn't choose to spend it on food?"

"Hard to say. If I hadn't volunteered to pay, she'd have tennis-shoed the place so I'd've been stuck either way. Bet she panhandled, too. Your age, you probably don't remember those days."

114

"Actually, I do. I was in my late teens."

"Point is, all those hippies hung out, cadging any change you had. Smoking these big fat joints. I forget now what they called 'em. Thumbs, I think. Me, I wasn't into that. Well, maybe a little grass, but never any LSD."

I murmured a response and then said, "Was she wearing jewelry?"

"Nope. Don't think so."

"No watch or bracelet? Maybe earrings?"

"Oh. I remember now. No earrings. Her left earlobe was torn through. Like somebody'd grabbed a hoop and ripped it right off."

"Was the injury recent?"

"Nope. It was all healed up, but it was definitely split."

"What about her fingernails?"

"Bitten to the quick. Nearly made me sick. She wasn't all that clean, and she'd picked at her cuticles until they bled. You ever see that? Nails so short the fingertips look all puffy. It's enough to make you lose your lunch."

"And you're sure you'd never seen her around town before?"

"Not before and not since."

"How'd you happen to get in touch with the Sheriff's Department?"

"I didn't 'happen' to do anything. I read about the

body in the paper and remembered she'd been in. Like I said before, the incident stuck in my mind because she tried to pull a fast one."

"What made you so sure it was the same girl?"

"Who else could it've been?"

"Ah. Well, this has been a big help. I appreciate your time." I reached out to shake her hand.

She complied reluctantly. "Don't you believe me? I notice you didn't take notes."

"I got it all up here," I said, tapping my head.

Once back in my car, I checked my road map. Roxanne was still on the porch looking out at me, probably wondering at the delay. Maybe she thought I was finally taking notes, recording the bullshit recollections she'd constructed over the years. I didn't think she'd lied. She'd simply told her story too often. By now, she was either vamping like crazy or remembering someone else. I folded the map in half, trying to gauge how far I might be from the ranch. If I continued south on Riverside and made a dogleg right, I'd hit the road that angled south and east, connecting with Highway 101 just about at Gull Cove. According to the map, the road was called Calle LeGrand, presumably named after my great-grandfather LeGrand, whose twenty-three thousand acres filled a sizeable chunk of the area. Twisting hair-like blue lines indicated creeks running through the land.

I started the VW and waved at Roxanne once as I pulled away. The last I saw of her she was sitting on the porch swing, a fresh cigarette in hand, taking yet another sip of beer.

I picked up Calle LeGrand and followed the road south, through low rolling gold hills that would turn as green as Ireland when the rains returned. In the areas where there were no structures in sight, I fancied I was looking through the eyes of the early settlers, marveling at the acres of untouched land, bare and silent except for the cries of birds. I missed the turn to the ranch and had to circle back when I realized I'd gone too far. On the return, I saw the side road where Stacey and Dolan and I had met Arne Johanson. The gate now stood open and a haze of dust on the gravel road suggested that a vehicle had recently passed that way.

I turned in, driving slowly, my attention drawn to the gulley where Jane Doe's body had been found. I could see now that a section of the road angled off to the left, ending in a cul-de-sac, and I remembered the passing reference to the VW van that was seen parked in the turnaround. Also, a red convertible with out-of-state plates. Offhand, I couldn't remember the name of the fellow who'd called it in, but the report might bear revisiting, as Arne had suggested. Somebody Vogel. I'd have to look it up. I eased the car up the hill, following the route Arne had taken in his Jeep. I was really hoping the No Trespassing signs didn't apply to me.

The house came into view, looking like something in an old horror film. I parked in the driveway and approached with a curious mix of anxiety and excitement. Bare wooden trellises affixed to the porch rails at intervals suggested that roses or morning glories might have climbed there once. Now the beds were overgrown. I climbed the front porch stairs, which seemed remarkably sound. The house, though a shambles, had been built to last. I remembered talk at some point of moving the house into the city limits, restoring it as a possible tourist attraction. I could see where the city would be reluctant to make a claim. Even the idea of renovating the house in situ would be an expensive proposition. To what end?

I tried the front door and to my surprise I found it unlocked. I pushed it open and went in, assaulted by the dense smell of soot and mildew. I spent the next thirty minutes wandering from floor to floor, sometimes awed at the grandeur that remained. High ceilings, the sweeping staircase in the foyer, all the marble and mahogany still gracing the rooms. A large butler's pantry opened into a vast kitchen with servants' quarters built on behind. A second staircase led up to the second floor from there. I could feel memory stir. Vague images, shapeless and filled with shadows, moved at the edge of my vision. I could hear sounds, talking and laughing in another room, without being able to distinguish the words.

I was standing on the wide second-floor landing when I heard someone walking in the hall below. From the bottom of the stairs, someone called, "Kinsey?"

For one wonderful moment, the voice was my mother's and she'd returned from the dead.

SEVEN

I crossed to the banister and peered over the railing.
Tasha stood in the stairwell, looking up. "I saw your
car parked outside."

"I'll come down."

I descended the stairs, embarrassed that I'd been
caught poking around the house uninvited. She'd taken
a seat on the third step up, leaning against the wall. I
settled on the same step, sitting close to the rail.

"How'd you know I was here?"

"Arne saw your car pull in and called me. My office
isn't that far." She was dressed in lawyer clothes: a crisp
navy-blue pantsuit with a white silk shell under the two-
button jacket. She wore pearls. I'd always heard you
could tell real pearls from fake by running them across
your teeth, but I wasn't clear what information that was
meant to impart. I thought it'd be rude to ask if I could
bite her necklace. She had dark eyes, delicately enhanced
with a smoky eyeliner, a straight nose where mine was

ever so faintly bumpy from having been broken twice. Her dark hair was tastefully highlighted with blond and pulled into a rope at the nape of her neck. I could see a bow of red chiffon peeking into view from the hair clip behind.

It's odd to see someone you know looks like you. The face we see in the mirror is always reversed so that our impression of ourselves is flipped left to right. If you stand in front of a mirror and put your right index finger against your right cheek, the mirror will tell you you're touching left to left. The only way you can see yourself as you appear to others is to hold a mirror to the mirror and check your image in that. What I saw now of Tasha was what others saw of me. Already, I liked her face a lot better than mine. I usually ignore my own looks, not from distaste, but from a sense of despair. So many women have mastered an arsenal of beauty products: foundation, powder, blusher, eye shadow, pencils for lining their eyes, brows, and lips. As a rule, I avoid makeup, having little experience with the selection and application process.

It was clear at a glance that Tasha knew her stuff. I couldn't identify all the kinds of goop on her face, but she'd tinted herself with care. Her skin had a healthy glow, her cheeks showed a hint of pink, and her eyes looked enormous because her lashes were so thick. I could see her assessing me while I assessed her. We smiled at the same time, which only furthered the notion we were looking at ourselves. We had identical teeth.

She said, "After our telephone conversation, I had a long talk with Mom. Her version of events is different."

"Oh, really. How so?"

"She says your parents made that trip to meet with Grand and Granddaddy in hopes of a reconciliation. They were killed on the way. Grand blamed herself. Aunt Gin blamed her, too. Mom says Grand tried to keep in touch, but Gin was having none of it. Finally, Grand gave up, but only after years of trying to make contact."

"Bullshit. I don't believe it."

"I'm not asking you to *believe*. I'm telling you what Mother said."

"Well, of course she'd say that. She's still tied into Grand. How can you afford to think ill of someone who has the power to pull the rug out from under you? You'd do just about anything to see them as good no matter what they've done."

"Kinsey, if you really want to find out what went on back then, you can't start by rejecting the messages you don't want to hear. There are two sides to every story. That's why we have the courts. To settle disputes."

"Oh, right. Compare this to litigation. That'll win you points," I said. "Most people can't stand lawyers. I'm one of the few with any respect for the trade." I stopped. I stared down at the floor for a moment and then shook my head. "I'm sorry. Forget it. I didn't mean to get into it with you again."

Tasha smiled slightly. "I told you we couldn't talk without hassling."

"You set me off."

"That's not my intent."

"I know. The hard part is that neither of us has any concrete proof. We can do this 'Did too! Did not!' routine until the cows come home. It's Grand's word against Aunt Gin's, or my mother's word against your mom's. There is no *fact* of the matter."

"Probably not. Just keep an open mind. That's really all I ask."

"I'm afraid it's too late for that. My mind's been made up since the day I met Liza. I wasn't interested then and I'm probably not interested now."

"At least you use the word 'probably.' That's progress, isn't it? You used to be adamant. Now you're obdurate."

"Which means what?"

"Resistant, but less flinty. It's a big improvement."

The comment seemed patronizing, but I shrugged it off. Why take offense when she might not have actually meant it that way? I said, "It feels like unfinished business and that bothers me. Regardless of how it comes out, I'd like to think I'm doing the right thing."

"That works both ways. We're having to go back and revisit the past, which is good for all of us. The point is, we have time to work this out."

"Thirty-two years of it so far."

"So what's thirty-two more? We can't settle a long-standing quarrel in a few casual talks." She glanced at her watch and then rose. "I have to get back to work. Did you finish the tour?"

I pulled myself up. "Essentially. I hoped I'd remember something, but I'm drawing a blank." The two of us paused simultaneously to brush off the backs of our pants.

We crossed to the front door, our shoes making scratching sounds in the grit that had accumulated on the marble floor. She said, "What do you think of the place?"

"It must have been beautiful in its day."

Tasha turned back, letting her eyes travel across the foyer and up the stairs. "You know Grand moved out shortly after Aunt Rita's death." Rita Cynthia Kinsey was my mother's maiden name.

"I didn't know that."

"Granddaddy Kinsey was fit to be tied, but she finally got her way. That's when they bought the house in town. You remember him at all?"

I shook my head.

"Maybe I can find some family photographs."

"I'd like that. I don't think I've ever seen pictures of anyone. Aunt Gin discounted sentiment as a form of sniveling. She refused to let either of us sink to such depths."

"She was tough."

"That she was."

"Well. I better go."

"Me, too," I said. "I do have one request. I know you've already talked to your mother about me, but please don't bring Grand into this."

"My lips are sealed."

It was 4:35 by the time I reached Santa Teresa. I made a stop at the public library, leaving my car in the adjacent four-story parking structure. My conversation with Roxanne Faught had raised unsettling questions, namely, what did she know and when did she know it? I wondered if there was any way to check. I trotted down the carpeted stairs to the periodicals room, where I asked the reference librarian for the microfilm records of the *Santa Teresa Dispatch* from the week of August 3, 1969. Since the body was found that Sunday, I didn't expect the news to hit the paper for another day or two. Once I had the box of film in hand, I sat down at the machine and unreeled the strip, which I threaded under the lens, catching the sprocket holes. I hand-cranked it until the strip caught properly and then pressed a button and watched the Sunday paper speed by in a blur. My eyes picked up a remarkable amount of information on the fly. I bypassed the sports, the business section, and the classified ads. I slowed now and then just to see what was going on. The oil spill off the Santa Teresa coast was in its 190th day. *Funny Girl* and *Goodbye, Columbus* were playing at the local movie theater along with *Planet of the Apes*. There was talk that Don Drysdale's fourteen-year pitching career might be coming to an end because of a recurrent injury, and a Westinghouse 2-Speed Automatic Washer was selling for $189.95.

When I reached Monday's paper, I slowed to a dead stop and scanned it page by page. On Monday, August 4, five column inches were devoted to the discovery of the body near the Grayson Quarry in Lompoc. Con Dolan and Stacey Oliphant were both mentioned by name, but there was little to report. The next day, August 5, in a column called "North County Events," I caught the second squib. By then the autopsy had been done and the cause of death was detailed. The same few physical traits were noted—hair and eye color, height and weight—in hopes of identifying the girl. I cranked the reel forward, through Wednesday and Thursday of the same week. Thursday's paper included a brief follow-up, with the same information I'd read in the initial account. Both gave a brief description of the girl's clothing, detailing the dark blue voile blouse and the daisy-patterned pants. Neither article specified the color of the pants. I knew from police reports that the daisies were dark blue, a red dot at each center, on a ground of white, but if you relied strictly on this data, it would be natural to assume the daisies were "daisy-colored," as Roxanne Faught had so aptly summed it up. Factoring in her certainty about the torn earlobe, the big feet, the big-boned wrists, and the closely bitten nails, I doubted the girl she'd dealt with was actually our Jane Doe. It was always possible, of course. Eyewitness testimony is notoriously shaky, easily influenced, subject to subtle modification with each telling of the tale. Roxanne had admitted she'd gone back to reread the very clippings I was looking at myself. I didn't wholly discount what she said, but I wondered at its relevance to our investigation. Stacey had hoped to establish a timeline, working backward from Roxanne's encounter to Cloris Bargo's sighting of the girl hitchhiking outside Colgate. Now Cloris had recanted and I suspected Roxanne's observations were too tainted to be of use. I fast-forwarded. That same week, on August 9, five people, including film and television actress Sharon Tate, were found slain in a Bel Air home. Two days later, Leno and Rosemary LaBianca were discovered murdered in a manner similar to the Tate slayings. I tracked forward again, but there was no further mention of Jane Doe. I jotted a few notes on my index cards and then made copies of the news stories, paid for them at the counter, and returned to my car.

It was just after 5:00, and Con was doubtless at CC's, knocking back Happy Hour drinks on a two-for-one deal. For my sake, I hoped he hadn't been at it long. I spotted his car as soon as I pulled up in front, but the area was otherwise deserted. Across the street at the bird refuge, two women in sweats were just starting a walk, chatting with animation. Closer to the water, a mother looked on placidly as her five-year-old child fed day-old bread to the gulls under a sign that read: PLEASE DO NOT FEED THE BIRDS.

I went into CC's, pausing in the doorway to let my eyes adjust. A plank of daylight had fallen in the open door, enhancing the contrast between CC's and the outside world. The place was dark. There was no one in the front room except the bartender and a waitress engaged in intimate conversation. Stacey and Dolan were seated in a booth in the rear. Stacey got up when I appeared. He was looking better today. I said, "Hi. Am I late?"

"Not at all," Dolan said. Both had glasses in front of them. Dolan's contained whiskey dark enough to pass for iced tea. Stacey's was empty except for the ice cubes and a wad of freshly squeezed lime. Dolan hauled himself to his feet just as Stacey sat down. "What can I get you?"

"Water's fine for now. I may switch later."

"I'll take another Tanqueray and tonic."

Dolan frowned. "You just had one. I thought the doc didn't want you mixing meds with booze."

"Or else what, I drop dead? Don't worry. I'll take full responsibility. I'd be doing myself a favor."

Dolan gestured impatiently and then moved off to the bar. I slid into the booth and put my shoulder bag on the seat beside me.

He said, "How'd your day go?"

"So-so. I'll tell you about it as soon as he gets back."

Stacey reached into his vest pocket and removed a pipe and a tobacco pouch, then filled the bowl. He fished around in another pocket for a pipe pick and tamped down the tobacco before he took out a wooden kitchen match and slid the head along the underside of the table. I waited while he puffed at the pipe. The smoke was sweet-smelling, like a meadow full of dried hay.

I said, "You're as bad as he is."

Stacey smiled. "On the other hand, suppose I only have a few months left? Why deny myself? It's all in your perspective."

"I guess it is."

We engaged in idle chitchat until Dolan returned,

bearing a tray with my water and two fresh drinks for them. He'd added napkins, a bowl of popcorn, and a tumbler of nuts.

"Look at this guy, buying dinner for us," Stacey said.

"Hey, I got class. More than I can say for you."

The air was cool and free of cigarette smoke, which Dolan corrected for as soon as he sat down. I didn't bother to complain. Stacey's pipe tobacco and Dolan's cigarette smoke masked the faint whiff of noxious gases from the excavation site outside. Dolan helped himself to a handful of nuts, popping them in his mouth one by one while he looked at me. "What'd you get?"

"You're not going to like it." I went on with a summary of my travels, starting with Cloris Bargo and the lie she'd told.

Stacey said, "I talked to her twice myself and she never said a word about that."

"It's my charm and finesse."

"Well, shit. I didn't realize she was married to Joe Mandel. He worked with us on this."

"I know. I remembered the name."

Dolan said, "I can't believe she was blowing smoke up our skirts. She actually admitted that?"

"Well, yeah. She said at the time she couldn't see the harm."

Stacey said, "Let's leave that one alone. No sense butting into their business. I tell you what we might do though is ask Joe if he could locate Jane Doe's effects for us. It'd be good to take a look. Might spark an idea. I'll make a call and clear it with the sheriff. Don't think he'd object, but you never know about these things." He made a note to himself and turned back to me. "What else?"

"After I left her, I drove on up to Lompoc, stopping off at Gull Cove, which is closed, by the way." I laid out my conversation with Roxanne Faught, what she'd said, and where the story she'd told me varied from what we knew. I gave them copies of the news clippings to demonstrate my point. "I think she lifted the details from these, which means we can't rely on her. I believe she encountered someone, but it wasn't necessarily our Jane Doe."

"Too bad. It sounds like a dead end," Dolan said.

Stacey said, "Dead ends are a given. That's how these things go. We're bound to run into a few along the way. All that tells us is to back up and look somewhere else. Lucky we found out about it now before we wasted any more time on it."

"Knocks our hitchhiking theory all to hell," Dolan said.

"Maybe so, maybe not. She could have gone to Lompoc by train or bus and hitched a ride from there."

I said to Dolan, "What about the vehicles seen in the area? Any way to check those out?"

"Johanson said something about a hippie van. We could track down that guy—what's his name . . ."

"Vogel."

"Right, him. Why don't we see what he remembers."

"It's a long shot," I said.

"So's everything else we've come up with so far."

Stacey let that remark pass, still fixating on his original point about where the girl had come from. "Another possibility is she bummed a ride to Lompoc with a friend, someone she stayed with 'til she hit the road again."

Dolan made a sour face. "Would you quit obsessing? We went over that before. If she'd had friends in the area, they'd have wondered what happened as soon as she disappeared."

"Not if she'd told 'em she was on her way north. Suppose she stays in Lompoc a couple nights and then leaves for San Francisco. She goes out the door, has a run-in with the Devil, and ends up dead."

"They'd still put two and two together as soon as the story broke."

Stacey stirred irritably. "We're not going to find answers to every question we ask."

"So far we haven't found answers to anything," I remarked.

Stacey waved that aside. "Maybe our mistake is assuming she's from somewhere else. Suppose she's local? Someone kills her and then makes up a story explaining where she's gone. That's why she wasn't reported missing. It's part of the coverup."

Dolan was shaking his head.

"What's wrong with that?"

Dolan sat back in the booth. "No one exists in a vacuum. She must've had family and friends. She worked, went to school. She did some damn thing. *Somebody* must have wondered. Essentially, this girl dropped off the face of the earth and you're telling me no one noticed? There's something off about that."

I said, "But, Dolan, think of all the kids who disappeared in those days. There must be dozens unaccounted for. Families probably still fantasize they'll show up one day."

Stacey said, "Why don't we forget that angle and come at it from the other direction?"

"Which is what?" I asked.

"What we talked about before, assume Frankie killed her and see if we can find a way to make it stick."

"Based on what? Make that leap and we could end up spinning our wheels," I said.

"We're doing that anyway. The exercise is only pointless if it turns out we're wrong. What do you say, Con?"

"I'm with you on that one. We'd be no worse off. I've always thought Frankie had a hand in it."

Stacey turned to me. I said, "You're the boss."

"My thought exactly. Let me show you what I got."

He opened a manila folder and removed two connected sheets of computer paper with perforated edges.
I peered at the pale print. There, in abbreviated form,
was Frankie Miracle's criminal history, starting with his
first arrest in Venice, California, in January of 1964.
Stacey picked up the paper and began to rattle off the
long string of his offenses. "I love this guy. Look at this.
1964. Kid's twenty-one years old, arrested for drunkenness and resisting arrest. Fined twenty-five bucks and
put on a year's probation. Well, okay. No problem. His
first contact with the law . . ."

"That we know of," Dolan said.

Stacey smiled. "That's right. But boys will be boys.
They're not going to execute the lad for public drunkenness. In May that same year, he was arrested for
burglary and contributing to the delinquency of a minor.
Probably screwed a thirteen-year-old. That'd be about
his speed. Put on probation. In February of '65, he was
arrested for another burglary. He pleaded guilty; sentence was six months in jail and probation. Judge is
really cracking down on him," he said, tongue in cheek.
"June 1965. Burglary again. This time, his probation's
revoked and he's sentenced to state prison, six months
to fifteen years; released after serving ten months.
December 1965. Drunk and disorderly, assault, and

marijuana possession. Admitted for psychiatric evaluation and treatment of drug and alcohol dependency."
Stacey snorted derisively. "The guy's a creep. We all
know that. April 1966—burglary and escape. November
1966—robbery, kidnapping, attempted rape. This time
they threw in assault and possession of a dangerous
weapon. March 1967—another burglary. Oh, and here's
a good one. I can't believe this guy's back on the street.
In January 1968, Frankie abducted a woman from a
supermarket parking lot. He was later arrested on
charges of kidnap, assault, robbery, oral copulation,
sodomy, and attempted murder. You better believe she
hasn't had a good night's sleep since she ran into *him*.
January 1969—attempted kidnap, statutory rape, contributing to the delinquency of a minor. Now we're
getting down to business. In March 1969, he was picked
up on charges of armed robbery, assault, and attempted
murder. Case dismissed. Cops probably beat a con-
fession out of him, and the public defender had the
whole thing thrown out. Sometime in June, he met a
sixteen-year-old girl named Iona Mathis. He was married to her briefly—six months I think. About as long as
some of his jail time, as it turns out. Which brings us to
Venice, California, late July, when Frankie killed Cathy
Lee Pearse." Stacey shook his head. "God bless the
courts. If they'd done their job right, they could have
saved her life."

I said, "How'd he manage to get away with all that shit?"

"Easy," Dolan said. He stubbed out one cigarette and fired up the next. "He knew how to work the system. Every time he was charged with multiple crimes, he'd plead guilty to one in exchange for the others being dropped. You haven't met Frankie. He can be as charming as all get out. He had judges and prosecutors bending over backwards, trying to give him a chance to straighten up and fly right."

Stacey returned the report to the manila folder. "Lot of times he was sentenced to state prison under the old indeterminate sentence system. Other times he was released on automatic parole. Longest he ever went between crimes was this period between March of '67 and November of '68."

Dolan said, "Bet you a dollar he just didn't get caught. He hasn't gone that long between crimes since he started out."

"Probably right about that. If you look at the pattern, you can see the stakes go up. Violence escalates. The stretch between crimes starts getting shorter and shorter until he killed Cathy Lee. For that one, he only served seventeen years on a life sentence so he's still lucking out. If I were her parents, I'd be pissed as hell."

I said, "What else do we have?"

Dolan pulled a battered notebook from his jacket

pocket and began to leaf through the pages. He clicked his ballpoint pen. "Frankie's cellmates. Turns out there were twelve altogether, but half the last known addresses are incorrect. We got two in state prison and one serving time in a federal prison camp in Yankton, South Dakota. I know the whereabouts of three for sure: Lorenzo Rickman, Pudgie Clifton, and John Luchek."

Stacey said, "Scratch Luchek. He was killed in a two-car accident in 1975. Drunk hit him head on."

"Right. That's the information I have." Dolan drew a line through the name. "Rickman's out on parole. Word has it he's been a real good boy of late, working as an auto mechanic at a place out in Colgate. I got the name here somewhere. Stacey'll stop by Monday to have a chat with him. Which leaves Clifton, who's currently at the tail end of ninety days on a misdemeanor possession. I picked up mug shots on all these guys in case you need something to refresh people's memories. I mixed in some unrelated photos so we can't be accused of biasing the witnesses—assuming we find a few."

"Let's be optimistic. It doesn't cost anything," Stacey said.

Dolan passed one pack of photos to me and one to Stacey, who said, "We'll let Kinsey talk to Pudgie. He's the type who'd respond to her feminine wiles."

"Like I got some."

"Don't underestimate yourself."

Dolan said, "That leaves Frankie."

"You and I can draw straws, but let's hold off on that until we contact the other two." Stacey winced and then stood up abruptly, saying, "Shit! Hang on a sec."

Dolan said, "What's wrong?"

Stacey groaned, then sucked in air through his teeth, his face tense. "Damn back's seizing up. *Jeez, that hurts.* Pain's shooting all the way down my leg."

"What's the doctor say?"

"How do I know? This ain't Death at my door. I told you—I pulled a muscle. I can't call the oncologist for every little thing." He leaned sideways, stretching. After a moment, he stood upright, taking a long, slow, deep breath.

"Better?"

"Much. Sorry to interrupt. Damn thing caught me by surprise."

"Would you quit the self-diagnosis and call the guy?"

"The doctor's a woman, you sexist prick. You ought to give some serious thought to the assumptions you make."

"Quit the bullshitting, Stace. This is all a big smoke-screen. You keep acting like you've only had the back pain for the past two days when you've complained of it for weeks. You should have had the docs take a look while you were in the hospital."

"It wasn't hurting me then."

"Oh, for heaven's sake. You know what? This is called 'denial.' This is you trying to minimize a problem that could be damn serious. Hell, give me the gal's name and I'll call her myself."

"No, you won't."

"Then *you* call."

"I will. I was going to do that."

"Now."

"Con, cut it out! It's past five. She's probably left for the day."

"Then call the service, leave CC's number, and have her paged. We can wait. You don't call her, I will. I'm sick of hearing you bellyache."

"You don't even know her name."

"I'll find out."

"Don't be ridiculous."

"Quit arguing. Maybe she'll give you some Valium to help you sleep at night."

Stacey shook his head. "I hate making a fool of myself because of you." Despite his grumbling and protests, he did go off to find a phone.

Dolan and I sat without looking at each other. I didn't like the sound of it any more than he did. Finally, I said, "Are the two of you okay? You seem testy."

"We're fine. He's just pissing me off. It's not about his back. The man's depressed. He thinks the cancer's spread and that's why he doesn't want to get it checked."

"I missed that, I guess. He seemed fine as far as I could tell. I mean, aside from his back."

"That's because he puts on an act for your benefit. You should've heard him before you showed. The shit's wearing him down. If he'd had a gun on him, he'd have blown his brains out. He's that close." Dolan held up his thumb and index finger a quarter of an inch apart.

"You're not serious."

"I am. He wasn't even going to do the chemo until I talked him into it. As far as he's concerned, this is the end of the line so why play it out? Get the damn thing over with is his attitude."

"But suppose the cancer's moved into his bones?"

"Now, damn it, don't you start. Don't be so negative."

"I'm just saying I can understand where he's coming from."

"Well, keep your opinion to yourself."

"My opinion's not relevant. He can do anything he wants. It's his life."

"Wrong. He could use a pep talk. He needs someone to make him realize how selfish it is."

"To kill himself? How so?"

"People who commit suicide are the ultimate narcissists. What makes him think everything revolves around him? I'm in this, too. Thirty years down the drain and all because he's a cowardly damn chickenshit and won't see this through."

"But what if he's terminal? I don't understand what you want."

"I want him to think about someone else for a change."

"If you don't get to think about yourself when you're dying, when do you?" I said.

Stacey reappeared moments later and we dropped the conversation. He declined to sit, remaining by the table with his fists pressed into the small of his back.

Dolan fired up another cigarette, pausing to cough into his fist. "What'd she say?"

Stacey waved the cigarette smoke away from his face. "She'll see me first thing tomorrow morning; maybe take an X-ray or do a CT scan."

"What's the matter with her? Did you tell her how bad it is? She should see you right now and find out what the hell's going on."

"Goddammit. Quit nagging. This isn't an emergency so lay off that stuff. Anyway, I'm tired and it's time to go home. I can't be sitting here drinking all night like some I could name."

"Sit down. You haven't had dinner yet. You have to eat. It's my treat."

"I got food at my place. You two stay. I can get a cab."

"I'll take you," I said. "My car's right outside."

"You don't have to do that. I can manage on my own."

"Really, I don't mind. I need to get home myself."

I reached for my shoulder bag and took out the keys. Stacey was already moving toward the door as I slid out of the booth.

Dolan stubbed out his cigarette. "I'll take care of it."

In the end, we left at the same time; Stacey in Dolan's car and me in mine. I watched Dolan turn off, heading toward the freeway. I took a right on Cabana Boulevard and followed the road as it wound along the beach. It was not quite dark, but a fog was rolling in off the ocean, enveloping the shore. I parked in Henry's driveway. He'd be home tomorrow in the late afternoon. I let myself into his place where I did a quick tour, making sure all was in order. No broken water pipes, no power outages, and no sign of disturbances. For a moment, I stood in his kitchen, drinking in the lingering scent of yeast and cinnamon—Henry's home-baked sweetrolls. Surely, I could survive one more day.

I was home minutes later, safely tucked away for the night. 5:56 on a Friday evening and I had no plans. I made an olive-and-pimento-cheese sandwich on whole-wheat bread, which I cut into quarters. I poured myself a glass of wine and settled on the couch where I took up the Jane Doe file and started back at page one. Sometimes you work because there's nothing else to do.

EIGHT

At 1:35 that morning, I was awoken from a sound sleep: Dolan on the phone, calling from the ER at St. Terry's.

"Stacey's back got worse after I dropped him off. He called me at midnight and asked me to bring him in. They took one look at him and rounded up the doc on call. I'm waiting to hear what the fellow has to say."

"You want me to come over?"

"Hang on a second." He put a hand over the mouthpiece and conducted a muffled conversation with someone else, then returned to the line. "I'll call you back in a bit. Soon as I find out what's going on."

I replaced the handset, now wide awake. If Dolan intended to phone again, there was really no point in going back to sleep. I flipped on the light and fumbled for my running shoes. Given my new efficiency measures, I was fully suited up in sweats and crew socks. I needed only brush my teeth and run wet hands through my mop and I was ready to go.

I parked on a side street across from the hospital emergency entrance. I love the town at that hour. Traffic is sparse, the streets are empty, most businesses are shut down. The temperature had dropped into the forties and the lights in the emergency room looked inviting. Apparently, the usual weekend traumafest hadn't gotten under way as yet, because the front desk was deserted and all was quiet. I found Dolan reading a magazine in the reception area. He rose when he saw me.

Without even thinking, I gave his cheek a buss. "How's he doing?"

"They're in the process of admitting him. I could have saved you a trip. I tried calling you back, but I guess you'd already left by then."

"Don't worry about it. I was up anyway. What now? Will they let you see him again?"

"They gave him something for the pain and he's out of it. He probably won't know the difference, but I'll feel better if I do. After that, I thought I'd make a run over to his place and pick up some of his things. Toothbrush and comb, stuff like that."

"Why don't I find us a cup of coffee? There's bound to be a vending machine on the premises somewhere."

We sat together for half an hour, sipping treacherous-smelling lukewarm coffee from thick paper cups with

SUE GRAFTON

handles like flat-folded butterfly wings. He said, "What
were you doing home? I was all set to leave a message.
I figured you'd be out on a date."

"People don't *date* anymore; at least I don't," I said.

"Why not? What's wrong with it? How else are you
going to meet someone?"

"I don't want to *meet* anyone. I'm fine, thanks so
much. What about you? You're single. Are you dating
these days?"

"I'm too old."

"Me, too," I said, peering over at him. "How long
ago did your wife die?"

"Ten months today." He was silent for a moment.
"I'll tell you what's been hard. She bugged me for
years to go on a cruise. I hated the whole idea. Tahiti.
Alaska. She'd bring me color brochures full of these
pictures of happy couples, all of 'em thirty years old,
standing on the deck, holding champagne flutes. Sunset.
Romance. Inside'd be a picture of this mountain of
food you could stuff yourself with twenty-four hours a
day. Just the sight of it's enough to make your ulcers
perforate. I hate being cooped up, and I was worried
I'd be stranded with a bunch of fools. Does that sound
unreasonable?"

"You think it was a cruise she wanted or just a trip
someplace?"

Dolan turned and gave me a look. "I never thought to ask."

I got back to my place at 2:45 A.M. and then slept restlessly until 10:00. The Santa Teresa County Jail is housed in a 25,000-square-foot building, two stories, 120 beds, designed to be staffed by only two corrections officers, one of whom monitors the state-of-the-art security panel with its bank of television screens.

Still feeling half-dead from lack of sleep, I pulled the VW into one of the slots out front and went through the main entrance doors, where I picked up a copy of the visitation request form. I filled in my name and gave it to the clerk at the counter, then hung out in the lobby area while the word went down to Pudgie that he had a visitor. I could picture his puzzlement, as I was reasonably certain he'd never heard of me. Curiosity (or boredom) must have gotten the better of him because the clerk returned and said he'd agreed to see me. She gave me the booth number where I could meet him.

Ten of us entered the elevator: two lone women and three mothers with assorted small kids. I pressed DOWN, wondering if I looked like the sort of person who'd have a boyfriend in jail. The elevator descended by inches while we all secretly worried about getting stuck. Once

the doors opened on the floor below, we spilled into a
room that was probably twenty feet by twenty. Molded
beige and gray plastic armchairs, chunky and square,
were arranged in a double row down the middle of the
room, with additional seats around the perimeter. The
floor was a glossy beige vinyl tile. The walls were cinder
block, painted a matte two-tone beige. A posted sign
read KEEP FEET OFF WALL, though there was nothing
to suggest how one might accomplish violating such a
... well, feat. In the visitors room, eight stationary
stools, with a handset at each place, were lined up on
either side of a large glass-enclosed aisle. I sat down and
placed my shoulder bag at my feet. I rested my elbows
on the counter, feeling as if I were seated at the lunch
counter of an old five-and-dime.

I knew from the police report that Pudgie was born
Cedric Costello Clifton in 1950, the same year I was.
He had a birthday coming up, June 7, so I'd aced him
by a month and two days. The door opened on the jail
side and a few inmates straggled in on the other side of
the glass, hands linked behind their backs, a requirement
any time they were moved from place to place. Pudgie
appeared and took a seat on a stool that was a match
for mine. His face was moon-shaped, and he wore
glasses with big round frames perched on a surprisingly
dainty nose. His facial hair was disorganized—rough
mustache and a beard that ran from patchy to thick as

it drifted across his cheeks. There were miscellaneous whiskers scattered almost to his eyes. His dark hair looked jangled, a texture that on a woman would be attributed to a bad home permanent. He wore the usual jail garb: a white T-shirt, blue cotton elastic-waisted pants, and rubber shoes. I've seen similar outfits on surgical residents in the corridors of St. Terry's. He was bulky through the shoulders, his chest and biceps bulging from years of pumping iron. The hair on his left forearm only partially masked an entire gallery of elaborate tattoos: a spiderweb, a skull wearing a sombrero, and a graphically portrayed sex act. There was also a big-breasted woman with flowing black tresses whose torso was laid out between his elbow and wrist. His right arm seemed to be bare of art. He studied me for a long time. Through sheer effort, I held his gaze without breaking eye contact. Finally, he lifted the handset on his side of the glass and said, "Hey, how you doin'?"

I held the handset loosely against my ear. "I'm good, Mr. Clifton. How about yourself?"

"I'm doing okay. I know you?"

"My name's Kinsey Millhone. I'm a private investigator. I appreciate your seeing me."

"Why don't you skip the 'mister' shit and tell me what you want." Behind the round lenses of his glasses, his eyes were a mild hazel under ill-kempt brows.

"I was wondering if you'd answer a few questions."

A slight smile appeared. "About what?"

"Something that happened in 1969."

"Why ask me?"

"This isn't about you. It's about someone else."

"Goody. And who's that?"

"You remember being arrested in Lompoc in August of '69?"

"Yeah." He replied with all the caution of someone who's not quite sure what he's agreeing to.

"You gave the officer a home address in Creosote, California. Can you tell me where that is? I never heard of it." I'd looked it up on the map, but in the manner of a polygraph, I thought I'd start with baseline questions, whose truth value was easily verified.

"Little town out near Blythe. Two miles this side of the Arizona line."

"How'd you end up in Lompoc?"

"I was traveling to San Francisco. I had a buddy who'd just come back from six months living on the streets up there. He told me you could buy dope right out on Haight. 'Ludes, grass and hash, peyote, acid. Free sex and free clinics to treat crabs and the clap if you picked up a dose. Sounded like a good deal to me. Still does, come to think of it. Anymore, you lay a hand on a chick, she blows the whistle on you."

I glanced at the sheet of paper I'd taken from my bag, though I knew what it said. "According to this, you were picked up for vagrancy and possession of an illegal substance."

He loosened up at that, face creasing into a smile. Apparently, he'd made an entire career out of substance abuse and denial. "What a crock of shit *that* was. I'm standing on the side of the road, thumbing a ride, when this cop car comes by. 'Couple rednecks in uniform. Fuckin' pigs. These two pull over and pat me down. Turns out I had some pot on me. One fuckin' joint. And for this I'm locked up. I should've sued for harassment and false arrest."

"You'd hitchhiked?"

"I'se nineteen years old. You don't have a car, that's what you do."

"We're interested in anyone who might have seen a young girl hitchhiking in the area. Seventeen, eighteen years old. Dyed blond hair, blue eyes. She was probably five foot three, a hundred twenty-five pounds."

"That's half the girls I knew. All of 'em looked like that except the ones porked up on grass. Ever notice that? Girls'd smoke too much dope and munch themselves up to twice their normal weight. Either that or all the fat ones were on the street in those days, hoping to get laid. Who else would have 'em?"

"That's a wholesome attitude."

Pudgie laughed at that, genuinely amused while I was not.

I said, "Can we get back to the subject?"

"Which is what now? I forget."

"The girl I described."

"Sure. What'd she do?"

"She didn't do anything. Her body was found dumped off the side of the road."

His attitude shifted slightly. "Sorry to hear that. You never said she was dead or I wouldn't have smarted off."

"The point is, she had no ID and her body was never claimed. We'd like to find out who she is."

"Yeah, but 1969? Why worry about it now after all these years?"

"It's someone's pet project. 'Couple of guys I work with. What about you? What happened when you got out of jail?"

"I had to call my old man to come pick me up. He was royally pissed. Soon as we got home, the shit-head threw me out; flung my clothes in the yard and broke my dinner plate on the porch. Fucking drama queen. Had to make a big scene, make sure all the neighbors knew he'd busted my ass."

"At least he was willing to drive all the way from Creosote."

"Yeah, but not before I'd spent the worst three days of my life in a cell with a bunch of freaks," he said and shrugged. "Worst until then. I've seen a lot worse since."

"You remember Lorenzo Rickman or Frankie Miracle?"

He snorted. "Lorenzo? What kind of name is that? What's the guy, some kind of fruit?"

"You shared a cell with those two and a guy named John Luchek. You remember him?"

"Not especially. I guess. Any reason I should?"

"What about Rickman?"

"Is this about him? Mean, it'd be nice if I knew what you were going for."

"We'll get to that. Did the two of you talk?"

"Jail's a bore. You talk just to keep from going out of your gourd. Food stinks, too, until you get used to it. Here, it's not bad; you know, heavy on the starch. Macaroni and cheese tastes like library paste. You ever eat that stuff?"

I wasn't sure whether he was referring to the jail cuisine or library paste. I'd dined on both, but I didn't think that was any of his business. I wasn't here to compare exotic foods. "What about Frankie? You have a conversation with him?"

"Must have. Why not? I'm a friendly little fuck. 'Course, I probably wouldn't recognize those guys now if I saw 'em on the street."

"Would it help if you saw pictures?"

"Might."

I shifted the handset from my right ear to my left, tucking it between my cheek and shoulder so I could free my hands. I removed assorted mug shots from the file folder and placed them by twos against the glass in front of him. There were twelve in all; names, aliases, and personal data, wants and warrants carefully blocked out. Pudgie subjected the black-and-white photos to the same careful scrutiny he'd lavished on me. He pointed to Frankie. "That one? That's Frankie. I remember him. Coked up and jumpy. He talked up a storm until the high wore off."

"What about the others?"

"Maybe him. I'm not sure." He pointed to Lorenzo Rickman, his memory better than he realized.

"Anyone else?"

"Don't think so."

"Did Frankie talk about his arrest?"

"What, you mean the chick he whacked? I guess he cut her up bad and then he fucked it up big time."

"Like what?"

"Stole her car, for one thing. What's he think? The cops aren't going to put out a fuckin' APB? Then he takes her credit card and uses that to pay for his entire escape. He left a paper trail a mile wide. Guy's dumb as he is mean. You kill a girl, you ought to have more sense." He stopped and stared. "I bet you know all this stuff, right? What's the story, is he out?

"You're full of questions."

"How can I help if you won't say what you're after?"

"Did he indicate how long he'd been in Lompoc before his arrest?"

Pudgie smiled. "I don't get your fascination with a little puke like him."

"I'm not fascinated with anything, except the truth."

"Hey, come on. Tell me the game and I can play for keeps."

I broke off eye contact. "Well, thanks for your time. Actually, I think that's it." I pinned the handset against my ear again while I gathered the mug shots and tucked them in the folder.

"Wait! Don't go. We're not done yet. Are we done?"

I paused. "Oh, sorry. I was under the impression you'd told me everything you knew. I didn't want to waste your time."

"It's like this: I might remember more if we could sit and chat awhile. You know, small talk and like that. Ask another question. Maybe it'll stimulate my brain."

I smiled at him blandly, getting to my feet. "Why don't you get in touch if you think of anything useful?"

"About what exactly? At least put me in the ballpark here."

"I'm not going to feed you lines. If you don't know anything, that's fine. We'll let it go at that."

"Naw, now don't get mad. How's this? I'll think real hard. Meanwhile, you come back later and bring a carton of smokes."

"I'm not buying you cigarettes. Why would I do that?"

"It's the least you can do, compensation for my time."

I glanced at my watch. "Four minutes' worth."

"Smoking helps me think."

I adjusted my shoulder bag, the handset still at my ear. "Bye now."

He said, "Okay. Skip the carton. Three packs. Any kind except menthol. I really hate those things."

"Buy your own," I snapped.

"I'm out tomorrow. I can pay you back."

"Quit while you can. That's my advice."

"What's your name again?"

"Millhone. I'm in the book. If you can read." I returned the handset to the cradle.

"I love you," he mouthed.

"Yeah, right. I love you too."

He winked and wiggled his tongue, a gesture I pretended not to see.

*

On my way home from the jail, I stopped at the supermarket to pick up items for Henry's return. Traffic permitting, he was due back in town sometime between five and six. He'd left his car in long-term parking at the Los Angeles airport. I'd offered to take them down, but Henry, ever independent, had preferred driving himself. He and Rosie and William had flown to Miami, where they were joined by their older sister, Nell, age ninety-seven, and brothers Lewis and Charles, ages ninety-five and ninety, respectively. This morning, after two weeks in the Caribbean, they'd dock in Miami and three of them would catch a plane to L.A. while the three older siblings returned to Michigan.

I loaded my shopping cart with milk, bread, bacon, eggs, orange juice, bananas, onions, carrots, a four-pound roasting chicken, new potatoes, and fresh asparagus, along with salad mix and a fifth of Jack Daniel's, Henry's beverage of choice. Briefly I considered fixing dinner for him myself, but my repertoire is limited and I didn't think pouring skim milk over cold cereal was that festive. Shopping done, I stopped at a corner kiosk a block from the market and bought a bouquet of zinnias and dahlias, a mass of orange and yellow with a ribbon tied around the stems. I could feel my energy lifting the closer I got to home, and by the time I unloaded groceries in Henry's kitchen and put away the perishables, I was humming to myself. I arranged the flowers in a silver coffee server and set them in the middle of the kitchen table.

I did a quick circuit of the house. His answering machine was blinking, but I figured he could pick up any messages as soon as he came in. I went into his cleaning closet and hauled out the vacuum cleaner, a dust mop, a sponge mop, and some rags. I made a second circuit of the house, dusting and vacuuming. All I needed were the singing mice to keep me company. After that, I scrubbed the kitchen and bathroom sinks and ran the sponge mop across the kitchen floor until it gleamed. Then I went home and took a serious world-class nap.

I woke at 5:25, at first reluctant to leave the cozy swaddling quilt in which I'd wrapped myself. It was still light outside. The spring days were getting longer, and we'd soon have the equivalent of an extra half-day at our disposal. People getting off work still had time to walk the dog or to sit on the front porch with a drink before supper. Mom could take a moment to read the paper. Dad could mow the lawn or wash the family car.

I pushed the covers back and moved into the bathroom, where I peered out the window, angling my face so I could catch a glimpse of Henry's back door. The kitchen light was on and I was energized by the idea that he was home. I put on my shoes, washed my face, tidied my bed, and trotted down the spiral stairs. I went out, locking the door behind me, noting with satisfaction that Henry's station wagon was now sitting in the drive where I'd parked the day before yesterday.

He had his back door open, the screen door latched but unlocked. There was no immediate sign of him, but I knocked on the frame and heard his "Yoo hoo" coming at me from the hall. He appeared half a second later in his usual T-shirt, shorts, and flip-flops. Before he could get the door open, his wall phone rang. He motioned me in and then snatched up the receiver. He had the briefest of conversations and then said, "Let me switch to the other phone. Hang on a minute. Don't go away." He held out the handset and whispered, "Be right back. Help yourself to a glass of wine."

I took the phone, waiting while he went into the bedroom and picked up in there. As soon as I knew he was on the line, I replaced the handset in the wall-mounted cradle. He'd already opened a bottle of Chardonnay, which sat in a frosty cooler with a stemmed glass close by. I poured myself half a glass of wine. I could smell chicken baking and I peered through the oven window. The plump hen I'd bought was already turning brown, surrounded by onions, carrots, and rosy new potatoes. He'd set the kitchen table for four, and I knew it wouldn't be long before William and Rosie popped in. It'd take them a day or two to get the tavern up and running. I wondered if Rosie's Hungarian dishes would take on the flavors of the Caribbean. I tried to imagine her pork stew gussied up with coconut, pineapple, and plantains.

Henry returned to the kitchen moments later and poured a drink of his own. He looked tanned and fit, his cheeks wind-burned, his eyes a lustrous blue. William and Rosie arrived at that point, William in a straw boater, Rosie with a tote made of woven fibers that looked like a cross between corn husks and grass. William was two years Henry's senior and blessed with the same silky white hair and the same lean frame. To my mind, he isn't quite as handsome as Henry, but he looks good nonetheless. William is a recovering hypochondriac who still can't resist a good story about inexplicable illness and sudden death. Rosie, by way of contrast, is stocky and solid, bossy, opinionated, insecure, humorless, and generous at heart. The tropical sun had rendered her dyed red hair a singular salmon hue, but she was otherwise unchanged. While Henry took out lettuce and tomatoes, I asked the newlyweds how they'd liked the cruise.

Rosie made a face. "I din't like the food. Too blend. No taste and what there was is no good."

William poured them each a glass of wine. "You ate more than I did! You were gluttonous."

"But I din't enjoy. That's what I'm say. Is forgettable. I don't remember nothing I ate."

"You forgot that pineapple pie? Delicious! Extraordinary. You said so yourself."

"I make twice as good if I want, which I don't."

"Well, I can't argue with that, but you were there to be pampered. The point of the whole vacation was not having to cook."

"What about activities? What'd you do with yourselves all day?"

William pulled out a chair for Rosie and then took a seat at the table. "It was terrific. Wonderful. We docked at various ports, maybe seven in all. When we weren't off seeing the sights, we had lectures and movies, swimming, shuffleboard, aerobics—you name it. They even had a bowling alley. At night, there was gambling and ballroom dancing. Bridge, chess tournaments. Never an idle moment. We had a ball."

"Good for you. That sounds great. How about the other sibs? Did they enjoy it?"

William said, "Well, let's see now. Charlie finally got his hearing aids adjusted and he's a changed man. You can hardly shut him up. Used to be he kept to himself since he never had a clue what anyone was saying to him. He and Nell played bridge and beat the socks off their opponents."

"And Lewis?"

"You put him around a bunch of women and he's happy as a clam. Men were outnumbered ten to one. He was the cock of the walk."

Rosie held up an index finger. "Not quite." She gave Henry a sly smile. "Tell what you did."

"No, no. Unimportant. Enough about us. What about you, Kinsey? What are you working on? Something interesting I'm sure."

"Come on, Henry. You haven't finished telling me about the trip. I've never been on a cruise. I really want to know what it was like."

"Just what William said. Little bit of everything. It was nice," he said, busy with oil and vinegar and his whisk.

Rosie leaned forward, her tone confidential. "He's pose for calendar and now all the old womens calling him night and day."

"Don't be silly," he said over his shoulder to her.

"What kind of calendar?"

"Oh, you know, the usual. The crew thought it'd be a good way to commemorate the trip. They do this all the time. It's nothing. Just a joke."

Rosie nodded, lifting one brown-penciled brow. "The 'nothing' I agree. Is what he's wearing. Our Mr. February, Kings of Heart."

"He wasn't wearing *nothing*," William said. "You make it sound like he was *nude* when he was no such thing."

She reached in her tote and pulled out a glossy calendar filled with color photographs. "I heve right here. You take a look and see for yourself. The man's got no clothes. Only underpents." She flipped to the month of February and turned the page so I could see it. The candid shot showed Henry on the upper deck, leaning against the rail with his back to the ocean. A distant palm-dotted island was visible to his right. He wore red shorts, no shoes, a white dress shirt hanging loose and unbuttoned down the front. A captain's hat was tilted forward at an angle. His grin was unaffected, showing a flash of white teeth against the tan of his face. The effect was rakish, the perfect combination of charisma and sex appeal. Henry, in the kitchen with us, blushed from ear to ear.

"Ooo, I love this. I have to have a copy of my own," I said.

"Is yours. You keep. I heve more for ladies in the neighborhood."

"Thanks." I flipped through the pages, checking the other entrants. While some of the photographs showed moderately attractive men—all octogenarians, by the look—not one was as dashing as Henry. I laughed with pleasure. "I never knew you were so photogenic. No wonder the phone's ringing. You look fabulous."

"The phone's not ringing," he said.

At that moment, the phone did, in fact, ring.

"I get," Rosie said, heaving herself to her feet.

"No, you won't. That's what machines are for."

We waited out the three additional rings until Henry's answering machine kicked in. From the other room, we heard the outgoing message, followed by the usual beep. "Henry? This is Bella, *'ma petite belle.'* Remember me? I promised I'd call you so here I am. I just wanted to say how disappointed I was we didn't have a chance to visit again before you left the ship. You bad boy. When you have a chance, you can reach me at . . ."

Dinner was punctuated by two additional calls, which Henry ignored. He kept his eyes on his plate, cutting his chicken with a concentration he rarely lavished on his food. The third time the phone rang, he left the table and went into the living room, where he turned off the ringer and lowered the volume on the answering machine. None of us said a word, but Rosie and William exchanged a look as she smirked at her plate. I could see her shoulders shake, though she pretended to cough, a napkin pressed to her lips.

"It's not *funny*," Henry snapped.

NINE

With Stacey back in the hospital for a second time in five days, I volunteered to take the Monday interview with Lorenzo Rickman. Dolan had offered to do it, but I knew he was eager to be on hand when the doctors talked to Stacey about this latest round of tests. As it turned out, my chat with Rickman was brief and unproductive. We stood in the service bay of an import repair shop that smelled of gasoline fumes, motor oil, and new tires. The floor, work benches, and all available countertops were littered with a jumble of tools and equipment, parts, manuals, blackened spark plugs, cracked cylinder heads, valves, fan belts, drive shafts, alternators, and exhaust manifolds.

Rickman was in his late thirties with an angular face and a neck that appeared too thin to hold his head upright. His dark hair was receding, a few feathers combed down on his forehead to form a fringe of sparse bangs. A beard, closely trimmed, ran along the line of his jaw, and he stroked it reflexively with fingers black-ened by oil. His uniform probably wasn't any different than the outfits he'd worn in prison, except for the machine-embroidered name above his left shirt pocket. He made a show of being cooperative, but he had no memory of incarceration with Frankie Miracle.

He shook his head. "Can't help. Name doesn't ring a bell. I was only in jail the one night. First thing the next morning, a friend of mine bailed me out, but only after I promised to join AA. I've been on the wagon—well, more or less—ever since." He smiled briefly while he smoothed his hair toward his forehead. "I still get in trouble with the law, but at least I'm clean and sober—condition of my parole. Right now, I do, you know, five, six meetings a week. Not that I like hanging out with dudes hyped up on coffee and cigarettes, but it sure beats incarceration." He put his hands in his back pockets and then changed his mind and crossed his arms, fingers drifting back to his beard, which he stroked with his thumb.

"What about the other guys in the cell that night? You remember anything about them?"

"Nope. Sorry. I was eighteen years old, drunk and stoned the night they picked me up. My second or third blackout, I forget which. Third, I think. I could've been in with Charlie Manson and you couldn't prove it by me."

I tried priming the pump, claiming we had a witness who was there at the same time and said Frankie'd bragged about a killing. This generated no response. I handed him the packet of photographs, which he shuffled through carelessly. He shook his head and handed them back. "Look like a bunch of thugs."

I tucked the photos in my bag. "I know this is none of my business, but what'd you do to warrant a prison sentence?"

His fingers became still and then he pulled at a thatch of beard growing under his chin. "What makes you ask?"

"No reason. I'm just curious."

"I don't really care to say."

"Ah. My fault. Sorry. It's your business, of course. I didn't mean to step on your toes." I gave him my card, offering the standard line. "Thanks for your time. If you think of anything, will you let us know?"

"Sure."

"Can I ask one more thing? You think you're out for good?"

He considered my question and then smiled to himself. "I doubt it."

I stopped off at the hospital on my way into town. Stacey was back on 6 Central, in another private room located down the hall from the room he'd had before. When I glanced in, his bed was empty. Beside it, a wide window looked out on a view of the ocean, maybe two miles away, across the shaggy treetops. An occasional glimpse of a red-tile roof punctuated the thick expanse of green. The room was airy; spacious enough to accommodate a forty-eight-inch round table and four captain's chairs, where I found Dolan sitting with a tattered copy of *Road & Track*.

"Oh, hi. Where's Stace?"

"In X-ray. He should be back in a bit."

"How's he doing?"

"Don't know yet. What'd Rickman say?"

"Regrettably, not much." I filled him in on my conversation. "I think we can safely write him off. Probably Pudgie as well. He's cagey, but dumb, and I don't trust the combination. So now what?"

Dolan set his magazine aside. He wore a dark blue windbreaker and a Dodgers baseball cap. "Stacey never got a chance to call Joe Mandel to see if he can lay hands on Jane Doe's effects. Soon as he's got a minute, he's going to do that. Meantime, we thought you might have a phone chat with this C. K. Vogel fellow that Arne was talking about. You might try Directory Assistance—"

"Dolan, this is what I do for a living."

"Oh, right. Sorry."

"I'll go down to the lobby and find a public phone. You want anything while I'm there?"

"I don't suppose they sell Camels in the gift shop."

"I don't suppose they do." When I got to the door, I hesitated. "What was Rickman in prison for?"

Lieutenant Dolan picked up his magazine and wet his index finger. He turned the page, paying close attention to a full-page ad for a fuel additive that required the presence of a blond in a bathing suit. "Well, let's see. Molestation, sodomy, oral copulation, lewd and lascivious acts with a child. I'm surprised he wasn't killed in prison. As a rule, inmates don't have a lot of tolerance for guys like that."

Geez, I'd been picturing a bit of B&E.

I took the elevator down and made my way through the maze of corridors to the lobby. I found a bank of public phone kiosks outside the front entrance, sheltered by a marquee that extended from the lobby door to the passenger loading ramp. While I looked on, a young nurse's aide helped a new mother out of a wheelchair and into a waiting van. I couldn't see the baby's face, but the bundle wasn't much bigger than a loaf of bread. I scrounged around in the bottom of my bag and came up with a handful of coins. Lompoc was in the same area code as Santa Teresa, so I knew it wasn't going to require much. I dialed directory assistance while the young husband loaded flower arrangements into the back of the van, along with a cluster of bobbing pink and silver helium balloons.

I got C. K. Vogel's number and made a note of it before I dialed. When he picked up on his end, I identified myself. Judging from the sound of his voice, he was in his eighties and possibly in the midst of an afternoon nap. I said, "Sorry to disturb you."

"No, no. Don't worry about that. Arne called on Friday and said someone might be in touch. You want to know about the van I saw, is that correct?"

"Yes, sir. It is."

"Tell you the truth, I didn't say much at the time. I had a brother-in-law worked for the Sheriff's Department—this was my sister Madge's husband, fella named Melvin Galloway. He's since died. Two of us never did get along. He's a damn know-it-all. Had an opinion about everything and hear him tell it, he's always right. I couldn't abide the man. Might not sound Christian, but it's the truth. I told him twice about that van, but he pooh-poohed the idea, said if he stopped to track down every half-assed theory the John Q. Public volunteered, he wouldn't get anything else done. Not that he did much to begin with. He's the laziest son of a gun I ever came across. After 'while, I figured I'd done what I could and said to hell with him. What struck me afterward was not the hippie van so much as that other car I saw. Snappy-looking red convertible with Arizona plates."

"Arne mentioned the red car, but I got the impression it was the van you thought was suspicious. Did I get that wrong?"

"No, ma'am. I noticed the van on account of the paint job—peace symbols and that sort, in the wildest colors imaginable. It was parked right there in that fork in the road when I first became aware of it."

"I know the location."

"Reason the other car caught my attention was because I later read in the paper they recovered a stolen car matching that description."

"You remember the make?"

"I don't, but I saw that car on three occasions. First time near the quarry, just a little piece down the road, and the second time over town. I was driving to the doctor's office to have a cyst removed and passed the wrecker pulling it up out of the ravine, all banged up. Looked like whoever took the car let the handbrake loose and pushed it down a hill into a bunch of brush. Must have hit a goodly number of trees on the way, judging from all the scratches and dents. Wasn't spotted for a week, but the fella where I take my car for repairs was the one the Sheriff's Department called when they needed it towed. I saw it at the repair shop the next day when I was having work done on my carburetor. That was the third time. Never saw it again after that."

"I remember mention of a stolen car. Was there anybody in it when you saw it the first time?"

"No, ma'am. It was setting on the side of the road just inside the entrance to your grandma's property. Top down, sun beating hard on those fine black leather seats. I slowed as I went by because I wondered if someone'd had engine trouble and had wandered off to get help. I didn't see a note on the windshield so I drove on. Next time I passed, the car was gone."

"Did you tell Melvin about that one?"

"I told Madge and she told him, but that's the last I heard. I didn't want to force my observations on a fella doesn't want to hear. He'd have pooh-poohed that, too. Trouble with Melvin is he didn't believe a thing unless it come from him. He's the type if he didn't know something, he made it up. If he didn't feel like doing something, he claimed he did it anyway. You couldn't pin the man down. Ask him a question, he'd act like he'd been accused of negligence."

"Sounds like a pain."

"Yes, he was. Madge, too."

"Well. I appreciate the information. I'll mention this to the guys and see if it's something they want to pursue." Inwardly, I was still hung up on the fact that he'd mentioned my "grandma." I never thought of Grand that way. I had a grandmother. How bizarre.

As though reading my mind, he said, "I knew your mama once upon a time."

"Really."

"Yes ma'am. You know Arne Johanson worked for the Kinseys from the age of seventeen. He was sweet on her himself, but Rita wouldn't give him the time of day. He figured it's because he was too old for her and then she up and marries your dad, the same age as him. He got his nose out of joint, I can tell you that. I told him don't be ridiculous. In the first place, she was never going to take up with a cowpoke. Second place, she'd rather die than get stuck where she is. She was wild, that one, and pretty as they come. Restless as all get out. She'd have taken up with anyone to get off the ranch."

"That's flattering," I said. In truth, this was the first concrete image I'd ever had of her. In that careless vignette, he'd captured the entire story of her life. My cousins, Liza and Tasha, had spoken of her in ways that seemed larger than life. She'd taken on the aura of family myth, a symbol of that legendary clash of wills. "I understand she and my grandmother didn't get along."

"Oh, they tangled, those two. Rita was Cornelia's pride and joy. I felt sorry for her in a way . . ."

"Who, my mother?"

"Your grandma. She liked to maintain she didn't have a favorite among the five girls, but Rita was her firstborn and Cornelia doted on her. You know the story, I suppose."

"Well, sure. I heard it once," I said, lying through my teeth. Somehow gossip seems less pernicious if the person telling the tale thinks it's one you've already heard.

"Cornelia married Burton Kinsey when she was seventeen, exactly half his age. That's one more reason she didn't want Rita to marry young like she did. She lost three babies in a row, all of them boys and not a one went to term. Rita was the first of her children to survive. Cornelia's boys were stillborn. Only the girls made it through alive."

"What was that about?"

"I don't think the doctors determined the cause. In those days, medicine was largely good luck and guesswork. People died of diabetes until those two fellows discovered insulin in 1923. Folks died of anemia, too, until liver therapy came along in 1934. Think of it. Eating liver was a cure. We forget things like that; forget how ignorant we were and how much we've learned." He stopped to clear his throat. "Well, now. I didn't mean to run on at the mouth. Trouble with getting old is you lose all the people you tell your stories to. You let me know if that red car turns out to be anything. I'd like to have a laugh at Melvin's expense after all these years."

"Thanks for your time. I'll be in touch."

I replaced the handset in the cradle and headed for the elevator, which I took to 6 Central. The doors slid open and I stepped off just as Dolan approached, having exited Stacey's room. He took a seat on a couch positioned under a window. The area wasn't designated as a waiting room, but it probably served as a getaway for friends and family members who needed a break. He rose when he caught sight of me.

"Don't get up," I said. "What are you doing out here? I thought you'd be down the hall with Stace."

Dolan sat down again on the couch. "The doctors are in there. Oncologist, radiologist, and another specialist nobody bothered to introduce."

"What's going on?"

"Beats me. All three had on those long medical faces so the news couldn't be good. How'd the phone call go? Did you talk to Vogel?" He scooted over on the couch to make room for me. "Here. Have a seat."

I perched on the near arm and propped my hand on the back of the couch. "For starters, in the small-world department, it turns out C. K. Vogel was Melvin Galloway's brother-in-law." I went on, summarizing the information C.K.'d given me about the red convertible.

"He could be confused. Frankie's car was red."

"I know, but he was very specific about it's being a convertible with black leather seats."

"Let's run that by Stacey and see what he says. It can't hurt to check."

Out of the corner of my eye, I saw the three doctors emerge from Stacey's room. I pointed in their direction as they rounded the far corner and disappeared. "Looks like they're done. You want to go down and find out what they said?"

"No. But I will."

I let Dolan take the lead as we entered Stacey's room, thinking that if Stace was upset, I could ease out without calling undue attention to myself. He was in bed, having cranked up the head so he could see the view. He had his knit cap off and I was disconcerted by the sight of his bare head. His hair was wispy, a cross between duck down and baby fuzz, scarcely half an inch long. The watch cap had given him an air of manliness. Without it, he was just a sick old man with a scrawny neck and ears that protruded from the bony shell of his skull. He turned from the view with a smile that came close to merriment unless you knew him. "Never let it be said God doesn't have a sense of humor."

Dolan said, "Uh-oh."

"It's really not too bad. No meningioma or neurofibroma; in other words, there're no metastatic tumors along my spine. The business with my back's benign. Probably a herniated disc, which is the result of degenerative changes not uncommon in a man my age. I'm quoting the doc here just in case you think I've started talking strange. The treatment of choice is bed rest, which is something I'm already well acquainted with. Analgesics, a mild tranquilizer, possibly Valium as you suggested. That doesn't work, they go to plan B, which they haven't laid out as yet. I'm guessing surgery, but they haven't actually said as much. Doctor did suggest exercises to strengthen my back once the pain subsides. Fair enough. Unfortunately, the very same X-ray that showed my back problem's no more than a pain in the ass also revealed a lesion. I'm supposed to be in remission, free and clear."

"What's he think it is?"

"She, goddammit! And don't interrupt. I was just getting to that. Doc says it could be scar tissue, it could be the remains of a dying tumor, or it might be our old friend lymphoma cropping up again. They can't tell from the film. So first thing tomorrow morning, I'm scheduled for a biopsy. Lucky I'm here is how they put it to me. Lucky my back feels like shit, they said. Without back pain, no X-ray. Without the X-ray, this whatever I've got would have gone undetected until the next follow-up appointment, which isn't on the books for months." He pointed at Dolan. "And don't say 'I told you so' because I don't want to hear it."

"I'd never say that—though I'll admit I did mention it."

I thought he was pushing his luck, but Stacey laughed.

Dolan said, "So when do you get out?"

"They haven't told me yet. Meantime, I'm not lying here idle. I put in another call to the Sheriff's Department. Joe Mandel's made detective so I'm hoping he'll let us take a look at the Jane Doe evidence."

"Kinsey and I can do that."

"Not without me. You want to keep me alive, you better do what I say."

"Bullshit. That's blackmail."

"That's exactly right. So tell me about Rickman. I could use a good laugh about now."

I had dinner that night at Rosie's, so grateful to have her home I could have kissed the hem of her muumuu. Since the tavern had been closed for two weeks, the smell of beer and cigarette smoke had nearly faded from the air. In her absence, she'd had a cleaning crew come in and scrub the place down. Floors now gleamed, wood surfaces were polished, and the mirror behind the bar reflected the rows of liquor bottles with a sparkle that suggested expensive handblown glass. The crowd that night was light, the usual patrons perhaps still unaware that the restaurant was open for business again.

William stood behind the bar, pulling beers and pouring drinks for the smattering of customers. Henry sat at his usual table, amusing himself with a book of anagrams. At his invitation, I took a seat across from him. I looked over as Rosie emerged from the kitchen with an armload of what appeared to be slim binders. She crossed the room, heading in our direction, clearly pleased with herself. She handed a binder to me and a second to Henry. I thought they might be picture albums, but I opened the front cover and found myself staring at a handwritten menu done in a calligraphic script.

"This is different," I remarked.

"Is new menu. So I don't hef to tell every dish what I'm cooking. William wrote by hand and then went to photo copy shop and hed them print. You order anything you want and what you can't say in Henglish you point." She stood and looked at us expectantly. Since she'd returned from the cruise, her Henglish seemed to have gotten worse.

Henry surveyed his menu, a curious expression crossing his face. I glanced at mine, running my gaze down the page. The dishes were listed first in Hungar-

ian, complete with letter combinations and accent marks
I'd never seen before. Under the Hungarian name for
each dish there was the translation in English:

Versenyi Batyus Ponty
Carp in a Bundle

Csuka Tejfeles Tormaval
Pike Cooked in Horseradish Cream

Hamis Oztokany
Mock Venison

Diszno Csülök Káposztával
Pig's Knuckles and Sauerkraut

I couldn't wait to see what the crowd of softball rowdies
was going to think about this.

"You've outdone yourself, Rosie," Henry said.

"Really," I said. "I can hardly choose."

She seemed to wiggle with pleasure, order pad in
hand. For a minute I thought she intended to lick her
pencil point.

Henry smiled at her blandly. "Why don't you give us
a few minutes? This is a lot to take in."

"You keep and I come beck."

"Good idea."

She moved away from our table and began to circle
the room, distributing a menu at each booth and table

along the way. Henry stared after her with something close to wonderment. "I guess this is what happens when you take someone on a cruise. She's come home inspired. If I didn't know her better, I'd say she was putting on airs."

I set my menu aside. "That's the least of our worries. What are we going to do? I don't want to eat a pig knuckle with sauerkraut. That's disgusting."

He looked at his menu again. "Listen to this one. 'Mazsolas es Gesztenyés Borjunyelv.' You know what that is? Calf's Tongue with Chestnuts and Raisins."

"Oh, that can't be true. Where do you see that?" I peered over at his menu, hoping it was somehow completely different.

He pointed at an item under a column entitled "Specialities of the House." "Here's another one. Lemon Tripe. I forget what that is. Could be stomach or bowel."

"What's the big deal with organ meats?"

Rosie had completed her circuit and she now headed back to our table. "I hef idea. I prepare for you special. Big surprise."

"No, no, no," Henry said. "I wouldn't want to put you to any trouble. We'll just order from what's here. My goodness. So many interesting dishes. What are you having, Kinsey?"

"Me? Oh. Well, actually on a night like this, I'd love

a nice big bowl of soup and maybe noodles on the side. Could you do that for me?"

"Easy. Of course. I give Shepherd's Soup. Is already make," she said, pausing to pencil an elaborate note on her order pad. She turned to Henry.

"I think I'll hold off for now. I just had a bite before I came over here."

"Little plate of dumplings? Jellied pork? Is fresh. Very good."

"Don't tempt me. Maybe later. I'll just keep her company for now," he said.

Rosie pursed her lips and then shrugged to herself. I thought she'd insist, but apparently decided to let him suffer. Neither of us said a word until she'd disappeared.

I leaned forward. "Why didn't you tell me you were doing that? I could have said the same thing."

"I blurted out the first thing that occurred to me. You were quick about it, too. Soup and noodles. That's safe. How can you go wrong?"

My gaze strayed toward the kitchen. Mere seconds had passed, and Rosie was already using her backside to push her way through the swinging kitchen doors into the dining room, bearing a wide tray that held a shallow bowl of steaming soup.

I said, "Oh, geez. Here she comes. I hate service this quick. It's like eating in a Chinese restaurant. You're in and out on the street again twenty minutes later."

She crossed the room, setting the tray on the adjoining table, then placing the bowl in front of me. She tucked her hands under her apron and looked at me. "How you like?"

"I haven't tried it yet." I fanned some of the steam toward my face, trying to define the odor. Burnt hair? Dog hide? "Gee, this smells great. What is it?"

She peered at my bowl, identifying some of the diced ingredients. "Is parsnip, ongion, carrot, kohlrabi—"

"I love vegetable soup!" I said, with perhaps more enthusiasm than I'd ordinarily express. I tipped my spoon down into the depths, bringing up a rich cargo of root vegetables.

She was still peering. "Is also head, neck, lungs, and liver of one lamb."

The spoon was already in the air by then, soup sailing toward my mouth as though of its own accord. As the spoon reached my lips, I caught a glimpse of porous gray chunks, probably minced lobe of lung, along with some floaters of something I was too fearful to ask about. I puckered my lips and made a slurping sound, sucking up the broth while deftly avoiding the little knots of offal. I made insincere *Mmm* noises.

"I come right beck with noodles."

"Take your time."

As soon as she left, I put my spoon down, craning to check all four corners of the room. "I wonder if I have

183

time to scoot to the toilet and put this back where it belongs. She doesn't even have planters where I can dump the stuff."

Henry leaned closer to the bowl. "Is that a nostril? Oh no, sorry. It's probably just a little cross-section of heart valve. Head's up. Here she comes again."

Rosie was returning to the table with a dinner-sized plate in hand. I made a big display of stirring my soup and wiping my mouth with a napkin as she set the noodles in front of me. I patted my chest as though overwhelmed, which I was. "This is filling. Really rich."

I stole an apprehensive look at the dish as she placed it on the table beside my soup bowl, experiencing a flash of relief. "What's that, manicotti?"

"Is call *palacsinta tészta*. Like what you call crepes."

"Hungarian crepes. Well, that sounds wonderful. I can do that."

"I fill with calf's brains scrembled with egg. Very dainty. You'll see. I can teach you to make."

"Okay then, I'll just chow down," I said. She stood by the table, as though prepared to monitor my every bite. I leaned to one side, focusing my gaze on the far side of the room. "I think William's calling you. It looks like he needs help."

Rosie crossed to the bar where she and William engaged in a baffled conversation. Meanwhile, I'd grabbed up my shoulder bag and I was rooting through the contents. Earlier that day, I'd spotted an outdated grocery list done on a sheet of yellow legal paper. I kept one eye on Rosie while I folded the note paper into a cone, pointed at the bottom with a wide mouth at the top. I turned the pointed bottom up to form a seal. I forked up crepes in rapid succession, ignoring the gnarly bits that fell back on the plate. I folded the top down, wrapped the cone in a paper napkin, and shoved the bundle in my purse.

By the time Rosie glanced in my direction, I was bent over my plate, making fake chewing motions while trying to look entranced. Another couple entered the bar and her attention was distracted. I put a twenty on the table near Henry's plate. "Tell her I was called away on an emergency."

Henry pointed to my soup, most of which was still in the bowl. "I'll have her put that in a jar and bring it over to you later tonight. I know how you hate to see food go to waste."

TEN

I was home earlier than I'd intended, concerned that calf brain would leak out of the makeshift container and contaminate the interior of my shoulder bag. As I passed Henry's garbage can, I removed the bundle from my purse and dumped it. I lifted my head, alerted by the dim ringing of a phone somewhere. I banged down the lid and hurried to my front door, unlocking it in haste. Three rings. Four. I slung my bag on a kitchen chair and snatched up the receiver. My answering machine had already kicked in and I was forced to override my own voice, singing, "It's me. I'm here. Don't go away. I'm answering."

"Kinsey?"

The caller was male and he spoke against the dull murmur of background conversations. I put a hand against one ear. "Who's this?"

"Pudgie."

"Well, hi. This is a surprise. I didn't think I'd hear from you. What's up?"

"You said call if I thought of something, but you have to promise you won't let this get back to him."

I found myself straining to hear. "Back to who?"

"Frankie. You ever meet him?"

"Not yet."

"He's a crazy man. You can't tell it right off because he's good at faking it . . . like he's normal and all, but believe me, you don't want to mess with him."

"I didn't realize you knew him."

"I don't, but it doesn't take a genius to figure out the guy's a freak."

"Is that why you called, to say how nuts he is?"

"Nuhn-uhn. I'll get to that, but lemme ask you something first. Suppose someone tells him I called you?"

"Come on. I can't control that. Besides, who's going to tell? I can promise not a word of this will come from me."

"You swear?"

"Of course."

I could hear him cup a hand over the mouthpiece, lips so close to the phone I thought he'd slobber in my ear. "He talked about stabbing some chick to death."

"Oh, for heaven's sake, Pudgie. That's why he went to prison. For killing Cathy Lee Pearse."

"Not her. Another one. This was after he killed her."

"I'm listening."

SUE GRAFTON

"He's bragging about what happens to any bitch tries to cross him. He said he picked up this chick in a bar. She had some dope on her and the two of them got loose. They go out to the parking lot to play grab ass, but she turns all sour on him and starts giving him a hard time, which pisses him off. When she refuses to put out, he offs her and sticks her in the trunk of Cathy Lee's car. He drives around with her two days, but he's worried she'll start to stink, so he dumps her when he gets to Lompoc."

"Where'd he pick her up?"

"What bar? Don't know. He never said. He didn't mention the town, either. I'd guess Santa Teresa. It had to've been before he hit Lompoc because that's where he got caught."

"What about the dump site? Did he say where that was?"

"Some place outside town where she wouldn't be found. I guess they managed to nail him on Cathy Lee, but nobody knew about the other one, so he was free and clear on that."

"What made you suddenly remember? This doesn't sound like something that would slip your mind."

"It didn't 'slip my mind,'" he said, offended. "You're the one came to me. I never offered to snitch. I didn't 'suddenly' do anything. I remembered the minute his name came up."

188

"Why didn't you tell me then?"

"We'd only just met. How'd I know I could trust you? I had to think about that."

"What made you decide to tell me?"

"I probably should've kept my mouth shut if it comes right down to it. Frankie's a bad-ass. Word leaks out and my sorry butt is fried. He's not a guy you fuck with and expect to live."

"Fair enough," I said. "Did he say anything else?"

"Not that I remember offhand. Time, I didn't pay much attention. Jail, everybody brags about stuff like that. It's mostly bullshit, so I didn't attach anything to it. I mean, I did, but then that's the last I ever heard of it. Now you're saying some girl's body was dumped and right away I think about him."

"You're sure about this."

"No, I'm not *sure*. He might've made the whole thing up. How the hell should I know? You said call and I did."

I thought about it briefly. This could be a hustle, though for the life of me, I couldn't see what Pudgie was getting out of it. "That's not much to go on."

"Well, I can't help you there."

"How'd he kill her?"

"Knife, I guess. Said he stabbed her, wrapped her up, and stuck her in the trunk. Soon as he got to Lompoc, he pitched her off the side of the road and hightailed it out of there. By the time the cops picked him up he figured he was safe. All they cared about was nailing him for Cathy Lee."

"Did he know the girl?"

"I doubt it. He didn't talk like he did."

"Because I'm curious about his motive."

"You gotta be kidding. Frankie doesn't need a *motive*. She could've looked at him funny or called him a pencil dick. If she knew he was on the run, she might've threatened to turn him in."

"Interesting," I said. "I'll have to give this some thought. Where are you calling from?"

"A place I hang out in Creosote. My sis drove up from the desert and brought me back to her house."

"Is there any way I can reach you if I need to get in touch?"

He gave me a number with an area code.

I said, "Thanks. This could be a big help."

"Where's Frankie now?"

"I'm not sure. We've heard he's in town."

"You mean the fucker's *out*?"

"Sure, he's been paroled."

"You never said that. Oh, shit. You have to swear you won't tell him where you heard this. And don't ask me to testify in court because I won't."

"Pudgie, you couldn't testify in court. This is all

hearsay. You didn't see him do anything so quit worrying. I'll tell the two cops I'm working with, but that's the end of it."

"I hope I haven't made a mistake."

"Relax. You're fine."

"You buy me those cigarettes?"

"No, but I owe you a bunch."

Dolan picked me up at the office Tuesday morning at 10:00. I'd managed my usual 6:00 A.M. run, after which I'd showered and dressed. I had coffee and a quick bowl of cereal, making it into the office by 8:35. By the time I heard Dolan's car horn, I'd finished catching up on all the odds and ends on my desk. Dolan had the good grace to toss his cigarette out the window as soon as I got in. Stacey's biopsy had been scheduled for 7:45, but neither of us wanted to talk about that. After I'd wrenched open the car door on the passenger side and hauled it shut again, I told Dolan about Pudgie's call.

He said, "Don't know what to make of it. What do you think?"

"I'd love to believe him, but I'm not sure how credible he is for a jailhouse snitch. He did seem to have a couple of the details right."

"Like what?"

"Well, he knew she'd been stabbed and he knew she'd been wrapped in something at the time she was dumped."

"It's possible he took a flyer, guessing at the fine points to make himself seem important."

"To me? Why would he care?"

"Because he's flirting with you. Gave him an excuse to call."

"Is that it? Well, I'm thrilled."

"Point is, what he says is useless. It's all air and sunshine."

"And hearsay as well."

"Right."

The next stop was Frankie's to see what we could shake loose from him. Dolan had talked to Frankie's parole officer, Dench Smallwood, who'd given him the address.

On our way across town, Dolan told me he'd gone through the murder book again. Early reports had made reference to three stolen vehicles, one of which was the red 1967 Chevrolet in which Frankie'd been stopped. Melvin Galloway had been asked to follow up on the other two, but gauging from the paperwork, it was impossible to tell what he'd actually done. Miracle was a fugitive and his arrest was a feather in Galloway's cap. Given his reputation for laziness, the routine aspects of the investigation probably didn't have much appeal. It was possible he'd simply claimed he'd handled the query when he'd let the matter slide. The red convertible C. K. Vogel had seen turned out to be a 1966 Ford Mustang, owned by a man named Gant in Mesquite, Arizona, just across the California line. Stacey had asked Joe Mandel to run the VIN and license plate to see where the vehicle was now. If Mandel could determine the current whereabouts, it might be worthwhile to track it down and take a look.

The room Frankie rented was located in the rear of a frame house on Guardia Street. We picked our way down the drive, avoiding a cornucopia of spilled garbage from an overturned can. Surrounding orange and red hibiscus shrubs had grown so tall that the narrow wooden porch was cold with shade. Dolan knocked on the door while I stood to one side, as though worried I'd be fired on through the lath-and-plaster wall. Dolan waited a decent interval and knocked again. We were on the verge of departing when Frankie opened the door. At forty-four, he was baby-faced and clean-shaven. He wore a T-shirt and loose shorts, with a sleep mask pushed up on the top of his head. His feet were bare. He said, "What."

"Mr. Miracle?"

"That's right."

Dolan moved his windbreaker aside, exposing the badge on his belt. "Lieutenant Dolan, Santa Teresa Police Department. This is Kinsey Millhone."

"Okay." Frankie had mild brown wavy hair and brown eyes. His gaze was direct and tainted with annoyance. I was surprised to see he had no visible tattoos. He'd been in prison for the past seventeen years and I expected him to look as though he'd been rolling naked and wet across the Sunday funnies. He wasn't overweight by any means, but he looked soft, which was another surprise. I picture prison inmates all bulked up from lifting weights. His eyes caught mine. "I suit you okay?"

I declined a response.

Dolan said, "You have a late night? You seem cross."

"I work nights, if it's any of your business."

"Doing what?"

"Janitorial. The Granger Building on the graveyard shift. I'd give you my boss's name, but you already have that."

Dolan smiled slightly. "Matter of fact I do. Your parole officer gave it to me when I talked to him."

"What's this about?"

"May we come in?"

Frankie glanced back across his shoulder. "Sure, why not?"

He stepped away from the door and we crossed the

threshold. His entire living quarters consisted of one room with a linoleum floor, a hot plate, an ancient refrigerator, an iron bedstead, and little else. In lieu of a closet, he had a rack made of cast iron pipe on which he'd draped his clothes, both dirty and clean. I could see a cramped bathroom through a door that opened off the rear wall. In addition to an ashtray full of butts, there was a tumble of paperback books on the floor by his bed, a mix of mystery and science fiction. The room smelled of ripe sheets and stale cigarette smoke. I'd have killed myself if I were forced to live in a place like this. On the other hand, Frankie was used to prison, so this was probably an improvement.

There was no place to sit so the two of us stood while Frankie crawled back in bed and pulled the sheet across his lap. The ensuing conversation seemed bizarre, like a visit with Stacey in his hospital room. I'd never seen anyone other than the chronically ill opt to be inter-viewed prone. It suggested a wary sort of self-confidence. He straightened the sheet and folded the top over once. "You can skip the small talk. I'm working again tonight and I need my sleep."

"We'd like to ask you about the time you spent in Lompoc before you got picked up."

"What about it?"

"How you got there, what you were doing before your arrest?"

"Don't remember. I was stoned. I had shit for brains back then."

"When the officers pulled you over, you were six miles from the spot where a young girl's body was found."

"Wonderful. And where was that?"

"Near Grayson Quarry. You know the place?"

"Everybody knows Grayson. It's been there for years."

"It seems like quite a coincidence."

"That I was six miles away? Bullshit. I have family in the area. My dad's lived in the same house forty-four years. I was on my way to visit."

"After killing Cathy Lee."

"I hope you aren't here coughing up that old hair ball. I'll tell you one thing, they never should have nailed me for murder one. That was strictly self-defense. She came at me with a pair of scissors—not that I need to justify myself to you."

"Why'd you run? Hardly the actions of an innocent man."

"I never said I was innocent. I said—oh hell, why should I tell you? I was in a panic, if you want to know the truth. You do meth, you don't think straight. Temper runs hot and you think everybody's after you."

"No need to be defensive," Dolan said.

"Please forgive me. I beseech you. People wake me up, I get cranky sometimes."

Dolan smiled. "You get cranky, you fly off the handle, is that it?"

"You know what? I've done my time. Not a mark on my record in seventeen years. Credit for time served, good behavior, the whole shootin' match. Now I'm out, I'm clean, and I'm gainfully employed so you can go fuck yourself. No offense."

"Prison did you good."

"Yes, it did. See that? Rehabilitation works. I'm living proof. Went from bad to good and now I'm free as a bird."

"Not quite. You're still on parole."

"You think I don't know that? All the fuckin' rules they lay down? Tell you something, you won't catch me in violation. I'm way too smart. I'm willing to play fair because I don't intend to go back in. And I mean, ever."

"You know the problem with you, Frankie?"

"What's that, Lieutenant? I'm sure you'll spell it out in great detail."

"You may be righteous today, but back then you didn't know enough to keep your big mouth shut."

"Come on. What *is* this?"

"I told you. We have an unsolved homicide with circumstances similar to Cathy Lee's."

"Yeah, well, I can't help you there. I don't know jack about that. You want anything else, you can talk to my attorney."

"And who's that?"

"Haven't hired one yet, but I'll let you know. Where's this horseshit coming from, or is that classified?"

"We got somebody willing to put the ju-ju on you."

"Ju-ju, my ass. What have you got, some ex-con having lunch on my expense account? I didn't kill the chick. You're full of shit."

"That's not what our witness says. He says you bragged about it afterward."

"You're blowin' smoke and you know it. You had anything on me, you'd've showed up with a warrant instead of this hokey song-and-dance routine."

Dolan shook his head. "I don't know, Frankie. I figure you had a hard-on for the girl and when she wouldn't put out, you lost control of yourself."

"Yeah, yeah, yeah." Frankie made a gesture like he was whacking off.

"Why don't you own up to it? You could really help us out. Show your heart's in the right place now that you've turned over this new leaf."

Frankie smiled, shaking his head in disbelief. "You think I'd be dumb enough to sit here and confess? To what? You got nothing on me. I don't even know who the fuck you're talking about."

"I'm not here to hassle you."

"Good, because I'm trying not to lose my cool. You want a urine sample, I'll piss in a cup. You want to search the place, have at it. Whatever it is, just be quick about it. Otherwise we're done. Pull the door shut behind you on your way out." He slid the mask down over his eyes and turned his back to us.

"Well, that was unproductive," I said when the two of us were back in the car again.

"I wanted you to have a look at him. It's always best if you know the players firsthand. Besides, it's good to let him sweat a bit, wondering what we have."

"That won't take long. We don't have anything, do we?"

"No, but he doesn't know that."

Dolan was going to go back over to St. Terry's as soon as he dropped me at the office, but when we pulled onto Caballeria Lane, we caught sight of Stacey sitting on the curb in front of my place, a brown paper bag at his feet. He wore his red knit watch cap, short-sleeve shirt, chinos, and shoes with no socks. His perforated plastic hospital bracelet still encircled his wrist. His arms were bone thin, his skin translucent, like the pale tissue overlay on a wedding invitation. Dolan parked two cars away. While we walked back to Stacey, Dolan took out a pack of cigarettes and his matches and paused to light up. He tossed the match aside and drew deeply, sucking smoke down as though he were using an asthma inhaler. "How'd you get here?"

Stacey shaded his eyes, looking sideways at him. "Called a cab. They do that. Pay 'em money, those guys'll take you anyplace you want."

"I didn't think you'd be released until they ran more tests."

Stacey waved that notion aside. "Hell with 'em. I got tired of waiting for the doc to pull a thumb out. I packed my things and took a hike. I don't have time for nonsense. It won't change anything. Meantime, I got a call from Mandel and he says come on out. He's pulled the Jane Doe evidence and we can take a look. Speaking of which, what'd our friend Frankie have to say for himself?"

"Don't change the subject. How'd the biopsy go?"

"Piece of cake. They've stuck me so often, it's like a bug bite."

"How soon do you get the results?"

Stacey's hand was so small he managed to ease his bracelet off without breaking it. "Day or so. Who cares? We got work to do. Now give me a hand here. My age, you get down, you can't get up again. Tell me about Frankie."

"He's completely innocent."

"Of course. We should have known."

Dolan extended a hand and pulled Stacey to his feet. He seemed to totter fleetingly and then he regained his balance. Dolan and I exchanged one of those looks, which Stacey caught.

"Quit that. I'm fine. I'm tired is all. I've been in bed too long."

The Santa Teresa County Sheriff's Department is located near Colgate off El Solano Road in the same general vicinity as the county dump. I guess land out there is cheap and there's room to expand. Behind the building, I could see rows of black-and-whites, county cars, and assorted personal vehicles belonging to the Sheriff's Department personnel. The one-story structure is a creamy beige and white stucco, with a series of arches across the front. The main jail is just across the road. We parked and went in the front entrance, letting Stacey lead the way. I could tell he missed working. Just the sight of the facility seemed to give him strength.

To the left, in the tiny lobby, was a counter with a glass partition, probably bulletproof, though it was impossible to tell. The civilian clerk, a woman, looked up when we came in. Stacey said, "We're here to see Sergeant Detective Joe Mandel."

She pushed a clipboard across the counter. "He said he'd be right out."

SUE GRAFTON

All three of us signed in and she gave us each a visitor's badge, which we fastened onto our shirts. There were three chairs available, but we elected to stand. Through the locked glass door, I could already see someone approaching from the far end of the corridor. He pushed the door open from his side and let us in. There were the usual introductions and a round of handshakes. From the flicker in his eyes, I could tell he recognized me from our meeting in his kitchen, but if he thought it odd, he never let on. He knew Stacey well, but I gathered he hadn't seen Dolan for many years. They exchanged pleasantries as he held the door open and let us into the corridor.

We turned left and followed him down a long hallway, a dogrun of beige carpeting and beige walls, with offices opening up on either side. Joe introduced us to Sergeant Steve Rhineberger, in the Sheriff's forensics unit. He unlocked a door and showed us into a room that looked like a tract-housing kitchen without the stove. There were counters on three sides and some sort of ventilation apparatus at the rear. A large battered-looking brown paper bag sat on the table in the center of the room.

Sergeant Rhineberger opened a lower cabinet door, tore off a length of white paper from a wide roll inside, and took out a pair of disposable latex gloves. "I asked the coroner's office to send over the mandible and

202

maxilla. I thought you might want to look at those, too."

He placed the sheet of protective paper on the table, pulled on the gloves, and then broke the seal on the evidence bag. He removed the folded tarp and various articles of clothing, which he spread on the paper. Mandel removed a handful of disposable gloves from the cardboard dispenser on the counter. He passed a pair to Stacey, a pair to Dolan, and a pair to me. The guys had been chatting about department business, but we all fell into a respectful silence. Eighteen years after the violence of her death, there was only the crackle of white paper and the snap of gloves.

It was strange to look at items I'd only seen before in faded photographs. The shirt and daisy-print pants had been cut from the body and the garments seemed sprawling and misshapen laid out across the tabletop. The fabric was soiled and moist, as though permeated with damp sand. The bloodstains resembled nothing so much as smudges of rust. Her sandals were leather, decorated with brass buckles linked with leather bands. A narrow thong would have separated her big toe from the remaining toes on each foot. The sandals looked new except for faint stains on the sole where her heel and the ball of her bare foot had left indelible marks.

Rhineberger opened a container and removed Jane Doe's upper and lower jawbones. Her teeth showed extensive dental work, sixteen to eighteen amalgam fillings. When he set the maxilla on the mandible, matching the grooves and worn surfaces where they met, we could see the extent of her overbite and the crooked eyetooth on the left. "Can't believe nobody recognized her by the description of the teeth. Charlie says it was all probably done a year or two before she died. You can see the wisdom teeth haven't erupted yet. He says she probably wasn't eighteen." He placed the bones back in the container, leaving the lid off.

Her personal effects scarcely covered the tabletop. This was all that was left of her, the entire sum. I experienced a sense of puzzlement that any life could be reduced to such humble remnants. Surely, she'd expected far more from the world—love, marriage, children, perhaps—at the very least a valued presence among her friends and family. Her remains were buried now in a grave without a headstone, its location marked by lot number in the cemetery ledger. In spite of that, she seemed curiously real, given the sparse data we had. I'd seen the black-and-white photograph of her where she lay on the August-dry grass, her face obscured by the angle of her body and the intervening shrubs. Her midriff, a portion of her forearm, and a section of her calf were all that were visible from the camera's perspective, her flesh swollen, mottled by decomposition as though bruised.

I picked up the plastic bag that contained a lock of her hair, which looked clean and silky, a muted shade of blond. A second plastic bag held two delicate earrings, simple loops of gold wire. The only remaining evidence of the murder itself was the length of thin cable, encased in white plastic, with which her wrists had been bound. The tarp was made of a medium-weight canvas, the seams stitched in red, with metal grommets inserted at regular intervals. It looked like standard-issue—a painter's drop cloth, or a cover used to shield a cord of firewood from rain. In one corner, there was a red speck that looked like a ladybug or a spot of blood, but on closer inspection I realized it was simply a small square of red stitches, where the thread had been secured at the end of the row. From these few tokens, we were hoping to reconstruct not only her identity but that of her killer. How could she be so compelling that eighteen years later the five of us would assemble like this in her behalf?

Belatedly, I tuned into the conversation. Stacey was laying out our progress to date. Apparently, Mandel had gone back and reviewed the file himself. Like Stacey and Dolan, who'd actually discovered the body, he'd been involved from the first. He was saying, "Too bad Crouse is gone. There aren't many of us left."

Dolan said, "What happened to Crouse?"

"He sold his house and moved his family to Oregon.

Now he's chief of police in some little podunk town up there. Last I heard he was bored to tears, but he can't afford to come back with housing prices here. Keith Baldwin and Oscar Wallen are both retired and Mel Galloway's dead. Nonetheless, it's nice to have a chance to revisit this case. You have to think after all these years, we might shake something loose."

Stacey said, "What's your take on it? You see anything we missed?"

Mandel thought about that briefly. "I guess the only thing I'd be curious about is this Iona Mathis, the gal Frankie Miracle was married to. She might know something if you can track her down. I hear she came back and sat through the trial with him. She damn near married the guy again she felt so sorry for him."

Stacey made a pained face. "I don't get the appeal. I can't even manage to get married once, and I'm a law-abiding citizen. You have an address on her?"

"No, but I can get you one."

ELEVEN

Dolan dropped me off at the office before he took Stacey home. Stacey's energy was flagging and, in truth, mine was, too. As I unlocked the door, I noticed a Mercedes station wagon parked in the narrow driveway that separated my bungalow from the next in line. The woman in the driver's seat was working on a piece of needlepoint, the roll of canvas resting awkwardly against the steering wheel. She looked up at me and waved, then set her canvas on the seat beside her. She got out of the car, reached into the rear seat, and pulled out a shopping bag, saying, "I was beginning to think I'd missed you."

I waited while she locked the car door and headed in my direction. She looked familiar, but I couldn't remember how I knew her. I placed her in her early sixties, trim, attractive, nicely dressed in a lightweight red wool suit. Her hair was medium length, tinted a deep auburn shade and brushed loosely off her face.

I hesitated on the threshold, still scrambling through my bag of memories, trying to connect a name to the face. Who was this? A neighbor? A former client? "Are you waiting for me?"

She smiled, showing a row of square even teeth. Before she managed to say another word, I felt a silvery note of fear pluck at the base of my spine, like a sandcrab picking its way erratically across guitar strings. She held out her hand. "I'm your Aunt Susanna."

I shook hands with her, trying to compute the term "aunt." I knew the meaning but couldn't for the life of me figure out what to do with it.

"Tasha's mother," she added. "I hope I didn't catch you at a bad time. She did tell you I'd stop by, didn't she? How embarrassing for me if she forgot."

"Sure. Of course. Sorry I drew a blank, but I was thinking of something else. Come on in and have a seat. You want coffee? I was just about to put a pot on for myself."

She followed me through the front door and into the inner office. "Thank you. I'd like that." She set down her shopping bag and took a seat in the client chair across the desk. Her eyes were hazel like mine. The air around her was scented with cologne. The fragrance suggested citrus—grapefruit, perhaps—very fresh and light.

"How do you take it?"

208

"I'm not fussy. Black's fine."

"It'll take me a minute."

"I'm in no hurry," she said.

I excused myself and went through the outer office and into the kitchen, where I leaned against the counter and tried to catch my breath. I'd been faking composure since the moment she'd announced herself. This was my aunt, my mother's sister. I was acquainted with Tasha and Liza, the oldest and youngest of Susanna's three daughters. The third girl, Pam, I'd heard about but never met. My introduction to the family had been thoroughly disconcerting as I'd known nothing of their existence. A fluke in an investigation three years previously had turned them up like a nest of spiders in the pocket of an old overcoat. In the absence of my parents and Aunt Gin, Susanna had to be one of my closest living relatives.

I patted myself on the chest. This was so bizarre. I don't remember my mother and I've never had a concrete image of her. Even so, I sensed the kinship. All the Kinsey women bore a strong resemblance to one another, at least from what I'd heard. I certainly looked like Tasha, and she'd told me that she and her sister Pam looked enough alike to be mistaken for twins. I looked much less like Liza, but even there, no one could deny the similarities.

I picked up the coffeepot and filled it with water,

which I poured into the reservoir of the machine. Filter paper, coffee can. I couldn't see my hands shake, but the counter near the coffeemaker became gritty with grounds. I grabbed a sponge, dampened it, and wiped the surface clean. I set the pot in the machine and flipped the button to ON. I didn't trust myself to talk to her, but I couldn't hang out here until the coffee was done. I took a couple of mugs from the cabinet and set them on the counter. If I'd had brandy on the premises, I'd have downed a slug right then.

I walked back to my office, trying to remember what "normal" felt like so I could imitate the state. "It'll be ready in a minute. Hope you didn't have to wait for me long. I was tied up on business."

She smiled, watching me take my seat across the desk from her. "Don't worry about that. I'm always capable of amusing myself." She was pretty; a straight nose, only the slightest touch of makeup to smooth out the palette of her complexion. I could see sun damage or faded freckles and a series of fine lines etched around her eyes and mouth. The red suit was becoming, the jacket set off by the white shell underneath. I could understand where Tasha had developed her taste in clothes.

She held up a finger. "Oh, I nearly forgot. I brought you something." She leaned down and reached into her shopping bag, coming up with a black-and-white photograph in a silver frame. She held it out and I took it, turning it over so I could see what it was. "That's me with your mother the day of her coming-out party, July 5, 1935. I was nine."

"Ah." I glanced down, but only long enough to take in a flash of the eighteen-year-old Rita Cynthia Kinsey in a long white dress. She was leaning forward, laughing, her arms around her youngest sister. My mother looked unbelievably young, with dark curly hair falling across her shoulders. She must have worn dark red lipstick because the black-and-white photo made her mouth look black. Susanna was done up in a long frothy dress that looked like a miniature version of Rita's.

I felt my face get hot, but I kept it averted until the rush of feeling passed. The pain was sharp, like the lid of a box being slammed on my fingertips. I wanted to howl with surprise. By sheer dint of will, I put myself in emotional lockdown. I smiled at Susanna, but my face felt tense. "I appreciate this. I've never had a photograph of her."

"That's my favorite. I had a copy made so that one's yours to keep."

"Thanks. Are there any pictures of my father?"

"I'm sure there are. If I'd thought of it, I could have brought the family album. We have everyone in there. Maybe next time," she said. "You know, you look like your mother, but then so do I."

I said, "Really," but I was thinking, *This is all too weird.* In my dealings with Tasha, it was easy to keep her safely at arm's length. We used words to hack at each other, establishing a comfortable distance between us. This woman was lovely. For ten cents, I'd have scampered around the desk and crawled up in her lap. I said, "From what I hear, all the Kinsey women look alike."

"It's not the Kinseys so much as the LeGrands. Virginia had some of Daddy's features, but she was the rare exception. Grand's features dominate. No surprise there since she dominates everywhere else."

"Why do you call her Grand?"

She laughed. "I don't know. We've called her that ever since I can remember. She didn't want to be 'Mummy' or 'Mommy' or any of those terms. She preferred the nickname she'd always had and that's how we were raised. Once we got to school, I became aware that other kids called their mothers 'Mama' or 'Mom,' but by then it would have seemed odd to refer to her that way. Maybe, on her part, it was a form of denial— ambivalence about motherhood. I'm not really sure."

The smell of coffee began to permeate the air. I didn't want to leave the room, but I got up and circled the desk. "I'll be right back."

"You want help?"

"No, I'm fine."

"Just yell if you need me."

"Thanks."

Back in the kitchen, I was businesslike, though I noticed, pouring coffee, I was forced to use both hands. How was I going to pass her the mug without spilling coffee in her lap? I took a deep breath and mentally slapped myself around. I was being ridiculous. This was a virtual stranger, a middle-aged woman on a mission of goodwill. I could do this. I could handle it. I'd simply deal with her now and suffer the consequences later when I was by myself again. Okay. I picked up the two mugs, my gaze fixed on the coffee as I walked. I really didn't spill that much and the rug was so gross it wouldn't show, anyway.

Once in my office, I placed both mugs on the desk and let her claim hers for herself. I took my seat again and reached for my mug, sliding it toward me across the desk. I wondered briefly if I could just lean down and slurp instead of lifting it to my lips. "Can I ask you something?"

"Of course you can, sweetie. What do you want to know?"

Sweetie. Oh dear. Here came the tears, but I blinked them back. Susanna didn't seem to notice. I cleared my throat and said, "Liza mentioned nephews the first time we met, but that's the last I've heard of them. Arne told me Grand had three sons, all stillborn, but wasn't there a boy who died in infancy? I thought Liza made reference to that."

She made that dismissive gesture so familiar to me. I'd used it myself and so had my cousin Liza on the day we met. "She never gets that right. Really, family history isn't her strong suit. Technically, it's true. Mother had three boys before Rita was born. The first two were stillbirths. The third lived five hours. All the other boys in the family— nine nephews—are part of the outer circle. Maura's husband, Walter, has two sisters, and they both have boys. And my husband, John, has three brothers, with seven boys among them. I know it's confusing, but since most of those peripheral family members also live in Lompoc, they're included in all the Kinsey gatherings. Grand doesn't like to share us with our husbands' families, so at Thanksgiving and Christmas she makes sure her doors are open and the celebrations are so lavish no one can resist. What else do you want to know? Ask me anything you like. That's why I'm here."

I thought for a moment, wondering how far I dared go. "I've been told you and Aunt Maura disapproved of my mother." The topic made me feel mean, but that was easier than feeling frail.

"That was Maura and Sarah, both of whom were older than me. Maura was twelve and Sarah fifteen when the 'war broke out,' for lack of a better term. Both sided with Grand. I was the baby in the family so I could get away with anything. I just pretended I didn't know what was going on. I always adored your mother. She was so stylish and exotic. I think I mentioned I was nine when she made her debut. I was always more concerned about my Mary Janes than the larger family issues. I like to think I'm independent, but I'm not the maverick your mother was. She took Grand head on. She never shied away from confrontation. I use diversionary tactics myself—charm, misdirection. For me, it's more effective to conform on the surface and do as I please when I'm outside Grand's presence. It might be cowardice on my part, but it makes life easier on everyone, or that's what I tell myself."

"But why did Sarah and Maura object to my mother's marriage? What business was it of theirs?"

"Well, none. It really wasn't the marriage so much as what that did to the family. Once the battle lines were drawn, Grand was unyielding, and neither your mother nor Virginia would give in."

"But what was that about? I still don't get it. It's not as if my father was a bum."

"I don't think Grand had any personal objections to your father. She saw the age difference as a problem. He was what, thirty-five years old to your mother's eighteen?"

"Thirty-three," I said.

Susanna shrugged. "Fifteen years. That really doesn't seem like much. I think Grand's problem was Rita's marrying on impulse. Grand did that, too—married Daddy on a whim the day she turned seventeen. He was twice her age, and I think they'd known each other less than a month. I suspect she may have regretted her haste, but divorce wasn't an option in those days, at least for her. She never likes having to admit she's wrong so she stuck it out. They were devoted to each other, but I'm not sure how long her infatuation survived. I know it's an old story, but I suspect Grand was hoping to express an unlived part of her life through Rita."

"I can understand that. What you're saying makes sense."

"What is it that bothers you? That's part of what I'd like to address."

"I'm thirty-six years old . . . thirty-seven in three weeks. I've lived all my life without a clue about this stuff. From my perspective, it sure seems like somebody could have let me know. I've said this before to Tasha and I don't mean to harp, but why didn't anyone ever get in touch? Aunt Gin's been dead now for fifteen years. Grand didn't even come down for the funeral, so what's that about?"

"I'm not here to argue. What you're saying is true and you're entirely correct. Grand should have come down here. She should have sent word, but I think she

216

was afraid to face you. She didn't know what you'd been told. She assumed Virginia turned you against her, against the whole family. At heart, Grand's a good person, but she's proud and she's stubborn—well, face it, she can be impossible sometimes—but Rita was stubborn, too. The two of them were so much alike it would have been comical if it hadn't been so destructive. Their quarrel tore the family to shreds. None of us have ever been the same since then."

"But Grand was her mother. She was supposed to be the grownup."

Susanna smiled. "Just because we're old doesn't mean we're mature. Actually, Grand did reach out. I can remember half a dozen times when she made a gesture toward your parents only to be ignored or refused. From what I understand, your father stayed out of it as nearly as he could. The fight was Rita's, and while he was certainly on her side, she was the one who kept the game alive. Virginia was even worse. She seemed to relish the split, and I'm really not sure why. She must have had issues of her own. In my experience, any time someone makes such a big deal about autonomy, it's probably a cover for something else. So, Grand tried to include them, especially after you were born, but they'd have nothing to do with her. If she and Daddy were out of town, the three of them would come to visit and, of course, they'd bring you, but there was always a stealthy feel to it. I remember thinking they enjoyed it, sneaking around behind her back."

"Why?"

"Because it forced the rest of us to declare ourselves. Every time we welcomed them—which we did on numerous occasions—it put us squarely in their camp. Maura and Sarah felt guilty about deceiving Grand. She'd come home from a trip and none of us would say a word. Sometimes I have to wonder what she knew. She has her network of spies, even to this day, so someone must have told her. She never let on, but maybe that was her way of making sure there was contact even if she couldn't enjoy it herself."

I thought about it for a moment, turning her comments over in my mind. "I'd like to believe you, and I guess I do in some ways. I know there are two sides to every story. Obviously, Aunt Gin took it seriously enough to maintain silence on the subject until the day she died. I never knew any of this until three years ago."

"It must be difficult to cope with."

"Well, yes. In part because it's been presented to me as finished business, a done deal. To you, it must be old news, but to me it's not. I still have to figure out what to do with my piece of it. The breach had a huge impact on how I turned out."

"Well. You could have done worse than having

Virginia Kinsey for a role model. She might have been an odd duck, but she was ahead of her time."

"That about covers it."

Susanna looked at her watch. "I really should go. I don't know about you, but I find conversations like this exhausting. You can only take in so much and then you have to stop and digest. Will you call me sometime?"

"I'll try."

"Good. That would make me happy."

Once she was gone, I locked the office door and sat down at my desk. I picked up the photo of my mother and studied it at length. The picture had been taken at the ranch. The background was out of focus, but she and her sister were standing on a wooden porch with railings like the ones I'd seen at the Manse. By squinting, I could make out a group of people standing to one side, all holding champagne flutes. The young men wore tuxedos and the girls were decked out in long white dresses similar to the one Rita Cynthia wore. In many ways, hair and clothing styles hadn't changed that much. Given any formal occasion, you could lift these people out of their decade and set them down in ours without dramatic differences. The only vintage note was the white shoes my mother wore with their open toes and faintly clunky heels.

My mother was slim, and her bare shoulders and arms were flawless. Her face was heart-shaped, her complexion smooth and clear. Her hair might have been naturally curly—it was hard to tell—but it had been done up for the occasion, tumbling across her shoulders. She wore a white flower behind one ear, as did Susanna, who was loosely encircled by my mother's arms. It looked like my mother was whispering some secret that both of them enjoyed. Susanna's face was turned up to hers with a look of unexpected delight. I could almost feel the hug that must have followed once the picture was snapped.

I placed the frame on my desk, sitting back in my swivel chair with my feet propped up. Several things occurred to me that I hadn't thought of before. I was now twice my mother's age the day the photograph was taken. Within four months of that date, my parents would be married, and by the time she was my age, she'd have a daughter three years old. By then my parents would have had only another two years to live. It occurred to me that if my mother had survived, she'd be seventy. I tried to imagine what it would be like to have a mother in my life—the phone calls, the visits and shopping trips, holiday rituals so alien to me. I'd been resistant to the Kinseys, feeling not only adamant but hostile to the idea of continued contact. Now I wondered why the offer of simple comfort felt like such a threat. Wasn't it possible that I could establish a connection with my mother through her two surviving sisters? Surely, Maura and Susanna shared many of her traits— gestures and phrases, values and attitudes ingrained in them since birth. While my mother was gone, couldn't I experience some small fragment of her love through my cousins and aunts? It didn't seem too much to ask, although I still wasn't clear what price I might be expected to pay.

I locked the office early, leaving the photo of my mother in the center of my desk. Driving home, I couldn't resist touching on the issue, much in the same way the tongue seeks the socket from which a tooth has just been pulled. The compulsion resulted in the same shudder-producing blend of satisfaction and repugnance. I needed to talk to Henry. He'd offered counsel and advice (which I'd largely ignored) since the Kinseys had first surfaced. I knew he'd be quick to see my conflict: the comfort of isolation versus cloying suffocation; independence versus bondage; safety versus betrayal. It was not in my makeup to imagine emotional states in between. I saw it as all or nothing, which is what made it difficult to risk the status quo. My life wasn't perfect, but I knew its limitations. I remembered Susanna's comment about a passion for autonomy serving as a cover for something else. When she'd said it, I'd been too startled to wonder what she meant. She'd been referring to Aunt Gin, whose hard heart I'd assimilated as a substitute for love. Had she been alluding to me as well?

Once I reached my neighborhood, I spotted an Austin Healy parked in my favorite place. I did a U-turn and found a space across the street. I pushed through my squeaking gate and down the driveway to Henry's back-yard. He'd hauled his lawn furniture out of storage, hosed off the chairs, and added a set of dark green cushions with the tags still attached. Two glasses and a pitcher of iced tea rested on a small redwood table, along with a plate of homemade oatmeal cookies with raisins. At first I thought he'd meant them for me, but then I spotted him in the far corner of the yard, showing off his garden to a woman I'd never seen. The tableau bore an eerie similarity to an earlier occasion when a woman named Lila Sams had waltzed into Henry's life.

He smiled when he saw me, gesturing me over so he could make the introductions. "Kinsey, this is Mattie Halstead from San Francisco. She stopped off to see us on her way to L.A." And to Mattie, he said, "Kinsey rents the studio . . ."

"Of course. Nice to meet you. Henry's talked quite a bit about you."

"It's nice meeting you, too," I said, with a sly glance

at him. He'd had his hair trimmed, and I noticed he was wearing a white dress shirt and long pants. I didn't think he'd ever gotten that spiffed up for a woman before. Mattie was easily his height and just as trim. Her silver hair was cut short and layered in a wind-blown mop. She wore a white silk shirt, gray slacks, and stylish low-heeled shoes. The jewelry she wore—matching earrings and a bracelet—were custom-made, hammered silver and amethysts.

She regarded me with intelligent gray eyes. "I was afraid he might be away so I called from Carmel when I arrived there last night. I'm taking my time, stopping to see friends as I travel down the coast."

"Is this business or pleasure?"

"A little bit of both. I'm delivering some paintings to a gallery in San Diego. I could've crated them for shipping, but I needed a break."

"You were on the cruise Henry took?"

"Yes, but I'm afraid that was work. This is my time off."

"Mattie teaches drawing and painting, and she lectures on art. Nell took her watercolor class and ended up doing quite well."

"Better than Lewis," Mattie said, with a smile. "I felt so bad for him. I've never seen anyone quite so enthusiastic."

"He was flirting," Henry said reprovingly before

turning to me. "Why don't you join us? We were just about to sit down and have a glass of iced tea."

"I better pass on that, thanks. I've got some reading to do and then I thought I'd sneak in a run. My schedule's been horsed up and I owe myself one."

"What about supper? We're heading up to Rosie's at six."

"No way. I don't intend to go until she gets off this kick of hers. Gourmet entrails. Did Henry mention that?"

"He warned me, but I'm actually a fan of liver and onions."

"Yeah, but the liver of what beast? I won't risk it myself. You ought to have him do the cooking. He's terrific."

She smiled at him. "Maybe another time. I've been looking forward to reconnecting with William and Rosie. They were dear."

"How long will you be here?"

"Just one night. I have a reservation at the Edgewater, my favorite hotel. My husband and I used to come here for anniversaries," she said. "I'll take off in the morning as soon as it's light. With luck, I can avoid the rush-hour traffic through Los Angeles."

"Well, it's too bad we won't have time to chat. Do you plan to stop by on the return trip?"

"We'll see how it goes. I don't want to be a nuisance."

"Maybe you can talk him into cooking for you then."

I let myself into the apartment, tossed my bag on the kitchen counter, and headed up the stairs. I didn't have any reading to catch up on and I'd done my three-mile run at six A.M. I told those tiny fibs to make sure Mattie and Henry had some time alone. I peered out the bathroom window, taking in the truncated view of the two of them down below. It was not quite four o'clock. I managed to kill an hour and a half and then thought about where to go for supper that night. I was serious about boycotting Rosie's until she abandoned her new-found passion for animal by-product cookery. As it was currently Happy Hour, I knew Dolan would be at CC's. I could have joined him, but I didn't want to sit and count his drinks while inhaling his secondhand smoke. I returned to the bathroom window and peered down at the backyard. Henry and Mattie were gone, but their two lawn chairs remained, pulled slightly closer together than they'd been when I'd first arrived home. I could see the lights on in his kitchen, so they were probably fortifying themselves with Black Jack on ice before braving Rosie's food.

Now that the coast was clear, I grabbed my shoulder bag and a jacket and scooted out the front door. I retrieved my car and drove to the McDonald's on lower Milagra Street. I'm at the drive-through lane so often, the take-out servers recognize my voice and deal with me by name. On impulse, I ordered extras and went to Stacey's house. In my opinion, there's no condition in life that can't be ameliorated by a dose of junk food.

When I knocked on his screen door, I could see him perched on a cardboard carton in the living room. His desk drawers were open and a shredder was plugged into an extension cord that trailed across the room. He motioned me in.

I held up the white bag. "I hope you haven't eaten supper. I've got Cokes, french fries, and Quarter Pounders with Cheese. Very nourishing."

"I don't have much appetite, but I'll be happy to keep you company."

"Fair enough."

I left the bag on the desk and moved into the kitchen where I found a package of paper plates and a roll of paper towels. I returned to the living room, put the dinnerware on the floor, and hauled over two boxes from the stack against the wall. I sat on one box and used the second as a table that I arranged between us. I unpacked Cokes, two large cartons of fries, packets of ketchup and salt, and a paper-wrapped QP with Cheese for each of us. I squeezed ketchup on the fries, salted everything in sight, and then downed my QP in approximately eight bites. "I'm going for the land speed record here."

Stacey lifted the top of his bun and eyed his burger with misgivings. "I've never eaten one of these."

I paused in the midst of wiping my mouth. "You're joking."

"I'm not." He tried a cautious bite, which he chewed with suspicion, letting the flavors mingle in his mouth. He wagged his head from side to side. With his second bite, he seemed to get the hang of it, and after that he ate with the same dispatch I did.

I reached into the bag and took out another burger that I passed to him. This time, halfway through, a nearly subliminal moan escaped his lips. I laughed.

"Where'd you get that?" I asked, pointing to the shredder with a french fry.

"Fellow next door," he said, pausing to swallow his bite. "I'm cleaning out my desk. Can't quite bring myself to shred my receipts. I don't intend to file a tax return. I figure I'll be dead before the IRS catches up with me. Even so, I worry about an audit without the proper paperwork on hand." He licked his fingers and wiped his mouth. "Thank you. That was great. I haven't had an appetite for weeks."

"Happy to help."

He gathered all the trash and put it back in the bag, then turned and made a free throw, tossing it in the wastebasket. He reached into the bottom drawer and took out a cardboard box filled with black-and-white photographs. He set the box in his lap, picked up a handful, and fed them to the machine.

I watched while six images were reduced to slivers. "What are you *doing*?"

"I told you. Cleaning out my desk."

"But those are family photographs. You can't do that."

"Why not? I'm the only one left."

"But you can't just *destroy* them. I can't believe you'd do that."

"Why leave the job for someone else? At least if I do it, there's a personal connection." He sang, "Good-bye, Uncle Schmitty. Bye Cousin Mortimer . . ." Two more images were converted to confetti in the shredder bin.

I put a hand on his arm. "I'll take them."

"And do what? You don't even know these folks. I can't identify the better half of 'em myself. Look at this. Who's he? I swear I never saw this guy before in my life. Must have been a family friend." He touched the edge of the photo to the shredder teeth and watched it disappear before he picked up the next.

"Don't shred them. Aren't those your *parents*?"

"Sure, but they've been dead for years."

"I can't stand this. Give me those. I'll pretend they're mine."

"Don't be ridiculous. You're alone just like me. If I let you take 'em, someone else will end up throwing them in *your* trash."

"So what? Come on, Stace. Please."

He hesitated and finally nodded. "Okay. But it's dumb."

He handed me the box of photos, which I placed near my bag out of his reach. I was worried he'd change his mind and shred someone else. He turned his attention to a file folder marked AUTO INSURANCE and fed its contents into the shredder. Idly, he said, "I almost forgot to mention, Joe Mandel called with an address for Iona Mathis. She's living in the high desert, little town called Peaches."

"Which is where?"

"Above San Bernardino, off Highway 138. There's no phone in her name so she might be bunking in with someone else. Did I tell you Mandel got a line on the red Mustang? This guy Gant, the original owner, died about ten years ago, but his widow says the car was stolen from an auto upholstery shop in Quorum, California, where he'd taken it to get the seats replaced. Gant had the car towed back from Lompoc, but it was such a mess he turned around and sold it to the guy whose shop it was stolen from—fellow named Ruel

229

McPhee. According to our sources, the car's now registered to him. I've left him four messages, but so far I haven't heard back. Con thinks it's worth a trip down there just to see what's what."

"Where's Quorum? I've never heard of it."

"Well, neither had I, but Con says it's just south of Blythe near the Arizona line. Now here's the kicker on that. Turns out Frankie Miracle grew up in Quartzsite, Arizona, which is just a few miles from Blythe in the same neck of the woods. Con wants to take a detour through Peaches and talk to Iona Mathis on his way to Quorum."

"When?"

"Tomorrow morning he says. I thought I better warn you in case you want to make up an excuse."

"Not at all. I'll go. I could use a change of scene. What about you? Are you feeling up to it?"

"You two go on. I'll wait and see what the doc has to say. They may want me back in the hospital for the third time this month. Talk about tedious."

"How're you holding up?"

"I'm not thrilled with this new development, but I don't see that I have much choice."

"I'll hold good thoughts for you."

"I could use a few," he said. He hesitated. "This may be out of line, but I'm wondering if Con's told you about his wife's suicide."

"I knew she had cancer, but he never said a word."

"That's why he gets so pissy on the subject. He thinks he could have saved her."

"Could he?"

"Of course not. When it comes right down to it, you can't save anyone except yourself. Sometimes, you can't even do that. Anyway, I thought you should know."

He smiled to himself for reasons I suspect were unrelated to me. I watched while his army discharge papers disappeared into the shredder with a grinding sound.

TWELVE

My packing for the trip took all of five minutes. At most, I figured we'd be gone for two days, which meant a toothbrush, toothpaste, two clean T-shirts, a sweatshirt, two pairs of socks, four pairs of underpants, and the oversized T-shirt I sleep in. I shoved it all into a duffel the size of a bolster pillow. Since I was wearing jeans and my Sauconys, the only other items I'd need were my running sweats, my windbreaker, and my little portable Smith-Corona. Dolan had opted for an early start, which in his terms translated to a 9:30 departure. This gave me time to sneak in a three-mile run, followed by a supersetting weight session at the gym. I was racking up virtue points in case I didn't have the chance to exercise while I was on the road.

By the time Dolan pulled up, I was sitting on the curb, reading a paperback novel with my shoulder bag, typewriter, and duffel. At my side, I had two rubber-band-bound stacks of index cards in my bag.

He must have run his vehicle through a car wash because the exterior was clean and the floorboards were free of gas receipts and discarded fast-food wrappers. Now that we were cohorts, he didn't feel required to escort me around the car and let me in. I hauled the door open, while he reached over the seat and shoved his suitcase to one side. "You can put your things back there with mine unless you'd rather leave 'em in the trunk."

"This is fine." I tucked my Smith-Corona on the floor, tossed my duffel in the rear seat, and got in. I tried hauling the door shut, but the hinges responded sluggishly and refused to budge. Dolan finally reached across me and gave the door a yank. It closed with a thunk. I wrestled with the seat belt, jerking until I'd pulled sufficient length to reach the catch and snap it down. I spotted a fresh pack of cigarettes on the dash. "I hope you don't intend to smoke."

"Not with the windows closed."

"You are so considerate. You have a map?"

"In the side pocket. I thought we'd go the back way. I'd take the 101 to the 405 and hit the 5 from there, but I with my bum ticker, I don't want to risk the freeway in case I die at the wheel."

"You're really making me feel good about this."

Dolan turned onto the 101 heading south while I flapped at the California map and refolded it into a manageable size. By my estimate, Peaches was ninety miles away, roughly an hour and a half. Happily, Dolan didn't like chitchat any more than I did. I sat and stared out the window, wondering if love would blossom between Henry and Mattie.

The coastline looked smoky. There was a harsh light on the ocean, but the surf was calm, advancing toward the shore in long, smooth undulations. The islands were barely visible twenty-six miles offshore. Steep hills sloped down to the highway, the chaparral a dark mossy green, flourishing after a wet autumn and the long damp winter months.

In many sections of the hillside, the vegetation had been overtaken by thick patches of cactus shaped like Ping-Pong paddles, abristle with thorns. I've always thought California prisons could discourage escape by seeding the surrounding landscape with vicious plants. Missing prisoners could be located by their howls of dismay and could spend their stay in solitary confinement picking thorns out of their heiniebumpers.

After twenty minutes, I glanced at Dolan. "You have kids?"

"Naw. Grace used to talk about it, but it didn't interest me. Kids change your life. We were fine as is."

"Any regrets?"

"I don't spend a lot of time on regrets. How about you? Are you planning to have kids?"

"I can't quite picture it, but I won't rule it out. I'm not exactly famous for my relationships with men."

At Perdido, we caught the 126 heading inland. The power lines disappeared. There was a dusting of snow on the distant mountain peaks, an odd contrast to the vivid green in the fields below. In the citrus groves, oranges hung on the trees like Christmas ornaments. The roadside fruit stands were boarded up, but they'd be open for business in another month or so. We passed through two small agricultural communities that hadn't changed in years. This section of the road was known as Blood Alley: only two lanes wide with an occasional passing lane in which the fiery crashes usually occurred. I kept a close eye on Dolan in the event he was on the verge of conking out on me.

He said, "Quit worrying."

At Palmdale, we turned east off Highway 14, picking up the 18. Ancient, cranky-looking billboards indicated land for sale. I saw a sign for 213th Street with a dirt road shooting off to a vanishing point. We passed a hand-painted sign that read PAIRALEGALS AVAILABLE: WILLS, CONTRACTS, DIVORCES, NOTER REPUBLIC. According to the map, the road we were on skirted the western border of the Mojave Desert at an altitude of 4,500 feet.

I checked the map again and said, "Wow. I never understood the size of the Mojave. It's really big."

"Twenty-five thousand square miles if you include

the portions in Nevada, Arizona, and Utah. You know much about the desert?"

"I've picked up the occasional odd fact, but that's about it."

"I've been reading about scorpions. Book claims they're the first air-breathing animal. They have a rudimentary brain, but their eyesight's poor. They probably don't perceive anything they can't actually touch first. You see two scorpions together, they're either making love or one of them is being eaten by the other. There's a lesson in there somewhere, but I can't figure out what. Probably has to do with the nature of true love."

I don't know why, but the information made me smile. We passed a sign that read PEACHES, POP. 897. The town was marked by a scattering of Joshua trees and was notable for its abundance of abandoned businesses. The San Gabriel Mountains loomed on our right, antiqued with snow, which had settled into all the crevices, defining them in white. Timbers formed a windbreak along the crest, while below them, I could see stands of evergreens laden with white. A freak spring storm had left mounds and patches of aging snow on the ground. Five cars had pulled over and parked on the berm where five sets of parents stood by chatting while their respective children played in the drifts. Most of the kids looked underdressed. As with the ocean, they'd frolic in the elements until their teeth were chattering and their lips had turned blue.

We passed a Liquor Mart that sold gas, tires, beer, and sandwiches. There were two cafés, one saloon, and no motels that I could see. There was a cluster of six single-wide trailers surrounded by chain-link fence and two real estate offices in double-wides with empty asphalt parking lots out front. What possessed people to move to Peaches in the first place? It seemed mysterious to me. What dream were they pursuing that made Peaches, California, the answer to their prayers?

Dolan did a U-turn, using the wide apron of gravel beside a service station, its gas pumps missing and its plate glass windows boarded up. The ground glittered with broken glass. Forlorn tatters of plastic wrap were caught in the bushes along the road. He backtracked as far as the enclave of mismatched trailers, which had the letters *A, B, C, D, E,* and *F* on small painted signs in front. A sign announced PEACH GROVE MOBILE HOME PARK, which was actually not a "park" so much as two rows of trailers with space remaining in the event a seventh trailer decided to pull in. Dolan nosed his car into a graveled area near a row of battered mailboxes and the two of us got out. I waited while he went through the ritual of tucking his gun in the trunk. "Looks like F's down that way," he said.

I followed him along the rutted two-lane dirt drive. "Wonder what she's doing up here?"

"We'll have to ask."

The door to F stood open, with a flimsy sliding screen across the frame to allow fresh air to circulate. A small handmade plaque said NAILS BY IONA with a telephone number too small to read in passing. A faded width of awning formed a covered porch, complete with bright green indoor-outdoor carpeting underfoot. The trailer was old and small. Two women were seated in the kitchenette, one on a banquette and the other on a chrome dinette chair pulled close to a hinged table that was supported by one leg. Both turned to look at us. The younger of the two continued to paint the older woman's nails.

Dolan said, "Is one of you Iona Mathis?"

The younger said, "That's me." She went back to brushing dark carmine polish on the thumbnail of the other woman's left hand. On the table between them, I could see an orange stick, emery boards, a bottle of cuticle remover, cotton balls, a nail brush, and a plastic halfmoon bowl filled with soapy water. To the right of the older woman, there was a pack of Winstons, with a book of paper matches tucked under the cellophane. The ashtray was filled with butts.

The older woman smiled and said, "I'm Iona's mom, Annette."

"Lieutenant Dolan with the Santa Teresa Police Department. This is Miss Millhone. She's a private detective."

Iona slid a look at us before she started work on her mother's index finger. If she was sixteen when she married Frankie, she'd be close to thirty-five now, roughly my age. Oh, hey, I was a little older, but who was keeping track? I tried to put myself in her place, wondering what might persuade me to live here and make my living nipping someone else's cuticles and massaging their toes. She was just shy of pretty. I watched her with interest through the softening haze of the screen door, trying to figure out where her looks fell short. Her hair was a lustrous brown, wavy, shoulder-length, and in need of a trim. She kept it parted in the center, which made her face look too long. She had full lips, a strong nose, brown eyes, and dark brows that were a shade too thick. She had a mole on her upper lip and one on her left cheek. In many ways, she still looked sixteen—lanky and round-shouldered. Her feet were bare, and she wore faded knee-ripped jeans and an India-print tunic in shades of rust and brown.

Annette leaned toward her daughter and said, "Baby, if you're not going to ask the man I will." When Iona made no response, she looked back at Dolan. "Hon, I wish you'd tell us why you're here because you're scaring me to death." Iona's mother, surely in her fifties, looked closer to thirty-five than Iona did. She had the same strong nose, but she'd had hers surgically reduced to something thinner and more sunken. Her hair, which she wore pulled up in a pony tail, was the same shade of brown, but of a uniformly intense hue that suggested she was dyeing it to cover gray. A sleeveless white knit top emphasized her big boobs, cantilevered over a thick waist and slightly rounded tummy. She wore red shorts and red canvas wedgies. Her toenails had been polished in the same red Iona was using on her fingernails. I thought she'd have been wise to cover more of herself than she had.

Dolan said, "We have a few questions about Iona's ex. You mind if we come in?"

"Door's open," Annette said.

Dolan slid open the screen door and stepped into the trailer, then sidestepped to his left so I'd have room to enter. Once inside, I moved to the right and perched on the near end of the blue plastic-padded bench where Annette was sitting. There was a long padded cushion across the back of the bench, and I was guessing at the presence of a mechanism that would allow the couch to level out into a double bed once the hinged table had been flattened against the wall. Did the two women share the trailer, or did Mom have her own? Dolan and I had agreed that he'd conduct the interview as it was confusing to have questions lobbed from two directions at once. I was there primarily to observe and to take mental notes.

Beyond the kitchenette, I could see a sliding door on the right that I assumed was the bathroom. Dead ahead, I saw the double bed that filled the only bedroom. I'm a sucker for small spaces, and I wouldn't have minded living in a place like this, though I'd have held out for something clean. I did love the diminutive sink and the half-size oven, the four-burner cooktop, and the wee refrigerator tucked under the counter. It was like a playhouse, designed for dollies, tea parties, and other games of make-believe. I focused my attention on Iona, whose bad posture was probably a side effect of hunching over her table all day.

Annette said, "You haven't said which ex, but if you're a police lieutenant, you must be talking about Frank. Her second husband, Lars, never broke the law in his life. He wouldn't even cross the street without a crosswalk. He drove Iona crazy. Here, she went out and found a fellow as different from Frank as you could possibly get and then it turns out he's worse. He suffered from that obsessive-compulsive syndrome? Shoot. Everything he did, he had to repeat six more times before he'd allow himself to move on. Getting anything accomplished took hours. I about went insane." She peered closely at her pinkie. "Baby, I think you got outside the line there. You see that?"

"Sorry." Iona used her thumb nail to eradicate the line of red that had encroached on Annette's cuticle.

Dolan said, "Mind if I smoke?"

Annette's eyes flicked briefly to Lieutenant Dolan's left hand. He wasn't wearing a wedding ring and it must have occurred to her that he might be a bachelor. "Only if you light one for me," she said. "Iona has a fit if I mess up a nail before she's done with all ten."

Dolan reached over and picked up Annette's pack of Winstons. He shook one free and placed it between her lips. She rested her hand seductively on his while he lit her cigarette. He then extracted and lit one from his own pack, apparently scorning her brand.

Annette inhaled deeply, blew a stream of smoke upward, and then removed the cigarette and placed it on the ashtray, being careful with her fingertips. "Lord, that tastes good. It just bores me to tears people get so tense about smoking these days. What's the big whoop-dee-do? It's no skin off their nose." Her eyes slid to me. "You smoke?"

"I did once upon a time," I said, hoping I didn't sound quite as pious as I felt.

To Dolan, she said, "What's Frank up to? We haven't heard from him in years, have we, baby?"

Iona ignored her mother and concentrated on her work.

Dolan said, "You know he's out on parole."

Annette made a face as though afflicted by a mildly spasming bowel. "I guess it was bound to happen. I never did care for the man myself. I hope you're not going to tell us he knows where she is."

"We talked to him yesterday and he didn't mention her."

"Well, thank god for that."

"Are you worried he'll make contact?"

"I wouldn't say 'worried,' but I don't like the idea."

Dolan focused on Iona. "When did you see him last? Do you remember the date?"

Annette stared at her daughter and when Iona failed to speak up, she said, "Iona, answer the man. What's the matter with you? I didn't raise you like that."

Iona shot a dark look at her mother. "You want me to mess these up or not?"

Annette smiled at Dolan. "She felt sorry for him. Frank's parents disowned him. His father's an oral surgeon, makes big bucks cutting on people's gums, but he's a stick-in-the-mud. His mother isn't much better. They had three other boys who did well, so naturally Frank lost out by comparison. Not that he wasn't a little shit from birth. Iona always said he was sweet, but you couldn't prove it by me. I thought he was kind of clinging, if you want to know the truth. He certainly became possessive toward the end of their marriage. Six months."

"Why'd the two of you break up?"

"I don't have to answer that," Iona said.

"He ever knock you around?"

This time when Iona declined to answer, Annette seemed happy to fill in. "Only twice that I know of. He was stoned all the time back then—"

"*Most* of the time, not *all*, Mom. Don't exaggerate."

"Oh, pardon. I stand corrected. He was stoned *most of the time* and when he was, he got mean. She told him if he didn't straighten up his act she'd kick his butt out the door. They were living in Venice then, right on one of the canals down there. All these little baby ducks. Didn't smell so nice, but they were cute as it could be. Frank kept on drinking and he refused to budge, so I sent her the money to get out."

"Is that when he connected with Cathy Lee Pearse?"

"Oh, that was awful, wasn't it?" Annette said. "I still get the shivers when I stop and think of it. He'd only known her a week before the incident."

"Is that what you call it, *an incident*?" Dolan asked. I could tell he was trying to suppress the outrage in his voice.

Iona put the brush back in the polish bottle and screwed the top shut. "You don't have to take that tone. For your information, Cathy Lee came onto him. She was a gold digger, pure and simple. All moody and temperamental. Frankie said she was violent, especially when she drank, which she'd been doing that night. She turned on him just like that." Iona snapped her fingers. "Came at him with a pair of scissors, so what was he supposed to do, let her jam the blades through his throat?"

Dolan's expression was bland. "He could have grabbed her wrist. It seems somewhat excessive to stab her fourteen times. You'd think once or twice would have done the job."

Iona began to tidy up her work space. "I don't know anything about that."

"Did you know Cathy Lee yourself?" Dolan was clearly working to maintain the contact now that she'd decided to talk.

"Sure. Frankie'd picked up a job painting this house for a friend of his so we'd moved in next door to her the week before. She was a tease, hanging out in her bikini, shaking her tits at him when he was out in the yard. Frankie felt terrible about what happened. He said he wished he could undo it, but by then it was too late."

"I heard you went back to him when the case went to trial. What was that about?"

"He needed me, that's what. Everybody else turned their backs on him."

"Iona's just like me. Can't resist a wounded bird.

Lars was the pits. Had to count everything. He was great for chopping onions—one, two, three, four, five . . ."

"Is that it, Iona? You see Frankie as a wounded bird?"

"He's a good person when he's sober and off drugs."

"Did he ever talk to you about what happened after Cathy Lee was killed?"

"Like what?"

"I'm wondering what he did between the time he killed Cathy Lee and the time the cops picked him up. There's a two-day gap when we don't know where he was."

Iona shrugged. "Beats me. Frankie and I were busted up by then."

Annette said, "Shortest marriage on record. Divorce took six times longer, didn't it?"

Iona declined a response, speaking to Dolan instead. "I don't know what he did or where he went after I moved out."

"Baby, I thought you said he ended up at your place. 'Member that? You'd moved into that studio apartment in Santa Teresa . . ."

"Mom."

"Well, why can't you tell him that if it's the truth? Believe me, Lieutenant, Iona knows better than to aid and abet. She fed him a meal and let him stay the night and then said he had to hit the road. I begged her to call the sheriff, but it was no, no, no. She was scared if she turned him in, he'd come back and retaliate."

"Mother, is there any way you could just shut the fuck up?"

"I'm trying to be helpful. You might think about that yourself. Now what's this about, Lieutenant?"

"We think he had contact with a young girl hitchhiking in the Lompoc area. It's possible he picked her up on his way to see his dad."

"Oh my lord. You don't mean to tell me he killed someone else?"

"That remains to be seen. Her body was dumped in a quarry on the outskirts of town. Right now, we're trying to find out who she is."

Iona stared at him. I thought she was on the verge of volunteering information, but she seemed to catch herself. "Why didn't you ask him, if you saw him yesterday?"

Dolan smiled. "He said he couldn't remember. We thought he might've said something about her to you."

Iona focused her attention on her mother's nails. "First I've heard."

When it was clear she wasn't going to say more, Dolan glanced at Annette. "I'm curious how the two of you ended up in Peaches."

She took another drag of her cigarette. "Originally,

we're from a little town out near Blythe. Iona's grand-parents—I'm talking now about my mom and dad—invested in sixty acres; must have been 1946. What we're sitting on right now is the only parcel left. I was the one had the idea for a trailer park after they passed on. It seemed like a smart move since we already owned the land. We each have our own place and the four other tenants pay rent. I work part-time over at the café; Iona has this business, so the two of us get by."

"What town?" I asked.

She looked at me with surprise, as though she'd forgotten I was there. "Come again?"

"What town are you from?"

"Oh. Little burg called Creosote. You probably never heard of it. Two miles this side of the Arizona line."

"You're kidding. I met someone else from Creosote just two days ago. A guy named Pudgie Clifton."

Iona's dark gaze strayed to mine.

Annette perked right up. "Oh, Iona's known Pudgie since elementary school. Isn't he the fella you dated before Frank?"

"We didn't *date*, Mom. We hung out. There's a big difference."

"Looked like dating to me. You went off and stayed weekends with him if memory serves." When Annette reached for her cigarette again, her hand brushed

248

against the edge of the ashtray, dinging her freshly painted nail. "Oh, shit. Now lookit what I've done."

She held her hand out to Iona, who studied the smudge. She wet her index finger and rubbed it lightly on the smear of red polish, effectively smoothing it out.

Dolan said, "You must have known Pudgie well."

"He mostly messed around with kids from somewhere else."

"Except for weekends when he went off with you," he said.

She looked up sharply. "We took some road trips, okay? He liked driving my car. Doesn't mean I screwed him. We were friends."

"Did he and Frankie know each other back then?"

"How would I know? I'm not in charge of either one of them."

There was a tap at the door. "Iona, honey? Sorry to interrupt." A woman stood on the porchlet, peering in at us.

Iona said, "My next appointment. I hope you don't mind."

"Not at all. We'll wait and talk to you when you get off work."

Annette scooted over from behind the table, her bare thighs creating fart sounds against the plastic seat. I stood up to make room for her while Dolan stepped outside. Annette was already chatting with Iona's client, wagging her fingers in the air. "Hey, sugar, take a look. This is called Cherries Jubilee. The shade would look gorgeous with your coloring."

The other woman, in her forties, didn't seem that excited by the prospect, as her coloring was blah.

Annette clomped down the trailer step on her canvas wedgies and tucked her hand through Lieutenant Dolan's arm. "Iona won't be long. I'm working lunch today. Why don't you walk me over to the Moonlight and have a bite to eat. It's on me."

I said, "Great. Let's do that. What hours do you work?"

She said, "Usually lunchtime on. We're open from five in the morning until ten at night. The only other restaurant is the Mountain View so people go back and forth, depending on their mood."

The three of us walked down the rutted driveway and across the two-lane road. Once in the café, we had our pick of the empty tables. Annette said, "It's mostly drinks and cold sandwiches. I can fry up some burgers if you want something hot."

"Sounds good to me. How about you, Kinsey?"

"Fine."

"What about something to drink? We have coffee, tea, Coke, and Sprite."

Dolan said, "Coke, I guess."

"Make that two."

Annette took her place behind the counter. She turned on the gas burner under the griddle, removed two hamburger patties from the refrigerator, and slapped them on the grill. "It'll just be a minute."

Dolan said, "Things slow today?"

"Things are slow every day."

She made a quick return trip with a dish of celery, carrot sticks, and green olives. She'd tucked a bottle of ketchup and a squeeze bottle of yellow mustard in her apron pocket and she placed those on the table as well. By the time she got back to the griddle, the patties were done and she assembled our plates. "I forgot to ask how you wanted these," she said as she unloaded her tray.

"This is fine," I said. I was busy doctoring my burger with mustard, ketchup, pickle, and onion. Not up to QP standards, but it would have to do.

Dolan said, "What are the chances she's been in touch with Frank?"

"You think he might've had something to do with that young girl's death?

"I have no idea. We were hoping Iona could help us fill in some blanks."

Across the road at the trailer park, we could see a car pull onto the highway, turn left, and speed off with Iona at the wheel. Annette leaned toward the window, frowning slightly to herself. "Wonder what that's about?"

Dolan bit into his burger. "Guess she doesn't want to talk to us."

THIRTEEN

We left the tiny town of Peaches at 2:00, when it finally became apparent Iona wouldn't return. The ever-loquacious Annette had nattered away, answering every question we asked, though most of the information consisted of her own attitudes. It was clear she was no friend of Frankie's, and I was reasonably certain she'd told us as much as she knew. Iona, on the other hand, had clearly left the vicinity to avoid being pressed. Annette wanted to believe she was done with Frankie Miracle, but I wasn't so sure.

From Highway 14, we took Highway 138 as far as the 15, then angled our way down to the eastbound 10, otherwise known as the San Bernardino Freeway. Despite Dolan's worries about his heart, there is quite literally no other way to get to Blythe. This 175-mile stretch of highway extends from the eastern edges of Los Angeles and crosses the state line into Arizona at Blythe. For close to three hours, Dolan kept his foot pressed to the accelerator while the road disappeared beneath us. The scenery became monotonous, the typical urban sprawl of tract housing, billboards, industrial plants, shopping malls, and railroad tracks. The highway was lined with palms, evergreens, and eucalyptus trees. We passed recreational vehicle "estates," an RV country club, and an RV resort and spa. This was a long stretch of land where no one intended to put down roots. We stopped once for gas in Orocopia and I picked up a copy of the *Mobile Home Gazette*; sixteen pages of coupons for discount dinners, cruise specials, golf lessons, custom dentures, and early-bird bingo.

After Palm Springs, the land flattened and the color faded from the landscape. For mile after mile, there was only sand and rock, chaparral, power lines, and passing cars. On either side of the road, at the horizon, the land rose to a fringe of foothills that confined the view. Everything was beige and gray and a pale dusty green. California deserts consist, in the main, of pale soils— fawn, cinnamon, sepia, and pink. We passed the state prison, its presence underlined by signs that advised us not to pick up hitchhikers. The speed limit was seventy, but the landscape was so vast that we scarcely seemed to move. Aside from the Salton Sea to the south of us, the map showed only dry lakes.

I said, "How does anything manage to grow out here?"

Dolan smiled. "The desert's a marvel of adaptability. California desert has one rainy season where southern Arizona has two. The rest of the year, you have drought. If you had seeds that germinated right after the rains, the young plants wouldn't survive the hard sun and heat. Lot of seeds are covered with wax that prevents them from absorbing water until a period of time has passed. Once the wax wears off, they germinate, and that's where the food chain originates. Rabbits and desert rats turn the vegetation into animal flesh and that provides dinner for the predators. Snakes eat the rodents and then the bobcats eat snakes."

"Very nice," I said.

"Efficient. Like crime. Everybody's busy eating someone else."

He went on in this fashion, regaling me with the mating and egg-laying habits of various desert insects, including the black widow, the brown widow, and the tarantula hawk, until I sang, "I'm getting sick here." That shut him up.

At Blythe, we turned south, taking the two-lane state road that ran twelve miles to the community of Quorum, population 12,676. On the map, the town was little more than a circle. Dolan slowed as the outlying residential properties began to appear. The houses were plain and the yards were flat. We reached the central business district less than a minute later on a main street six lanes wide. Buildings were low, as though by hugging the ground, the inhabitants could escape the penetrating desert sun. Palm trees seemed to flourish. There were numerous motels along the thoroughfare, most with wistful-sounding names, like the Bayside Motor Court and the Sea Shell Motel. Among the commercial establishments, many seemed travel-related: gas stations, car dealerships, tire sales, car washes, camper shells, and automotive repair. Occasionally, I'd catch sight of a locksmith or a beauty shop, but not much else. Here, as in Peaches, there were numerous boarded-up businesses; signs with the glass punched out, leaving only the frame. Jody's Café, Rupert's Auto Radiator, and a furniture store were among those that had failed. Glancing to my right, I could see that even the secondary streets tended to be four lanes wide. There was clearly nothing out here but space.

As we drove through town, we made a brief detour, stopping in at the Quorum Police Department and the Riverside County Sheriff's substation, which were next door to each other on North Winter Street. I waited in the car while Dolan talked to detectives in both agencies, letting them know he was in the area and what he was working on. Technically, neither visit was required, but he didn't want to step on any toes. It was smart to lay the groundwork in case we needed local assistance later. When he got back in the car and slammed the door, he said, "Probably a waste of time, but it's worked in my favor often enough to make it worthwhile."

It was close to 5:30 by then and the afternoon temperatures were dropping rapidly. Dolan's plan was to find a motel and then cruise the town, looking for a place to eat. "We can have supper and turn in early, then scout out the auto upholstery shop first thing in the morning."

"Fine with me."

Most of the motels seemed equivalent, matching rates posted on gaudy neon signs. We settled on the Ocean View, which boasted a pool, a heated spa, and free TV. We checked in at the desk, and I waited while Dolan gave the clerk his credit card, picking up the tab on two rooms and a key for each of us. We hopped back in the car, driving the short distance so he could park in the slot directly in front of his room. Mine turned out to be right around the corner. We agreed to a brief recess during which we'd get settled.

I let myself into my room. The interior smelled like the Santa Teresa beach, which is to say, faintly of damp and less faintly of mildew. I placed my shoulder bag on the desktop and my duffel on the chair. I christened the facilities, shrugged into my windbreaker, and met Dolan at his door. Not surprisingly, his goal was to find a restaurant with a cocktail lounge attached. Failing that, he'd opt for a decent bar somewhere, after which we could eat pizza in our rooms. We stopped in the motel office, where the desk clerk recommended the Quorum Inn, two blocks down, on High Street. I'd miscalculated the chill in the desert air at night. I walked with my arms crossed, hunched against the brisk wind whipping down the wide streets. The town seemed exposed, laid open to the élements, low buildings the only hope of shelter from the desert winds.

The Quorum Inn was already packed when we arrived: the late-afternoon martini crowd firing up cigarettes, alternating bites of green olives with the mixed nuts on the bar. The walls were varnished pine and the booths were upholstered in red Naugahyde. The free-standing tables were covered with red-and-white checked cloths. Most of the menu choices were either steak or beef. The side dishes were french fries, fried onion rings, and batter-fried zucchini. You could also order a foil-wrapped baked potato smothered in butter, sour cream, bacon, and/or cheese.

We sat at the bar for the first hour while Dolan downed three Manhattans and I sipped at a puckery white wine that I diluted with ice. Once we retired to a table, he asked for a well-done twenty-two-ounce sirloin and I settled for an eight-ounce filet. By 8:00, we were back at the motel, where we parted company for the night. I read for a while and then slept the way you do with a tummy full of red meat and a shitload of cholesterol coursing through your veins.

At breakfast, I had my usual cereal while Dolan had bacon, eggs, pancakes, four cups of coffee, and five cigarettes. When he pulled out the sixth, I said, "Dolan, you have to quit this."

He hesitated. "What?"

"The booze and cigarettes and fatty foods. You'll trigger another heart attack and I'll be stuck doing CPR. Haven't you read the Surgeon General's report?"

He gestured impatiently. "Nuts to that stuff! My granddaddy lived to ninety-six and he smoked hand-rolled cigarettes from the time he was twelve until the day he died."

"Yeah, well I'll bet he hadn't had two heart attacks by the time he was your age. You keep ragging on Stacey and you're worse than he is."

"That's different."

"It is not. You want him alive and that's exactly what I'm bugging *you* about."

"If I'm interested in your opinion, I'll be sure to ask. I don't need a lecture from someone half my age."

"I'm not half your age. How old are you?"

"I'm sixty-one."

"Well, I'm thirty-six."

"The point is, I can do anything I want."

"Nah, nah, nah. I'll remind you of that next time Stacey threatens to blow his brains out."

Dolan crushed out his cigarette butt in the ashtray. "I'm tired of jawing. Time to go to work."

McPhee's Auto Upholstery was located on Hill Street in the heart of town. We parked across from the shop and took a moment to get our bearings. The morning was filled with a flat, clean sunlight. The air felt pleasant, but I was guessing that by afternoon the heat, while dry, would feel oppressive. By the time the sun went down, it'd be as cold as it had been the night before. Behind the shop, we could see a small lot where six cars had been parked, each shrouded in an automobile cover. That part of the property was enclosed by heavy chain-link fence topped with razor wire. The building itself was constructed of corrugated metal with three bays on one side, the doors rolled up to reveal the shop's interior. It looked like a gas station, surrounded with the usual cracked asphalt. We could see two men at work.

"You really think the car we're after is the one C. K. saw?"

"That's what we're here to find out," he said. "We know it was stolen from here."

"If it was parked near the quarry, then what?"

"Then we'll see if we can establish a connection between the car and Jane Doe."

We got out and crossed the street to the front entrance. Under the big plate glass window, a large concrete planter sat empty except for packed dirt. To the right of the shop there was a lumberyard; to the left, a long-distance hauling company with a lot full of tractor rigs and detached semitrailers. This was a commercial neighborhood made up of businesses that catered to customers in pickups and vans.

The showroom was an extension of the shop area out back. The floor was done in black-and-white vinyl tile. Behind a glass case filled with service manuals, there was a metal desk, metal file cabinets, and a Rolodex. The top surface of the glass case was piled high with sample books showing automobile and marine vinyls, "Performance-rated fabrics for heavy-duty application." Rear and side camper windows in a variety of styles had been mounted on pegboard and hung on the wall. We picked our way through a cluster of bench and bucket car seats still exhibiting their torn upholstery. A display board was set up to show the leather/vinyl match for Ford, GM, Chrysler-Jeep Eagle, Honda, and Toyota interior upholstery. You could order any number of convertible tops, tonneau covers, floor mats, and glass or plastic window curtains.

An open door led from the showroom into the first of the three connecting bays, where one of the two men looked up. I pegged him in his mid-thirties. He was medium height, clean-shaven, his complexion ruddy. His hair had the kind of blond streaks that women pay money for. He wore it parted in the middle with strands falling loosely on either side of his face. Most of his teeth were good. There were creases around his mouth where his smile had made inroads. His hands were dirty, his nails permanently underlined with black like a lady's French tip manicure in reverse. Blue-plaid flannel shirt, jeans, desert boots. He was built like a high school football player—which is to say, some guy who'd get creamed if he played football today. I tried to decide whether I'd have been attracted to him when I was sixteen. He looked like the type I'd have had a crush on from a distance. Then again, most guys in high school were like that as far as I was concerned.

He was using a crescent wrench and a pair of pliers to dismantle a car seat that was propped up in front of him. The workbench, which extended the length of the wall behind him, was stacked with bolts of vinyl, hoses, coffee cans, sheets of foam rubber, toolboxes, cans of latex paint, tires. Two fans were blowing, thus circulating the smell of synthetics. Beside him there was a garbage bin full of scraps. A second ripped and cracked auto seat sat on a counter nearby. He was smoking a cigarette, but he put it out casually before he spoke to us. "Help you?"

Dolan put his hands in his pants pockets. "We're looking for Ruel McPhee."

"That's my dad. He's retired. Who are you?"

"Lieutenant Dolan, Santa Teresa Police Department. This is my colleague, Ms. Millhone. I didn't catch your name."

"Cornell McPhee. Are you the one who left the phone message?"

"That's my partner, Detective Oliphant. As a matter of fact, he left four and says your father never called him back."

"Sorry. I didn't realize it was urgent. I gave Dad the messages and he said he'd take care of it. I guess it slipped his mind."

The second man in the shop was older, possibly in his fifties. He'd returned to his work as soon as he figured out the conversation had nothing to do with him.

"Your dad still in town?"

Cornell put down his crescent wrench and wiped his hands on a rag. "Sure. What's this about?"

"We're hoping to track down a vehicle stolen from his shop in 1969."

Cornell's brow shifted slightly. "That car was recovered. It belonged to a guy in Arizona."

Dolan smiled briefly. "We know about him. DMV says the car's now registered to Ruel McPhee."

"What brought this up again?"

"We're looking at the possibility of a link between the car and a homicide back then."

"A homicide?"

"That's right," Dolan said. "We're taking another run at it."

"I'm still not clear why you want to talk to him."

"We have a witness who says he saw a red Mustang in the area shortly before the body was found. We're wondering if the vehicle's the same one stolen from his shop."

"You can ask him if you want. He and Mom live on Fell. 1520. It's just a few blocks away. You go down two blocks, take a left at Ruby. You'll find Fell five blocks down. You want me to call and make sure he's there?"

"That's fine. We can swing by later if he's out somewhere," Dolan said. He indicated the seat Cornell was working on. "How long's it take to do a job like that?"

"'Couple of days. Depends on the condition. You have some work you need done?"

"Might."

"What kind of car?"

"Chevy. 1979."

"Leather seat?"

"No, cloth."

Cornell smiled. "Throw a bedspread over it. You'd be better off."

"That's my idea. I just wondered what you'd say. Appreciate your help."

"Sure, no sweat. I wish you luck."

The house at 1520 Fell was a red-brick ranch with detached two-car garage on the righthand side of the drive. Behind the house, at a distance, I caught sight of the rear of an outbuilding that looked like a large storage shed or second garage. A basketball backboard was still planted in concrete on a wide asphalt apron set aside for guest parking. Cornell probably spent his leisure time in high school practicing his free throws. I imagined him lettering in three sports, elected pep king or treasurer of his senior class. A check of the yellow pages had indicated that McPhee's was the only game in town, so he must be doing well financially even if his job lacked glamour and pizzazz.

Dolan parked at the curb out in front and we made our way along the walk to the porch, where we rang the bell. The door was opened by a girl who was probably six years old, judging by the number of missing teeth. Her hair was still a white blond that would probably darken over time. She wore glasses with pink plastic frames and a pair of barrettes with a row of pink and blue flowers. Her dress was pink-and-blue plaid with rows of white smocking across the bodice.

Dolan said, "Hey there, young lady. Is your grandpa at home?"

"Just a minute." She shut the door and a moment later her grandmother opened it, wiping her hands on a kitchen towel. A mild, vanilla-smelling breeze wafted out from behind her. She was heavy-set and wore small rimless glasses and a knee-length striped apron over a loose floral-print housedress. Her gray hair had a fringe of curls around her face while the rest was cut short. "Yes?"

"Good morning. We're looking for Ruel McPhee. Cornell, over at the shop, gave us this address."

"Ruel's out back. Won't you come in? I'm Edna, his wife."

She opened the door for us. We did a round of introductions that included the McPhees' granddaughter, Cissy, who skipped on ahead of us in her Mary Janes. Edna led us through the house, saying, "We're about to frost cupcakes for Cissy's birthday. Six years old today. She's having a little party with her kindergarten class this afternoon."

Cissy said, "My grammaw made me this dress."

Dolan said, "Well, that's real cute. I like that."

As usual, I played the silent sidekick, prepared to fly into action if Edna or the child suddenly went berserk.

Cissy had climbed onto a kitchen chair and was now perched on her knees, inspecting the baking project. On the table, there were two muffin tins, each containing twelve freshly baked cupcakes in paper liners with little golden-brown domed heads. I could see the yellow-cake mix box on the counter by the sink where the mixing bowl sat.

The room was decorated in a patriotic flurry of red, white, and blue. The kitchen paper was done in Revolutionary War motif, a repeating pattern of battle scenes, complete with cannons, ships, and soldiers in various heroic poses. The woodwork was white, the counters red, and a window seat built into a side bay was filled with plump pillows and a neatly folded quilt, all in coordinating hues.

Crayon and fingerpaint projects were fixed to the refrigerator with magnets shaped like fruit. There were also school pictures of two additional girls, ages about eight and ten, who might have been Cissy's sisters. All three had the same blond hair and features reminiscent of Cornell's. Cissy lowered her face, her nose a mere centimeter from a cupcake.

Edna said, "Cissy, don't touch. You wait until they're

cool and don't pick at them. Why don't you take these nice folks to see Grandpa? I'll have the frosting ready as soon as you get back."

That job would be quick. I could see the container of ready-to-use fudge frosting on the table with a photo of a shiny chocolate swirl, like an ocean wave, on the side. As a kid, I'd imagined that's what real Grannies did—sewed and made cakes. Aunt Gin always said, "I'm not the cookie-baking type," as though that excused her from cooking of any kind. Now I wondered if that's why I was so bent—because I lacked the homely services she'd so proudly repudiated.

Cissy got down off the chair and took Dolan by the hand. Behind Edna's back, he shot me a look that said, *Help*. I trailed after them, crossing a section of grass that butted up against the garages. A side door stood open and Cissy took us that far before scampering back to her post.

Ruel McPhee sat on a wooden desk chair inside the door. A small color TV set had been placed on a crate and plugged into a wall-mounted outlet. He was smoking a cigarette while he watched a game show. Ruel was half the size of his wife, gaunt-faced and sunken-chested, with narrow bony shoulders. He wore a broken-rimmed straw hat pushed back on his head while his bifocals were pulled down on the bridge of his nose. He smelled a teeny, tiny bit like he hadn't changed his socks this week. Dolan handled the introductions and a quick explanation of why we were there. At the sight of Ruel's cigarette, Dolan was inspired to take out one of his own.

Ruel was nodding, though his attention was still fixed on the television set. "That was years ago."

"DMV tells us the vehicle's registered to you."

"That's right. Fella from Arizona brought it over here to have the seats redone. I had it parked behind the shop. Someone must have broken in and hotwired the ignition because when I came to work Monday morning, it was gone. Don't know when it was taken. Saw it Friday afternoon, but that's the last I know. I reported it right off and it wasn't but a week later someone called from the Sheriff's Department up north to say it'd been found. This fellow Gant, who owned the car, paid to have it towed back but it was worthless by then. Car looked like it'd been rolled—doors all messed up, front banged in. Gant was pissed as hell." He flicked me an apologetic look for the use of the word. "I told him to file a claim with his insurance company, but he didn't want anything more to do with it. He'd already been in a couple fender-benders and the engine froze up once. He was convinced the car was jinxed. I offered him a fair price, but he wouldn't take a cent. He said good riddance to bad rubbish and signed it over to me." Ruel's gaze returned to the screen where contestants were pressing buttons while the prize money they'd racked up was being flashed on monitors. I couldn't answer even one of the questions they responded to with such speed.

Dolan said, "What happened to the car?"

"Someone pushed it down a ravine is what I heard."

"I mean, where is it now?"

"Oh. It's setting right out back. Cornell and I intend to do the restoration as soon as we have time. I guess you met him. He's married with three girls, and Justine lays claim to any spare time he has. We'll get to it in due course."

"Justine's his wife?"

"Going on fifteen years. She's difficult to get along with. Edna has more patience with the situation than I do."

"You have any idea who might have stolen the car?"

"If I did, I'd've told the police back then. Joyriders is my guess. Town this size, it's what the kids do for fun. That and throw paint balloons out the back of their trucks. Not like when I was young. My dad would've pounded me bloody and that'd've been the end of that."

"You ever had a car stolen from the shop before?"

"Not before and not since. I put up a fence with concertina wire and that took care of it." He turned his attention from the TV. "What's your interest?

Dolan's expression was bland. "We're cleaning out

our files, doing follow-up on old crime reports. Most of it's administrative work."

"I see." Ruel stepped on his cigarette and then placed the flattened butt in a Miracle Whip jar that was nearly filled to the brim. He held the jar out to Dolan who stepped on his cigarette and added it to the collection. Ruel was saying, "I'm not allowed to smoke inside, especially when the granddaughters visit. Justine thinks it's bad for their lungs so Edna makes me come out here. Justine can be moody if she doesn't get her way."

"Why'd you hang on to the car?"

Ruel drew back and made a face as though Dolan were dense. "That Mustang's a classic. 1966."

"Couldn't have been a classic then. The car was only three years old."

"I told you I got the car for free," he said. "Once we finish the restoration, it'll be worth somewhere in the neighborhood of fourteen thousand dollars. Now I'd call that a profit, wouldn't you?"

"Mind if we take a look?"

"Help yourself. I got five of them back there; one sweet little GT Coupe, silver frost with the black vinyl top torn up. Doesn't run yet and the body needs work, but if you're interested, we could talk money and maybe make a deal."

"My car's fine, thanks."

Dolan lit another cigarette as the two of us trooped

through high grass to a rutted dirt lane overgrown with weeds that led to the second of Ruel McPhee's garages. The entire area had been undercut by gopher tunnels, and my foot occasionally sank into a softly crumbling hole. The garage was positioned so that its backside was to us, its double doors facing a flat field beyond. We could see the faintly defined path where the lane had originally been laid out, possibly in anticipation of a second house on the property. Three additional vehicles were visible in the area immediately in front of us. We checked those cars first, lifting their respective car covers like a series of ladies' skirts. The two I peeked at were in poor shape, and I didn't think they'd ever amount to more than yard ornaments. While we made our inspection, I said, "You think someone used the vehicle to drive the body to Lompoc?"

"Hard to say. She could have been alive when she left, assuming she was ever in Quorum at all. Just as likely someone stole the car and picked her up along the way."

"But what if she was killed here? Why drive the body all the way up there to dump? Seems like it'd be easier to go out in the desert and dig a hole."

Dolan shrugged. "You might want to put some distance between the body and the crime scene. It'd make sense to take off and go as far as you could. Then you'd have to find a place to pull off and unload, which's not

272

as easy as you'd think. If the body was in the trunk much more than a day, it'd start to decompose and then you'd have a big problem on your hands. You'd have to figure the car'd been reported stolen, which means you couldn't risk a traffic stop in case the officer became curious about what you had back there. At least Lompoc's off the main highway and if you found an isolated spot, you'd dump her while you had the chance."

"What about the original owner? How do we know he didn't have a hand in it?"

"It's always possible," he said, "though Gant's been dead the last ten years. Ruptured abdominal aneurysm, according to the information I received."

When we reached the garage, Dolan tried the side door, but a combination of warping and old paint had welded it shut. We went around to the double doors in front. Both were closed, but there were no locks in the hasps. Dolan gave the one on the right a hefty yank and the three-section door labored up, trailing spider webs and dead leaves. Sunlight washed in, setting a cloud of dust motes ablaze. The two cars inside were both covered with canvas tarps and the space was crammed with junk. In addition to old cars, McPhee apparently saved empty cans and jars, stacks of newspapers bound with wire, wood crates, boxes, shovels, a pickax, a rusted tire iron, firewood, sawhorses, and lumber. The garage had also been made home to an ancient mower, automotive parts, and dilapidated metal lawn furniture. The air smelled stale and felt dry against my face. Dolan paused to extinguish his cigarette while I raised a corner of the nearest tarp. "This looks a lot like the tarp the body was wrapped in."

"Sure does. We'll have to ask McPhee if one was taken the same time the car was."

I looked down, catching sight of the battered right rear fender of the red Mustang. "Found it."

Together we removed the car cover and folded it like a flag. To my untutored eye, the car looked as though it hadn't been touched since the day it was hauled out of the ravine back in '69. At best, the exterior had been hosed off, but dried dirt still clung to the underbelly of the car with its scraped and dented right side and its banged-in driver's door. Both sides were rumpled. A portion of tree branch was caught under the left rear fender. Something about it made my heart thump. Dolan took out a handkerchief and gingerly pressed the trunk lock. The lid swung open. Inside, the spare tire was missing from the mount. A couple of dusty cardboard boxes filled with old *National Geographic* magazines had been shoved into the space. Dolan removed the boxes and set them aside. The exposed matting looked clean except for two large dark smudges and two smaller ones near the back. Dolan peered closer. "I think we better call the local sheriff's department and get the car impounded."

He crossed to the single door and tested it again. Satisfied that it was frozen shut, he said, "Wait here. I'll be back in a minute."

I stood just outside, staring at the untilled pasture with its tangle of wildflowers while Dolan headed off toward his car. I noticed he steered a wide path around the backside of the garage, where I assumed McPhee was still sitting. I couldn't see the old man, but the occasional drift of frenetic music suggested he'd remained in his wooden chair, watching TV. I returned to the Mustang and circled it, hands behind my back, peering in the windows with their cracked and broken glass. The black leather seats, while gray with dust, seemed to be in good shape.

Dolan returned six minutes later carrying a Polaroid camera, his pant legs covered with burrs. He handed me the camera while he took out a pen and a packet of seals he'd retrieved from his car. He jotted his initials, the date, and the time on four seals and affixed one across each of the two doors, one to the hood, and the remaining seal across the trunk opening. Then he clicked off a series of Polaroid shots while he circled the car. As each photograph emerged from the slot, Dolan handed it to me. I waited for the image to appear and then wrote a title across the bottom. Dolan added his name, the date, and the time, and tucked them in an envelope he placed in his jacket pocket.

I said, "Does McPhee know we're doing this?"

"Not yet."

"What now?"

"I'll go back to the motel and call Detective Lassiter. He can send out a deputy to secure the car until a tow truck arrives. I'll also put in a request to the Santa Teresa Sheriff's Department to send down a flatbed as soon as possible. They can load the car at the local impound lot and tow it back."

"How long will that take?"

Dolan checked his watch. "It's ten thirty now. They should be able to get someone here by six tonight. Meantime, I'll call Judge Ruiz in Santa Teresa and ask him to issue a telephonic warrant. We'll return the affidavit with the Mustang and have Stacey file the paperwork up there. I'll be back within the hour."

FOURTEEN

I hadn't sat surveillance for ages and I'd forgotten how long an hour could feel. At least the car wasn't going to move. I took off my watch and slipped it in my pocket so I wouldn't be tempted to keep peeking at the time. I settled in the shade, leaning against the garage while I added a few notes to my index cards and then slipped the paperback from my shoulder bag and found my place.

Half a chapter later, I heard a car door slam, and when I peered around the corner, I saw Cornell getting out of a white truck. He was crossing the parking pad, heading for his parents' back door, possibly to have lunch. I was starving and had to take my nourishment in the form of an ancient Junior Mint I'd tossed in the bottom of my shoulder bag. I figured the fuzz on it would supply my quota of fiber.

The day had warmed up considerably and the air smelled of wildflowers and weeds. An occasional bumblebee lumbered by, a black-and-yellow gumball in flight. A swarm of gnats danced in the light and a horsefly zipped around, looking for a place to land. This was entirely too much wildlife for my purposes. I'm an indoor kind of person, and I prefer my contact with Nature reduced to the front of a picture postcard.

I heard someone trampling through the grass. I got to my feet, dusted off my jeans, and tucked the book back in my bag. I was expecting to see Dolan. Instead, Cornell appeared, smoking a cigarette he'd cupped in the palm of his hand. He didn't seem all that happy to see me. His gaze shifted to the open garage door, where the Mustang sat in plain view, its tarp removed, a seal affixed across the opening of the hood.

I said, "Hi. I'm Kinsey. We met this morning." I flicked a look toward the driveway, hoping to see the deputy arriving, but no such luck.

"I know who you are. What's all this?"

"A sheriff's deputy should be here shortly. Lieutenant Dolan thinks this might be the vehicle used to transport our victim. He wants to have it checked."

"What's that mean?"

I put a casual shrug in my voice. "It's no big deal. He wants the evidence technicians to go over it."

"And Dad knows about this?"

"I'm assuming so," I said, lying through my teeth. "I'm not sure what the lieutenant told him. You'd have to ask him."

Cornell frowned. He dropped his cigarette and stepped on it. "How long's this going to take?"

"Probably no more than a couple of days." I was hoping it wouldn't occur to him we'd be removing the Mustang from the premises. Also, hauling it north where he probably wouldn't see the car again for months. I didn't want to deal with him if he raised a big stink.

He hunched his shoulders. "The law allows you to just waltz in this way? You're on private property out here, same as the house. My dad owns everything as far as that fence."

I turned and followed his gesture. "I wasn't aware of that. Lot of land," I said. "Actually, we had a chat with your father and asked to see the Mustang. He told us to help ourselves."

"I don't think he understood what you meant. He didn't mention it to me."

"Is that a problem?"

"Well, no. Not at all. It just seems weird."

I looked down at the ground, snubbing the tip of my right Saucony in the dirt. "I don't know what to tell you. Maybe Lieutenant Dolan can explain it when he gets back. He asked me to secure the car until the deputy arrives. Did you need something out here?"

"I came out to see what was going on. Dad saw you head in this direction, but then you never came back. Where's Lieutenant Dolan?"

"Ah. I guess he went around the other way. He probably didn't want to bug your dad while he was watching his show." I let a silence settle. I didn't want to manufacture small talk and I wasn't interested in continuing the conversation on its present course.

"I better let Dad know. He's not going to like it, but that's your look-out."

"Go ahead. Do anything you like."

Cornell backed up a step and then took off for the house. By the time he reached the driveway, a black-and-white unit was pulling in. When the deputy got out, he and Cornell shook hands. I watched the two men confer, joined moments later by the old man himself. He had his straw hat set square on his head, the rim shading his face. Even from a distance, I could see he'd taken on the air of a bandy rooster whose barnyard was under siege. The conversation continued with a lot of hand waving on Ruel's part. The three faces turned in my direction. Behind them, Lieutenant Dolan pulled up and parked at the curb. The three of them waited for Dolan and then another discussion ensued, at the end of which the four of them formed a little ragtag parade and trudged toward me.

Dolan introduced the deputy, whose name was Todd Chilton. He seemed to be acquainted with Ruel, and I gathered their relationship predated the current meeting. Chilton was in his late thirties, with dark hair clipped short on the sides and curling slightly on top. He'd loosened his tie, and he took a moment to rebutton his collar before the two of us shook hands.

Ruel peered at me and then turned to Lieutenant Dolan. "This the technician you were talking about?"

"She's a private investigator. We'll tow the car to Santa Teresa and do the evidence search up there."

Ruel turned and stared. "You mean to take the car *away*?" He looked from Dolan to the deputy in disbelief. "He can't do that, can he?"

"Yes, sir."

"But I hold title to that car and it's registered in my name. He never said what he was up to or I'd've told him to get lost."

Chilton said, "We understand that, Mr. McPhee, and I'm sure Lieutenant Dolan appreciates the inconvenience."

"Inconvenience, my foot! That car's been setting out there for the past eighteen years. If the cops thought it was so all-fired important, they should have taken it back then."

Dolan said, "The information came in a week ago. That's the first we'd heard of it, or we'd have done just that."

"This's private property. The car belongs to me. You can't sashay in here and walk off with what's mine." He turned to the deputy. "I want him out of here."

Chilton said, "I can't help you with that. He has the right to take it."

"Then you clear off, too! What good's that gall-dang badge of yours if you can't protect us any better than this?"

Chilton's manner was beginning to shift. Where at first his tone had been conciliatory, now it was turning flat. "Excuse me, sir, but that car's considered evidence in a criminal investigation. You don't have a choice. Techs don't find anything, you get the vehicle back and there's no harm done."

"I'm calling my lawyer."

Lieutenant Dolan said, "Mr. McPhee, we have a legitimate search warrant. You can call anyone you want, but it won't change what's happening. No disrespect intended, but you might as well save your breath."

"I'm entitled to one call."

"That's only if they put you in jail," Chilton said, exasperated. "No one's proposing to arrest you. It's the car he wants. He's talking about a homicide. You interfere here and you're only making trouble for yourself. None of us want that."

Cornell said, "Let it go, Dad. Come on. They're going to do it anyway."

Ruel gave way suddenly. He took his hat off and slapped his thigh with it. "People been telling me we live in a police state, but I never thought I'd see the day.

It's a damn shame when a law-abiding citizen gets treated like dirt."

He walked away from the group. Cornell glanced back with a dark look and then followed his father to the house.

We heard a quick horn toot at the street and saw the local towing company with a flatbed truck idling at the curb. Chilton whistled to catch the driver's eye and then gestured him in our direction with a series of arm rolls. The driver shifted gears, pulling the truck forward. He then backed into the driveway and eased up the long dirt lane toward the garage where we were standing.

Dolan and I acted as sideline supervisors while the chain was attached to the Mustang's front axle and the car was winched up the ramp. Cornell's truck was gone by then and there was no sign of Ruel. Once the Mustang was loaded, we tagged after the moving tow truck as far as the street. The driver waited while we got in Dolan's car. We followed him, keeping the Mustang in view.

I said, "By the way, you talked to Stace? What's he heard about his biopsy and X-rays? They must know something by now."

Dolan looked at me blankly. "Completely slipped my mind. He wanted to come down here and I was so busy trying to talk him out of it I forgot to ask."

"He's joining us?"

"Not if I can help it. I'd rather have him up there where he can do some good."

At the impound lot, we waited while the Mustang was unloaded and the rolling gate was locked. Dolan took care of all the paperwork and then he returned to the car. We headed for the motel. He was whistling idly to himself, tapping out a rhythm on the steering wheel.

"You seem chipper."

"I am. I got a good feeling about this."

"How long until the forensics guys can get back to us?"

"Soon, I hope. Things are quiet at the moment, so Mandel said he'd ask them to get right on it."

"And in the meantime, what?"

"Nothing. If they can connect our victim to the Mustang, we'll use her dental chart to canvas the local dentists. Teeth that bad, someone might remember her."

"Can't we do that while we wait? I hate sitting around. We know someone stole the car and drove it up to Lompoc. C. K. spotted it near the quarry . . ."

"We still don't know for sure this is the car he saw. It could've been something similar; some guy stopping near the quarry to take a leak. Don't be so quick off the mark."

"But suppose this *was* the car, doesn't it seem safe to assume it was used to move the body?"

"Where do you get that, unless they find trace evidence?"

"Oh come on, Lieutenant . . ."

"I'm serious. Even if we're right about the car, it still doesn't prove the girl was from Quorum. Killer could have picked her up and stabbed her when he was on the road."

"Okay, I'll grant you that one. So what now, we just sit?"

"Yep."

"But it could take *days*."

"I can put you on a bus and send you home," he said mildly.

"That's not what I'm getting at."

"Then what?"

"Why don't you do the sitting while I start nosing around?"

He shook his head. "There's no point going off half-cocked."

"How about this? I'll work with the meter off, but keep a running tab of my hours. If I manage to track her down, pay me, and if I don't, oh well."

Dolan thought about it, taking up his finger tapping as he studied the street ahead. "Maybe."

"Come on, Dolan. Please, please, pretty please with sugar on it? Let me take a crack at it. I'll be good. I swear."

"Begging's unbecoming. You're not the type." He stopped tapping. "I suppose I could borrow your type-writer and catch up on the paperwork. I want to get some of this down while the details are fresh."

"Good. I'm glad. Makes it a lot more fun."

Once in my room again, I opened the bed-table drawer and took out the pint-sized Quorum phone book, look-ing for the address of the public library. The Quorum Branch of the Riverside County District Public Library was on High Street. According to the minimap in the front of the directory, it was only five blocks away. I tucked the book into my bag, left my typewriter with Dolan, and then headed off on foot.

At the library, I went straight to the reference room and pulled the city directories for 1966, '67, '68, and '69. I took the phone book from my shoulder bag and turned to the yellow pages under the heading "Den-tists." There were ten listed. I checked the current names against those of dentists in practice during the years in question. Two past dentists, Drs. Towne and Nettleton, had disappeared, which I was guessing meant they'd retired, died, or left the area. Four names carried over and six were new. Most seemed to be generalists, judg-ing from their full-page ads, which trumpeted crowns,

286

dentures, fillings, periodontal work, bridges, root canals, cosmetic dentistry, and oral surgery. With my dental phobia, this was making my palms sweat. Already I favored the fellow who offered "Nitrous oxide: Dentistry while you sleep." I wouldn't be opposed to postponing my next appointment 'til I was dead.

Of the carryovers, the fourth dentist, Dr. Gregory Spears, had listed himself twice, once under the general heading and again under the listing for orthodontists, of which there was one, namely him. The word "straightening" had been added in parentheses for those who didn't know what an orthodontist did. I jotted down the four names and addresses, returned to the city map, and charted my route. Given the size of the town, it was no big deal to walk from the library to the first dentist on my list.

Spears's office was located in a storefront on Dodson. There was no one in the waiting room. His front office "girl" was in her sixties, a Mrs. Gary, according to her name tag. Her desktop was orderly and the surrounding office space was laid out with efficiency; charts filed on the vertical. A random band of color-coded labels formed an irregular line across the flaps. A small sign in cross-stitch hung on the wall: PLEASE PAY AT TIME SERVICES ARE RENDERED. I was sure she'd be sympathetic when she heard your front cap came off in the middle of a ladies' lunch, but she probably wouldn't take any guff from you if your check should bounce.

When she opened the sliding glass window that separated her office from the waiting room, I placed a copy of my PI license on the counter. Dolan had given me the file containing Jane Doe's dental chart, showing the number and location of her fillings. I placed that on the counter as well. In the background, I could hear the high-pitched squealing of a drill, a sound that was sometimes sufficient to cause me to pass out. I ran a dampened palm across the seat of my pants and said, "Hi. I'm hoping you can give me some information."

"I can certainly try."

"I'm currently working with two Santa Teresa homicide detectives on a Jane Doe case that's been on the books since 1969. This is a chart of her dental work. There's an off chance she lived in this area and we're wondering if she might have been a patient of Dr. Spears's. She was most likely a minor when the work was done."

She glanced at the file. "He's with a patient right now. Can you come back in half an hour?"

"It's easier if I just wait," I said. "How long have you worked for him?"

"Since he opened his practice in 1960. What did you say the patient's name was?"

"I don't know. That's the point. She was never identified. She had numerous fillings and the forensic odontist who examined the maxilla and mandible thought the work was probably done in the two years before her death. It's a long shot, I know."

"I doubt we'd have a chart on someone we haven't seen in nearly twenty years."

"What happens to the old charts? Are they destroyed?"

"Usually not. They're put on inactive status and retired to dead storage. I'm not sure how far back they go. You're talking about hundreds of patients, you know."

"I'm aware of that. The charts are here in town?"

"If you're suggesting a hand search, that's something you'd have to talk to Dr. Spears about. I'm not sure he'd agree to anything without a court order."

"We'll only be in town for two days and we were hoping to avoid delay."

"Wait and see what he says. It isn't up to me."

"I understand."

I took a seat in the corner, where I sorted through the magazines. I chose the current issue of *Architectural Digest* and entertained myself trying to imagine a color spread on my studio apartment, all eight hundred and fifty feet of it.

Fifteen minutes later, a woman with a puffy lip

emerged, pausing at the desk while she wrote out a check for services. I waited until she'd left and then set the magazine aside and returned to the counter.

"Shall we try again?"

Mrs. Gary went into the examining room. I could hear the murmur of voices as she explained my request.

Dr. Spears came out to meet me, still wearing his white coat, wiping his hands on a paper towel he then tossed in the trash. He was gray-haired and blue-eyed and after we shook hands, mine were left smelling like soap. While he seemed to appreciate my problem, he wasn't much help.

Before I could even get through the details, he was shaking his head. "I couldn't do that without a name. Inactive charts are filed alphabetically. I've got hundreds of them. From what Mrs. Gary's said, the girl was a minor, which further complicates matters. I don't see how you'd find her."

"She had tons of fillings, buckteeth, and a crooked eyetooth on the left," I said.

"Most of my patients have crooked teeth. I'd like to help, but what you're asking is impossible."

"That's too bad. I'd hoped for more, but I can see your point. What about the other dentists in the area back then? Can you tell me anything about Dr. Towne or Dr. Nettleton? I noticed both were in practice in the late sixties."

"Dr. Towne died two years ago, but his widow might be willing to help if his records are still in her possession. Dr. Nettleton's over ninety. He's reasonably sharp, but I doubt you'll get much." He turned to Mrs. Gary. "You know the family, don't you? Where's he living these days?"

"With his daughter. She goes to my church."

"Why don't you give Miss Millhone the information. Maybe he'll remember. It's worth a try, at any rate."

"Thanks. I'd appreciate that."

Mrs. Gary checked her Rolodex and made a note of the daughter's name and address. From her expression, I was guessing I'd be lucky if Dr. Nettleton could remember how to tie his own shoes.

I left the office, pausing on the sidewalk out front. I consulted my map and my list, moving on to the next name. I repeated the same conversation, with variations, in my chats with the three remaining dentists. The response was polite but discouraging. They seemed willing to help, but all of them were busy and no one was interested in searching dead files on the off chance of finding her. Not only was I unable to supply them with a name, but I couldn't prove she'd ever lived in Quorum or that her dental work was done there. My only hope had been that the meager facts in my possession might have triggered a recollection. I did have Dr. Nettleton's address, but I was too tired by then to pursue the point.

It was close to 6:00 by the time I walked the ten blocks back to the motel where Dolan waited. I hated admitting I'd bombed out, but that's what I did as soon as he answered his door.

He seemed unusually magnanimous. "Don't worry about it. You covered a lot of ground."

"For what it's worth."

"Let it go for now. Start again tomorrow. You might have better luck. Right now, it's time for drinks and dinner. Are you up for that?"

"Sure, but you'll have to give me half an hour. I want to check in with Henry and then I'm grabbing a shower. If you're going to the Quorum Inn, I'll meet you there."

"Good."

My call caught Henry just as he was going out the door. I gave him a hasty summary of the trip and the lack of progress, and he was properly consoling. "By the way, you received a package from Lompoc. It was on your doorstep this morning. I brought it in."

"Who's it from?"

"Doesn't say."

"What's it look like?"

"About the size of a shirt box, two pounds. Probably not a bomb. I'm holding it to my ear and it doesn't tick."

"Now you've got me curious. Open it and peek."

"I refuse to open your mail. I'll keep it 'til you get back."

"If you change your mind, I'm giving you permission to see what's there," I said. "How's Mattie?"

"She's fine. She ended up staying an extra day so she could hike Diamondback Trail. There's a hot springs up there she used to visit with her husband. She's thinking about a painting of the scene if she can find it again."

"Sounds like fun. Did you go?"

"No, no. My knees wouldn't take it so I sent her on alone. Besides, I'd agreed to do a tea for Moza and I ended up making finger sandwiches and cookies all day." Henry had been a commercial baker during his working life, and he was still smitten with the process. He catered the occasional luncheon or tea and worked a deal with Rosie, trading homemade breads for occasional free meals.

"I liked her. She seems nice."

"I hate to cut this short, but I'm late as it is. When will you be home?"

"I'm not sure yet. I'll let you know."

I hung up the phone, stripped off my clothes, and hopped in the shower, thinking *Late for what?* He'd been in a hurry to get off the phone, but I couldn't tell if it was me he was avoiding or the subject of Mattie. I'd hoped to find out if he was interested in her and she in him. She and Henry had been cute together and I was feeling proprietary. I'd thought it was a good sign she stayed the extra day, but then the mention of her husband didn't sit well with me. I'd assumed she was a widow, but she might be divorced. In either case, she'd referred to her husband twice, so maybe she was still emotionally connected to him. Not a good sign.

FIFTEEN

At breakfast, drinking my second cup of coffee, I said, "I'll track down Dr. Nettleton this morning to get some closure on that." I watched Dolan eat his eggs Benedict. The yellow of the sauce was suspiciously bright, suggesting that the "chef" had used a packet of powdered Hollandaise.

He mopped up a puddle of poached egg with a fragment of buttered sweetroll. "I thought you covered all the dentists when you were out yesterday."

I shook my head. "Didn't get to him. This guy's retired. I got his address from Dr. Spears but haven't been there yet. Are you interested in coming?"

"Sounds like something you can handle on your own. Why don't you drop me at the Sheriff's Department. I asked them to go through their dead files looking for any missing-persons reports that might sound like our girl. After that, I'll walk back to the motel, see if we've heard from Mandel. I talked to him late last night and he said the guy who picked up the Mustang did a quick turnaround and headed right back. He and his wife were leaving on vacation this morning so that worked in our favor. Mandel said the evidence techs'll get on it first thing this morning. He'll call as soon as he has anything to report. I don't hear soon, I can call him again."

"Sounds good. I'll report in after I've talked to Dr. Nettleton."

At the Sheriff's Department, Dolan put the car in neutral and pulled on the emergency brake, then slid from the driver's seat while I emerged from my side, went around the front, and took his place at the wheel. He'd fired up a cigarette before I could get my bearings. He fished his key out of his pocket and let himself into his room. I spent a few seconds adjusting the seat and the rearview mirror, trying to get a feel for the old Chevy, which had the bulk of a tank after my snub-nosed VW. As soon as I was set, the engine conked out on me. I turned the key in the ignition and pressed the gas pedal lightly, coaxing and cajoling until the engine caught hold again. I felt like a little kid. I peered down the length of the hood, wishing I were perched on a New York City telephone book, though my feet barely touched the pedals as it was.

I pulled my bag onto my lap and checked my notebook for the address I'd been given, then consulted the minimap. The town of Quorum was roughly twenty-five streets wide, transected by five big boulevards that ran east and west. A series of smaller east-west streets further defined a grid that made navigation easy. Dr. Nettleton's daughter lived on Banner Way in a small subdivision on the northern outskirts. I released the hand brake and backed out of the space with caution, then eased the car through the lot and onto the main drag. Drive time was approximately four minutes.

The house number I was looking for turned out to be another one-story brick ranch set among full-grown trees. The two-car garage had been incorporated into the main structure, and I was guessing it now served as guest quarters. Large tubs of pink begonias were lined up across the porch with its wide overhang.

I rang the bell and waited. The door was opened by a woman in her late forties. I'd caught her in the middle of her morning exercise, pink-faced and out of breath. In the background, I could see Jane Fonda doing leg lifts.

"I'm looking for Dr. Nettleton. Are you his daughter?"

"That's right. I take it you're the private detective. Alana Gary told me you might be stopping by. Come on in."

"I'm Kinsey Millhone."

"Vonda Landsberg," she replied. "Dad's in his room down the hall, the last door on the right. If you don't mind, I'll let you find your own way."

"Sure. Is he expecting me?"

"Hard to say. His mind is sharp, but his memory comes and goes. He can still beat the pants off my husband at chess, but he's easily exhausted, so please don't stay long."

"Fifteen minutes tops."

Vonda returned to her exercise mat while I went down the hallway to the back bedroom. The door was ajar. I pushed it open. Dr. Nettleton was sitting in a bentwood rocker, staring out the window, which was open about six inches. On the sill outside, someone had scattered sunflower seeds. A squirrel was perched up on its haunches peering in at him.

The old man looked ninety; frail and bent, hunched in his chair with a shawl across his knees. His face was long and his earlobes drooped like melting candle wax. Most of his hair was gone, but what he had was pure white and clipped close to his head. Flesh-colored hearing aids filled his ear cavities like flattened wads of bubble gum.

"Dr. Nettleton?"

Rheumy-eyed, he turned in my direction and cupped a hand behind one ear. "What say?" His voice was powdery and dry, as though dust had accumulated on his windpipe.

"May I join you?"

"Are you the visiting nurse?"

"I'm a private detective." I spotted a small wooden desk chair that I pulled close to his. I sat down. He seemed perfectly accepting of my appearance on the scene. Perhaps at his stage in life, he'd given up the notion of personal boundaries and privacy. In a slightly elevated voice, I explained who I was and what I needed from him. As I talked, Dr. Nettleton kept his head tilted, his trembling right hand cupped behind his ear. "Come again?"

I pulled my chair closer and went through it again, speaking louder this round. I could see the intelligence in his eyes, though I wasn't at all certain he was following me. When I finished, the ensuing silence went on so long I wondered if he'd caught any of what I'd said. The squirrel picked up a sunflower seed and nibbled rapidly, cracking the shell, tail twitching. Dr. Nettleton smiled with such sweetness I nearly wept.

"Dr. Nettleton?"

He turned his head. "Yes?"

"I was wondering about the girl. Did you ever have a patient like her?"

He pulled himself upright, staring at a spill of sunlight on the floor. "The last year I had my practice, there was one girl fits that description. I was forced to retire when I was seventy-five. Hands weren't steady and I couldn't take standing on my feet all day. I forget her name now, but I remember the fuss I made when I saw her teeth. Told her, 'Cavities like that can undermine your health.' "

I blinked at him. Maybe he'd misunderstood. "She had the buckteeth I mentioned?"

"Oh, yes. Occlusion was pronounced and her upper left cuspid was pointed anteriorly and slightly outward. That's this one right here," he said, pointing to his eyetooth. "Left third molar hadn't yet erupted and I warned her she might have a problem with it if it didn't come through shortly. She had considerable plaque, of course, and her gums tended to bleed. Teeth spoiled her looks. Pleasant-looking girl otherwise, though if I remember rightly, she had behavioral problems."

"Like what?"

"Not sure. Something off about her. She'd been taken from her natural parents and placed in foster care. Must've had their hands full with her. Boisterous. Inappropriate. I believe she had a tendency to take things that weren't hers. She'd come in for an appointment and the next thing we knew, the stapler'd be missing or the paper clip dispenser. I took care of her fillings and then referred her to Dr. Spears for orthodontic evaluation. Don't know what happened to her after that. Doubt she had the work done. Didn't seem the type. Pity, if you ask me."

"Can you remember the name of the foster family?"

His focus shifted to the wall. "Not offhand. They weren't patients of mine. I forget now who they went to."

"What about the girl? Do you remember her name—first, last? Anything that might help?"

He gave his head a shake like a horse irritated by a fly. "I had to sedate her to get the work done and that affected her badly. Sometimes happens. Made her wild. I did one quadrant at a time, but she fought me every step. Novocaine didn't seem to take either. I must have stuck her four times for every tooth I filled."

I wiped my damp palm casually against my jeans, my dental phobia and my needle phobia having collided midair. "Did she attend the local high school?"

"Must have. State law. Pretty girl I'd say until she opened her mouth. Bad teeth spoil your looks and I told her so. Uncooperative. Missed two appointments and she came late for the ones she made. My hygienist could have told you the name, but she died. Can't believe I outlived her. Fit as a fiddle; worked for me thirty-two years and never took a sick day."

"What'd she die of?" I said, sidetracked.

"Heart. Weeding a pansy bed and toppled over sideways. She was out like a light. Yard work'll do that.

Wretched way to spend time. I prefer indoors. Always have."

"Anything else about the girl?"

He squinted at me, shifting in his chair. "What's that?"

I said, "Anything else about the girl?"

He studied his hands, which seemed to move of their own accord, plucking at the shawl. "I remember the foster mother raised a fuss about the bill. Sent to her in error; a simple clerical mistake. You should have heard her carry on. Had my office girl in tears. I never liked the woman after that. She'd bring the girl in, but I wouldn't go out to greet her like I did everyone else. Figured she could sit there by herself. My hygienist was the one who said the woman drank. Can't understand how Social Services considered her fit. She wasn't, in my opinion, but then they never asked me what I thought." He was silent for a moment. "That's all."

I touched his arm. "Thanks so much. This has been a big help. I'll leave my phone number with your daughter. You can have her call me if you think of anything else."

His wandering gaze met mine. "You play chess?"

"I don't, but I hear you're good at it."

"I should be. My pa taught me when I was seven and now I'm ninety-three years old. Son-in-law plays badly.

302

Hasn't got the head for it, if you know what I mean. Requires you to think. You have to plan in advance, maybe ten to fifteen moves. I'd be happy to teach you if you have a desire to learn."

"I'm afraid not, but thanks."

"All right." He was silent briefly and then pointed a dancing index finger at a jar on the chest of drawers. "You might fetch a few more sunflower seeds for that squirrel. Good company for me. More personality than some folks I've known and he's easily amused."

I sprinkled a handful of seeds on the ledge. Dr. Nettleton was already sinking, the energy fading from his face. As I opened the door, he said, "Don't remember your name, but I thank you for the visit. I enjoyed the conversation and hope you did, too."

"Believe me, I did." I wanted to put him in the car and take him with me. I waved from the door, but I don't think he caught the gesture.

I headed back to the motel. Surely we were on the right track. While Dr. Nettleton couldn't supply the name, the details he'd given me were consistent with what we knew. A thought struck me—a quick stop I could make before I reconnected with Dolan. I slowed the car and then pulled over to the curb. I picked up my map and looked for a small black square with a tiny flag on top. I did a U-turn on Chesapeake and drove back in the direction I'd been coming from.

Quorum High, which was part of the Unified School District, occupied a flat, two-block stretch of land on the northeast side of town. The grass looked patchy and the flagpole was bare. The classrooms were dispersed among a number of low-slung outbuildings that appeared to be prefabricated, with walls you could probably pierce with an X-Acto knife. I counted six trees on campus; not enough to pass for landscaping, but sufficient to offer the occasional shallow puddle of shade. The administration building looked like the first story of something far more grand. Maybe the school was in the process of raising funds, driving everyone insane with endless telethons on the local TV station. People will pay big bucks to get their regular programs back: sitcoms and soaps instead of all those amateur rock bands playing songs they've written without training of any kind.

I parked in the lot in a space marked VISITOR. I locked the car and trotted across the flattened grass to the entrance, pushing through the double glass doors and into the main corridor. It was dead quiet, though there must have been students somewhere on the premises. The portable classrooms outside weren't large enough to house the auditorium or the gym. I was guessing that a goodly number of classes were held in this building as well. I could smell sweat and hair spray, hormones and hot gym shoes—the scents of teen misery. Bad skin, no power, too few choices, too much sexual pressure, and not enough wisdom to see you through until you reached eighteen. How many lives were out of whack by then? Girls pregnant, guys dead in cars before the beer cans had quit rolling across the floorboards.

Ahead of me, down the hall, I spotted a sign indicating the principal's office. I could feel my anxiety mount as it had every day of my life during my high school years. I'd been so out of it, such a dork. I'd survived by rebelling—smoking dope and hanging out with other misfits like me. Here I was again, only all grown up (allegedly), crossing the threshold voluntarily, looking for answers to questions I'd never even dreamed of when I was young.

The school secretary was in her early thirties with brown eyes and short silky hair the color of pecan shells. A gossamer array of freckles lay across her nose and upper cheeks. She was casually dressed: beige slacks, short-sleeve brown sweater, and flat-heeled shoes. Her laminated name tag read ADRIANNE RICHARDS, and under that, in smaller letters, ADMINISTRATIVE ASSISTANT. She got up when she saw me and came to the counter. "May I help you?"

"I hope so," I said. "I'm a private investigator from

Santa Teresa. I'm working with a couple of police detectives trying to identify a homicide victim, who died in August of '69."

"You mean here?"

"We're not sure." I took a brief time-out, giving her a verbal sketch of the girl we were trying to identify. "We've been down here talking to local dentists, hoping to locate her through her old dental records. I just talked to Dr. Nettleton. He thinks she was a patient, but he can't remember her name. I thought if I could talk to a couple of teachers, my description might ring a bell. Do you have any idea who was on the faculty back then?"

She stared at me blankly. I could almost see her compute the possibilities. I thought she might speak, but her expression shut down and she dropped her gaze. "You'd have to talk to Mr. Eichenberger. He's the principal. All our student records are confidential."

"I don't want her *records*. I just want to know her name."

"Mr. Eichenberger doesn't allow us to give out information like that."

"You mean you know her?"

Her cheeks had begun to color. "Of course not. I'm talking about school policy."

I stared at her, annoyed. Maybe as administrative assistant she was unaccustomed to people talking back.

I'd be lucky if I didn't end up in detention myself. "I don't understand the problem."

"Mr. Eichenberger's the only one authorized to discuss the students' files."

"Fine. Is he available?"

"I'll check, but I'd have to see proper identification first."

I removed my wallet from my shoulder bag and opened the flap to show the photocopy of my license. I passed it across the counter.

"May I take this?"

"As long as I get it back."

"Just a moment."

She crossed the office, approaching a closed door that bore the name plate LAWRENCE EICHENBERGER, PRINCIPAL. She knocked once and went in. After perhaps a minute, the door opened and Mr. Eichenberger emerged with Adrianne Richards right behind him. She handed me my wallet and then returned to her desk, where she busied herself with paperwork so she could eavesdrop without appearing interested.

Mr. Eichenberger was a man in his early sixties with sparse, soft-looking white hair, glasses, and a bulbous nose. His complexion looked sunburned, and I picked up the scent of his aftershave, which smelled like incense. He wore a vivid blue dress shirt, a dark sweater

307

vest, and a hand-tied bow tie. His manner was officious, his expression suggesting he was hellbent on thwarting me. "I understand you have a problem with one of our students."

"Not quite," I said. Mentally, I could feel my eyes cross. No wonder I'd hated high school, where I'd been wholly at the mercy of guys just like him. I went through my entire explanation again, feigning a patience I didn't really feel.

Mr. Eichenberger said, "Ms. Millburn, let me make something clear. I've been here since the mid-sixties. As a matter of fact, I'm retiring in May. I came to the job when I was forty and I've enjoyed every minute of it. I don't mean to brag, but I remember just about every student who's come through those doors. I make it my priority to know who they are and what they're about. That's what these kids need—not a buddy or a pal, they need guidance from adults with their best interests at heart. We're in the business of getting these kids shaped up to face the real world. They need skills—reading and writing primarily—all in preparation for productive, well-paid work. If they're not college material, we make sure they find trades. Truancy, gangs, drug problems— we don't see much of that here, despite our proximity to Los Angeles."

I flicked a look over my shoulder. Were we being

filmed? It's not that his sentiments weren't admirable, but the spiel sounded canned and had nothing to do with me. "Excuse me, but is this relevant?"

He seemed to collect himself, as though recovering from a momentary lapse of consciousness. "Yes. Well. You were talking about a student. It would help if you'd give me the details. I can't be of assistance without that."

Ever obliging, I repeated my tale while his assistant moved papers randomly across her desk. Before I could finish my account, Mr. Eichenberger shook his head. "Not here. Not during my administration. You might try Lockaby. That's the alternative high school."

"Really. I didn't know there was one."

"It's over on the Kennedy Pike; a white frame building across from the town cemetery. You can't miss it."

"Is there someone in particular I should ask for?"

"Mrs. Bishop is the principal. She might be able to help."

"You didn't know the girl yourself?"

"If I had, I'd say so. I wouldn't withhold information in a murder investigation."

"What about your assistant?"

"Mrs. Richards wasn't working here back then."

"Too bad. I thought it was worth a try," I said. I took out a business card and made a note of the motel number on the back. "I'm at the Ocean View for the next couple of days. I'd appreciate a call if you think of anything that might help."

"You mentioned a foster family. I'd try Social Services."

"Thanks. That's a good suggestion. I'll do that."

I decided not to make another move until I'd brought Dolan up to speed. For the second time that morning, I was headed back to the motel. I left the car in the parking space in front of his room and gave a rap at his door. From inside, I caught the muffled sounds of the blaring television set. Dolan must not have heard me because he didn't answer my knock. Head tilted against the door, I waited and then tried it again. No deal. I turned and stared off across the parking lot toward the office. I let my eyes stray to the alcove that housed the soft-drink and Coke machines. No sign of him. I knocked again, this time sounding like the ATF at the outset of a drug raid. Maybe he was in the shower or otherwise indisposed.

I crossed the parking lot to the office and poked my head in the door. The desk clerk, a girl in her twenties, was sitting on a swivel stool, flipping through a copy of *People* magazine. I'd interrupted her in the middle of an article about Princess Di. The clerk was dark-haired, pretty in a sulky sort of way, with a mouth way too wide. Her lipstick was dark red and her lashes were so thick I thought they must be false. She was wearing a navy skirt and white blouse, topped by a smart red blazer with a phony crest on the patch pocket. The outfit must have been provided by the motel because it didn't look like anything she'd have worn without the threat of being fired. To compensate, she'd shortened the skirt and left the top three buttons of her blouse undone. She was chewing gum, a habit I'd been warned against when I was in tenth grade. My French teacher swore it made you look like a cow and I haven't chewed gum since. I hadn't even liked the teacher, but the admonition stuck.

I said, "Sorry to bother you, but I'm wondering if you've seen the fellow from room 130? I know he's expecting me, but he doesn't answer his door."

She leaned over and checked the register, flipping back a page. While she did this, she pushed her tongue through the wad of gum until it bulged like a small pink lung being extruded through her lips. "You're talking about the old guy?"

"He isn't *old*," I said, offended.

"Yeah, right. The day he checked in? He got an AARP discount. Fifteen percent off. You can't get that unless you're old. You have to be fifty at least."

"I'm fifty myself."

She said, "Far out. You look forty." She blew a bubble and popped it to punctuate her point. She looked at me. "Oops, sorry. You were kidding, right?"

"Never mind. I asked for that," I said. "Did he leave the motel for some reason?"

"He went out for cigarettes, but I saw him come back."

"How long ago was that?"

"Hour. He stopped by to pick up messages and then he went to his room."

"Had any calls come in?"

"Ask him yourself, you're such a pal."

"Ring his room for me, okay?"

"Sure." She picked up the phone, blowing another bubble as she punched the number in. It must have rung fifteen times. "He must have gone out again. Lotta old people get antsy. Too much energy. Have to be on the go or it drives 'em nuts."

"I appreciate your assessment. Can you come with me to his room and use your key?"

"Nope. I'm here by myself and I can't leave the desk. Why don't you go around the back and bang on his bathroom window? He might be on the pot."

I didn't like this at all. I returned to his room and knocked again about as loudly as the villagers at Frankenstein's castle door. Nothing. I circled the building, counting off the intervening rooms until I reached one I assumed was his. All the bathroom windows were too high off the ground to do me any good. I went back to his front door and stood there, undecided, while I thought about life. Why wasn't he answering? I reached for my shoulder bag and pulled out my wallet. In the windowed compartment under my driver's license, I keep a simple set of lock picks. This was not the battery-operated device I own that opens just about anything. I'd left that one at home, primarily because if I happened to get caught with it, the cops would take a dim view. What I had in hand was a set of the old-fashioned picks, a little hook and a tiny torque wrench, for occasions such as this. In my bag, I also carry a pin light and a folding screwdriver, neither of which would be necessary for today's B&E.

I knocked one more time and called Dolan's name in bullish tones. The guy in the next room opened his door and stuck his head out. "Hey! Keep it down, for cripes sake? And while you're at it, you can tell that jerk to turn off his TV set. It's been blasting since ten o'clock and I'm sick of it. Some of us have to work."

"Sorry. He's handicapped," I said, and tapped my ear. "Severe hearing deficit, the poor guy."

The man's expression shifted from annoyance to something less. "Oh. I didn't realize . . ."

"That's okay. People treat him badly all the time. He's used to it."

I waited until he'd disappeared and then I set to work. In movies, thieves tend to pop the locks in no time flat, often with the use of a credit card, a method I avoid. I don't trust the process. I knew a guy once whose credit card snapped off in the door he was trying to open. A neighbor spotted him breaking in and called the cops. When he heard the sirens approach, he high-tailed it out of there, leaving half his card behind. The cops picked up his surname and the last six digits of his account. He was busted within a day.

In reality, picking locks takes practice, great patience, and no small measure of dexterity. Though most lock mechanisms are similar, there are variations that would drive the novice burglar insane. It usually takes me a few tries. I manipulated my little torque wrench with one eye on the parking lot. If Dolan was out, I didn't want him to catch me breaking into his room. And I was not all that keen on having the cops called if one of the other occupants was watching me from behind the drapes. At the same time, if he was in there, it was time to find out what was going on. I felt the last gate give way. I turned the knob, pushed the door open, and stepped in. "Lieutenant Dolan?"

He was lying on the bed, fully dressed, his shoes off. He turned toward me. His breathing was shallow and his face was a pasty gray. I flipped off the TV and crossed the room.

His voice was hoarse and raspy. "Heard you knocking, but I was in the bathroom being sick. I'm not doing so good."

"I can see that. You look awful. Are you having chest pains?" Up close, I could see a fine sheen of clammy sweat on his forehead and cheeks.

He shook his head almost imperceptibly. "Tightness across here. Hard to breathe. Feels like an elephant sitting on my chest."

"Oh, shit." I picked up the phone and dialed 911.

SIXTEEN

The Emergency Medical Services crew seemed to take forever, though in truth it was no more than six minutes. I alerted the front desk and then waited in the parking lot so I could flag them down. I heard the sirens before I saw the Fire Department Rescue van speed into view. I waved and the vehicle veered toward me and pulled in with a chirp of brakes. The woman driver and two other EMS techs emerged, wearing bright yellow jackets with FIRE DEPARTMENT written across the backs. They carried their equipment with them as they followed me into Dolan's room.

I stood to one side, watching as the two guys moved the furniture aside, clearing space to work. Their manner was efficient but conversational, taking care not to further alarm Dolan, who was doubtless already aware of the depth of trouble he was in. One tech loosened his shirt and then placed a stethoscope against his chest. He took Dolan's pulse and jotted notes on his clipboard, then attached a blood pressure cuff, pumped it, and took a reading, his gaze fixed on his watch. He asked Dolan a series of questions designed to assess the symptoms and events preceding the episode. I was surprised to hear Dolan admit he'd experienced something similar the night before, though the feeling had been less pronounced and had passed within minutes. The woman tech stepped in. She administered two sublingual tabs of nitroglycerin, and then started an IV line while the third technician secured an oxygen cone across Dolan's nose.

I went outside. A minute later, the crew emerged from the room. Dolan had been loaded onto a gurney. They rolled him as far as the back doors of the ambulance, which they opened to slide him into the rear. A few people passing through the parking lot paused to stare, but most moved on as soon as they realized what was happening. I appreciated their discretion. It's hard enough to be ill without feeling as though you've made a spectacle of yourself.

One tech climbed into the van with Dolan. The rear doors were slammed shut. The hospital was seven blocks away. I got directions from the second tech before he got in the cab of the van on the passenger side. The woman took the wheel again. She backed out and made a beeline for the street, sirens warbling, bar light flashing. I made sure Dolan's motel room door was locked and followed in his car.

When I arrived, the ambulance had already pulled into the emergency entrance. I parked in the main lot and by the time I entered the waiting room, he'd been rolled into the rear. I spoke to the desk clerk, telling her who I was. She asked me a few questions about Dolan, making me aware how little I really knew about him. I told her he had insurance coverage through the STPD and she said she'd pick up the remaining data from him. She got up and left her desk, clipboard in hand, indicating that the ER doctor would be out as soon as she was finished with him.

I took a seat in the waiting room, which was spare and reasonably pleasant: pale green carpet, fake plants, and piles of tattered magazines. An assortment of children's toys was scattered on the floor. Lines of interlocking chairs had been arranged, cotillion-fashion, around the edges of the room. In the corner, the face of a television set was blank. Someone had brought in Easter decorations; a basket filled with plastic eggs nestled in impossibly green paper grass. I wasn't even sure when Easter fell this year, but it was doubtless coming up soon, unless these were left from last year. Two patients came in while I was waiting: a man with superficial contusions and abrasions from a bike accident (judging from his shaved legs and his bun-hugging Spandex shorts), and a woman with her right ankle sandwiched between ice packs. Both were taken into examining rooms in the rear, but probably placed on hold while the doctors dealt with Dolan.

Outside, the sun was shining and the town of Quorum was going about its business as though nothing unusual had occurred. It was odd having a medical emergency in the middle of the day. Somehow, in my life, crises of this sort always seem to happen in the dead of night. I couldn't tally the number of times I'd been sitting in waiting rooms like this one while outside, city streets were deserted and shrouded in darkness.

Restless, I left my seat and wandered into the hall, where I asked a passing nurse for the nearest pay phone. I was directed to the hospital lobby, two long corridors away. I dialed Stacey's home number, charging the call to my credit card. Two rings later, he was on the line and I was filling him in.

"How's he doing?"

"Don't know. I haven't talked to the doctor yet. I wish I'd busted into his room when I first got there. I'm telling you, Stacey, his face was gray. He should have dialed 911 himself, but I think he was in denial. You know him."

"This is ridiculous. You can't do this alone. I'm coming down."

"Don't be silly. You're not well yourself. Just stay where you are. I've got enough on my hands."

"I'm fine. Didn't Dolan tell you? The docs showed

my X-rays to some big muckety-muck and she says the shadow's insignificant. I forget now what they call it, but it's bullshit. Biopsy came back negative too so I got a clean bill of health."

"Are you serious?"

"Of course. Why would I lie about a thing like that? I'm in remission. At least for now."

"Lucky you didn't blow your brains out last week. Wouldn't you be pissed?"

"I just wish I hadn't gotten rid of my all personal possessions."

"I could have told you as much."

"Speaking of which, I'd like to have my family photos back."

"Forget it. Find another bunch. Those are mine."

"Come on now, Kinsey. I'll get duplicates made."

"Quit wheedling. I don't want duplicates. I want those. Anyway, you shredded Cousin Mortimer and he was my favorite."

"You never even met him."

"I know, but he had a good face."

"You're tough."

"A deal's a deal."

"How about joint custody. Shared visitation. One week on, one week off."

"Maybe," I said. "You shouldn't have been in such a hurry."

"At least I had the good sense not to shred my tax returns. I could be in jail for life, however much of it I got left."

"What about your clothes?"

"Those went last week. I'll have to scour the Goodwill thrift store and buy 'em back."

"Oh ye of little faith. Dolan swore you'd be fine. You should have listened to him."

"What does he know? The man's a mess. Didn't I tell you he was heading for another heart attack? Talk about a time bomb."

"I know. I told him the same thing, but there was no stopping him. What about you, are you really feeling okay?"

"Terrific. Full of beans. I'm determined to come down. Don't know how I'll get there, but I'll find a way."

"The doctor's letting you drive?"

"Of course. It's no business of hers. Problem is, I sold my car and let my license lapse."

"Oh, no."

"Well, I didn't want to take the test again. I was sure I'd be dead."

"What about the lease on your house?"

"Shit, I'd forgotten about that. Healthy, but homeless. What a turn of events. By the way, did Dolan tell you what happened here?"

"We never had a chance to talk."

"Triple homicide this morning—woman, her boyfriend, and her kid shot to death. The ex-husband's fled into the backcountry, where he's hiding out. All the SO guys have been pulled into the search. This guy's a wilderness expert, a paramilitary type. No telling how long it's going to take to flush him out. Forensics is still at the crime scene, which means they won't get to us again until they wrap that up. Could be days."

"So why hang around down here? Once Dolan's out, I can drive us home in his car and that'll save you the trip."

"No way. I'm bored to tears up here. I got cabin fever so bad, I'm about to go insane. Besides, if you two come home, we'll just have to turn around and go back again."

"Assuming there's a link between the Mustang and Jane Doe," I said.

"Trust me, it's there and Dolan thinks so, too. You been in business as long as we have, you develop a feel for these things. We're getting close."

"Actually, I'd agree. I talked to a dentist this morning who remembered her—someone like her, at any rate. He thinks she was one of the last patients he treated before he had to retire. The guy's ninety-three now and couldn't give me the name, but everything else he says seems to fit. I checked with the principal at Quorum

322

High and he referred me to the alternative high school for problem kids. I haven't had a chance to deal with that—I'd just stopped by the motel to give Dolan the news when I found him in the throes of this heart attack."

"You hang on 'til I get there. Then we'll put our heads together and decide what's next. How will I find you?"

"I'll be around somewhere. If I'm not at the motel, you can try me here. You know Dolan's car. Just keep an eye out for that. This town's so small you can hardly miss."

"Let me get a pencil and paper and you can give me that address. As soon as I find wheels, I'll be on my way."

I gave him the name and address of the motel.

He said, "Do me a favor and reserve a room in my name."

"Why not take Dolan's? He's already forked out the bucks for it."

"Good plan. Let's do that."

"While we're at it, I need you to do me a favor. Could you stop by my apartment and pick up my leather jacket before you hit the road? It's hanging in my downstairs closet. I'll tell Henry to let you in and he can show you where it is."

"It's that cold?"

"To me it is. You better be prepared." Out of the corner of my eye, I saw a woman in scrubs come out of the treatment area with a manila folder in hand. "I think the doc just showed. I'll call you back if there's anything to report."

Dr. Flannery, the ER physician, was in her late forties, small, with short, pale brown hair, a broad forehead, thin lips, and deep lines in her face. Her nose was a raw pink, as though she'd blown it a few times since she'd applied her makeup. She had a tissue in her pocket and she dabbed at it before she held her hand out. "Sorry. Allergies. I'm Dr. Flannery. Are you Mr. Dolan's friend?"

We shook hands. "Kinsey Millhone. It's actually Lieutenant Dolan."

She checked his chart. "So it is."

"How's he doing?"

"He's been stabilized, but he has a serious left coronary arterial blockage. We'll be admitting him as soon as his paperwork's done. I've spoken to his cardiologist in Santa Teresa and he's suggested a cardiac surgeon he knows in Palm Springs. Dr. Bechler's on his way now. As soon as he's seen the patient and reviewed the EKG, the two of them will talk. I'm guessing they'll insert a stent. The choice is Lieutenant Dolan's, but that's what I'd do if I were in his shoes."

I made a face. "They'll open his chest?"

The doctor shook her head. "They'll run a catheter through a small incision in his left inguinal area and go up through the vein."

"How long will he be in?"

"That depends on his progress. Not as long as you'd think. Two days."

"Can I see him?"

"Of course. I've plugged him full of morphine so he's feeling no pain. The effect is about the same as a four-martini lunch."

"Not unusual for him."

"So I gathered. We had a little chat about that. I told him the smoking and heavy drinking would have to stop. He has to clean up his act around food as well. If you eat like he does, you should do the same yourself. QP's with Cheese?"

"He ratted me out?"

She smiled. "Make sure we know how to reach you. He's listed you as next of kin, which means you're cleared for visits if you keep it brief. You want to follow me?"

I tagged after her as she pushed through the door and padded down the highly polished corridor. When we reached Dolan's cubical, she pulled aside the curtain on its overhead track. "I have a visitor for you."

Dolan mumbled a reply. Dr. Flannery held up five

fingers, signaling a five-minute visit. I indicated I understood and she withdrew. I looked down at Dolan.
"How're you feeling?"

His eyes were closed and he had a goofy smile on his
face. His color had improved. He was stretched out on
the table, his upper body draped with a cotton coverlet.
His shoes were off and the toe of one sock was pulled
up to form a little cap, which made him look like a kid.
He was still on oxygen; attached to a bank of machines
that monitored his vital signs. He had an IV line in each
arm. A bag of clear liquid had been hung on one pole
and I counted fifteen drips. He began to snore.

I took his hand, wagging it. "How're you doing?"

He opened his eyes. "I'm good."

"You were in big trouble, you dork. You should have
called for help."

"Heard you knock. Couldn't move. Glad you got
in." He spoke carefully, as though his lips had been
injected with novocaine.

"Me and my little key picks. Don't tell."

His eyes closed again and he put a finger to his lips.

I said, "I put a call in to Stacey and told him where
you were. He says his X-rays are clear and he's coming
down."

"Said the same to me. No point arguing."

"Tell me about it. I tried to talk him out of it, but he
was adamant. I figured as long as you're stuck in here,

he might as well pitch in. We can't do much for now, but maybe we can stir things up. I'm hoping Forensics will come up with something good. I think we'll put him in your room if I can have the key."

"Hang on." Dolan revived himself long enough to fumble in his pants pocket and extract his key. I tucked it in my shoulder bag, thinking I'd stop by and pick up my typewriter before Staccy arrived.

The desk clerk appeared at the curtain with a plastic hospital bracelet and a sheaf of documents affixed to a clipboard. "I have your jewelry, Lieutenant Dolan. I just need your signature and you'll be on your way."

He roused himself, lazily gestured her in. "Sign away my life." He turned to me. "You okay on your own?"

"Don't worry about me. You take care of yourself and get some rest. I'll stop by this evening. You behave."

"Good deal."

Before I left Quorum General, I put a call through to Henry. He was out. I left a message on his machine, telling him about Dolan's heart attack. I also mentioned that Stacey'd be stopping by. I told him where my jacket was and said I'd call later when there was more to report. It was 1:35 when I emerged from the hospital and returned to the parking lot. I hadn't realized how tense I was until I'd unlocked the car door and slipped behind the wheel. I took a good deep breath and did a neck roll. Anxiety was roiling through my body now that I was on my own. I hadn't realized how dependent I'd become on Dolan. It was nice to compare notes, nice to share meals, even fun to knock heads. My attachment didn't contain a shred of romance, but it did trigger a longing to be connected to someone. I'd trained with two old guys, who'd taught me the business many years before. Maybe it was them I missed.

I flipped through my note cards. The next obvious move was to chat with the principal at the alternative high school. I wished Dolan were on hand so he could handle it. Though I hated to admit it, he'd be subjected to a lot less guff. *Mano a mano*. Once he flashed that badge of his, people tended to respond. I picked up my minimap and located the Kennedy Pike, then fired up the Chevy and pulled out of the lot. On the way down Main Street, I detoured into a filling station and pumped gas into the tank. I stood there clutching the pump, watching the gallons go in while the total sales price went up. The process took so long I thought the tank must have sprung a leak. I'm accustomed to my VW with its gas tank the size of a bucket of paint. $29.46 later, I nosed out of the station and turned right.

Once I reached Kennedy Pike, I drove west, scanning for sight of the cemetery and the white frame structure across the street from it. This section of Quorum was made up of endless flat, empty fields stitched together with lines of trees that served as windbreaks. When I finally spotted the cemetery, it looked as flat as the fields around it. There was only a smattering of visible head-stones. Most were laid flat in the ground. I could see a few concrete benches and a sparse assortment of plastic bouquets that had been left near graves. The surround-ing fence was iron and without ornament. Square brick support posts appeared at fifteen-foot intervals. There were seven full-sized trees of an indeterminate type, but the branches hadn't leafed out yet and the limbs looked frail against the April sky.

Just beyond the cemetery entrance and across the street, I saw the Lockaby Alternative High School. I wondered if the students made the same melancholy association: from Youth to Death with only a stone's throw between. When you're of high school age, the days go on forever and death's little more than a rumor at the end of the road. Dolan and I knew death was just a heartbeat away.

I parked in the lot and followed the walkway to the front porch, up a flight of wide wooden steps. This must have been a farmhouse once upon a time. It still carried an air of small rooms and cramped hopes. I let myself into the foyer, where eight kids were sprawled on the floor with sketchbooks, doing pencil drawings of the staircase. The teacher glanced up at me and then continued moving from student to student, making brief suggestions about perspective. From upstairs, I could hear another class in progress. Laughter trickled down the treads like leaking water. I don't remember anything funny from my high school days.

To my right, the former parlor served as the main office, complete with the original fireplace. The hearth and surround were dark red brick and the whole of it was topped with a dark mahogany mantelpiece. There was no counter separating the reception area from the office secretary, whose desk had been arranged facing the wide bay window. She interrupted her typing to turn and look at me. She seemed pleasant; dark-haired, plump, probably in her forties, though it was hard to tell. When she said, "Yes, ma'am?" several dimples appeared in her cheeks. She pulled out a chair and patted the seat.

I crossed the room and sat down, introducing myself. "I'm looking for Mrs. Bishop."

"She's in district meetings all day, but maybe I can help. I'm Mrs. Marcum. What can I do for you?"

"Here's the problem," I said, and launched into the tale. I'd told it so often that I had it down pat; the search for Jane Doe's identity in fifty words or less. For the umpteenth time, I described Jane Doe and the series of interviews that had led me to Lockaby. "Do you remember anyone like that?"

"Not me, but I've only been here ten years. I'll ask some of the teachers. Mrs. Puckett, who teaches typing, doubles as the guidance counselor. She'd be the one who'd recognize the girl if anyone did. Unfortunately, she's out today—we all get a mental-health day every couple of months. She'll be in first thing tomorrow morning if you want to come back."

"If she does recognize the girl, would you have her records somewhere?"

"Not going back that far. We had a fire here eight years ago. Between the smoke and water damage, we lost the majority of our files. It's a wonder the whole place didn't go up in flames. The fire department saved us. They were here in seven minutes and knocked it down in thirty before it had a chance to spread."

"How'd it happen?"

"Fire chief said electrical. We had wiring that dated from the original construction—1945. He said it was a wonder it hadn't happened before. Now we have smoke detectors, heat detectors, and a sprinkling system—the works. We're lucky we weren't wiped out. Happily for us, there weren't any injuries or loss of life. Paperwork, who cares? It accumulates faster than I can file it."

"The kids like it here?"

"They seem to. Of course, we're a magnet for the troublemakers—dropouts, truants, delinquents. We get them when everyone else gives up. We only have a

SUE GRAFTON

handful of teachers and we keep the classes small. Most
of our students do poorly in an academic setting. Basi-
cally, they're good kids, but some are slow. Short attention spans. They're easily frustrated and most of them
suffer from poor self-image. With a regular high school
curriculum, they lose heart. Here the emphasis is practical. We cover the basics—reading, writing, and math—
but we teach them how to write a résumé, how to dress
for a job interview, simple etiquette. Art and music, too,
just to round them out."

"Sounds like something every school should do."

"You'd think so, wouldn't you?"

The phone on her desk rang, but she made no move.

"You want to answer that?"

"They'll try back. I'm often out of the office and
they've learned. You have a business card?"

"Sure."

"Why don't you give me a number. I'll try to reach
Betty Puckett and have her give you a call."

"That'd be great." I took out a card and jotted down
the name of the motel, the phone number, and my room
number on the back. "I appreciate this."

"I can't swear she'll know the girl, but if she was ever
a student here, I promise you, Betty dealt with her."

"One more question: Dr. Nettleton seemed to think
this girl was in a foster home, so I'm wondering if Social
Services might help?"

332

"I doubt it. They closed that office years ago, and I have no idea how you'd locate the old files. It'd be Riverside County, but that's as much as I know. You'll have a battle on your hands. They're worse than schools are about access to records, especially on a juvenile."

"Too bad. I had hopes, but I guess not."

"Sorry."

"I'll figure it out eventually. It's just a question of time."

When I left Lockaby, I was no better informed, but I was feeling encouraged. Once in the car again, I sat for a moment, beating out a little rhythm on the steering wheel. Now what? In the confusion of the moment, I hadn't thought to ask Dolan what he'd learned from the Quorum PD and the sheriff's office about the old missing-persons reports. I'd ask him when I went to visit. I did a mental check of our list. The only item we hadn't covered yet was the issue of the tarp and whether one had been stolen at the time the Mustang was taken. I started the car and backed out of the slot, took a left on the Kennedy Pike, and returned to town.

The McPhee's red-brick ranch house looked deserted when I arrived—doors shut, curtains drawn, and no cars in the drive. I passed the house, cruising slowly, and at the next intersection, did a U-turn and drove back. I parked across the street. I disliked the idea of seeing Ruel again, but who else could I ask about the tarp? While I'd remained largely in the background during the impounding of the Mustang, he'd still associate me with his loss of face.

I sat and studied the house, wondering if I could handle the question by phone. Chickenshit idea. Where possible, it's always better to deal in person. I was on the verge of taking off, postponing the visit until later in the day, when an approaching car slowed and turned into the drive. Edna.

Once she turned off the engine, I could see her fussing in the front seat, gathering packages. After a bit of maneuvering, she got out with her purse over her shoulder, a grocery bag in one hand, and two department store carryalls clutched in the other. She pushed the door shut with one hip and moved to the rear of the car, setting down the carryalls while she opened the trunk. She placed her purse and the grocery bag on the driveway, reached into the trunk, and removed several additional grocery bags. I could see her debate whether she could manage everything in one trip or if she'd be forced to make two. I took the opportunity to get out of my car and cross the street at a trot. "Hi, Edna. Kinsey. Can I give you a hand?"

She looked up with surprise, coloring slightly at the sight of me. "I can manage."

"There's no sense in making two trips. Why don't I take these and you can handle the rest?" I leaned forward and picked up her purse, one grocery sack, and the two large paper carryalls. "You must have spent all morning running errands."

"The family's coming for supper and I'm running late. I want to get a pot roast in the oven." Her demeanor had softened, though she seemed ill at ease. Good manners apparently took precedence over any discomfort she felt at my reappearance on the scene. Ruel would have cut me dead, but the removal of the Mustang had little to do with her. It'd been sitting in the garage for years, anyway, and she was probably tired of his procrastination. His collection of classic cars must have seemed like a lousy investment since he'd apparently made no effort to restore even one of them.

I followed her along the driveway to the back gate and then, since she didn't protest, I continued up the porch steps and through the back door. I put her purse on the Formica counter, waiting to see where she wanted the other bags. The red, white, and blue color scheme was like a tone poem to Americana. I took the time to let my gaze rest on every surface. "What time will Ruel be home?"

She'd placed her bags on the kitchen table. "Soon, I'd guess. The rest of them—Cornell and his wife and kids and my daughter—are supposed to come at six. You can put those over there," and she gestured toward the window seat.

SUE GRAFTON

I left the grocery sack on the kitchen table and crossed to the window seat, where I placed the department store carryalls. I moved aside a couple of pillows and the patchwork quilt and perched, uninvited. I glanced at my watch. "It's almost two now. Do you mind if I wait?"

"I'm not sure that's a good idea. Ruel's been upset and I don't want anything to set him off again." She began to put groceries away, leaving out the items she intended to use: a mammoth cellophane-wrapped chuck roast that looked like the whole back end of some unidentified beast, onions, carrots, potatoes, fresh green beans, brown-and-serve rolls. She looked at me. "Did you need him for anything in particular? You know he's madder than spit. There's nothing he hates more than someone trying to put one over on him. You and that detective should have told him the truth."

"We told Cornell why we were here. He could have mentioned it himself. We're talking about a murder. What difference does it make if Ruel's mad?"

"Nonetheless."

"Nonetheless, what?"

"He won't be happy if he finds you here."

"Maybe you can help me and I'll be on my way."

"What do you want?"

"We're wondering if someone took one of his tarps at the time the car was stolen."

336

She paused to think about that and then shook her head. "Not that I recall. He never said anything. I suppose I could ask him and get in touch with you later on."

"You'd be doing him a service, especially if it turns out the Mustang was used to abduct the girl."

Edna laid a hand against her chest. "You can't seriously believe he had anything to do with it."

"It's not up to me." Her anxiety was infectious. I stood up, suddenly eager to be gone. As I picked up my shoulder bag, my glance fell on the red, white, and blue quilt folded neatly on the seat. The pattern consisted of a series of patches stitched together in a traditional log cabin pattern. In repeat rows, running along the diagonal, the fabric was a print of dark blue daisies, a dot of red in each center, on a white background.

I must have made a sound because Edna looked at me, saying, "What?"

"Where did you get this?"

"That was given to me by Justine's mother, Medora—Cornell's mother-in-law. Why?"

"I need to talk to her."

SEVENTEEN

I stood on the front steps of Medora Sanders's house, a modest stucco box with a shallow overhang that served to shield the small concrete porch. The exterior was painted dark gray. The wood trim had shed flakes of white paint, like dandruff, on the shrubs planted along the foundation. At the end of the dirt drive there was a detached single-car garage with its door padlocked shut. Edna had allowed me to borrow the quilt and I carried it draped over one arm. The daisy-print fabric had been pieced into the quilt in seven adjoining sections. While it was true that the fabric might have been sold across the country, the coincidence was too striking to imagine it was unrelated.

I couldn't find a bell so I opened the wood-framed screen and knocked on the glass pane in the front door. A moment passed and then a woman peered out. She was thin and unkempt, with pale green eyes and pale fly-away hair. Her cheeks and the rim of her nose were patterned with spider veins. She smoothed her hair with a knobby-fingered hand, tucking a loose strand into a disordered chignon before she opened the door a crack. "Yes?"

"Mrs. Sanders?"

She wore faded jeans and a red nylon sweater with a runner up one sleeve where a loop of yarn had come loose. I could smell whiskey fumes seeping through her pores like toxic waste. She hesitated, apparently unwilling to confirm or deny her identity until she knew why I asked. "I don't buy door-to-door," she said.

I held up the quilt. "I'm not selling anything. I came to talk to you about this."

Her gaze shifted, though her manner remained fuzzy and her eyes were slightly out of focus. She looked like someone chronically inebriated. "Where'd you get that?"

"Edna McPhee let me borrow it. I'm returning it later, but I have some questions for you first."

"Why'd she send you over here?"

"She said since you made the quilt, you might have some information. May I come in?"

Medora thought about that briefly, probably wishing I'd go somewhere else. "I hope this won't take long. I got other things to do."

She opened the door and I stepped directly into the living room, which was small and cramped, with an

SUE GRAFTON

acoustic-tile ceiling and a stingy-looking brick fireplace.
On the mantel there was a cluster of statuettes: angels,
milkmaids, and coy-looking kids with the toes of their
shoes turned in.

Medora closed the door, saying, "That Edna's a pill.
I don't know how Justine manages to put up with her."

"The two of you don't get along?"

"I never said that. Edna's a good person and I know
she means well, but she's holier-than-thou. You know
the type—doesn't drink, doesn't smoke, and doesn't
hold with those who do."

"Cornell smokes."

"Not around his mother. He's pure as the driven
snow," Medora said. "She disapproves of cards, too.
Devil's handiwork, she says. Granddaughters come here,
we play Canasta, War, Fish, Slap Jack. Doesn't seem
like the Devil's work to me."

She returned to the couch and sat dead center, causing the cushions to rise on either side of her. A crocheted
green-and-black afghan was bunched haphazardly at
one end. There was an ashtray full of butts on the coffee
table, a cluster of prescription pill bottles, a fifth of
Early Times, and a highball glass half-filled with melting
ice cubes. Many surfaces looked sticky, and there was a
fine haze of dust over everything. "I was taking a little
nap. I haven't been feeling well the last couple days.
What's your name again?"

340

"I should have introduced myself. I'm Kinsey Millhone."

"Medora Sanders," she said, "but I guess you know that. What's your connection to Edna? I hope it's not through her church. She's always trying to get me roped in."

"Not at all. Mind if I sit?"

She waved me into a chair. I moved aside a stack of newspapers and took a seat, keeping the quilt on my lap. There were a number of crafts projects in the room, most from kits, by the look: a wall-hung quilt, embroidered pillows on the couch. In front of the hearth there was a hand-hooked rug bearing the image of a Scottie. There were several framed cross-stitched pieces voicing corny sentiments. She followed my survey. "I used to do a lot of needlework until my joints flared up." She lifted her right hand, displaying a twisted thumb and fingers that did a slow curve outward. It looked like she'd been tortured for information she'd refused to give. "I don't quilt anymore in case you want one for yourself."

I folded a section of the quilt until the daisy-print fabric was foremost. "Actually, I'm curious about this fabric. Do you remember where you got it?"

She glanced at the print. "I used to make clothes for my daughter." She reached for a pack of Camels and extracted one. She flicked her lighter, but it took her two tries to make the flame touch the tip of the cigarette.

341

"That was a remnant. Cheaper to buy that way. I used to check the bin at the fabric shop in town. It's gone out of business now so you can save yourself a trip. Same time I bought that, I picked up six yards of royal blue taffeta that I offered to run up for Justine's prom dress. She about had a cow. Said she'd kill herself before she wore anything homemade. She insisted on store-bought, so I made her pay for it. It's like I told her, 'Money doesn't grow on trees, Justine.' Kids these days don't appreciate that."

"They're embarrassed," I said. "They want exactly the same clothes every other teenager has. That's how they express their unique individuality."

"I guess. I had to make do with precious little once her dad ran out."

"When was that?"

"Summer of 1969, somewhere around in there. Who keeps track? Fellow wants to take a hike, it's good riddance." She reached for one of her pill bottles and shook out a white tablet that she placed on her tongue. She picked up her highball and took a swallow, frowning slightly when she realized how watered down it was. "I'm on pain medication. Whiskey gives the codeine a little boost. Any rate, what's this in relation to?"

"I'm trying to identify a young woman who was murdered during that same period. When the body was found, she was wearing home-sewn pants made of this same daisy print."

Medora's laugh was like a cough, hacking and full of phlegm. "I don't know about a murder, daisy print or no, but I can tell you one thing. You got a big job ahead. Company must've made thousands of yards of that print."

"I'm sure you're right, but I thought it was worth a shot. The girl I'm referring to would have been somewhere between fifteen and eighteen. This was late July, early August, of 1969. About five foot four, a hundred and twenty-five pounds. Brunette hair she probably dyed blond. She had prominent teeth and the eyetooth on this side was twisted. She'd had a lot of dental work done."

Her smile had begun to fade.

"Does any of that sound familiar?"

Medora crossed her arms and squinted against the smoke, cigarette held close to her face. "Years ago, I had a girl living with me sounds like that. Name was Charisse Quinn."

I felt my heart thump twice from the hit of adrenaline that shot through my veins. I'd run across the name before, but I wasn't sure where. "What happened to her?"

"Nothing as far as I know, except she flew the coop. I went in her room one morning and found her bed hadn't been slept in and half her stuff was gone. She'd helped herself to my best suitcase, too. Of course, she stole just about anything wasn't nailed down."

"The murdered girl I'm talking about was found in Lompoc. You know the area?"

"Up near San Francisco?"

"Not that far north. Closer to Santa Teresa."

"Couldn't prove it by me. I don't travel. Used to, but now I prefer to stay put."

"Why was she living in your home?"

"I was a foster mom—something like that. Reason she ended up with me is I had this woman lived next door asked if I'd help. She'd had a whole string of foster kids trooping through her place. County wanted her to take Charisse, but her husband wasn't well and it was more than she could manage. She asked if I could open my home—that's how she put it—'open my home to someone less fortunate than myself.' What a joke. Wilbur barely gave me enough to cover all the household expenses. At any rate, my neighbor told me Social Services paid close to a hundred and eighty dollars a month, so that's why I agreed. Doesn't sound like much, but every little bit helped."

"How'd the arrangement work out?"

"Not that good. Girl was foul-mouthed and disrespectful, though, at that age, I'll be the first to admit,

Justine was the same. Her and me had troubles enough without Charisse sticking in her two cents' worth."

"How long was she was with you?"

"Five, six months, I'd guess. I believe she came here early March."

"Can you remember the date she disappeared?"

Medora made a sour face. "I never said she disappeared. I said she took off."

"Sorry. That's what I meant. When did she take off?"

"July, I'd say. Doesn't surprise me to hear she came to a bad end. She's a wild one, that girl. Had a bad case of hot pants. Picked up boys every chance she got. Out until all hours. She'd come waltzing in here three in the morning, smelling like crème de menthe and marijuana. I warned her and warned her, but would she listen to me?"

"What happened to her parents?"

"Don't know. I never laid eyes on that pair. Must've been druggies or something if the State had to step in."

"How old was Charisse?"

"Seventeen. Same as Justine. Girls were both seniors. Of course, Charisse got kicked out of regular high school and sent over to Lockaby. That's the school for dummies and delinquents."

Bemused, I thought back to my conversation with Eichenberger, the principal of Quorum High, who'd

SUE GRAFTON

sworn up and down he remembered every student who'd ever passed through his doors. What a pompous old windbag. Charisse had not only been there, but she'd caused enough trouble to get tossed out.

"You have other children?"

"Just the one."

"And you were living here at the time?"

"I lived here ever since Wilbur and I got married in 1951. We only have the two bedrooms, so the girls had to share. Imagine how popular that was."

"Must have been hard."

"Oh, they went through every kind of conflict—spats over clothes and boyfriends—the two went round and round like alleycats, spitting and hissing, fur flying. You never heard the like. Justine didn't want Charisse hanging out with her friends and I could see her point. Always had to raise a fuss. Always had to have her way."

"Not much of a charmer from the sound of it."

"She could be charming once she put her mind to it, but only if she wanted something."

"What about your husband? Where was he?"

"Well, he lived here in theory, but he was gone half the time."

"What sort of work?"

"He hired on at Sears in major appliances—dishwashers, refrigerators, things like that. Worked nights,

346

weekends, and every holiday. Never got us a deal, but that was him in a nutshell. You'd think he could've got me a portable dishwasher at the very least. I had to do everything by hand. Probably why my joints went bad. Made my back hurt, too."

"So he left about the same time she did?"

"I suppose so, though I never thought of it like that." She frowned at me, taking a drag of her cigarette. "I hope you're not saying he went off with *her*."

"I don't know, but it does seem odd. If she was so hot for guys, why not him?"

"He was close to fifty years old, for one thing. And I can't think why he'd take an interest in someone her age. He never paid any attention to her as far as I could see. He's a skunk, that's for sure, but I can't believe he'd sink *that* low. That's—what do you call it?—statutory rape."

"Did he give you any explanation when he left?"

She took another drag of her cigarette. "None. He went off to work one day and he never came home. He left before she did, now I think of it. I remember because he missed seeing Justine in her prom dress and that was June fourteenth."

"What'd you do when he left?"

"Nothing. Gone is gone," she said.

"What about Charisse? Did you talk to the police when you realized she'd left?"

"I went to see them that day. Police and the sheriff. I got county funds for her and I knew the social worker would have a fit otherwise. As it was, I had to return the next month's check and with Wilbur gone, I came up short on the bills. Justine tried to tell me Charisse wasn't to blame, but it was typical of her. She'd do anything she could to screw it up for someone else."

"But you did file a missing-persons report?"

"I told you, that day, though the deputy didn't offer much encouragement. He found out she'd run off half a dozen times before. And like he said, with her eighteenth birthday coming up she'd be on her own, anyway. Said they'd do what they could, but he couldn't promise much. He as good as told me to go home and forget about her."

"Which you did."

"What else could I do? I didn't even know her mother's name. I guess the social worker called the mother."

"You think that's where she went, back to her mom?"

"Don't know and didn't care. With Wilbur gone, I had my hands full just trying to make ends meet. In case you intend to ask, I never heard from her again. Him either. Far as I know, we're still married, unless he's dead. That'd be something, wouldn't it?"

"You have reason to think something might have happened to him?"

"I'm saying, if he's alive, you'd think he could have dropped us a card. Thirty-six years married, that's the least he could do."

"What about Charisse's social worker? What was her name?"

"Don't remember. It's been too many years. Tinker, Tailor—something along those lines. I called and talked to her, and you know what she said? Said she never expected the arrangement to last; Charisse was such a pain. Not those words exactly, but that's the gist of it. I thought, Oh, thanks. Now she pipes up, after all I went through."

"You must have felt terrible."

She coughed a thick laugh into her fist, pausing then to cough in earnest. She took a sip of watery bourbon and then recovered herself. "Especially when I found out Wilbur'd emptied all the bank accounts. Excuse me, are you about done here? Because if not, I intend to fix myself another drink—see if I can get some relief from this cough. That was my mother's remedy—whiskey and honey—though you ask me, it wasn't the honey that helped."

"Just a few more questions and then I'll let you get some rest. How did Charisse travel? Do you have any idea?"

"Wasn't by bus. I know because police checked on that. I suppose she hitched a ride with one of those hoodlums she ran around with once she got to Lockaby."

"You remember any of their names?"

"Couldn't tell one from the other. They were all the same—skanky-looking boys with bad skin."

"You heard about the car that was stolen from the back of Ruel's shop?"

"Everybody heard. He was fit to be tied."

"Is there any chance Charisse took it?"

"I doubt it. She didn't drive. Never passed the test. I offered to help her get her license, but she didn't get around to it. Afraid to fail, you ask me; worried she'd end up looking like a fool."

"How'd she get around if she didn't drive?"

"Bummed rides with Justine and Cornell and everyone else. That's another thing got on people's nerves. She was a mooch."

"Did she work?"

"Her? That's a laugh. I couldn't even get her to pick up after herself."

"I know I asked you this before, but is there any way you could pinpoint the date she left?"

Medora shook her head. "I was just glad to have her gone. Does seem queer to think she's been dead all these years. I pictured her married with kids. That or living on the street. Wonder who killed her."

"That's what we're trying to find out. Do you have a photograph by chance? I'd be interested in seeing how she looked."

"I don't, but you might ask Justine." She paused, coughing again with such vigor it brought tears to her eyes. "I can't stand it. My throat's killing me. You want a drink?"

"No, thanks."

I watched Medora pour herself some whiskey, her hands shaking so badly she could scarcely lift the glass to her lips. She swallowed with relief and then took two deep breaths. "Whoo! That's better. Whiskey'll cure just about anything."

"Well, I guess that's it. I can't tell you how much I appreciate your help."

"You want my opinion, whatever happened to her? She brought it on herself."

I was on my way down her walkway, heading for Dolan's car with the quilt over my arm, when I noticed a sedan had pulled in and parked at the curb. The door on the driver's side opened and a woman got out. She tucked her keys in her purse and she was halfway up the walk when she caught sight of me and stopped. Her gaze flicked to the quilt and then back to me. This had to be Justine. She and Medora shared the same body type and the same pale flyaway hair. Though their features were unremarkable, I could see the resemblance; something in the shape of their narrow chins and their pale green eyes. Like her husband, Cornell, she appeared to be in her mid-thirties.

"Excuse me. Are you Justine McPhee?"

"Yes?"

"My name's Kinsey Millhone. I'm a private detective—"

"I know who you are. I believe we have you to thank for the foul mood my father-in-law's been in." Her manner was an odd mixture of composure and agitation, her tone giving vent to something prickly lurking under the surface.

"I'm sorry about that, but it couldn't be helped."

She glanced toward the house. "What are you doing here?"

"I was just chatting with your mother about Charisse."

Her expression was vacant for an instant and then I could see recognition spark. "Charisse?"

"That's right. I don't know if Cornell mentioned this, but we're investigating a murder . . ."

"That's what he told me, but surely you're not talking about her?"

"We don't have a positive ID yet, but it does look that way."

"I don't believe it. What happened?"

"She was stabbed and her body was dumped outside of Lompoc. This was August of '69. The sheriff's detectives worked the case for months without progress. Now they've decided it's time to try again."

"But what brought you to Quorum? She was only here a few months."

"Following our noses. We were lucky to get some breaks."

"Like what? I'm sorry for all the questions, but none of this makes sense."

"I know it's tough to absorb," I said. "When I was at Edna's, I spotted the quilt and realized the dark blue daisy print was a match for the victim's home-sewn pants. Edna told me your mother made the quilt, so I came to see her. You thought she'd run away?"

"Well, yes. It certainly didn't occur to me the poor girl was *dead*. I'm sure Cornell and his dad would have helped you if they'd known who it was."

"Let's hope that's true. At this point, we're trying to pin down events between the time she took off and the time her body was found."

"When was that again?"

"August third. Your mother said she left in July, but she couldn't remember the exact date."

"Charisse came and went as she pleased. I didn't even realize she was gone until Mom started screaming about her suitcase. The pants you mentioned must've been the pair my mother made for me."

"Did you give her the pants or did she take those, too?"

"I wouldn't have *given* them to her. She always helped herself to my stuff."

"What about the other items she stole?"

"I don't remember anything specific. She had no scruples at all. She didn't care who she hurt as long as she got what she wanted. The kids at Quorum didn't want to have anything to do with her." She adjusted the watchband on her wrist, glancing at the time as she did.

"You have to go?"

"I'm sorry, but we're due at my in-laws for supper and I still have to pick up the girls. I stopped by to see Mom because she hasn't been feeling well."

"What about tomorrow? I'd love to talk to you again."

"Oh, I don't think so. I wish I could help, but Ruel's mad enough as it is. He'd have a fit if he knew I'd even said this much."

"You said he'd've been cooperative himself if he'd known it was her."

"I meant if he'd known about it up front. He's hard to predict, especially now that he thinks you've made a fool out of him."

"Well, give it some thought and let me know."

"I'd have to talk to Cornell. He's pissed off, too, because his dad blames him about the car."

"That's dumb. Ruel's the one who took title and let it sit all those years."

"True, but I don't want to give him reason to come down on me. He complains enough as it is. He thinks I'm controlling. Ha. Like he's not."

"He doesn't have to know. That's entirely up to you. I don't want you getting into trouble on my account."

"Trust me. I won't. You have to watch your backside around him. He might seem harmless, but he's a snake."

"Well. I better let you go. I'm staying at the Ocean View. I'd appreciate your calling once you've talked to Cornell. He might have something to contribute even if you don't."

"I doubt it. He really only knew Charisse because of me."

"Speaking of that, your mother told me Charisse hung out with a bunch of hoodlums at Lockaby. You might ask if Cornell remembers anyone in particular. We could use a few names."

"You really expect to find her killer after all these years?"

"We've made it this far," I said. "I hope to hear from you.

"I can't promise anything, but I'll do what I can."

I went back to the motel and put a call through to Dr. Spears. I told Mrs. Gary, his assistant, what I'd learned from Medora Sanders. She remembered Charisse Quinn as soon as she heard the name. She made a note and said she'd pass the information along to him. She assured me that if he had time, he'd search the dead storage boxes for her chart. If he couldn't do it himself, she promised she'd pitch in. I thanked her profusely. Once I hung up, I sat on the edge of the bed, grinning from ear to ear, finally allowing myself a moment to celebrate. I couldn't wait to tell Dolan. A match on dental records would confirm my hunch. I was convinced this was her, but we needed concrete proof.

EIGHTEEN

I went in through the front entrance of Quorum General and asked the volunteer at the reception desk for directions to the CCU. The facility wasn't large, but it seemed up-to-date, at least judging by the portions of it I saw en route. As it turned out, Dolan had been taken into surgery by the time I reached the floor. The Palm Springs cardiologist had blown in an hour before, and he'd kicked butt in six directions getting the procedure under way. I got a cursory briefing from the charge nurse, who checked with the OR. She assured me everything was going fine, though it'd be a while before Dolan was out of post-op. She suggested I call her at 7:00 to make sure he'd returned.

Leaving the hospital, I could feel my exhilaration fade. It was 4:30 by then. I had no access to Dolan and no way to know when Stacey Oliphant would appear. At best, I wouldn't hear from Justine until some time the next day, if I heard from her at all, which left me with no one to talk to and nothing to do. I retreated to the Ocean View. I parked the car in the motel lot and bought a can of Diet Pepsi from the vending machine. I used Dolan's key to let myself into his room, where I retrieved my Smith-Corona. Once ensconced in my own room, I set up a minioffice, using the motel desk. I typed up my notes, a process that took the better part of an hour and a half.

At 6:15 I opened the phone book and consulted the yellow pages for the nearest pizza joint. I called and ordered a medium sausage-and-pepperoni pizza with jalapeño peppers and extra cheese on top. Given Dolan's diet restrictions, there was no way I'd be able to eat such fare in front of him. As a courtesy, I decided to indulge now. While I waited for delivery, I popped out to the vending machine and bought another Diet P. I ate supper sitting on my bed, my back propped against the pillows, watching the news and feeling completely decadent.

I called the hospital shortly after 7:00 and talked to the ward clerk in CCU. She said Dolan was in his room if I wanted to visit, which, of course, I did.

It was fully dark outside and the temperature had dropped precipitously by the time I emerged from my room and headed back to the hospital. Despite the halo of light pollution hovering over the town, the stars were as distinct as pinpricks in black construction paper, light shining through from the other side. The moon hadn't yet risen, but I could see where the darkness would lift and the desert would glow like a silver platter once it mounted the sky. I parked in the hospital lot and walked through the entrance doors for the second time that day.

All of the interior lights were ablaze, and it lent the premises a warm, cozy air. The lobby was filled with evening visitors. I passed the gift shop and the coffee shop and continued to the elevators, heading for the second floor. In all the semiprivate rooms I peered in, the curtains were drawn and the corner-mounted television sets were tuned to reruns. Dinner had probably been served at 5:30 or so, and the trays were now in the meal carts that still sat in the corridor. I caught glimpses of partially consumed foodstuffs: canned green beans and Salisbury steak (which is a fancy name for meatloaf) and countless packets of saltines still secured in cellophane. Plastic cups of taut red Jell-O squares sat untouched, and I suspected the hospital dietitian would find herself in a state of despair. These meals, like those in elementary schools, look better on paper than they do to the hapless participants. Half the items end up in the trash.

CCU was quiet and the lights were subdued. Dolan was in a private room attached by tubes and wires to a bank of monitors. His vital signs were flashed on a digital read-out, like the time and temperature bulletins outside a bank. The decor had been designed to minimize stress. The color scheme consisted of restful blues and pale, soothing greens. There was a bank of windows and a wall-mounted clock, but no television set and no newspapers trumpeting the day's quota of economic woes, murders, disasters, and fatal accidents.

One of Dolan's IV lines had been removed and I could see the bruising in the crook of his arm. His one-day growth of beard already looked like the splayed white bristles on a toothbrush used to clean the bathroom grout. Two clear-plastic oxygen prongs extended from his nose. That aside, he was alert, his color was good, and some of his friskiness had been restored. He seemed tired, but he didn't look half-dead. Any minute now, he'd get cranky about the absence of booze and cigarettes.

"Hey, Lieutenant, you look great. How're you feeling?"

"Better. Almost human, as a matter of fact."

There was a murmur behind me and I turned to find a nurse standing in the doorway. She was in her forties, with dark eyes and shiny brown hair streaked with gold. She wore civilian clothes, but her shoes were crepe-soled and her name tag announced her as CHRIS KOVACH, RN. She said, "Sorry to bother you, but there's a fellow at the nurses' station claiming he's related to you. I checked your chart, but you don't have him listed as an emergency contact or your next of kin."

Dolan's face went blank.

Chirpily, I said, "It must your brother, Stacey. When I called and told him about your heart attack, he said he'd hop in the car and head right down." I turned to Ms. Kovach. "I know the lieutenant's not supposed to have more than one visitor at a time, but his brother's just finished chemo for non-Hodgkin's lymphoma, and it'd be great if we could be together after all these months."

I thought the medical angle was a nice touch, but the look she gave me indicated she heard tales like that, on average, three times a day. "His brother? I don't see the family resemblance."

"That's because he's bald. With his hair grown in, they look enough alike to be mistaken for twins."

"And you're *his* daughter," she said, indicating Dolan with a tilt of her head.

"Uh-huhn."

"So the fellow in the hall is your uncle Stacey, is that correct?"

"On my mother's side."

She wagged a warning finger. "Just this once, but not for long. I've got my eye on the clock. No cheating on the time."

Piously, Dolan said, "Thank you, Nurse."

His tone was what finally netted us the smile she'd been trying to suppress.

Stacey appeared in the doorway moments later. I was happy to see he'd doffed his watch cap, exposing an endearing patchwork of bald spots and fuzz. At least the nurse would know I hadn't lied about that.

Dolan said, "How'd you get here? I thought you sold your car."

"Rented one—a spiffy little Ford I drove like a bat out of hell. I'm surprised I didn't get a ticket. How are you?"

"Especially driving without a license."

Stacey pulled over a chair, offering it to me. "You want to sit?"

"You take that. I prefer to stand."

Since the visit was being limited, we truncated polite talk in favor of a Jane Doe update. I said, "I think I may have a line on her." I told them about the quilt with the daisy-print patches that led me to Medora Sanders. "From what Medora says, the girl's name is Charisse Quinn. She was apparently a ward of the State, fostered out through Riverside County Social Services. Both Medora and her daughter said she was a pain in the ass: dishonest, promiscuous, and foul-mouthed. According to Medora, she lived with 'em five months or so and then took off without a word. This was in the summer of '69. I should also mention that Wilbur Sanders, Medora's husband, disappeared at about the same time. I asked if the two events could be related, but she hated that idea. Let's hope Dr. Spears can confirm the ID when he pulls her old chart."

"You know the date this girl left?"

"I'm still trying to pin that one down. The timing's close enough to work, or so it appears. I hope to talk to Justine again and maybe she can narrow the frame. By the way, she's married to Ruel's son, Cornell, if that's significant."

Stacey piped up. "The auto upholstery guy?"

Dolan said, "That's him. The Mustang was recovered from his shed."

Stacey was squinting. "And this runaway. You're sure the name's Charisse Quinn?"

"Fairly sure," I said. "Why?"

"Because she shows up in one of the old reports. You can check for yourself. Her mother called the Sheriff's Department here a week or so into the investigation. She'd heard her daughter'd been reported missing and wanted us to know she was alive and well."

"I remember now. You're right. I knew I'd read the name, but I couldn't think where."

Dolan said, "Well, she couldn't be Jane Doe unless she rose from the dead. You said she called in a week or so after the body was found."

"The caller *said* she was Quinn's mother. Might have been someone else," Stacey said.

"I don't guess those old phone records still exist," I said.

"Probably not," Dolan replied. "Too much time's elapsed. All we can hope is the deputy took down her number when the call came in."

Stacey said, "Let's see what this dentist says. If the records match, then we know the victim's Quinn and the call's a fake."

"Any word on the Mustang?" Dolan asked.

Stacey smiled, holding up three fingers. "Three blond hairs caught in the hinge of the trunk. Characteristics are similar to Jane Doe's hair. Not conclusive, of course, but it shores up the theory she was stowed in the Mustang for transport. Someone made an effort to wipe the car clean, but the techs picked up a few latent fingerprints, including a partial palm print on the jack. The guy must have moved it when he was clearing space in the trunk."

I said, "What about the stains, were those blood?"

"We sent the carpet to the DOJ lab in Colgate, but we won't get results on that for weeks. We're lucky we have the technology now we didn't have back then. The blood might be all hers, or we might have some of the killer's mixed in."

"Seems like the other question is whether the stains

in the trunk match the ones on the tarp. A bloody stabbing like that, she might have put up a fight," I said.

Stacey's tone was dubious. "Maybe so, but don't forget, her hands were bound and the coroner's report doesn't make mention of defensive wounds."

Dolan said, "Even so, the guy might have been nicked."

"Let's hope. Problem is, we don't have a suspect for comparison."

"Correction. We don't have a suspect *yet*."

I raised my hand. "Could one of you ask Ruel about the tarp? I want to know if it was his."

Dolan snorted. "Why should *we* ask? Why not you?"

"Come on. You know he's going to yell at me. He'd never yell at the two of you."

"Chickenheart."

"What a wuss."

I smiled. "I thought that's what you tough guys were for. To do the dirty work."

"I'll tackle him," Stacey said. "He won't pick on a guy as sick as me."

Dolan said, "Wait a minute, Stace. Don't pull rank. You said you were well. I'm the sick one. Lookit where I am."

"So you can ask him. Who cares? Point is, we ought to see if we can find out where the tarp came from."

"How're you going to do that? Damn thing doesn't

even have a tag with the manufacturer's name. Besides which, I don't see the relevance."

I said, "The killer might have been a long-distance hauler. They sometimes use tarps to secure a load." I stopped. "Uh-oh."

"Uh-oh, what?"

"I just had a flash."

"Of what?"

"If the victim turns out to be Charisse and the body was transported in the Mustang, then your theory about Frankie Miracle is really screwed."

Dolan frowned. "How you figure that?"

"We know Frankie stole Cathy Lee's Chevy. So how could he have driven two cars, one from Quorum and one from Venice, and have both arrive in Lompoc at the same time?"

I could see him calculate. "He could have made two trips."

"Oh, please. What's he do—he kills Charisse, drives the Mustang to Lompoc, dumps the body, abandons the car, and then hitchhikes to Venice so he can stab someone else?"

"So he had an accomplice," Dolan said.

"To do what? There's no link between the two murders, unless I missed a beat somewhere."

Stacey said, "Dolan hates the idea Frankie's innocent."

"I don't hate the idea, it's Frankie I hate," Dolan said, irritably. "But what you say makes sense. How'd you come up with that?"

"I don't know. It's like one of those thought problems in high school math. The minute I'd see that sentence about the two trains, one leaving Chicago at sixty miles an hour, and the other blah, blah, blah, I'd start blacking out. I abandoned math the minute I was allowed."

"You didn't believe 'em when they said math would be useful later in your life?"

"Not even a little bit."

In the doorway, Chris Kovach cleared her throat and pointed to her watch.

"We're just going," Stacey said, rising from his chair.

"You can come back tomorrow, but only one at a time."

Stacey followed me to the motel in his rental car and we parked in adjoining slots. I walked with him to Dolan's room and gave him the key. He unlocked the door and put his duffel on a chair. The room had been made up and the furniture was back in place. It was 9:25 and I was ready to say good-night, assuming he was tired and wanted to hit the sack. "If you like, we can have breakfast together. What time do you get up?"

"Not so fast. I drove straight to the hospital after hours on the road. I haven't had my dinner yet. Wasn't that an Arby's I saw out on Main?"

"Sure, but the Quorum Inn's still open. Wouldn't you prefer a regular sit-down meal?"

"Arby's has tables. I've never had an Arby-Q. Isn't that what they're called? Now you've introduced me to fast food, I have some catching up to do."

I sat with Stacey, watching him plow through an Arby-Q, two orders of Curly Fries, and a Roast Beef sandwich, oozing a yellow sauce that was rumored to be cheese. He looked as if he'd picked up a few pounds in the days since I'd seen him last. "You do this often?"

"'Couple times a day. I found a cab company that delivers fast food, sort of like Meals on Wheels. Geez, this is great. I feel like a new man. I never would have known if you hadn't turned me on to this stuff."

"Happy to be of help. Personally, I never thought of junk food as life-affirming, but there you have it."

Stacey wiped his mouth on a napkin. "Forgot to mention this to Con. I got a call from Frankie's PO. Dench says he may be in violation. Looks like he left the county without permission."

"When was this?"

"Yesterday."

"That surprises me. To hear Frankie talk, he knew

all the rules and regs and wasn't going to be caught out. Wonder what set him off?"

"Might have been your visit. Con said he seemed cool, but you never know about these things. What's on for tomorrow?"

"Let's talk to Ruel. I've got the perfect excuse. I still have Edna's quilt. We can ask him about the tarp when I take it back it to her."

Stacey leaned forward. "Kinsey, we're cops. We don't need excuses. That's for them to give us."

Sheepishly, I said, "Oh. You've got a point."

When we reached the motel again it was 10:15. The wind had kicked up and I had my arms crossed, trying to protect myself from the cold.

Stacey said, "Hang on a minute. I have your jacket in my trunk."

I stood by his rental car while he opened the trunk and extracted my bomber jacket, along with a bulky mailing pouch he handed to me. "What's this?"

"Henry sent it. He said he found it on your doorstep and didn't think you'd want to wait. What is it?"

I turned the package to the light. "Beats me. Postmark's Lompoc, which means it's probably something from my aunt Susanna."

"I didn't think you had folks."

"I don't. Well, sort of. The jury's still out."

"Got it," he said. "I'll leave you to open it. Good-night."

"'Night," I said.

In the privacy of my room, I turned on the light and set my jacket aside. I left my shoulder bag on the chair and then I sat on the bed, turning the mailing pouch over in my lap. On the back, there was a pull tab that opened a seam along one edge. I pulled the strip and peered in. I removed the leather-bound album she'd sent. I remembered her mentioning family pictures, but never imagined she'd actually send them to me. I leafed through page after page of heavy black paper on which black-and-white photographs had been mounted by means of paper seals affixed to the corners and glued into place. Some of the pictures had come loose and the photos were tucked into the spine of the book. Under each, someone had written in white ink, identifying the subject, the date, and the circumstance.

There they were. All of them. My mother. Various uncles and aunts. The wedding of my grandfather Kinsey and my grandmother Cornelia Straith LeGrand. Babies in white christening dresses that trailed to the floor. Group photos, complete with cousins, servants, and family dogs. In most, the faces were solemn, the poses as stiff as paper dolls assembled on the page. A Christmas at the ranch with everyone gathered in front of an enormous pine tree laden with ornaments, garlands, and lights. A summer picnic near the house, with wooden harvest tables set out on the grass. Long dresses, pinafores, straw hats with wide brims freighted with artificial flowers; women looking buxom and broad-shouldered, their waists pinched by corsets that made their ample hips look twice as wide. Two men had been photographed in the army uniforms of World War I. One of the two appeared at later family gatherings while the other was never seen again. Sometimes the men were in shirt sleeves, dark vests, and black bowlers; sometimes striped summer jackets and white straw boaters. I could see the passing years reflected in women's rising hems, their arms increasingly bare. Thanksgiving of 1932, suddenly all the little girls were decked out like Shirley Temple. Nothing of the Great Depression seemed to have touched the house or its occupants, but time did march on.

Many of these people were dead by now. The adults had grown old. The children had married and given birth to children of their own. There was my mother in that long white dress again at her coming-out party, July 5, 1935. There were other snapshots of the occasion. In one, I could have sworn the photographer caught my father in the background, his eyes fixed on her. I'd never actually seen a picture of him, but I felt I'd recognized him nonetheless. After that, the pages were abruptly blank, the entire last third of the album empty. That was odd. I thought about it, puzzled that the family history so carefully recorded up to that point should suddenly be abandoned.

Oh. Could that be right?

My parents had eloped. I'd seen a copy of their marriage license dated November 18, 1935. My grandmother had been horrified. She'd had her heart set on Rita Cynthia marrying someone she considered worthy of her firstborn daughter. Instead, my mother had fallen in love with a common mail-carrier, who was moonlighting as a waiter on the day of her debut. There was apparently no Thanksgiving that year. And precious little in the way of celebrations since.

NINETEEN

Saturday morning after breakfast, Stacey and I drove to the McPhees'. The day was clear and sunny. The wind had died down and the desert stretched out in a haze of beige and mauve. Cactus, mesquite, and creosote bushes grew at neatly spaced intervals, as though planted by an arborist. Out there, unseen, the bobcats, foxes, owls, hawks, and coyotes were feeding on the smaller verte-brates. I'd read that jackrabbits constitute half the diet of breeding coyotes, so that when hard times reduce the rabbit population, the coyote population shrinks as well, thus maintaining the balance in Nature's culinary scheme.

We paused briefly on the street and I pointed across the pasture to the shed where we'd found the Mustang. Stacey said, "I wonder why he got himself in such a lather when the car was impounded?"

"Territorial, I guess. You'd do the same in his place."

"I'm not so sure about that. Sounds like a man who knows more than he's letting on."

"Maybe he's just another cranky old geezer, used to having his way."

"Nothing wrong with that."

"Stace, I wasn't talking about you."

I rang the bell and the two of us stood on the porch, waiting for someone to respond. From the backyard, I could hear children giggling and shrieking while a dog barked.

When Edna finally opened the door, she seemed somewhat taken aback. "Oh. I didn't expect to see you here again," she said. She averted her gaze politely from Stacey's patchy head.

"Hi, Edna. How are you? This is Detective Oliphant from the Santa Teresa Sheriff's Department. Have we caught you at a bad time?"

"I have my Baptist Church Auxilliary Committee here and we're busy."

I held out the quilt. "We won't take long. I wanted to return your quilt."

She took it, murmuring "Thank you," and then moved to shut the door.

I put a restraining hand on the frame. "We were hoping to see Ruel. Is he here?"

"He's in the garage."

"Mind if we talk to him?"

With a tiny flicker of irritation, she gave in. "You might as well come through the house and I'll send you out the back. It's quicker than going all the way around."

The two of us stepped inside while she closed the door and then we followed her down the hall.

She said, "Did you talk to Medora?"

"I did. She was great. Thanks so much."

In the kitchen, there were five women sitting at the table, which was stacked high with flyers and long white envelopes. All five glanced up at us, smiling expectantly as we moved toward the back door. Edna did a brief detour, returning the quilt to its place on the window seat. I noticed she didn't stop to introduce us, probably reluctant to explain the arrival of an out-of-town sheriff's detective and a private eye.

On the counter, she'd set up a big Thermos of coffee, a plate of sweetrolls, and a pile of paper napkins. The one empty chair was clearly hers. Two women folded the flyers, while another two stuffed them in the envelopes. The last woman in line licked the flaps and applied the stamps. I recognized this one: the light brown hair, brown eyes, the sprinkling of freckles across her nose. I'd seen her at Quorum High, where she worked as Mr. Eichenberger's assistant.

I paused, saying, "Hi. How're you?"

"Fine."

"I'm Kinsey Millhone. I'm sorry, but I've forgotten your name."

"Adrianne Richards."

Edna hesitated and then said, "Adrianne's my daughter."

"Ah. Well, it's nice seeing you again. This is Detective Oliphant," I said, thus forcing a round of introductions. I really hate to be pushy, but what's a poor girl to do?

One of the women piped up and said, "I'm Mavis Brant. This is Chalice Lyons, Harriet Keyes, and Adele Opdyke."

Stacey tipped an imaginary hat, which the ladies seemed to like.

I smiled at them briefly, my attention returning to Adrianne. "You're Cornell's sister? I didn't realize that. Small world."

"Isn't it?" She offered me a thin smile before she turned to the woman at the end of the table. "Excuse me, Harriet, could you pass me some envelopes?"

Harriet handed a batch of envelopes to Adele who passed them on to Adrianne, who was busy being busy. She must have been married, because if her office name tag had read "McPhee," I'd have asked if she was related. She flicked a look in my direction and then engaged the woman next to her in conversation.

"Well, we don't want to hold you up," Edna said to us, ushering us on.

Stacey and I went out the back door and trooped down the stairs, heading for the garage. Edna's granddaughter, Cissy, and her two older tow-headed sisters were racing across the yard in the throes of hysteria, a little yappy dog bouncing after them, nipping at their heels. As we watched, the dog caught a mouthful of Cissy's sock. Growling, he tugged, trying to dig in his paws while she dragged him across the grass. I envisioned dog bites, blood, and tetanus shots later in the afternoon. There was no sign of Justine, so I was guessing the girls had been parked with the grandparents while she was off somewhere.

I smelled Ruel's cigarette before we caught sight of him. He was in the same wooden desk chair with the same straw hat pushed to the back of his head. He looked small and harmless, and I could sense that Stacey was perplexed that I'd expressed any uneasiness about him. He was close to Stacey's age, in his early seventies I'd guess. He was watching another television show with all the concentration of a kid. This time, it was a cartoon so completely asinine that even the little girls preferred being chased and bitten by a dog.

Without looking up, Ruel said, "Back again, I see. Who's your friend?"

Stacey stepped forward, extending his hand. "Stacey Oliphant, Mr. McPhee. I'm a homicide detective with the Santa Teresa Sheriff's Department. Nice to make your acquaintance."

Ruel gave him an obligatory handshake. "Suppose you're here to confiscate something else. It's a damn shame you can walk in and take anything you want."

"I can understand your point. Then again, the law's the law. We don't make it up; we just carry it out," Stacey said.

"True enough," Ruel said. "Nothing I can do about it now. You just be sure that car comes back without a scratch."

I said, "Wait a minute. How's that supposed to happen? The car was banged up to begin with."

Ruel rolled his eyes with annoyance. "I meant, no damage aside from that."

Stacey eased back in. "Mr. McPhee, I only drove in last night so I'm new on the scene. If it's not too much trouble, I wonder if I can ask you to bring me up to speed."

"Ask her, she's so smart. I got better things to do."

"She tells me you made quite a deal on that car."

Like a recording, Ruel recited the details of his good fortune. "I got that Mustang free of charge back in 1969. Fella left it at the shop to have the seats repaired.

Car was stolen and once it came back, he didn't want anything to do with it."

"Is that right? Good deal," Stacey said, as though impressed. "And what inspired you to keep the car all these years?"

"My son and I intended to restore it, though now they've as good as told me it was used in some kind of criminal enterprise. Homicide, is that right?"

"Yes, sir. Naturally, we're interested in taking a closer look."

"You ought to talk to the previous owner. Feller name of Gant. He could've stolen the car himself. Have you ever thought of that?"

"I don't believe we have. Wonder why he'd steal his own car and then turn around and give it to you?"

"Why does anyone do anything? Man might've been nuts."

"Always possible. Happens he's dead now."

"Too bad. Otherwise, you could pester him instead of me," Ruel said. He paused to light a cigarette with a wood match that he dropped in his jar. "Point is, I don't know beans about a murder and my son knows less. Cornell should be here shortly to fetch the girls and that nasty dog of theirs. Talk to him yourself. Waste of time, you ask me."

"That could well be. Police work, we pursue a lot of

lines that don't pan out. For instance, we've been curious about a tarp that was dumped with the girl's body.
Anybody mention that?"

"What kind of tarp?"

"Canvas. Looks like a car cover or a drop cloth. Ms.
Millhone saw a couple tarps at the shop and wondered
if one of yours might've come up missing at the time."

"Nope. Can't help. Happens I own a bunch of tarps,
but I never had one taken and couldn't care less if I did.
Tarps are cheap. Take a stroll through the Kmart, if you
doubt my word."

"What about a car cover? You remember if there was
one on the Mustang when it was taken?"

"I already answered that. All my tarps and car covers
are accounted for."

"You buy those in town?"

"You think I send off with box tops? Two of you are
like dogs, chasing your own tails. Try something new.
I'm tired of tarps."

Stacey and I exchanged a look while Ruel returned
his attention to the TV set. Stacey shifted his weight.
"Do you happen to remember a young woman in town
by the name of Charisse Quinn? Same age as your kids,
so you might have met her through them."

"Doesn't sound familiar. She the one who got
killed?"

"Yes, sir."

"I don't remember things like that."

I touched Stacey's arm, leaning close so I could murmur a question of my own. He nodded, saying, "What's the story on Justine's father? Medora told us yesterday the man deserted her."

"Poor specimen of a fella, if you want to know the truth."

"We heard he was a womanizer."

"Everybody knew that . . . except his wife. Not to speak ill of the woman, but she has a serious drinking problem, has had for years. Edna and I, we don't hold with hard liquor or spirits of any sort. It's one thing Justine's always appreciated about us."

"You were talking about her dad's womanizing. What's the story on that?"

"He used to drive up to Palm Springs to meet the ladies. He'd tell Medora he was working late and go keep company with floozies."

"You know this for a fact or was that just the gossip around town?"

"He told me so himself. Wilbur was as fond of drink as Medora, and once he imbibed, he had a tendency to brag about himself. Homely as a monkey, but he must've had his ways. Claimed he could walk into a bar and the women'd fall all over him. Married or single didn't matter to him. He'd order a drink and offer to buy one for the gal sitting next to him. Once she said

381

yes, he'd pull out his wallet and all he'd have on him was a hundred dollar bill. She'd end up paying, assuming he'd pony up by the end of the evening. Next thing you know he'd be getting in her panties and she'd be out that, too. I never figured women for such nitwits, but that's how he told it."

"This Quinn girl I mentioned was a ward of the court. A social worker placed her with the Sanders."

Ruel turned and stared at Stacey. "That who you mean? Well, I'll be. I hadn't thought of her in years. Quinn. That sounds right. You should have said so in the first place."

"We heard her name for the first time yesterday. How well did you know her?"

"I knew her to speak to, but not otherwise. Cornell said she fooled around with any boy she met. 'Free with her favors' is how he put it. She'd take 'em up to the Tuley-Belle and misbehave."

"The Tuley-Belle?"

"Construction site outside town. Big condominium complex some fellas started building in 1968. Leon Tuley and Maurice P. Belle. Got it half-done and went bankrupt so the place's sat there since. Kids like it because in parts there's a roof overhead and the walls are up. Plumbing and electrical are torn out, but given what they're up to, I guess you don't need that."

"Wilbur Sanders ever say anything to you about the Quinn girl?"

"I didn't know him well, except as Justine's dad. Cornell was dating her and the families would get together every now and then. Medora wasn't often sober. I felt sorry for Justine. She'd sit there trying to cover up her shame and embarrassment. Meanwhile, Wilbur would excuse himself, come out here, and bend my ear about his sexual exploits. Ask me, he should have paid more attention to his wife."

"And Charisse?"

"I don't know anything about that. Hear Wilbur tell it, he was too much the gent to mention names. Minute they arrived, he'd make excuses and head out here. Always brought a flask of dark rum and we'd smoke our cigarettes. Once he got talking, you could hardly shut him up. Best of my knowledge, he kept his escapades to Palm Springs so Medora wouldn't get wind."

"If she was drinking so much, would she have cared?" I asked.

"Of course she'd have cared! Infidelity doesn't sit well with the ladies. They're apt to tear your head off."

I heard a car pull into the driveway and I turned in time to see Cornell park his white pickup. As he came through the back gate, his three daughters made a run at him and piled into his legs, the pup bouncing along behind them like a basketball. Much squealing and hugging, punctuated by the dog's shrill barks. Cornell extracted himself and headed in our direction, combing his hair with his fingers, tucking in the tail of his shirt where the girls had pulled it loose. He said, "Hey, Dad," with some enthusiasm. To me, he said hi in a tone as flat as a tumbler of two-day-old Coke.

I introduced him to Stacey and the two men shook hands. Stacey said, "We've just been chatting with your dad about Charisse."

Cornell seemed embarrassed by the subject. "Justine told me about that. I was sorry to hear."

"Was she a friend of yours?"

"Well, no, but I'd see her at school. This was before she got kicked out and went over to Lockaby."

"Did she have a boyfriend?"

"She never went steady with anyone I knew. She dated quite a few guys, various classmates of mine."

"Who would you say offhand?"

Cornell thought about it briefly. "I guess Toby Hecht and George Baum. You might start with them."

Stacey made a note of the names while Cornell peered over his shoulder and pointed. "That's *B-A-U-M*, not *B-O-M-B*."

"Got it. And how could I go about getting in touch with these birds? They still around somewhere?"

"George is your best bet. He sells new and used cars over in Blythe. Toby, I don't know about. I haven't talked to him in years."

Ruel had been following the conversation, but now he rose to his feet. "You fellers will excuse me, I got to go see a man about a dog. Nice talkin' to you."

"Same here," Stacey said, touching his head as though tipping his hat.

Ruel took off across the grass, heading for the house while Stacey was saying to Cornell, "How about Wilbur Sanders? You ever see her with him?"

Cornell shifted his weight. He reached in his shirt pocket and took out a pack of cigarettes. He shook one loose and lit it, glancing back to make sure neither Edna nor Ruel was watching him. "I'm sorry, but I don't want to say anything bad about my wife's dad."

Stacey said, "We're not asking you to tell tales. I'm sure he's a fine man."

Cornell didn't seem prepared to go that far. "All I know is she doesn't want to think ill of the man even if he's gone."

"Good point. She doesn't want to think what, that Wilbur cheated on her mom?"

"Now I never said that. He put up with a lot."

"You're talking about Medora's drinking? That'll certainly throw a family into disarray. At the same time, people have been telling us Charisse was so interested in

385

men, we can't help but wonder was she interested in him?"

"I think I've said enough. If I were you, I wouldn't mention this to Justine. She gets touchy on the subject."

After that, Cornell stubbed out his cigarette, resisting any further attempts to probe. I watched Stacey come at the matter from a number of directions, but, try as he might, he couldn't weasel anything more out of him.

Later, with Stacey at the wheel of the rental car, I said, "What was that about? Talk about resistance."

Stacey shook his head. "I can't decide if he was lying about something and doing a piss-poor job, or trying not to tattle and making a sore botch of that."

"How could he be lying? He didn't say anything."

"Maybe you should talk to Justine—you know, woman to woman."

I rolled my eyes. "Oh yeah, right. Like she'd break down and confide in me."

"Well, she might. Meanwhile, I think we better go by the hospital and see Con. First day without a smoke, he'll be climbing the walls."

"What about you? I haven't seen you light your pipe since you arrived."

"I gave it up; part of the deal I made, hanging on to life."

*

The CCU nurse we'd been dealing with the night before was off duty and wouldn't be back on the floor until 3:00. Winsome as we were, the current charge nurse, Meredith Snow, couldn't be persuaded to let us break the rules. I sat in the waiting area, with its bare end table and four upholstered chairs, while Stacey went in to Dolan's room for the requisite ten-minute visit. In the absence of magazines, I amused myself by cleaning all the woofies, loose hair, and tatty tissues from the bottom of my shoulder bag. In the process, I came across the Quorum phone book that I'd been toting around for days. I sat and thought about the tarp, wondering how to figure out where Ruel bought his. As the entire phone book, white and yellow pages combined, was about the thickness of a modest paperback, I tried the obvious, looking under "Tarpaulins" first. There were two subheadings: "Renting" and "Retail." I wasn't sure anyone would rent a tarpaulin to wrap up a corpse, but I suppose stranger things have happened. Dolan's theory about the killer involved haste and improvisation, so it was always possible a rented tarp was the closest at hand. Ruel didn't rent his, but someone else might.

"Tarpaulins—Renting" referred me to "Rental Service Stores" and "Yards." Of the seven companies listed, four offered heavy equipment: lifts, loaders, backhoes, hand tools, paint sprayers, scaffolding, generators, air compressors, and related items. The remaining three

companies were devoted to party supplies, including
canopies and tents. I turned a corner of the page down,
thinking I might check into them later.

Under "Tarpaulins—Retail," there was one company
listed, Diamond Custom Canvas. The boxed advertise-
ment went on at some length in the teeniest print
imaginable, listing their products, which included:
asphalt, lumber, lumite, mesh, polyethylene, steel haulers, vinyl-coated polyester, vinyl laminates, tarps, weld-
ing curtains, screens, blankets, roll systems, and drop
cloths. The address was on Roberts, one block over
from Main. I was still staring at the ad when Stacey
reappeared.

I tucked my finger in the book to mark my place.
"You were in there ten minutes? It didn't seem that
long."

"Lady came in with a tray to draw blood so I
hightailed it out of there." He noticed the phone book.
"Good reading."

"Actually, it is," I said. "Are you going back in?"

"Nah, he's grouchy as all get out. I knew he'd turn
sour if he didn't get his fix. I think I'll take a little trip
to Blythe and see if I can find this Baum fellow.
Shouldn't take long; it's twelve miles. You want to come
along?"

"Nah, I'm going to try something else. Why don't
you drop me at the motel and I'll pick up Dolan's car?

If you're finished by noon, we can hit the Burger King in town and pig out on Whoppers."

"Sounds like a good plan to me."

Diamond Custom Canvas was part of a block of two-story brick buildings, constructed with shared walls, that ran between Twenty-third and Twenty-fourth. There were several warehouses, an abandoned furniture wholesaler, and a discount clothing outlet. Some of the businesses were padlocked shut and the few that were open looked as though they'd fallen on hard times. Diamond was the single exception. Though the location wasn't a magnet for the walk-in trade, both phones were busy. I stood at one end of the counter, listening idly to one of the two clerks, who was engaged in a lengthy discussion about the volume discount on a shipment of lumite asphalt solid tarps. The second clerk finished her conversation, got up, and disappeared through a side door. While I waited for assistance, I took a visual tour of the place.

The interior was one vast, gloomy room, twice as long as it was wide. The pressed-tin ceiling was two stories high, with long banks of hanging fluorescent lights. On the left, an ornate wooden stairway, painted an odd shade of turquoise, curved upward to the second floor. Across the back wall, two courses of glass blocks let in a muted light. I could see water marks streaking down the wall, some long-ago plumbing leak or possibly a hole in the roof.

I picked up and studied a pamphlet that listed the part numbers, cut size, UPC codes, and weights of various twelve-ounce olive-drab tarpaulins. The twenty-by-thirty weighed seventy-nine pounds—tough to tote around, I thought. The tan ten-ounce tarps seemed to be lighter, but I was already worried they wouldn't hold up as well.

The second clerk came out of the back room. Glancing up, she spotted me and crossed to the counter. "May I help you?"

She was probably in her fifties, with heavy eye makeup and dyed black hair that she'd pulled up in a swirl on top. She wore jeans, a sweatshirt, and a pair of black spike-heel boots. Her fingernails were long, perfect ovals, painted dark red with a thin white stripe across each. I was reminded briefly of Iona and I wondered if she'd developed an expertise in nail art.

I said, "I know this is a weird request, but I hope you'll bear with me." I told her about Jane Doe and the tarp that was found when the body came to light. I did a quick summary of our reasons for believing the victim was local and our suspicion that the murder and/or abduction might have taken place down here. "I keep thinking if we could find out about the tarp, we might get a line on the guy."

"You mean what kind of work he did?"

"Something like that. If he did painting or drywall . . ."

"Not drywall," she said. "Those guys usually use a big roll of paper. It would help if I knew the material the tarp was made of. Are you talking about duck, cotton, acrylic, or a blend?"

"Well, I don't really know and that's the point. Looking at this brochure, I can see you make hundreds of tarps, so the question's probably absurd."

"Not really. Many of our products fall into other categories, like cargo control—lumber tarps and steel haulers. I don't think you'd mistake either for a painter's drop cloth. They're too big. Too bad you don't have it with you. At least I could tell you if it's one of ours."

"Sorry. They've got it in the property room up north, under lock and key."

"In that case, let's think how else we might help. Most drop cloths are standard, though we do make two grades—eight- or ten-ounce natural. If I showed you, do you think you'd recognize the difference?"

"I could try."

"My name's Elfreida."

"I'm Kinsey. I appreciate your time."

I followed as she came out from behind the counter and *clip-clopped* across the bare concrete floor to a big worktable where two stacks of folded canvas tarps were sitting side by side. She grabbed a tarp from each stack and opened both across the tabletop, flapping them like bedsheets to shake the folds loose. "Look familiar?"

"It's that one, I think," I said, pointing to the lighter of the two.

"Here's the trick," she said. She held up one edge, showing me the red stitched seam with a tiny square of red in the corner. "This is not a trademark per se, but we use it on everything."

"Oh, wow. I remember that red square from the tarp we have."

"It's actually not a square. It's a diamond."

"The company name," I said.

She smiled. "Of course, that doesn't tell you anything about where it was purchased. Might have been here in Quorum or it might have been somewhere else. Problem is, we distribute to paint stores and hardware stores all across the country, plus places like Target and Kmart. There's no way you'd ever track the outlet. We don't code for things like that."

"Who buys them?"

"Painting contractors, for the most part. The average homeowner usually buys a plastic tarp he can dispose of when he's finished. Makes the job easier. You toss it in the trash and you're done. Do commercial or residential work, you need something you can use more than once. These things are sturdy. They last for years." She went on talking, but I found myself snagged again on the issue of painting contractors. Where had I run across mention of a paint contractor? I was sure I'd seen it in one of the county sheriff's reports. She said, "Looks like I lost you back there."

"Sorry. I'm fine. I just remembered where I'd seen mention of a painting contractor. I should go check that out. Thanks so much. You've been more help than you can know."

TWENTY

After I left Diamond's, I returned to the motel. The housecleaning cart was parked on the walk outside my room. The maid had stripped off my sheets and she was using the pile of soiled linens to prop the door open while she went about her work. I peered in, trying to get a sense of where she was in the process. My plastic-covered mattress was bare and a flat stack of clean sheets rested at the foot of the bed. I could hear her in the bathroom with her portable radio tuned to a Spanish-language station. On the night table the message light was blinking on my phone. I heard the toilet flush and the maid emerged with my damp towel across her arm. She toted her carryall of cleaning products.

I said, "Oh, hi. Sorry to interrupt. How much longer will you be?"

She smiled broadly and nodded, saying, "*Hokay. Sí. Una momento.*"

"I'll come back," I said. I trotted across the parking lot to the office and went in.

The desk clerk was perched on her swivel stool, still chewing bubble gum, her skirt hiked up, swinging one foot while she read the inner pages of the *National Enquirer*.

"My message light's blinking. Can you tell me who called?"

"How should I know? Pick up the phone and dial 6."

"The maid's in my room so I'm here to ask you."

The look she gave me said she was feeling put-upon. "What room?"

"125."

With exaggerated patience, she set the paper aside, swiveled her stool to face her computer, tapped on the keyboard, and read from the screen. She chewed her gum briefly and then her face brightened. "Oh, yeah. I remember now. You got a call from a dentist, Dr. Spears. What's the problem with your teeth?"

"Did he leave a number?"

She blew a bubble and curled it back into her mouth on the end of her tongue, waiting to pop it after she'd closed her lips. "He did, but I didn't bother to write it down. It's in the book."

"When you first took this job, did they train you?"

She stopped chewing. "To do what?"

"Simple clerical skills, phone etiquette, manners— anything like that?"

"Nah. Know what I'm paid? Minimum wage. Three dollars and thirty-five cents an hour. Besides, I don't need manners. My uncle owns the place. My name's Geraldine, in case you feel like filing a complaint."

I let the matter drop.

I went out the office door and turned right, moving to the bank of pay phones I'd seen near the ice machine. I opened my bag and fished out the Quorum phone book and a handful of change. I looked up the dentist's number and dialed, receiver tucked between my shoulder and my tilted head while I put the directory back in my bag.

When Mrs. Gary picked up, I said, "Hi, Mrs. Gary. Kinsey Millhone here. I can't believe I caught you in the office on a Saturday."

"I'm just catching up on insurance claims. This is about the only time I have."

"Dr. Spears left me a message. Is he there by any chance?"

"He's off playing golf, but I can tell you why he called. He found the chart you asked about. I've got it sitting on my desk."

"Tell him I'm in love."

"He'll be thrilled to death," she said.

I laughed. "Could you do me a favor? Could you slip

it in a manila envelope and mail it to Sergeant Detective Joe Mandel at the Santa Teresa County Sheriff's Department? He'll talk to the forensic odontologist and they'll handle it from there." I gave her the address, adding my copious thanks to her and to Dr. Spears. I hung up the phone, offering up small, fervent prayers.

I had to believe that a comparison of his records with the Jane Doe maxilla and mandible would confirm Charisse Quinn's identity. At the same time, I knew reliance on such records could prove inconclusive. A chart might contain errors, or it might be incomplete if details of previous or subsequent dental work had been omitted for some reason. A positive ID might take weeks, but once it was confirmed, the guys could chase down the paperwork on Charisse's birth parents through Riverside County Social Services. In the meantime, I was feeling good. We seemed to be making progress in spite of the odds.

When I returned to my room, my door was closed and the maid's cart was halfway down the corridor. I let myself in and tossed my purse and jacket on the bed. I retrieved my duffel from the closet and took it over to the desk, digging deep to the bottom, where I'd stashed my copy of the murder book. I sat and went through it page by page. I knew what I was looking for, but not where it was. Twenty pages in, I came across the report, dated August 1, 1969, detailing the arrest of Frankie

Miracle, who'd given the deputy his home address in Blythe, California. No mention of Venice, where the murder had taken place. Under occupation, he'd classified himself as a handyman/helper. For his employer, he'd listed Lennie Root, R&R Painting, with an address and phone number in Hazelwood Springs. I turned down a corner of the page and moved on. I was curious about the purported call from Charisse's mother that Stacey'd mentioned earlier.

Fifty pages further on, I found the follow-up report, dated 8-9-69/Approx. 1400 hrs., in which Deputy Joe Mandel had entered information about a call he received from the Riverside County Sheriff's substation in Quorum. A Detective Orbison had contacted the Lompoc substation in response to the teletype regarding the Jane Doe homicide victim whose description matched that of a missing juvenile named Charisse Quinn. She'd left home on July 27. The Riverside County Sheriff's Department noted her DOB as 4-10-52; height: 5'3"; weight: 120 lbs. Blond hair, blue eyes, pierced ears, and extensive dental work. Her foster mother was listed as Medora Sanders, at the address where I'd had my conversation with her. According to Orbison, she'd come in the morning of August 9, to file the missing-persons report.

After Orbison's call, Mandel had made two attempts to contact Medora without success. Then on 8-11-69/

Approx. 1855 hrs., RCSD phoned again, this time tell-ing Mandel they'd received a call from a woman who stated she had a daughter named Charisse Quinn, whom she understood was believed to be a murder victim. She wanted to let them know the girl had come home and she was alive and well. She gave the River-side County Sheriff's deputy a phone number where she could be reached, and Orbison passed the number on to Mandel. In his typed account, Mandel indicated that he'd attempted contact, but the number was listed as out of service. If he'd tried tracing the party, there was no notation of the fact. I continued leafing through the book, but I found no other reference to Medora or Charisse. I made a few notes and then sat, playing idly with my index cards, laying them out randomly in rows.

It was odd to see how the pieces realigned. When Dolan had first given me my copy of the murder book, I'd read these same reports, many of them more than once. The entry about the missing girl had been only one of a number of items that had meant nothing outside the current context. The name itself didn't seem significant until Stacey remembered it. It was the same with Frankie Miracle's place of employment. In early readings, the note had seemed incidental. Now the information fairly leapt off the page.

Three things struck me: First, in filing the missing-persons report, Medora hadn't been quite as prompt as she'd led me to believe. She'd implied she'd gone straight to the police, when she'd actually waited more than a week. I'd have to go back and ask her about the delay. Secondly, Charisse's July 27 departure from Quorum would place her in easy range of Frankie Miracle's road trip after the murder of Cathy Lee Pearse on July 29. I still couldn't figure out how the Mustang ended up in Lompoc, unless Charisse had stolen it herself. Despite Medora's claim that she had no license, she might have known how to drive. If so, she might have gone as far as Lompoc, abandoned the vehicle, and tried hitching a ride from there. And finally, I wondered who'd made the call pretending to be Charisse's mother. If Frankie'd had anything to do with Charisse's murder, Iona could have made the call to cover for him. By August 11, when that call came in, Charisse's body had been discovered and attempts were under way to determine who she was. What better way to eliminate the link than to claim the missing girl was home? As nearly as I could tell, that call had effectively removed Charisse's name from the loop.

I put the murder book and my index cards in the desk drawer and pulled out my trusty pint-sized phone book, which covered Quorum, Blythe, Mesa Verde, Hazelwood Springs, Palo Verde, Ripley, Creosote, and eight towns in Arizona. I flipped to the yellow pages and found the listing for paint contractors. There were only four in the area—two in Blythe, one in Palo Verde, and one in Hazelwood Springs. According to his boxed ad, Lennie Root of R&R Painting was a residential painting specialist who also did condominiums, apartments, and commercial accounts. He was insured, bonded, and state licensed, promising reasonable rates, prompt work, and free estimates. There was a phone number, but no street address, which probably meant he operated on an answering machine from his home. I checked the white pages under "Root" and, sure enough, there he was. I was becoming quite fond of these small towns for the ease of access to their citizens. Big-city paranoia with its unlisted phone numbers only made my job tougher. I had ways of acquiring the information, but not as readily as this. I picked up my bomber jacket and got in the car.

When I got to the Burger King it was 12:15 and Stacey's rental car was already parked in the side lot. I went in, scanning the crowd until I spotted him at a table on the far side of the room. Even here, there were Easter decorations—big posterboard eggs and posterboard Easter bunnies. Stacey waved when he saw me.

I slid in across from him, saying, "Sorry to keep you waiting."

"Who said anything about waiting? I already had a Whopper and an order of fries."

"Well, good for you. I hope you don't mind sitting while I grab a bite myself."

"Oh, I'll be eating again. The Whopper was good, but it didn't fill me up. I've been thinking we should do a study—purely scientific—a side-by-side tasting, a Whopper and a Big Mac, to see which we prefer. Or go vertical—McDonald's hamburger, cheeseburger, a QP with Cheese, and a Big Mac. What do you think?"

"You sit. I'll go. You want a Coke with that Whopper?"

"I'd prefer a chocolate shake."

Over lunch (my first, his second), I brought Stacey up to date on my visit to the canvas shop and my review of the murder book with its reference to Lennie Root. "How was your interview with George Baum?"

"What a pain," he said. "He's the consummate sales-man—all capped teeth and phony charm. He tried talk-ing me into a BMW, but I nixed that idea. Point is, when I asked him about Charisse, he sidestepped the whole subject. He thought he was being slick; like I never heard a guy equivocate. I'm guessing he diddled her, but now that he knows she was murdered, he'd like to distance himself. He nearly shit when I told him where I got his name. He's maneuvering like crazy, doing anything he can to get me off his back, so he gives me some information I think you'll find interesting. He tells me Charisse and Cornell's *sister* were thick as thieves."

"Well, that's a new one."

"Isn't it? He says he used to see the two of them all over town. He swears Charisse had the hots for Cornell and sucked up to Adrianne to get close to him."

"Kind of makes you wonder why Adrianne didn't speak up. To hear Cornell tell it, he barely knew Charisse. Justine certainly gave me that impression."

"It's worth a chat with Adrianne if not the other two."

"You want to do that while I talk to the painting contractor?"

"I'd rather you take care of both. My energy's running low. I need a nap. As soon as you finish, stop by the motel. I should be up, and if not, feel free to wake me. We'll go back to the hospital and let Dolan know what's going on."

Once Stacey and I parted company, I sat in my car debating which interview to do first. At the moment, I was more interested in hearing about Adrianne's friendship with Charisse than I was in talking to Justine, Cornell, or the painting contractor. However, when I consulted the phone book, there were eight "Richards" listed, and Adrianne didn't seem to be among them. I had no idea what her husband's name was. Since it was Saturday, I knew she wouldn't be at the school. *Quelle bummeur.* This brought the matter down to a toss-up between the painting contractor and the younger Mc-Phees. Again, according to the phone book, I was only four blocks from Cornell and Justine's, so they won by default.

Their house turned out to be a bright yellow board-and-batten, with white trim and diamond-paned windows flanked by dark green shutters. Pink geraniums grew in flower boxes across the front. The yard was enclosed by a white two-board fence. The two-car garage stood open, and I could see six-year-old Cissy and her two older sisters arranged in a cluster around Cornell's workbench.

I parked in front and approached, moving up the driveway past a tangle of bikes. Cornell looked up, greeting me without interrupting his work. "Hey, how're you?"

"I'm great. Is that a doghouse you're building?"

"You bet, and I'm almost done as soon as I finish this roof. Girls are all set to paint it. You meet my daughters?"

"I met Cissy on Thursday. I saw all three of them at your parents' house this morning."

"Oh, that's right. So you did. This is Amelia and Mary Francis."

I said, "Hi." I couldn't tell which was Amelia and which was Mary Francis, but it probably didn't matter. Most children seem interchangeable to me, anyway. "Is Justine at home?"

"Doing laundry. You can go in through there. Utility room's just inside the door. Cissy, why don't you show her where it is."

I hesitated, tempted to ask him about Charisse before I broached the subject with Justine, but with his children present, it didn't seem like a good idea. Cissy was tugging at my hand so I allowed her to lead me through the rear of the garage and into the utility room. She skipped back to her dad and his Saturday-morning project.

I found Justine in her sock feet, wearing an olive green sweatsuit. Her back was to me and she was cramming filthy blue jeans and work shirts into the washing machine. Beside her, the dryer was already in service, filling the room with a rich, damp heat while a garment with buckles clattered endlessly as it tumbled in the drum. I said, "I hope you don't mind my dropping by without notice."

She jumped and gave a yelp. "Shit, you scared me to death. I didn't hear you come in."

"Sorry. I didn't mean to sneak up on you. Cornell

suggested I come in this way. I guess he figured you'd never hear me if I rang the front bell."

"What are you doing here?"

"The usual. I'm nosing around. Mind if we talk?"

"I've already told you everything I know."

"Indulge me, okay?"

She stared at the floor, curbing her annoyance, but I could see her relent, albeit unhappily. "Let me finish this and we'll go into the kitchen."

She shoved in the last of the load of clothes, added liquid detergent and bleach, then closed the lid and set the program knob. She pushed the Start button. She washed her hands at the utility sink, drying them on a terry cloth towel she retrieved from the pile of soiled linens.

I followed her into the kitchen, which was immaculate, a far cry from her mother's house with its grunginess and knickknacks. I don't know how women with active kids manage to keep a house picked up. She offered me coffee, probably to atone for her snappishness. I accepted with an eye to stringing out the visit. She poured me a mug and popped it in the microwave to heat. She was not a pretty girl. There was something washed-out about her looks, as though vital blood supplies had been suppressed for years, leaving her pale and depleted. The green sweatsuit added more color to her eyes than I'd seen before, but it still wasn't much. The microwave pinged and she removed the mug.

When she set it in front of me, a wave of coffee slopped over the rim. She handed me a paper napkin. "Did you want something in particular? We haven't eaten lunch. I need to go to the market to pick up some bread."

"This shouldn't take long," I said, busy cleaning the spill. I decided to take an indirect route getting to the subject of Adrianne and Charisse. "Did you have a chance to talk to Cornell?"

"About what?"

"You were worried he'd get mad at you if you talked to me."

"He got over that. He said he saw you at his dad's so I guess all's forgiven. Lucky you," she said. She brought sugar and half-and-half to the table and then sat down, tucking her hands under her thighs.

"That's because Detective Oliphant was there. He and Ruel seemed to hit it off. Did you meet Stacey?"

She shook her head. "I heard there was a second detective in town, but I haven't met him yet. They must be going all out."

"They are. They're very serious about this."

"Well, good, though I don't get why it matters after all these years."

"Cops are funny that way. They never really give up. They just wait."

"Look, I don't mean to be rude about it, but I really have to scoot. The kids'll get cranky."

"Sorry. I'll get down to it," I said. "This morning, when Stacey spoke to Cornell, he mentioned a high school classmate of yours named George Baum."

"Sure, I know George. Why was he talking about him?"

"Cornell seemed to think he was involved with Charisse."

"Involved?"

"That's a dainty way of saying he screwed her."

"Oh, for heaven's sake. He did not. George had a girlfriend, a cheerleader named Swoozie Franks. They went together for years, since junior high at least. They got married a month after graduation."

"Swoozie?"

"It's a nickname. I forget her real one."

"Maybe Swoozie wouldn't put out so George got relief from Charisse instead."

Justine made a face. "That's a tacky idea."

"Why? You've all been saying what a slut she was."

"Well, yes, but I can't believe George would do something like that. Did he admit it?"

"Not as far as I know, but he did tell Stacey that

Charisse and Adrianne were close. I was curious why no one mentioned that to us."

"That's not true at all. Why would he say that? He's crazy."

Dubiously, I said, "I don't know, Justine. He says Charisse had a crush on Cornell and hung out with Adrianne to have access to him. You'd think Adrianne would've volunteered the information as soon as she heard Charisse was dead."

"You said you weren't even sure it was her."

"Well, the ID isn't positive, but now we have her dental records so we're getting close. I would have mentioned it this morning, but it didn't seem appropriate in front of Edna's church group. Besides, that was the first time I realized who Adrianne was. You can imagine my surprise. I see her at Quorum High. I find out she's Cornell's sister, and then I hear she and Charisse were such good pals."

"They weren't *pals*. George doesn't know what he's talking about. Charisse's so-called pals were a bunch of losers from Lockaby. They were more her speed."

"Really. Your mother said she made a real pest of herself, wanting to hang out with the two of you."

"We took her with us sometimes, but she was an embarrassment."

"Did you know Charisse was so smitten with him?"

"Oh, please."

"Why would George lie to us?"

"I didn't say he *lied*. I said he got it wrong. The guy's a dimwit. Besides, even if she had a crush on Cornell, what difference did that make? A lot of girls had crushes. He was the most popular guy in our high school class."

"But how'd you feel about it? Didn't it bother you?"

"I knew we'd end up together, so who cared about them?"

"I mean Charisse in particular."

"She was nothing. A pig. I couldn't have cared less about her."

"Geez, that's amazing. When I was in high school, I was insecure. You must have had a lot more self-confidence."

"I wouldn't say that. It just seemed like fate. The minute I saw Cornell, that was it for me. That was grade school. We went to different junior high schools and reconnected in high school in our senior year."

"Love at first sight."

"Right."

"So really, it didn't matter if Charisse and Adrianne were friends—in terms of its effect on you."

"Charisse could do anything she liked. No skin off *my* back." She glanced at her watch, signaling time was up. She could have been a shrink, given her skill in silent communication.

I held up a hand. "Just one other thing and then I'll let you go. Doesn't it seem a trifle coincidental that your father disappeared just about the same time she did?"

Justine stared at me. "I don't get what you mean."

"Come on, Justine. You're not that naive."

"You're implying the two of them went off *together*?"

"Didn't it ever cross your mind?"

"Of course not. Daddy left in June. She was with us for months and months after that."

"Actually, it was only until the end of July. Maybe six weeks or so. What if they were having an affair?"

Justine laughed. "Oh, that's gross. I don't like to think he had sex with my mother, let alone with someone like her. That's disgusting."

"Disgusting to you perhaps, but in the annals of human history it's not exactly a first. I said the same thing to your mom. Charisse was promiscuous, so why not him?"

Justine clamped her mouth shut, staring at the floor. Agitated, she tucked a strand of pale hair behind one ear.

I said, "Look, I'm not making any claims here. None of us have the facts. This is purely speculation."

"Well, it's in bad taste," she said. She stood up.

"I guess I better let you go. Maybe I should have a chat with Cornell."

"I'm not sure he's interested."

"He didn't seem opposed to my talking to you."

"He was being polite."

"A quality I've always admired in a man. Anyway, you needn't fret because I can't do it now. I have something else to do."

Hazelwood Springs on my California map was a micro-dot on Highway 78 ten miles south of Quorum. The town turned out to be so small that I drove straight through without realizing it. I made a three-point turn, using the next convenient driveway, and then doubled back. The entire town consisted of a minimart, two side roads, a scattering of houses, and a two-pump gas station of the old-fashioned variety, where some guy actually came outside, filled your tank, cleaned the windshield, and passed the time of day. I ended up putting another twenty bucks' worth of gas in Dolan's boat, but in return, the fellow was kind enough to point out Lennie Root's place, which was just across the road.

Lennie Root's small white frame house sat on pylons of raw cinder block, thus creating the crawl space he used to store his miscellaneous painting equipment.

There was a flowery ceramic plaque affixed to the wood frame above the front door that read THE ROOTS, MYRA AND LENNIE.

Lennie responded to my knock. He was a man in his sixties with a narrow, sagging face and heavy bags beneath his eyes. His bushy gray hair was peppered with tiny specks of dried red paint. Over his chinos and white T-shirt he wore a full-length apron with a ruffle around the bib. He held a wrinkled white dress shirt like an errant tomcat he intended to boot out the door.

"Mr. Root? My name's Kinsey Millhone. I'm hoping you can answer a few questions about a former employee. You remember Frankie Miracle?"

"What makes you ask? Because if you're working for OSHA or state disability insurance, I want it on record—the injury was fake."

"I'm not here about that. I'm actually a private investigator, doing follow-up on a homicide investigation. This was August of '69. Frankie says he worked for you shortly before that."

He blinked. "How much do you know about ironing?"

"Ironing?"

"My wife's out of town at her mother's until next Monday and I'm supposed to be at my daughter's for supper tonight. I need to iron this shirt, but I don't know how. My wife always sprinkles 'em with water and leaves 'em in a wad, but I never paid attention to what comes next. You show me how to do this and I'll tell you anything you want to know."

I laughed. "Mr. Root, you're in luck. You got a deal."

He handed me the shirt and I followed him through a modest living room to the kitchen at the rear. There were dirty dishes piled in the sink, and the counter was littered with additional glasses, flatware, and plates. On the breakfast table, there was a large broken-rimmed plastic basket piled with freshly laundered clothes. The door to the utility room stood open and Lennie crossed the kitchen to retrieve an ironing board with a floral padded cover and scratched metal legs. When he opened it, the sustained screech of metal on metal sounded like the mating call of an exotic bird. He plugged in the iron. I moved the setting to Cotton and waited for the iron to heat.

"My aunt Gin taught me to do this when I was seven years old, primarily because she hated to do the ironing herself." I licked an index finger and touched it to the hot iron. It made a spatting sound. "Watch this." I took the dampened shirt by the yoke, holding it between my hands, and straightened the puckered seams with one efficient snap.

"That's first?"

"Unless your shirt doesn't have a yoke. Then you

414

start with the collar." I placed the shirt on the ironing board and explained the strategy: the yoke, followed by the collar, then the cuffs, the two sleeves, and finally the body of the garment.

He watched with care until I'd finished the shirt and buttoned it onto a wire hanger. I handed him a second shirt from the basket and had him try his hand. He was slow and a bit clumsy, but he did a credible job for his first time out. He seemed pleased with himself, and I had a brief vision of him whipping through the entire basket of ironing as the afternoon wore on. He turned off the iron, moved the basket aside, and gestured me into a chair.

As soon as we were seated, he said, "Now. What can I tell you about Frankie, aside from the fact he's the biggest punk who ever lived?"

"How long did he work for you?"

"Six months. Drunk most days; incompetent the rest."

"Did you hire him or did your business partner?"

"I don't have a partner."

"I thought your company was called R&R Painting. I figured it was your brother, your son, or your dad."

"No, no. It's just me. I put that other R in there to reassure the public. One-man painting company, people worry you don't have the manpower to get the job done. This way I give the estimate and get the contract signed and then when it turns out it's just me, well, what's it to them. I'm fast, I'm thorough, and I'm meticulous."

"How'd you end up hiring Frankie?"

"Did someone a favor. Biggest mistake I ever made. This fellow knew Frankie's brother and he asked me if I'd give him a job. He'd just gotten out of jail and no one else would take a chance. I wasn't all that crazy about the idea myself, but I'd just taken on a big project and I was desperate for help."

"What year was this?"

"Between Christmas of '68 and the summer of '69. He claimed he had experience but that was a lie. Worst excuse for a helper you ever saw, him and that friend of his. It's people like that give prison a bad name."

"What friend?"

"Clifton. Big guy. Had a funny first name . . ."

"Pudgie."

Lennie pointed at me. "Him."

"I didn't realize Frankie and Pudgie were such buddies back then."

"Were when they worked for me."

That was an unexpected nugget of information. I couldn't wait to tell Stacey, though for the moment I wasn't sure what it meant—if anything. "From what you said earlier, I gather Frankie filed some kind of worker's comp claim. Was he injured on the job?"

"Said he was. Oh, sure. Said he fell off a scaffold, but

he was working by himself and it was bull. I got notice of the claim and next thing I knew, he was back in jail, this time on a murder rap. Is that the homicide you mentioned?"

"This was a second murder—a young girl stabbed to death within days of the first. Her body was dumped in Lompoc, which is where he was arrested. You remember when he left your employment?"

"June. How I know is because Myra's and my twenty-fifth wedding anniversary fell on the fifteenth and he was gone by then."

"How'd he end up in Venice?"

"I heard he got a job in Blythe, doing landscape work—in other words, a grown man cutting grass for minimum wage. He met some sixteen-year-old girl and three weeks later, the two of them got married. He was fired from that job so they moved up to Venice, where he did some painting for a friend."

"Got it."

"That other homicide you mentioned, is he a suspect in that?"

"Let's put it this way. The cops have been taking a long, hard look at him. Unfortunately, at this point, there's no proof he even knew the victim and nothing to link him to the crime itself."

"How'd you end up at my door?"

"A drop cloth at the scene was made by the Diamond

Custom Canvas Company in Quorum. I was over there a while ago looking at their tarps when I remembered mention of a painting contractor on his arrest sheet. He listed you as his employer."

"Nah, he was long gone by then. I was all set to fire his butt if he hadn't quit, which I'm sure he knew. Shortly afterward, the project I was working on went belly-up. It was a bad year for me."

"I don't suppose you'd recognize the drop cloth if you saw it again?"

"Should. I've used the same ones for years. I buy them in Quorum at the hardware store on Main. You have it with you?"

"I wish I did. It's in the property room at the Santa Teresa County Sheriff's Department."

"Well, you might have 'em check for paint spots. During the time Frankie worked for me, the only exterior color we used was something called Desert Sand. I forget the company—Porter most likely, though it might have been Glidden. Get a match on the paint and it might help tie the tarp to him. I'd be willing to testify."

"Thanks. I'm impressed. You've got a good memory."

"Desert Sand turned out to be a bad luck color. Biggest job I ever bid. At least to that point," he said. "I'd've made thousands if the complex hadn't gone in the tank."

I felt a minor jolt in my chest. "Are you by any chance talking about the Tuley-Belle?"

"How'd you hear about that?"

"Ruel McPhee mentioned it earlier today."

"Oh, I know Ruel. I've done many jobs for him over the years."

"Where is this place? I'd like to take a look."

"You passed it on your way in. It's on 78, halfway between here and Quorum. On the west side of the road. From a distance, it looks like a prison. You can't miss it."

TWENTY-ONE

The faded billboard on the side of the road read THE TULEY-BELLE LUXURY CONDOMINIUMS — TOMORROW'S LIVING FOR TODAY. The project had been ambitious, accompanied by hype designed to create a buying frenzy. The banner pasted across one corner of the sign trumpeted ONLY TWO UNITS LEFT UNSOLD! If true, the lawsuits were doubtless still in the courts. I slowed and turned off the highway, following the deteriorating four-lane blacktop that was divided by concrete planting beds as empty as the surrounding landscape. The builders must have intended to create a lavish entrance with lush grass and palm trees lining the parkway, but the project had been abandoned long before the plans were executed. Vegetation was minimal. The flat terrain gave way to foothills stretching upward to form the Palo Verde Mountains. Distances were deceptive, the clear, dry air apparently functioning as an atmospheric zoom lens. The complex, which appeared to be a short quarter mile away, turned out to be closer to a mile and a half.

When I finally pulled into the dirt parking area and cut the engine, the silence enveloped the car like an invisible shield. In the harsh afternoon light, the partially constructed buildings looked as bleak as cliff dwellings. Piles of trash had blown up against the edifices. The surrounding acreage was flat and still. Dolan had told me that despite torrential desert rains, the runoff is usually swift and results in little saturation. Even from the car, I could see numerous deep channels cut into the porous soil, where flash floods had carved runnels, baked now to the hardness of poured concrete.

I got out and slammed the car door. The sound was muffled, as though absorbed by the very air itself. The subdivision was sprawling. Some portions had been completed; others had been framed in and deserted where they stood. Farther out, I could see where a series of foundations had been poured but the slabs remained untouched. There were numerous tire tracks, and I pictured a steady stream of teenagers slipping through the darkness, escaping from the raw night into the relative warmth of insulated walls. Out here, the wind was constant—a strong, whistling presence that whipped my hair across my face. Behind me, sand gusted across the road.

Two hundred feet away, a gaunt gray dog was

SUE GRAFTON

stretched out on its belly, lazily tearing flesh from the carcass of a recent kill. It took me a moment to realize I was looking at a coyote. He regarded me without interest, but he did rise and pick up his prized bone before he trotted off. His coloring was so close to the muted desert hues that he vanished like a wraith.

I turned back to the nearest building and went in. The windows were gone and the doors had been removed from their hinges. The squatters hadn't penetrated far. In what must have been intended as a lobby, mattresses now lined the walls like a hospital ward. Some sported ratty blankets, but most were bare. Cardboard boxes had been carted in and now served as bed tables for an assortment of ashtrays, drug paraphernalia, and empty beer cans. I toured, checking out the pharmaceutical fare. These kids were doing grass, hash, and cocaine, but the addiction of choice was still nicotine, with cigarette butts outnumbering the roaches four to one. A used rubber, draped across the toe of a lone high-top basketball shoe, just about summed it up. I tried to imagine the poor teenaged girls whose introduction to sex took place under such sorry circumstances. Maybe they were too drunk or too stoned to care what they were doing or what was being done to them.

Outside, I heard a racket like a flock of birds lifting

422

into the air. I listened, struggling to identify the noise. It sounded like plastic flapping, as though a dust barrier had torn loose and was being blown by the wind. The rattle was unsettling, like someone shaking open a fresh garbage bag after taking out the trash. I crossed to the nearest doorway and ventured down the corridor, peering in all directions. There was no sign of the errant sheeting, only rooms opening off rooms, filled with merciless sunlight. I stopped, my senses acute. It occurred to me then what I should have realized right away: The Tuley-Belle was the ideal setting for a murder. The cries of the victim wouldn't carry a hundred yards. If the killing took place outside, any blood could be concealed by turning the soil under with a spade. And if the killing took place inside, the floors could be swabbed down and the rags subsequently buried like strange soil amendments.

The Tuley-Belle reminded me of grand and ancient ruins, as though some savage civilization had inexplicably come and gone. Even in broad daylight, I could smell defeat. I knew I was alone. Because of the isolation, anyone approaching by car would be visible for miles. As for vagrants, they might be anywhere on the premises. There were countless places to hide, ways to remain concealed if the necessity should arise. I retraced my steps, trying not to run, scarcely drawing a breath until I'd tucked myself safely in the car. Stacey had to see this.

When I got back to the motel, he was pacing up and down in front of my door. I figured he was ready for another fast-food binge because I couldn't think what else would generate such excitement. The minute he saw me, he scurried to the car. I rolled down my window. He leaned on the sill while he grinned and pointed to his face. "Well, am I glad to see you! I thought you'd never get here. Know what this is? This is me being as happy as I'm ever going to get."

"What's up?"

He stepped back, opening the car door so I could emerge. "Joe Mandel called. The fingerprint techs are working overtime. I told you, it looks like someone made an effort to wipe down the Mustang? Well, it turns out the job wasn't very thorough because the techs picked up two sets of prints: one on the emergency brake, the gas cap, the inner rim of the spare tire, and the outside of the glove compartment. Looks like the driver leaned over to get something out and then pushed it shut. They lifted the second set of latents from a California road map shoved under the front seat."

"They managed to get good prints after all these years?"

Stacey gestured dismissively. "These guys can do anything. It helps that the car's been out of circulation and locked in that shed."

"Whose prints?"

Stacey's expression was pained. "Quit being so pushy and let me tell it my way. They compared both sets of prints with Charisse's, but no luck on that score. It's my theory she was already dead and in the trunk by then. The spare tire had been removed, probably stowed in the backseat to make room for her. Whoever wiped down the car actually did us a favor. All the incidental prints were eliminated and the ones he overlooked were as clear as a bell. Mandel got a pop on the first set within minutes. Guess who? You'll never guess. This is so good."

"Frankie Miracle."

"That's what I said, but I was wrong. Guess again."

"Stacey, if you don't spit it out, I'm going to fall on you and beat you to death."

"Pudgie."

I felt myself blinking. "You think Pudgie was involved?"

Stacey laughed. "I don't know yet, but there's a good possibility. When Mandel first told me, I nearly dropped my teeth. However, if you think about it, it does make sense. When you talked to Pudgie at the jail, he must have started to sweat. He probably assumed the business was forgotten, but eighteen years later, it's coming up again. He couldn't have been sure how much we knew or how close we'd come to establishing his connection. He must have pondered his options and decided it'd be smart to implicate someone else. That's how he knew the little details to seed into the tale. Doesn't mean he killed her, but I think he knows who did."

I said, "He was subtle about it, too. I remember when he mentioned that the body had been wrapped, he was so offhand about it, I thought it was just a minor part of Frankie's jailhouse talk. The same with the fact she'd been stabbed."

"You didn't mention it yourself?"

"Of course not. He was fishing for information, but I never gave him that. No wonder he was so worried about word getting back. Frankie'd go berserk if he thought Pudgie pointed a finger at him. I take it the second set of prints wasn't Frankie's."

"Nah, what a pisser. I felt bad about that."

"Me, too. I just talked to the painting contractor, a guy named Lennie Root. He says Frankie and Pudgie both worked for him in early '69. After six months, Frankie quit—this was approximately mid-June. Apparently, after that, he worked in Blythe for three weeks. That's where he met and married Iona Mathis."

"What about Pudgie? Where was he?"

"Don't know, but I can go back and ask. I was focusing on Frankie."

"So Root puts him in Quorum at the same time as Charisse?"

"Not Quorum, but Blythe, which is close enough," I said. "By the end of July when she disappeared, Frankie'd moved to Venice, a five-hour drive. Here I was, just about to swing over to your view, thinking Frankie's our guy, and now Pudgie surfaces, so there goes that."

"Not necessarily. They could've been in it together. Pudgie told you they didn't know each other, but that was clearly horseshit."

"Yeah, right. Pudgie knew Iona, so why wouldn't he know Frankie? She could have introduced them," I said. "Or maybe it was the other way around and Pudgie was the one who introduced Iona to Frank."

"Well, it doesn't make much difference since the second set of prints wasn't his. Personally, I hate to see him off the hook for this."

"Well, someone was in the Mustang with Pudgie. Iona maybe?"

Stacey frowned, scratching at the underside of his chin. "Well now, wait a minute. Hold on. That's a leap we can't make. We're putting Pudgie in the Mustang when the girl was killed, but the prints might have been sequential instead of simultaneous. Did Pudgie know the McPhees?"

"If he stole the car it wouldn't matter if he knew them or not."

SUE GRAFTON

"Problem is, if Pudgie knew Cornell or any one of them, he might've had legitimate access to the vehicle. The car came back in poor condition. Ruel might have asked him to move it into the shed or hose it down. Or he and Cornell might have gone out to the shed to sneak a smoke. There could be all kinds of explanations for his prints being there."

I said, "Assuming they knew each other."

"Right."

I thought about that briefly. "Pudgie did grow up in Creosote, which is only sixteen miles south. I think it's down below Hazelwood Springs."

"That's my point."

"But even if they knew each other, it still could've been Pudgie who stole the Mustang. When he was arrested in Lompoc, he was thumbing a ride. He could have stolen the car, driven it to Lompoc, dumped the body, and pushed the car into that ravine."

"Why don't we ask him? You said his sister brought him down here after he got out of jail. You have an address for her?"

"No, but we can probably get one."

We picked up Pudgie's home address from the administrator at the Santa Teresa county jail. We decided to take the rental car since Dolan's smelled like cigarette

428

smoke. Driving south on Highway 78, I pointed out the Tuley-Belle, telling Stacey what I'd seen. As I'd predicted, he was interested in seeing it and we decided to stop off as soon as time allowed.

Creosote wasn't as big as Quorum, but it was ten times larger than Hazelwood Springs, which we passed through en route. The sign said POP. 3,435, but the Chamber of Commerce might have been inflating the facts. Given its close proximity to the Arizona state line, the town had opted for a Western look and resembled nothing so much as a cheap movie set where, at any moment, a cowboy might be shot and sail, tumbling, from the roof of the saloon. The commercial properties on the narrow main street were all wood frame, two- and three-story structures built side by side, with tall, fake facades, steep outside wooden stairs, and plank walkways between buildings instead of the usual sidewalks. It might have been an actual mining town or it might be masquerading as a place with a more interesting history than it had.

Stacey'd donned his red knit watch cap, claiming his head was cold. I suspected he was suffering a rare moment of vanity, but I could have been wrong. Pudgie's sister's house was on A Street near the corner of Third, a small, square box set on a square patch of lawn. Three concrete steps led to a small porch. From inside, we could hear a vacuum cleaner droning away.

Stacey rapped smartly to no particular effect. He knocked again, and this time we could hear the vacuum cleaner being turned off. Felicia Clifton opened the door, barefoot, dressed in jeans and a T-shirt, with a dust rag hanging from a belt loop. She was a tall, big-boned redhead with a blue bandanna tied around her head, Cinderella-style. Her eye makeup was dramatic. Both her upper and lower lids were lined with kohl. A fringe of false lashes set off the blue of her eyes. "Yes?"

"We're looking for Felicia Clifton. Is that you?"

"Yes."

"I'm Stacey Oliphant, with the Santa Teresa Sheriff's Department, and this is Kinsey Millhone . . ."

Felicia closed her eyes. "If this is about Cedric, I'll kill myself. I swear to god, I will."

"He's not in trouble, Ms. Clifton—at least as far as I know—but we'd like to have a word with him if he's here."

"Well, he's not. He went out late last night or first thing this morning. I'm really not sure which. He didn't even leave a note about where he was going or when he'd be back."

"Would you mind if we stepped into the house?"

Felicia hesitated, scanning the street as though the neighbors might be peering through their curtains at us. "I guess I can't have you standing in the yard."

We found ourselves stepping directly into the living

room, which was probably ten feet by ten. We could see the kitchen from where we stood, and I was guessing the rest of the house consisted of two small bedrooms with a bath between. The air was scented with cleaning products. I could see where she'd swabbed a wet mop across the kitchen floor, leaving residual streaks of Pine-Sol. I picked up whiffs of Pledge furniture polish, Comet, Lysol toilet bowl cleaner, and perhaps a soup-çon of household bleach.

"Have a seat," she said.

Stacey settled on the couch while I chose a bright yellow molded-plastic chair to his left. Felicia couldn't quite settle down, and I wondered if she cleaned to calm her anxieties, as I sometimes did. She'd worked hard to make the place attractive though the furnishings seemed to be an odd assortment of seconds, thrift shop finds, and discount sales.

"What sort of work do you do?" Stacey said, trying to strike a friendly tone.

"I manage a dry-cleaning establishment. My whole life's about that—cleaning up other people's messes."

Stacey said, "I imagine Cedric's been a problem."

"Oh, go ahead and call him Pudgie. Everybody else does. I don't know why I insist on 'Cedric.' It's ridiculous given the sort of person he is." She perched on a plastic chair that was a mate to mine. She reached out and straightened a stack of magazines, then idly took out her dust rag and ran it around the table, picking up unseen particles of dust.

Stacey cleared his throat. "Is it just the two of you?"

"Just us. He's been a source of aggravation as long as I remember. Our parents split when he was only eighteen months old. Mom ran off with this guy who sold galvanized pipe. Daddy drank himself to death a little over two years ago. I was eight when my brother was born. Daddy was useless by then so I raised him myself. You can imagine how that went."

"Tough job at that age."

"You can say that again. I must not've done too good a job because Cedric's been in trouble since he was nine. I know I should quit coming to his rescue, bailing him out, trying to get him on his feet again. It doesn't do any good. His only talent is avoiding work; plus he sometimes steals cars."

I said, "What's he been doing since he got out of jail?"

"Same thing he always does. Drinks, smokes, borrows money from me, and lies around on his butt. Occasionally he helps out, but only if I scream loud enough. Then he'll sometimes do dishes or he'll grocery shop. I guess I've been waiting for the other shoe to drop."

"Has he been looking for work?"

"Says he has, but in this town, there isn't much to

do. There's an opening at the Dairy Queen, but he thinks that's beneath him. I don't know where he got that. He's down so low, there's nothing under him as far as I can see. It's only a matter of time before he blows it again. I don't get how that works. Every time a guy screws up, there's always some gal around to feel sorry for him. In this case, it's me."

"I know one of those," I said, thinking of Iona.

"It's guilt," Stacey said.

"Is that it? Well, I guess. He always seems so sincere. Every time I look at him, I see him at nine. He got caught when he stole two silver picture frames from a neighbor lady across the street. What in hell did he want with two silver picture frames? Then he cried like a baby and swore up and down he'd never do it again."

"How long did that last?"

"About a month. I forget what he stole next—something equally useless. I can lecture him all I like; scream and yell. He knows exactly what to say to reel me in again. He's not dumb by any stretch, but he's lazy as all get out. He does whatever works in the moment without a thought in his head about the consequence. I'm sorry, I don't know how I got off on that. You want me to have him call you when he gets back?"

"If you would, that'd be great," Stacey said, taking out a ballpoint pen. "You have a piece of paper? I can give you the number."

"You can write it on the cover of that *Cosmopolitan*. I never throw those out."

Stacey jotted down the name of our motel, the number, and our two room numbers on the cover of the magazine.

"You might write your names down so I don't forget," she said, meaning that she already had.

Stacey scribbled our names, then clicked his pen and tucked it away. "When he goes out, do you have any idea where? We'll be happy to scout around and see if we can find him ourselves."

"There's a tavern—just a little hole-in-the-wall—over on Vine. You might try there. I can't think where else he might be, unless he drove into Blythe."

"Who's he hang out with?"

"No one that I know. He's been in jail so many times, he doesn't have many friends left. He did get a couple of phone calls Thursday night. The first, I don't know about. He took that himself. The second time I answered and it turned out to be a woman he dated years ago . . ."

"Not Iona Mathis," I said.

"That's exactly who. You know her?"

"I met her a few days ago."

"She's nice. I like her. Too bad he didn't end up with her. I hear she married someone else."

"Why'd she call him?"

"I don't know, but she must have been pissed because I heard him backpedaling like crazy, swearing up and down he didn't do whatever it was she was so aggravated about. Then some guy got on the line and it started all over again."

"Frankie Miracle?"

"Could be. I think so. I wasn't paying that close attention. Phone's in the kitchen. The call came during my favorite TV show, so after a few minutes of his yammering, I got up and shut the door."

"After the call, he didn't say anything about going out last night?"

"No, but then it's not like he tells me half of what he does."

"You think he might have gone off to meet Iona?"

"Oh god, no. I sincerely hope not. As mad as she was? He'd be smart to keep his distance."

"I don't like the sound of that," I said when Stacey and I were in the car again. "Why don't you find a gas station and we'll see if there's a pay phone."

"Who're you going to call?"

"Annette up in Peaches. Iona's mom."

There were two gas stations on the main drag; a Chevron at the corner of First and Vine and an Arco station at the corner of Hollywood and Vine. Somebody had a sense of humor here, at any rate. Stacey pulled in at the Arco. The two of us emptied our pockets and came up with a handful of change. He waited in the car while I dialed Directory Assistance and got the number for the Moonlight Café. Within minutes, I had Annette on the other end of the line.

"Hi, Annette. This is Kinsey Millhone. Lieutenant Dolan and I . . ."

"I remember you," she said. "How's that lieutenant? I forget his first name . . ."

"Conrad. People call him Con. As a matter of fact, he had a heart attack yesterday. He's in the hospital in Quorum."

"Well, forevermore. I'm so sorry to hear that. The poor man. How's he doing?"

"Well, he's got good doctors and they seem to think he'll be okay."

"Thank goodness. You tell him I intend to keep him in my prayers."

"I'll do that. In the meantime, I have a question for Iona. Is she working today?"

"Honey, don't I wish. She left Peaches shortly after you did and drove straight to Santa Teresa. She called later that same day to say she was at Frank's. I can't believe my own flesh and blood's so dumb. I told her to stay away from him, but would she listen? Of course not."

"How'd that happen? Last I heard he didn't even know where she was."

"Baby, that was daydreaming on my part. Now I find out she was in touch with him the whole time he was in prison. They're on the phone with each other just about every day."

"What sent her running to him?"

"You don't know how protective she is where he's concerned. She's worse than a mama bear. She's sure he didn't have anything to do with that other poor girl's death—you know, the one you were here asking about? If he did, she'd be first in line volunteering an alibi for him."

"Could she do that?"

"Do what?"

"Provide him an alibi for the two days after Cathy Lee's death? She was awfully vague on that score."

"Iona's convinced there's an explanation, but so far I haven't heard a word of it. I think that's why she went, to find out where he was for that two days. I know she was fretting about the quarry where the girl was dumped."

I held the receiver out and squinted at the mouth-piece. "Why would Iona fret about that?"

"Oh, she knows the place well. She used to play there as a kid. She has a couple cousins—this is my sister's two kids. Iona stayed with them every summer for two weeks. They'd ride their bikes over to the quarry and have rock fights."

"In Lompoc?"

"What did I just get through saying to you?"

"Why didn't you tell Lieutenant Dolan?"

"I must not've been thinking or I'd have spoken right up."

"Are you sure it's the same one? There must be others in the area."

"I guess that's what Iona's trying to find out."

"Did she mention Pudgie at all?"

"In regard to what?"

"I'm wondering if she said anything to Frankie about him?"

"Well, she must have. You know Pudgie and Frankie were in jail together right around that same time. If anybody pointed a finger, it almost had to be him. She figures Pudgie threw Frankie's name in the hat, hoping to make some kind of deal for himself."

"Oh geez, that's not true. There wasn't any deal," I said. "Look, do me a favor. If she gets in touch, will you have her call me? I'm in Quorum at the Ocean View Motel, room 125."

"I don't expect to hear from her, but if I do, I'll be happy to tell her. Of course, you're closer to her than I am."

"Excuse me?"

"Well, hon, she's in Creosote. I told you that. After she left Santa Teresa, she went looking for Pudgie to see if she could straighten this out."

"Did Frankie come with her?"

"Lord, I don't know. I hope not. She never said."

I didn't actually groan, but I probably should have. "Let's don't worry about that now. Thanks, Annette. You've been a big help."

"Honey, you tell Lieutenant Dolan I'm sending him a big old sloppy kiss."

"I'll do that. Just please have Iona call me if you hear from her. You don't know where she's staying?"

"Of course not. I'd have said if I did."

"Great. I thought I better check in case I missed that part."

TWENTY-TWO

We cruised Vine, which was the main street of Creosote and all of ten blocks long. There was only the one tavern, done up in the ubiquitous Western theme. We parked and went in, pausing to get our bearings: low ceilings supported by heavy beams, a wooden floor dense with sawdust, rough-hewn log walls chunked with stucco or its equivalent. There was a long, polished mahogany bar with the requisite brass foot railing, eight tables with captain's chairs, and a Foosball table. The place was deserted, so it didn't take long to figure out that Pudgie wasn't there. At one end of the bar, there was an old Orange Julius machine with a perpetual fountain of juice laving the square, glass tank. Behind the bar, there was a rotisserie where old-fashioned hotdogs on skewers circled past a heat source, throwing off an irresistible cheap scent.

Stacey and I made a beeline for the bartender, ordering and consuming two hot dogs each, decorated with a

440

squiggle of mustard, and piled high with a nasty sweet pickle relish and onions minced so fine our eyes were watering. Neither of us said a word until the last bite of bun had been munched and swallowed. I was gratified to hear Stacey making the same low whimpering sounds that accompanied most of my meals.

He chased his lunch down with a Coke and then used a paper napkin to scrub his mouth and fingers. "I'll be burping weenies for the rest of the day, but it's worth it. Don't know how I worked up such an appetite."

"Well Stacey, we haven't eaten since noon and it's after three o'clock."

"Can I get you anything else?" The bartender was a man in his late fifties, with an egg-shaped face, balding head, and a gap between his two front teeth.

Stacey said, "We're looking for Pudgie Clifton. His sister, Felicia, thought he might be here."

"Haven't seen him today. He usually shows up at eleven when we open the place. He'll be in later. Happy Hour for sure. He never misses a chance to get his two for one."

"When he comes in, would you have him get in touch with us? We're out running around, but he can reach us later at the Ocean View Motel in Quorum." Stacey made a note on a paper napkin, which the bartender set on the ledge of liquor bottles behind him. I waited while

441

Stacey paid for lunch (my second, his third) and then we returned to the car.

Heading north again on Highway 78, I pointed out the hazy outlines of the Tuley-Belle in the distance, off to the left. "You want to do the tour now or come back?"

"No time like the present."

Stacey turned into the paved four-lane entrance, noting as I had its deteriorating state. We drove the mile and a half, the desert stretching out on every side of us. When we reached the complex, he parked and we got out. It was still afternoon, and the sun overhead was like a pitiless spotlight, revealing every crack and flaw in the abandoned site. Somehow in my memory, I'd tidied it up a bit, forgetting the garbage and blowing sand, the gaping windows and ruts in the surrounding dirt parking area. I sensed movement and shifted my gaze. I reached out and put a hand on Stacey's arm and both of us stood stock still. Two coyotes had appeared at a trot. Both were pale gray and scrawny, bony-legged, taller than the average German shepherd, but with the same prominent ears. The first coyote stopped and regarded us with a certain leisurely arrogance. These were desert coyotes, smaller than the ones we saw in Santa Teresa. There, when the drought years eliminated small rodents and ground game, coyote packs were forced down out of the foothills into urban neighborhoods. I'd heard them calling to one another, chilling, high-pitched yelps, when they'd cornered their quarry and were closing in on the kill. I'd seen countless handmade signs stapled to telephone poles, usually displaying photographs and phone numbers, offering plaintive appeals for the return of "lost" cats and small dogs. I knew where they were. In dawn light, in my travels around town, I'd spotted the occasional lone coyote crossing the road with a bundle in its jaws. Out here in the desert, where the heat was extreme and even less rain fell, coyotes ate anything: lizards, insects, carrion, snakes.

The second coyote had trotted on, but now circled back to the first. This must have been the female of the pair, her sides rounded by a litter of pups. The two animals stared up at us with an eerie intelligence. I was aware of their cold yellow eyes and the fathomless round, black pupils. I had no sense that they feared us. This was their territory, sparse and untamed, and their survival rates would always be better than ours out here. Stacey clapped his hands and the two continued on to the road at the same unhurried pace. He turned and watched them, as I did, until they disappeared from view.

The wind picked up. Despite the sun and even in my bomber jacket, I found myself huddled against the cold. "Let's go inside before I freeze to death."

We wandered the empty corridors. With Stacey close by, I was willing to venture farther afield. We explored together at first and then separated. While he inspected the partially completed condominium next door, I stumbled across an unfinished wood staircase and picked my way carefully to the second floor. I crossed to a wide, frameless window and looked out at the land; mile after mile of scrub dotted with tumbleweeds. Again, the sound of rapidly flapping plastic. I leaned out, peering to my right. At ground level, I could see a cloudy corner of the sheeting dance forward and back from beneath a pile of rocks. Ghost stories originate from such phenomena. I was surprised the locals hadn't already generated legends about the place.

Across the way, Stacey emerged from the adjacent building into full sunlight. He saw me and waved. I returned his wave, watching as he rounded the corner of that building and disappeared again. I left the window and joined him down below.

It was close to 4:00 when we pulled in at the motel. I felt we'd done enough for one day and I voted for a break. Stacey said he'd go back to the hospital and spend time with Dolan. Once he dropped me at the room, I changed into my sweats and Sauconys and went jogging. My last run had been Wednesday, before Dolan and I left town. As this was now Saturday, I thought it was high time I did something in my own behalf. For once I was happy about the chilly desert air. Humidity was low and I managed to do the entire three miles scarcely breaking a sweat.

Back again, I found the message light blinking on the face of my phone. I dialed 6 and the operator told me I had a message from Betty Puckett. I wrote down the name and number, but it took me a beat to remember her—the guidance counselor slash typing teacher at Lockaby Alternative High School. I thought about showering but decided to place the call before I got myself cleaned up.

When she picked up on her end, she was already sounding most annoyed with me. "I'm sorry to be peevish, but I've called you three times and I expected a call back."

"Mrs. Puckett, my apologies, but this is the first and only message I've ever had from you. When did you call before?"

"Twice yesterday afternoon and again first thing this morning."

"It must be the desk clerk. She's terrible with messages and just about everything else. Believe me, I'd have called you if I'd known."

"Well. I suppose these things happen," she said, mollified. "Patsy Marcum called me shortly after you left the office yesterday. I don't think I can help, but Patsy thought I should get in touch."

"We've actually made some progress since I talked to her. It now appears possible our murder victim is a girl named Charisse Quinn. Do you remember her?"

"That name doesn't ring a bell. When was she at Lockaby?"

"This would have been April or May of 1969. She started at Quorum High in March, but she got expelled fairly soon from what I've heard. She must have transferred to Lockaby close to the end of the school year."

"I was afraid you'd say that. I was out during that period on medical leave. I know because I went back through my records and checked my calendar for that year. Otherwise, I'd have done the intake interview."

"So you didn't meet with her."

"I didn't. I wish I could help."

"I do, too. We've been hearing a lot about her, but most of it's derogatory. I was hoping to get something more objective from you."

"Sorry to disappoint. Was the family local?"

"Not as far as I know." I took a moment to explain the situation with Medora Sanders and her fostering of Charisse.

"I do know the Sanders, or I should say I did. I'm not familiar with Medora's current circumstances, but in those days, she had a serious drinking problem."

"How much to you know about Wilbur?"

"Well, I knew him to speak to. We went to the same

church, at least when Medora was sober enough to attend."

"She says he left her mid-June and she hasn't heard from him since. We've been wondering if there's a link between Charisse's disappearance and his."

"Oh, I wouldn't think so. He did run off with someone, but it wasn't her. This was a woman he worked with at Sears."

"How do you know that?"

"Rumors were flying. That's all anybody ever talked about."

"I can't believe Justine and Medora didn't know," I said.

"I guess no one was willing to be the bearer of bad news. I heard just recently—and I forget now who told me—that Wilbur married that woman and he's living in Sacramento under a fictitious name. Sandy Wilburson, or some variation."

"Really. That's interesting, because Medora thinks he's dead."

"To all intents and purposes, he is."

"One more thing while I have you on the line. This is probably a long shot, but I'm wondering if you remember a kid named Cedric Clifton. He's originally from Creosote, but he's been in trouble since he was nine and he might well have ended up at Lockaby."

"Yes, I know Cedric, though it's odd you should ask.

He was a student of ours in 1968, a year before the period you were talking about."

"What's odd about that?"

"Well, you mentioned the Sanders. He dated their daughter. He was older than she—probably nineteen or so to her sixteen."

"Justine and Pudgie Clifton? I don't *think* so. Didn't she date Cornell McPhee?"

"Yes, but she dated Cedric first. The two of them broke up after she started dating Cornell and 'set her cap for him,' as they used to say. They were both in my daughter's class at Quorum."

"Oh for heaven's sake," I said. "What's the deal around here? Everybody knows everybody."

Betty Puckett laughed. "Welcome to Smalltown, America. What else can I tell you about Cedric?"

"Did he ever do time for Grand Theft Auto?"

"Oh, sure. Among other things," she said.

"Such as what?"

"Theft by deception, forgery, bad checks."

"Not violent crime?"

"Not while he was at Lockaby. I have no way of knowing what he's done since then."

"Thanks. You've been a big help. Sorry you had so much trouble getting through to me," I said.

*

I showered and washed my hair, wishing I could rinse off my confusion as easily with the water running down the drain. All the little bits and pieces, the subterranean links. It was like looking for a pattern in the Milky Way. After I was dressed, I sat down at the desk, where I hauled out a pack of index cards and started making notes. Once I'd jotted down everything that seemed relevant, I organized the cards in roughly chronological order, set the Smith-Corona on the desk, and typed up a report. Both Stacey and Dolan were capable of doing the same work and would have done so if pressed, but I was eager to see how the facts would arrange themselves. I could see the connections form and separate, though they made no particular sense: Pudgie working with Frankie; Frankie married to Iona; Pudgie dating Justine before her marriage to Cornell. Iona had grown up in the same town as Pudgie and had hung out with him in her youth. Cornell's sister, Adrianne, had been friends with the murdered girl, always assuming, of course, that Charisse and Jane Doe were one and the same. Then there were Pudgie's fingerprints on the stolen car. Now that was an interesting development. I sat and stared at the cards, thinking about the players.

It occurred to me that in 1969, I was only two years older than these "kids" were then. I'd fumbled my way through high school without once achieving academic excellence. I was never elected to class office, never

played a sport, and never participated in extracurricular
activities. I wasn't a member of the band, the pep squad,
or the chorus. Mostly, I walked around feeling glum
and disenfranchised. I made unremarkable to mediocre
grades, smoked dope, and hung out with other low
sorts, undistinguished and unnoticed. Had I attended
Quorum High School, Pudgie would more likely have
been a friend of mine than Justine or Cornell. While
Cornell was no longer a varsity hero, he was a decent,
hard-working guy with a wife and kids to support.
Justine was a full-time wife and mom; Adrianne now
worked as an administrative assistant in the very high
school she'd attended. And Pudgie was still busy getting
sent to jail. As for me, I was now a (more or less)
respectable, law-abiding citizen who shunned illegal
drugs and refused to place burning objects of any sort
between my lips. I wondered how Charisse had figured
into the grand scheme of things. At least the rest of us
had enjoyed the option of making better choices in later
life than we'd made in our teens. All of her opportunities
had ended in 1969, and one of the decisions she'd made
had been her last.

Once I finished typing the report, I sat and shuffled
the cards, playing the little game I always play. I laid
them out randomly, then like a hand of Solitaire, watching to see how events would look when the chronological order became jumbled. The truth isn't always

immediately apparent, especially when it comes to murder. What appears to be a logical series of incidents might look entirely different when the sequence is turned on its head. The police are always working backward from the homicide itself to events leading up to the fatal blow. Except for random killings, which have become increasingly common these days, murders happen for a reason. There is motive—always motive. In nine cases out of ten, if you know why something happens, you'll know the "who" as well.

I sorted through the cards again just to see if I'd missed anything. Of course, I'd forgotten to go back to Medora and ask why she'd waited a week to file the missing-persons report on Charisse. I placed that card on top of the stack, turning it upside down as a reminder to myself before I secured them with a rubber band. The point was minor and there was probably an explanation, but it was still a question that needed covering.

At 5:00, I tossed the pack of index cards in the drawer on top of the murder book, stacked the pages of my typed report, tucked them in a folder, and drove them to the local print shop, where I had two copies made. On my way back to the motel, driving east on Main Street, I caught a glimpse of Adrianne Richards heading for the local supermarket. She'd just parked her car and was walking from the side lot to the front entrance. I braked, glancing belatedly in the rearview mirror in hopes the car behind me wouldn't climb up my tailpipe. I made a hard left-hand turn to the annoyance of several motorists, one of whom shook his fist at me and mouthed a naughty word. I made a sheepish gesture and blew him a kiss.

I parked and went in. I did a quick walking survey, canvassing the store aisle by aisle. I finally spotted her in the produce section, grocery list between her teeth while she picked through a display of cantaloupes. In her cart, she had a plastic basket of cherry tomatoes, two bunches of green onions, and a cauliflower that looked like a brain wrapped in cellophane.

I said, "Hi. I've been hoping to talk to you, but I didn't know how to get in touch. What's your husband's first name?"

"Peter. We're divorced. He's in Reno."

"Mind if I tag along?"

"Fine with me," she said. She was wearing jeans, tennis shoes, and a twin set of smoky blue cashmere. Her hair was pulled back at the nape of her neck, secured with a barrette. She selected a cantaloupe, sniffed it, and then tucked it in her cart. She moved on, pausing at the dairy case to check the expiration date on a carton of skim milk, which she then placed in her cart. "What can I help you with?"

"Well, I'm curious. When I showed up in the office

at Quorum High, didn't it occur to you I might have been talking about Charisse?"

"Not at all. Why would it? She's been gone for years."

"I heard you were good friends."

"I don't know about 'good' friends. We hung out together some."

"Did she say anything to you about leaving town?"

"I didn't even know she was gone. It's not like I saw her every day."

"But once you figured it out, didn't you worry about her?"

"Not particularly. I figured she could take care of herself."

"Did you ever hear from her again?"

"No, but I didn't expect to. That's not how it was. I was a couple of years younger and we didn't have much in common. I've lost touch with a lot of classmates I was closer to than her. Such is life."

"You don't seem upset about the murder. Doesn't that bother you?"

"Look, I'll be honest. I'm sorry for what happened, but I'm not *sad*. Why would I be? I knew her four months at best."

"Tell me about the friendship, such as it was."

"I don't know what to say. I thought she was funny.

She didn't care what she said and she really didn't care what other people thought. I was feeling rebellious. She did things I didn't have the nerve to do. I was a good girl. She was bad. I guess opposites attract."

We turned left, ambling down an aisle stocked with canned vegetables, dried pasta, white and brown rice, and dried legumes. She picked up a package of lentils.

I said, "Do you know Pudgie Clifton?"

"Sure. He dated Justine."

"How long did they go together?"

"A year or so, less. Personally, I thought he was a bum, but she liked him. Even after they broke up, they stayed friends."

"He seems like an odd choice for her."

"You should have seen the guy I dated. Talk about a misfit."

"Did Pudgie know Cornell?"

"We all knew each other."

"What about Frankie Miracle and Iona Mathis?"

"I've heard the names, but I don't know either one."

"Did Pudgie spend much time at your house?"

She seemed mildly baffled. "A fair amount. What makes you ask?"

"Do you think he could have stolen the Mustang from your father's shop?"

I could see her consider. "It's possible. He stole other cars back then." She moved over to the shelves, choosing a can of tomato sauce and two cans of pork and beans.

"Did you suspect him at the time?"

"It might have crossed my mind."

"Did you ever mention that to your dad?"

"No. I didn't *see* Pudgie do it so why get him in trouble when I didn't know for sure. I figured he was trying to impress Justine."

"Hadn't they broken up by then?"

"Well, yes, but he was hoping to get her back."

"Did she know he took the car?"

"*I* don't even know that. It's just a guess on my part. I don't understand what you're getting at."

"I think he not only stole the car, but drove up to Lompoc with Charisse." I didn't mention "dead in the trunk."

"So what?"

"You never asked him if he knew what happened to her?"

"I'm sure if he'd known something he would have spoken up."

"Didn't anybody seem concerned?"

"Not really. Medora reported her missing so we all assumed the police would take care of it. I'm sorry if that sounds mean."

By now she'd turned onto an aisle lined on both sides with freezer cases: ice creams, frozen pies, pizzas, and bags of frozen vegetables. Adrianne opened a glass door and removed a bag of baby peas.

I studied her with puzzlement. "Why do I have the feeling you know something you're not telling me?"

"I'm sure I know lots of things I haven't told you."

"About Charisse."

"I don't want to make trouble. I told you that before."

"Who would you be making trouble for?"

"I'm speaking in generalities, not about anyone specific."

"Let's hope that's true. Thanks for your time."

She moved on and I remained where I was, watching the efficiency with which she went about her business.

I stopped by the motel. Stacey's car was gone. He hadn't left me a note, so I figured I'd catch him later. I drove on over to Quorum General, where I found Dolan sleeping, his dinner tray pushed to one side. I tiptoed to his bedside and tucked one copy of the report, sealed in a manila envelope, under the edge of the blanket folded at his feet. On my way past the nurses station, I had a quick chat with Ms. Kovach, who told me he was being transferred out of CCU and onto a regular medical floor. I told her to tell him I'd been in and had left him an update at the foot of his bed.

"I'll be sure and tell him," she said.

As I eased out of the parking lot, Stacey was just pulling in. We both rolled down our windows and had a chat, car to car. I passed him the second copy of the notes I'd typed and included a quick account of my conversation with Adrianne, plus the gossip I'd picked up from Betty Puckett regarding Wilbur Sanders's decampment and his subsequent bigamy.

Stacey said, "Sorry to hear Pudgie spent so much time at the McPhees. I hate rooting against the guy, but we could use a break about now."

"So what if he knew them? He still could have stolen the car, don't you think?"

"How're we going to prove it? I thought the prints would turn out to be significant," he said. "Oh, well. I'll ask the boys to get to work on Wilbur. Shouldn't be hard to track him down. Might as well cook his goose while we're at it."

"Yeah, Medora's in bad shape. It'd be nice to see him taking some responsibility. Meanwhile, where were you? I stopped by the motel and you were gone."

"I went over to the sheriff's office and talked to a couple of detectives. They said they'd take a set of elimination prints on the McPhees if I can talk them into it."

"You think they'll agree?"

"I can't think why not. By the way, I want you to go

to the Baptist Church with me. It's Easter and Edna tells me the McPhees will all be there. Two services tomorrow, but I think the nine o'clock's our best bet. Afterward, they're going back to Edna's for a big Sunday dinner. Easter, I bet she does a spiral-cut ham."

"What makes you say that?"

"She's just like my mother. We had ham every Easter, along with yams and green beans. We'll follow them to the house and have a quick chat with them while they're all there together."

"I don't know, Stacey. Maybe you should go alone. I'll only end up irritating Ruel."

"I want you with me. I promise we'll keep it brief."

A car pulled up behind me and the driver gave a quick, polite beep of his horn.

I said, "I'll catch you later at the motel."

"Give me fifteen minutes."

We ate supper in Dolan's room, which Stacey had by now adopted as his own. Both of us sat on the king-size bed, sharing a bucket of franchised fried chicken, mashed potatoes, gravy, and watery corn on the cob. Once we finished, I gathered the chicken bones, empty cartons, and used plasticware and tossed everything in the trash. Stacey wanted me to stay and watch a movie, but I was ready for a break. I'm not accustomed to spending so much time in the company of others. "If you need me, I'll be in my room. Otherwise, I'll see you in the morning."

"Great. I'll knock on your door at eight. That'll give you time to shower and get dressed."

"Oh shoot. I just remembered. The only thing I have with me are blue jeans."

"No problem. We don't have to go in. We can wait in the parking lot and follow them home."

"Why not go straight to the house?"

"What if they change their minds and decide to go out for Sunday lunch? This may be the only chance we have to talk to them together."

"You think she'd give up the chance to cook her big Easter dinner?"

"Probably not, but I want to see the congregation all dressed up," he said. "We used to do that as kids."

"You're not going to let me get out of this, are you?"

He smiled benignly. "Enjoy your evening."

TWENTY-THREE

The phone was ringing as I unlocked my door. I dropped my bag and plucked the handset from the cradle on what must have been the fourth or fifth ring. A woman said, "Is this Kinsey?"

"Sure, who's this?"

"Iona. My mom said you called looking for me."

"Where are you, in Creosote?"

"Peaches. I just got in. What do you want?"

"Did you talk to Pudgie Clifton Thursday night?"

"I might have called him," she said, cautiously. "Why do you ask?"

"Did you make arrangements to see him?"

"Why would I do that? He's a low-life punk."

"His sister said you were pissed at him. What was that about?"

"None of your business. That's between him and me."

"All right. Let's try this one. Your mother tells me

you spent time in Lompoc as a kid. I'm wondering if
you told Pudgie about the quarry up there."

Dead silence.

"You remember telling him about that? I'm talking
about the one where the girl's body was found."

"How would I know where the body was found?"

"Oh come on, Iona. Don't play games with me. I
don't care if you told him. I just want the information."

"I might have."

"You might have, or you did?"

"All right, I did, but that was years ago. I even took
him to see it once when we were out on the road."

"Did you know Charisse Quinn?"

"No."

"Aren't you going to ask who she is?"

"I'm not stupid. I assume she's the dead girl they
found after Cathy Lee was killed. I asked Frankie about
that and he says he had nothing to do with that. He
didn't even know her."

"You know, he's not stupid, either. If he killed the
girl, he's hardly going to tell you."

"Why are you so against him? Can't you give the guy
a break? He hasn't done anything to you."

"This isn't about me, Iona. It's about Charisse. Is
Frankie there by chance? I'd like to talk to him myself."

"He took off Friday morning. He was scheduled to
work Friday night and had to get back."

"Short visit, wasn't it?"

"So what?" she said, annoyed.

"What'd you tell him about Pudgie?"

Another silence, during which I could hear her breathing in my ear.

"Iona?"

"If you must know, I told him Pudgie's a fuckin' snitch. He knew somebody had pointed a finger at him. The minute you mentioned Pudgie, I figured it was him."

"Is that why you were so pissed at him?"

"I'm not the only one. Frankie's pissed about it, too. Pudgie cut a deal for himself by blaming Frankie for what happened to that girl."

I felt a whisper of fear, like a millipede, running down my back. "Where'd you get that?"

"Well, it's true, isn't it?"

"No."

"Yes it is, because Frankie checked it out. He knows this guy at the county jail who's serving thirty days? The guy told him Pudgie had a visitor—this woman private eye, who was asking about the murder—that was you, right?"

"Of course, but Pudgie never made a deal."

"Yes, he did. You know how I know? He got out of jail the very next day. The guy said."

"Because his *sentence* was up. He'd served his time and he was released."

"Nuhn-un. No way. Pudgie went back to his cell block and bragged to everyone. He said you were doing something special for him. Next thing you know, he got out."

"He asked me for cigarettes and I said *no*. That's all it was. There wasn't any *deal*."

"Ha, ha, ha. Tell me another one."

"Would you listen to me? Iona, think about this. I don't have the authority to get him out. How would I do that?"

"That's not what the guy said."

"Well, the *guy* got it wrong. I don't have the power to make a deal with anyone. I'm not a cop. I'm a private citizen just like you."

She said, "Oh."

"Yeah, '*oh*,'" I snapped. "Next time you talk to Frankie, would you set him straight? If he needs to hear it from me, he can call. In the meantime, lay off Pudgie. He didn't do a thing."

Exasperated, I returned the handset to the cradle. All we needed was Frankie Miracle on a rampage. I had to admit I was really splitting hairs on this one. Pudgie had most certainly pointed a finger at Frankie, but not in order to make a deal for himself. He was hoping to divert our attention, which he'd succeeded in doing, but only temporarily. Now that his fingerprints had showed up on the stolen vehicle, the focus had shifted back to him. His attempt to implicate Frankie only made his own behavior the more suspect, so in the end, his scheme backfired. Unfortunately, I didn't credit Frankie with an appreciation of the finer points of finking. To him, a rat was a rat. I checked my notes and picked up the phone again, dialing Felicia Clifton's number in Creosote. I didn't even hear the line ring on her end before she said, "Hello?"

"Felicia? Kinsey Millhone. How are you?"

"Not good. Cedric hasn't come home and I'm worried sick about him."

"He hasn't been gone that long, has he? You said he left the house this morning. That's only a few hours."

"Or he could have gone out last night. All I know is he wasn't here when I got up. Either way, he should have checked in by now. This is not like him."

"Did you call the tavern? The bartender said he was always there for Happy Hour."

"Jerry hasn't seen him either. I don't know where he could have gone."

"Maybe he met a girl and went home with her."

"I don't think so. I didn't give him any money so he didn't even have enough to buy drinks. My car's still here so he has to be on foot. He could have walked to the tavern, but not anywhere else. You've seen this town. We're out here in the middle of nowhere and everything shuts down at six."

"Have you tried the police?"

"I suppose I could do that," she said reluctantly. "I tried the two hospitals—the one in Quorum and the other one in Blythe—but neither has a record of him."

"Well, that's good news, isn't it?"

"I guess."

"Would he skip town without telling you?"

"You mean take off for good? Why would he do that?"

"Ah. He's in a bit of trouble with Frankie Miracle, Iona's ex."

"Shit. Does Pudgie know that?"

"I'm sure he's well aware of it. So maybe he decided to lay low."

"Without any money, where could he go?"

"Good question. Look, why not try the police? Maybe he was picked up. For all you know, he's sitting in jail."

"Trust me, if that was true, he would have hit me up for bail."

"Well, I hope he shows soon, but if he doesn't, let me know. Maybe we can come up with another idea."

"You really think he's okay?"

"I'm sure he's fine, but I agree it's worrisome," I said.

We chatted briefly, trying to boost each other's confidence. Once I hung up, I thought, *Who am I trying to kid?* I couldn't believe Frankie would risk jail time on a charge of assault and battery (or worse), but he wasn't exactly famous for his impulse control. Now that Iona had set him off, who knew what he'd do?

Sunday morning at 8:45, Stacey and I were staked out in the parking lot of the Quorum Baptist Church. It was Easter and most of the women and children we'd seen were decked out in pastel suits and floral dresses, wearing fresh corsages, their hats atremble with artificial flowers. The McPhees pulled into the church parking lot in three separate cars. We'd been there for half an hour, the rental tucked discreetly behind a three-foot hedge. I was still arguing it made more sense to go straight to the house, but I think Stacey preferred the drama of doing it this way. The elder McPhees arrived first. They parked and got out, waiting while Adrianne turned in behind them and parked her car close by. Shortly afterward, Justine and Cornell arrived with their three girls. Dressed in their Sunday best, the eight of them looked like a picture-book family. Edna wore a hat. Ruel's hair was slicked down with gel, and his light-blue suit was only slightly too big. The three girls, in matching outfits, complete with hats and white cotton gloves, bypassed the sanctuary and went into the Sunday School building attached at one end.

Stacey and I remained where we were. Some of the church windows were open, and we were treated to organ music and an assortment of hymns. The sermon itself didn't carry that far. Stacey had bought a copy of the *Palo Verde Valley Times*, and while the service went on, we occupied ourselves with the local news. He said, "What'd you hear from Pudgie?"

"Not a word. I called last night, but Felicia said he hadn't showed. I'll call again this afternoon. With luck, he'll be back and we can talk to him. I'll bet you money he has a story cooked up to explain his prints on the Mustang."

I read the front section and the funnies, and Stacey entertained himself by reading aloud ads for cheap desert real estate. I looked up. "You ought to do it, Stacey. Now that you're a homeless person, you could live down here."

"Too hot. I've been thinking to ask Dolan about moving in with him."

"Hey, I like that. He needs someone to ride herd on his profligate lifestyle."

"I'd have to sneak out for junk food. That's the only thing worries me." With a rattle, Stacey flipped the page, his attention shifting to sports.

"It wouldn't hurt you to cut down."

"Speaking of which, what would you like to try next? Taco Bell, Long John Silver's, or Jack in the Box?"

"I thought we were going to McPhee's."

"I'm talking about later. A fella has to eat."

After the church service ended, we waited until the family headed out, and we followed them to the house. Ruel and Edna turned off a block early. "What's that about? Are they ducking us?" I asked, peering back at them.

"They do that every week—visit a shut-in before Sunday lunch."

"You're too much," I said. "Is there anything you don't know?"

Justine let us in. She and Adrianne were apparently in charge of the kitchen until Edna got home. The house smelled of the baked ham she must have put in the oven before she left for church. I detected whiffs of pineapple and brown sugar and the burnt sugar smell of baking sweet potatoes oozing sap onto the oven floor. Justine's girls had settled at the coffee table in the living room, playing a board game with only minor squabbling. I could see their Easter baskets on the floor where they'd left them. Judging from the bits of crumpled foil, it looked as though the girls had already begun to sample the hollow chocolate bunnies and foil-wrapped chocolate eggs. All three had received bright yellow plush ducks. The dining room table had been set with the good china. The centerpiece was an enormous arrangement of Easter lilies I could smell from where I stood.

Justine proceeded down the hall ahead of us. "We're out here in the kitchen putting the finishing touches on lunch."

"No problem," Stacey said as we followed her.

The kitchen was densely heated, in part by the kettle of green beans simmering on the stove. Of course, I was starving, hoping to get on with this so Stacey and I could hit the junk food circuit. I'd already decided it wasn't my job to help Stacey reform. I'd set him on this path so I might as well keep him company while he stuffed himself.

Adrianne stood at the counter, twisting plastic ice cube trays so the cubes dropped neatly into a big clear-glass pitcher. She passed each empty tray to Cornell, who refilled it after she handed it to him. He delivered the last tray to the freezer and then picked up a dish towel and dried his hands. In the meantime, Justine was setting out salad plates, arranging a lettuce leaf on each. She opened the refrigerator and removed a Tupperware Jell-O mold, which she ran briefly under hot water at the sink. Over her shoulder she said to Stacey, "What did you want?"

"I was hoping your parents would be here so I

wouldn't have to repeat myself. I don't know if Lieutenant Dolan mentioned this, but we're going to need a set of fingerprints from each of you. Detective Bancroft at the Sheriff's Department said she'd look for you first thing tomorrow morning."

Cornell leaned against the counter and crossed his arms. He'd taken off his sport coat and loosened his tie. "What's this about?"

"Elimination purposes. Any one of you might've left prints on the Mustang. This way, if we come up with latents, we'll have something to compare 'em to. Saves time and aggravation."

"We're supposed to get inked and rolled like a bunch of criminals?" Cornell asked.

"Well, no sir. Not at all. This is strictly routine, but it's a big help to us. Lieutenant Dolan would have told you himself, but he ended up at Quorum General. I suppose you heard about that."

Cornell wasn't to be distracted by Dolan's medical woes. "What if we say no?"

"I can't think why you would. It's common practice."

"Well, it's not common for me."

Adrianne looked at him. "Oh, just do it, Cornell. Why are you kicking up a fuss?"

"He's not *kicking up a fuss*," Justine said. "He's asking why we have to agree to this crap."

"I wouldn't go so far as to call it 'crap,'" Stacey said. "Left up to me, I'd let the matter slide, but Dolan seems to think it's a good idea. He's the boss on this one. Only takes a couple minutes and the place can't be any more than ten blocks away. If you want, I'll drive you over and bring you back when you're done."

"It isn't that," Cornell said.

"Then what?" Adrianne said. "Why are you acting like this?"

"I wasn't talking to you. I want your opinion, I can ask."

"Excuse the heck out of me."

"Look, I'll go down there, okay? I just don't like being told what to do."

Stacey said, "Tell you what. I've got an inkless pad in the car. Inked prints are superior, but I can see your point. We can take care of it right now if you'd prefer."

"Skip it. I'll go. It just bugs me, that's all."

"We appreciate that. I'll tell the detective the family's coming in."

"Wait a minute. Mom and Dad have to go, too?"

"Since the vehicle belongs to your dad, it wouldn't be unusual to find his prints on it. It's the same with your mom. No point in chasing our tails if there's an obvious explanation."

"Oh, for Pete's sake," Cornell said. He tossed the

dish towel on the counter and went out the back door, letting it bang shut behind him. I'd have bet serious money he'd be lighting a cigarette to calm himself.

His sister stared after him. "What's his problem?"

"Just drop it. He's in a bad mood," Justine said.

Adrianne caught my eye briefly and then looked away.

Stacey and I went to Long John Silver's for lunch, this time swooning over crisp-fried fish and chips doused in puckery vinegar the color of iced tea. Afterward, we stopped by Quorum General to visit Dolan. I hadn't seen him since Friday night and I was amazed at his progress. He was out wandering the hall, wearing a pair of paper slippers and a light cotton robe over his hospital gown. He was freshly showered and shaved, his hair still damp and neatly combed to one side.

As soon as he saw us he said, "Let's use the waiting room at the end of the hall. I'm sick of being cooped up."

I said, "You look great."

"I'm lobbying the doc to let me out of here." Dolan seemed to shuffle, but it may have been the only way to keep the slippers on his feet.

"What's the deal at this point?"

"Possibly tomorrow. I'm supposed to start cardiac

rehab and he thinks I'm better off doing that on home turf," he said. "Joe Mandel called me this morning with good news. They picked up the guy on that triple homicide."

Stacey said, "Good dang deal. Now they can concentrate on us."

We had the waiting room to ourselves. Up in one corner, a wall-mounted color TV was tuned to an evangelist, the sound turned down low. There was a white-robed choir behind him and I watched the vigor with which they sang. Lieutenant Dolan seemed restless, but I thought it was probably the lack of cigarettes. For him, work and the act of smoking were so closely connected it was hard to do one without the other. We chatted about the case. None of us ever tired of rehashing the facts, though there was nothing new to add.

He said, "Right now, Pudgie's our priority. Time to lean on that guy."

"Waste of time," Stacey said. "He's an old family friend. His prints are easy to explain. Might be bullshit, but nothing we can prove either way."

We moved on to idle chitchat until Dolan's energy began to flag. We parted company soon afterward.

Stacey and I spent the remainder of Sunday afternoon in our separate rooms. I don't know how he occupied his time. I read my book, napped, and trimmed my hair with my trusty pair of nail scissors. At 6:00, we went out for another round of junk food, this time Taco Bell. I was beginning to crave alfalfa sprouts and carrot juice; anything without additives, preservatives, or grease. On the other hand, the color had returned to Stacey's cheeks and I'd have been willing to swear he'd gained a pound or two since he arrived.

Dolan was released from the hospital late Monday afternoon just as the dinner trays were coming out. Stacey and I arrived on the floor at 5:00 and waited with patience while Dolan's doctor reviewed his chart and lectured him at length about the importance of staying off cigarettes, eating properly, and initiating a program of moderate exercise. By the time we saw him, he was dressed in street clothes and eager to be gone.

We tucked him in the front seat of Stacey's rental car while I climbed in the back. He carried a manila envelope with copies of the ER report, his EKGs, and his record of treatment. As Stacey turned the key in the ignition, Dolan said, "Bunch of bunk. They exaggerate this stuff, trying to keep you in line. I don't see what's so bad about an occasional smoke."

"Don't start on that. You do what they say."

"How about I'll be as compliant as you were? As I remember it, you did what suited you and to hell with them."

Stacey turned off the key and threw his hands up. "That's it. We're going right back upstairs and talk to the doctor."

"What's the matter with you? I said I'd do as I'm told . . . in the main. Now start the car and let's go. I'm not supposed to be upset. It says so right here," he said, rattling his envelope.

"Does not. I read that myself."

"You read my *medical* records?"

"Sure. The chart was in the slot on your door. I knew you'd lie about things."

I leaned forward, resting my arms on the front seat between them. "Guys, if you two are going to bicker, I'll get out and walk."

All three of us were silent while they thought about that.

Finally, Dolan said, "Oh, all right. This is making my blood pressure go up."

At the Quorum Inn over dinner, Dolan's mood improved and the tension between them eased. Dolan made a pious display of ordering broiled fish with lemon, steamed vegetables, a plain green salad, and a glass of red wine, which he swore he was allowed. After our day of junk food, Stacey and I both ate broiled chicken, salad, and the same steamed vegetables. We all pretended to enjoy the dinner more than we did. By the time our decaf coffee arrived, it was clear we'd run out of conversation. In the morning, Stacey would drive Dolan back to Santa Teresa in the rental car, leaving Dolan's for me. The case had sailed into one of those inevitable calms. We were waiting for paperwork, waiting for test results, waiting for comparison prints; in short, waiting for a break that might never come. I probably should have headed home at the same time they did. I'd certainly join them in a day or two, if nothing further developed.

I said, "In the meantime, what's left? I don't want to sit here idle."

Dolan said, "Just don't get in trouble."

"How could I do that? There's nothing going on."

Tuesday morning, I saw them off at 8:00, giving a final wave as Stacey turned out of the parking lot. I went back to my room, feeling a mild depression mixed with relief at being on my own again. I usually experienced a similar reaction after Robert Dietz had been with me and finally hit the road. It's hard to be the one left behind. If I were home, I'd clean house, but in the confines of the motel, I couldn't even do that. I gathered my wee pile of laundry, rooted in the bottom of my bag for loose change, and walked to the Laundromat half a block away. There's no activity more profoundly boring than sitting in a Laundromat, waiting for the washer and dryer to click through their cycles from beginning to end. If you dared leave your clothes, thinking to return later when the load was done, someone would steal them or pull them out of the machines and leave them in a heap. I sat and did surveillance on my own underwear. It beat doing a records search, but not by much.

TWENTY-FOUR

I hadn't been back from the Laundromat for more than ten minutes when I heard a knock on my door. I peered through the fisheye and saw Felicia Clifton standing outside, staring off across the parking lot. I opened the door. The face she turned to me was pale and undefined, free of makeup. Her eyes, without the black liner and false lashes, were actually prettier, though not nearly as large or as vivid. She wore jeans, a sweatshirt, and running shoes without socks, as though she'd dressed in haste. Her red hair was pulled back in a jumbled ponytail.

"This is a pleasant surprise. Come in."

She stepped in, reaching out a hand to steady herself. At first I thought she was drunk, but I realized within seconds, she was shaken and upset. "Felicia, what's wrong? Is it Pudgie?"

She nodded mutely. I moved her to one side and closed the door after her, saying, "Hey, you're safe. You're fine. Take your time."

She sank onto the desk chair, putting her head between her knees as though on the verge of passing out.

So far, I didn't like the way the conversation was shaping up. I went into the bathroom and grabbed a washcloth. I rung it out with cold water and carried it back to her. She took it and pressed it to her face. She made a sound that was half-sigh and half-moan.

I sat down at the foot of the king-size bed, almost knee to knee with her. "Is he all right?" From the way she was behaving, I suspected he was dead, but I was unwilling to voice that possibility until she did.

"They called at seven. They think it's him. They need someone to look, but I can't."

"What happened?"

"I don't know. They told me to come in."

"Where, the Sheriff's Department downtown?"

She nodded. "This is bad. He's been gone for days. If he was hurt, they wouldn't ask me to come in, would they? They'd tell me where he was."

"You don't know that for sure. Did they call you at work?"

"I was still at home. I don't start until eight. I was having a cup of coffee in my robe when the phone rang. I don't even know how I got here. I remember getting in the car, but I don't remember the drive."

"We'll go. Leave your car where it is and we'll take

mine. Just let me grab my things. In the meantime, breathe."

I breathed in and out for her, demonstrating the process. I knew her anxiety was such that she'd end up holding her breath. Jacket and bag in hand, I ushered her out and pulled the door shut behind us. She didn't have a purse and her hands were shaking so badly the car keys she carried jingled like a length of chain. I put a hand out to still them. She looked at me in surprise and then stared down at the keys as though she'd never seen them before. She tucked them in her jeans. I opened the passenger door for her, then circled the car and slipped in under the wheel. Once I started the car, I turned the heat on full blast. The day wasn't cold, but she was so tense I knew she'd be feeling chilled. She sat, shoulders hunched, pressing her hands between her knees, while she shook like a dog on the way to the vet's.

The Police Department and Sheriff's Department were housed together in a two-story brick building, which, like everything else in Quorum, was hardly more than seven blocks away. I found parking on the street and went around to the passenger door to help her out. Once she was on her feet, she regained some of her composure. I knew she was still rattled, but something about being in motion helped her assume control. So far, she really hadn't heard any bad news. It was the anticipation that was crushing her.

We went into the station. I had Felicia take a seat on a wooden bench in the corridor while I went into the office. This was strictly no-fuss decor: a counter, plain beige floor tile, gray metal desks, rolling swivel chairs, and government-issue gray filing cabinets. Cables and connecting wires ran in a tangle from the backs of the computers and down behind the desks. A cork bulletin board was littered with memos, notices, and official communications I couldn't read from where I stood. There were also framed color photographs of the Riverside County sheriff, the governor of California, and the president of the United States.

I told the uniformed deputy at the desk who Felicia was and why we were there. He referred me in turn to a Detective Lassiter, who emerged from the inner office to have a chat with me. He was in his forties, clean-shaven, trim, and prematurely gray. He was dressed in civilian clothes, gun and holster visible under his dark gray sport coat. He kept his voice low while he detailed the information he'd received. "We got a call from a woman who lives out on Highway 78, four miles this side of Hazelwood Springs. Are you familiar with the area?"

"I know the section of the road you mean."

"There are coyotes in the hills near her property, so

she leaves her dog inside unless she can be in the yard to keep an eye on him. Yesterday, the trash haulers left the gate open and the dog escaped. He was gone all night and when he came back this morning he was dragging a bone. Actually, an arm. The deputy remembered Felicia's call about Cedric. Most of us know him, but we want someone else to take a look."

"I really only met him once and I'm not sure I'd recognize his *arm*. Unless it's the one with all the tattoos," I added. I had a quick vision of his left arm from the one and only time I'd seen him at the Santa Teresa county jail. On it, he'd had a tattoo of a big-breasted woman with long, flowing black hair. In addition, he had a spiderweb, the sombrero-clad skull, and a pornographic sex act he would have been well advised to have tattooed on his butt.

"We had a warrant out on him for a traffic-related felony—this was 1981. Along with his mug shot we have a description of his tattoos that seems to match."

"Can't you use the hand to roll a set of prints?"

"Most of the fingers have been chewed, but we'll try that as soon as the coroner's done whatever he needs to do."

"Where's the rest of him?"

"That's just it. We don't know."

I stared at him, blinking, startled by the notion that had just popped into my head. "I might."

482

Intuition is odd. After one of those gut-level leaps, you can sometimes go back and trace the trajectory— how this thought or observation and yet another idea have somehow fused at the bottom of your brain to form the insight that suddenly rockets into view. On other occasions, intuition is just that—a flash of information that reaches us without any conscious reasoning. What I remembered was the sound of plastic being flapped by the wind, and a coyote leisurely stripping flesh from what I'd assumed at the time was a recent kill. "I think he's at the Tuley-Belle. The scavengers have been dining on him for days."

Felicia and I sat in the car for an hour on the upwind side of the abandoned complex. By now, the odor of putrefying flesh was unmistakable, as easily identified as the smell of skunk. We waited while the coroner examined the remains. The coyotes must have picked up on the scent of blood within hours, and many of Pudgie's facial features had apparently been ravaged. It was that aspect of his death that seemed to offend even the most cynical of the officers present. Pudgie's troubles with the law had occurred with a frequency that had created something of a bond with many of the deputies. Granted, he was a screwup, but he was never vicious or depraved. He was simply one of those guys for whom crime came more easily than righteous effort.

Eventually, Detective Lassiter came over to the car and asked Felicia if she wanted to see the body. "He's not in good shape, but you're entitled to see him. I don't want you left with any doubts about this."

She glanced at me. "You go. I won't look if it's that bad."

It was.

Pudgie's body had been covered with a length of opaque plastic sheeting, weighted with rocks, and left in a shallow depression out behind the very building I'd toured. Even as I approached the area with Detective Lassiter, I could hear the wind pick up a corner of the plastic and flap it like a rag.

I said, "Where'd the plastic come from?"

"It was tacked across a doorway at the rear of this wing. You can still see the remnants where it was torn from the door frame."

The glimpse I had of the body was sufficient to confirm that it was Pudgie. No surprise on that score. The cause of death was blunt-force trauma: repeated blows to the head that had fractured his skull and left a lot of brain matter exposed.

"What about the murder weapon?"

"We're looking for that now."

There was no immediate estimate as to time of death.

That would wait until the coroner did the postmortem. Felicia had last seen him Friday night between 9:30 and 10:00 when she'd turned off the TV and had gone to bed. He might well have been killed that night, though it was unclear how he got to the Tuley-Belle. Odds were someone had picked him up in Creosote and had driven him out here—probably someone he trusted, or he wouldn't have agreed to go. I wondered how long it had taken the coyotes to arrive, their knives and forks at the ready, bibs tucked under their little hairy chins. The hawks and crows, foxes, and bobcats would have waited their turns. Nature is generous. Pudgie, in death, was a veritable feast.

The area had been secured. Anyone not directly involved was kept at a distance to preclude contamination of the scene. The coroner's van was parked close by. Detective Lassiter had organized the deputies and they'd started a grid search, looking for additional bones and body parts as well as the murder weapon and any evidence the killer might have left behind. Deputy Chilton, whom I'd met at the McPhees', was one of the men combing the surrounding area. Felicia and I sat in Dolan's car. Technically, she wasn't required to be there at all, and I suspect the detective would have preferred that I ferry her home. At the station, while we'd waited, they'd sent a unit out to the Tuley-Belle to check my guess. The deputy had spotted Pudgie's body and called in the report. Felicia had been given a vague accounting, enough to know it was her brother and the condition of his body poor. She'd insisted on coming. He was far beyond rescue, but she kept her vigil nonetheless.

I watched the crime scene activity as if it were a movie I'd already seen. The details sometimes varied, but the plot was always the same. I felt sick at heart. I avoided thinking about the coyotes and the sounds I'd heard on the two occasions I'd been at the Tuley-Belle. There was no doubt in my mind that he was dead by then. I couldn't have saved him, but I might have prevented some of the mauling that came later. The fact that Pudgie was killed here lent support to my suspicion that Charisse had been killed at this location as well.

At 2:00, Detective Lassiter crossed the wide unpaved parking area and again headed in our direction. I got out of the car and went to meet him midway. "They're getting ready to transport the body. You might have Felicia call the mortuary in Quorum. Once the autopsy's done, we'll release the body to them unless she's made other arrangements. You might ask if she has a pastor she wants us to notify."

"Sure. I'll see what she says."

"You're down here with Stacey Oliphant?"

"Right. He and Lieutenant Dolan are on their way back to Santa Teresa. I was scheduled to follow, but under the circumstances, I'll stay."

"We'll operate on the assumption the two murders are related unless we find out otherwise. I imagine Santa Teresa will want to send down a couple of their guys."

"Most certainly," I said. I gave him my summary of what had brought us to Quorum and what we'd learned. Since Stacey had relayed much of the same information, I skimmed across events, only filling in details when I came to something he hadn't heard, Frankie Miracle being prime. I said, "Lieutenant Dolan and I dropped in on his ex-wife in Peaches as we were heading down to the desert. Her name's Iona Mathis."

"We're familiar with her," he said. "She and my niece belong to the same church, or at least they did."

"Yeah, well her mom says she drove to Santa Teresa to see Frankie as soon as we left. I thought he drove back with her, but I'm not sure. She claims he was at work Friday night in Santa Teresa."

"Easy enough to check. You know the company?"

"I don't, but I'm sure Stacey or Dolan will know. You might want to talk to Iona as well. She called Pudgie Thursday night and was really pissed off from what Felicia said." I made a verbal detour, telling him about Iona's belief that Pudgie'd made a deal for himself at Frankie's expense. "Felicia doesn't know if Pudgie went out late Friday night or first thing Saturday morning. She told me a call came in before Iona's, but she has no idea who it was. He answered that one himself."

"I'll talk to Iona soon . . . maybe later today. Where will you be?"

I told him where I was staying. "I'll call the guys as soon as I get back to the motel. This business with Pudgie will be a blow. I'm sure Stacey told you they found his prints on the Mustang. We all assumed he either killed her himself or else knew who did. Now it looks like someone killed him to shut him up."

"The downside of being an accessory," Lassiter said. "Meanwhile, if anything comes up, let us know."

I drove Felicia back to the motel. She was quiet, leaning her head against the seat with her eyes half-closed. She had a tissue in one hand, and I could see her dab at her eyes occasionally. Her lids were swollen and her face was splotchy, her red hair lusterless as though dulled by grief. Whatever weeping she did was silent. Now that she knew the worst, there was something passive in her response, a resignation she must have harbored for years, waiting for the blow.

Finally, I said, "If it's any consolation, people did care about him."

She turned and smiled wanly. "You think? I hope you're right about that. He had a sorry life; in jail more times than he was out. Makes you wonder what it means."

"I've given up trying to figure that out. Just don't blame yourself."

"I do in some ways. I'll always think I could have done a better job with him. Trouble is, I don't know if I was too tough on him or not tough enough."

"Pudgie made his choices. It's not your responsibility."

"You know something? I don't care what he did. He was decent to me. He might have sponged, but he never ripped me off, you know? He's my baby brother and I loved him."

"I know. You belong to a church? I'd be happy to make some calls."

"In a town this size, the word's already out. The minister will probably already be there by the time I get home. I just hope I don't fall apart. This is hard enough."

At the motel, I parked near her car and the two of us got out. I gave her a hug. She clung to me briefly. Then she pulled back, eyes brimming, and wiped her nose on a tissue. "Don't be too nice. It only makes it worse," she said.

"You're okay to drive?"

"I'll be fine."

"I'll call you tomorrow."

"Thanks. I'd appreciate that."

I let myself into my room. The maid had come and gone, so my towels were fresh and my bed had been neatly made. I stretched out, reaching for the phone next to my book on the bed table. Stacey's number was a disconnect. I had to smile at that. Since he'd been convinced he was dying, he probably hadn't worried much about utility bills. I called Dolan's number and left a message, asking one or the other of them to give me a call as soon as they rolled in. It was 3:00 by then and even if they'd stopped for lunch, they should arrive in Santa Teresa within the hour. I didn't dare leave the room, for fear I'd miss their call. I tried reading, but I found myself, not surprisingly, brooding about Pudgie's death. I thought about my conversation with Iona Mathis, wondering how she'd come up with that cock-amamie notion that I'd made a deal with Pudgie to get him out of jail. I hoped her misconceptions hadn't contributed to his death. If so, then I bore a certain responsibility for what had happened to him. The thought made me ill.

I took my shoes off and slid under the covers, pulling the spread over me. I picked up my book and read for a while, hoping to distract myself. I was warm. The room was quiet. I found myself dipping into sleep so that when the phone finally rang, I jumped, snatching up the handset while my heart thumped. The surge of adrenaline peaked and receded. It was Dolan.

I sat up and trailed my feet over the side of the bed, rubbing my face while I suppressed a yawn. "How was the trip? You sound tired."

"I've felt perkier," he said. "Stacey dropped me off half an hour ago. He's taking a run to the Sheriff's Department to talk to Mandel. On his way back, he plans to stop by his apartment and pick up his things. I guess we'll think about dinner after that."

"Is he staying with you?"

"Temporarily. You know the lease is up on his place and he has to be out by the end of the month. He assumed he'd be six feet underground by then, but I guess the gods fooled him. I asked if he wanted to stay here until he finds some place else. I can use the company."

"Nice. That should benefit both of you if you can keep from quarreling."

Dolan had the good grace to laugh. "We don't quarrel. We disagree," he said. "What about things on your end? We felt bad you got stuck holding the proverbial bag. Did you manage to amuse yourself?"

"Funny you should ask." And then I told him about Pudgie's death, which we discussed in detail. In the midst of dissecting events, Dolan said, "Hang on a second. Stacey just came in. I want to tell him about this."

He put his hand across the mouthpiece to spare me the replay while he brought Stacey up to speed. Even in its muffled form, I could hear Stacey's expletives.

He took the handset from Dolan. "That's the last time I'm leaving you. What the hell's going on?"

"You know as much as I do."

He had his own set of questions about Pudgie, and then we chatted about Frankie. He said they'd do what they could to track him down and see if he could account for his whereabouts from Friday morning on. "Good news on this end. Charisse's dental chart is a match for Jane Doe's, so at least we nailed that down. Forensics is just about willing to swear the hairs we recovered belong to her as well. Now all we need is a match on that second set of prints and we may be in business. Have the McPhees gone in?"

"I assume so. I'll check tomorrow morning to make sure," I said. "When are you planning to drive back?"

"Soon as I can. I'll hit the road the minute things here are under control."

I heard Dolan rumbling in the background.

Stacey said, "Oh, right. Dolan left his gun in the trunk of his car. He wants to know if it's still there."

"I haven't had occasion to open the trunk, but I'll look when I can. What's he want me to do with it?"

Dolan said something to Stacey.

"He says just make sure you get it back to him as soon as you get home."

"Of course."

Dolan said something else to him that I couldn't make out.

Stacey said, "Hang on a minute." And to Dolan,

"Damn it! Would you quit talking to me when I'm on the phone with her?"

More mumbling from Dolan.

"Horsepucky. You will not." Stacey returned. "Guy's driving me nuts. He says he'll do fine on his own, but he's full of shit. Minute my back is turned, he'll run out and buy himself a pack of cigarettes. They oughta lock him up."

I heard a door slam in the background.

"Same to you, bub!" Stacey yelled. "Anyway, I'll call and let you know when I'm hitting the road. You can talk to the desk clerk and reserve a room."

After we hung up, I put a call through to Henry. His machine picked up. I left a message, telling him I missed him and that I'd call back. I read for another hour or so and then ordered a pizza. I didn't have the heart to go out and eat a proper meal by myself. Ordinarily, I like eating in a restaurant alone. But with Stacey and Dolan gone, the idea seemed alien. Pudgie's murder had left me spooked. It was one thing dealing with a murder that had happened eighteen years before. Whatever the motivation, time had provided a lengthy cooling-off period. Life had gone on. The killer had managed to strike once and get away with it. I'd assumed there wouldn't be a reason to kill again, but Pudgie's death made it obvious how wrong I was. The stakes were still high. In the intervening years, someone had enjoyed a life that was built on a lie. Now we'd come along threatening the status quo.

I ate my supper and tossed the box in the trash. I watched a couple of television shows with annoying laugh tracks. At 9:00, I decided I might as well work. Keeping a systematic set of notes has its soothing side effects. I sat down at the desk and opened the drawer.

Things had been moved.

I stared and I then looked around the room, wondering if someone had come in. Not *if*. I wondered *who*'d come in and handled the contents of the drawer. The last time I'd taken notes must have been Saturday afternoon. Stacey and I had been to Creosote, stopping off at the Tuley-Belle on the way home. Once at the motel, we'd decided to take a break. I'd had a phone chat with Betty Puckett from Lockaby and then I'd showered, dressed, and started jotting down the tid-bits—events, questions, and conversations. At the end of that session, I'd put a rubber band around my index cards and tossed them in the drawer on top of the murder book. Now they were underneath. It seemed a small matter, but my memory was distinct.

I picked up a pen and used it to lift one corner of the murder book so I could slide the cards out. I held the stack along the edges while I peeled off the rubber band. I'd left the top card upside down as a reminder to myself to have a second chat with Medora Sanders. Now the card was reversed, lined up in the same direction as all the other note cards.

Someone had been in here. Someone had handled the murder book and read my notes.

I got up abruptly, almost as though a shock had been administered through the seat of the chair. I circled the room, carefully scrutinizing every square foot of it. My duffel and the family photo album were in the closet untouched. Except for what was in the drawer, everything else was as I remembered it. Had the maid tidied up? If so, why would she stop and read the index cards? The maid I'd chatted with had barely spoken English. It could have been another employee. There were probably different women who worked weekday and weekend shifts. Maybe the last maid who'd cleaned my room had been curious and had helped herself, thinking I'd never know. I had trouble believing it, but I couldn't prove otherwise.

I rebanded the cards and returned them, using the tip of my pen to push the drawer shut. I didn't think it would occur to anyone that I'd have such a clear recollection of how the contents of the drawer had been left. If it wasn't the maid, then how had entry been effected? The room door was kept locked. I went into the bathroom and pulled a tissue from the box, then moved to the door and used the tissue to turn the knob. I examined the exterior of the door, the escutcheon and the face plate, but there were no gouges or scratches, and no evidence of forced entry. The windows were latched on the inside and showed no indications of tampering.

On the other hand, the means of access could have been simple. While the maid had been cleaning the room on Saturday, she'd left my door propped open with the pile of dirty sheets. She'd had her radio on in the bathroom, music blaring while she cleaned the toilet and the sink. Anyone could have slipped in and searched the desk, which was just inside the door. There wouldn't have been time to read the murder book itself, but the cards were more important. My notes reflected everything I knew about the case and everything I considered relevant. By perusing my notes, someone could figure out where I'd been, who I'd talked to, and what I intended to do. There was an obvious advantage to anticipating my next move. Someone could step in before I'd had the chance to get the information I needed.

I closed the door and went back to the desk. I studied the stack of cards with Medora's name on top. I didn't think she knew anything she hadn't told me before, but it might be smart to check with her. Briefly, I considered calling Detective Lassiter or someone else at the local Sheriff's Department, but what was I supposed to say? My stack of index cards has been moved an inch? Gasp!

I didn't think they'd rush right out and dust for prints. At best, they'd come up with the same suggestion I had, that the maid had opened and closed the drawer in the process of cleaning my room. Big deal. Aside from the rearrangement of my belongings (which they'd have to take my word for), there wasn't any evidence of a break-in. The room hadn't been vandalized and nothing had been stolen, so from their perspective, no crime had been committed.

I grabbed my bag and my bomber jacket, preparing to leave. I was almost out the door when something occurred to me. I retrieved my family album from the closet and then crossed to the desk drawer and removed the murder book and the index cards. I went out, making sure the door was secured behind me. I locked my armload of valuables in the trunk of Dolan's car and then headed for Medora's house. I was heartened by the lingering image of Dolan's Smith & Wesson in the trunk.

TWENTY-FIVE

The night was cold and windy, but the drive was so brief, there wasn't time enough for Dolan's heater to kick in. There was scarcely a building in Quorum more than two stories tall, so there wasn't much protection from the blasts of chill air sweeping in off the desert. The sky was a brittle black and the presence of stars wasn't as comforting as one might hope. Nature has her little ways of reminding us how small and frail we are. Our existence is temporary while hers will go on long after our poor flesh has failed.

I parked in Medora's driveway. The house was dark except for one lamp in the living room. As I crossed the patchy stretch of grass I realized the front door was standing open. I could see the vertical strip of dull light expand and contract as the wind ebbed and flowed. I hesitated and then knocked on the screen door frame. "Medora?"

There was no sound from inside. I opened the screen door and called through the opening. "Medora?"

I didn't like the idea of intruding, but this was odd, especially given my suspicions about an intruder of my own. If someone had read my notes and spotted her name, her house might well be the next stop. I pushed the door open and eased in, closing it behind me. The room was dark except for a small table lamp. I could see Medora on the couch, lying on her back, her hands folded across her chest. I drew closer. She was snoring, her every exhalation infused with the fumes of metabolizing alcohol. If she woke to find me hovering she'd be startled, but I didn't want to leave until I knew she was okay. A half-smoked cigarette, resting on the lip of the ashtray, had burned down to an inch of ash before it had gone out. The ice in her highball glass had long since melted away. Her prescription pill bottles appeared to be full and the caps were in place. At least she hadn't overdosed in any obvious way, though I knew her practice of mixing whiskey with painkillers was dangerous.

The house was cold and I could feel a breeze stirring. I crossed to the kitchen and flipped on the light. The back door stood open, creating a cross-ventilation that had drained all the heat from the rooms. I lifted my head and scanned the silence for any hint of sound. I remained where I was and did a visual survey. The back door was intact—no splintered wood, no shattered framing, and no broken glass. The windows were shut and the latches turned to the locked position. The kitchen counters were crowded with canned goods, boxes of cereal and crackers, packages of paper napkins, toilet tissue, paper towels, and cleaning products. It looked as if the dishes hadn't been done in a week, though all she seemed to eat was cereal and soup. The trash can was overflowing, but aside from the mess, it didn't appear that anything had been disturbed.

I glanced over at Medora, chilled by the notion of how vulnerable she was. Anybody could have walked in, robbed her, assaulted her, killed her where she lay. If a fire had broken out, I doubt she'd have been aware. I closed the back door and locked it. I toured the rest of the house, which comprised no more than one small, dingy bathroom and two small bedrooms. Her housekeeping habits, such as they were, made it impossible to tell if anyone else had been in the rooms doing a quick search.

I returned to the living room and leaned toward her. "Medora, it's Kinsey. Are you all right?"

She didn't stir.

I placed a hand lightly on her arm, saying, "Hey."

Nothing. I shook her gently, but the gesture didn't seem to register. She was submerged in the murky depths of alcohol, where sound couldn't penetrate and no light reached. I shook her again. She made a grunting noise, but otherwise remained unresponsive. I didn't think I should leave her in her present state. I looked for a telephone and finally spotted one in the kitchen, mounted on the wall near the hall door. I searched one drawer after another until I found the phone book. I looked up Justine's number and called her. She answered after four rings.

"Justine? This is Kinsey. I'm really sorry to bother you, but I stopped by your mother's house just now and found both doors standing open. She seems to have passed out. I think she's okay, but I'm having trouble rousing her. Could you come over here? I don't think I should leave her until you've seen for yourself."

"Damnation. Oh, hell. I'll be there as soon as possible."

She hung up abruptly. I was sorry I'd annoyed her, but such is life. I returned to the couch and perched on the edge of the coffee table. I took Medora's hand and slapped it lightly. "Medora, wake up. Can you wake up?"

Groggily, she opened her eyes. At first, she couldn't seem to focus, but she finally coordinated her eyes and looked around the room, disoriented.

"It's me, Kinsey. Can you hear me?"

She mumbled something I couldn't understand.

"Medora, did you take something for the pain? Let's get you up, okay?" I slid an arm under her head, trying to lift her into a sitting position. "I'm going to pull you up here, but I need your help."

She seemed to gather herself, pushing up on one elbow, which enabled me to haul her upright. Her gaze settled on mine with an expression of confusion. "What's happening?"

"I don't know, Medora. You tell me. Let's get you on your feet and take a walk. Can you do that?"

"What for? I'm fine. I don't want to walk."

"Well, sit then and let's talk. I don't want you falling asleep again. Did you take something?"

"A nap."

"I know you took a nap, but your doors were wide open and I was worried about you. Did you take any pills?"

"Earlier."

"How many? Show me what you took, was it this?"

"And the other ones."

I checked the labels on the bottles: Valium, Tylenol with Codeine, Percocet, Xanax. "This is not a good idea. You're not supposed to take all of these at the same time, especially if you've had a drink. It's not safe. Are you feeling okay?"

"Dr. Belker gave me those."

"But you shouldn't take them when you drink. Didn't he explain that?"

"That case I couldn't take 'em at all. I drink every

day." She smiled at my goofiness, having settled that point.

We went on in this fashion, with Medora offering short declarative sentences in response to my continued questions. While it was hardly scintillating conversation, it did serve its intended purpose, which was to keep her in contact with reality. By the time Justine arrived, fifteen minutes later, Medora was more alert and in control of herself.

Justine shed her coat and tossed it on the back of a chair. "Sorry it took so long, but I was waiting for Cornell. I finally called my next-door neighbor and she came over to watch the girls."

Medora had focused on Justine with an air of humility and embarrassment. "I didn't tell her to call you. I wouldn't do that."

Justine sat down beside her mother and took her hand. "How many times have we been through this, Mother? You can't keep doing this. I have a life of my own."

"All I had was one drink and a pain pill."

"I'm sure you did. How many?"

"The usual."

"Never mind. Just skip it. I shouldn't waste my breath. Are you all right?"

"I'm fine. You didn't have to leave the girls and come over."

"She says the doors were wide open. What was that about?"

"I closed them. I did. I remembered what you said."

"Let's just get you into bed. We can talk about this later when you're more yourself."

"I'm myself," she said blearily, as Justine assisted her to her feet. Medora was a bit tottery.

"You need help?"

Justine shook her head, intent on maneuvering her mother around the sharp-cornered coffee table, across the room, and into the short hallway that led to her bedroom. I could hear the two of them murmuring, Medora apologizing while Justine went about the business of getting her to bed.

Five minutes later, Justine returned, rubbing her arms reflexively. "I swear she's getting worse. I don't know what to do with her. Geez, the place is *freezing*."

"It's warmer than it was."

She went over to the thermostat. "It's turned off. What's she doing, trying to save money on the heating bill? No wonder she gets sick. She had pneumonia two months ago." She adjusted the lever and within seconds, I could hear the furnace click on.

She sat down on the couch with a sigh that was laden with irritation. "I can't tell you how many times I've talked to her about this. She takes out the garbage or goes to pick up the newspaper from the drive and then she either locks herself out or forgets to latch the door again. On a windy night like this, the doors bang and blow open. She never even knows."

"I'm not sure that's what happened here, but it's giving me the creeps. Could you take a look around and make sure nothing's missing? Suppose someone's been here."

"Why would anybody bother? There's nothing worth stealing."

"I understand, but I don't like the feel of it. Can you make a quick circuit for my sake?"

"All right. You might as well follow me. This won't take long, but you can see for yourself." She leaned over and picked up the whiskey bottle from the coffee table. "Here."

I took the bottle and waited while she snagged the highball glass and the pill bottles lined up nearby. "Her doctor's out of his mind. I've had this discussion with him a hundred times. They're old friends, so she comes along right after me and talks him into it."

She gave the kitchen a cursory look while she poured her mother's whiskey down the drain. She emptied all the pills into the trash, where I heard them rattling toward the bottom like a cupful of BB's. She tossed in the empty whiskey bottle. "I'll take care of this later," she said, referring to the overflowing trash can and the pile of dishes in the sink. "Things look fine in here. The place is a pigsty, but no more than usual."

I trailed after her while she looked into the bathroom and the second bedroom. The latter must have been her room as a kid, the one she'd been forced to share with Charisse. The twin beds were still in place, but most of the remaining space was taken up with piles of clothing, boxes, and miscellaneous junk. I nearly confided my suspicion about someone having entered my room, but I thought better of it. I didn't have proof and I didn't want to sound completely paranoid. Besides, it would only encourage her to ask questions I didn't want to answer.

As we were returning to the living room, she said, "I heard about Pudgie. It's horrible."

"News travels fast."

"Trust me, everybody knows by now."

"Who told you?"

"Todd Chilton called. He's a deputy—"

"I met him. Why did he call you?"

"Oh, right. He remembered I dated Pudgie and he thought I should know. From what he said, it was gross. At least I got that impression reading between the lines. He says you're the one who figured it out."

"Someone would have noticed before long," I said, thinking about the smell. I filled in a few brush strokes, avoiding anything of substance. I was certain Detective Lassiter would limit the information that reached the public.

"Why'd you stop by?"

"I had a question for your mom. I know this seems minor, but I was curious. The first time I talked to her, she said she'd gone to the police the day Charisse disappeared. But according to the police report, she waited a week. I was hoping she'd explain the discrepancy."

"She didn't tell you about the note?"

"From Charisse? Not that I remember."

"She probably forgot to mention it. Her mind's completely shot from all the crap she takes. The note said she'd decided to go see her mother and she'd be back in three days. We thought she'd show up, but a week passed and Mom started getting worried. That's when she talked to the police."

"You saw the note yourself?"

"Sure. She'd left it on the bed."

"And the handwriting was hers?"

"As far as I could tell."

"Did your mother save it?"

"I doubt it. Why would she do that?"

"Could you ask her please?"

"Right now?"

"I'd appreciate it."

507

She left the living room and returned to her mother's bedroom, where I could hear her insistent questioning and Medora's foggy response. I heard drawers being opened and shut. Moments later, Justine returned. "I don't believe this. She says she saved the note because she didn't want Social Services blaming her when Charisse took off. She thought if they ever asked, she could show the note as proof that Charisse left of her own accord."

"Amazing. That's great. I'd love to see it."

"Well, that's just it. She can't remember where she put it. She thought it was in the chest of drawers, but it's not there now. Knowing her, it could be anywhere. She's such a slob."

"Maybe we can look again when she's on her feet."

Justine gave me a look. "Yeah, right. Listen, I need to get back to the girls. Cornell must be home by now, but just in case. Let me turn off some lights and I'll walk you to your car. It's dark as pitch out there."

I waited while she double-checked, making sure the back door was locked. She turned off the lights, except for one in the hall. She tested the thumb lock on the front door, flipped it to the locked position, and pulled it shut behind her. She took her keys from her coat pocket and crossed the yard to her Ford sedan, which was parked in the driveway behind Dolan's car.

"Did you guys go down and have your fingerprints taken?"

508

"Edna went Monday, but I haven't had a chance. I'll pop in tomorrow while I'm out running errands."

"What about the others?"

"Adrianne said she'd try later in the week."

"What about Ruel and Cornell?"

"Don't look at me. I don't want to be the one to nag them. It's not my job."

"You're right. Thanks anyway. I'll bug them myself."

I drove to the motel with an eye on my rearview mirror. The wide streets were deserted. Businesses were shut down and most of the houses were dark. Once in my room, I spent a few minutes assuring myself everything was exactly as I'd left it. My book was facedown on the bed where I'd placed it, the bedspread still rumpled where I'd pushed it aside. The table lamp was on and the warm light made the room seem cozy. The windows were latched and I made sure the drapes were properly closed. Didn't want any boogermen to peek in at me. After that, I stripped out of my clothes and into the oversize T-shirt I use as a nightie. I washed my face, brushed my teeth, and slid into bed. I thought my paranoia might keep me awake, but since I'm a person of no depth whatever, I fell asleep right away.

At 2:06, the phone rang. I reached for the handset

automatically, noting the time as I placed it against my ear. "What."

"Kinsey?"

"What."

"This is Iona."

"Okay."

"Frankie wants to talk to you."

"About what?"

"Pudgie."

"Put him on."

"In person."

I leaned over and flipped on the table lamp, which made me squint painfully and probably put permanent wrinkles on my face. "Why are you calling me in the dead of night? I'm asleep."

"I would've called earlier, but he just got here."

"Got here where?"

"Quorum. He wants you to meet us at the all-night diner. Know the one I mean? On Main Street. It's called the Chow Hound."

I closed my eyes. "No offense here, but there's no way I'm going out at this hour to talk to Frankie Miracle, so scratch that idea."

"What if he comes there? We're calling from a pay phone. We're not far."

"Like how far?"

"A block."

"Why isn't he on the phone instead of you?"

"He's afraid you'll say no."

I laughed. "He's worried about me? Iona, the guy's a *killer*. He stabbed a woman fourteen times."

"But he's paid for his crime. He went to prison and now he's out."

"Oh, crap. Why am I arguing with you? If you want to come over, I'll open the window and talk to him through the screen. That's as much as I can offer."

"Okay."

I hung up and went into the bathroom to brush my teeth. This was not the kind of hotel that offered complimentary robes (hell, I felt lucky they offered complimentary toilet paper!), so I pulled on a sweatshirt. I thought about it briefly and pulled on my jeans. By then, I could see headlights arc across the drapes. I turned off the lamp and crossed to the window, peering out as Frankie's white pickup pulled into a slot two doors down. Iona was at the wheel. She waited in the truck with the engine running, probably trying to keep warm, while Frankie got out on the passenger side and slammed the door. I said, "Great. Wake everybody up. I'll feel safer that way."

I watched him check room numbers until he got to mine. As soon as he was close, I slid the window open a crack. "Hello, Frankie."

"Hi. Can I come in?"

511

"No."

"Come on. I can't stand around out here. It's fuckin' cold."

"I don't need a weather report. I know it's cold. You want to talk, I'm listening, but get on with it."

"All right," he said, irritably. He paused to light a cigarette. Despite the low-watt outside lighting, I could see him clearly—the brown wavy hair, the smooth baby face. He peered over his shoulder, his manner embarrassed. "I heard about Pudgie. I just wanted you to know I had nothing to do with it."

"Good for you."

"Don't you want to know the rest?"

"Sure."

"The cops have already been around—Lieutenant Dolan and some pal of his. I thought my landlord was talking about you, but he said it was a old guy."

"Stacey Oliphant."

"That's him."

"They're good guys. They're fair. You should be talking to them."

"I hate cops. What pigs. I'd rather talk to you."

"What for? I'm just going to turn around and ask you the same questions Lieutenant Dolan would have asked."

"You want to know where I was Friday night, right?

I was in Santa Teresa, working my regular shift. Eleven to seven. And that's the truth."

"I thought you were down here with Iona."

"Who told you that?"

"Weren't you with her when she called and talked to Pudgie Thursday night?"

"Sure, but I left Friday morning and drove back to Santa Teresa."

"Anybody see you at work?"

"Two-thirty in the morning, I'm moppin' floors, not entertaining the troops. Reason I like the job is it's quiet and nobody's there to hassle me."

"You were completely alone."

"At that hour? Of course. Who's going to be there? The place's all locked up."

"I don't know. Someone else on the cleaning crew? A lawyer working late? A building that size can't be empty."

"For starters, there's nobody else on the crew. I'm it. And second, even if there was someone in the building, how would I know? Six floors is tough. I got a lot of ground to cover. Some lawyer's workin' late, he's not going to stop and make small talk with the likes of me. So. Nobody saw me. You'll have to take my word that I was there all night."

"You drove all the way down here to tell me this?"

"Hey, I could've had her alibi me, which she'd've done in a heartbeat, but I wanted to play straight."

"Good boy. Now what?"

"Iona thought you might put in a good word for me."

"Frankie, come on. You know better than that. No one gives a shit what I think. My opinion carries no weight at all. It's like Iona thinking I had the clout to offer Pudgie a deal. It's ridiculous."

"Those cops like you."

"Sure they do, but so what? Look, I'm perfectly willing to pass the story along, but trust me, without an alibi, my big, hot endorsement won't help."

"But you believe me?"

"Let's put it this way; nothing would make me happier than your telling the truth. I'm sure the cops will be crazy about the idea, too."

He dropped his cigarette and stepped on the ember with the toe of his boot. "You try, okay?"

"I'll call Lieutenant Dolan tomorrow. Meantime, if I were you I'd get back to town before your PO gets wind of what's going on."

"I'll do that. And thanks."

"You're welcome."

I closed the window and had it latched again before Frankie reached the truck. I heard the door slam and she backed out, the headlights doing a reverse angle on the draperies as she pulled away. I shook my head. What a baby. Gone was the tough guy I'd met the first time around. As for his story, I wasn't sure whether to believe him or not. Sincerity aside, he was capable of manipulation if it suited his purposes.

In the morning, I changed rooms. There were far too many people who knew where I was and I didn't feel safe. I chose an innocuous location on the second floor in the middle of a stretch of rooms. No ice machines. No vending machines. No reason to be up there unless you were a paid motel guest. At ground level, I figured I was a sitting duck for Peeping Toms or guys with a penchant for picking locks. Up here, even if the house-keeper propped my door open for hours on end, it would take nerve for someone to climb the stairs and pretend to be wandering around lost. From the second floor I had a nice view of the parking lot. I'd left Dolan's car in a row of cars to one side so there was no way to associate the vehicle with my whereabouts.

At 9:15, I called Dolan's house. Stacey picked up. I told him my concern that someone had entered my room and had taken a long hard look at my notes. He told me to change rooms, which I told him I'd done. He told me Dolan had left for an appointment with the cardiologist. I told him about Medora's house, the note, and Frankie's late-night visit. He told me I better watch my step and I said I would. Then he said, "What have we picked up in the way of elimination prints?"

"We're not doing so well. Last I heard Edna had gone in, but none of the other four."

"What's up with that? I don't like them thinking they can bypass us. Go back and threaten. Tell them it looks bad, like maybe one of them has something to hide."

"So how's Dolan doing?"

"He's good. I'd say good. Doing better than I thought."

"You think the living arrangements are going to work?"

"Jury's still out on that. I could probably do worse—though, frankly, the guy's a colossal pain in the ass. Of course, he says the same thing about me."

"Makes you the perfect pair," I said. "Better than some of the marriages I've seen."

"Amen to that. What's the latest down there?"

"I haven't heard anything since I was at the Tuley-Belle last night, but I can stop by the sheriff's office and talk to Lassiter."

"Do that and call me back. I've been trying to get in touch with him, but so far no luck. Meantime, we'll see what we can find out about Frankie's whereabouts on Friday night."

"Great. Tell Dolan I said hi. I really miss you guys."

Stacey said, "Ditto. And you take care of yourself."

I retrieved Dolan's car and drove the few short blocks to the Sheriff's Department. Todd Chilton and a civilian clerk seemed to be the only ones in. He was chatting with one of the church ladies I'd seen at Edna's. She was in her seventies, wearing a pale green leisure suit. Her hair had just been done and it puffed out as nicely as a dandelion. She'd placed a parking ticket on the counter, and I waited politely while she wrote out a check and tore it from her register. I flicked a quick look at the name printed on the face of the check: Adele Opdyke.

"How are you, Adele? We met at Edna's on Saturday. Nice seeing you again."

"Nice seeing you, too." She seemed flustered to realize I was standing close enough to see what she was doing. "Don't go thinking this ticket's mine. It's my husband's. He parked in a fire lane Friday night, late going to a movie. He's always doing that. Doesn't matter how many times I tell him not to."

Deputy Chilton said, "Why are you the one paying? He'll never learn this way."

"You're right, you're right. I'm entirely too good to him. I should make him take care of it. It would serve him right." She glanced at me. "You're that private detective, but I forget your name. Edna told us all about the fabric in her quilt."

"Kinsey Millhone," I said. "Did you get that mailing out?"

"It's done and it's been delivered by now." She turned back to Chilton. "How's the investigation? That poor Cedric had a sorry life and what a terrible end."

"We're all working overtime, doing everything we can. Quorum PD's pitching in so we're on it."

"That's good." She tucked her checkbook in her handbag. "Well, I'm off to run my errands. I wanted to get this done first before I forgot. Nice talking to you."

As soon as she left, I said, "I was looking for Detective Lassiter, but I gather he's not here."

"He's at the Tuley-Belle. The coroner thinks Pudgie was killed with a tire iron, which hasn't turned up yet. Detective Lassiter thinks it's possible it's still out there— dumped or buried. Detective Oliphant left a couple of messages for him, but they'll have to wait. I know he's concerned about this business with the McPhees' fingerprints, but we've got all our personnel at the crime scene, so even if they came in there's nothing we could do."

"Well. First things first. I'll tell Stacey someone will get back to him later in the day. I'm sure he'd like an update."

TWENTY-SIX

I sat in the car in front of the Sheriff's Department, thinking about tire irons. As murder weapons go, the lowly tire iron has the virtue of being genderless and easily obtainable. Lots of people have tire irons. They're probably not as common as a set of kitchen knives, but they're cheap, readily available, have no moving parts, and no one would think to question your possessing one. You don't need a license to buy one and you don't have to worry about a three-day waiting period while your local hardware salesman runs a background check.

I'd seen a tire iron in the past week. I knew it was only one of millions in the world, and the chances were remote that I'd seen the very tire iron used on Pudgie's head. Still, it seemed like a good mental exercise. Where had I seen tools? McPhee's automobile upholstery shop, both in the two-car garage where he sat to smoke and in the second garage where Dolan and I had found the Mustang. Also Cornell's garage where I'd seen him at work constructing a dog house for his daughters' pup. The question was, did any of these locations warrant another look? It seemed like a waste of time except for the fact that I had nothing else to do. While Detective Lassiter and the deputies were out combing the area surrounding the Tuley-Belle, the killer might have scrubbed the blood and brains off the murder weapon and put it back where it'd been. So finding it wouldn't mean anything and not finding it wouldn't mean anything, either. Well, that was dumb. I decided to try something more productive.

I started the car and went back to the Ocean View. I wanted to call Felicia and see how she was doing. I was also interested in the arrangements she'd made for Pudgie's funeral. My message light was blinking. I dialed 6 and picked up a message indicating that Lieutenant Dolan had called at 10:00. It was only 10:20 now, so I was hoping I'd catch him before he left the house again. He picked up on the first ring.

"Hey, Lieutenant, this is Kinsey. How are you?"

"I'm fine. Sorry I missed your call earlier."

"That's okay, though with all these phone calls flying back and forth, Stacey really doesn't need to come back. I think I'm talking to you guys more now than I did when you were here."

"Don't tell him. He can't wait to get down there and back to work."

"So what's up?"

"Nothing much. We're restless and bored. Hang on. Here's Stacey. He has something he wants to say."

He handed the phone to Stacey, and we went through an exchange of pleasantries as though we hadn't spoken in days. Then, he said, "I've been thinking about this Baum guy and he bothers me. I got sidetracked and left without asking him for leads. Stands to reason she was killed by someone she knew, so let's broaden the search. Can you check it out for me?"

"Sure. Give me the address of the car lot and I'll pay him a visit."

Before I left for Blythe, I put in a call to Pudgie's sister. She sounded better; subdued, but not weepy. She probably found it therapeutic to be caught up in the clerical work that follows in the wake of a death. I could hear the murmur of voices in the background. "You have people there?"

"Friends. Everybody's been great. A cousin stayed with me last night and another one's driving in from Phoenix."

"Are you having services?"

"On Friday. I'm having his body cremated as soon as the coroner releases him, but people are stopping by this evening if you'd like to join us. The memorial on Friday probably won't amount to much, but I thought I should do something. The pastor keeps calling it 'a celebration of his life,' but that doesn't seem right to me with him in jail so much."

"Up to you," I said. "What time tonight?"

"Between five and eight. I've borrowed a big coffee urn and there's tons of food."

"I'll aim for seven. Can I bring anything?"

"Please don't. I'm serious. I've already got far more than I can use," she said. "If you run into anyone who knew him, tell them they're invited, too. I think he'd be happy if people turned out for him."

"Sure thing."

The Franks Used Cars lot looked like just about every other car lot I'd ever seen. The business was housed in what must have been a service station once upon a time, and the showroom now occupied one of the former service bays. An assortment of gleaming cars was lined up street-side with slogans painted in white on the windshields. Most were spotless and polished to a high shine, making me glad I'd parked Dolan's half a block away.

George Baum was the only salesman on the premises. I caught him sitting at his desk, eating a tuna sandwich, the open packet of waxed paper serving as a handsome lunch plate. I hated to interrupt his feeding process—I tend to get cranky when someone interrupts mine—but he seemed determined to do business. I sat down in the visitor's chair while he rewrapped half his sandwich and tucked it in the brown paper bag he'd brought from home. I detected the bulge of an apple and imagined it held cookies or a cupcake as well.

On his desk, he had a formal family portrait in a silver frame: George, Swoozie (who still looked perky as could be), and three stair-stepped adolescent boys wearing jackets and ties. The color photograph was recent, judging by hair and clothing styles. While only in his mid-thirties, George was already portly, wearing a brown suit of a size that made his head look too small. Stacey was right about his teeth—even, perfectly straight, and bleached to a pearly white. He wore his hair short and the scent of his aftershave was fresh and strong.

I introduced myself, watching his enthusiasm fade when he realized I was there to pump him for information. "This is your father-in-law's place? I didn't realize you worked for him."

"You know Chester?"

"No, but I heard you were married to Swoozie Franks. I put two and two together."

"What brings you here? I already talked to someone about Charisse Quinn."

"That was my partner, Detective Oliphant. He's the one who thought we should have another chat."

"What now?"

"We need the names of the guys who were involved with her. 'Involved' meaning screwing, just so you know what I'm talking about."

He smiled uncomfortably. "I can't do that."

"Why?"

"What's the point in asking me? Why don't you go over to the high school and get names from the yearbook? It'd be the same list."

"I could do that," I said, "but I'd rather hear it from you. And skip what's-his-name—Toby Hecht. Cornell says nobody's heard from him in years."

"That's because he's dead. He was killed in Vietnam."

"Sorry to hear that. Who else would you suggest?"

George shook his head. "I don't see the relevance. So maybe a few classmates had sexual relations with her. What bearing does that have on where they are now in life?"

"I'm not worried about where *they* are. I'm worried about Charisse. Somebody killed her. That's what I'm here to discuss."

"I understand that. Of course. And if I thought any one of them was capable of murder, I'd speak up."

"Let me tell you something, George. The person who

killed her turned around and killed Pudgie Clifton. And you want to know why? Pudgie knew something he shouldn't have. I'm not sure what, but it cost him his life. You keep quiet and you could end up putting yourself at risk. That's not a smart move, especially if your only motive is to protect a bunch of horny high school dudes."

"I do business with a lot of those *dudes*. Honest, I don't mean to be uncooperative, but I don't like being put on the spot."

I was watching him, fascinated, because he'd started to perspire. I'd never really seen that, a man breaking out in a sweat while he talked. I said, "All right. Try this. Let's just talk about you. Were you intimate with her?"

"Swoozie would have killed me."

"You never made it with Charisse?"

"I'd rather not answer that."

"Which means yes."

He paused, taking out a handkerchief to mop at a trickle of sweat running down the side of his face.

"George?"

"Okay, yes, but that's just between us. If it ever got out, my marriage would be over. Swoozie thinks I was a virgin. I told her she was the first. She hated Charisse. All the girls did."

"I'm listening."

"I was kind of nerdy. You know the type—smart and earnest and inexperienced. I'd pretend I'd made out. The guys'd be talking about sex and I'd act like I knew what they meant when I didn't have a clue. Then Charisse came along and she was really nice to me. I liked her—I mean that sincerely—so when she offered to, you know, I just figured what the hell, no harm was ever going to come of it. I felt better about myself after that, a lot more confident."

"How many times?"

"Three. Swoozie and I had been dating since we were kids. I knew we'd get married and then I'd never have a chance to be with anyone else. I didn't want to live my whole life only knowing one girl."

"And afterwards?"

"I wasn't sorry I'd done it, but I was scared Swoozie would find out. I already had a job lined up with her dad."

"You must have been relieved when Charisse disappeared."

"Well, hey, sure. I'll admit that, but so were a lot of guys, including Mr. Clean."

I smiled. "Mr. Clean?"

"Sure. Cornell. We called him that because he worked for his dad and his hands were always dirty. He used to scrub 'em with lye soap, but it never did any good."

My smile had faded because I'd blocked out his explanation and tuned into what he'd actually said. "Cornell was screwing Charisse?"

"Sure. Justine was holding out for marriage. She came up from nothing. And I mean her family was for shit—"

"I know about that," I said, cutting him off.

"She saw Cornell as the answer to her prayers. She wasn't about to put out unless he married her."

I thought about that. "I did hear Charisse had the hots for him."

"Oh, sure. She was also jealous of Justine. Compared to her life, Justine's already looked better, so she got competitive."

"And Justine knew about this?"

"Oh, no. No, no. Charisse knew better. After all, she was living at Justine's. She wasn't about to get herself thrown out on the street."

"You're telling me Cornell was in the same jeopardy you were."

"Big time. Even more so. He was everybody's hero— scholastics, sports, student government, you name it. We all looked up to him."

"Who else knew about this, aside from you?"

"Adrianne, I guess. She walked in on 'em once over at the Tuley-Belle. That's how she found out."

"How do you know that?"

527

"Because she told me."

"Why? Were you a close friend of hers?"

"No, not really. We were in the same church youth group. We went on a weekend retreat and I could see she was upset. I asked and she told me what was going on. She thought she should talk to our pastor, but I disagreed. I said it wasn't her job to save Cornell's soul. He was a big boy and he could work it out for himself."

I arrived at Felicia's house in Creosote at precisely 7:00 that Wednesday night. Cars were lined up at intervals along the darkened street. I didn't think I could manage to parallel park in Dolan's tank so I was forced to leave his car around the corner and walk back. Cornell's white pickup truck was parked in front of the house, behind Justine's dark Ford sedan. The moon had been reduced to the size of a fingernail paring. The air was dry and cold. The usual wind whiffled through the trees, making the shaggy palms sway, fronds rustling like rats running through an ivy patch. Lights shone from every room of Felicia's small house. Despite her admonition, I'd brought a dense chocolate cake in a pink bakery box.

A neighbor answered the door, introducing herself while relieving me of the box, which she carried to the kitchen. I stood for a moment and surveyed the room. I counted eight flower arrangements, about half of them containing leftover Easter lilies. Felicia had dimmed the lights, using votives and candles to illuminate the rooms. The effect was nice, but the air had been warmed to a feverish temperature. I suppose the gathering could have been called a wake, though there was certainly no corpse present. Perhaps "visitation" was the better term. That's how Felicia had referred to it.

On a purely self-centered note, I hadn't thought I'd need to pack my illustrious all-purpose dress. That long-sleeve black garment is tailor-made for such occasions, but how could I have known? Cheap shit that I am, earlier in the day I'd ducked into a Goodwill thrift store, where I'd found a pair of serviceable black wool slacks and a short black jacket of another fabric altogether. I'd also bought preowned black flats and a pair of (new) black pantyhose. My shoulder bag was brown, probably a fashion faux pas given the rest of my ensemble, but it couldn't be helped. I'd looked better in my day, but I'd also looked a lot worse.

I had no way of guessing how many people had come and gone in the hours before my arrival, but the number of mourners I saw was embarrassingly small. I wouldn't have referred to them as "mourners," either. They came closer to being talkers, Nosy Parkers, and consumers of free food. Clearly some of those assembled were Pudgie's relatives. I could tell because they all looked faintly surprised he hadn't been shot to death in the process of an armed robbery. I caught sight of Cornell talking to his sister, but both avoided eye contact, and I got the impression neither was eager to talk to me. I didn't see Justine, and the rest of those gathered were total strangers, except for Felicia, who was standing in the kitchen talking to a fellow I'd never seen before. I'd hoped to see George Baum, to whom I'd given the address before I'd left the car lot. Maybe he didn't want to risk running into Cornell, having tattled on him.

Since I didn't recognize anyone except people who didn't seem to want to talk to me, I crossed to the buffet table on the far side of the room. Felicia hadn't fibbed about the copious amounts of food folks had brought. There was every kind of casserole known to man, platters of cold cuts, crackers and cheeses, chips and dips, plus an assortment of cakes, pies, and cookies. A big pressed-glass punch bowl had been filled with coral liquid that looked suspiciously like Hawaiian Punch. There was one lone bottle of white zinfandel. I unscrewed the top and filled a clear plastic cup to the brim, then drank it down an inch so it wouldn't look like I was hogging more than my share.

I moved through the smattering of people, hoping to corner Adrianne so the two of us could have a chat. I saw Cornell go out to the front yard to grab a cigarette, so at least I didn't have to worry about him. I drifted through the living room and into the kitchen. Felicia passed me with a plate of cookies in hand. I touched her arm and said, "How're you doing?"

Her red hair was pulled away from her face. "I'm all right for now. I think the hard part comes later when everyone goes home. I'll try to catch you in a bit. I have to get back with this."

"Have you seen Adrianne?"

"I think I saw her go out there," she said. "Cedric would have been glad you came."

"I wouldn't have missed it," I said, and she was gone.

I set my wine cup on the counter and pushed the kitchen screen open. Adrianne was on the back porch, sitting on the top step. I took a seat beside her, my shoulder bag between us. "Are you okay?"

"I'm fine. This depresses me, that's all."

"I have a question for you."

"Geez, would you give it up already? This is hardly the time."

"You can talk to me or you can talk to the cops. Take your pick."

"Oh hell. What do you want? I'm sick of this business."

"So am I. Unfortunately, it isn't over."

"It is as far as I'm concerned. So ask me and get it over with. I'm about to go home."

"Did you know Cornell was fooling around with Charisse?"

She looked at me sharply and then she looked away. She was quiet for a long time, but I decided to wait her out. Finally, she said, "Not at first."

"And then what?"

"Do we really have to talk about this? That was eighteen years ago."

"I hear you were at the Tuley-Belle and walked in on them."

"Thank you, George Baum. If you knew the answer, why'd you ask?"

"Because I wanted to hear it from you. Come on. Just tell me what happened. Like you said, it was years ago so what difference does it make?"

"Oh, for heaven's sake," she said, with disgust. "A bunch of us had gone out there. We used to do these big scavenger hunts and play stupid games. That Friday night, it was Hide-and-Seek. Cornell and Charisse were in a room on the second floor. I stumbled in, looking for a place to hide, and there they were. I was horrified and so was he."

She stopped. I thought that was the end of it, but she picked up again. "I guess I was naive, but I genuinely liked Charisse. I didn't know she was using me to get to him."

"What'd she say to you?"

"What could she say? I'd caught them in the act. Not that she was ever one to apologize for what she did. I told her she was a shit, but she shrugged it off. She didn't care for my opinion or anyone else's. Afterward, I begged her to stay away from him, but she was obsessed. I hated her for that. She nearly ruined his life."

"How?"

Silence again. "Ask him. It's really his business, not mine."

"Let me guess," I said. "She told him she was pregnant."

Again, she was quiet.

"Am I right?"

"Yes. She was determined to marry him. She told me about it before she told him."

"Why?"

"Because she thought I'd help. I told her to blow it out her butt, but she threatened to tell Mom and Dad unless I talked him into it."

"Did anyone else know?"

"No. She was sure he'd marry her to avoid the embarrassment. Once he did that, it'd be too late for anyone else to interfere—meaning Justine, of course."

"And he was willing to go along with this?"

"He didn't have any choice. You know how straight-laced my parents are, especially Mom. If they found out, they'd have forced him to marry her anyway."

"So what was the plan?"

"There wasn't a *plan*. She had it all figured out. They were going to run off together. She knew a place where they could get a marriage license even if they were underage."

"He must have been in a sweat."

"He was really scared. I told him he was being dumb. How could he even be sure the kid was his? All he had to do was get five or six of his buddies to swear they'd screwed her too and he'd be off the hook."

"Nice move, Adrianne. Did you come up with that yourself?"

"Well, what was I supposed to do? I couldn't let her wreck my brother's life! Besides, it was true. Why should he pay? He only did what every other guy was doing. Why's that so wrong?"

"Oh sure. I can see your point. There's only one tiny problem."

"What."

"She wasn't pregnant."

"Yes, she was."

I shook my head. "I read the autopsy report."

She stared at me, a hand lifting to her mouth as though pulled by strings. "Oh, shit. She made it up?"

534

"Apparently. So when she disappeared, what'd you think? That she'd gone off on her own to spare him the disgrace?"

"I didn't know she was lying. I thought she might have decided to have an abortion."

"If she'd been pregnant in the first place."

There was another long silence and I stepped in again. "When you heard Medora'd filed a missing-persons report, weren't you worried they'd find her?"

"I hoped they wouldn't, but it did worry me."

"But there might have been a way to head them off."

"Head who off?"

"The cops who were looking for her."

"I don't know what you're getting at."

"The phone call."

She looked at me blankly, but I didn't know her well enough to know if she was faking.

I said, "Someone called the Sheriff's Department, claiming to be Charisse's mother, saying she was home again, alive and well. The Lompoc Sheriff's Department and the one down here were on the verge of linking the two—the missing girl and Jane Doe. Then the call came in and that was the end of that."

"Well, it wasn't me. I swear. I didn't call anyone."

"I'm not the one you have to persuade." I got up and brushed off the back of my pants. "I'll talk to you later."

"I sincerely hope not."

I went into the kitchen, feeling hyped up and tense. I was treading dangerous ground, but I couldn't help myself. These people had been sitting on their secrets far too long. It was time to kick in a few doors and see who'd been hiding what. I wondered where Cornell was the night that Pudgie was killed. That was a subject worth pursuing.

In my absence, someone had drained off my entire cup of wine. I tossed the empty plastic in a trash can. As I went into the hall, I glanced into the bedroom Pudgie must have occupied. There was a single bed, covered with a plain spread, the blanket and pillow stacked together at the foot. The room had all the cozy charm of a jail cell. There were no curtains at the window, and the plain white shade had been pulled down halfway. No pictures, no personal possessions. The closet door stood open, revealing an empty hanging rod. Felicia must have swept through, boxing up everything he owned, and then called the Goodwill. I felt a pang of disappointment. Given my curious nature, I'd hoped for the opportunity to search his things. I wasn't even sure what I thought I'd find—some sense of who he was, some feeling for why he'd died. I didn't imagine he'd left a note about his final rendezvous, but there might have been a hint of what he'd meant to do in life.

"Bleak," someone said.

I turned. Justine was standing to my left, making the same sad assessment of the room that I had. I saw her gaze linger on my jacket. "What."

"Nothing. I used to have a jacket just like that."

"Really? I've had this old thing for years." I felt a spark of fear and a second lie sprung to my lips. "Hey, what was Cornell up to Friday night? I thought I saw him downtown about ten."

She gave me a little smile of negation and bafflement. "He was home with the kids. I was out doing stuff for church."

"He was home alone?"

"Not at all. The kids were there. I told you that."

"Well, that's odd. You sure he didn't pop out to get a video? I could have sworn it was him."

"It couldn't have been. I went out at nine after the girls were in bed. He was folding laundry when I left and sacked out on the couch when I got home at midnight."

"The church is open that late?"

"I wasn't at the church. I was over at Adele's, working on a mailing. That's why he ended up baby-sitting."

"I thought they did the mailing Saturday at Edna's."

"They finished it then. We started Friday night."

I didn't point out that Cornell could have driven to Creosote and back in an hour, with plenty of time left for a stop at the Tuley-Belle to deliver forty whacks to

Pudgie's head. She could have done it, too. Three hours would have been more than adequate. I tried to remember what Adele had said when she paid her husband's parking citation. He'd been ticketed Friday night because he was late for a movie, but I couldn't remember if she said she'd been with him or not. Changing the subject, I said, "You want some wine? I'm out. I'll be happy to bring you some."

"No, thanks. I don't drink. I've seen enough of that."

"I'll be right back."

I bumped into someone as I entered the living room. I said, "Pardon me," and looked up to find Todd Chilton. He wasn't in uniform and it took me an instant to realize who he was. I said, "Hey, how are you? I didn't realize you'd be here. Can I talk to you a minute?"

"Sure."

We stepped to one side. Music had started up. Someone had apparently put together a tape of Pudgie's old favorites, starting with Chubby Checker. "*Come on, baby, let's do the twist . . .*" Nobody seemed to think it was inappropriate. I was just happy to have the noise to cover my conversation with the deputy. He bent his head, a hand cupped to his ear.

I said, "Have they found the murder weapon yet?"

He shook his head. "We searched until six and then we had to give it up. No point fumbling around in the

538

dark. Detective Lassiter did say he'd return Detective
Oliphant's call first thing tomorrow morning. Lot of
paperwork's piled up since we've been out in the field."

"I'm assuming Pudgie's murder hit the news."

"Oh yeah. Big spread this morning, asking for vol-
unteers. I was just talking to Cornell. We got a lot of
desert out there and a weapon like that's easy to hide.
We've searched that whole area behind the Tuley-Belle
and now we'll head toward the highway. You're welcome to join us. We could use the help."

"Thanks. I may do that."

Chilton moved away. I scanned the room, looking
for Cornell. Adrianne had reappeared and she gave me
a look of dark distaste before she walked away. I'd
probably overplayed my hand with her. I didn't want to
think she'd tell her brother what I knew, but she was
capable of that.

Felicia passed me again. "They're about to cut that
chocolate cake if you're interested. It looks great."

"I'll have some in a bit. Have you seen Cornell?"

She glanced around. "He was here a while ago. He
might be in the kitchen. I saw him talking to Adrianne.
He might have left to pick up the kids at the babysitter's. I hear he's a doll about things like that."

"I'm sure. Thanks."

I crossed to the front window and peered out to
the darkened street. Justine's sedan was still there but

Cornell's truck was gone. I didn't like that. His departure seemed abrupt. Maybe it was true he'd gone to pick up his kids, but it was also true he knew the search for the murder weapon was heating up. I let myself out the front door, struck by the chill night air after the suffocating level of artificial heat inside. My thrift store jacket, which had probably belonged to Justine once upon a time, was too light to offer much protection from the cold. I readjusted my shoulder bag and broke into a trot, heading for Dolan's car.

I unlocked the door and slid in under the wheel. I jammed the key in the ignition and turned it. The car coughed and died. I tried again. No deal. I pumped the gas pedal twice and then realized I was only flooding the engine. I sat and waited and then tried again. The starter ground and turned over. I gave it way too much gas and the engine roared to life. I pulled out, tires chirping as I took off. I turned on the heat, hoping to warm up. My sense of urgency coupled with the dry cold was making me shiver.

Half a minute later, I was on Highway 78, driving north toward Quorum. At this hour of the evening, traffic was light. I thought I caught a glimpse of Cornell's truck up ahead. There were four cars on the road between us and I was having to peer around and through them to keep an eye on him. Approaching the Tuley-Belle, the car in front of me slowed and I realized that, at the head of the line, Cornell had slowed to a stop. His turn signal winked merrily and he turned left as soon as oncoming traffic allowed.

I slowed as I passed the entrance, watching his tail-lights disappear into the dark. I drove on a hundred yards and pulled over to the side of the road. I doused the headlights, set the handbrake, and let the car idle while I debated with myself. I'd be foolish to follow him. The Tuley-Belle was a mile and a half from the main road, not only isolated, but riddled with hiding places better known to him than they were to me. I peered over my shoulder and stared into the darkness, picking up the parallel rounds of his headlights, now facing me. He hadn't driven to the complex. For some reason, he'd turned the truck around and was now parked by the road, facing the highway. I saw the headlights go out. Soon after that, I picked up a faint smudge of light off to the right of the four-lane blacktop. What was he doing out there? Burying the murder weapon? Digging it up to move it? But why take that risk? Simple. He knew the sheriff's investigators had been and gone. He also knew they'd return the next morning to start the search again. Todd Chilton had described the terrain the deputies had covered. If the weapon was out there, he could either move it into an area they'd already searched or remove the weapon from a section yet to be combed. Why would the tire iron be out there in the first place? Because he didn't want the damn thing hidden anywhere close to home? Because he hadn't had time to dispose of it anywhere else? Whatever he was up to, he must have decided this was his only opportunity to act.

I reached up and snapped the cover from the dome light and unscrewed the bulb. I got out, pushing the door closed without snapping it shut. I walked to the rear of the car and opened the trunk. I wasn't worried about the trunk light. Nothing on the back end of Dolan's vehicle worked, including the taillights. I felt my way across the darkened space until my hand came down on Dolan's Smith & Wesson, snug in its holster. I picked up the gun and the holster, eased down the lid of the trunk, and returned to the driver's seat. I slipped under the wheel again, leaving the car door ajar. I fumbled in my bag until I found my pen light. I snapped it on and placed it on the passenger seat, keeping my inspection process well below the level of the dashboard. This was the gun Dolan carried on duty; a 9mm Parabellum, with a clip that held fifteen rounds. I hit the clip release button and checked the magazine—fully loaded—and then smacked it back into place. I pulled the slide back and released it, then checked to see that the safety was on. I hefted the weight of the gun, close to twenty-eight ounces, feeling its clumsiness in a hand as small as mine. At least it was an equalizer, wasn't it?

I stripped off my jacket. Dolan's shoulder holster had a Velcro and leather strip shoulder strap that I adjusted and secured under my left arm, the gun tucked snugly in place. I pulled on the jacket again, tugging at the front until it lay flat. I kept an eye on the rearview mirror, waiting for a break in the flow of cars. As soon as I was clear in both directions, I made a wide U-turn, swinging across the two-lane highway and onto the berm on the far side of the road. I eased the car along on the berm until I found a spot that seemed to provide at least a modicum of cover. I was now facing in the direction of Creosote instead of Quorum on the same side of the road as the entrance to the Tuley-Belle. Cornell was laboring away somewhere to my right, though I couldn't really see him from where I sat.

I killed the engine, tucked the keys in my jacket pocket, and got out of the car. It wasn't my intention to do anything dumb. I wasn't going to tackle the guy or try to make a citizen's arrest. I just wanted to see what he was up to and then I'd slip back to the car and be on my way. Even so, if there'd been a public phone in a five-mile radius, I would have bagged my scheme, called the Sheriff's Department, and let them handle him.

The entrance to the abandoned property had been blocked by bright orange plastic cones and a sign mounted on a sawhorse designating the entire area as a crime scene. Someone had moved the No Trespass warnings aside and the sawhorse now lay toppled on its side.

The thin crescent moon worked to my advantage. The road itself was dark, but the sky was a muted gray. The landscape—largely sand and gravel basins—gradually came into focus as my eyes adjusted to the dark. I could make out a number of features: clusters of tumbleweeds, like giant beach balls, creosote bushes, bayonet cactuses, yuccas, and the leggy branches of the palo verde trees. Ahead of me, I caught glimpses of a stationary light, possibly a lantern or a good-sized flashlight. I was getting closer, but as I'd noticed before, distances were difficult to calculate.

I could hear the peeping of ground frogs, probably poisonous, and the intermittent hooting of an owl. Unbidden, my brain suddenly played back in excruciating detail Dolan's earlier recital about Mojave insect life, specifically the tarantula hawk, a species of desert wasp, the female of which sniffs out a tarantula, stings it into a state of paralysis, drags it back to her burrow, and lays an egg in its abdomen. Once hatched, the tiny grub feeds daintily until its final moult, then rips open the spider's abdomen, thrusts its head and part of its thorax inside and devours everything in sight. Sometimes the tarantula is even dead by then. I was grossing myself out. This is the very same Nature that some people find spiritually uplifting. I picked up my pace,

trying to block the interminable list of other insects he'd
mentioned, scorpions and fire ants among them. Whatever else happened out here, I wasn't going to sit down.

The road made a slight bend, and I found myself not
ten yards away from Cornell's white pickup truck, its
engine still ticking as the metal cooled. Tucked in behind
Cornell's truck was Justine's dark Ford sedan. I stared
in disbelief. The last time I'd seen it, it was parked in
front of Felicia's house. Apparently, while I was struggling to get Dolan's car started, Justine left the house in
her car and followed him. By the time I was finally
under way, it hadn't occurred to me to glance back and
see if her car was still there. She must have caught up
with him, passed him, and turned off the highway before
he did. She was the one who'd moved the barrier from
the entrance to the place. She'd been back in her car and
heading up the road before I'd caught sight of him
making his turn.

I reached out and laid a hand on the hood of the
truck, steadying myself, then eased to my left, using the
cab as cover. I could hear the persistent chunking of a
spade. He was digging. Were they burying the weapon
or digging it up? I lifted on tiptoe. He'd set the flashlight
on the ground. I saw the occasional distorted shadow as
one or the other crossed the path of the light as the
work progressed. I could hear them arguing, but the
subject wasn't clear. I wasn't sure if they'd collaborated

from the first or if Cornell had done the killing and she'd finally figured it out. My heart began to bang and a cloud of fear, like indigestion, burned in my chest. I tried to get my bearings, noting two nearby Joshua trees and a clump of sagebrush on my left that formed a mound the size of a pup tent. Directly across the road, there was a massive flowering shrub where white moths the size of hummingbirds had gathered to feed. Their wings beat audibly in the still night air, like the far-off thrumming of helicopter blades.

I turned back, suddenly aware that the chunking sound had stopped. I looked again. Cornell was on his knees, reaching into the hole. He hauled out the tire iron and wrapped it in a fold of cloth. The two of them started kicking soil back in the hole, intent on eradicating any evidence of their work. Justine picked up the spade and used the flat of the blade like a spatula, smoothing the sand like frosting. He bent and picked up the flashlight and gave a cursory sweep to make sure they hadn't left anything behind. They headed toward me.

I pivoted and ducked, silently retracing my steps, hoping to gain the bend in the road before the two reached Cornell's truck. If they climbed into their respective vehicles and returned to the highway, their two sets of headlights were going to pick me out of the dark like a startled bunny rabbit. I heard the slamming of two doors. I left the pavement and scurried out into the dark. I spotted a furrow in the earth, a channel where flash flooding had cut a shallow trench. I dropped flat and propelled myself on my elbows, belly-crawling, until I reached the shallow ditch and rolled into it. I put my head down, my arms folded under me, and waited. Only one engine sparked to life. I expected the flash of passing headlights, but none appeared. Cautiously, I lifted my head and peered in time to see the taillights of the pickup truck. One or both of them were on their way to the Tuley-Belle. I scrambled to my feet and ran. If I was mistaken and she'd been left behind, posted by the sedan, I was in bigger trouble than I thought. I slowed my pace as I rounded the bend. The Ford was still parked by the side of the road and there was no sign of her.

I reached her Ford and snatched at the door on the driver's side. She'd left her keys behind, dangling in the ignition. I got in and started the car. I released the hand brake, left the lights off, and made a wide sweeping turn, bumping off the road and back, this time driving, as they had, toward the sprawling complex ahead. If they intended to hide the tire iron at the Tuley-Belle, it might never turn up.

When I was as close as I dared drive, I took my foot off the gas pedal and let the sedan coast to a stop. I turned the engine off and put her car keys in my pocket, again reaching up to disable the dome light before I opened the car door. I took out Dolan's Smith & Wesson. I moved off the road, circling out and to my left so that I was approaching the complex at an angle across raw land. Cover was better out here. The huddled shadows tended to form and reform, shifting, as the wind pushed the tumbleweeds across the uneven ground. I spotted the truck, which Cornell had parked between the two half-finished buildings, looming silent and dark. In the second building, upstairs, I saw a glimmer of light. I moved forward with caution, hoping Cornell had left his keys behind as she had. If I could steal their only means of transportation, it would force them to walk the mile and a half to the main highway. By the time they reached the road, I could be speeding back to Creosote and return with help. Let them explain to Todd Chilton what they'd been doing out there. There was no motion in the patch of darkness immediately surrounding the truck.

I circled the vehicle, noting that the window was rolled down on the driver's side. I peered in, catching the glint of his keys right where I'd hoped they'd be. In my mind's eye, I was already opening the truck door, sliding under the wheel. I'd turned the key in the ignition, slammed the gear lever into drive, and sped off, leaving the two of them behind. As it turned out, I celebrated my achievement prematurely. I heard a scuffling behind me and a little voice inside piped up, saying "Uh-oh," but by then it was too late. I turned, expecting to see Cornell, but it was Justine sailing toward me. With her pale flyaway hair and her icy pale green eyes, she looked like a banshee sweeping out of the dark. Cornell must have left her to stand watch, acting as a sentinel in case a horny pack of teenyboppers showed up at the Tuley-Belle for a midweek Screwfest. Maybe I hadn't been as quiet as I'd thought. Perhaps, given the peculiarities of desert acoustics, she'd heard my every step and simply waited for me.

She had the shovel in her hands. I saw her lifting her arms, raising the shovel overhead like an axe. I had to admire her strength. What she was doing wasn't easy. The shovel looked heavy and I hadn't thought she'd developed that much upper-body strength. Still, from her perspective, this was an emergency, so she might have been calling on reserves she didn't know she had.

As with many moments of crisis in life, the swiftness with which the ensuing events unfolded created the reverse effect, emerging with the soft, dreamy qualities of slow-motion footage. Like a sequence of time-lapse photographs, Justine's arms continued to rise until the shovel reached its apex. I saw the first shimmering instant of its descent. I curled to my left and lifted my right arm, trying to aim and fire Dolan's S&W before the shovel hit its mark. If she'd brandished the shovel with the blade perpendicular, striking me side-on, she probably would have chopped my arm to the bone. As it was, the flat of the shovel collided with my forearm and the gun spun off into the dark. I never even heard it land. The shovel came down again. A ringing pain radiated outward from my left shoulder and disappeared. It was odd. I knew she'd landed a blow, but I was so flooded with adrenaline the pain vanished. I staggered, my knees buckling, nearly felled by the impact.

I spotted the Smith & Wesson lying six feet away. The shovel came down again, this time clanging against the top of the truck cab with a force that wrenched the tool from her grip. I ran at her and shoved her as hard as I could. She stumbled backward but managed to catch herself before she hit the ground. She was making guttural sounds, probably trying to marshal her forces to yell for Cornell. I grabbed the shovel and used it like a scythe to crack her across the shins. She screamed. I looked back and saw she was down. Cornell came running from the building. Just as he spotted me, I saw Justine scramble to her feet and reach the truck door. She yanked it open and got in on the driver's side, screaming at him, "Get in the truck! Get in the truck!"

I scrambled forward, snatched up the gun, and pushed off the safety.

He flung himself at the tailgate as she started the

truck. She backed up and shifted gears, gunned the engine, and turned the wheel, peeling out. I watched him haul himself over the side and into the truck bed, disappearing from view. I turned and extended my arms, both hands on the gun as I aimed. It helped that I was pissed off. I was talking aloud, admonishing myself to take my time. There was no reason to panic. The ground was flat and I'd be able to see them for a long time. I located one of the rear taillights between the niche in the gun's rear sight and the niche in the foresight as I squinted down the barrel. I hadn't paid attention to Dolan's choice in ammunition, but if I remembered correctly, the baseline 9mm 100-grain slug moves out at muzzle velocities of between 1,080 and 1,839 feet per second, depending on slug rate. My figures might have been off, but not by much. I fired. The recoil was like a quick sneeze, kicking the barrel up and back. I missed, corrected, fired again, and heard a tire blow. Cornell had flattened himself in the bed of the truck. I altered my sights slightly and fired again, missing. I took aim again and fired four more rounds, trying to make each one count. By the time I paused, both back tires were flat. After that, the truck veered off course and came to a stop almost of its own accord. I approached on foot, taking my time, knowing I had sufficient rounds left to take care of business if Justine and Cornell still felt like arguing.

EPILOGUE

Justine was arrested and charged with two counts of first-degree murder, with a string of related offenses thrown in to sweeten the pot. Edna and Ruel prevailed on Cornell to hire a lawyer of his own, and his lawyer, in turn, persuaded him to make a deal with the DA. After all, he'd had nothing to do with the murder of Charisse Quinn and he'd had no part in Pudgie Clifton's death. That Saturday after I'd gone to the house to talk to Justine, she'd panicked and begged for his help in moving Pudgie's body and subsequently burying the tire iron with which she'd killed him. Cornell pled guilty to being an accessory after the fact, for which he's serving one year in the county jail. Edna and Ruel have taken on the responsibility for Amelia, Mary Francis, and Cissy McPhee until their father's release.

Justine's motivation wasn't difficult to fathom. She'd killed Charisse for seducing Cornell and trying to steal the life she'd envisioned for herself. It was indeed Pudgie who'd stolen the Mustang and loaded Charisse's body in the trunk. While Justine packed the dead girl's clothes and forged the note explaining her fictional departure, Pudgie drove the body to Lompoc and dumped it at the quarry Iona'd told him about. Justine waited a week and then called the Riverside County Sheriff's Department, pretending to be Charisse's mother and claiming her daughter was safely home again.

Once Pudgie reappeared in Quorum with news that the investigation had been reactivated, Justine had been forced to eliminate him. She'd enlisted Cornell's aid in disposing of Pudgie's body as she'd once enlisted Pudgie's aid in disposing of Charisse. His was certainly too unwieldy a corpse for her to manage on her own. The day I'd startled her in the laundry, it was his blood and brains she was washing from her clothes. It dawned on me later that the business with Medora's doors standing open was Justine's doing as well, affording her the opportunity to pump me for information about the progress I'd made.

For once in his life, Frankie Miracle was innocent of any complicity in these crimes, a fact that went some way toward brightening his outlook.

With the trial date approaching, Justine's attorney is insisting on a change of venue, maintaining she'll never get a fair trial in Riverside County after the media circus generated by her arrest. I love it when killers want to argue about what's fair.

SUE GRAFTON

On a more homely note, Stacey's still living with Dolan, an arrangement that suits them surprisingly well. Both are currently in good health, limiting their consumption of tobacco and junk food, and continually grousing about each other, as good friends are sometimes inclined to do. As for me, I'm back in my office in Santa Teresa, unpacking my moving boxes while I wait to see what else life has to bring.

Respectfully submitted,
Kinsey Millhone

AUTHOR'S NOTE

About this novel . . .

There is one additional, quite lengthy note about the writing of this novel. *Q is for Quarry* is based on an unsolved homicide that occurred in Santa Barbara County in August 1969. The catalyst for the book was a conversation I had with Dr. Robert Failing during a dinner party at the home of our friends Susan and Gary Gulbransen in early September of 2000. Dr. Failing is a forensic pathologist who worked, under contract, for the Santa Barbara County Sheriff's Department from 1961 until 1996. I had just completed and submitted the manuscript of *P is for Peril*, and the dinner conversation turned, not surprisingly, to what I might do next. Bob mentioned the Jane Doe victim, whose body had been dumped near a quarry in Lompoc, California, about an hour north of Santa Barbara. He had performed the autopsy, and, in passing, he remarked that the Coroner's Office had retained her maxilla and mandible. It was his feeling that Jane Doe's distinctive dental features should have sparked public recognition. Unfortunately, at the time, she was either never reported missing or the missing-persons report somehow failed to reach the detectives working this case. Despite months of tireless effort, they were never able to identify Jane Doe, and her killer was never caught. To this day, no one knows who she is, where she came from, or who murdered her.

As a novelist, I've been offered countless plot ideas, stories, personal anecdotes, "real life" events, and "true" murders—experiences that were important to those who suggested them, but which, for one reason or another, didn't stimulate or excite me. This idea took root. I expressed an immediate interest, knowing full well that the survival of an idea is unpredictable. I'd met the coroner's investigator, Larry Gillespie, retired now, on previous occasions while researching earlier books in the series. Bob offered to speak to Larry about rounding up the jaw bones. He also offered to introduce me to some of the Sheriff's Department detectives he'd worked with during his association with this law-enforcement agency.

I keep a journal during the writing of these books, a ritual I began in rudimentary form with *A is for Alibi* and have continued, with ever increasing breadth and depth, through the seventeen novels in the series to this point. The early portions of the journal for any given novel are usually a record of my fumbling attempts to find a workable story line. I ruminate, I chat with myself, I fret, I experiment. Oddly enough, from my perspective, the first journal note on the subject of Jane Doe didn't appear until November 8, 2000, some two months after my initial conversation with Bob Failing. I had, at that point, already accepted the subject matter as the basis for this book, though it took me many more months to work out the details. I loved the word "quarry" because its meaning, particularly in this instance, could do double-duty, referring to the place where the body was found and to the search for the killer.

On January 11, 2001, Bob Failing and I met with Sergeant Detective Bill Turner and then Commander Bruce Correll of the Criminal Investigations Division, Santa Barbara Sheriff's Department, and the four of us drove to Lompoc to see the quarry. I met with Bruce Correll and Bill Turner again on January 19, 2001. At that time, in a gesture of incredible generosity, they gave me a copy of the murder book for the Jane Doe case. It contained case notes, investigative reports, and both color and black-and-white photographs of the body and the area where she was found. I was also given photographs of her effects, including her leather sandals and the home-sewn pants with the daisy-print, dark blue with a dot of red on a white background.

Over the ensuing year, with the blessings of then-sheriff Jim Thomas, I met with these two detectives on numerous occasions. Bill Turner, in particular, became an invaluable resource, providing information about procedural issues, technicalities, and the myriad nuts and bolts of his work. He answered my many (sometimes stupid) questions with unfailing patience and enthusiasm, responding with the sort of detailed replies that make a writer's job a joy. Any errors, herein, by the way, are either the result of my faulty understanding or license I took in the interest of the story.

My fascination with the case rekindled the interest of the department, and the possibility arose of an exhumation of the body so that a facial reconstruction might be done, in hopes that Jane Doe might be identified. I wasn't privy to the discussions that must have gone on behind the scenes. In Santa Barbara County exhumations are uncommon, and budget considerations became an issue, not only because of the cost of the exhumation itself but for the expense of hiring a forensic sculptor, who would use Jane Doe's skull and jaw bones to re-create her likeness. There was also the matter of the reinterment, to accord Jane Doe the ultimate dignity of a proper burial, which we all considered essential. I offered to underwrite the plan because I, too, had become hopeful that something might come of it.

The exhumation was scheduled for July 17, 2001.

On that day, we traveled again to Lompoc, this time to the cemetery where Jane Doe was buried thirty-three years earlier. Dr. Failing flew in from his vacation home in Colorado. My husband, Steve Humphrey, made the journey with us, as did Sergeant Detective Bill Turner. Also present were Detective Hugo Galante, his wife, Detective Kathryn Galante, and Detective Terry Flaa, of the North County Detective Unit of the Criminal Investigations Division; Detective David Danielson; coroner's investigator Sergeant Darin Fotheringham; Sheriff's dispatcher Joe Ayala; his wife, Erin Ayala; the coroner's office secretary; Sheriff's trainee Danielle Goldman; Lieutenant Ken Reinstadler of the Santa Maria station, Patrol Division; Commander Deborah Linden, of the Santa Barbara Sheriff's Department, South Coast Patrol Division; and Mr. Mark Powers, the graveyard superintendent. The procedure took the better part of the day. Once Jane Doe's body was recovered, she was removed to the Santa Barbara County Coroner's Office.

In anticipation of the exhumation, Bill Turner had contacted Betty Gatliff in Oklahoma, whose work as a forensic artist is internationally recognized. Betty Gatliff is a retired medical illustrator who not only practices forensic sculpture but teaches workshops and seminars across the country. She is a Fellow of the American Academy of Forensics Sciences, an Emeritus Member of the Association of Medical Illustrators, and an Associate

Member of the International Association for Identification. Jane Doe's skull, maxilla, and mandible were sent to Ms. Gatliff, whose services had been engaged.

In the meantime, I had begun a re-creation of my own, constructing a wholly fictional account of a young girl whose fate was similar to Jane Doe's. Where possible, I used details from the Jane Doe murder book, including fragments from the autopsy report, case notes, and the investigative reports submitted by the detectives originally assigned to this case. There are two exceptions of note: (1) There was no tarp. I manufactured that detail to give my fictional detectives yet another means of pursuing their inquiries; and (2) there was, in fact, found at the scene a blood-soaked man's Western-style blue denim shirt with white-covered snaps, size 14½ neck. I omitted this detail in the interest of simplicity. That aside, I must assure the reader that every character in this novel is fictional. Every event is purely the product of my invention. Whatever the personality and nature of the "real" Jane Doe, my assertions are the figment of my imagination and are in no way purported to be real, true, or representative of her. I emphasize this point out of respect for her and out of consideration for those who must have loved her and wondered about her silence as the years have passed.

By mid-September of 2001, Betty Gatliff had reconstructed a likeness of Jane Doe and returned her skull with its mandible and maxilla. She also sent numerous color photographs of Jane Doe, four of which are reproduced here in black and white. Jane Doe was reinterred on Tuesday, February 26, 2002, with a uniformed Sheriff's Department Honor Guard accompanying her from the coroner's office to the cemetery, a sheriff's chaplain conducting the service, flowers, and the heartfelt prayers of those of us who have been a small part of her life. It is our hope that someone reading this novel and seeing the photographs will recognize this young woman and step forward with information about her. Though both Bruce Correll and Bill Turner retired in the summer of 2002, Bill Turner will be available to respond to queries by mail at: Sheriff's Department, County of Santa Barbara, 4434 Calle Real, P.O. Box 6427, Santa Barbara, CA 93160–6427, or through the Sheriff's Department's website, www.sbsheriff.org.

Respectfully submitted,
Sue Grafton

Jane Doe, Santa Barbara County,
August 1969. Forensic Reconstruction
by Betty Gatliff, September 2001.

R is for Ricochet

For my granddaughter, Taylor,

with a heart full of love

1

The basic question is this: given human nature, are any of us really capable of change? The mistakes other people make are usually patently obvious. Our own are tougher to recognize. In most cases, our path through life reflects a fundamental truth about who we are now and who we've been since birth. We're optimists or pessimists, joyful or depressed, gullible or cynical, inclined to seek adventure or to avoid all risks. Therapy might strengthen our assets or offset our liabilities, but in the main we do what we do because we've always done it that way, even when the outcome is bad ... perhaps *especially* when the outcome is bad.

This is a story about romance—love gone right, love gone wrong, and matters somewhere in between.

I left downtown Santa Teresa that day at 1:15 and headed for Montebello, a short ten miles south. The weather report had promised highs in the seventies. Morning cloudiness had given way to sunshine, a welcomed respite from the overcast that typically mars our June and

July. I'd eaten lunch at my desk, feasting on an olive-and-pimiento-cheese sandwich on wheat bread, cut in quarters, my third-favorite sandwich in the whole wide world. So what was the problem? I had none. Life was great.

In committing the matter to paper, I can see now what should have been apparent from the first, but events seemed to unfold at such a routine pace that I was caught, metaphorically speaking, asleep at the wheel. I'm a private detective, female, age thirty-seven, working in the small Southern California town of Santa Teresa. My jobs are varied, not always lucrative, but sufficient to keep me housed and fed and ahead of my bills. I do employee background checks. I track down missing persons or locate heirs entitled to monies in the settlement of an estate. On occasion, I investigate claims involving arson, fraud, or wrongful death.

In my personal life, I've been married and divorced twice, and subsequent relationships have usually come to grief. The older I get, the less I seem to understand men, and because of that I tend to shy away from them. Granted, I have no sex life to speak of, but at least I'm not plagued by unwanted pregnancies or sexually transmitted diseases. I've learned the hard way that love and work are a questionable mix.

I was driving on a stretch of highway once known as the Montebello Parkway, built in 1927 as the result of a fund-raising campaign that made possible the creation of frontage roads and landscaped center dividers still in evidence today. Because billboards and commercial structures along the roadway were banned at the same time, that section of the 101 is still attractive, except when it's jammed with rush-hour traffic.

Montebello itself underwent a similar transformation in

1948, when the Montebello Protective and Improvement Association successfully petitioned to eliminate sidewalks, concrete curbs, advertising signs, and anything else that might disrupt the rural atmosphere. Montebello is known for its two-hundred-some-odd luxury estates, many of them built by men who'd amassed their fortunes selling common household goods, salt and flour being two.

I was on my way to meet Nord Lafferty, an elderly gentleman, whose photograph appeared at intervals in the society column of the *Santa Teresa Dispatch*. This was usually occasioned by his making yet another sizable contribution to some charitable foundation. Two buildings at UCST had been named for him, as had a wing of Santa Teresa Hospital and a special collection of rare books he'd donated to the public library. He'd called me two days before and indicated he had "a modest undertaking" he wanted to discuss. I was curious how he'd come by my name and even more curious about the job itself. I've been a private investigator in Santa Teresa for the past ten years, but my office is small and, as a rule, I'm ignored by the wealthy, who seem to prefer doing business through their attorneys in New York, Chicago, or L.A.

I took the St. Isadore off-ramp and turned north toward the foothills that ran between Montebello and the Los Padres National Forest. At one time, this area boasted grand old resort hotels, citrus and avocado ranches, olive groves, a country store, and the Montebello train depot, which serviced the Southern Pacific Railroad. I'm forever reading up on local history, trying to imagine the region as it was 125 years ago. Land was selling then for seventy-five cents an acre. Montebello is still bucolic, but much of the charm has been bulldozed away. What's been erected instead—the condominiums, housing developments, and the big flashy starter castles of the nouveau riche—is poor compensation for what was lost or destroyed.

I turned right on West Glen and drove along the winding two-lane road as far as Bella Sera Place. Bella Sera is lined with olive and pepper trees, the narrow blacktop climbing gradually to a mesa that affords a sweeping view of the coast. The pungent scent of the ocean faded with my ascent, replaced by the smell of sage and the bay laurel trees. The hillsides were thick with yarrow, wild mustard, and California poppies. The afternoon sun had baked the boulders to a golden turn, and a warm chuffing wind was beginning to stir the dry grasses. The road wound upward through an alley of live oaks that terminated at the entrance to the Lafferty estate. The property was surrounded by a stone wall that was eight feet high and posted with No Trespassing signs.

I slowed to an idle when I reached the wide iron gates. I leaned out and pushed the call button on a mounted keypad. Belatedly I spotted a camera mounted atop one of two stone pillars, its hollow eye fixed on me. I must have passed inspection because the gates swung open at a measured pace. I shifted gears and sailed through, following the brick-paved drive for another quarter of a mile.

Through a picket fence of pines, I caught glimpses of a gray stone house. When the whole of the residence finally swept into view, I let out a breath. Something of the past remained after all. Four towering eucalyptus trees laid a dappled shade on the grass, and a breeze pushed a series of cloud-shaped shadows across the red tile roof. The two-story house, with matching one-story wings topped with stone balustrades at each end, dominated my visual field. A series of four arches shielded the entrance and provided a covered porch on which wicker furniture had been arranged. I counted twelve windows on the second floor, separated by paired eave brackets, largely decorative, that appeared to support the roof.

I pulled onto a parking pad sufficient to accommodate ten cars and left my pale blue VW hunched, cartoonlike, between a sleek Lincoln Continental on one side and a full-size Mercedes on the other. I didn't bother to lock up, operating on the assumption that the electronic surveillance system was watching over both me and my vehicle as I crossed to the front walk.

The lawns were wide and well tended, and the quiet was underlined by the twittering of finches. I pressed the front bell, listening to the hollow-sounding chimes inside clanging out two notes as though by a hammer on iron The ancient woman who came to the door wore an old-fashioned black uniform with a white pinafore over it. Her opaque stockings were the color of doll flesh, her crepe-soled shoes emitting the faintest squeak as I followed her down the marble-tiled hall. She hadn't asked my name, but perhaps I was the only visitor expected that day. The corridor was paneled in oak, the white plaster ceiling embossed with chevrons and fleurs-de-lis.

She showed me into the library, which was also paneled in oak. Drab leather-bound books lined shelves that ran floor to ceiling, with a brass rail and a rolling ladder allowing access to the upper reaches. The room smelled of dry wood and paper mold. The inner hearth in the stone fireplace was tall enough to stand in, and a recent blaze had left a partially blackened oak log and the faint stench of wood smoke. Mr. Lafferty was seated in one of a pair of matching wing chairs.

I placed him in his eighties, an age I'd considered elderly once upon a time. I've since come to realize how widely the aging process varies. My landlord is eighty-seven, the baby of his family, with siblings whose ages range as high as ninety-six. All five of them are lively, intelligent, adventurous, competitive, and given to good-natured squabbling among themselves. Mr. Lafferty, on the other hand, looked as though he'd been old for a good twenty years. He was inordinately thin, with knees as bony as a pair of misplaced elbows. His once sharp features had at least been softened by the passing years. Two small clear plastic tubes had been placed discreetly in his nostrils, tethering him to a stout green oxygen tank on a cart to his left. One side of his jaw was sunken, and a savage red line running across his throat suggested extensive surgery of some vicious sort.

He studied me with eyes as dark and shiny as dots of brown sealing wax. "I appreciate your coming, Ms. Millhone. I'm Nord Lafferty," he said, holding out a hand that was knotted with veins. His voice was hoarse, barely a whisper.

"Nice to meet you," I murmured, moving forward to shake hands with him. His were pale, a tremor visible in his fingers, which were icy to the touch.

He motioned to me. "You might want to pull that chair close. I've had thyroid surgery a month ago and more recently some polyps removed from my vocal cords. I've been left with this rasping noise that passes as speech.

Isn't painful, but it's irksome. I apologize if I'm difficult to understand."

"So far, I'm not having any problem."

"Good. Would you like a cup of tea? I can have my housekeeper make a pot, but I'm afraid you'll have to pour for yourself. These days, her hands aren't any steadier than mine."

"Thanks, but I'm fine." I pulled the second wing chair closer and took a seat. "When was this house built? It's really beautiful."

"1893. A man named Mueller bought a six-hundred-forty-acre section from the county of Santa Teresa. Of that, seventy acres remain. House took six years to build and the story has it Mueller died the day the workers finally set down their tools. Since then, the occupants have fared poorly . . . except for me, knock on wood. I bought the property in 1929, just after the crash. Fellow who owned the place lost everything. Drove into town, climbed up to the clock tower, and dived over the rail. Widow needed the cash and I stepped in. I was criticized, of course. Folks claimed I took advantage, but I'd loved the house from the minute I laid eyes on it. Someone would have bought it. Better me than them. I had money for the upkeep, which wasn't true of many folks back then."

"You were lucky."

"Indeed. Made my fortune in paper goods in case you're curious and too polite to inquire."

I smiled. "Polite, I don't know about. I'm always curious."

"That's fortunate, I'd say, given the business you're in. I'm assuming you're a busy woman so I'll get right to the point. Your name was given to me by a friend of yours—fellow I met during this recent hospital stay."

"Stacey Oliphant," I said, the name flashing immediately to mind. I'd worked a case with Stacey, a retired Sheriff's Department homicide detective, and my old pal Lieutenant Dolan, now retired from the Santa Teresa Police Department. Stacey was battling cancer, but the last I'd heard, he'd been given a reprieve.

Mr. Lafferty nodded. "He asked me to tell you he's doing well, by the way. He checked in for a battery of tests, but all of them turned out negative. As it happened, the two of us walked the halls together in the afternoons, and I got chatting about my daughter, Reba."

I was already thinking skip trace, missing heir, possibly a background check on a guy if Reba were romantically involved.

He went on. "I only have the one child and I suppose I've spoiled her unmercifully, though that wasn't my intent. Her mother ran off when she was just a little thing, this high. I was caught up in business and left the day-to-day raising of her to a series of nannies. If she'd been a boy I could have sent her off to boarding school the way my parents did me, but I wanted her at home. In retrospect, I see that might've been poor judgment on my part, but it didn't seem so at the time." He paused and then gestured impatiently toward the floor, as though chiding a dog for leaping up on him. "No matter. It's too late for regrets. Pointless, anyway. What's done is done." He looked at me sharply from under his bony brow. "You probably wonder what I'm driving at."

I proffered a slight shrug, waiting to hear what he had to say.

"Reba's being paroled on July twentieth. That's next Monday morning. I need someone to pick her up and bring her home. She'll be staying with me until she's on her feet again."

"What facility?" I asked, hoping I didn't sound as startled as I felt.

"California Institution for Women. Are you familiar with the place?"

"It's down in Corona, couple of hundred miles south. I've never actually been there, but I know where it is."

"Good. I'm hoping you can take time out of your schedule for the trip."

"That sounds easy enough, but why me? I charge five hundred dollars a day. You don't need a private detective to make a run like that. Doesn't she have friends?"

"Not anyone I'd ask. Don't worry about the money. That's the least of it. My daughter's difficult. Willful and rebellious. I want you to see to it she keeps the appointment with her parole officer and whatever else is required once she's been released. I'll pay you your full rate even if you only work for a part of each day."

"What if she doesn't like the supervision?"

"It's not up to her. I've told her I'm hiring someone to assist her and she's agreed. If she likes you, she'll be cooperative, at least to a point."

"May I ask what she did?"

"Given the time you'll be spending in her company, you're entitled to know. She was convicted of embezzling money from the company she worked for. Alan Beckwith and Associates. He does property management, real estate investment and development, things of that type. Do you know the man?"

9

"I've seen his name in the paper."

Nord Lafferty shook his head. "I don't care for him myself. I've known his wife's family for years. Tracy's a lovely girl. I can't understand how she ended up with the likes of him. Alan Beckwith is an upstart. He calls himself an entrepreneur, but I've never been entirely clear what he does. Our paths have crossed in public on numerous occasions and I can't say I'm impressed. Reba seems to think the world of him. I will credit him for this—he spoke up in her behalf before her sentencing. It was a generous gesture on his part and one he didn't have to make."

"How long has she been at CIW?"

"She's served twenty-two months of a four-year sentence. She never went to trial. At her arraignment—which I'm sorry to say I missed—she claimed she was indigent, so the court appointed a public defender to handle her case. After consultation with him, she waived her right to a preliminary hearing and entered a plea of guilty."

"Just like that?"

"I'm afraid so."

"And her attorney agreed to it?"

"He argued strenuously against it, but Reba wouldn't listen."

"How much money are we talking?"

"Three hundred fifty thousand dollars over a two-year period."

"How'd they discover the theft?"

"During a routine audit. Reba was one of a handful of employees with access to the accounts. Naturally, suspicion fell on her. She's been in trouble before, but nothing of this magnitude."

I could feel a protest welling but I bit back my response.

He leaned forward. "You have something to say, feel free to say it. Stacey tells me you're outspoken so please don't hesitate on my account. It may save us a misunderstanding."

"I was just wondering why you didn't step in. A high-powered attorney might have made all the difference."

He dropped his gaze to his hands. "I should have helped her . . . I know that . . . but I'd been coming to her rescue for many, many years . . . all her life, if you want to know the truth. At least that's what I was being told by friends. They said she had to face the consequences of her behavior or she was never going to learn. They said I'd be enabling, that saving her was the worst possible action under the circumstances."

"Who's this 'they' you're referring to?"

For the first time, he faltered. "I had a lady friend. Lucinda. We'd been keeping company for years. She'd seen me intercede on Reba's behalf on countless occasions. She persuaded me to put my foot down and that's what I did."

"And now?"

"Frankly, I was shocked when Reba was sentenced to four years in state prison. I had no idea the penalty would be so stiff. I thought the judge would suspend sentence or agree to probation, as the public defender suggested. At any rate, Lucinda and I quarreled, bitterly I might add. I broke off the relationship and severed my ties with her. She was much younger than I. In hindsight, I realized she was angling for herself, hoping for marriage. Reba disliked her intensely. Lucinda knew that, of course."

"What happened to the money?"

"Reba gambled it away. She's always been attracted to

card play. Roulette, the slots. She loves to bet the ponies, but she has no head for it."

"She's a problem gambler?"

"Her problem isn't the gambling, it's the losing," he remarked, with only the weakest of smiles.

"What about drugs and alcohol?"

"I'd have to answer yes on both counts. She tends to be reckless. She has a wild streak like her mother. I'm hoping this experience in prison has taught her self-restraint. As for the job itself, we'll play that by ear. We're talking two to three days, a week at the most, until she's reestablished herself. Since your responsibilities are limited, I won't be requiring a written report. Submit an invoice and I'll pay your daily rate and all the necessary expenses."

"That seems simple enough."

"One other item. If there's any suggestion that she's backsliding, I want to be informed. Perhaps with sufficient warning, I can head off disaster this time around."

"A tall order."

"I'm aware of that."

Briefly, I considered the proposition. Ordinarily I don't like serving as a babysitter and potential tattletale, but in this case, his concern didn't seem out of line. "What time will she be released?"

2

On my way back into town, I picked up my dry-cleaning
and then cruised through a nearby supermarket, picking
up odds and ends, which I intended to drop off at my place
before I returned to work. I was hoping to touch base with
my landlord before the arrival of his lady visitor later in
the day. I was running the errands to provide myself with
props to explain my unexpected midafternoon appearance.
Henry and I confide in each other on many issues, but his
love life isn't one. If I wanted information, I knew I'd do
well to proceed with finesse.

My studio apartment was originally the single-car
garage attached to Henry's house by way of a now glass-
enclosed breezeway. In 1980 he converted the space to the
snug studio I've been renting ever since. What began as a
basic square fifteen feet on a side is now a fully furnished
"great room," which includes a living room, a bump-out
galley-style kitchen, a laundry nook and bathroom, with a
sleeping loft and a second bathroom up a set of spiral
stairs. The space is compact and cleverly designed to

exploit every usable inch. Given the pegs and cubbyholes, walls of polished teak and oak, and the occasional porthole window, the studio has the scale and feel of a ship's interior.

I found a parking spot two doors away and hauled out my cleaning and the two grocery bags. My timing couldn't have been more perfect. As I pushed through my squeaky metal gate and followed the walkway around to the rear, Henry was just pulling into his two-car garage. He'd taken his bright yellow five-window Chevy coupe for its annual checkup and it was back now, the exterior polished to a fare-thee-well. The interior was probably not only spotless, but scented with faux pine. He bought the vehicle new in 1932 and he's taken such good care of it you'd swear it was still under warranty, assuming cars had warranties back then. He has a second vehicle, a station wagon he uses for routine errands and the occasional trip to the Los Angeles airport, ninety-five miles south. The coupe he reserves for special occasions, today being one.

I have trouble remembering that he's eighty-seven years old. I also have trouble describing him in terms that aren't embarrassingly laudatory given our fifty-year age difference. He's smart, sweet, sexy, trim, handsome, vigorous, and kind. In his working days, he made a living as a commercial baker, and though he's been retired now for twenty-five years, he still makes the best cinnamon rolls I've ever eaten. If I were forced to accord him a fault, I'd probably cite his caution when it comes to affairs of the heart. The only time I'd seen him smitten, he was not only deceived, but nearly taken for every cent he had. Since then, he's played his cards very close to his chest. Either he hadn't run into anyone of interest or he'd looked the other way. That is, until Mattie Halstead appeared.

Mattie was the artist-in-residence on a Caribbean cruise he and his siblings had taken in April. Soon after the cruise ended, she'd stopped in to see him on her way to Los Angeles to deliver paintings to a gallery down there. A month later, he'd made an unprecedented trip to San Francisco, where he spent an evening with her. He'd kept mum on the subject of their relationship, but I noticed he'd spiffed up his wardrobe and started lifting weights. The Pitts family (at least on Henry's mother's side) is long-lived, and he and his siblings enjoy remarkably good health. William's a bit of a hypochondriac and Charlie's almost entirely deaf, but that aside, they give the appearance of going on forever. Lewis, Charlie, and Nell live in Michigan, but there are visits back and forth, some planned and some not. William and my friend Rosie, who owns the tavern half a block away, would be celebrating their second wedding anniversary on November 28. Now it looked like Henry might be entertaining similar thoughts . . . or such was my hope. Other people's romances are so much less hazardous than one's own. I was looking forward to all the pleasures of true love without suffering the peril.

Henry paused when he caught sight of me, allowing me to fall into step with him as he proceeded to the house. I noticed his hair had been freshly trimmed, and he wore a blue denim work shirt with his crisply pressed chinos. He'd even traded in his usual flip-flops for a pair of deck shoes with dark socks.

I said, "Hang on a second while I drop this stuff off."

He waited while I unlocked my door and dumped my

armload on the floor just inside. Nothing I'd bought would go funky in the next thirty minutes. Rejoining him, I said, "You had your hair trimmed. It looks great."

He ran a self-conscious hand across his head. "I was passing the barbershop and realized I was long overdue. You think it's too short?"

"Not at all. It shaves years off your age," I said, thinking Mattie would have to be an idiot if she didn't understand what a treasure he was. I held open the screen door while he pulled out his keys and unlocked his back door. I followed him inside, watching as he set his groceries on the kitchen counter.

"Nice that Mattie's coming down. I'll bet you're looking forward to seeing her."

"It's only the one night."

"What's the occasion?"

"She did a painting on commission for a woman in La Jolla. She's delivering that one plus a couple more in case the woman doesn't care for the first."

"Well, it's nice she can manage a visit. When's she getting in?"

"She hoped to be here by four, depending on traffic. She said she'd check into the hotel and call once she's had a chance to freshen up. She agreed to supper here as long as I didn't go to any trouble. I said I'd keep it simple, but you know me."

He began to unload his sack: a packet wrapped in white butcher's paper, potatoes, cabbage, green onions, and a big jar of mayonnaise. While I watched, he opened the oven door and checked his crock of soldier beans bubbling away with molasses, mustard, and a chunk of salt pork. I could see two loaves of freshly baked bread resting on a rack on the counter. A chocolate layer cake sat in the middle of the kitchen table with a glass dome over it. There was also a bouquet of flowers from his garden— roses and lavender he'd arranged artfully in a china teapot.

"Cake looks fabulous."

"It's a twelve-layer torte. I used Nell's recipe, which was originally our mother's. We tried it for years, but none of us could duplicate her results. Nell finally managed, but she says it's a pain. I ended up tossing half a dozen layers before I mastered the thing."

"What else are you having?"

Henry took out a cast-iron skillet and set it on the stove. "Fried chicken, potato salad, coleslaw, and baked beans. I thought we'd have a little picnic on the patio, unless the temperature drops." He opened his spice cabinet and sorted through the contents, taking down a bottle of dried dill. "Why don't you join us? She'd love to see you."

"Oh please. Socializing is the last thing she needs. After six hours on the road? Give the woman a drink and let her put her feet up."

"No need to worry about her. She has energy to spare. She'd be delighted, I'm sure."

"Let's just see how it goes. I'm on my way back to the office, but I'll check in with you again as soon as I get home."

I'd already decided to decline, but I didn't want to seem rude. In my opinion, they needed time to themselves. I'd pop my head in and say hi, primarily to satisfy my curiosity about her. She was either widowed or divorced, I wasn't sure which, but during her last visit, I'd noticed she'd made a number of references to her husband. At one point, when Henry was nursing a bum knee, she'd gone hiking alone, taking her watercolors with her so she could paint a spot in the mountains she and her husband had enjoyed for years. Was she still emotionally entrenched? Whether hubby was dead or alive, I didn't like the idea. Henry, meanwhile, was busy being nonchalant, perhaps in denial of his feelings or in response to covert signals from her. Of course, there was always the possibility that I was imagining all this, but I didn't think so. At any rate, I intended to have my supper at Rosie's, resigned to my usual weekly allotment of her bullying and abuse.

I left Henry to his preparations and went back to the office, where I put a call through to Priscilla Holloway, Reba Lafferty's parole agent. Nord Lafferty had given me her name and phone number at the end of our appointment. I was already back at my car, opening the driver's side, when the elderly housekeeper had called from the front door and then hurried down the walk, a photograph in hand.

Winded, she'd said, "Mr. Lafferty forgot to give you this. It's a photograph of Reba."

"Thanks. I appreciate that. I'll return it as soon as we get back."

"Oh, no need. He said to keep it if you like."

I thanked her again and tucked the photo into my bag. Now, while I waited for Parole Agent Holloway to answer her phone, I plucked out the photo and studied it again. I'd have preferred something recent. This had been taken when the woman was in her mid- to late twenties and almost puckish in appearance. Her large dark eyes were intent on the camera, her full lips half-parted as though she were on the verge of speaking. Her hair was shoulder-length and dyed blond, but clearly at considerable expense. Her complexion was clear with a hint of blush in her cheeks. After two years of prison fare, she might have packed on a few extra pounds, but I thought I'd recognize her.

On the other end of the line, a woman said, "Holloway."

"Hi, Ms. Holloway. My name is Kinsey Millhone. I'm a local private investigator—"

"I know who you are. I had a call from Nord Lafferty, telling me he'd hired you to pick up his daughter."

"That's why I'm calling, to clear it with you."

"Fine. Have at it. It'll save me the trip. If you're back in town before three, bring her over to the office. Do you know where I am?"

I didn't, but she gave me the address.

"See you Monday," I said.

I spent the rest of the afternoon taking care of paperwork, mostly sorting and filing in a vain attempt to tidy up my desk. I also did some boning up on parole regulations from a pamphlet printed by the California Department of Corrections.

Returning to my apartment for the second time that day, I saw no sign of picnic items on the patio table. Perhaps he'd decided the meal was better served indoors. I crossed to his back door and peeked in. As it turned out, my hopes for their romantic interlude were squelched by William's presence in the kitchen. Looking aggrieved, Henry sat in his rocking chair with his usual glass of Jack Daniel's while Mattie nursed a goblet of white wine.

William, two years Henry's senior, has always looked enough like him to be his twin. His shock of white hair was thinning where Henry's was still full, but his eyes were the same hot blue and he carried himself with the same erect military bearing. He wore a dapper three-piece suit, his watch chain visible across the front of his vest. I tapped on the glass and Henry motioned me in. William rose to his feet at the sight of me, and I knew he'd remain standing unless I urged him to sit. Mattie rose to greet me, and though we didn't actually hug, we did clasp hands and exchange an air kiss.

She was in her early seventies, tall and slender, with soft silver hair she wore pulled into a knot on the top of her head. Her earrings glinted in the light—silver, over-size, and artisan-made.

I said, "Hey, Mattie. How are you? You must have arrived right on time."

"Good to see you. I did." She wore a coral silk blouse and a long gypsy skirt over flat-heel suede boots. "Will you join us in a glass of wine?"

"I don't think so, but thanks. I've got business to take care of so I have to run."

Henry's tone was morose. "Have a glass of wine. Why not? Stay for supper as well. William's invited himself so what's the difference? Rosie couldn't tolerate having him underfoot so she sent him over here."

William said, "She had a small conniption fit for no reason at all. I'd just returned from the doctor's office and I knew she'd want to hear the results of my blood work, especially my HDLs. You might want to take a look yourself." He held the paper out, pointing with significance at the long column of numbers down the right side of the page. My gaze slid past his glucose, sodium, potassium, and chloride levels before I caught the expression on Henry's face. His eyes were crossed so close to the bridge of his nose I thought they'd trade sides. William was saying, "You can see my LDL-HDL risk ratio is 1.3."

"Oh, sorry. Is that bad?"

"No, no. The doctor said it was excellent . . . in light of my medical condition." William's voice carried a hint of feebleness suggestive of a weakened state.

"Well, good for you. That's great."

"Thank you. I called our brother Lewis and told him as well. His cholesterol is 214, which I think is cause for alarm. He says he's doing what he can, but he hasn't had much success. You can pass the paper on to Mattie once you've studied it yourself."

Henry said, "William, would you sit down? You're giving me a crick in my neck." He left his rocker and took another wineglass from the kitchen cabinet. He poured wine to the brim and passed the glass to me, slopping some liquid on my hand.

William declined to sit until he'd pulled out my chair. I settled myself with a murmured "Thank you" and then I made a show of running a finger down the column of reference and unit numbers from his doctor's report. "You're in good shape," I remarked as I passed the paper to Mattie.

"Well, I still have palpitations, but the doctor's adjusting my medication. He says I'm amazing for a man my age."

"If you're in such terrific health, how come you're off to the urgent care center every other day?" Henry snapped.

William blinked placidly at Mattie. "My brother's careless with his health and won't acknowledge that some of us are proactive."

Henry made a snorting sound.

William cleared his throat. "Well now. On to a new subject since Henry's apparently unable to handle that one. I hope this is not too personal, but Henry mentioned your husband is deceased. Do you mind my asking how he was taken?"

Henry was clearly exasperated. "You call that a different subject? It's the same one—death and disease. Can't you think of anything else?"

"I wasn't addressing you," William replied before returning his attention to Mattie. "I hope the topic isn't too painful."

"Not at this point. Barry died six years ago of heart failure. I believe cardiac ischemia is the term they used. He taught jewelry making at the San Francisco Art Institute. He was a very talented man, though a bit of an eccentric."

William was nodding. "Cardiac ischemia. I know the term well. From the Greek, *ischein*, meaning 'quench' or 'seize,' combined with *haima*, or 'blood.' A German pathology professor first introduced that term in the mid-1800s. Rudolf Virchow. A remarkable man. What age was your husband?"

"William," Henry sang.

Mattie smiled. "Really, Henry. I'm not sensitive about this. He died two days shy of his seventieth birthday."

William winced. "Pity when a man's struck down in his prime. I myself have suffered several episodes of angina, which I've miraculously survived. I was discussing my heart condition with Lewis, just two days ago by phone. You remember our brother, I'm sure."

"Of course. I hope he and Nell and Charles are all in good health."

"Excellent," William said. He shifted in his chair, lowering his voice. "What about your husband? Did he have any warning prior to his fatal attack?"

"He'd been having chest pains, but he refused to see the doctor. Barry was a fatalist. He believed you check out when your time is up regardless what precautions you take. He compared longevity to an alarm clock that God sets the moment you're born. None of us knows when the little bell will ring, but he didn't see the point in trying to second-guess the process. He enjoyed life immensely, I'll say that about him. Most folks in my family don't make it to the age of sixty, and they're miserable every minute, dreading the inevitable."

"Sixty! Is that right? That's astonishing. Is there a genetic factor in play?"

"I don't think so. It's a little bit of everything. Cancer, diabetes, kidney failure, chronic pulmonary disease . . ."

William put his hands on his chest. I hadn't seen him so happy since he'd had the flu. "COPD. Chronic obstructive pulmonary disease. The very term brings back memories. I was stricken with a lung condition in my youth—"

Henry clapped his hands. "Okay, fine. Enough said on that subject. Why don't we eat?"

He moved to the refrigerator and took out a clear glass bowl piled with coleslaw, which he plunked on the table with rather more force than was absolutely necessary. The chicken he'd fried was piled on a platter on the counter, probably still warm. He placed that in the center of the table with a pair of serving tongs. The squat little crockery pot now sat on the back of the stove, emitting the fragrance of tender beans and bay leaf. He removed serving utensils from a ceramic jug and then took down four dinner plates, which he handed to William, perhaps in hopes of distracting his attention while he brought the rest of the dinner to the table. William set a plate at each place while he quizzed Mattie at length about her mother's death from acute bacterial meningitis.

Over supper Henry steered the conversation into neutral territory. We went through ritual questions about Mattie's drive down from San Francisco, traffic, road conditions, and matters of that sort, which gave me ample opportunity to observe her. Her eyes were a clear gray and she wore very little makeup. She had strong features, with nose, cheekbones, and jaw as pronounced and well proportioned as a model's. Her skin showed signs of sun damage, and it lent her complexion a ruddy glow. I pictured her out in the fields for hours with her paint box and easel.

I could tell William was reflecting on the subject of terminal disease while I was calculating how soon I could make my excuses and depart. I intended to drag William with me so Henry and Mattie could have some time alone. I kept an eye on the clock while I worked my way through the fried chicken, potato salad, coleslaw, baked beans, and cake. The food, of course, was wonderful, and I ate with my usual speed and enthusiasm. At 8:35, just as I was formulating a plausible lie, Mattie folded her napkin and laid it on the table beside her plate.

"Well, I should be on my way. I have some phone calls to make as soon as I get back to the hotel."

"You're leaving?" I said, trying to cover my disappointment.

"She's had a long day," Henry said, getting up to remove her plate. He took it to the sink, where he rinsed it and set it in the dishwasher, talking to her all the while.

"I can wrap up some chicken in case you want some later."

"Don't tempt me. I'm full but not stuffed, which is just the way I like it. This was wonderful, Henry. I can't tell you how much I appreciate the effort that went into this meal."

"Happy you enjoyed it. I'll get your wrap from the other room." He dried his hands on a kitchen towel and moved off toward the bedroom.

William folded his napkin and scraped back his chair. "I should probably run along as well. Doctor urged me to adhere to my regimen—eight full hours of sleep. I may engage in some light calisthenics before bed to aid the digestive process. Nothing strenuous, of course."

I turned to Mattie. "You have plans for tomorrow?"

"Unfortunately, I'm taking off first thing in the morning, but I'll be back in a few days."

Henry returned with a soft paisley shawl that he laid across her shoulders. She patted his hand with affection and picked up a large leather bag that she'd set beside her chair. "I hope to see you again soon," she said to me.

"I hope so, too."

Henry touched her elbow. "I'll walk you out."

William straightened his vest. "No need. I'll be happy to see her off." He offered Mattie his arm, and she tucked her hand through the crook with a brief backward look at Henry as the two went out the door.

3

Saturday morning, I slept in until 8:00, showered, dressed, made a pot of coffee, and sat at my kitchen counter, where I ate my ritual bowl of cereal. Having washed both bowl and spoon, I returned to my stool and surveyed the place. I'm inordinately tidy and I'd just done a thorough house-cleaning earlier in the week. My social calendar was unblemished and I knew I'd spend Saturday and Sunday alone as I did most weekends. Usually this doesn't bother me, but today I felt an unsettling sensation. I was bored. I was so desperate for something to do, I thought about returning to the office to set up the files for another case I'd taken on. Unfortunately, my office bungalow is depressing and I wasn't motivated to spend another minute at my desk. Which left me to do what? Damned if I knew. In a moment of panic, I realized I didn't even have a book to read. I was on the verge of leaving for the bookstore to stock up on paperbacks when my telephone rang.

"Hi, Kinsey. This is Vera. I'm glad I caught you. You have a minute?"

"Of course. I was on my way out, but it's nothing pressing," I said. Vera Lipton had been a colleague of mine at California Fidelity Insurance, where I spent six years investigating arson and wrongful-death claims. She was the claims manager while I worked as an independent contractor. She had since left the business, married a doctor, and settled into life as a full-time mom. I'd seen her briefly in April with her husband, a physician named Neil Hess. Also in tow was a rowdy golden retriever pup, and her eighteen-month-old son, whose name I forgot to ask. She was massively pregnant and due to deliver her second child within days, judging by her belly. I said, "Tell me about the baby. You looked ready to drop one the day I saw you at the beach."

"No kidding. I was sway-backed as a mule. I had shooting pains in both legs, and the baby's head pressing on my bladder made me dribble in my pants. I went into labor that night and Meg was born the next afternoon. Listen, the reason I called, we'd love to have you over. We never see you these days."

"Sounds good to me. Give me a toot and we'll set something up."

There was a pause. "That's what I'm doing. I just invited you to come over and have a drink with us. We're putting some people together for a barbecue this afternoon."

"Really? What time?"

"Four o'clock. I know it's short notice, but I'm hoping you're free."

"As it happens, I am. What's the occasion?"

Vera laughed. "No occasion. I just thought it'd be nice. We've invited a few neighbors. Strictly casual and low-key. If you have a pencil handy, I'll give you the address.

Why don't you plan to be here a little early and we can catch up."

I took down the information, not at all convinced. Why would she call like this out of the blue? "Vera, are you sure you're not up to something? I don't mean to sound rude, but we chatted for five minutes in April. Before that, there was a gap of four years. Don't get me wrong. I'd be happy to see you, but it does seem odd."

"Mmm."

I said, "What," not even bothering to make a question of the word.

"Okay, I'll level with you, but you have to promise you won't scream."

"I'm listening, but this is making my stomach hurt."

"Neil's younger brother, Owen, is in town for the weekend. We thought you should meet him."

"What for?"

"Kinsey, occasionally men and women are introduced to each other, or haven't you heard?"

"Like a blind *date?*"

"It's not a blind date. It's drinks and a few snacks. There'll be tons of other people so it's not like you'll be stuck with him one-on-one. We'll sit on the back deck. Cheez Whiz and crackers. If you like him, that's swell. If you don't, no big deal."

"The last time you fixed me up, it was with Neil," I said.

"My point exactly. Look how that turned out."

I was silent for a moment. "What's he like?"

"Well, aside from the fact that he walks with his knuckles barely grazing the floor, he seems to do okay.

Look, I'll have him fill out an application. You can do a background check. Just be here at three-thirty. I'm wearing my only pair of jeans that haven't been split up the back."

She hung up while I was saying, "But . . ."

I listened to the dial tone in a state of despair. I could see now I was being penalized for shirking my job. I should have gone in to work. The Universe keeps track of our sins and exacts devious and repugnant punishments, like dates with unknown men. I went up the spiral staircase and opened my closet so I could stare at my clothes. Here's what I saw: My black all-purpose dress—which is the only dress I own, good for funerals and other somber occasions, not suitable for meeting guys, unless they're already dead. Three pairs of jeans, a denim vest, one short skirt, and the new tweed blazer I bought when I had lunch with my cousin, Tasha, eighteen months before. Also, an olive-green cocktail dress I'd forgotten about, given to me by a woman who was later blown to bits. In addition, there were castoffs from Vera, including a pair of black silk pants so long I had to roll 'em up at the waist. If I wore those, she'd ask to have them back, thus forcing me to drive home essentially naked below the waist. Not that I thought harem pants would be suitable for a barbecue. I knew better than that. Shrugging, I opted for my usual jeans and turtleneck.

At 3:30 promptly I was ringing Vera's doorbell. The address she'd given me was on the upper east side of town, in a neighborhood of older homes. Theirs was a ramshackle Victorian painted dark gray with white trim and an L-shaped wooden porch complete with frou-frou along the rail. The front door had a stained-glass rose in the center that made Vera's face look bright pink when she peered out at me. Behind her, the dog barked with excitement, eager to jump up and slobber on someone new. She opened the door, holding the dog by its collar to prevent its escape.

She said, "Don't look so glum. You've been given a reprieve. I sent the guys out to buy Pampers and beer, so it's just us for twenty minutes. Come on in." Her hair was cropped short and streaked with blond. She still sported her glasses with wire frames and enormous pale blue lenses. Vera's the type of woman who attracts admiring glances wherever she goes. Her figure was substantial, though she'd already dropped much of the weight she gained with Meg. She was barefoot, wearing tight jeans and an oversize tunic with short sleeves and a complicated cut to the top. All the toddler and baby toting had firmed her biceps.

She held the door for me, angling her body so the dog couldn't lunge at me just yet. He'd doubled in size since I'd seen him on the beach. He didn't seem like a mean mutt, but he was exuberant. She leaned close to his face, put a hand around his muzzle, and said, "No!" in a tone that had no particular effect. He seemed to like the attention and licked her in the mouth the first chance he got.

"This is Chase. Ignore him. He'll settle down in a bit."

I made an effort to ignore the dog while he pranced around, barking happily, and then snagged the hem of my pant leg and began to tug. He emitted a puppy growl, his feet braced on the hall carpet so he could rip my jeans to shreds. I stood there, captive, and said, "Gee, this is fun, Vera. I'm so glad I came."

She gave me a look, but let the sarcasm pass. She snagged the dog by the collar and dragged him toward the kitchen while I followed. The foyer ceiling was high with a set of stairs to the right, the living room on the left. A short hall led straight to the kitchen across the back. The passage was the usual land mine of wooden blocks, plastic toy parts, and abandoned doggie bones. She shoved Chase into a kennel the size of a steamer trunk. This didn't dismay the dog, but I felt guilty nonetheless. He placed a baleful eye to one of the air vents in the kennel and stared at me with hope.

The kitchen was large and I could see a wide deck accessible through a set of French doors. The cabinets were dark cherry, the counters dark green marble, with a six-burner stove-top built into a central island. Both the baby and Vera's son, whom she introduced as Peter, were already bathed and dressed for bed. Near the kitchen sink, a woman in a pale blue uniform was piping a star of yellow filling into each of a dozen hard-boiled egg halves.

"This is Mavis," Vera said. "She and Dirk are helping to save the wear and tear on me. I've got a babysitter on her way."

I murmured greetings and Mavis smiled in response, hardly pausing as she squeezed the filling from a pastry bag. Parsley had been tucked around the platter. On the counter nearby there were two baking sheets of canapes ready for the oven and two other serving platters, one arranged with fresh cut vegetables and the other an assortment of imported cheeses interspersed with grapes. So much for Cheez Whiz—which I personally adored, being a person of low tastes. This party had clearly been in the works for weeks. I now suspected the designated blind date had come down with the flu and I'd been elected to take her place . . . a B-list substitute.

Dirk, in dress pants and a short white jacket, was

working near the walk-in pantry where he'd set up a temporary bar with a variety of glasses, an ice bucket, and an impressive row of wine and liquor bottles.

"How many are you expecting?"

"Twenty-five or so. This is strictly last minute so a lot of people couldn't make it."

"I'll bet."

"I'm still off the booze because of Twinkletoes here."

The baby, Meg, was strapped in an infant seat in the middle of the kitchen table, looking around with a vague expression of satisfaction. Peter, aged twenty-one months, had been secured in a high chair. His tray was littered with Cheerios and green peas that he captured and ate when he wasn't squishing them instead.

Vera said, "That's not his dinner. It's just to keep him occupied until the babysitter shows. Speaking of which, Dirk can fix you a drink while I take Peter upstairs." She removed the tray from the high chair and set it aside, then lifted the boy and set him on one hip. "I'll be back shortly. If Meg cries, it's probably because she wants to be picked up."

Vera disappeared down the hall with Peter, heading for the stairs.

Dirk said, "What can I get for you?"

"Chardonnay's fine. I'd appreciate that."

I watched while he removed a bottle of Chardonnay from an ice tub behind him. He poured me a glass and added a cocktail napkin as he passed the wine across the makeshift bar.

"Thanks."

Vera had set out Brie and thinly sliced French bread, bowls of nuts and green olives. I ate one, being careful not to crack my teeth on the pit. I was curious to tour the rest of the downstairs rooms, but I didn't dare leave Meg. I had no idea what a baby her age was capable of doing while strapped in an infant seat. Could they hop in those things?

One end of the kitchen had been furnished with two sofas upholstered in a floral fabric, two coordinating chairs, a coffee table, and a television set built into an entertainment center that ran along the wall. Wineglass in hand, I circled the periphery, idly studying the silver-framed photos of family and friends. I couldn't help wondering if one of the fellows pictured was Neil's brother, Owen. I imagined him, like Neil, on the short side and probably dark-haired as well.

Behind me, Meg made a restless sound of the sort that suggested more to follow at twice the volume. I tended to my responsibilities, setting down my wineglass so I could free the child from her infant seat. I picked her up, so unprepared for how light she was I nearly flung her through the air. Her hair was dark and fine, her eyes a bright blue with lashes as delicate as feathers. She smelled like baby powder and maybe something fresh and brown in her pants. Amazingly, after staring at me briefly, she laid her face against my shoulder and began to gnaw on her fist. She squirmed and the little oinking sounds she made hinted at feeding urges I hoped wouldn't erupt before her mother returned. I jiggled her a bit and that seemed to satisfy her temporarily.

I had now exhausted my vast fund of infant-care tricks.

I heard a manly trampling outside on the wooden deck. Neil opened the back door bearing a grocery sack bulky with disposable diapers. The guy who came in behind him carried two six-packs of bottled beer. Neil and I exchanged greetings and then he turned to his brother and said, "Kinsey Millhone. This is my brother, Owen."

I said, "Hi." The babe in my arms precluded anything in the way of handshakes.

He responded with hey-how-are-you-type things, talking over his shoulder while he delivered the beer into Dirk's capable hands.

Neil set the sack on a kitchen stool and removed the package of disposable diapers. "Let me run these on up. You want me to take her?" he asked, indicating Meg.

"This is fine," I said, and surprisingly, it was. After Neil left, I peered down at her and discovered that she'd gone to asleep. "Oh, wow," I said, scarcely daring to breathe. I couldn't tell if the ticking I heard was my biological clock or the delayed timing device on a bomb.

Dirk was in the process of making a margarita for Owen, ice clattering in the blender. With his attention occupied I had an opportunity to study him. He was tall, compared with his brother, over six feet while Neil topped out closer to my height at five-feet-seven. His hair was sandy, lightly dusted with gray. He was lean, an ecto-morph, where Neil's build was stocky. Blue eyes, white lashes, a good-size nose. He glanced over at me and I dropped my gaze discreetly to Meg. He wore chinos and a navy short-sleeved shirt that revealed the light downy hair along his forearms. His teeth were good and his smile seemed sincere. On a scale of 1 to 10—10 being Harrison Ford—I'd place him at 8, or maybe even 8 plus plus.

He moved to the counter where I was standing and helped himself to a canape. We chatted idly, exchanging the sort of uninspired questions and answers that tend to pass between strangers. He told me he was visiting from

New York, where he worked as an architect, designing residential and commercial structures. I told him what I did and how long I'd done it. He feigned more interest than he probably felt. He told me he and Neil had three other brothers, of which he was the second from the bottom of the heap. Most of the family, he said, was scattered up and down the East Coast with Neil the lone holdout in California. I told him I was an only child and let it go at that.

Eventually, Neil and Vera came downstairs. She took the baby and settled on the couch. Vera fiddled with her shirt, popped a boob out, and began to breast-feed while Owen and I made a point of looking somewhere else. Eventually several other couples arrived. There were introductions all around as each new twosome was incorporated. The kitchen was gradually taken up with guests, standing in small groups, some spilling into the hallway and out onto the deck. When the babysitter arrived, Vera took Meg upstairs and returned wearing a different shirt. The noise level rose. Owen and I were separated by the crowd, which was all right with me as I'd run out of things to say to him.

I made an effort to be friendly, chitchatting with any poor soul who caught my eye. Everyone seemed nice enough, but social gatherings are exhausting to someone of my introverted nature. I endured it as long as I could and then eased toward the foyer where I'd left my shoulder bag. Good manners dictated that I say thank you and good-bye to host and hostess, but neither were in sight and I thought it'd be expedient to tiptoe away without calling attention to my escape.

As I closed the front door and made my way down the wooden porch stairs, I caught sight of Cheney Phillips coming up the walk in a deep red silk shirt, cream dress pants, and highly polished Italian loafers. Cheney was a local cop, working vice last I heard. I tended to run into him at a dive called the Caliente Café—also known as CC's—off Cabana Boulevard by the bird refuge. Rumor had it he'd met a girl at CC's and the two had taken off for Vegas to get married a scant six weeks later. I remembered the pang of disappointment with which I'd greeted the news. That was three months ago.

He said, "Leaving so soon?"

"Hey, how are you? What are you doing here?"

He tilted his head. "I live next door."

I followed his gaze to the house, another two-story Victorian that appeared to be a twin of the one I'd just left. Not many cops can afford the tab on a Santa Teresa residence of that size and vintage. "I thought you lived in Perdido."

"I did. That's where I grew up. My uncle died, leaving me a great whack of dough so I decided to invest it in real estate." He was probably thirty-four, three years younger than I, with a lean face and a mop of dark curly hair, five-eight or so, and slim. He'd told me that his mother sold high-end real estate and his father was X. Phillips who owned the Bank of X. Phillips in Perdido, a town thirty miles to the south. He'd clearly been raised in an atmosphere of privilege.

"Nice house," I said.

"Thanks. I'm still getting settled or I'd offer you a tour."

"Maybe another time," I said, wondering about his wife.

"What are you up to these days?"

"Nothing much. A little this and that."

"Why don't you return to the party and have a drink with me? We should talk."

I said, "Can't. I have to be someplace and I'm late as it is."

"Rain check?"

"Of course."

I waved, walking backward for a moment before I turned and headed to my car. Now why had I said that? I could have stayed for a drink, but I couldn't face another minute in that crowd. Too many people and too much chitchat.

I was home again by 6:15, relieved to be alone but feeling let down nonetheless. Given that I hadn't wanted to meet Vera's brother-in-law in the first place, I was disappointed—the blind date had turned out to be a bland date. Nice guy, no sparks, which was probably just as well. Sort of. It was entirely possible the regrets were attached to Cheney Phillips instead of Owen Hess, but I didn't want to deal with that. What was the point?

4

I left for the prison at 6:00 Monday morning. The drive was boring and hot, my route taking me from Santa Teresa down the 101 as far as Highway 126, which cuts inland at Perdido. The road runs between the Santa Clara River on the right and a fencework of power lines on the left, skirting the southern reaches of the Los Padres National Forest. I'd seen contour maps of the area, which detailed numerous hiking trails through that bleak and mountainous terrain. Dozens of creeks are threaded along the canyon floors. There are a surprising number of public campgrounds distributed throughout the 219,700 acres that constitute the wilderness. If I weren't preternaturally opposed to bugs, black bears, rattlesnakes, coyotes, heat, stinging nettles, and dirt, I might enjoy seeing the rumored sandstone cliffs and pines growing at odd angles along the boulder-strewn hills. In years past, even from the safety of the highway, I sometimes spotted one of the last of the California condors circling in the sky, its ten-foot wingspan stretched out as gracefully as a soaring kite.

I passed countless avocado orchards and citrus groves laden with ripening oranges, with produce stands set up every two to three miles. I caught a red light in each of three small communities of newly constructed housing and lavish shopping malls. An hour and a half later, I reached the junction of the 125 and Highway 5, which I followed to the south. It took me another hour to reach Corona. The incarceration-prone family couldn't do much better than to serve their separate bids in this area, which has the California Youth Authority, the California Institution for Men, and the California Institution for Women all within shooting range of one another. The land was flat and dusty, interrupted by power lines and water towers, parcels separated by low barbed-wire fences. A thin line of trees appeared at intervals, but it was hard to see the point. They provided no shade and only the sparsest screening from the cars speeding by. The houses had flat roofs and looked shabby, with dilapidated outbuildings. There were thick, knobby trees, whose amputated branches were, if not dead, devoid of foliage. As is true of most raw acreage in California, housing developments were taking root like a slew of weeds.

By 8:30 I found myself sitting in my car in the parking lot adjacent to the Processing Center at the California Institution for Women. For years, the CIW was known as Frontera, the feminine derivative of the word frontier. The 120-acre campus (as they referred to it back then) opened in 1952, and until this year, 1987, it was the only facility in California housing female felons. I'd already been inside the building where I showed the officer my photo ID and told him I was there to pick up Reba Lafferty, whose CDC number was, by an amusing coincidence, the same as my birthdate. The officer checked his roster, found her name, and then called Receiving and Release.

He'd suggested that I wait in the parking lot, so I'd hoofed it back to my VW. So far, the community of Corona seemed a bit grim for my taste. A trail of yellow smog hung on the horizon like something a crop-dusting plane might have left in its wake. The mid-July heat was as thick as soured milk and smelled of feedlots. A buffeting wind was blowing and there were flies everywhere. My T-shirt was sticking to my back and I could feel a sheen of moisture on my face—the sort of clamminess that wakes you from a dead sleep when you've just come down with the flu.

The view through the ten-foot chain-link fences was an improvement. I could see green lawns, walkways, and hibiscus plants with showy red and yellow blossoms. Most of the buildings were dun-colored and built close to the ground. Female inmates strolled the yards in groups of two and three. I knew from reading I'd done that construction had just been completed on a 110-bed Special Housing Unit. Total staff was 500, give or take a few, while the prison population varied between 900 and 1,200. Whites were in the majority, with ages bunched in the thirty-to-forty range. The prison provided both academic and vocational programs, including computer programming. Prison industries, largely textiles, produced shirts, shorts, smocks, aprons, handkerchiefs, bandannas, and fire-fighting clothing. Frontera also served as a hub for the selection and training of firefighters, who would be assigned work in the forty-some conservation camps across the state.

For the umpteenth time, I looked at the snapshot of Reba Lafferty taken before her legal ills and her felony quarantine. If she'd abused alcohol and drugs, the excess didn't show. Restlessly, I returned the photo to my shoulder bag and fiddled with the tuner on the radio. The morning news was the usual disheartening mixture of murder, political shenanigans, and dire economic predictions. By the time the news anchor cut to the station break, I was ready to cut my own throat.

At 9:00 A.M. I glanced up and caught sight of activity near the vehicle sally port. The gates had been rolled back and an outbound sheriff's department van now idled while the driver presented his paperwork to the sally port officer. The two of them exchanged pleasantries. I got out of my car. The van pulled through the gate, made a wide right-hand turn, and then slowed to a stop. I could see a number of women onboard, parolees headed for the real world, their faces turned to the window like a row of plants seeking light. The doors to the van hissed open and closed, and then the vehicle moved off.

Reba Lafferty stood on the pavement in prison-issue tennis shoes, blue jeans, and a plain white T-shirt without benefit of a brassiere. All inmates are obliged to surrender their personal clothing on arrival at the prison, but I was surprised her father hadn't sent her something of her own to wear home. I knew she'd been compelled to purchase the outfit she wore since the articles were considered government property. She'd apparently declined the prison-issue bra, which was probably about as flattering as an orthopedic brace. Inmates are also required to leave prison without anything in hand, except their two hundred bucks in cash. Startled, I saw that she looked exactly like the photo. Given Nord Lafferty's advanced age, I'd pictured Reba in her fifties. This girl was barely thirty.

Her hair was now cropped short and looked damp from

a shower. During her incarceration, the blond had grown out and the natural dark strands were spikey, as though she'd stiffened them with mousse. I expected her to be heavy, but she was trim almost to the point of looking frail. I could see the bony hollows of her collarbones beneath the cheap fabric of her T-shirt. Her complexion was clear but faintly sallow, and her eyes were smudged with dark shadows. There was something sensual about her; a defiance in her posture, a touch of swagger in her walk.

I lifted my hand in greeting and she crossed the road, moving in my direction.

"You here for me?"

"That's right. I'm Kinsey Millhone," I said.

"Great. I'm Reba Lafferty. Let's hit the friggin' road," she said as we shook hands.

We walked to the car and for the next hour, that was the extent of our conversation.

I prefer silence to small talk so the lack of chitchat wasn't awkward. I varied my route, catching Highway 5 south until it intersected the 101. A couple of times I thought of asking her a question, but I didn't think the ones that came to mind were any of my business. *Why'd you steal the money* and *How'd you screw it up and get caught* being foremost.

It was Reba who finally broke the silence. "Pop told you why I was in?"

"He said you took money, but that's all," I said. I noticed that I'd bypassed the word "embezzlement," as though it might be rude to name the crime that resulted in her prison term.

She rested her head against the back of the seat. "He's a love. He deserves a lot better than me."

"May I ask how old you are?"

"Thirty-two."

"No offense, but you look about twelve. How old was your dad when you were born?"

"Fifty-six. My mother was twenty-one. There's a match made in heaven. No telling what her deal was. She dropped me like a litter of kittens and hit the road."

"Does she keep in touch?"

"Nope. I saw her once, when I was eight. We spent one day together— well, half a day. She took me to Ludlow Beach and watched me splash in the waves until my lips turned blue. We had lunch at that snack stand, you know the one near High Ridge Road?"

"Know it well."

"I had a milk shake and ate fried clams, which I haven't eaten since. I must have been hyper. I remember my stomach was full of butterflies from the minute I woke up, knowing she'd be there. We were on our way to the zoo when I got sick in the car and she ended up taking me home."

"What'd she want?"

"Who knows? Whatever it was, she hasn't wanted it since. Pop's been great, though. I'm lucky in that regard."

"He feels guilty about you."

She turned and looked at me. "How come? None of this is his fault."

"He thinks he neglected you when you were young."

"Oh. Well, he did, but what's that got to do with it? He made his choices and I made mine."

"Yeah, but generally speaking, it's better to avoid the ones that are going to land you in jail."

She smiled. "You didn't know me back then. I was either drunk or stoned or sometimes both."

"How'd you hold down a job?"

"I saved the drinking for nights and weekends. I smoked dope before and after work. I never did the hard stuff—heroin, crack, or speed. Those can really mess you up bad."

"Didn't anyone ever notice you were stoned?"

"My boss."

"How'd you manage to take the money? Seems like that would necessitate a clear head."

"Trust me, I was always clear about some things. Have you ever been in jail?"

"I did an overnight once," I said, making it sound like an outing with my Girl Scout troop.

"For what?"

"Assaulting a cop and resisting arrest."

She laughed. "Wow. Who'da thunk? You look like a real button-down type. I'll bet you cross the street with the light and never fudge the numbers on your tax return."

"Well, true. Is that bad?"

"No, it's not *bad*. It's just boring," she said. "Don't you ever want to cut loose? Take a risk and maybe blow yourself through the roof?"

"I like my life as it is."

"What a drag. I'd go nuts."

"What makes me nuts is being out of control."

"So what do you do for laughs?"

"I don't know . . . I read a lot and I jog."

She looked at me, waiting for the punch line. "That's *it?* You read a lot and you *jog?*"

I laughed. "It does sound pathetic when you think of it."

"Where do you hang out?"

"I don't do any 'hanging out' as such, but if I want dinner or a glass of wine, I usually go to a tavern in my neighborhood called Rosie's. The owner's a mama bear, which means I can eat without being hassled by guys on the make."

"You have a boyfriend?"

"Not so's you'd notice," I said, slipping into the vernacular. Better not to let her venture too far down that path. I glanced over at her. "If you don't mind my asking, have you been in trouble before?"

She turned to look out the passenger-side window. "Depends on your point of reference. I went through drug rehab twice. I did six months in county jail on a bad-check charge. By the time I got out, my finances were in the shitter so I declared bankruptcy. Here's the weird part. Once I filed? I got a ton of credit card offers in the mail and all of them were preapproved. How could I resist? Of course, I ran those up, too. Thirty thousand bucks' worth before the gates clanged shut."

"Thirty thousand for what?"

"Oh, you know. The usual. Gambling, drugs. I blew a bunch at the track and then went to Reno where I played the slots. I sat in on some high-stakes poker, but the cards were running cold. Not that I'd quit because of that. I figured I could only lose so many times before the game turned around and started working my way. Unfortunately, I never reached that point. Next thing you know, I was broke and living on the streets. That was 1982. Pop moved me into his house and then he cleaned up my debts. What about your vices? You must have *one*."

"I drink wine and the occasional martini. I used to smoke cigarettes, but then I gave that up."

"Hey, me, too. I quit a year ago. Talk about tough."

"The *worst*," I said. "What made you quit?"

"Just to prove I could," she said. "What about other stuff? You ever do coke?"

"Nope."

"Ludes, Vicodan, Percocet?"

I turned and stared at her.

"I'm just *asking*," she said.

"I smoked dope in high school, but then I straightened up my act."

She flopped her head to one side and said, "Snore."

I laughed. "Why snore?"

"You live like a nun. Where's the friggin' joy?"

"I have *joy*. I have a lot of joy."

"Oh, don't be so defensive. I wasn't *judging* you."

"Yes, you were."

"Well, okay, maybe a little bit. I'm mostly curious."

"About what?"

"How you make it in this world if you give up living on the edge."

"Maybe you'll find out."

"I wouldn't bet on *that*, but one can always hope."

As we approached Santa Teresa, a drifting fog had curled across the landscape, wispy and pale. I drove along the beach, palms standing out darkly against the soft white of the Pacific. Reba'd been staring at the ocean since it came into view south of Perdido. As we passed the Perdido Avenue off-ramp, she turned her head, watching it recede into the mist. "You ever hear of the Double Down?"

"What's that?"

"Perdido's only poker parlor—scene of my downfall. Had some great times there, but that's over and done with. Or so I hope."

The highway angled inland and she watched the ebb and flow of citrus groves on either side of the road. Houses and businesses began to accumulate until the town itself appeared—two- and three-story white stucco buildings with red tile roofs, palm trees, evergreens, the architecture defined by the Spanish influence.

"What'd you miss most?" I asked.

"My cat. Long-haired orange tabby I've had since he was six weeks old. He looked like a little powder puff. He's seventeen now and a great old guy."

As I took the Milagro off-ramp, I glanced at my watch. It was 12:36. "Are you hungry? We have time for lunch if you want to eat before you meet your PO."

"That'd be great. I've been hungry since we hit the road."

"You should have spoken up. You have a preference?"

"McDonald's. I'd kill for a Quarter Pounder with Cheese."

"Me, too."

Over lunch, I said, "Twenty-two months. What'd you do with your time?"

"I learned computer programming. That's a hoot and a half. Also, I memorized prison stats," she said.

"Sounds like fun."

She began dunking her fries in a lake of ketchup, eating them like worms. "Well, it was. I spent a lot of time in the library reading all the studies they've done on female inmates. Used to be, I'd pick up an article like that and it had nothing to do with me. Now it's all relevant. Like in 1976? There were eleven thousand women in state and federal prisons. Last year, the number jumped to twenty-six thousand and you want to know why? Women's Liberation. Judges used to take pity on women, especially those with little kids. Now it's equal-opportunity incarceration. Thank you, Gloria Steinem. Only something like three percent of convicted felons do any prison time anyway. And here's something else. Five years ago half the killers released from prison had served less than six years. Can you believe that? Murder someone and you're back on the street after six in the can. Most parole violations, you end up doing a bullet, which is a lot if you look at it proportionately. I flunk one drug test and I'm back on the bus."

"A bullet?"

"A year. I'm telling you, the system's really screwed. I mean, what do you think parole's about? You serve your sentence on the street. What kind of punishment is that? You have no idea how many vicious guys you got walking around out here." She smiled. "Anyway, let's go meet my PO and get it over with."

5

The parole offices were housed in a low yellow brick building of a style popular during the sixties—lots of glass and
aluminum and long horizontal lines. Dark green cedars
grew under an overhang that ran the length of the façade.
The parking lot was generous and I found a spot without
difficulty. I shut down the engine. "Want me to go with
you?"

"Might as well," she said. "Who knows how long I'll
have to wait. I could use the company."

We crossed the parking lot and hung a right, moving
toward the entrance. We pushed through the glass doors
and found ourselves facing a long drab hallway lined with
offices on both sides. There was no reception area that I
could see, though at the far end of the corridor there were
a few folding chairs where a smattering of men were seated.
As we entered, a big woman with red hair and a fat file in
hand peered out of an office and called to one of the guys
loitering against the wall. A sorrowful-looking man in his
sixties stepped forward, dressed in a shabby sport coat and

pants that were none too clean. I'd seen guys like him sleeping in doorways and picking half-smoked cigarette butts out of the sand-filled ashtrays in hotel lobbies.

She glanced over at us, catching sight of Reba. "Are you Reba?"

"That's right."

"I'm Priscilla Holloway. We spoke on the phone. I'll be with you in a sec."

"Great." Reba watched them depart. "My parole officer."

"I figured as much."

Priscilla Holloway was in her forties, strong-featured, big-boned, and tan. Her dark red hair was pulled back in a French braid that extended halfway down her back. Her dark slacks were wrinkled from sitting. Over them she wore a white shirt, hem out, and a zippered red knit jacket that was open down the front, discreet concealment for the firearm she wore holstered at her side. Her build was athletic, and my guess was she played the fast, hard-sweating sports: racquetball, soccer, basketball, and tennis. When I was in grade school a girl her size would have scared the crap out of me, but I learned, in those days, that if I cultivated a friendship, I'd end up with playground protection for life.

Reba and I staked out our claim on a tiny section of the hallway where we variously leaned and slouched, trying to find a comfortable position in which to wait. There was a pay phone mounted on the wall nearby and I could see Reba's focus sharpen at the sight of it. "You have any change? I need to make a phone call. It's local."

I opened my shoulder bag and did a quick search along the bottom, fishing for stray coins. I passed her a handful of change, watching as she moved to the phone and picked up the handset. She dropped in the coins, punched in a number, and then turned her body at an angle so I couldn't read her lips while she talked. She was on the line for three minutes and when she finally put the handset back in the cradle, she was looking happier and more relaxed than I'd seen her so far.

"Everything okay?"

"Sure. I was touching base with a friend." She sank down along the wall and took a seat on the floor.

Ten minutes later, Priscilla Holloway appeared, walking her fusty-looking client to the front door. She issued him an admonition and then turned to Reba. "Why don't you come on back?"

Reba scrambled to her feet. "What about her?"

"She can join us in a bit. We've got a couple of things we need to talk about first. I'll come get you in a minute," she said to me.

The two moved down the bleak hallway, Reba looking half Holloway's size. Reconciled to the wait, I leaned against the wall, my shoulder bag on the floor. The glass doors opened and Cheney Phillips came in, passing me on his way down the hall. I saw him tap on Priscilla Holloway's open door and stick his head in. He chatted briefly with her and then turned, walking in my direction. He still hadn't recognized me, which gave me a moment to study him.

I'd known Cheney for years, but we hadn't had occasion to interact until a murder investigation two years before. Over the course of several conversations, he'd told me he'd grown up in circumstances of benign neglect and fixed his sights early on a career in law enforcement. He'd been working undercover vice the last time our paths crossed, but by now his face was probably too well known for anything covert. He was dressed to the nines, as usual: dark slacks and a pin-stripe sport coat, wide in the shoulders and nipped at the waist. His dress shirt was midnight blue worn with a midnight blue tie with a sheen of lighter blue. His dark hair was curly, his dark gaze revealing a curious mix of cop-think and come-hither. When I heard he'd gotten married, I'd moved his name, in my mental Rolodex, from a prominent place near the front to a category I labeled "expunged without prejudice" near the back of the file.

His gaze connected briefly with mine and when he realized it was me, he stopped in his tracks. "Kinsey. I don't believe it. I was just thinking about you."

"What are you doing here?"

"Getting a bead on a parolee. What about you?"

"Babysitting a gal until she gets on her feet."

"Missionary work."

"Hardly. I'm getting paid," I said.

"When I ran into you Saturday I meant to ask why I haven't seen you at CC's. Dolan told me the two of you were working a case. I figured you'd be in."

"I don't 'do' bars at my age except for Rosie's," I said. "What about you? Last I heard, you were off in Las Vegas getting married."

"Geez, word gets around. So what else did you hear?"

"That you met her at CC's and only knew her six weeks before the two of you ran off."

Cheney's smile was pained. "Sounds so crass when you put it that way."

"What happened to your other girlfriend? I thought you'd been dating someone else for years."

"That wasn't going anywhere. She realized it before I did and dumped my sorry butt."

"So what'd you do, marry on the rebound?"

"That would cover it, I guess. What about you? How's your friend Dietz?"

"Kinsey, would you like to join us?"

I glanced up to see Priscilla Holloway approaching.

Cheney turned his head, following my gaze. His eyes flicked from the parole officer to me. "I better let you go."

"Nice seeing you again," I said.

"I'll give you a call as soon as I'm free," Priscilla said to him as he turned to go.

I glanced back, watching him as he pushed out the glass doors and turned toward the parking lot.

"How do you know Cheney?" she asked.

"Through a case I worked. Nice guy."

"He's good. Did the drive go okay?"

"Piece of cake, but it was hot down there."

"And way too many bugs," she said. "You can hardly open your mouth without swallowing one."

Her office was small and the furniture was plain. A window overlooked the parking lot, the view cut into slices by a dusty venetian blind. There was a Polaroid camera resting on the windowsill and two instant photos of Reba lay on top of a stack of thick files. I assumed Priscilla kept current photos in the file in case Reba took off without notice. There were file cabinets on her side of the desk and two metal chairs on ours. Reba sat in the one closest to the window. Priscilla took a seat in her swivel chair and looked at me. "Reba says you'll be squiring her around town."

"Just for a couple of days, until she's settled."

Priscilla leaned forward. "I've been over this with her, but I think it bears repeating so you know the score. No drugs, no alcohol, no firearms, no knife with a blade longer than two inches, except knives in her residence or in her place of employment. No crossbow of any kind." She paused to smile, directing the rest of her remarks to Reba as though for emphasis. "No consorting with known felons. Any change of residence has to be reported within seventy-two hours. No traveling more than fifty miles without authorization. You will not be out of Santa Teresa County for more than forty-eight hours and not out of California at all without my written consent. Cops pick you up and you don't have the magic piece of paper, you'll be back in the clink."

"I'm cool with that," Reba said.

"One thing I forgot to mention. If you're seeking employment, a special condition of your parole prohibits a position of trust: no handling of payroll, taxes, no access to checks—"

"What if the employer knows about my record?"

Holloway paused. "Under those circumstances, maybe, but talk to me first." She turned back to me. "Any questions?"

"Not me. I'm just along for the ride."

"I've given Reba my number if she should need me. If I'm not available, leave a message on my machine. I check four or five times a day."

"Right."

"In the meantime, I have two concerns. The first is

54

public safety. The second is her successful reentry. Let's not screw up on either count, okay?"

"I'm with you," I said.

Priscilla stood up and leaned across her desk to shake first Reba's hand and then mine. "Good luck. Nice meeting you, Ms. Millhone."

"Make it Kinsey," I said.

"Let me know if there's any way I can be of help."

Once we were in the car again, I said, "I like Holloway. She seems nice."

"Me, too. She's says I'm the only female she handles. Every other parolee she has is a 288A or a 290."

"Which is what?"

"Registered sex offenders. 288A signifies a child molester. A couple of 'em are considered sexually violent predators. Nice company. You'd never guess just from looking at those guys," she said. She took out a folded pamphlet with "Department of Corrections" printed on the front. I could see her scanning the information as she turned the page. "At least I'm not classified as High Control. Those guys really have to jump through hoops. I see her once a week at first, but she says if I behave myself, she'll move me to once a month. I'll still have to attend AA meetings and I'll be subjected to weekly drug tests, but that's just peeing in a jar and it's really not so bad."

"What about employment? Will you be looking for a job?"

"Pop doesn't want me to work. He thinks it stresses me out. Besides, it's not a condition of parole and Holloway doesn't care as long as I keep my nose clean."

"Then let's get you home."

At 2:30 I dropped Reba off at her father's estate, making sure she had both my home and office numbers. I suggested she take a couple of days to get settled, but she said she'd been cooped up, idle and bored, for the past two years and wanted to get out. I told her to call in the morning and we'd work out a time to pick her up.

"Thanks," she said, and then opened the car door. The elderly housekeeper was already standing on the front porch, watching for her arrival. Near her sat a big long-haired orange cat. As Reba slammed the car door, the cat stepped down off the porch and strolled toward her at a dignified pace. Reba leaned down and swept the cat into her arms. She rocked him, her face buried in his fur, a display of devotion the cat seemed to accept as his due. Reba carried him to the porch. I waited until she'd hugged the housekeeper and disappeared inside, cat tucked under one arm, and then I put the car in gear and headed back to town.

I stopped by the office and put in the requisite time returning phone calls and opening the mail. At 5:00, having taken care of as much business as I intended to do, I closed up the office and retrieved my car for the short drive home. Once there, I opened my mailbox and pulled out the usual assortment of junk mail and bills. I pushed through the squeaky gate, engrossed in an ad from a Hong Kong tailor soliciting my business. I had another offer from a mortgage company suggesting ready cash with one simple call. Wasn't I the lucky one?

Henry was in the backyard hosing down the patio with

a steady stream of water as fat as a broom handle. With it, he forced leaves and grit across the flat stones and into the grass beyond. The late afternoon sun had broken through the overcast and we were finally experiencing a touch of summer. He wore a T-shirt and cutoffs, his long, elegant bare feet tucked into a pair of worn flip-flops. William, in his usual natty three-piece suit, stood just behind him, carefully avoiding any spatter from the hose. He was leaning on a black malacca walking stick with a carved ivory handle. The two were arguing but paused long enough to greet me civilly.

"William, what'd you do to your foot? I've never seen you with a cane."

"The doctor thought it would help keep me steady."

"It's a prop," Henry said.

William ignored him.

I said, "Sorry to interrupt. I must've caught you in the middle of a chat."

William said, "Henry's feeling indecisive about Mattie."

"I'm not indecisive! I'm being sensible. I'm eighty-seven years old. How many good years do I have left?"

"Don't be absurd," William said. "Our side of the family has always lived to be at least a hundred and three. Did you hear what she said about *hers?* I thought she was reciting from the *Merck Manual.* Cancer, diabetes, and heart disease? Her mother died of meningitis. Of all things! Take my word for it, Mattie Halstead will go long before you."

"Why worry about that? None of us are 'going' anytime soon," Henry said.

"You're being foolish. She'd be lucky to have you."

"What in heaven's name for?"

"She'll need someone to see her through. No one wants to be ill and alone, especially toward the end."

"There's nothing wrong with her! She's healthy as a horse. She'll outlive me by a good twenty years, which is more than I can say for you."

William turned to me. "Lewis wouldn't be this stubborn—"

"What's Lewis have to do with it?" Henry asked.

"He appreciates her. If you'll remember, he was most attentive to her on the cruise."

"That was months ago."

"You tell him, Kinsey. Maybe you can get through to him."

I could feel uneasiness stir. "I don't know what to say, William. I'm the last person in the world who should give advice about love."

"Nonsense. You were married twice."

"But neither one worked out."

"At least you weren't afraid to commit. Henry's being cowardly—"

"I am not!" Henry's temper was climbing. I thought he was going to turn the hose on his brother, but he moved over to the faucet and wrenched the water off with a squawking sound. "The idea's preposterous. For one thing, Mattie's entrenched in San Francisco and my roots are down here. I'm a homebody at heart and look at the way she lives—always taking off on cruises, sailing around the world at the drop of a hat."

"She only cruises the Caribbean so it doesn't present a problem," William said.

"She's gone for weeks on end. There's no way in the world she's going to give that up."

"Why should she give it up?" William said, exasperated. "Let her do anything she wants. You can live six months up there and the other six months down here. We can all benefit from a change of scene—you more than most. And don't give me that song and dance about 'roots.' She can keep her place and you can keep yours, and you can go back and forth."

"I don't want to go anywhere. I want to stay right here."

"I'll tell you your problem. You don't want to do anything that involves risk," William said.

"Neither do you."

"Not so! No sir. You're completely incorrect. By golly, I got *married* at the age of eighty-six and if you don't think that's taking a risk, then ask *her*," he said, pointing to me.

"Really, it is," I murmured dutifully, my hand in the air as though swearing an oath. "But guys? Excuse me . . ." They both turned to stare at me. "Don't you think Mattie's feelings count? Maybe she's no more interested in him than he is in her?"

"I didn't say I wasn't *interested*. I'm discussing the situation from her point of view."

"She's interested, you dolt!" William said. "Look at this. She's coming back to town in a day. She said so herself. Didn't you hear her say that?"

"Because it's right in her *path*. She isn't stopping off to see *me*."

"Oh yes she is, or why wouldn't she drive straight on through?"

"Because she has to buy gas and stretch her legs."

"Which she could do without taking the time to see you."

"William has a point. I'm with him," I said.

Henry began to coil the hose, his hands picking up bits of grit and cut grass. "She's a wonderful person and I value our friendship. Let's just leave the subject. I'm tired of it."

William turned to me. "That's how this started. All I did was point out the obvious, that she's a wonderful person and he'd better get a move on and snap her up."

Henry said, "Nuts!" waving William off as he returned to the house. He opened the screen door and banged it shut.

William shook his head, leaning on his walking stick. "He's been like this all his life. Unreasonable. Stubborn. Having temper tantrums at the slightest hint of disagreement."

"I don't know, William. If I were you, I'd back off and let them work it out for themselves."

"I'm only trying to help."

"Henry hates to be helped."

"Because he's mulish."

"We're all mulish when it comes right down to it."

"Well, something has to be done. This may be his last chance at love. I can't bear to see him make a hash of it." There was a gentle pinging sound and William reached into his vest pocket and checked his watch. "Time for my snack." He took out a small cellophane packet of cashews that he opened with his teeth. He popped two in his mouth, chewing them like pills. "You know I'm hypoglycemic. The doctor says I shouldn't go more than two hours without eating. Otherwise I'm subject to faintness, weakness, clamminess, and palpitations. Also, tremulousness, which you've doubtless observed."

"Really. I hadn't noticed."

"Precisely. The doctor's encouraged me to instruct

friends and family in recognizing the symptoms because it's imperative to render *immediate* treatment. A glass of fruit juice, a few nuts. These can make all the difference. Of course, he wants me to undergo tests, but in the meantime, a diet high in protein, that's the trick," he said. "You know, with deficient glucose production, an attack can be triggered by alcohol, salicylates, or in rare cases, by ingesting the ackee nut, which produces what's commonly known as the Jamaican vomiting sickness . . ."

I cupped a hand to my ear. "I think that's my phone. I'd better run."

"Certainly. I can tell you more over supper since you're interested."

"Great," I said. I began to edge toward my door.

William pointed at me with his walking stick. "As for this business with Henry, isn't it better to feel something intensely even if you're wounded in the process?"

I pointed at him. "I'll get back to you on that."

6

I had a brief debate with myself about working in a three-mile jog. I'd had to skip my morning run in the interest of reaching CIW by nine. I usually run at 6:00 when I'm still half-asleep and my resistance is down. I've discovered that as the day wears on my sense of virtue and resolve both rapidly diminish. Most days, by the time I get home from work, the last thing I want to do is change into my running clothes and drag myself out. I'm not so fanatic about exercise that I don't occasionally let myself off the hook; however, I'd noticed a growing inclination to seize any excuse to sit on my butt instead of working out. Before I thought too much about it, I went up the spiral stairs to change my clothes.

I kicked off my loafers, peeled out of my jeans, and pulled my T-shirt over my head, tugging on my sweats and my Sauconys. In circumstances like this, I make a little deal with myself. If I jog for ten minutes and really really hate it, I can turn around and come back. No shame, no blame. Usually by the time the first ten minutes have elapsed, I'm into the swing of it and enjoying myself. I tied my house key in the laces of one shoe, locked the door behind me, and set off at a brisk walk.

Now that the marine layer had burned off, the neighbors were out in their yards, mowing lawns, watering, and pruning deadheads from the rosebushes massed along the fences. I could smell ocean brine mingled with the scent of freshly clipped grass. My block of Albinil Street is narrow. Aside from vehicles parked on either side, there's barely room for two cars to pass. Eucalyptus trees and stone pines provide shade for the assorted stucco and frame houses, most of them small, dating back to the early forties.

By the time I reached the jogging path, I was sufficiently warmed up to break into a trot. After that, I only had to cope with my protesting body parts, which gradually melded into the smooth rhythms of the run. I was home again forty minutes later, winded, sweating, but feeling virtuous. I let myself into the apartment, stripped off my sweats, and took a short hot shower. I was out and drying myself when the telephone rang. I took the call while turning the towel into a makeshift sarong.

"Kinsey? This is Reba. Did I catch you at a bad time?"

"Well, I'm standing here soaking wet, but I should be good for a minute until the chill sets in. What's up?"

"Not much. Pop was feeling bad so he's gone to bed. The housekeeper just left and the home-care nurse called to say she'd be a little late. I was just wondering if you were free for dinner?"

"Sure. I could do that. What'd you have in mind?"

"Didn't you mention a place in your neighborhood?"

"Rosie's. That's where I was headed. I wouldn't call it fancy, but at least it's close."

"I just need to get out. I'd love to join you but only if it doesn't interfere with your plans."

"What plans? I don't mind a bit. You have transportation?"

"Don't worry about that. As soon as the nurse arrives, I'll meet you down there. About seven?"

"That should work."

"Good. I'll be there as soon as I can."

"I'll grab a good table and see you there," I said, and then gave her the address.

After she hung up, I finished my routine, putting on fresh jeans, a clean black T-shirt, and a pair of sneakers. I went downstairs and spent a few minutes tidying my already tidy kitchen. Then I flipped on the lights and sat in the living room with the local paper, catching up on the obituaries and other current events.

At 6:56, I walked the half block to Rosie's through the lingering daylight. Two sets of neighbors were having cocktails outside, enjoying conversation from porch to porch. A cat crossed the street and eased its slim body through the palings in a picket fence. I could smell jasmine.

Rosie's is one of six small businesses on my block, including a laundromat, an appliance-repair shop, and an automobile mechanic, who always has clunkers lined up along his drive. I've been having supper at Rosie's three to four nights a week for the past seven years. The exterior is shabby, a building that might have served as the neighborhood market once upon a time. The windows are plate glass, but the light is obscured by sputtering neon beer signs, posters, announcements, and faded placards from the health department. As nearly as I can remember, Rosie's has never been awarded a rating higher than a C.

Inside, the space is long and narrow, with a high, darkly painted ceiling that looks like it was made of pressed tin. Crudely constructed plywood booths form an L on the right. There's a long mahogany bar on the left, with two swinging kitchen doors and a short corridor leading to the restrooms located at the rear. The remaining floor space is occupied by a number of Formica dinette tables. The accompanying chairs have chrome legs and upholstered marbleized gray plastic seats, variously split and subsequently mended with duct tape. The air always smells of spilled beer, popcorn, ancient cigarette smoke, and Pine-Sol.

Monday nights are generally quiet, allowing the day-drinkers and the usual sports rowdies to recover from their weekend excesses. My favorite booth was empty, as were most of the others, as a matter of fact. I slid in on one side so I could watch the front door for Reba's arrival. I checked the menu, a mimeographed sheet inserted in a plastic sleeve. Rosie runs these off on a machine at the back, the blurred purple lettering barely legible. Two months before, she'd instituted a new style of menu, closely resembling a leather-bound portfolio with a handscripted list of the Hungarian Specialties du Jour of the Day, as she referred to them. Some of these menus had been stolen and others had served as hazardous flying missiles when opposing soccer teams enjoyed a hot dispute about the last big match. Rosie had apparently given up her pretensions to haute cuisine and her old mimeographed sheets were back in circulation. I ran an eye down the list of dishes, though I'm not even sure why I bothered to check. Rosie makes all my food decisions for me, compelling me to dine on whatever Hungarian delicacies come to her mind when she's taking my order.

William was now working behind the bar. I watched him pause to check his pulse, two fingers of one hand pressed to his carotid artery, the other hand holding aloft his trusty pocket watch. Henry came in and flicked a look in his direction. He chose a table near the front, pointedly turning his back to the bar. As I watched, Rosie moved out from behind the bar bearing a glass of lip-puckering white wine that she passes off as Chardonnay. I could see an inch of gray hair growing in along her parting. In the past, she's claimed to be in her sixties, but now she's so quiet on the subject I suspect she's slipped over the line into her seventies. She's short, pigeon-breasted, and the red portion of her red hair is dyed to a hue somewhere between cinnabar and burnt ocher.

She placed the glass of wine in front of me. "Is new. Very good. You sip and tell what you think. I'm saving two dollar a bottle over other brand."

I sipped and nodded. "Very nice," I said. Meanwhile, enamel was being eaten off my teeth. "I see Henry and William aren't speaking."

"I'm telling William to mind his own business, but he's no listen to me. I'm shock to see a woman can come between them two brothers."

"They'll get over it," I said. "What's your take on the situation. You think Mattie has designs on Henry?"

"What do I know? That Henry's a catch. You should hev seen little old ladies flirt with him on cruise ship. Was comical. On other hand, her husband die. Maybe she don't want to connect with some guy. Meybe she want freedom all to herself and Henry for a friend."

"That's what I've been worried about, but William's convinced there's something more going on."

"William's convince she won't be living two more years. He wants Henry to hurry in case she's dropping dead already."

"That's ridiculous. She's barely seventy."

"Very young," Rosie murmured. "I myself hope to look so good when I'm getting her age."

"I'm certain you will," I said. I picked up the menu and pretended to study it. "I'm expecting a friend so I'll hold off on ordering. Actually this all sounds pretty good. What do you recommend?"

"Lucky you esk. For you and your friend, I'm fixing Krumpli Paprikas. Is stew made of boil potato, ongion, and what you call weenies cut in pieces. Is always serve with rye bread and on the side you hev choice of cucumber salad or sour pickle. Which you want? I'm think pickle," she said, scribbling a note on her pad.

"Sour pickle, my favorite. So perfect with the wine."

"I'm bring you food as soon as he come."

"It's a 'she' friend, not a 'he.'"

"Is pity," she said, shaking her head. She added an emphatic mark to her pad and then returned to the bar.

At 7:15 Reba appeared, pausing at the door to scan the room. She saw me waving from my booth and made her way toward the back. She'd changed out of her jeans and T-shirt into slacks, a red cotton sweater, and sandals. Her color had improved and her eyes looked enormous in the perfect oval of her face. The spikes were gone from her hair, strands of which she'd tucked behind her ears,

causing them to protrude like an elf's. When she reached
the booth, she slid in on her side, saying, "Sorry I'm late,
but I ended up taking a cab. Turns out my driver's license
expired while I was in the can. I was worried I'd be pulled
over if I tried driving without one. I could have applied for
a renewal from prison but never got around to it. Maybe
tomorrow we can go to the DMV."

"Sure. No problem. Why don't I pick you up at nine
and we can take care of your license and then run any
other errands you have in mind."

"Maybe some clothes. I can use a few things." Reba
craned her head, doing a quick survey of the room behind
her where the patrons were starting to trickle in. "Would
you mind switching seats? I hate sitting with my back to
the room."

I slid out on my side of the booth and traded places
with her, though in truth I wasn't any fonder than she was
about sitting with my back to the room. "How'd you
manage in prison?"

"That's where I learned to keep an eye on my ass. I
trust what I can see. The rest is way too scary for my
taste." She took up a menu and ran her eye down the page.

"Were you scared?"

She lifted her enormous dark eyes to my face, her smile
fleeting. "At first. After a while, I wasn't scared so much
as cautious. I didn't worry about the staff. It took me about
two full seconds to figure out how to get along with them."

"Which was what?"

"Compliance. I was nice. Polite. I did as I was told and
I obeyed all the rules. It was really no big deal and it
made life easier."

"What about the other inmates?"

"Most of them were okay. Not all. Some of the girls were mean, so you didn't dare let 'em see you as weak. You backed down on anything, they'd be all over you like flies. So here's what I learned. Some bitch gets in my face? I get right back in hers. If she escalates, I do the same and keep on upping the ante until it finally dawns on her she'd better leave me alone. What made it tricky was you didn't want to be written up, especially for anything involving violence—there was hell to pay for that—so you had to find a way to stand your ground without calling attention to yourself."

"How'd you manage it?"

She smiled. "Oh, I had my little ways. The truth is I never messed with anyone who didn't mess with me first. My goal was peace and quiet. You go your way and I'll go mine. Sometimes it just didn't work out that way and then you had to move on to something else." She glanced down at the menu. "What *is* this stuff?"

"Those are all Hungarian dishes, but you don't need to fret. Rosie's already decided what we're having. You can argue with her if you like, but you'll lose."

"Hey, just like prison. What a happy thought."

I saw Rosie approach, bearing another glass of second-rate wine. Before she could put it down in front of Reba, I reached for it, saying, "Thanks. I'll take that. What about you, Reba? What would you like to drink?"

"I'll have iced tea."

Rosie made an officious note to herself like a proper journalist. "Sweet or no sweet?"

"I prefer plain."

"I'm bring lemon on the side in little diaper so you squeeze in your tea with no seeds come out."

"Thanks."

Once Rosie left, Reba said, "I would have turned that down. It really doesn't bother me to see you drink."

"I wasn't sure. I don't want to be a bad influence."

"You? Not possible. Don't worry about it." She set the menu aside and clasped her hands on the table in front of her. "You have other questions. I can tell."

"I do. What were they in for, the mean ones?"

"Murder, manslaughter. A lot for selling drugs. The lifers were the worst because what did they have to lose? They'd get thrown in detention? Whoopee-do. Big deal."

"I couldn't stand having all those people around. Didn't that drive you nuts?"

"It was terrible. Really bad. Women living in close proximity always end up on the same monthly cycle. I guess there must be primitive survival advantages— females fertile at the same time. Talk about PMS. You tack a full moon on top of that and the place turned into a loony bin. Moodiness, quarrels, crying jags, suicide attempts."

"You think being among hardened criminals corrupted you?"

"*Corrupted* me? Like how?"

"Didn't you pick up new and better ways to break the law?"

She laughed. "Are you kidding? All of us were in there because we got caught. Why would I take instruction from a bunch of fuckups? Besides which, women don't sit around trying to teach other women how to rob banks or fence stolen property. They talk about what lousy attorneys they had and how their case is going on appeal. They talk about their kids and their boyfriends and what they want to do when they get out, which usually involves food and sex—not necessarily in that order."

"Was there an upside?"

"Oh, sure. I'm clean and sober. The drunks and druggies are the ones who end up back in the can. They go out on parole and the next thing you know, they're on the bus again, coming through Reception. Half the time they can't even remember what they did while they were out."

"How'd you survive?"

"I walked the yard or read books, sometimes as many as five a week. I did tutoring. Some of the girls barely knew how to read. They weren't dumb; they'd just never been taught. I did their hair and looked at pictures of their kids. That was hard, watching them try to maintain contact. The phones were a source of conflict. You wanted to make an afternoon call, you had to get your name on a list first thing in the morning. Then when your turn came, you had twenty minutes max. The big beefy dykes took as long as they liked and if you had objections, tough patooties to you. I was a shrimp compared to most. Five-two, a hundred and four pounds. That's why I learned to be devious. Nothing sweeter than revenge, but you don't want to leave your fingerprints all over the deed. Take my advice: never do anything that points back to you."

"I'll remember that," I said.

Rosie returned with a tray bearing Reba's iced tea, the lemon swaddled in cheesecloth, and an order of Krumpli Paprikas for each of us. She set down rye bread, butter, and sour pickles, and disappeared again.

Reba leaned close to her bowl. "Oh. Caraway seeds. For a minute, I thought I saw something move."

The potato stew was tasty, served in big porcelain bowls

flecked with caraway seeds. I was using my last piece of buttered rye bread to sop up the remaining traces of gravy when I saw Reba glance over my left shoulder toward the front of the restaurant, her eyes widening. "Oh my goodness! Look who's here."

I leaned left, peering around the edge of the booth so I could follow her gaze. The front door had opened and a guy had come in. "You know him?"

"That's Beck," she said as though that explained everything. She pushed herself out of the booth. "I'll be right back."

7

I waited a decent interval and then peered at the two of
them standing near the door. The guy was tall, lean, and
rangy in jeans and a supple black suede jacket. He had
his hands in his jacket pockets and his collar turned up,
which didn't look as thuglike as it sounds. His hair was a
tawny mix of blond and brown, and his half-smile created
a deep crease on either side of his mouth. Beside him,
Reba was diminutive, a full head shorter than he, which
forced him to lean toward her attentively as the two of
them talked. I went back to cleaning my bowl—food, in
this instance, taking precedence over idle speculation.

A moment later they appeared and Reba gestured at
him. "Alan Beckwith. I used to work for him. This is
Kinsey Millhone."

He held his hand out, his wrist thin, his fingers long
and slim. "Nice to meet you. I'm Beck to most."

I put him in his thirties—fine lines on his face, but no
pouches anywhere. "Nice meeting you, too," I said, shaking hands with him. "Are you joining us?"

"If you don't mind. I don't want to butt in."

"We're just chatting," I said. "Have a seat."

On their side of the booth, Reba slid in first, scooting over to make room for him. He sat down, half-slouching, his long legs outstretched. He was clean shaven, but I could see the shadow of a beard. His eyes were the dark, rich brown of Hershey's Kisses. I picked up the scent of cologne, something spicy and light. I'd seen him before . . . not here, but somewhere in town, though I couldn't imagine why our paths would have crossed.

He tapped on the back of Reba's hand. "So. How've you been?"

"Fine. It feels great to be home."

I tuned them out, watching as the two exchanged pleasantries. For people who'd once worked together, both seemed ill at ease, but that might have been because he'd turned her over to the cops, a move that would put a damper on most relationships.

"You look good," he said.

"Thanks. I could use a decent haircut. I did this myself. What about you? What have you been up to?"

"Not much. Traveling a lot on business. I just got back from Panama last week and I may be heading out again. We're in the new building, part of the mall that was finished last spring. Restaurants and shops. It's really slick."

"That was in the works when I left and I know what a pain in the ass it was. Congratulations."

"Have you seen it?"

"Not yet. Must be convenient for you, working right downtown."

"Dynamite," he said.

She smiled. "How's the office gang? I hear Onni took my old job. Is she doing okay?"

"She's fine. It took her a while to learn the system, but she's doing great. Everyone else is pretty much the same."

What did I sense? I tested the air with my little feelers, trying to identify the nature of the tension between them.

Idly, I listened while Beck continued. "I got a new deal in the works. Commercial property up near Merced. I just met with some guys who have capital to invest so we may pull something together. I stopped in here for a good-luck drink before I headed home." His attention shifted in an effort to include me in the conversation. A smooth move, I thought. He wagged a finger between Reba and me, like a windshield wiper. "How do you two know each other?"

I'd opened my mouth to speak, but Reba got in first. "We don't. We just met this morning when she picked me up and brought me home. I was going nuts, stuck at the house. Pop went to bed early and I was too hyper to sit still. The silence was really creeping me out so I called her."

His gaze settled on mine. "You live around here?"

"Half a block down. I rent a studio apartment. Matter of fact, that's my landlord over there," I said, gesturing toward Henry at his table near the front. "The bartender's his older brother William, who's married to Rosie, the gal who owns this place, just to fill you in."

Beck smiled. "A family affair." He was one of those guys who understands the power of being totally focused on the person he's talking to. No barely disguised glances at his watch, no surreptitious shifts in his gaze to see who's coming in the door. Now he seemed as patient as a cat staring at a crack in a rock where a lizard has disappeared.

"You live in the area?" I asked.

He shook his head. "I'm in Montebello, right where East Glen and Cypress Lane intersect."

I rested my chin on my hand. "I've seen you someplace."

"I'm a native, Santa Teresa born and bred. My folks had a place in Horton Ravine, but they've been gone now for years. My dad owned the Clements," he said, referring to a three-story luxury hotel that folded in the late seventies. Subsequent ownerships had failed as well and the building had been converted to a retirement facility. If I remembered correctly, his father had been involved in numerous businesses around town. Major bucks.

I glanced over to see Rosie moving toward us with an empty tray, her sights fixed on Beck, her approach as direct and unwavering as a heat-seeking missile. When she reached the table, she made a point of directing all her comments to me, a minor eccentricity of hers. She seldom looks a stranger in the eye. Male or female, it doesn't matter to her. Any new acquaintance is treated like an odd appendage of mine. The effect, in this instance, was coquettish, which I thought was unbecoming in a woman her age. "Your friend would like something to drink?"

I said, "Beck?"

"You have single-malt Scotch?"

She fairly wriggled with pleasure, shooting an approving look at him out of the corner of her eye. "Special for him, I hev MaCallum's. Is twenty-four years old. You want neat or wit ice?"

"Ice. A double with a water back. Thanks."

"Of course." She cleared the table, loading our dinner

plates and silverware onto her tray. "He's want supper, perhaps?"

He smiled. "No, thanks. It smells wonderful, but I just ate. Maybe next time. Are you Rosie?"

"Yes, I em."

He rose to his feet and offered his hand. "An honor to meet you. Alan Beckwith," he said. "This is quite a place."

In lieu of an actual handshake, Rosie allowed him temporary possession of her fingertips. "Next time, I'm fix something special for you. Hungarian like what you've never had until I give."

"You got a deal. I adore Hungarian cuisine," he said.

"You hev been to Hungary?"

"Budapest, once, about six years ago . . ."

Covertly, I watched the interplay between the two of them. Rosie became more girlish as the exchange went on. Beck was too slick for my taste, but I had to give him credit for making the effort. Most people find Rosie difficult, which she is.

As soon as she went off to fetch his drink, Beck turned to Reba. "How's your dad? I saw him a couple months ago and he wasn't looking good."

"He's not doing well. I really had no idea. I was shocked to see how much weight he's lost. You know he had surgery for a thyroid tumor. Then it turned out he had polyps on his vocal cords so he had to have those removed. He's still shaky on his feet."

"I'm sorry to hear that. He's always seemed so vigorous."

"Yeah, well, he's eighty-seven years old. He's bound to slow down at some point."

Rosie returned, bringing Beck a hefty glass of Scotch

over ice with a small carafe of water on the side. She set his drink on a cardboard coaster and handed him a dainty paper cocktail napkin. I noticed she'd found a doily to put on her tray. If the guy had been with me, she'd have been measuring the inseam for his wedding tuxedo.

He picked up his drink and took a measured sip, sending her a smile of approval. "That's perfect. Thanks."

Rosie departed reluctantly, at a loss for any other service to perform.

Beck turned back to me. "Are you a local as well?"

"Yep."

"Where'd you go to high school?"

"S.T."

"Me, too. Maybe that's where we knew each other. What year did you graduate?"

"1967. What about you?"

"A year ahead of you—1966. Odd I don't remember you. I'm usually good about those things."

I upgraded his age to thirty-eight. "I was a low-waller," I said, indicating my association with the badass kids who sat on the low wall at the rear of the school property where the hillside sloped down to meet the street behind. We smoked cigarettes and dope and occasionally mixed vodka in our bottles of orangeade. Tame by later standards, but considered wicked in our day.

"Really," he said. He gave me a brief searching look and then reached for the menu. "How's the food?"

"Not bad. Are you really fond of Hungarian cooking, or were you making that up?"

"Why would I lie about something like that?" He delivered the line lightly, but he could have meant anything—perhaps that he'd never bother to lie about the trivial or mundane in life. "Why do you ask?"

"I'm surprised you haven't been in before."

"I've seen the place in passing, but frankly, it always looked like such a dive I never had the nerve. I had a meeting with some guys and thought I'd give it a try since I was in the neighborhood. Nicer inside than out, I'll say that."

My antennae went up with a little whining sound. That was the second time he'd explained how he happened to come in. I picked up my glass and took a sip of bad wine. Really, it tasted like a product you'd use to clean tar off your feet after a day at the beach. Reba was playing with the straw in her iced tea.

Looking from her face to his, I realized what a dunce I'd been. She'd arranged this in advance. Dinner with me was just a cover for her meeting with him, but why the subterfuge? I rearranged myself so I was sitting with my back against the side wall, my feet on the seat, keeping my demeanor casual while I watched the scenario play out. "You're in real estate?" I asked.

He downed half the whiskey remaining in his glass, adding water to the residue. He swirled the glass, rattling his ice cubes. "That's right. I have an investment company. Development, mostly. I do property management on occasion, though not a lot these days. And you?"

"I'm a private investigator."

He smiled, bemused. "Not bad for someone who started her career loitering behind the school."

"Hey, the training was good. Hang out with a bunch of budding crooks, you get to know how they think." I made a display of looking at my watch. "Ah. I don't know about you, Reba, but it's time for me to head out. My car's just half a block down. Give me a minute to go get it and I can drive you home."

Beck looked at Reba with feigned surprise. "You don't have wheels?"

"I've got a car, but no license. Mine expired."

"Why don't I give you a lift and save her the drive?"

I said, "I don't mind doing it. I've got my car keys right here."

"No, no. I'll be happy to take her. No point in your having to go out of your way."

Reba said, "Really. It'd be easier for him than it would be for you."

"You're sure?"

Beck said, "Absolutely. It's right on my way."

"Okay with me. You two stay if you like and I'll take care of the bill. It's my treat," I said, as I slid out of the booth.

"Thanks. I'll take care of the tip."

"Nice meeting you." I shook hands with Beck again and then glanced at Reba. "I'll see you in the morning at nine. You want me to call first?"

"No need. Just come up to the house whenever you like," she said. "Actually, I ought to be heading home myself. It's been a long day and I'm bushed. You mind?"

"Anything you want." Beck finished his drink, swallowing the watered-down whiskey that remained in his glass.

I moved over to the bar and paid the bill. Glancing back, I saw that Beck was already on his feet, fishing in his pocket for his money clip. I watched him peel off two bills for the tip, probably fives since he was so eager to impress. They waited for me to join them so we could walk out together. Henry had disappeared by then, but the shank-of-the-evening drinkers were straggling in.

Outside it was dark, the moon not yet visible. The air was clear and still except for the chirping of crickets. Even the sound of the surf seemed diminished. The three of us ambled toward the intersection, chatting about nothing in particular.

"I'm down there," Beck said, pointing toward the shadowy side street to our right.

"What do you drive?" I asked.

"'87 Mercedes. The sedan. And you?"

"'74 Volkswagen. The bug. See you later."

I waved and continued walking while the two of them turned off. Fifteen seconds later, I heard the double report of their respective car doors slamming shut. I paused, waiting for the sound of an engine turning over. Nothing. Maybe they'd decided to sit and talk. When I reached my gate I pushed through, listening to the familiar squeaking of its hinges. I followed the walk around to the rear. Once I reached my front door, I hesitated, debating about Reba and Beck. Maybe I was wrong about them. Curiosity got the better of me. I left my shoulder bag on the porch and took off across the grass, crossing Henry's flagstone patio to the chicken-wire fence that ran along the rear property line. I felt my way from post to post, tracing the length until I reached his garage. I stooped and pushed the fencing aside, slipping through the gap where the fittings had come loose.

My heart was thumping merrily and I could feel my gut contract with anticipation. I love these nighttime adventures, easing in silence across darkened backyards.

Fortunately, none of the neighborhood mutts caught wind of me, so my passage was completed without a chorus of shrill warning barks. At the mouth of the alley, I veered right, emerging onto the side street. I moved forward, scanning the shapes and sizes of the cars parked on either side. A single streetlight cast only the faintest illumination, but once my eyes adjusted to the dark, I had no trouble identifying Beck's Mercedes. Every other vehicle was a compact, a minivan, or a pickup truck.

I could discern his profile where he slouched in the driver's seat half-turned so that he was facing Reba. I stood there for ten minutes and when nothing transpired, I backed up with caution and retraced my steps.

I let myself into my place and set my bag on a kitchen stool. It was 8:05. I flipped on the TV and watched the front end of a movie that actually seemed amusing, despite all the annoying commercial interruptions. I kept notes so I wouldn't buy anything I saw. At 9:00 I muted the set and went into the kitchenette, where I opened a bottle of Chardonnay and poured myself a glass. On impulse, I pulled out a saucepan, the lid, and a bottle of corn oil. I turned on the front burner, set the pan in place, and added a puddle of oil to the bottom of the pan. I scrounged through my cupboard for the bag of popcorn I'd bought months before. I knew it would be stale, but it was chewier that way. I measured out a jigger of kernels and tossed them in the pan. I kept an eye on the TV screen while the sound of the popcorn accelerated like the finale to a fireworks show. Happily for me, the size of my studio is such that I can cook, watch TV, start a load of laundry, or use the john without moving more than eight or ten feet.

I returned to the couch with my wine and the bowl

of hot popcorn, propped my feet on the coffee table, and watched the remainder of the movie. At 11:00, when the news came on, I left the apartment and followed the same circuitous route through the alley until I reached the shadowy street where I'd hovered before. Beck's Mercedes was still visible, parked at the curb. The rear window was fogged over with condensation as pale as gauze. Instead of Beck in silhouette, I saw Reba's legs. Her head was apparently down near the steering wheel, one foot propped on the dashboard, the other on the passenger-side door, thus providing her leverage while Beck labored in the confines of the leather-bound front seat. I went back to my place, and when I checked again at midnight, the car was gone.

8

The gates to the Lafferty estate were open, and when I cruised up the drive, I saw Reba waiting on the porch step, the cat at her feet. She had a brush in her hand and she groomed the cat while he strutted back and forth, arching his back against the bristles. When she caught sight of me, she kissed him and set the brush aside. She crossed to the front door, opened the screen, and leaned in to tell her father or the housekeeper she was on her way out. I couldn't help but smile as she bounded down the walk. She was happy, in high spirits, and I remember thinking, *That's what sex will do for you, kid.* She wore desert boots, jeans, and a nubby dark blue sweater with a large cowl neck. She looked as giddy as a young girl. Her father had said she was difficult—"reckless" was his word—but I'd seen no hint of it in my dealings with her. She possessed a natural exuberance and it was hard to picture her drunk or stoned. She opened the car door and slid onto the passenger seat, smiling and out of breath.

"What's the cat's name?"

"Rags. He's a love. Seventeen years old and he weighs in at eighteen pounds. The vet wants him on a diet, but pooh on that." She put her head back. "You don't know how good it feels to be out. Like coming back from the dead."

I pulled away from the house, shifting gears as I headed down the drive and through the gates. "Did you sleep well?"

"I did. Talk about a treat. Prison mattresses are about this thick, like lawn-chair pads, and all the sheets are gross. The pillow was so flat I had to roll it up and wad it under my head like a towel. I'd get in bed at night and my body heat would activate this strange smell in the bedding." She wrinkled her nose.

"What about the food?"

"Not too bad. I'd say the food ranged from passable to gross. What saved us was they let us have these electric coils in our cells. You know the ones you use to heat up a single cup of tea? We figured out all kinds of things to make with ours—Top Ramen, soups, stewed tomatoes in a can. I never even *liked* stewed tomatoes until I got down there. Some days, the cells stank; scorched coffee or bean sludge crusted on the bottom of the pan. Most of the time I disconnected and blocked everything out. I created this invisible force field that I kept between me and the rest of the world. Otherwise, I'd've gone bonkers."

"Did you have friends?"

"A couple and that helped. My best friend was Misty Raine, with an *e* on the end. She's a stripper—big surprise with a name like that—but she's an absolute hoot. Before California, she lived in Vegas, but after she was released and got off parole, she moved to Reno. She says the action there is better than in Vegas. She's been good about keeping in touch. God, I miss her."

"What was she in for?"

"She had a boyfriend who taught her how to lift credit cards and forge checks—'hanging paper' as they say. They'd go on these big spending sprees, stay in a bunch of fancy hotels, and charge anything they liked. Then they'd dump that card, steal another one, and mosey on down the road. Then they branched out into phony IDs. She has this artistic streak and it turns out she's a whiz at replicating passports and driver's licenses and shit like that. They made so much dough she bought herself a new set of tits. Before the boyfriend, she'd been working for one of those mobile-maid-type cleaning services for a minimum wage. She said she'd've never gotten anywhere on what she made even if she worked all her life.

"My other friend, Vivian, was mixed up with this drug dealer. You don't know how many times I heard that one. He was pulling in a thousand bucks a day, and they lived like kings until the cops showed up. That was her first offense and she swears it's her last. She's got another six months to serve and then I'm hoping she'll come here. Her boyfriend's been sent up five times and he'll be in for years, which is just as well. She's still crazy about the guy."

"True love is like that."

"You really think?"

"No. That was meant to be tongue in cheek," I said. "I take it you don't have friends here in town."

"Just Onni, the woman I used to work with. I talked to her earlier, hoping I could see her this afternoon, but she was tied up."

"Isn't she the one who took your old job?"

"Right. She feels guilty about that, but I said don't be dumb. She used to do front desk, but this was an opportunity she couldn't pass up. Why would I begrudge her the chance? She said she'd have driven me around today if she didn't have to work."

I turned into the parking lot of the Department of Motor Vehicles. "If you want, you can run in and pick up a booklet and study in the car before you take the test."

"Nah. I've been driving for years so how hard can it be?"

"Well, it's your choice. I prefer to bone up myself. Cuts the flop sweat."

"I like anxiety. It keeps me awake."

I waited in the car while Reba went in. She was gone forty minutes, some portion of which I spent hanging over the seat, trying to tidy all the crap that I keep back there. I generally motor around town with an overnight case stocked with toiletries and clean underpants. This, in the event I'm presented with a pressing reason to hop on a plane. In addition, I have assorted articles of clothing that I sometimes wear while pretending to be a public servant. I can do a pretty good imitation of a postal employee or meter reader from the gas-and-electric company. It pays to look like I'm doing official business when I'm standing on a front porch, idly scanning someone's mail. I also keep several reference books in the backseat—one on crime scene investigation, *Deering's California Penal Code*, a Spanish-language dictionary left over from a class I took years ago—an empty soda can, a bottle opener, an old pair of running shoes, a pair of badly snagged panty hose, and a lightweight jacket. While my apartment is tidy, I'm a slob when it comes to my car.

I glanced up in time to catch Reba's emergence from the DMV office. She half-skipped across the lot, waving a piece of paper that turned out to be her temporary license. "Aced it," she said, as she got into the car.

"Good for you," I said. I turned the key in the ignition, shifted into reverse, and backed out of the space. "Where now?"

"I know it's only ten forty-five, but I wouldn't object to another QP with Cheese."

We ordered from the drive-through window, found a space in the parking lot, and ate in the car. We'd opted for two large Cokes, two Quarter Pounders apiece, and a large order of fries, which we doused in ketchup and ate as fast as we could. I said, "I had a friend regained his health eating shit like this."

"I'm not surprised. I like how flat the pickles are, all mooshed in there. Pop's got a personal chef who's really great, but she's never been able to duplicate this. I can't figure it out, how they do it. Doesn't matter where you are, a QP with Cheese tastes exactly the same and so does everything else. Big Macs, fries."

"Nice to have something you can count on," I said.

After lunch we drove out to the La Cuesta shopping mall, where Reba worked her way from store to store, flashing her father's credit card and trying on clothes. Like other women I've known, she seemed to have an inborn sense of what would look good on her. In most stores, I made a point of finding the nearest chair from which I watched her like a good mom while she moved from rack to rack. Sometimes she'd take out a garment, study it critically, and put it back. Other times, she'd lay the item on top of those she'd draped over her arm. At intervals, she'd head off to the dressing room and then appear twenty minutes later with her choices made. Some pieces she'd leave behind and the rest she'd pile on the counter while she looked for something else. In the course of two hours, she bought pants, skirts, jackets, underwear, knit tops, two dresses, and six pairs of shoes.

Once in the car again, she put her head back against the seat and closed her eyes. "I used to take so many things for granted, but never again. Where next?"

"Up to you. Where do you want to go?"

"The beach. Let's take our shoes off and walk in the sand."

We ended up at Ludlow Beach, not far from my house. Santa Teresa City College was perched on the bluffs above us. The sky was gray as far as the eye could see, and wind was whipping the waves, blowing spray toward the beach. We left our shoes locked in the car, along with my shoulder bag and Reba's purchases. The picnic tables in the grassy area had been abandoned except for a foursome of gulls squabbling over a bread bag that had been tied shut and left on the edge of a trash bin. Reba picked up the bag, tore through the cellophane, and tossed the crumbs across the grass. Gulls began to wheel in, shrieking, from all directions.

We trudged through a hundred yards of soft sand between the parking lot and the surf. At the water line, icy waves tumbled perilously close to our bare feet, but the sand was damp and packed hard, easier to walk on. I said, "So what's the deal with Beck?"

She flashed me a smile. "That blew me away, running into him like that."

"Really. That's odd. I was under the impression you'd arranged it in advance."

She laughed. "No, not at all. Why would I do that?"

"Reba." I got the big brown eyes turned on me.

"Honest. He's the last person in the world I expected to see."

I shook my head. "Nope. Not honest. Lying through your teeth. That's why you sat on the far side of the booth so you could watch for him."

"That's not *true*. I had no idea he'd be there. I was totally surprised."

"Wait, wait, wait. Just hold on a second and I'll bring you up to speed. I've been telling lies for years and believe me, I know when someone's maneuvering the truth. I got a bullshit meter working 'round the clock. I watched the two of you last night and it was *ding ding ding!* I was strictly window dressing, the person, in the olden days, they referred to as a 'beard.' You called him from the parole office and told him where you'd be."

She was quiet for a moment. "Maybe. But I wasn't sure he'd come."

"Oh, he came all right, if his behavior in the car was any indication."

Her head whipped around and she looked at me in disbelief. "You were *spying* on us?"

"That's what I'm paid for. You don't want to be seen, you shouldn't do it in public."

"What a *bitch*!"

"Reba, your father cares about your welfare. He doesn't want you to end up in the shit again."

She clutched my arm, looking at me earnestly. "Don't tell Pop. Please. What purpose would it serve?"

"I haven't decided what I'm going to do. It might help if you told me what's going on."

"I don't want to talk about it."

"Oh, give it a whirl. You want me to keep quiet, you better fill me in." I could see how tempted she was. Who can resist talking about a guy that they're so smitten with?

"I'm not sure how to explain. I worked for him for years and he's always been supportive . . ."

"Not the long version, dearie, just the salient points. You're having an affair, right?"

"It's much more than that. I'm crazy about him and he's crazy about me, too."

"The crazy part I'll buy. Since when?"

"Two years. Well, four if you count the two I was gone. We've been writing back and forth and talking on the phone. We planned to get together tonight, but there's an AA meeting I'm supposed to attend. I thought I better show up in case Holloway checks. Beck called me at Pop's and said he couldn't stand the wait. I thought of Rosie's because her place is so out of the way I couldn't imagine running into anyone we know. I guess I should have told you up front, but I wasn't sure you'd approve so I just went ahead and did it."

"What'd you need me for? You're big boys and girls. Why not go to a motel and get it over with?"

"I was scared. We haven't been together for so long, I was afraid the chemistry might be gone."

"I don't get it. What's the timing on this? Were you bonking the guy while you were ripping him off?"

"It isn't 'bonking.' We make love."

"Oh, sorry. Were you 'making love' while you were making off with all his hard-earned cash?"

"I guess you could put it that way. I mean, I knew it

was *wrong*, but I couldn't help myself. I felt awful. I still do. He knows I'd never do anything to hurt him."

"Losing that much money didn't hurt? I'd be cut to the quick."

"It wasn't personal. I took money from the company—"

"Which he owns."

"I know, but I didn't look at it that way. It was just *there* and nobody seemed to notice. I kept thinking I'd score big and then I'd put it all back. I never meant to keep it and I certainly wouldn't *steal*."

"Reba, that's what stealing *is*. You pocket someone else's money without their knowledge or consent. If you use a gun, it's called robbery. Either way, it's not behavior that's designed to endear."

She shrugged uncomfortably. "I saw it as a loan. It was just a temporary thing."

"The guy must have a big heart."

"He does. He tried to help me. He did everything he could. I know he's forgiven me. He said it all again last night."

"Hey, I'll take your word for it, but it's weird. I mean, it's one thing to forgive, but then to go on with the affair? How does he rationalize *that*? Doesn't he feel used?"

"He understands I have a self-destructive streak. That doesn't mean he condones it, but he doesn't hold it against me."

"Is that why you never went to trial? Because of him?"

"Partly. When I got arrested, I knew I'd hit bottom. I was guilty as shit. I just wanted to take my licks and get it over with. A trial would've been an embarrassment for Pop. I didn't want him to suffer another public spectacle. I've caused enough trouble as it is."

"Your father tells me Beck's married. Doesn't his wife figure into the equation somewhere?"

"That's a marriage of convenience. They haven't been intimate for years."

"Oh, come *on*. Every married guy says *that*."

"I know, but in his case, it's true."

"What a crock of shit. You think he'll leave her for you? It doesn't work that way."

"Wrong. You are so wrong," she said. "He has it all set up."

"Like what?"

"This is all part of his game plan, but he has to bide his time. If she finds out about me, she'll take him for everything."

"I know *I* would."

"He told me last night he's close to pulling it off."

"Pulling what off?"

I got the double whammy—the big imploring eyes, plus the arm clutch denoting her earnest intent. "Promise you won't tell."

"I can't promise you that! What if he's planning to rob a bank?"

"Don't be dumb. He's getting his finances in shape. Once he has his assets under wraps, he'll broach the subject of divorce. By then, it'll be a done deal and what's she going to do? She'll just have to face facts and accept reality."

"Would you listen to yourself? You're telling me he's worked out a way to cheat his wife. What kind of man *is* he? First he runs around on her and then he rips her off? Oh wait. Skip that. Just occurred to me that you ripped him off first so maybe you're the perfect pair."

"You don't even know what love is. I bet you've never been in love in your life."

"Don't change the subject."

"Well, it's true, isn't it?"

I rolled my eyes, shaking my head in despair. "You are such a nincompoop."

"So what? It's not hurting anyone."

"Oh, right. What about his wife?"

"She'll come around eventually, once it's out in the open."

"Are there any kids?"

"She never wanted kids."

"That's a blessing at any rate. Look, babe. I know where you're coming from. I was once involved with a married man myself. At the time they were separated, but they were married all the same. And you know what I learned? You have no idea what goes on between a husband and wife. I don't care how he represents the relationship, you shouldn't tread on sacred turf. It's the same as walking on hot coals. Doesn't matter how much faith you have, your feet are going to *burn*."

"Tough. It's too late. It's like playing craps. Once the dice leave your hand, you can't do anything but watch."

"At least break it off until he's free," I said.

"I can't. I love him. He's everything to me."

"Oh shit, Reba. Go see a shrink and get your head on straight."

I watched her face shut down. She turned abruptly and started walking away, addressing her comments to me over her shoulder as the gap between us widened. "You don't have a clue what you're talking about. You only met the man *once* so you can keep your friggin' opinions to yourself. It's none of your business and it's none of Pop's." She walked on, heading toward the parking lot. I was left with no choice but to trot along behind.

We barely spoke during the drive to her father's house. By the time I dropped her off, I figured that was the end of the line for me. She was out of prison. She was home. She had her driver's license back and a closet full of clothes. Nothing she'd done—namely, screwing—was in violation of her parole so her actions and behavior were no concern of mine.

She got out of the car and retrieved her packages from the backseat. "I know you mean well and I appreciate your concern, but I've paid for my sins and now my life belongs to me. If I make bad choices, it's my tough luck. It has nothing to do with you."

"Okay by me. Have a good life," I said.

She closed the car door. She paused and leaned in the window briefly. I thought she meant to say more, but she decided to let it ride. I watched her until the front door closed behind her and then I headed for the office. Once there, I typed up an invoice, billing Nord Lafferty the five hundred dollars a day for the two days I'd worked. I put the bill in an envelope, which I sealed and addressed. On the way home, I drove past the post office, where I slowed to a stop and dropped it in the box at the curb.

9

For supper, I fixed myself a hot hard-boiled-egg sandwich slathered with mayo and heavy on the salt, vowing in a vague and insincere way to rectify my diet, which is woefully short of fruits, vegetables, fiber, grain, and nutrition of any sort. I'd intended to make an early night of it, but by seven I was feeling restless for reasons I couldn't name. I decided on a quick trip to Rosie's, not so much for the bad wine as for a change of scene.

To my surprise, the first person I saw was Henry's older brother Lewis, who lives in Michigan. He stood behind the bar with his suit jacket off, his arms bare to his elbows and plunged in soapy water while he washed assorted glasses and beer mugs. I crossed to the bar, saying, "Well, this is a surprise. Where did you come from?"

He looked up with a smile. "I flew in this afternoon. William picked me up at the airport and put me straight to work."

"What brings you to town?"

"Nothing in particular. I needed a change. I came up

with the plan on the spur of the moment. Charlie was busy and Nell wasn't in the mood, so I booked a seat and made the trip by myself. Travel's invigorating. I'm full of beans," he said.

"Well, good for you. That's great. How long will you be here?"

"Until Sunday. William and Rosie are putting me up. That's why he's teaching me to tend bar, so I can earn my keep."

"Does Henry know you're here?"

"Not yet, but I'll call him as soon as William lets me take a break."

He rinsed the last of the beer mugs and set it on a rack to drain, then dried his hands on the white towel he'd tucked in his waist. He put a cocktail napkin on the bar in front of me and shifted into bartender mode. "What are you drinking? If memory serves, you prefer Chardonnay."

"Better make that a Coke. Rosie's changed 'vintners,' though the term hardly applies. The wine she's serving has all the subtlety of solvent."

He hosed me a Coke and placed it in front of me. For a gentleman of eighty-nine, he was the picture of efficiency, his manner brisk and relaxed. Watching him, you'd have thought he'd been tending bar all his life.

"Thanks."

"You're entirely welcome. My treat."

"Well, aren't you nice! I appreciate that."

I watched him amble toward the far end of the bar to wait on somebody else. What was going on? I'd never known Lewis to fly out unannounced. Had William put him up to it? That seemed like a bad idea. I turned and glanced over my shoulder at the smattering of patrons. My favorite booth was occupied, but there were numerous other seats available. I carried my Coke and crossed to a table near the entrance. Fresh air wafted in with each opening and closing of the door, thus dispelling some of the accumulated cigarette smoke, which lay on the air like fog. Even so, I knew I'd get home smelling like soot and have to hang my clothes on the shower rod overnight to eliminate the stink. My hair was doubtless already reeking, though I wear it too short to hold a strand to my nose. Smokers listen to these prissy-ass complaints as though the charges were trumped up simply to annoy and offend.

I was scarcely settled when I sensed the welcomed shift in air current that signaled someone entering the place. Cheney Phillips stood in the doorway. I felt one of those lurches you experience on a plane that leaves you wondering if the flight will be the last you take. I watched him scan the assembled patrons, apparently looking for someone who hadn't yet arrived. His clothing was the usual mix of expensive fabrics and fine tailoring. He favored crisp white dress shirts or soft-collared silk in shades of cream or buttermilk. On occasion, he shifted to a tone-on-tone, usually in dark hues that lent him a faintly sinister air. Tonight, he wore a cinnamon sueded silk sport coat over a rust-colored cashmere turtleneck. I lifted my hand in greeting, wondering if the sweater was as soft as it looked. He sauntered over to my table and pulled out a chair. "Hey, how's by you? Mind if I sit?"

I gestured assent. "Our paths cross again. I haven't seen you for months and now I've run into you three times in the past four days."

"Not entirely accidental." He pointed to my glass. "What the hell is that?"

"Coke. A soft drink. It's been around for years."

"You need something stronger. We have to talk." Without waiting for my response, he caught Lewis's eye and gestured, indicating the need for service.

I turned in time to see Lewis hustle out from behind the bar and head toward our table. "Yes, sir."

"Two vodka martinis, straight up. Stoli if you have it, Absolut if not. And a side of olives." Glancing at me, he said, "You want ice water?"

"Oh, why not?" I said, ever the bon vivant. "This is Lewis Pitts, my landlord's brother. You've met Henry, haven't you?"

"Of course. Cheney Phillips," he said. He rose to his feet and shook hands with Lewis, who said a few pleased-to-meet-you-type things with the usual pleasantries thrown in. I found myself noting the texture of Cheney's hair, springy dark brown curls that looked as soft as a poodle's coat. I'm not a dog lover at heart. Doggies tend to bark their bad breath in my face, preparatory to jumping up and parking their cumbersome paws on my chest. Despite numerous sharp commands, most dogs behave any way they please. There's the occasional exception. The week before, in a rare moment of goodwill, I'd stopped to chat with a woman who was walking a breed I'd never seen before. She introduced me to Chandler, a Portuguese water dog who sat on command and gravely offered to shake hands. The dog was quiet and well mannered with a coat so curly and soft I could hardly keep my hands to myself. Why was I thinking about that *now?* Having missed the bulk of the conversation, I tuned in as Lewis was saying, "Be right back." It was like waking up in the middle of a TV movie. I had no clear idea what was going on.

As soon as he was gone, I turned to Cheney. "I take it you're here to meet someone."

His attention was focused on faces halfway across the room, his gaze shifting at precise intervals like a corner-mounted camera. He'd been a vice cop for years and he had a letch for hookers and dope dealers the way some guys are fixated on the size of a woman's boobs. His eyes flicked to mine. "Actually, I came in looking for you. I stopped by your apartment and when I didn't find you there, I figured you'd be here."

"I didn't realize I was so predictable."

"Your best trait," he said. His gaze caught on mine again and the effect was unnerving. I glanced at the bar, the front door, anywhere but him. Where was Lewis and what was taking him so long?

Cheney said, "Don't you want to know why I'm here?"

"Sure."

"We have an interest in common."

"Oh, really. And what would that be?"

"Reba Lafferty."

The answer was unexpected and I could feel my head tilt with curiosity. "What's your connection to her?"

"That's why I went to see Priscilla Holloway. I heard someone was driving down to CIW to bring Reba back. I didn't know it was you until I saw you that day."

Cheney glanced up at Lewis, who'd appeared with our martinis on a tray. He set them down with great care, watching the liquid tremble. The stemware was so cold I could see ice flakes sliding along the outer surface of the glass. The vodka, just out of the freezer, looked oily in the light. I hadn't drunk a martini in ages and I remembered the sharp, nearly chemical taste.

I can never decide what makes Cheney's face so appealing—wide mouth, dark brows, eyes as brown as old pennies. His hands are big and it looks like he busted his knuckles pounding someone in the chops. I studied his features and then caught myself, thinking I should slap my own face. I'd just lectured Reba on the folly of a dalliance with a married man and here I was idly entertaining the very thought myself.

Cheney said, "Thanks, Lewis. Can you run a tab for us?"

"Of course. Just let me know if you need anything else."

Once he was gone, Cheney lifted his glass and tapped its edge against mine. "Cheers."

I took a sip of my drink. The vodka was smooth, forming a column of heat that sank down my spinal cord and into my shoes. "I hope you're not saying she's in trouble."

"I'd say she's teetering on the brink."

"Oh, no."

"How well do you know her?"

"You can make that past tense. I did the job I was hired for and now I've moved on."

"As of when?"

"We parted company this afternoon. What's she done?"

"Nothing so far, but she's close."

"So you said. Meaning what?"

"She's been seeing Alan Beckwith, the guy you met in here Monday night."

"I know when I met the guy, but what's that to you?" I could hear hostility creep into my tone at the implications of what he'd said. Someone was apparently watching me the same night I was watching Reba carry on with Beck.

"Don't be crabby."

"Sorry. I didn't mean for it to come out that way." I took a deep breath, willing myself into a more sanguine place. I said, "I don't understand where you fit in. And don't make me guess. I really hate that shit."

Cheney smiled. "I'm talking to some guys who have an interest in him. Her, too, by association. You have to understand this is all highly confidential."

"I'm crossing my heart," I said, and made an X on my chest.

"You know anything about Beck?"

"I'm an innocent. Well, wait. That's not entirely true. I know his father owned the Clements, so I'm assuming the man was a major player in his day."

"The best. Alan Beckwith Senior made a shitload of money in a number of franchises, mostly real estate. Junior's been successful, but he's worked all his life in the shadow of his dad. Beck never measured up. From what I've heard, it's not like his dad made judgments about him, but Beck was conscious of the gap in their accomplishments. His old man went to Harvard and graduated fifth in his class. Beck's academic career was undistinguished. His college was good, but strictly second tier. He ended up with an MBA, but gradewise, he wasn't even in the top twenty-fifth percentile. That's just how it went. His achievements were modest compared to his dad's and I guess the older he got the worse he felt. He's the kind of guy who swore he'd be a multimillionaire by the time he was forty. At thirty, he was stalled out and getting desperate to make good. You know the saying 'Money's just a way of keeping score'? Well, Beck took that to heart. Five, six years back, he decided his prime goal was to outearn his dad. Since he couldn't manage it playing straight, he took a left-hand turn. He realized he could make a lot more money if he offered his services to people who needed to have theirs washed."

"Money laundering?"

"Right. Turns out Beck has an aptitude for financial shenanigans. Since he deals in high-end real estate, the basic infrastructure was already in place. There are half a dozen ways to fiddle funds when you buy and sell property, but the mechanism's slow and there's too much paperwork. With money laundering, you want to minimize the paper trail and put as many fire walls as possible between you and the source. His early efforts were clumsy, but he's getting better at this stuff. Now he's set up an offshore company—a Panamanian dummy corp called Clements Unlimited. Places like Panama, you can hide a lot of dough because the bank secrecy laws have been tight there since day one. 1941, they took their cue from the Swiss and went to coded accounts. Unfortunately for the bad guys, the numbered account isn't what it once was. Swiss banks don't offer the same level of protection, because they've taken so much flak for providing cover for thugs. They've finally recognized the necessity for getting along in the international banking community and that's motivated their signing treaties with a host of other countries. In effect, they've agreed to cooperate where there's proof of criminal activity. Panama isn't as eager to please. They've got lawyers who create companies in bulk and sell them off to customers who want to sidestep the IRS."

"You're talking about shell corporations, right?"

He nodded. "You can create a sham company according to your specifications or you can buy one ready-made. Once you have a shell in place, you funnel money from the U.S. by way of the shell to any financial haven you choose. Or you can set up an offshore trust. Or you do what Beck did, which was to buy himself a bank-in-a-box and start accepting deposits."

"From whom?"

"He makes a point not to inquire too closely, but his primary client is a big-time Los Angeles drug dealer, ostensibly doing business in scrap gold. Beck also dry-cleans money for a major pornography mill and a syndicate that runs a network of hookers and whorehouses down in San Diego County. Guys in the sin trades accumulate millions in cash and what can they do with it? Live lavishly and your neighbors will start to wonder about the source of your wealth. So will the IRS, the DEA, and half a dozen other government agencies. There's never a shortage of folks who need to run dirty money through the sluice and have it come up clean. The neat thing from Beck's perspective is that, until recently, what he's doing wasn't illegal in and of itself."

"You're kidding."

"Nope. Last year Congress passed the Money Laundering Control Act. Before that, the same basic transactions might have been the focus of an investigation or subject to prosecution under some other statute, but the laundering itself wasn't a crime. Sorry to be so long-winded. Bear with me on this."

"Don't worry about it. Most of this is news to me."

"Me, too. From what I'm told, the groundwork was laid in 1970 when the Bank Secrecy Act was passed. The BSA established reporting regulations for financial institutions—banks, brokerage houses, currency dealers, anybody issuing traveler's checks, money orders, shit like that. They're required to report certain transactions to the Secretary of the Treasury within fifteen days on a form called the Currency Transaction Report—the CTR—for any transaction over ten thousand dollars. Are you following?"

"More or less. How do you know all this stuff?"

"Most of it I picked up from my IRS pal in the past couple of months. He says in addition to the CTR, there's something called a Currency and Monetary Instrument Report, the CMIR. This is for the people who physically receive or transport cash—carry it, mail it, ship it—again, that's in any amount over ten thousand dollars. There's another form for casinos, but we don't have to worry about that here. Far as we know, Beck doesn't have ties to any of the big gambling operations, though that's another nice way to scrub a load of cash and get it squeaky clean.

"The government relies on financial institutions to track the flow of cash through the system. Obviously, there's nothing illegal about dealing in large sums as long as all the proper forms get filed. Try to bypass that and you're subject to severe penalties—assuming you're caught, of course. Beck made a point of cultivating a bunch of banker pals and for a period, he was bribing one of them to look the other way. The bank officer would prepare the CTR as required and place a copy in the files, only instead of shipping the original to the IRS, he'd run it through a shredder. Problem is, the banks tend to move these executives from branch to branch, and Beck lost his co-conspirator. That's how he came to the attention of Internal Revenue. Some new VP at Santa Teresa Savings and Loan noticed a pattern of small deposits that he was pretty sure were all linked to Beck or Beck's company. He's been breaking the big deposits into a series of smaller

transactions, hoping to skirt the ten-thousand-dollar requirement for a government report. This is the fundamental
maneuver in any laundering operation. It's called structuring, or 'smurfing.' Beck employed a regular road crew of
smurfs, who'd go from bank to bank here in town—sometimes from city to city—buying cashier's checks or money
orders in the smaller dollar amounts—two grand, five,
sometimes as much as nine, but never over ten. The dribbles
and drabs were deposited piecemeal into a single account,
and then Beck would use wire transfers to move the whole
of it to a couple of offshore banks. After that, he'd funnel it
back to his clients in a more respectable form.

"Anyway, while all this was going on, the DEA was
following the money from the other end, tracking funds
through the system from a cartel importing marijuana and
cocaine into Los Angeles. At some point, the two paths
intersected and a red flag went up. I'd met the IRS
investigator at a conference in D.C. about four years back.
Shortly after that, he got assigned to the L.A. office to
coordinate the task force. Once Beck's name surfaced, the
focus shifted to him. The agent, Vince Turner, asked me
to act as the local interface. His guys are keeping a low
profile because the feds are trying to build a case without
Beck's getting wind of it."

"Oh, good luck. In this town?"

"We're well aware," he said. "So far they've initiated
mail and trash covers and they've been running surveillance, covering his movements in and out of the country.
What they need now is an informant, which is where Reba
Lafferty comes in."

I gestured impatiently. "You're kidding. She's in love
with the man. She'd never rat him out."

"Don't be so sure . . ."

"I *am* sure. She's smitten. That's how she's managed to hold herself together for the past two years. They wrote to each other and talked on the phone a couple of times a week. That's how she survived. I got it straight from her."

"Just hear me out," he said. "You know the background on this."

"Of course. She ripped off his company for megabucks over a two-year period—"

"While she and Beck were having an affair," he said.

"I know that. So what?"

"So under the circumstances, doesn't it seem strange he'd take up with her again the minute she gets out?"

"Well, yeah. Matter of fact, I asked her about that myself. She claims he's forgiven her. She says he knew she was self-destructive and couldn't help herself. Or words to that effect."

He was shaking his head. "Nope. Don't think so. It doesn't ring true."

"I'm not defending the point. I'm just telling you what she said. I agree with you. It's hard to believe Beck would turn the other cheek. So what's the deal? I gather you know something I don't."

Cheney leaned forward, lowering his voice. I tilted my head closer and felt the whisper of his breath against my cheek as he spoke. "She took the fall for him. He had her set up accounts for a couple of phony companies. She'd invoice for bogus goods and services, then write checks out of accounts payable. He'd sign 'em and she'd send 'em off to a post office box. Later, she'd pick 'em up and deposit the money to a phony account. Sometimes, he'd wire the money offshore or she'd withdraw the cash herself and pass it on to him."

"I don't get it. Why's he stealing from himself?"

"He has people to pay off and this is how he covers his butt. He can't siphon off large sums of cash without an explanation. If he's ever audited, the IRS will want to know where the money went. He figured he'd disguise the fact he's draining off the bucks by making it look like a legitimate business expense."

"Why not use money from one of his offshore accounts?"

"Who knows the rationale? By then he'd cooked up a couple new schemes anyway and he was anxious to shift gears. He talked Reba into going down for the three hundred and fifty thou and he came out smelling like a rose. Since she claimed she'd gambled all the money away, who could prove otherwise? Truth is, she's always had a gambling problem and she was already making trips to Vegas and Reno, which suited him to a tee."

"But how'd he talk her into it?"

"Same way guys talk women into anything. He promised her the moon."

"I can't believe she went to jail for him. What an idiot."

Cheney shrugged. "My IRS buddy says there was talk of approaching her back then, offering to cut her a deal, but at the time, they were just setting up shop and couldn't afford to take the risk. Now it's crunch time. They need the inside track and she's it."

"Beck must have a company comptroller and accountants. Why not one of them?"

"They're working on that angle as a backup plan."

"Well, you better tell 'em to work hard. If Reba spent two years in prison for Beck, why turn on him now?"

"You know he's married . . ."

I could feel my impatience mount. "Of course. And Reba knows it, too. He says it's a marriage of convenience. I think it's a crock and I told her so, but couldn't get her to budge."

"She's delusional in that case. You see Beck and his wife together—her name's Tracy, by the way—there's no suggestion whatever he's anything less than devoted. Could be an act on his part, but it doesn't look that way."

"That's how guys are . . ."

"Hey, women are the same. Percentagewise, women probably screw around more than men."

"Listen to us. That's sick. How'd we get so cynical?"

Cheney smiled. "It comes with the turf."

"You think Tracy knows about Reba?"

"Hard to say. Beck's got a ton of money and he treats her like a queen. Maybe from her perspective, it's smarter to look the other way. Or maybe she knows and doesn't give a shit."

"Yeah, well, Reba's convinced he's kept his wife in the dark, and furthermore, if Tracy finds out, she'll not only divorce his ass, but take him for everything he's got."

"How's she going to do that? He has money stashed in bank accounts all over the world. And some are banks he *owns*. She'd end up with the same nightmare we're facing, which is how to trace his assets. Reba's got that down cold. She knows where the bodies are buried if we can get to her."

"What makes you think he didn't change it all while she was gone?"

"Why would he do that? He may vary the game plan, but the accounts have been in place for years. Setting up an offshore bank is an expensive proposition. He's not going to go back and start from scratch unless he's forced to. That's why the feds are so worried about tipping him off. They don't want him to panic before they're ready to roll."

"What do they want from her?"

"Facts and figures, banks, account numbers—whatever she can get her hands on. Some of the information they have, but they need corroboration, plus whatever she knows that they haven't come up with yet."

"But what's her motivation? You've got nothing to offer. She's a free human being. Ask her for help and she'll run straight to him."

Cheney reached into the inner pocket of his sport coat and removed a manila envelope that he pushed across the table.

"What's this?"

"Take a look."

I undid the clasp. Inside I found a series of grainy black-and-white photographs of Beck, probably taken with a telephoto lens. In two, his companion's face wasn't clear, but she appeared to be the same woman. The pictures had been taken on five different occasions, judging from the date and time recorded in the bottom right-hand corner of each print. All had been snapped within the past month. The last photo was a shot of the two of them leaving a motel I recognized on upper State Street. I slid the photos back into the envelope. "Who's the woman?"

"Her name is Onni. She's Reba's best friend. He's been bedding her ever since Reba landed at CIW."

"What a shitheel," I said. "And I'm supposed to show her those in hopes of persuading her to turn on him?"

"Yes."

I tossed the photos and they skittered across the table to him. "You have the resources of the entire United States government at your disposal. Find someone else to do your dirty work."

"Look, I understand where you're coming from, but this isn't penny-ante stuff. What Beck's doing is—"

"I know what he's doing. Don't give me this 'Money laundering is evil' bullshit. I got that already. I don't see why I should be the one who talks Reba into rolling over on him."

"We're guys. We don't know her the way you do. Just call her and chat. The woman trusts you."

"She does *not*. She doesn't even *like* me. I'm telling you, she got really pissed off when I tried telling her the truth. How can I turn around and call? She'd know I was up to something. She may be an idiot, but she isn't unaware."

"Think about it—*please*—before you make up your mind."

I stood up and pushed back my chair. "All right. I'll think about it. In the meantime, I need to go home and take a bath."

10

I did not sleep well. My encounter with Cheney Phillips had generated a gloom that seemed to permeate my dreams. I woke often and stared up through my skylight at the overcast night sky. His proposal had at least served to diminish his appeal. Reba was vulnerable by nature and only marginally stable, given to veering off course in response to her own internal tumult. So far she seemed fine (sort of) but I didn't want to trip her into a downward spiral when she'd just reached solid ground. She'd been free for two days. What would she do if she heard about this? She'd go off the deep end. On the other hand, she'd pinned her hopes on a bum and what was I to do? Sooner or later, she was going to learn the truth. Was it better to tell her now while she still had an opportunity to redeem herself?

At 5:59 A.M. I shut down my alarm and pulled on my sweats in preparation for a run. I went through my usual bathroom routine—brushing my teeth, splashing water on my face, lamenting the state of my hair, which was sticking up every which way. I looped my housekey in my shoelace, locked the apartment, and started walking at a fast pace toward the bike path that runs parallel to the beach.

Gradually I broke into a trot, my muscles protesting. My feet felt leaden, as though someone had affixed ten-pound weights to the bottoms of my shoes. The sun had already risen and for once there was no evidence of fog. The day promised to be a good one, clear and sunny. Across the rumble of the surf, I could hear the barking of a sea lion, probably some hoary old guy who'd staked out a place for himself on a marker buoy. In hopes of shaking off my depression, I picked up the pace, my sights focused on the bathhouse where I made my turnaround. By the time I started back, I wasn't exactly light of heart, but I didn't feel quite so dead.

I finished my run and walked the last couple of blocks to cool down. When I reached home, I saw Mattie's car parked in Henry's drive. *Oh goody.* I let myself into my place, showered, dressed, and ate a bowl of cereal. As I left for the office, I picked up the tantalizing scent of bacon and eggs wafting across the patio. Henry's kitchen door was open and through the screen, I heard laughter and chatting. I smiled, imagining the two of them sitting down to breakfast together. I knew better than to think she'd spent the night with him. He's entirely too proper to compromise her reputation, but an early morning get-together was well within the purview of Emily Post.

I crossed the yard and tapped on the door frame. He responded, inviting me to come in, though his tone wasn't quite as chipper as I'd hoped. I let myself in, thinking *Uh-oh.* Henry had reverted to his usual dress code—flip-flops, white T-shirt, and tan shorts. The kitchen showed all the signs of a recent meal—dirty skillets and bowls, an array of spices near the stove. Dishes and utensils were piled in the sink, and the counter was gritty with toast crumbs. Henry was at the sink, running water for a fresh pot of coffee, while Mattie sat at the kitchen table engrossed in a conversation with William and Lewis.

I caught the dynamic in a flash and I could feel myself wince. William had set this up. He'd been infuriated by Henry's attitude where Mattie was concerned. Lewis had no such qualms. I knew William had been chatting with Lewis on the phone, but I hadn't thought much of it. Now I had visions of his maneuvering Lewis onto the scene, assuming Henry's competitive instincts would kick in. Instead, Henry was reacting like a schoolboy, withdrawn and insecure in the presence of his brother's cockiness. Maybe William didn't care which of his brothers snagged Mattie as long as one of them did.

From what I knew of the family history, Lewis—two years older than Henry—had always asserted his superiority in matters of the heart. Neither Lewis nor Henry had ever married, and though I hadn't quizzed them on the subject, there was one reference I remembered. In 1926 Henry had taken Lewis's girlfriend away from him. Henry claimed Lewis had never fully recovered from the insult. Now, to all appearances, Lewis was finally mounting a retaliatory campaign. He'd made a point of dressing smartly—starched white shirt, vest, suit coat, his shoes shined, his trousers sharply creased. Like his two younger brothers, Lewis had all his hair and most of his teeth. I saw him as Mattie must—handsome, attentive, with none of Henry's reticence. The two brothers had met her on the same Caribbean cruise and Lewis had pursued her relentlessly. He'd signed up for Mattie's watercolor class, and while his efforts were crude, she'd admired his enthusiasm and his doggedness. Henry claimed he was only flirting, but Mattie didn't see it that way. Now here he was again, stepping into the picture just as Henry was making headway.

"Coffee?" Henry asked me. Even his voice sounded bruised, though he was covering as well as he could.

"Sure, I'll take a cup. Thanks."

"Mattie? Fresh pot coming up."

"Love some," she said, distracted by the anecdote Lewis was in the midst of telling. Henry wasn't listening. The story was probably one he'd heard before and he knew how it would end. I was so focused on Henry I didn't hear much of it myself. Lewis reached the punch line and both William and Mattie burst out laughing.

I sat down at the table and when the merriment subsided, I glanced at Mattie. "So what's up today? The two of you have plans?"

"Oh, no. I can't stay. I've got responsibilities at home."

Lewis slapped the table. "Nonsense! There's a show at the art museum. I read about it in the paper and I know it's one you'd love."

"What sort of show?"

"Blown glass. Extraordinary. It's a traveling exhibit the reviewer called a 'must-see.' At least stay for that. Afterward, we could have a bite of lunch at a Mexican restaurant right there in the arcade. There's an art gallery across the court you really should see. You could talk to the owner about your work. Maybe she'd agree to represent you."

William chimed in. "Fabulous idea. Don't go rushing off. Take a little time for yourself."

I felt my head swivel. William was beaming like a mother at a dance recital.

I said, "Uh, Henry? Could I see you for a minute? I've got a problem at my place."

"What sort of problem?"

"It's just something I have to show you. It won't take long."

"I'll look into it later. Can't it wait?"

"Really not," I said, hoping to signal him with my tone.

He seemed resigned or annoyed, I couldn't tell which. He turned to Mattie. "You won't mind if I slip out for a minute?"

"Not at all. I can tidy up the kitchen while you're gone."

"That's not necessary," Henry said. "I'll take care of the dishes as soon as I get back."

"Take your time," Lewis said, airily. "We'll get the place all shipshape and then take a walk on the beach. Mattie needs some fresh air. Place is like an oven in here."

Henry turned a bleak eye on Lewis. "If it's all the same to you, I'd prefer to clean the kitchen myself."

Lewis made a face. "Oh, loosen up, for Pete's sake. You're like a little old lady. We're not going to mess with your precious things. I promise we'll keep all the spices in alphabetical order. Go on. Get out of here. We're fine."

Henry's cheeks flushed with embarrassment. I tucked my arm into his and steered him toward the door. I could tell he was torn between wanting to defend himself and wanting to escape the torment. I didn't think Mattie was being mean. Her affection for both brothers was doubtless genuine. She simply wasn't tuned into the rivalry between the two.

The screen door banged shut behind us and we crossed the yard. As soon as I let him into my apartment, I could see Henry scrutinize the premises, his expression sour, looking for the problem he was there to fix. "I hope it's not the plumbing. I'm not in the mood to crawl under the house."

"There isn't any problem. I had to get you out of there. You need to chill out. You can't let Lewis get under your skin like that."

He gave me a stony look. "I don't know what you're talking about."

I couldn't tell if he was actually that obtuse or feigning ignorance to avoid addressing the point. "Yes, you do. Lewis is flirting, but he flirts with every woman he sees. It doesn't mean anything. You've got twice his charm and twice his good looks. Besides, you're the one she came to see. You can't let him swoop in like that and sweep her off her feet."

"Swoop and sweep?"

"You know what I mean. She's taking the path of least resistance. That doesn't mean she likes him any better than you."

"I wouldn't be so sure. Mattie couldn't set aside time for me. Let him propose an outing and suddenly she's got all day."

"But you could have proposed something just as easily."

"I did. I suggested breakfast."

"And she agreed. The only thing I don't understand is how Lewis and William ended up over there as well."

"A remarkable coincidence. The two were taking their

morning constitutional and just 'happened' to be passing as she pulled into the drive. They stopped for a chat and naturally, she invited them to join us. Now she intends to spend the rest of the day with *him*."

"She never said that. What's the matter with you? So Lewis came up with a plan. Big deal. Think of a better one and stand your ground."

"It's not up to me. It's Mattie's call. Lewis is being pushy and competitive, vying for her attention. The way he's acting, he might as well be eight."

"Well, that's true," I said. "He is competitive with you."

"Precisely. And it's revolting—grown men scrapping over her like dogs with a bone. No gentleman should impose himself when it's a lady's right to choose."

"Mattie isn't choosing. She's being nice."

"Fine. She can be as nice as she pleases. Far be it from me to interfere."

"Oh, come on, Henry. Don't be like that."

"But that's how I am. That's exactly how I am."

"Stubborn and proud."

"I can't change my nature. I refuse."

"So don't change your *nature*. Change your attitude."

"I won't. If she's so easily swayed by his *flirtation*, as you so aptly refer to it, then perhaps I've misjudged her. I assumed she was a woman of integrity and common sense. He's vain and superficial and if she finds that appealing, then so be it."

"Would you get off your high horse? You're only taking that position to avoid a fight. You think if you go head-to-head with him, you'll lose out, but that's just not true."

"You have no idea what I think."

"Okay. You're right. I shouldn't speak for you. Why don't you tell me how it feels."

"It doesn't 'feel' like anything. This is all beside the point. Mattie has her preferences and I have mine."

"Preferences?"

"That's right. I prefer to be accepted for myself. I prefer not to dictate the behavior of others or have them dictate to me."

"What's that got to do with Lewis?"

"She thinks he's entertaining. I do not. In addition, I find his sudden appearance highly suspect."

"Really," I said. I was reluctant to communicate my own suspicions about William unless Henry voiced them first.

Henry went on. "I believe she spoke to Lewis on the phone and he flew out in response."

"Where'd you get that?"

"He didn't seem the least bit surprised at finding her here, which means he knew in advance. And how could he have known unless she told him herself?"

"He could have heard from someone else."

"Who?"

"Rosie."

"Rosie doesn't *chat* with Lewis. Why would she talk to him? She barely talks to me."

"William, then. He could have mentioned it in passing."

"I see you're determined to protect her."

"All I'm doing is injecting a note of reality. No one's plotting behind your back. Well, Lewis, maybe, but not Mattie. You know better."

"You're implying I'm paranoid, but this is not my imagination. Mattie's intention was to come for breakfast and then drive straight home. Lewis suggested something *off the top of his head* and now she's delaying her return. Yes or no?"

"No."

"Yes."

"Let's not argue. I don't think there's anything afoot, but you do, so let's drop the subject. My only point . . . well, I don't even know what my only point is. My only point is don't give up on her. And that's all I'm going to say."

"Good. Now if you'll excuse me, I have to get back to my kitchen and my little-old-lady ways."

I went to the office and locked myself in. Truly, it was more restful to ponder crime than human beings in love. Here I was trying to talk Henry *into* the very thing I was trying to talk Reba *out of*, and neither one would listen. Then again, why would they? I've bungled every relationship I've ever been in so it's not like my advice is worth much.

I opened the window in hopes of creating a little cross-ventilation. The thermometer outside on the window frame read 74 degrees. It felt hotter than that to me. I sat down, put my feet up on the desk, and rocked back in my swivel chair. I studied my surroundings with a sense of discontent. The windows were so dingy I could hardly see out. Grime on the windowsill. Dust on my fake plant. My desk was covered with junk and the trash can was filled to capacity. I still had boxes I hadn't unpacked since I moved in and that was five months ago. What a slattern I was.

I got up and went into my tiny kitchen, where I scrounged under the sink for a bucket, a sponge, and a quart of virulent yellow liquid that resembled toxic waste. I spent the morning scrubbing surfaces, vacuuming, dusting, shining, polishing, unpacking, and putting things away. By noon, while I was hot, tired, and sweaty, my mood had improved. But not for long.

There was a knock on the door. I opened it to find a courier standing on my doorstep with an envelope in hand. I signed for it and opened it, pulling out a check from Nord for $1,250 in response to the invoice I'd sent him the day before. The handwritten note that accompanied the payment indicated the $250 bonus was for a job well done.

I wasn't so sure. Psychologically, the bonus put me in his debt and triggered another round of peeps from my conscience, which I'd thought to pacify with all the cleaning I'd done. I was right back in the thick of my debate. Should I tell Reba what was going on or should I not? More important, should I bring her father into the loop? His single admonition—to which I'd agreed—was to keep him informed of any backsliding on her part. This hadn't happened yet (as far as I knew), but if I told her about Beck and Onni, what would she do? She was going to crash and burn. And if I *didn't* tell her and she somehow got wind of it—which was not out of the question in a town this size—much crashing and burning would ensue anyway. She'd begged me not to tell her father about Beck, but Reba wasn't the one who was paying my bills. Witness this check.

I tried to think of an overriding principle that might

apply—some moral code that would guide my decision. I couldn't think of *one*. Then I wondered if I had morals or principles of *any* kind, and that made me feel worse.

The phone rang. I picked it up and said, "What," rather more rudely than I'd intended.

Cheney laughed. "You sound stressed."

"Well, I *am*. Do you have any idea the bind you've put me in?"

"I'm sorry. I know it's tough. Would it help if we talked?"

"What's to talk about? Betraying that poor girl? Giving her the news about his screwing around?"

"I told you he's a bad man."

"But isn't it just as bad to go after her like that?"

"You have any other suggestions? Because we're open to just about anything. God knows, we don't want to pull out the big guns unless we have to. The girl's freaky enough."

"That's for sure. I notice you're using the term 'we,' so I assume you've thrown in your lot with the IRS."

"This is a law-enforcement issue. I'm a cop."

"Well, I'm not."

"Would you at least have a chat with my IRS pal?"

"So he can pile his bullshit on top of yours? That's a happy proposition. I feel like I'm going under as it is."

"Look, I'm just around the corner. You want to have lunch? He's on his way up from L.A. and said he'd join us. No hard sell. I promise. Just listen to him."

"To what end?"

"You know a place called Jay's? Hot pastrami sandwiches and the best martinis in town."

"I don't want to *drink* at lunch."

"Me neither, but we can eat together, yes?"

I said, "Hang on. There's someone at my door. I'm going to put you on hold. I'll be back in a second."

"Good deal. I'll wait."

I pushed the Hold button and laid the receiver on my desk. I got up and paced from the inner office to the outer one. What was wrong with me? Because I did want to see him. And it didn't have anything to do with Reba Lafferty. That subject was just a cover for another form of confusion I was wrestling with. I went into the bathroom and stared at myself in the mirror, noting that I looked like shit. This was ridiculous. I went back to the phone and pushed Hold, activating the line. "Give me ten minutes and I'll meet you there."

"Don't be silly. I can swing by. No point in taking two cars when we can make do with one. It's better for the environment."

"Oh, please."

I locked up the office and waited for him out on the street. There was no point worrying about my grubby jeans or my ratty tennis shoes. My hands smelled like bleach and my turtleneck was stretched out of shape. I needed a complete makeover, but I didn't think I could manage one in the next three to four minutes. Oh, to hell with it. This was business. What difference did it make if I were fresh as a daisy, wearing heels and panty hose? The more immediate problem was Cheney's IRS contact. I was already experiencing a low-level dread at the idea of meeting him. No hard sell, my ass. The man would grind me underfoot.

Cheney came around the corner in a sporty little red Mercedes convertible. He pulled in at the curb, leaned over, and opened the passenger-side door. I slid in. "I thought you drove a Mazda," I said, sounding faintly accusative.

"I left that at home. I also have a six-year-old Ford pickup that I use for surveillance. I took delivery on this baby in Los Angeles last week."

"Slick."

He turned right at the corner and headed across town. I liked his driving style. No speeding, no showing off, and no reckless moves. Out of the corner of my eye, I noted the matte finish on his red silk windbreaker—nothing shiny or vulgar—white dress shirt, the chinos, snappy Italian shoes that probably cost more than my monthly rent. Even in an open car, his aftershave smelled like spices, the scent of tiny blossoms on some night-blooming shrub. This was pitiful. I wanted to lean over and sniff deeply at the side of his face. He glanced at me, smiling, as though he knew what was going on in my head. This was not a good sign.

11

Santa Teresa has never been noted for its club scene or its wild nightlife. Most restaurants close soon after the last of the dinner orders have been plated and served. The bars are open until 2:00 A.M., but most don't provide dance floors or live music. Jay's Cocktail Lounge, downtown, is one of the few spots to offer both. In addition, from 11:30 A.M. until 2:00 P.M., lunch is served to a limited clientele who prefer the privacy and quiet for low-key business meetings and discreet liaisons. The walls are padded in gray suede, with a thick gray carpet underfoot that makes you feel you're walking across a mattress. Even by day, the place is so dark, you have to pause at the entrance until your eyes adjust. The booths are commodious, padded in black leather, and any ambient noise is dampened to a hush. Cheney gave his name to the hostess—Phillips, party of three.

He'd made reservations in advance.

I said, "God, you're cocky. What made you so sure I'd say yes?"

SUE GRAFTON

"I've never known you to turn down food, especially if someone else pays. Must feel like mothering."

"Well, it is, isn't it?"

"By the way, Vince called to say he's running late. He said to go ahead and order."

We spent the first part of the meal dealing with matters unrelated to Reba Lafferty. We sipped iced tea and picked at our sandwiches, unusual for me where food is concerned. I'm accustomed to eating fast and moaning aloud, but Cheney seemed to enjoy taking his sweet time. We chatted about his career and mine, the police department budget cuts, and the effects thereof. We knew a few cops in common, one being Jonah Robb, the married man I "dated" during one of his frequent separations from his wife, Camilla.

I said, "How's Jonah doing these days? Is the marriage off again or on?" I rattled the last of the ice cubes in my empty glass and, as if on cue, the busboy appeared to replenish my supply.

Cheney said, "Off, from what I hear. They had a kid. I should say, Camilla did. According to the scuttlebutt, the boy wasn't his."

"Yeah, but he's crazy about that baby all the same," I said. "I ran into him a couple of months ago and he was busting his buttons he was so proud of the kid."

"What about the two daughters? No telling what effect this is having on them."

"Camilla doesn't seem to care. I wish they'd just get back together and be done with it. How many times have they split?"

Cheney shook his head.

I studied him. "What about you? How's married life these days?"

"That's over."

"Over?"

"You know the word 'over'? As in done with."

"I'm sorry to hear that. When did this transpire?"

"Middle of May. Embarrassing to admit, but we were only married five weeks, which is one week less than we'd known each other before we eloped."

"Where is she now?"

"She's moved back to L.A."

"That was quick."

"Like ripping off a Band-Aid. Better to get it over with."

"Did you learn anything?"

"I doubt it. I was tired of feeling dead. Work we do, we take chances in the real world but not so much in here," he said, tapping on his chest. "What's love about if not risk?"

I studied my plate, which was littered with potato chip crumbs. I licked my index finger and captured a cluster that I laid on my tongue. "You're beyond my area of competence. These days, I seem to be surrounded by people who've got it wrong, Reba Lafferty being one."

He leaned forward, elbows on the table, holding his glass by the rim. "So let's talk about her."

"What's to talk about? She's fragile. It doesn't seem right to put the squeeze on her."

A flicker of irritation crossed his face. "Fragile, my ass. She's the one who elected to get involved with him. Turns out, he's a sleazebag in more ways than one. She should know what's going on."

"You're not doing this for her sake. You're doing it for yours."

"What difference does that make? She needs to be told. Or do you disagree?"

"What if the revelation pushes her over the edge?"

"If she goes off the deep end, we'll handle it." His gaze shifted to a point just over my shoulder. I turned my head and caught a glimpse of a man I assumed was Vince Turner approaching to my left. Cheney slid out of the booth and the two of them shook hands.

Vince Turner was a hefty man in his forties, round-faced, balding, wearing a tan raincoat. The wire stems on his frameless glasses had been bent at an angle that left them slightly askew. He toted a brown leather school bag that in sixth grade would have labeled him as hopelessly out of it. Now the scuffed handle and the buckles on the two exterior pockets marked him as self-assured.

Cheney introduced us. Turner peeled off his raincoat and tossed it across the back of the banquette before he sat down. His suit was mud brown, the jacket wrinkled across the back. His trousers had accordion pleats radiating from the crotch because he'd sat in them too long. He loosened his tie and tucked the ends in the pocket of his dress shirt, perhaps to keep them from flapping in his food.

"Have you eaten?" Cheney asked.

"I had a burger in the car coming up, but I could use a drink."

Cheney signaled the waiter, who appeared moments later with a menu in hand.

Turner waved it away. "Maker's on the rocks. A double."

"Would you like anything else?"

"That's fine. What about you, Cheney?"

"I'm good."

"By me," I said.

As soon as the waiter disappeared, Turner picked up his baton of napkin-wrapped flatware, unrolled the utensils, and set a place for himself. On his right hand he wore a heavy gold-and-garnet class ring, but there was no way to read the legend that encircled the stone. His face was shiny with perspiration, but his pale eyes were cold. He lined up the handles of his knife, his spoon, and two forks, then checked his watch. "I'm not sure how much Lieutenant Phillips has told you about me. It's one-fifteen now. At two-fifty, I'll be on a flight from here to LAX and then on to Washington, D.C., where I meet with a group of IRS investigators and the DEA. That gives us approximately one hour to conduct our business, so I'll get straight to the point. You have questions or comments, feel free to raise your hand. Otherwise, I'll talk until I get to the end. Is that agreeable?" He made another minute adjustment to the silverware.

"Fine with me," I said. I found it easier to watch his hands than to look him in the eye.

"I'm forty-six years old. Since 1972 I've worked in the Criminal Investigation Division of the Bureau of Internal Revenue. My first assignment was as assistant to the man who pursued the case against Braniff Airlines in the laundering of illegal corporate campaign contributions. Braniff, like American Airlines, needed the occasional government assist in those days and began to funnel money to the Nixon re-election committee by way of Maurice Stans. You remember him?"

He looked up at me long enough to see me nod.

"Having cut my teeth on Watergate, I developed an appetite for financial chicanery. I've never been blessed with a wife or children. My job is my life." He glanced down at his jacket and removed a tiny speck of lint. "A year ago, in May of 1986, Congress, in a rare moment of common sense, passed Public Law 99-570, the Money Laundering Control Act, which has provided us the hammer with which to pound the shit out of violators of the Bank Secrecy Act. The banking community is already feeling the effects. For a long time, banks in this country treated reporting requirements as a trivial matter, but that's changed. Many violations once considered misdemeanors have now been elevated to felony offenses with maximum prison sentences, fines, and civil penalties. Crocker National Bank has been fined $2,250,000; Bank of America was fined $4,750,000; and Texas Commerce Bancshares was fined $1,900,000. You can't imagine the satisfaction I've felt forcing these guys into line. And we ain't done yet."

He paused, looking up with a smile that warmed his face from within. His ice blue eyes suddenly contained a merriment impossible to resist. I think in that moment, my position shifted. I'd do what I could for Reba, but if she came up against this guy, she was in deeper shit than she knew.

The waiter arrived with his Maker's Mark, which was the color of strong iced tea. Vince Turner sucked down half without hesitation and then placed the glass carefully in front of him. He folded his hands and lifted his eyes to mine. "Which brings us to Mr. Beckwith. I've spent the past year assembling a comprehensive dossier on him. As I'm sure you know, his lifestyle looks clean and his social credentials are solid, largely because of his late father's standing in the community. He's considered by most to be an honest, law-abiding citizen, who'd never dream of trafficking in drugs, pornography, or prostitutes.

"He's what we call a market-based offender. He takes the profits from these same illegal activities, disguises their origin, and introduces them back into the system as legitimate earnings. For the past five years, he's been 'rehabilitating' funds for a man named Salustio Castillo, a Los Angeles jewelry wholesaler who also deals in scrap silver and gold. The business is just a cover for what he really does, which is to import cocaine from South America. Castillo bought a large property in Montebello through Mr. Beckwith's real estate firm. Mr. Beckwith brokered the deal, which is how they became acquainted. Mr. Castillo needed someone of Mr. Beckwith's professional reputation. His company is diverse and his financial dealings of sufficient magnitude to camouflage the funds Castillo was so eager to place. Mr. Beckwith saw the possibilities and agreed to help.

"At first, he employed the standard laundering techniques—structuring transactions, consolidating the deposits, and using wire transfers to move the money out of the country. By the time the money was routed through his company books and back to Castillo, the sources appeared to be legitimate. After six months, Mr. Beckwith got tired of paying his smurfs or maybe he got tired of keeping track of the myriad accounts he'd opened across Santa Teresa County. He began to make big deposits—two and three hundred thousand dollars at a clip, claiming these were the proceeds of commercial real estate ventures. This time he was the model of compliance, making sure all the appropriate CTRs were filed. In truth, he was counting on the fact that the IRS has to process so many millions of CTRs that his were in little or no danger of being flagged for scrutiny. Soon he was running a million a week through the system, taking one percent off the top as his service fee.

"Finally, deposits reached a level where the risks outweighed the benefits of doing business so close to home. Mr. Beckwith got nervous and decided to bypass the local banks and eliminate the paper trail. He acquired a Panamanian bank and an unrestricted banking license in Antigua, putting up the requisite one million in U.S. dollars as paid-in capital. He invested an additional five hundred thousand dollars for a second international banking license in the Netherlands Antilles, which doesn't have a tax treaty with the U.S. at this point."

I raised my hand. "A million and a half? Is it really worth that to him?"

"Absolutely. With his offshore banks, he can make deposits. He can write his own references, issue letters of credit to himself, all of this protected by complete privacy and with very little interference from the host countries. He doesn't even have to be there to handle management. Keep in mind, too, when people hear you own a bank, they tend to be impressed."

I said, "I'll bet." Cheney caught my eye fleetingly, probably thinking, as I was, about the banks his father owned.

Vince Turner paused and looked from Cheney to me.

I said, "Sorry. Go on."

He shrugged and continued as though his commentary

had been recorded in advance. "By law, an American citizen is required to declare all foreign bank accounts on their yearly tax returns, but these guys aren't any more scrupulous about that than any other aspect of their business. Mr. Beckwith, under the auspices of the banks he'd bought, established an international business corporation, an IBC, in Panama, with shares being held in a Panama Private Interest Foundation, allowing him to avoid both U.S. and Panamanian taxation. With the shell company in place, he began to move currency *physically* from the States to his offshore havens. You move cash, Customs requires a CMIR—a Currency and Monetary Instrument Report—but Mr. Beckwith doesn't much care for filling out these pesky little government forms. No forms means no more violations, at least to his skewed way of thinking. Once deposited in one of his offshore banks, monies are returned to Mr. Castillo in the form of business loans with a twenty-year balloon.

"Of course, the transport of currency generates difficulties of a different sort. Bills are not only bulky, but weigh more than you'd think. The foreign markets prefer the smaller denominations—twenties and fifties. A million dollars in twenty-dollar bills tops out at over one hundred twenty-five pounds. Try toting that through an airport. Not a problem for our boy. The ever resourceful Mr. Beckwith leased a Learjet and now he flies suitcases full of cash to Panama every couple of months. Panama's currency is the U.S. dollar, so he doesn't even have to worry about the exchange rate. Between plane trips, he's been taking his wife on a series of luxury cruises, moving the cash in a steamer trunk that he keeps in his stateroom."

Turner polished off his bourbon, signaling the waiter for another round. "Anybody ever tell you how much money gets laundered every year worldwide?"

I shook my head.

"One-point-five trillion dollars—that's a one, a five, and eleven zeros—just so you get the picture. In the U.S., the figure's somewhere in the neighborhood of fifty billion, but we're talking about revenue that's never taxed, so you see how serious it gets."

Cheney spoke up. "How much can you tell her about the investigation to date?"

"Broad strokes? Four years ago the IRS, the DEA, the FBI, Customs, and the Justice and Treasury departments put together a task force to investigate gold and precious metals dealers in Los Angeles, Detroit, and Miami, all of whom we suspect are laundering money for a Colombian drug cartel. So far they've managed to place, layer, and integrate sixteen million dollars, running the cash through four businesses, using multiple accounts, at ten different banks, one of which has a branch here in town. Alan Beckwith is responsible for processing a substantial portion of that sum.

"Ours is painstaking work. We're still sorting out the particulars, developing as much hard evidence as we can before we make our move. The trick is not to alert him until we have all our ducks in a row. A U.S. District Court judge in Los Angeles and another in Miami have recently approved electronic surveillance. That's allowed us to monitor Mr. Beckwith's phone conversations. We've also obtained authorization to seize and remove trash from his home and business premises. Right now we have our merry band of agents picking through his garbage. They've found invoices listing fictitious addresses for nonexistent businesses, assorted handwritten notes, canceled checks, discarded typewriter cartridges and adding-machine tape. Mr. Beckwith has legitimate dealings with financial institutions on a number of fronts, and he's skilled at mingling the profits from illegal activities with the mundane business he does from day to day. What he's apparently unaware of is that financial institutions are required to save signature cards, account statements, copies of checks written for any amount over a hundred dollars. The banks also retain a transaction log of wire transfers, so they can properly account for funds passing through the system. The information is all coded, but it's possible to use the sequence numbers to identify the source bank, the target bank, and the dates and times the money was sent on its way. We don't yet have access to these documents, but we're putting together the necessary paperwork to subpoena bank records."

The waiter appeared, setting down Turner's second drink. A silence fell until he'd moved away from the table and out of earshot. Turner picked up his glass of bourbon. His drinking had slowed to a sipping pace, and I could see him savoring the taste.

"What do you want from Reba? Surely you're not asking her to waltz in and lift all the pertinent files."

"Not at all. In point of fact, we can't instruct her to do anything that violates the law because we're not at liberty to do so ourselves. Even if she stole the files without our prior knowledge or approval, we couldn't even peek at them without jeopardizing our case. What we *can* ask for is an in-depth description of his records—the nature of the files he has and where they're located—which will allow us to prepare financial and document search warrants. I understand you feel protective of Ms. Lafferty, but we need her cooperation."

"Isn't there anybody else? What about his company comptroller?"

"The company comptroller's a fellow named Marty Blumberg. We've thought of him. The problem is he's so deeply implicated he might panic and run, or worse, panic and warn Mr. Beckwith. Now that she's not working for him, Reba's been removed from the line of fire and she might be more inclined to help. Lieutenant Phillips showed you the photographs?"

"Well, yeah, but I'm not sure what those are going to do for you. She finds out he's in trouble, she'll fall all over herself telling him whatever you tell her."

"I gathered as much. Do you have a suggestion about how to contain her reaction?"

"No. To me, it's like detonating a nuclear device. You risk as much destruction as you're hoping to unleash."

Turner adjusted a minute irregularity in the flatware he'd aligned. "Point taken. Unfortunately, we don't have much time. Mr. Beckwith has uncanny survival instincts. We've been discreet, but from the intelligence we've gathered, he may well suspect there's something afoot. He's consolidating his funds, picking up the pace, which we find worrisome."

"Reba mentioned that, but she's convinced he's doing it for her. He says once his assets are secure, he'll dump his wife and the two of them can hit the highway. Or that's what she hears. Who knows the truth of it?"

"There's no doubt he's preparing to make a run for it. Another week and he might succeed in placing the cash and himself beyond our reach."

"Does the money belong to him or Salustio Castillo?"

"Him, in the main. If he's smart, he'll keep his hands off Salustio's cash. Last guy who crossed Castillo got turned into a concrete popsicle in a twenty-gallon garbage can."

Once it was clear Vince was finished, Cheney said, "So. Who talks to Reba? You, me, or her."

There was a silence while all three of us stared at the tabletop. Finally, I raised my hand. "I've got a better shot at it than either one of you."

"Good. Give us a couple of days. As soon as I get back from Washington, I'll set up a meeting with our FBI contact and the DOJ. Customs will want to sit in as well. As soon as we decide how we want to proceed, we'll bring you in for a briefing, probably the beginning of next week. After that, we'll hope to talk to her."

"You better make it good. I don't look forward to delivering the news."

"Don't worry about that. We'll advise you in advance."

Cheney dropped me off at my office at 2:00 P.M. The afternoon temperature was climbing, a complete contradiction of the morning weather report that promised a moderate 74 degrees. Vince Turner had called a taxi to ferry him to the airport so he could catch his flight. I was hoping Cheney would have the good grace to deliver me without reference to Reba Lafferty or Beck, but as I got out of the car, he held up a manila envelope. "I had copies made for you."

"What am I supposed to do with 'em?"

"Whatever you like. I thought you should have a set."

"Thanks so much." I took the envelope.

"Call me if you need me."

"Trust me. I will."

I waited until he'd turned the corner and the sound of his little red Mercedes had faded in the turgid afternoon air. I let myself into the office, where the air felt stuffy and dead. I passed through the reception area to my desk. I tossed my shoulder bag on the client chair and sat down with the manila envelope. I used it to fan myself and then undid the clasp and removed the prints. The photographs were just as I remembered them—Beck and Onni emerging from various motels, he with his arm around her, the two holding hands, Onni with her head on his shoulder and her arm around his waist, the two hip-to-hip walking in lock-step. Poor Reba. She was in for a rude awakening. I opened my desk drawer and tossed the envelope inside. I didn't even want to think about the sorry task of breaking the news. In hopes of distracting myself, I did something I hadn't done for ages. I walked the four blocks from my office into downtown Santa Teresa and caught two movies, back-to-back, watching one of them twice. I thus succeeded in dodging the heat and dodging reality at the same time.

12

When I reached my apartment, I saw that Mattie's car was
gone and Henry's kitchen was dark. I wasn't sure what to
make of that. The temperature was somewhere in the
eighties, almost unheard of at this hour. It was still light
out and the sidewalks shimmered with accumulated heat.
The air felt sluggish, with no movement to speak of and
humidity probably hovering at 95 percent. You'd think it
would rain, but this was mid-July and we'd be stuck with
drought conditions until late November—if the weather
broke for us at all. My apartment was stifling. I sat on my
porch step, flapping a breeze at my face with the folded
newspaper. While most Southern California properties
have sprinkler systems, few have central air conditioning.
I was going to have to haul a fan out of the closet and set
it up in the loft before I hit the sack.

Nights like this little kids toss aside nighties and
pajamas and sleep in their underpants. My aunt Gin always
swore I'd be cooler if I did a 180-degree turn on the bed,
feet on the pillow, my head propped on the tangle of covers

wadded at the foot. She was remarkably permissive, this woman who raised me, having never given birth to any children of her own. On those rare California nights when it was too hot to sleep, she'd tell me I could stay up all night even if I happened to have school the next day. We'd lie there reading our books in our respective bedrooms, the trailer so quiet I could hear her turning the pages. What I treasured was the heady sense that we were breaking the rules. I knew "real" parents probably wouldn't tolerate such license, but I saw it as one small compensation for my orphaned state. Inevitably, I'd drift off to sleep. Aunt Gin would tiptoe in, slip the book out of my hands, and douse the light. I'd wake later to find the room dark and the sheet laid over me. Odd, the memories that linger long after a life is gone.

Finally, just as the streetlights came on, I heard the telephone ring. I pulled myself to my feet and scooted into the apartment, snatching up the handset. "'Lo?"

"This is Cheney."

"Well, hi. I didn't expect to hear from you. What's up?"

There was sufficient noise in the background I had to press a hand to my ear to hear what he was saying. "What?"

"Have you had dinner yet?"

I'd eaten a box of popcorn at the movies, but I didn't think that counted. "I wouldn't call it that."

"Good. I'll be there in two minutes and we'll go out and grab a bite."

"Where *are* you?"

"Rosie's. I figured you'd be here, but I was wrong again."

"Maybe I'm not as predictable as you thought."

"I doubt that. You own a sun dress?"

"Well no, but I have a skirt."

"Wear that. I'm tired of seeing you in jeans."

He hung up and I stood there, staring at the receiver. What a weird turn of events. Dinner sounded like a *date*, unless he'd heard something from Vince Turner about the briefing coming up next week. And why would I have to wear a skirt to receive information like that?

I took my time going up the spiral stairs, trying to figure out what to wear aside from the skirt. I sat down on the bed, pulled off my tennis shoes and shed my sweaty clothes. I showered and wrapped myself in a towel. When I opened my closet door there, sure enough, was my tan poplin skirt. I removed it from the hanger and flapped the wrinkles out. I put on fresh underwear and then stepped into the skirt, noting that the hem hit me just above the knee. I crossed to the chest of drawers where I pawed through a stack of shirts and selected a red tank top that I pulled over my head and tucked in at the waist. I put on a pair of sandals, went into the bathroom, and brushed my teeth. This was all my way of stalling while I decided how I felt.

I stood at the sink and studied my reflection. Why was I compelled to stare at myself in mirrors whenever Cheney called to say he was on his way? I ran water in my hands and ruffled up my hair. Eye makeup? Nah. Lipstick? Don't think so. That would look presumptuous if this were really IRS business. I leaned closer. Well, okay, just a touch of color. No harm in that. I settled for pressed powder, a quick sweep of eye shadow, mascara, and coral lipstick that I applied and wiped off, leaving my lips faintly pink. You see? This is the downside of relationships with men—you become a narcissist, obsessed with "beauty" issues that ordinarily you couldn't care less about.

I turned off the light, trotted downstairs, and picked up my shoulder bag. I left a lamp burning in the living room, locked the door behind me, and went out into the street. Cheney was already there, his little red Mercedes idling at the curb. He leaned across the seat and opened the door for me. The man was a fashion plate. He'd changed clothes again: dark Italian loafers, sand-washed silk pants in a charcoal brown, and a white linen shirt with the sleeves rolled up. He did a quick head-to-toe appraisal. "You look good."

"Thanks. So do you."

He smiled slightly. "Glad we got that settled."

"Me, too."

He turned right at the corner, heading over to Cabana Boulevard, where he took a left. With the top down, my hair was flying every which way, but at least the air was cool. I figured we were heading to the Caliente Café. The place is a cop hangout and all-around dive—cigarette smoke, beer smell, the constant rattle and howl of blenders whipping ice cubes into margarita mix, tasty faux-Mexican cuisine, and no discernible decor unless you count the six raggedy-ass Mexican straw hats nailed to the wall.

When we reached the bird refuge, instead of turning left as I expected, we sailed right on under the freeway and up the other side. We were now in what was known as "the lower village" of Montebello. The four lanes of divided road merged and narrowed into two, lined with elegant clothing and jewelry shops, real estate offices, and the usual assortment of businesses, including beauty salons, a tennis shop, and a high-priced art gallery. By then, it was fully dark and most places, while closed, were awash with light. The trees were wrapped in strands of tiny Italian bulbs, trunks and branches sparkling as though with ice.

We continued along the frontage road as far as St. Isadore. Cheney took a left. We passed through an area dubbed the "hedge row district" where pittosporum and eugenia shrubs grew ten to twenty feet high, shielding properties from the road. Until now, tax myself as I might, I hadn't thought of one word to say so I'd kept my mouth shut. This didn't seem to bother Cheney, and I was hopeful he disliked small talk as much as I did. On the other hand, we couldn't spend the entire evening without speaking. That would be too strange for words, as it were.

We wound along dark lanes, the little red Mercedes humming, Cheney downshifting until we reached the St. Isadore Hotel. Once a rustic working ranch that dated back to the late 1800s, the St. Isadore is now an upscale resort with luxury cottages dotted across fourteen acres of flower beds, shrubs, live oaks, and orange trees. Pets were permitted. For a mere fifty dollars per mutt, dogs were provided with doggie beds, "Pawier" mineral water, hand-painted personalized water bowls, and pet "room service" on request. I'd been here for dinner on occasion, but never as a paying guest.

Cheney pulled up at the main building and got out of the car. A parking attendant stepped forward and helped me extricate myself and then he spirited the car away. We bypassed the elegant second-floor restaurant and ducked into the Harrow and Seraph, a low-ceilinged bar located at ground level. The door stood open. Cheney stepped aside, allowing me to pass in front of him, and then he followed me in.

The walls were stone, whitewashed and cool. There were fewer than twenty tables, many empty at that hour. A small bar ran along the back wall. There was a stone fireplace on the left, the hearth dark, given that it was summer. There was banquette seating on the right with the remainder of the tables staggered across the space in between. Illumination was discreet but not so dim that you'd need a flashlight to read the menu. Cheney steered me to an upholstered bench seat backed with pillows so plump I had to push them aside. He sat across the table and then seemed to think better of it, got up and slid in beside me, saying, "No cop talk. I'm off duty here and so are you."

"I thought you wanted to chat about Reba."

"Nope. Don't want to hear a word."

I was only moderately distracted by the warmth of his thigh in proximity to mine. That's the thing about wearing poplin—the way it conducts body heat. The waiter appeared and Cheney ordered two vodka martinis, straight up, with extra olives on the side. As soon as the waiter left, Cheney said, "Quit worrying. We won't drink all the time. This is just to loosen our tongues."

I laughed. "I appreciate the reassurance. The notion did flit across my mind." I let my gaze travel briefly—mouth, chin, shoulders. His teeth were beautiful, white and straight—always a weakness of mine. Dark hairs shaded the curve of his forearms.

He studied me, his right elbow propped on the table, his chin resting in his palm. "You never answered my question."

"Which one?"

"At lunch. I asked you about Dietz."

"Ah. Well, let's see if I can be fair about this. He tends to drop out of sight. Last time I saw him was a year ago March. Where he's been since then I have no idea. He's not big on explanations. I guess you'd call it the 'Take it or leave it' school of relationships. I've left messages on his machine, but he hasn't returned my calls. It's possible he's dumped me, but how would I know?"

"Would it matter if he had?"

"I don't think so. I might feel insulted, but I'd survive. I think it's rude to leave me hanging, but such is life."

"I thought you were nuts about the guy."

"I was, but I knew what he was."

"Which is what?"

"An emotional drifter. The point is, I chose him anyway, so it must have suited me somehow. Now things are different. I can't go back to that. It's over and done." Which was, now that I thought about it, roughly how Cheney had described his marriage.

He seemed to be considering what I'd said. "You've been married once?"

I held up two fingers. "Both ended in divorce."

"What's the story on those guys?"

"The first was a cop."

"Mickey Magruder. I heard about him. You leave him or did he leave you?"

"I was the one who pulled out. I misjudged him. I left because I thought he was guilty of something. Turns out, he wasn't. I still feel badly about that."

"Because why?"

"I didn't have a chance to tell him I was sorry before he died. I'd have liked to clear that. Husband number two was a musician, a pianist, very talented. Also, chronically unfaithful and a pathological liar with the face of an angel. It was a blow when he left. I was twenty-four years old and probably should have seen it coming. Later I found out he'd always been more interested in men than he was in me."

"So how come I don't see you around town with other guys? Have you given up on men?"

I nearly made a smart remark, but I caught myself in time. Instead, I opened my mouth and said, "I've been waiting for you, Cheney. I thought you knew that."

He looked at me, waiting to see if I was making light of him. I returned his gaze, waiting to see what he'd do with the information. I couldn't imagine what would happen next. There were so many wrong moves, so many dumb things that might come out of his mouth. I was thinking, *Don't mess this up ... please, please don't ruin it ... whatever it is ...*

Here are two things I hate to have men do:

(1) Tell me I'm beautiful, which is bullshit manipulation and has nothing to do with me.

(2) Look into my eyes and talk about my "trust" issues because they know I've been "hurt."

Here's what Cheney did: He put his arm up on the seat back and picked up a strand of hair from the top of my head. He studied it with care, his expression serious. In the split second before he spoke, I heard a muffled sound, like gas jets igniting when a match is struck. Warmth fanned up along my spine and softened all the tension in my neck. He said, "I'll give you a proper haircut. Did you know I cut hair?"

I found myself staring at his mouth. "No. I didn't know that. What else do you do?"

He smiled. "Dance. Do you dance?"

"Not very well."

"That's all right. I can teach you. You'll improve."

"I'd like that. What else?"

"I work out. I box some and lift weights."

"Do you cook?"

"No, do you?"

"Peanut butter and pickle sandwiches."

"Sandwiches don't count, except for grilled cheese."

I said, "Any other talents I should know about?"

He ran the back of his hand down along my cheek. "I'm an especially good speller. Fifth grade, I came in second in the school spelling bee."

I could feel a hum forming in my throat, the same strange mechanism that causes cats to purr. "What'd you screw up on?"

"'Eleemosynary.' It means 'of or for charity or alms.' Should be e-l-e-e-m-o-s-y n a r-y. I left out the third e."

"But you haven't screwed up since. So you learned."

"Yes, I did. What about you? Any skills you want to talk about upfront?"

"I know how to read upside down. I interview some guy and he has a document on his desk? I can read every word while I'm chatting away with him."

"Excellent. What else?"

"You know that party game we played in elementary school? The mom brings out a tray, twenty-five objects covered with a towel? She lifts the towel and the kids study the items for thirty seconds before she covers them again. I can recite 'em back without missing one, except sometimes the Q-tips. I tend to mess up on those."

"I'm not good at party games."

"Neither am I, except for that one. I've won all kinds of prizes. Bubbles in a jar and paddles with the ball attached that goes bang-bang-bang."

The waiter brought our drinks. The connection between us faded, but the moment the waiter left, I could feel it start up again. He put his hand on my neck. I leaned toward him, tilting my head until my lips were close to his ear. "We're going to get in a lot of trouble, aren't we?"

"More than you know," he murmured in response. "Know why I brought you here?"

"Not a clue," I said.

"The macaroni and cheese."

"You're going to mother me?"

"Seduce."

"You're doing well so far."

"You ain't seen nuttin' yet," he said, and smiled. He kissed me then, but only once and not for long.

When I could speak again, I said, "You're a man of great restraint."

"And self-control. I probably should have mentioned that much earlier."

"I like surprises. Good ones," I said.

"That's all you get with me."

The waiter approached and took out his pad. We eased away from each other, both of us smiling politely as though Cheney's thigh wasn't locked against mine under the tablecloth. I hadn't taken the first sip of my drink, but I was feeling bleary-eyed, drowsy with the heat that was suffusing my limbs. I checked the other diners, but no one else seemed to notice the charged particles undulating between us.

Cheney ordered a salad for each of us and told the

waiter we'd share the macaroni and cheese, which was apparently served in a ramekin the size of a bread-and-butter plate. Didn't matter to me. He'd neatly shifted me off-center, away from my usual contentious and arbitrary self. I was already hooked into him. I could feel my boundaries dissolve, desire cleaving the barricade I'd erected to keep the Mongol hordes at bay. Who cared about that? Let them swarm over the walls.

As soon as the waiter left, Cheney put his hand, palm up, on the table and I laced my fingers through his. He was staring off across the room, his gaze shifting from face to face as he checked the other patrons. I sensed he'd detached himself, but I knew he'd be back. I studied his profile, the mop of curly brown hair, mine to touch if I liked. I could see the pulse beat in his throat. He turned and looked at me. His eyes moved from mine to the shape of my mouth. He leaned into me and we kissed again. Where the first kiss had been delicate, this kiss was promissory.

I nearly hummed aloud. "We have to eat dinner, right?"

"Food as foreplay."

"I'm starving."

"I'll do right by you."

"I know."

I'm not sure how we made it through the meal. We ate a salad that was cold and crisp, pungent with vinaigrette. He fed me macaroni and cheese, hot and soft, laced with prosciutto, and then he kissed the taste of salt from my mouth. How had we arrived at this place? I thought of all the times I'd seen him, conversations we'd had. I'd never caught a real glimpse of this man, but here he was.

He paid the bill. While we waited for the car, he pulled

SUE GRAFTON

me in against him with his hands on my ass. I wanted to climb his frame, shinny up his body like a monkey up a palm. The parking attendant averted his eyes, keeping his manner disinterested as he handed me into the car. Cheney tipped him, pulled his door shut, and shifted into first. As we sailed through the dark, I rubbed a hand along his thigh.

By the time we pulled into his driveway, I wasn't even sure where we were. His house, apparently. Dazed, I watched as he got out of the car on his side and came around to mine. He pulled me out of the seat and turned me until I was laid up against him, my back against his front, his lips moving along my neck. He pushed the strap of my tank top aside and kissed my shoulder, letting me feel the faintest nudge of his teeth. He said, "Let's slow down, okay? We can take as long as we want. Or do you have to be somewhere?"

"No."

"Good. Then why don't we go upstairs."

"Okay." I reached back and slid my fingers into his hair, gripping, as I turned my face toward his. "Please tell me you're not so sure of yourself you changed the sheets before you left the house tonight."

"I didn't. I wouldn't do that to you. I bought new."

13

Cheney drove me home at 5:45 through the early morning light. He'd go into the gym for his morning workout and then hit the department in time for a briefing at 7:00. I intended to crawl straight into bed. We'd finally untangled ourselves at dawn, just as streaks in the sky were turning from salmon to hot pink. It had taken me less than a minute to throw on my clothes, after which I'd watched him get dressed. He was more muscular than I'd imagined, his body sleek and well defined. Good pecs, good biceps, good abs. When I'd married Mickey I was twenty-one years old to his thirty-seven, a difference of sixteen years. Daniel had been closer to my age, but soft, with a boyish body, slender and narrow-chested. Dietz, like Mickey, had been senior to me by sixteen years, a connection I'd never made before. Something to ponder later. I hadn't devoted much thought to men's bodies, but then again I'd never made the acquaintance of one quite like Cheney's. He was just so beautifully built—skin as smooth as fine leather, pulled taut over an armature of stone.

On the street in front of my place, we kissed one last time before I got out of the car and watched him rumble away. With any other man, I might already be fretting about all the dumb things women worry about—would he call, would I see him again, had he meant even one small portion of what he'd said. With Cheney, I didn't care. Whatever this was and whatever came next, it was all fine with me. If the entire relationship ended up encapsulated in the hours we'd just spent, well, wasn't I the lucky one for the experience?

I slept until ten, skipped the run, lollygagged around the house, and finally drifted into the office shortly before noon in time to break for lunch. I was just about to unwrap my cheese and pickle sandwich when I heard someone open the outer door and slam it shut. Reba appeared in the doorway, her face suffused with rage, manila envelope in hand. "Did you take these?"

I felt a spurt of fear at the sight of the envelope, given that I had its identical twin in my drawer.

She leaned across my desk and slashed the air in front of my face with the corner of the envelope, shaking it so close to my eyes she could have taken one out. "Did you?"

"Did I what? I don't even know what you're talking about." This was world-class lying, me at my best, rising to the challenge, unflinching in the heat of battle.

She undid the clasp and snatched out the prints, which she slapped down in front of me. She leaned forward again, this time supporting her weight with both hands. "Some fucking little creep came to the house and asked to speak to me. I thought it was a parole officer doing a home visit so I take him in the living room and sit him down to have a chat, cheery as all get-out just to show what a good little citizen I am. Next thing I know he's handing me these and laying out a line of shit like you wouldn't believe. That's Beck, by the way, in case the light's too grainy."

I picked up the black-and-white prints and made a display of sorting through them, trying to decide how to play this. I placed them on the desk and looked up at her. "So he picks up some hooker. What do you expect?"

"Hooker, my ass." She took one photo by the edge and pointed at the woman with such viciousness she nearly ripped the page. "Do you know who that is?"

I shook my head, my heart thudding in my chest. Of course I *knew*. I just didn't want to admit it to her.

"That's Onni. My best friend."

"Ah."

She made a face. "I don't give a shit if he had *sex*, but with her?"

"Yeah, you'd think as a courtesy, he could have screwed his wife instead of your best friend," I said.

"Exactly. I didn't expect him to be celibate. I certainly wasn't."

Ooo, what did she mean by that? With whom had she done what? In prison, the options were limited, or so one would think.

"You know what pisses me off? I'm supposed to have dinner with Onni. Tonight. Can you picture it? I'd be chatting away, happy to be with her because I missed her so much. The whole time she'd be sitting there, laughing up her ass. The friggin' bitch. She knows I'm in love with him. She *knows* that!" Her face suddenly took on that pinched look that precedes tears. She sat down abruptly. "Oh god, what am I going to do?"

I waited for a moment, listening to the tight squeezed-up sound of her weeping. This went on for a while, but once the sobs had subsided, I said, "Are you okay?"

"No, I'm not okay. Does it look like I'm okay? I'm going out of my mind. I could have gone my whole life without this."

Like a shrink, I picked up the box of tissues from the corner of my desk and pushed it over to her. She took one and blew her nose. "Hell with it. I wasn't going to do this, but I really can't help myself." She opened her bag and took out a fresh pack of cigarettes. She tugged on the thin band of red, peeling away the top of the cellophane wrapper. She tore off one half of the foil and smacked the bottom of the pack on her hand to force a cigarette forward out of the tight pack. She reached for her gold Dunhill lighter and flicked it, bending to the flame with a rapt expression on her face. She inhaled, drawing smoke into her lungs like nitrous oxide, letting it out again in a soft stream. She leaned back in the chair and closed her eyes. This was like watching someone shoot up. I could see the sedative effect as the nicotine permeated her system. She opened her eyes again. "Better. That's awesome. I hope you have an ashtray."

"Flick it on the floor. The carpet's shit anyway."

She was probably light-headed, but at least the outrage had been erased and replaced by an artificial calm. She allowed herself a thin, mocking smile. "I should have known when I bought the pack I'd crack it within a day."

"Just don't drink."

"Right. I won't. One vice at a time." She took another drag from her cigarette, tension draining from her face. "It's been a year since I smoked. Shit, and I was doing so well."

"You were doing great." I was still picking my way across what felt like a minefield, wondering if I could tell her the truth without bringing down fire on my own position.

"What's sick is the damn thing tastes so good," she said.

The subject of Beck was beside the point, now that she had her smokes. "So now what?" I asked.

"Beats the hell out of me."

"Maybe the two of us can figure it out."

"Yeah, right. What's to figure? I've been had," she said.

"I'm puzzled about the fellow who came to the house. I don't get that. Who was he?"

She shrugged. "He said he was FBI."

"Really. The FBI?"

"That's what he claimed, all superior and smarmy. As soon as I saw the first photo, I told him to get the hell off the property, but he wanted to sit there and spell it out for me, like I was too dumb to get it. I picked up the phone and told him I'd call the cops if he wasn't out the door in five seconds. That shut him up."

"Did he show you his ID? Badge, business card? Anything like that?"

"He flashed a badge when I first opened the door, but I didn't pay attention. Parole officers carry badges. I thought that's who he was so I didn't bother to check his name. I mean, what's it to me? I didn't see what choice I had so I let him in. When he pulled out the envelope, I figured he had forms to fill out, like he'd be filing some report. By the time I realized what he was up to I was so damn mad I didn't care who he was."

"What are you going to do?"

"I'm sure as hell canceling my dinner date. I wouldn't sit down with Onni if I had a gun to my head."

"Don't you think Beck's the one you should be mad at? You went to jail for the guy and this is what he does in return."

"I never went to jail for *him*. Who told you that?"

"What difference does it make? That's the word around town."

"Well, I didn't."

"Come on, Reba. You might as well come clean. I'm the only friend you have. So you're crazy in love and took the fall for him. Wouldn't be the first time. Maybe he sweet-talked you into it."

"He didn't sweet-talk me into anything. I knew what I was doing."

"I have a hard time believing *that*."

"You want to argue the point? You ask me to be honest and then you sit there and make judgments? How fucked up is that?"

I raised a hand. "Right. You're right. I apologize. I didn't mean it that way."

She stared at me, assessing my sincerity. I must have looked like an honest woman because she said, "Okay."

"Anyway, whatever the motivation, you're saying you didn't embezzle any money from him?"

"Of course not. I have money of my own, or at least I had some back then."

"That being the case, how'd you end up in jail?"

"The discrepancies showed up on an audit and he *had* to account for the missing money somehow. He thought they'd let me off easy. Suspended sentence, probation—you know, something like that."

"That seems like a stretch. You'd been in jail once before on a bad-check charge. From the judge's point of view, this was simply more of the same."

"Well, yeah, I guess it might have looked that way. Beck did everything he could to soften the blow. He told the DA he didn't want to file charges, but I guess it's like a case of domestic violence—once the system gets hold of you, you don't have much choice. There's this big gap, three hundred and fifty thousand gone and him without an explanation."

"What happened to the money?"

"Nothing. He was socking it away, shifting the money to an offshore account so his wife couldn't get her hands on it. How was he supposed to know the judge would turn out to be such a hard-ass? Four years? My god. He was more shocked than I was."

"Really."

"I'm serious. He felt like a turd. He got in this big stinking argument with the prosecuting attorney. That went nowhere. Then he wrote to the judge, begging him to be lenient, but no such luck. He promised he'd have his attorney file an appeal—"

"An appeal? What are you talking about? Beck had no standing to file an appeal. The law doesn't work that way."

"Oh. Well, maybe I misunderstood. It was something like that. He said it was his responsibility and he'd take the blame, but by then, it was too late. He had more to lose than I did. How I looked at it, as long as he was free, he could work on getting the rest of the money set aside. Besides, he was taking all the risks. If somebody had to pay, better me than him."

"So you came up with the idea," I said, trying to keep the skepticism out of my voice.

"Sure. I mean, I can't exactly remember who mentioned it first, but I was the one who insisted."

"Reba—I don't mean to sound critical so don't blow your stack—but it looks like he set you up. Doesn't it look like that to you?"

That was a stumper. "You think he'd *do* that?"

"He did this," I said, pointing to the photographs. "You're the one who toughed it out down there, day after day for the past twenty-two months. Meanwhile, Beck's up here screwing around. Doesn't that bug you? It bugs me." ·

"Of course it bugs me, but it's not exactly news. He's a womanizer. I've always known that about him. It doesn't mean anything. That's just the way he is. The reason I'm mad at her is she should've had more loyalty or integrity or *something*."

"You don't even know when it started. He could have been involved with her when the alleged embezzlement first came to light."

"Thank you. That's nice. Once I get done choking her to death, I'll have her verify dates and times."

"I hope that's hyperbole."

"Whatever that is," she said. "The thing I can't figure out is what this has to do with the FBI? Why's this guy chasing around town snapping pictures of Beck? And why bring 'em to me? If he wanted to make trouble, why not show Tracy?"

"I can help with that," I said, mentally cursing the bumblefuck FBI agent who jumped the gun on us. I stopped, poised on the brink. There was still time to back up. This was like standing on a ten-meter platform, looking at the drop to the water below. If you're going to jump, get it over with. It doesn't get easier the longer you wait. I felt a thin mist of anxiety settle on my skin. "The feds are interested in Beck's relationship with Salustio Castillo."

She studied me. "Where'd you get that?"

"Reba, you worked for the guy. You have to be clued in."

She veered off that topic. "Did Pop put you up to this?"

"Don't be ridiculous. I haven't spoken to him since he hired me. Besides, he's an honorable man. He'd never stoop to sleazy photos. He's got way too much class."

She took another deep drag and blew the smoke straight up. "What's your source then?"

"I have pals in law enforcement. It was one of them."

"And the FBI's involved?"

"The IRS is interested as well. Plus Customs, plus the DOJ, plus the ATF for all I know. Lieutenant Phillips is the local liaison if you want to talk to him."

"I don't get it. Why me? What do they want?"

"They need help. They're putting a case together and need the inside dope. I guess the pictures were intended to get you in the mood."

"He screws me over so I turn around and screw him?"

"Why not?"

"What else have you heard?"

"About Beck? Nothing you don't already know. He takes the illegal profits and he runs the funds through his company to make them look legitimate. He takes a percentage off the top and then he returns clean money to the thugs he works for. Right?"

She was silent. Her gaze shifted an inch.

I said, "You had to have been in on it all along. You did the books for him, bank deposits, stuff like that, right?"

"The company comptroller handled most of it, but okay, maybe some."

"The FBI can use information if you're willing to play."

She was silent, her gaze tracking the dust motes settling through the air like fairy dust. "I'll think about it."

I said, "While you're at it, think about this. Onni has your old job, which means she knows as much about his business as you do, except her information's current. If he's planning to disappear, who's he going to take with him? More to the point, who's he leaving behind? Onni? Don't think so. Not if she's in a position to blow the whistle on him."

"I'm in that position, too," she said, as though feeling competitive about her ability to squeal. She held up the last inch of her cigarette. "I have to put this out."

"Give it to me."

I reached over and took the butt end, holding it with about as much enthusiasm as I'd feel for a freshly salted slug. I left the office and carried it down the hall to my tatty toilet with the permanent rust stains. I dropped it in the john and flushed. I could feel the tension between my shoulder blades. This was *work* and I had no way to tell if the pitch would be effective. If nothing else, I hoped she'd give up her fantasy of what Beck was.

When I returned to the office, she was standing by the window. I sat down at my desk. With the light coming in, she was almost entirely in silhouette. I picked up a pencil and made a mark on my blotter. "Where's your head at this point?"

She turned and smiled at me briefly. "Not as far up my butt as it was."

And that was where we left it.

I told her to take her time thinking about the situation before she decided what to do. Vince Turner might be in a hurry, but he was asking a lot and, one way or the other, she'd better be convinced. Once she'd agreed, he couldn't afford to have her changing her mind. I watched her through the window. She got in her car and sat there long enough to light up again and then she took off. Once I knew she was gone, I put a call through to Cheney and laid out the sequence of events, including the hapless FBI agent who'd put the plan at risk.

He said, "Shit."

"That was my reaction."

"Damn. And there's no name on this crud?"

"None, and no description of him, either. I'd have pressed her for details, but I was too busy trying to act like I didn't know the whole of it in advance."

"She buy it?"

"I'd say so. In the main. Anyway, I thought you'd want to call Vince and let him know where we stand."

"Which is where?"

"I'm not sure. Reba needs time. This is a lot to digest."

"Doesn't sound like she was that surprised."

"I think she's always known more than she lets on. Now that it's out in the open, we'll see what she does with it."

"Makes me nervous."

"Me, too. Let me know what Vince says."

"Will do. See you later."

"Okey-doke," said I.

14

I closed the office at 5:00, locked the door behind me, and retrieved my car. I drove the long way home so I could stop at my favorite service station and fill the tank with gas. As I cruised down State Street past the heart of town, I spotted a familiar figure. It was William in a dark fedora and a dark three-piece suit, walking briskly toward Cabana Boulevard, swinging his black malacca stick. I slowed and honked, pulling over to the curb. I leaned over and rolled down the window on the passenger side. "You want a ride?"

William tipped his hat. "Thank you. I'd appreciate that."

He opened the car door and angled himself in, his long legs sticking up awkwardly in the cramped front seat. He kept his cane between his knees.

"You can slide that seat back and get yourself more room. The lever's right down there," I said, pointing toward his feet.

"This is fine. It's not far."

I glanced over my left shoulder, waiting for a break in traffic before I eased into the flow. "I didn't expect to see you down here and you're all decked out. What's the occasion?"

"I attended a visitation at Wynington-Blake. Afterward, I had a cup of tea with the sole surviving family member. Lovely man."

"Oh, sorry. I didn't realize someone died. I wouldn't have sounded quite so chirpy if I'd known."

"That's all right. This was Francis Bunch. Eighty-three years old."

"Gee, that's young."

"My thought precisely. He was mowing his lawn Monday and blew an aneurysm in his brain. His second cousin Norbert is the only one left. At one count, there were twenty-six first cousins and now everybody's gone."

"That's a tough one."

"It is. Francis was quite the fellow—U.S. Army veteran, who fought in WW Two. He was a retired pipe-fitter and a Baptist. Preceded in death by his parents, his wife of sixty-two years—Mac was her name—seven children, and his brother, James. Norbert said Francis loved working in his yard so he went the way he would have wanted, except perhaps not quite so soon."

I turned the corner onto Cabana Boulevard and drove the three blocks to Castle, where I turned right again. "How long had you known him?"

William looked surprised. "Oh, I never met the man. I read about him in the paper. With so many of his family gone, I thought *someone* should be there to pay their respects. Norbert was most appreciative. We had a nice long chat."

"I thought you'd given up funerals."

"I have . . . in the main . . . but there's no harm in attending a service now and then."

I turned right onto my street, passing Rosie's. I spotted a space halfway between my apartment and the restaurant and then did a half-assed job of parallel parking. Close enough, I thought. I shut the engine down and turned to him. "Before you go, I've been wondering about something. Did you, by any chance, call Lewis in Michigan and talk him into coming?"

"Oh, he didn't require much persuasion. Once I mentioned Mattie's name, he was Johnny-on-the-Spot. I even had him thinking it was his idea. As I said to Rosie, 'This is just the ticket.'"

"William, I can't believe you did that!"

"Neither can I. In a moment of inspiration, the idea popped into my head just like that. I thought, Henry's complacent. He needs an incentive and this ought to do the trick."

"I didn't say I liked the plan. I think it stinks."

He frowned, somewhat taken aback. "Why do you say that? He and Lewis are jealous of one another. I'm surprised you weren't aware."

"Of course I'm *aware*. I'd have to be brain-dead to miss that. The problem is Henry's reaction is just the opposite. He's not going *after* her. He's backing away."

"He's a sly one, that Henry. Always has a little something hidden up his sleeve."

"That's not what I hear. He's saying he refuses to compete. He thinks it's tacky behavior so he's retiring from the field."

"Don't be fooled by that ploy. I've seen this a dozen times or more. He and Lewis set their caps for the same fair maiden and the jousting begins. It's actually working out even better than I'd hoped. You know Lewis talked Mattie into staying an extra day. You should have seen the look that came across Henry's face. That set him back on his heels, but he'll rally. It may take a bit of doing, but he'll prevail."

"Have you *talked* to him?"

"Not since yesterday. Why?"

"When I came home last night, her car was gone and his place was dark."

"He didn't come to Rosie's. I can assure you of that. You know Lewis invited Mattie to go with him to the art museum and then lunch afterward."

"William, I was sitting right there."

"Then you must have seen her response. She sparked to the idea, which Henry couldn't fail to notice. He probably came up with something special for the two of them last night."

"I don't think so. When I talked to Henry, he was adamant."

William waved the idea away. "He'll back down in the end. He'll never let Lewis get the better of him."

"I hope you're right," I said dubiously.

We opened our respective car doors and got out, taking leave of each other on the street. I wanted to say more, but it seemed wiser to let the subject drop. He seemed so sure of himself. Maybe Henry would come back fighting and William's meddling would be "just the ticket," as he'd referred to it. I watched him set off toward Rosie's, whistling and twirling his cane. As I went through the gate, I picked up Henry's afternoon paper, which was still lying on the walk.

I rounded the corner. Henry's back door was open. I went through a quick debate, then crossed the patio and tapped on the screen. "You there?"

"I'm here. Come in."

The overhead light was off and, though to all intents and purposes it was still broad daylight outside, the effect was gloomy. He sat in his rocker with his usual glass of whiskey in hand. The kitchen was spotless, appliances gleaming, the counters glossy. The oven was off and the stove top was bereft of any pots and pans. The air smelled blank. This was so unlike him. No sign of his daily baking project, no dinner preparations under way.

"I brought your paper in."

"Thank you."

I placed it on the kitchen table. "Mind if I join you?"

"Might as well. There's half a bottle of wine in the refrigerator if you're interested."

I took a wineglass from the cabinet and found the stoppered bottle of Chardonnay tucked in the refrigerator door. I poured myself half a glass and looked over at him. Henry hadn't moved. "Are you okay?"

"I'm fine."

"Ah. That's good because the kitchen looks kind of grim. I thought I'd turn on some lights."

"Suit yourself."

I crossed to the wall and flipped the switch, which didn't seem to help. The light seemed as dull and as flat as Henry's demeanor. I sat down and placed my wineglass on the table. "What happened last night? I saw Mattie's car was gone and you were out. The two of you go somewhere?"

"She left for San Francisco. I took a walk."

"What time did she leave?"

"I didn't pay much attention. Four thirty-two," he said.

"Pretty late start for a six-hour drive. If she stopped for supper, she probably didn't get home until close to midnight."

Silence from Henry.

"I take it she stayed for lunch. Did you go with them to the art museum?"

"You know we don't have to discuss this. There's really nothing to say. I'd just as soon drop the subject."

"Sure. No problem," I said. "Are you going to Rosie's for supper? I was thinking of doing that myself."

"And risk running into Lewis? I think not."

"We could go somewhere else. Emile's-at-the-Beach is always lovely."

He looked at me with such injury in his eyes, I couldn't bear to see it. "She broke it off."

"She did?"

"She said I was impossible. She said she really couldn't bear my bad behavior."

"What brought that on?"

"Nothing. It came out of a clear blue sky."

"Maybe she had a hard day."

"Not as hard as mine."

I sat staring at the floor, feeling a wave of disappointment washing over me. I'd had such high hopes for them. I said, "You know what I find hard? I want to believe nice things can happen to us. Not every day, maybe, but just now and then."

"Me too," he said. He got up and left the room.

I waited a minute and when it was clear he wasn't coming back, I dumped my wine in the sink, rinsed the glass, and then let myself out. I was ready to wring William's neck and I wouldn't have minded having a go at Lewis while I was at it. I could have handled pain of my own easier than Henry's. Part of my bleak mood was probably connected to my lack of sleep, but it didn't feel that way. It felt deep and permanent, a darkness being stirred up, like silt, from the very depths. Henry was a great guy and Mattie'd seemed perfect for him. He probably *had* been impossible, but so had she in her way. What would it have taken to be a little more sensitive to the situation? Unless she didn't care much to begin with, I thought. In that case, she'd cut and run the minute things got tough. As a person with cut-and-run tendencies myself, I could see her point. Life was difficult enough without having to put up with someone else's petulance.

I let myself into my apartment and checked the answering machine. I was hoping Cheney'd left a message, but the light wasn't blinking so I kissed that one off. Despite my earlier self-confidence, I wasn't keen on the idea of waiting around to see if he'd call. It was dinnertime, but I wasn't any more willing than Henry to venture into Rosie's. William would prance over, taking his own pulse and asking for the latest in the lovers' progress report. In case he was ignorant of the breakup, I didn't want to be the one to tell him. And if he'd heard it from Lewis, I didn't want to listen to him minimize the role he'd played. I suspected a run would cheer me up, but given my current mental state, I'd have had to jog all the way to Cottonwood, twenty miles round-trip.

This was one of those moments when you need a girlfriend. When you're down in the dumps, that's what you do—call your best friend—or so I've heard. You chat. You laugh. You tell her your sad tale of woe, she commiserates, and then you take off and go shopping like normal folk. But I didn't have a girlfriend, a lack I'd hardly noticed until Cheney appeared. So now, not only was I facing the fact that I didn't have him, I didn't have her either, whoever she was.

A voice said . . . *Ah, but you do have Reba.*

I thought about that one. If I made a list of desirable girlfriend traits, "convicted felon" wouldn't be one. On the other hand, I'd be a convicted felon myself if I'd ever been caught doing even half the things I'd done.

I picked up the phone and punched in the number for the Lafferty estate. When Reba answered, I said, "Reba, this is Kinsey. I need a favor. How good are you at giving fashion advice?"

Reba picked me up in her car, a two-year-old black BMW she'd acquired shortly before she'd been sent to CIW. "The DA was panting to seize the car on the premise I'd bought it with ill-gotten gains. Ha ha ha on him. My father gave it to me for my thirtieth birthday. Hopes dashed again."

"What'd you say to Onni when you canceled dinner?"

"I told her something came up and we'd make it another night."

"She was cool with that?"

"Of course. She probably hated the idea of having dinner with me. I was always pouring my heart out about

Beck. There wasn't anyone else I could talk to about him. Beck said this, Beck said that. When it came to our sex life, I'd be giving her a blow by blow, so to speak."

"That was your mistake. You made him sound too good."

"You got that right. She was always jealous of me. Minute my back is turned, she walks off with my job and then she walks off with the love of my life, or so I thought at the time. I hate women who get into that competitive shit."

"What's she like?"

"You can judge for yourself as long as you end up agreeing with me. I know where she hangs out. If you're interested, we can drop by later and I'll introduce you."

"Drop by where?"

"Bubbles in Montebello."

"That's been closed for two years."

"Nuhn-uhn. The place has changed hands. Name's the same, but it's been open for a month under new management."

"Where we headed now?"

"The mall."

Passages, the newly opened shopping plaza in the heart of Santa Teresa, had been designed to resemble an old Spanish town. The architecture featured a picturesque assortment of narrow shoulder-to-shoulder buildings of varying heights, arches, loggias, courtyards, fountains, and side streets, the whole of the three-block complex capped by red tile roofs. At ground level there were restaurants, clothing stores, galleries, jewelry stores, and other retail shops. The wide central esplanade was anchored at one end by Macy's and at the other end by Nordstrom's, with a large chain bookstore occupying a prominent spot. Pepper trees and flowering shrubs were planted throughout. In the taller structures, three and four stories high, office space had been leased to lawyers, accountants, engineers, and anyone else who could afford the staggering rents.

Given Santa Teresa's resistance to new construction, the project had taken years to push through. The city-planning commission and the architectural board of review, plus the city council, plus the county board of supervisors, plus the building and safety commission, all at odds with one another, had to be soothed, pacified, and reassured. Citizens' groups protested the razing of buildings five and six decades old, though most were otherwise unremarkable. Many were already slated for mandatory earthquake retro-fitting, which would have cost the owners more than they were worth. Environmental impact studies had to be approved. Numerous small merchants were evicted and displaced, with only one holdout, a funky little bar called Dale's that was still moored in the middle of the plaza like a tugboat in a harbor full of yachts.

We ate dinner at an Italian boutique restaurant located on one of the smaller avenues that connected the center esplanade to State Street on one side and Chapel on the other. Temperatures were still elevated, and we elected to eat on the patio outside. As the dark came down, the landscape lighting began to paint walls and vegetation in colors more vivid than their daylight shades. Details of wrought-iron fixtures were picked out in shadow, the plaster frieze along the roof outlined in black. If you squinted, you could almost believe you'd been transported to a foreign country.

While we waited for our salads, I said, "I appreciate your doing this—the clothes thing."

"No problem. It's obvious you need help."

"I'm not sure the word 'obvious' should come into play."

"Trust me."

Later, while she was winding spaghetti on her fork, she said, "You know this is Beck's project."

"What is?"

"The mall."

"He did Passages?"

"Sure. I mean, not on his own—in partnership with a guy in Dallas, another developer. Beck moved his office to the far end, down by Macy's. The fourth floor runs the full block between State and Chapel."

"I didn't realize the building covered that much ground."

"Because you didn't bother to look up. If you did, you'd see that there are covered walkways that join the second and third levels in places above the esplanade. Technically, in the rainy season, you could move from one building to the other without getting wet."

"You've got a better eye than I do. I missed that."

"I have the advantage. The mall's been in development for years so I've seen the plans at just about every stage. Beck moved his office in a couple of months after I went into CIW, so I never got to see it. Turned out great, or so I hear."

I took a sip of wine, finishing the last bite of eggplant parmigiana while I watched Reba use a chunk of bread to clean up her marinara sauce. I said, "Where are you going with this?"

She popped the bread in her mouth, smiling while she chewed. "You're the kick-ass private eye. You figure it out. In the meantime, let's go buy you some clothes and then we can make the run into Montebello."

15

We shopped until the stores closed at 9:00. Reba kept up a running commentary as I tried things on. In the interests of education, she let me make my choices without reference to her opinion. At first, I tried gauging her reaction as I lifted a garment off the rack, but she looked on with the same deadpan expression she must have donned at the poker table. With no guidelines whatever, I picked out two dresses, a pantsuit, and three cotton skirts. "Okay," I said.

Her brow went up about an eighth of an inch. "That's it?"

"Isn't this enough?"

"You like that green deal, that pantsuit thing?"

"Well, yeah. You know, it's dark and it won't show spots."

"All riiiight," she said, with a tone suggesting that you have to let kids make boo-boos in order for them to learn.

She trailed behind me as far as the line of dressing cubicles in the rear. She looked on idly while I tried door after door, looking for a room not in use. When I finally found an empty cubicle, she gave every impression of following me in.

"Hold on a sec. You're coming *in* here with me?"

"What if something doesn't fit? You can't stroll around out there in your underwear."

"I wasn't planning to. I was going to try on stuff back here and then decide."

"Deciding is my job. You try on clothes and I'll explain how misguided you are."

She sat on a plain wooden chair in a space that was six feet on a side with floor-to-ceiling mirrors on three. The fluorescent lighting guaranteed your skin would look sallow and every tiny body flaw would appear in bas relief.

I took my shoes off and began to strip down with the same enthusiasm I feel before a pelvic exam. "I can tell I have a better developed sense of modesty than you do," I said.

"Oh, please. Prison knocked that out of me. The shower stalls were a quarter this size with these skimpy canvas curtains designed to keep your head and feet in view. That was to prevent the inmates from having sex in private. Little did they know. Aside from that, you might as well forget privacy altogether. It was simpler to prance around nude like everybody else."

During these revelations, I was trying to step gracefully out of my blue jeans, but my foot caught and I nearly toppled sideways. Reba pretended not to notice. I said, "Didn't that bother you?"

"At first, but after a while, I thought, oh who gives a damn? All these naked women and pretty soon you've seen every possible body type—short, tall, skinny, fat, little tits, big ass, or big tits and no ass. Scar, moles, tattoos, birth defects. Everybody looks just about like everybody else."

I peeled my T-shirt over my head.

"Oh, bullet holes!" she said, nearly clapping her hands as she caught sight of mine.

"Do you *mind?*"

"Well, I think they're cute. Sort of like dimples."

I slid the first of two cotton dresses from the hanger and eased my arms up the interior and out the requisite armholes. I turned to the mirror. I looked about like I always did—not bad, but not that good. "What do you think?"

"What do *you* think?"

"Come on, Reba. Just tell me what's wrong with it."

"Everything. The color for starters. You should wear clear tones—red, maybe navy blue, but not that pukey shade of yellow. It makes your skin tone look orange."

"I thought that was the lighting."

"And look how loose it's cut. You've got good legs and a great set of boobs. I mean, they're not *huge*, but they're sassy so why cover them with something that looks like a pillowcase?"

"I don't like to wear stuff too tight."

"Clothes are supposed to *fit*, dear. That dress is one size too big and it looks—dare I say it—so matronly. Go ahead and try on the blue print skirt, but I can tell you right now it's another pass. You're not the big-ass Hawaiian palm-and-parrot type."

"If you already hate it, why should I try it on?"

"Because otherwise you'll never get the *point.*"

And so it went. Bossy women and I get along swimmingly as I'm a masochist at heart. I bypassed the blue print skirt and didn't bother trying on the green pantsuit, knowing she'd be right about that, too. She removed the offending garments, holding the hangers at arm's length like so many dead rats. While I waited in the dressing room, she went out to the floor and flipped through the racks. She returned with six items, which she exhibited one by one, creating the illusion that she was letting me choose. I resisted one dress and one skirt, but everything else she'd selected ended up looking great on me, even if I do say so myself.

"I don't understand how you know all this stuff," I said, getting dressed again. This is my perpetual complaint, that somehow other women have a flair for things that make me feel like a dunce. It was like thought problems in math. In high school, the minute I encountered one I'd feel like I was on the verge of blacking out.

"You'll get the hang of it eventually. It's really not that hard. At CIW, I was the resident styling expert. Hair, makeup, clothes, all of it. I could've taught a class." She paused to check her watch. "Let's get a move on. Time to party."

We sped south on the 101 with Reba at the wheel.

I said, "I'm not sure this is smart. Why go to a place where everyone's drinking?"

"I'm not going there to drink. I haven't had a drink for twenty-three months, fourteen and a half days."

"Then why put yourself in harm's way?"

"I told you. Because that's where Onni is. She goes out every Thursday night to hustle guys." I opened my mouth to protest, but she shot me a look. "You're not my mother, okay? I promise I'll call my sponsor the minute I get home. At least, I would if I had one, which I don't."

Bubbles was a Montebello wine-and-champagne bistro that had once done a lively business in concert with the Edgewater Hotel and another high-priced piano bar called Spirits. The three were in easy driving distance of one another and formed a triangle traveled by every rich, hot, single person on the market back then. All three places were heavy on atmosphere—glitz, glitter, live music, small dance floors, and low lights. Drinks were pricey, served in oversize glasses, and food was an afterthought, meant to get you home again without a fatal accident.

In the mid-seventies, for reasons unknown, Bubbles became a magnet for escort services, girls working high-end out-call and "models" from Los Angeles, who drove to Montebello cruising for love. Eventually cocaine became prevalent and the county sheriff's department stepped in and shut the place down. I'd been there on occasion because my second husband, Daniel, was a jazz pianist who played the three night spots in rotation. Early in the relationship, I realized if I didn't make a point of being there with him, I might not see him until breakfast the next day. He claimed he was out "jamming" with the guys, which turned out to be true, in both the literal and metaphorical senses.

We pulled up to the left of the entrance. Reba handed her car keys to the valet and we went in. Men in suits and sport coats stood five and six deep at the bar, checking out our boobs and butts as we passed. Reba did a quick search from table to table while I followed in her wake. Bubbles hadn't changed. Illumination was achieved primarily by way of massive fish tanks that lined the walls and separated one seating area from the next. In the main room, there was a bar with a U-shaped border of booths and a scattering of tables big enough for two. In the second room, through a wide arch, a jazz combo—piano, saxophone, and bass—was set up on a wide deck above a dance floor the size of a trampoline. The music was mellow—haunting melodies from the forties that stuck in your head for days. This was not a place where voices were raised or raucous laughter cut through the murmur of civilized conversation. No one got drunk and tumbled backward into other patrons. Women didn't weep or fling drinks on their dates. No one upchucked in the elegant restrooms with their marble floors and baskets of tiny terrycloth towels. Customers smoked, but the ventilation system was high-tech and a roving band of busboys whisked away dirty ashtrays and replaced them with clean ones every five minutes or so.

Reba put a hand out and slowed me to a halt. Like a pointer, she stood and pinned a look on Onni, who sat at a table by herself, smoking a cigarette with an air of indifference I suspected was fake. The presence of two half-filled champagne flutes and a bottle resting in a nearby cooler suggested a companion who'd left the table moments before. The "real" Onni bore only passing resemblance to the Onni I'd seen in the grainy black-and-white photos. She was tall and slim, with a long thin face, wide nose, thin lips, and small nearly lashless eyes. Her dark hair was dead straight and spilled across her shoulders with the high silky shine you see in ads for shampoos. Silver earrings dangled from her lobes and brushed against her neck with every move of her head. The jacket of her black business suit had been shrugged aside, revealing a white silk tank top that looked more like a slip than any blouse I'd seen. Taken feature by feature, she really wasn't pretty, but she'd managed to maximize her assets. Her makeup was artful and her breasts looked as hard as croquet balls inserted inexplicably under the skimpy flesh on her chest. Nonetheless, she presented herself as though she were beautiful and that was the impression that prevailed.

Reba moved forward with trumped-up exuberance. "Onni! How perfect. I was hoping you'd be here."

"Hello, Reba." Onni's manner was cool, but Reba didn't seem to notice as she slid into a chair. I sat down too, fully aware Onni wasn't at all happy to see us. Beside her, Reba seemed childlike, animated, petite, with dark tousled hair, the large dark eyes, perfect nose, and delicately rounded chin, where Onni's receded slightly. What Reba lacked was that air of self-containment that passes for breeding among middle-class pretenders.

Reba said, "This is my friend Kinsey. I've been telling her about you." Her gaze settled on the two champagne flutes as though she'd just noticed. "I hope we're not cutting in on your action. Big hot date?"

"It's actually not a date. Beck and I had to work late so he suggested stopping off for a nightcap. I don't imagine we'll stay long."

"Beck's here? That's great. I don't see him."

"He's chatting with a friend. I'm sorry you canceled dinner. When you said something came up, I pictured AA."

"I did a meeting already. I'm only required to do one a week." Reba helped herself to one of Onni's cigarettes and waggled it between her teeth. "You have a light for this?"

"Of course." Onni reached into a small bag and came up with a pack of matches. Reba took the pack, struck one, and cupped a hand around the flame. She inhaled with satisfaction and returned the matches with a sly smile that Onni seemed to miss. I knew Reba well enough by now that I could see the icy rage sparkling in her eyes. She pulled the ashtray closer and then put an elbow on the table and propped her chin on her hand. "So. How are things with you? You said you'd write, but then I never heard from you."

"I *wrote*. I sent you a card. Didn't you get it?"

Reba took a drag of her cigarette, her smile still in place. "That's right. So you did. It had bunnies on it as I remember. One measly card in twenty-two months. Hey, don't put yourself out."

"I'm sorry if that bothers you, but I was busy. You left the office in bad shape. It took me months to straighten it out."

"Yeah, well, the Department of Corrections had first claim. Whisk you off to prison, you don't have the option to stop by your workplace and tidy up your desk. I'm sure you have the situation well in hand."

"Finally. No thanks to you." Onni's gaze shifted slightly.

Reba turned her head in time to see Beck approaching from the bar. He caught sight of her and his forward motion halted for a split second, like a few frames of film missing from a sequence. Reba's face brightened. She pushed out of the chair and moved toward him. When she reached him, her arms slid around his neck as though she meant to kiss him on the mouth.

He extracted himself gently. "Hey, hey, hey, gorgeous. We're in public. Remember?"

"I know, but I missed you."

"Well, I missed you, too, but suppose one of Tracy's girlfriends is here." He steered her back to her chair, sending me a smile in the process. "Good to see you again."

"Nice seeing you," I said, though it wasn't nice at all. Not surprisingly, my view of him had changed radically. When I'd met him in Rosie's, I'd thought he was handsome—long-limbed, loose-jointed, with that lazy half-smile. Even his eyes, which I'd thought were a rich chocolate brown, now looked as dark as volcanic stone. Seeing him with Onni, I could sense the trait they shared—both were opportunists.

Of the three of them, Reba currently occupied the power position. Onni knew the intimate details of Reba's relationship with Beck, but neither Beck nor Onni were aware that Reba had been tipped off about their affair. To further complicate the situation, I was reasonably sure Onni didn't know that Beck and Reba had reactivated their sexual connection. I felt a frisson of tension ripple up my spine, curious how Reba intended to play the hand she'd been dealt.

Beck sat down in the remaining chair and slouched on his spine, extending his legs as though he were entitled to more space than we were. In the geography of body language, he and Onni were lined up in parallel, their bodies tracing the same angle while Reba sat across the table from them, her body an upright that cut across the slant of their respective postures.

Onni's attention was fixed on her champagne flute.

Beck sipped champagne, watching Reba above the rim of his glass. The blond highlights in his hair must have been professionally applied. Certainly, the haphazard thatch effect was no accident. "So how's it going?" he asked.

Reba said, "Not bad. I was actually thinking of coming back to work."

Onni's expression was incredulous, as though Reba had farted in the presence of Elizabeth II.

Reba ignored her reaction, addressing her remarks to Beck. "Yeah, I mentioned it to my parole officer and she was all for it as long as my 'prospective employer' knew about my past," she said, forming quote marks with her fingers. "I figured who better than you?"

Smoothly, he said, "Reeb, I'd love to help, but it doesn't seem smart."

"It's ridiculous," Onni snapped. "You robbed him blind."

Reba shifted her gaze. "Onni, I'm sorry, but you don't get it. Beck trusts me. He knows I'd do anything for him." She looked back at him. "Right?"

Beck rearranged his legs, pulling himself into an upright position, his tone mild. "It's not a question of trust. There's no position. It's as simple as that. I wish we had an opening, but we don't."

"You could make one, couldn't you? I remember you did that for Abner."

"Different situation. Marty was overloaded and needed the help. I had no choice in that case."

"But you have one with me, is that it? You could choose to help me, but you won't?"

He reached out and grabbed one of her fingers, giving it a shake. "Hey, babe, remember? I'm on your team."

Reba studied him with care, the lean, handsome face,

the hand touching hers. "You said you'd take care of me. You owe me."

"Hey, anything you want."

"Except work."

Onni snorted and rolled her eyes. "What gall! How do you have the fucking nerve to sit there and *argue* the point after what you did?"

Beck said, "Cool it, Onni. This is between her and me."

"Well, pardon the hell out of me. I just think someone should set this girl straight. She wreaked havoc on the company and for what? So she could go on indulging herself, blowing every nickel she could get her hands on at the poker table? My god!"

I half-expected Beck to belt her in the mouth, but he focused on Reba's face. He took her hand, placing her index finger against his lip. The effect was erotic, some intensely private communication taking place between them. "Forget about work. Take a little time for yourself. Do something nice, like that spa in Floral Beach. I can have Ed set it up. You've been through tough times, I understand that, but talk about work is premature."

"I have to do something with my life," she said, her eyes pinned on his.

"I know, babe. I hear you. All I'm saying is you need to take it slow. I don't want you rushing into anything you might regret."

Reba smiled. "Like what? Coming back to work for you?"

"Like getting stressed out, upset, when there's no reason to. You need to keep it low-key. Kick back and relax while you have the chance."

Onni said something under her breath. She shoved her

arms into the sleeves of her jacket and shrugged herself into it, straightening her lapels. She reached for her cigarettes and tucked them in her bag, then stood, saying, "Night, folks. I'm out of here." Her manner seemed to be matter-of-fact unless you knew what was going on.

"Give me five minutes and I'll drive you home," Beck said to her.

Onni's smile was brittle. "Thanks, but no thanks. I'd rather walk."

"You won't make it a block in those heels."

"Not your problem, champ. I'll figure it out."

"Cut the crap, Onni. Have Jack call you a cab. I'll square the fare with him on my way out."

"Not to worry. I'm a big girl. I think I can manage to call a cab on my own. Meantime, enjoy Panama. And thanks for the drink. It was really swell, you fucking jerk."

Reba turned her head, watching as Onni walked away. "What's her problem?"

"Forget it. She gets bored anytime the topic of conversation moves to something other than her," Beck said.

Reba said, "What's the deal with Panama? When did that come up?"

"It's just a quick trip. Couple of days."

"Why couldn't you take me with you? Like a minivacation. You could take care of business while I sit by the pool and get some sun. It'd be great."

"Baby, this is strictly solo. I've got wall-to-wall meetings. You'd be bored to tears."

"No, I wouldn't. I can amuse myself. Come on, Beck. We've hardly had a minute together. We could have a ball. Please, please, please?"

He smiled. "You nut. I'd do it in a heartbeat if I thought

we could get it past your PO. Trust me, if you're not allowed to leave the state, you sure as hell wouldn't be allowed to leave the continental U.S.A."

Reba made a face. "Oh, shit. You're right. I forgot about that. I don't even have a passport. It expired in June."

"So get your passport renewed and I'll take you to Panama as soon as you're out from under all the rules and regs." He took a hasty look at his watch. "Speaking of which, I gotta go. The limo's picking me up in an hour to drive to LAX."

"You're flying out tonight? Why didn't you tell me?"

Beck waved the idea away. "I'm down there so often, it's not worth mentioning. Anyway, I'll call you as soon as I get back."

"Couldn't I ride down in the limo with you and come back with the driver once he drops you off?"

"It's an L.A.-based company. The driver's coming up from Santa Monica. Once he leaves me at the airport, he's on his way home."

"Shoot. I wanted to spend time with you."

"Me, too. We'll take a rain check. Meantime, let's get you out of here. It's late."

16

The three of us went out into the chill night air together as we had at Rosie's earlier in the week. I kept my distance, feigning interest in the lighted window display in the shop next door. Beck and Reba had a murmured conversation, their heads bent together like co-conspirators. Reba seemed to drink in the sight of him, her face in profile looking childlike and trusting. The revelation about Beck's relationship with Onni had apparently done nothing to mitigate his hold on her. It looked as if Cheney and Vince would have to find another source for confidential information. I only hoped she'd keep her mouth shut and not blow the whole deal.

A valet pulled up in Reba's BMW. Beck slipped the guy a tip on her behalf and then turned as a second parking valet pulled his car in behind hers. Once Reba got in the car, she took out a lipstick and applied a fresh coat, checking her reflection in the rearview mirror. She caught sight of Beck behind her and waved to him, blowing him a kiss. She shifted into drive and turned right onto Coastal

Road. I glanced back in time to see Beck pull out after we did. He made a left-hand turn, heading toward West Glen Road. As soon as he was out of sight, Reba slowed, made a U-turn, and sped after him.

"What are you doing?" I said.

"I want you to see his house."

"What do I care? At this hour? It's dark."

"It won't take long. It's just about a mile down West Glen."

"It's your car so you can do as you please, but don't put yourself out on my account."

I couldn't get a fix on her mood. At first I'd thought she was flirting with Beck purely to infuriate Onni. I was anticipating the rehash, the two of us comparing notes about Onni's reaction, especially when she walked out in such a huff. By that point in the evening, however, Beck was really pouring on the charm and she'd fallen under his spell. I found it unnerving how deftly he'd drawn her back into orbit, exerting the same invisible pull as the earth on the moon. Just when I thought we'd won her over to our side, Beck had taken her back.

We turned right on West Glen. Beck was now out of sight, several curves in the road between our car and his. Even if he noticed our headlights behind him, he probably wouldn't give the matter much thought. We reached the straightaway and caught sight of him about a quarter mile ahead. His brake lights came on as he slowed and made a right-hand turn. His car disappeared from view. Reba sped up, closing the distance, and then she slowed as well. She peered across me and out the passenger-side window as we passed a gated estate. I caught a glimpse of a massive stone mansion in a fairyland of lights.

Fifty yards beyond the entrance to his property, she pulled onto the berm. She killed the lights, shut the engine down, and got out of the car. Before she eased the door shut, she said, "You coming or not?"

"Sure. Eleven o'clock at night, I could use a walk." I emerged from the car on my side. She'd made a point of not slamming her door and I certainly knew better than to slam my own. If we were on a search-and-seizure mission of some kind, there was no point in alerting him to our presence. I joined her as she backtracked along the darkened road. Having spent half an hour in a smoke-filled bar, we must have smelled like two cigarette butts out for a breath of fresh air. This section of Montebello was dark, no streetlights, no sidewalks, and no passing cars. We were accompanied by the chirring of crickets and the scent of eucalyptus trees. She halted at the entrance to Beck's driveway.

Through iron gates, I was treated to the full panoramic view. The ivy-covered stone façade looked as stately as a monastery, mansard roof, half-timbered, a long bank of mullioned windows aglow along the front. I was guessing three to four acres with a tennis court visible on one side and a swimming pool on the other. Reba moved to the right of the gate and eased herself between the hedge and the stone pillar, where a gap permitted passage despite the solid look of the shrubs. I followed, pushing through a turnstile of branches that nearly tore off my shirt. She proceeded with an air of calm familiarity as she veered off across the lawn. I gathered she'd made the walk many times before. She seemed confident about the absence of motion-detecting floodlights and attack-trained dogs. I was worried the automatic sprinkling system (complete with toe-busting sprayer heads) would suddenly spark to life and drench us in a downpour of artificial rain.

Closer to the house, a porte cochere spanned the driveway and served as a covered walkway, sheltering residents and guests as they moved to and from their cars. Reba skirted the entrance and took up a position between two squared-off clipped shrubs on the far side. The box-woods had been shaped to form an alcove about the size of a phone booth, easily big enough to allow the two of us to huddle. A wide slat of shadow shielded us from view.

We waited in silence. I love nighttime surveillance as long as my bladder isn't screaming for relief. Who wants to have to squat in the bushes where the high beams of any passing car can flash across the globes of your pearly hind-end? Add to that the likelihood of peeing on your own shoes and the notion of "penis envy" isn't tough to comprehend.

A set of headlights appeared at the bottom of the drive and a mechanical hum announced the slow parting of the wrought iron gates. A black stretch limousine swung into view and proceeded slowly up the drive, approaching the house with all the gravity of the lead car in a funeral procession. The driver pulled under the porte cochere and triggered the trunk lid, which seemed to pop up of its own accord.

As if on cue, the porch light went on and the front door was opened. I could hear Beck talking to someone over his shoulder as he carried out three large bags and set them on the porch. With the engine still idling, the driver got out in his tuxedo and chauffeur's cap and moved around to the rear where Beck waited with the luggage. The driver hefted the suitcases into the trunk one by one. He shut the trunk and then opened the rear limo door. Beck paused, looking toward the house as his wife stepped out onto the porch. She stopped, apparently to check the thumb lock before she pulled the door shut behind her. "Is that everything?"

"We're good. Bags are in the trunk."

She crossed to the limo and ducked into the backseat. Beck followed her in. The driver closed the limo door and then returned to the driver's seat and resumed his place at the wheel, shutting the car door. I could hear a slight pop as he released the emergency brake and then the limo glided down the drive toward the road. The lighted rear license plate read: ST LIMO-1, designating car number one of the Santa Teresa Limousine Service. The gates swung open, the limo disappeared, and the gates eased shut again.

Beside me, Reba flicked her Dunhill, the flame warming her face briefly as she took the first long drag from a fresh cigarette. She put the pack and lighter in her pocket and blew out a stream of smoke. Her eyes were remarkably large and dark, and her lips curved upward in a cynical smile. "Lying sack of shit. You know when I figured it out? Did you see the little hitch in his walk when he first caught sight of me? That said it all. I was the last person in the world he wanted to see."

"At least you managed to queer it for Onni. She was really pissed at him."

"I hope so. Anyway, let's get out of here before a sheriff's deputy decides to cruise by. Beck always notifies 'em when he's leaving town. They're quite attentive to him."

"Are you okay?"

"I feel great. How long will it take to set up the meeting with the feds?"

When I let myself into my apartment at 11:25, the light was blinking on the answering machine, a tiny red beacon in the dark. I flipped on the overhead light. I set my shoulder bag on the countertop and dumped my shopping bags on the floor. I crossed to the desk and stood there, staring at the *blink, blink, blink* as though it might be a message in Morse code. Either it was Cheney or it was not. The fact of the matter had already been entered into evidence so I might as well find out. If he hadn't called, that didn't necessarily mean anything. And if he had called, it didn't necessarily mean anything, either. The problem in the early stages of any relationship is that you don't know where you stand and you don't know how to interpret the other person's behavior.

So okay. All I had to do was push the button and I'd know.

I sat down. If he hadn't called, I sure didn't want to be the one to call him, though I was panting to tell him what had transpired between Beck and Reba. I could touch base with him for that purpose. In fact, I'd *have* to call him soon so he could set up the meeting between Reba and Vince. But aside from business—on a personal level— he'd have to make the first move. He looked like the kind of guy women called all the time—too cute and too sexy to have to expend much effort himself. I didn't want to place myself in the same category with his other women, whoever they were. How was it, though, that after only one day I was feeling insecure? Ruefully, I remembered my cockiness of the night before.

I pushed the button and listened to the brief high-pitched squeal as the tape rewound. *Beep.* "Kinsey, this is Cheney. It's ten-fifteen and I just got off work. Give me a buzz when you get in. I'll be up." He left his number. *Click.*

I checked the clock. Over an hour ago. I made a note of his home number, then suffered a fit of indecision. He said to call, so I'd call. Nothing tricky about that . . . unless he was already in bed and asleep. I hate waking people up. Before I felt any more squirrelly, I punched in the number.

He picked up on the first ring.

I said, "If you're asleep I swear I'm going to slit my wrists with a butter knife."

He laughed. "Not at all, babe. I'm a night owl. How about you?"

"Not me. I'm an early bird. I usually get up at six for my run. How come you were working so late? I thought you got off at five."

"We spent the day cooped up in a van over on Castle, taking videos of johns going in and out of a hot new whorehouse. Heavy weekend trade coming up. We'll do a sweep as soon as we have enough little fishies in the net."

"Nothing like sitting all day to wear you down."

"I'm trashed. How about you?"

"I'm pretty trashed myself," I said. "Though I did have a productive evening. You won't believe where I've been."

"Answer can't be Rosie's. Too easy."

"I was out with Reba. First we went clothes shopping and then we went to Bubbles where we ran into Beck and Onni. I won't plague you with the details—"

"Hey, come on. Don't be like that. I love the details."

"I'll tell you next time I see you. At the moment, I'm too bushed to go into a blow-by-blow. The upshot is Reba's ready to do business."

"She's agreed to talk to Vince?"

"That's what she told me half an hour ago."

"What brought this on? I know she was waffling, but this falls into the too-good-to-be-true category, don't you think?"

"No, I'm trusting her on this. Mostly because I was right there watching when the whole thing went down. Beck laid on a bunch of BS, three or four lies in a row, and Reba nailed him on all counts. I mean, not to his face. He was stringing her along and stringing her along. I think she could have dealt with that—she's probably used to his messing with her head. The kicker was, she realized he was taking Tracy to Panama when he'd implied he was going alone."

"How'd she find out?"

I hesitated. "We did some independent research."

"I don't want to hear this."

"I thought not. Bottom line is she'll meet with the feds as soon as you can set it up."

"Shit, that's great. I'll let Vince know as soon as I can track him down. Might take a couple of days. He's hard to reach on weekends."

"The sooner the better. We don't want her changing her mind," I said.

"While we're on the subject, Vince checked on that FBI guy who went to Reba's with the photos. Turns out he'd been transferred from another office and wanted to show how good he was at taking the initiative. He got his ears boxed but good."

"Glad to hear that," I said.

"So what are you doing at the moment? Are you down for the count?"

"Meaning what, am I in bed? No, I'm up."

"Meaning, I don't want to keep you on the phone if you're about to hit the sack."

"Not a bit of it. I just walked in the door. I was worried I wouldn't catch you before you went to bed yourself."

There was a moment of quiet.

I said, "Hello?"

"I'm here. I was wondering how you'd feel about company."

"Right now?"

"Yes."

I thought about exhaustion, both his and mine. "Good. I'd feel good— assuming it's yourself we're discussing and not someone else."

"Give me ten minutes."

"Make it fifteen. That'll give me time to change."

I took the spiral stairs two at a time, whipped off my clothes, jammed everything in the hamper, showered, shaved my legs, washed my hair, flossed and brushed my teeth, all in the space of eight minutes, which gave me plenty of time to pull on clean sweats (minus underwear) and change the sheets. Downstairs again, I was in the process of refolding sections of the newspaper when I heard his tap at the door.

I tossed the *Dispatch* in the wastebasket and let him in. His hair was curly and damp and he smelled like soap. He was holding a pizza box that smelled heavenly. He closed the door behind him. "I never ate dinner. The guy just delivered this. You hungry?"

"Of course. You want to take it up with us?"

He smiled, shaking his head fondly. "Always in a hurry. We have time."

———————————

At 1:00 A.M., he gave me the promised haircut, me sitting on a stool in the loft bathroom with a towel draped across my shoulders, Cheney with a second towel wrapped around his waist.

I said, "Most of the time I do this myself with a pair of nail scissors."

"So I see." He worked with ease and concentration, taking off very little hair, but somehow making the whole of it fall together in tidy layers.

I watched his reflection in the mirror. So serious. "Where'd you learn to cut hair?"

"I have an uncle who does this for a living. Salon on Melrose, 'Hair Cutter to the Stars.' Four hundred bucks a pop. I figured if I washed out of police academy I could do this instead. I'm not sure which option was more horrifying to my parents, my becoming a cop or a guy who does women's hair. They're otherwise decent folks, barring the inherent snobbery."

"Last time I had a really good cut, you know who did it?"

"Danielle Rivers. I remember that." Cheney's attention had shifted to the nape of my neck, where he was busy snipping away, trying to even out the line.

Danielle Rivers was a seventeen-year-old hooker he'd introduced me to. He'd recently been transferred to vice, part of the regular rotation system at the police department, while I'd been hired to track down the killer of Lorna Kepler, a beautiful young woman who was caught up in porno films and sex for hire. He'd put me together with Danielle because she and the victim had been cohorts.

I said, "Danielle was appalled when she heard how little I earned—half of what she made. You should have heard her riff on investment strategies, all of which she picked up from Lorna. I wish I'd taken her advice. Maybe I'd be rich."

"Easy come, easy go."

"Remember the sandwiches you bought in the hospital cafeteria the night she was admitted?"

He smiled. "Man, those were bad. Ham and cheese from a vending machine."

"But you added all the stuff that made them edible."

He gave me a hand mirror and kissed me on the top of the head, saying, "All done."

I turned, holding the mirror so I could check the cut in the back. "Oh, wow. It looks good. Thanks." I glanced down at his towel, the two ends of which had parted in front. "I like your friend. Must be showtime and he's popped his head out to check the audience."

Cheney glanced down. "Why don't we go in the other room and see if we can catch his act?"

Eventually we slept, curled together like cats.

17

Friday morning, we dragged ourselves out of bed at 10:00. We showered and dressed, and then walked over to Cabana Boulevard, where we had breakfast at a little beachside café. Cheney didn't have to go to work until later in the day, having been scheduled for another shift in the surveillance van. Back from breakfast, we stood and chatted at the curb until we ran out of things to say. We parted company at noon. He had errands to run and I was ready to be alone. I watched until his little red Mercedes disappeared from sight and then I followed the walkway around to the backyard.

Henry was kneeling in one of his flower beds, where nutgrass was popping up. He was barefoot, wearing cutoffs and a tank top, his flip-flops lying on the lawn nearby. Eliminating nutgrass requires patience. The weed multiplies by way of threadlike roots and tiny black rhizomes that spread underground, so simply yanking the stems free does nothing to the plant's underlying structure, which goes on merrily reproducing. The small pile of weeds Henry had successfully uprooted resembled nothing so much as a cluster of spiders with frail legs and bodies the size of blackened match heads.

"You need help?"

"No, but you can keep me company if you like. There's something satisfying about going after these things. Ugly-looking little buggers, aren't they?"

"Disgusting. I thought you got rid of all the nutgrass this spring."

"Ongoing process. You never really win." He sat back on his heels briefly, then shifted so he could tackle the next section.

I kicked off my tennis shoes and settled in the grass, letting the sunshine wash across my legs. Henry's dark mood had lifted, and while he was still subdued, he seemed almost himself again.

"I see you had company last night," he remarked, without looking at me.

I laughed, feeling the blush begin to mount in my cheeks. "That was Cheney Phillips. STPD. He's a friend of Lieutenant Dolan's," I said, as though that were relevant.

"Nice?"

"Very. We've known each other for years."

"I thought it must be something of the sort. I've never known you to be impulsive."

"Actually, I am. It just sometimes takes me a while to work up to it."

There was a companionable quiet, broken only by the sound of Henry's trowel chunking in the ground.

Finally, I said, "Is Lewis still in town?"

"He flies home tomorrow. I feel better about him, in

case you're wondering. I don't want to see him just yet, but we'll work it out in due course."

"What about Mattie?"

"Oh, that's probably for the best. I never expected the relationship to turn into anything serious."

"But it might have."

"'Might' doesn't count for much. I generally find it wiser to deal with what is than with what might have been. Having made it to the ripe old age of eighty-seven without a long-term romance, there's no reason to suppose I'm even capable of such a thing."

"Couldn't you at least call?"

"I could, though I'm not sure what that would accomplish. She made her feelings clear. I have nothing else to offer and nothing much to add."

"What if she called you?"

"That's up to her," he said. "I don't mean to sound like a sad sack. I'm really fine."

"Well, of course you're *fine*, Henry. It's not like you're crushed because you've dated her for years. On the other hand, I thought you were great together and I'm sorry things didn't work out."

"You were picturing . . . what? . . . a little trip down the aisle?"

"William got married at eighty-seven, why not you?"

"He's impetuous by nature. I'm a stick-in-the-mud."

I threw a handful of grass at him. "You are not."

Reba called at 5:00, interrupting what I realized in retrospect was an award-winning nap. I'd stretched out on the

bed with my favorite John le Carré spy novel. The light
was soft. The temperature was mild and the sheet I'd
thrown over me was the perfect weight. Outside I could
hear the dim buzz of a lawn mower, followed by the *pft-pft-
pft* of Henry's Rain Bird, firing jets of water across the
newly trimmed grass. Thanks to my sleep deprivation of
the past two nights, I sank out of consciousness like a flat
stone settling lazily to the bottom of a lake. I don't know
how long I might have gone on like that if the phone hadn't
rung. I put the handset to my ear and said, "Uh-huh."

"This is Reba. Did I wake you?"

"I greatly fear you did. What's the time?"

"Five minutes after five."

I checked the skylight, squinting in an attempt to
determine if the sun was coming up or going down. "A.M.
or P.M.?"

"It's Friday afternoon. I was just wondering what you'd
heard from your guys."

"Nothing so far. Cheney's currently on surveillance, but
I know he's trying to reach his contact in Washington,
D.C. It may take a few days to set up the meeting. With so
many agencies involved, the protocol's tricky to negotiate."

"I wish they'd get on with it. Beck's back Sunday
night. I don't want to have to deal with him if I'm doing
this."

"I can appreciate that. Unfortunately, Cheney's dependent on other people and he can only push so hard. Doesn't
help we have a weekend coming up."

"I guess. You want to go someplace later? We could
have dinner."

"That sounds good. What time?"

"Soon or right away, whichever one comes first."

"What'd you have in mind? You want to meet me somewhere?"

"You decide. All I know is I gotta get out before I lose my mind." I could hear her pause to light a cigarette.

"What's making you so itchy," I said.

"I don't know. I've been feeling anxious all day. Like maybe there's a drink or a poker parlor coming up real soon."

"You don't want to do that."

"Easy for you to say. I'm already back to smoking a pack a day."

"I could have told you not to start."

"I couldn't help myself."

"So you said. Personally, I don't buy it. You either take charge of your life or you might as well give up."

"I know, but I've been feeling so bad. I know Beck's a shit, but I really love the guy—"

"You *love* the guy?"

"Well, not now, but I *did*. Doesn't that count for something?"

"Not in my opinion."

"Also, you know, as odd as it sounds, I kind of miss being locked up."

"You're kidding."

"I'm not," she said. "In prison, I didn't have to make all these decisions, so that limited my chances of screwing up. Out here, what's the incentive to behave?"

I pinched the bridge of my nose in despair. "Where are you now, at your dad's?"

"Yeah, and you'll never guess who came waltzing in for a visit with him."

"Who?"

"Lucinda."

"That woman who hoped to marry him?"

"The very one," she said. "She'd love to see me violate parole. I get tossed in the can again, she'll whip back into Pop's life before the doors slam shut."

"Then you better pull yourself together."

"That'd be easier to do if I could have a drink. Or maybe I could drop in at the Double Down and just watch. No harm in that."

"Would you cut the crap? You can do anything you want, but don't kid yourself. You're just looking for an excuse to self-destruct."

"Yeah, it might be a relief."

"Look, why don't I hop in the car and come get you?"

"I don't know. Now that I think about it, maybe that's not such a hot idea. If I leave Lucinda alone with him, she'll find a way to make trouble."

"Oh, come on. What can she do? Your father told me he was done with her."

"She'll manage somehow. I've seen her do it before. Pop's like me, weak-willed and indecisive, only not as hell-bent. Besides, if he's so done with her, how come she's sitting in the other room?"

"Would you quit obsessing about her? She's the least of your worries. Look, give me a minute to throw on some clothes and I'll be up."

"Are you sure you want to go out?"

"Sure I'm sure. Why don't you start walking down the drive, and I'll meet you at the gate."

203

In the car on the way over, I tried to assess the situation. Reba was on the verge of coming unglued. Since the moment she'd fired up that first cigarette, I'd been waiting for signs of emotional decompression. After two years at CIW, she was unaccustomed to real-world conflicts and real-world consequences. Prison, while loathsome, apparently provided a form of containment that must have made her feel safe. Now there was too much to deal with and no way for her to assimilate the impact. Bad enough to find out Beck had hoodwinked her into taking the fall for him, worse still to discover he'd launched into an affair with the woman she'd thought of as her best friend. She was tough enough to acknowledge his deception, but perhaps not tough enough to make the break. I could see her ambivalence; she'd been dependent on him for years. What worried me was the fact she had so little tolerance for stress. If the meeting with Vince Turner had been scheduled right away, she might have sailed right on through, spilling everything she knew. With the delay of even three days, she was in danger of losing control. And while she wasn't my responsibility, I was party to the push that had her teetering on the brink.

When I arrived at the estate, she was perched on a big sandstone boulder to the right of the gate. In a navy blue windbreaker, jeans, and tennis shoes, she sat with her knees drawn up, cigarette in hand. When she saw me, she took one last drag and then scrambled to the ground. The moment she got in the car, I could feel the nervous energy pouring out of her like heat. Her movements were agitated and her eyes were too bright. "What'd you do to your hair?" she asked.

"Got it cut."

"It looks good."

"Thanks." I put the car in reverse and did a three-point turn.

She craned her neck and looked back at the gate. "I just hope she's gone by the time I get back. I couldn't believe she showed up like that unannounced."

"How do you know she didn't call him in advance?"

"That's even worse. If he agreed to see her, he's crazier than I am."

"Hey, take a deep breath and get a grip. You're all over the place."

"Sorry. I feel like there's someone inside trying to crawl out through my skin. I wish I had a guy. I'd rather have a drink, but getting laid would help."

"Call your sponsor. Isn't that what they're for?"

"I haven't found one yet."

"Then call Priscilla Holloway."

"I'm fine. Don't worry about it. I've got you," she said, and laughed.

"Yeah, right. This is way beyond me."

"Well, me too, you know? I'm just trying to muddle through the same as anybody else." She was quiet for a moment, staring out the window. "Fuck it. Never mind. I can tough it out on my own."

"As you've so amply demonstrated in the past," I said.

"Well, you're so smart, what do you suggest?"

"Find a meeting."

"Where?"

"How do I know? We'll go to my place and check the yellow pages. There's bound to be a listing for AA."

Once we reached my apartment, it took less than a minute to look up the number and make the requisite phone call. As it turned out, the closest meeting was at the city recreation center four blocks away. I drove her myself, not trusting her to make it on her own.

"I'll be back to pick you up in an hour," I said, as she got out of the car. The slamming of the door was as much as I received in the way of a reply. I made a point of waiting until I saw her walk in the door and then I waited another minute in case she intended to sneak out again. I could see how an alcoholic's family became ensnared in the game. I was already battling an urge to monitor her every move. That, or wash my hands of her altogether and be done with it. If I hadn't been intent on keeping her under wraps until she met with Vince, I might have cut her loose.

To kill time, I circled back to my neighborhood and parked outside of Rosie's. And yes, I recognized the irony of waiting for Reba in a bar while she struggled with the urge to have a drink. Lewis was there tending bar by himself, an apron tied around his waist. Two day-drinkers had taken up residence at the far end of the room. The color television mounted in the corner was tuned to a golf tournament being played someplace green. Rosie must have been back in the kitchen doing dinner prep because the place smelled like sautéed onions. She was also doing something with fried kidneys I didn't want to know about.

I perched on a bar stool and ordered a Coke. I honestly might have minded my own business, if Lewis hadn't seemed so chipper and oblivious. He gave no indication that he regretted, or even recognized, the trouble he'd caused.

He set my Coke on the bar, saying, "Where's Henry? I haven't seen him the last couple of days."

I studied him. "You really don't know."

"What? Is something wrong with him?"

I debated for half a second and then said, "Look, I know this is none of my business, but I think William was out of line when he talked you into flying out. Henry and Mattie were doing fine until you showed up."

Lewis blinked at me as though I were speaking in tongues. "I don't understand."

"You didn't have to barge in on breakfast and ask her for a date."

"I didn't ask her for a date. I suggested an art exhibit and a bite of lunch."

"Out here, we call that a date. Henry was upset and rightly so," I said.

Lewis seemed bewildered. "He was upset with *me?*"

"Sure he was. She was supposed to be spending time with him."

"Why didn't he speak up?"

"How could he? You called him a little old lady, in front of Mattie, no less. He was mortified. He couldn't speak up without looking even more foolish than he already felt."

"But that was just good-natured jostling. It was a joke."

"It's not a joke when you hustle in and try to beat him to the punch. Life's complicated enough."

"But we've always competed for the ladies. It's all in good fun. Neither of us takes it seriously. For heaven's sake, ask William if you doubt my word."

"He's never going to cop to it. He set the whole thing up. He had no business meddling, but what you did was worse. You knew Henry was interested in her."

"Of course he is and I am, too. That was obvious on the

cruise. I made my pitch and he made his. If he can't handle the challenge, why complain to me?"

"Mattie broke it off. She said she didn't want to see him again."

Disconcerted, Lewis said, "Oh. Well, I'm sorry to hear that, but it's got nothing to do with me."

"Yes, it does. You flew out to California and got right in the middle of something that was none of your concern. There's nothing 'good-natured' about that. You were being hostile."

"No, no. Not a bit of it. I can't believe you're saying this. I'd cut off my right arm before I'd do such a thing."

"But you did do it, Lewis."

"You're completely wrong. That wasn't my intention. Henry's always been my favorite. He knows I'm crazy about him."

"Then you better find a way to make amends," I said.

It was close to 8:00 when Reba emerged from her AA meeting and headed toward my car. It was still light out. A massive fog bank hovered on the horizon and the breezes coming off the ocean laid a chill in the air. "Feel better?"

"Not especially, but I'm glad I went."

"You still want to have dinner?"

"Shit, we have to go back to the house. I forgot the photographs."

"Why do you need those?"

"Visual aids," she said. "There's a guy I want you to meet. He has dinner the same place every Friday night at nine. I did some reconnoitering this morning just to satisfy a hunch. We'll make a run up to Pop's for the pix, have a heart-to-heart with my pal, and then take some time to explore."

"Isn't a nine o'clock dinner kind of late?"

"I hope so. Prison, you eat at five in the afternoon. Talk about depressing. Makes you feel like a kid." She turned in her seat. "Why're you going this way? You should have taken a right back there."

"Actually, we don't need to go to your house. I have a set of pictures at my office. Cheney gave 'em to me." I wondered if she'd question my having copies of the photos, but she was sidetracked by something else and gave me a speculative look.

I said, "What."

"I notice you're dropping Cheney's name every chance you get. Is that where you got that?" She pointed.

"Got what?"

"That hickey on your neck."

I put a hand against my neck self-consciously and she laughed. "Just teasing," she said.

"Very funny."

"Well, I'd like to think you have a sex life."

"I'd like to think my sex life is private," I said. "So who's this guy you're so hot for me to meet?"

"Marty Blumberg. Beck's company comptroller."

18

I drove over to my office. I left Reba in the car, the VW idling, while I ran in and grabbed the manila envelope from my desk drawer. In the car again, I passed her the envelope and watched her out of the corner of my eye as I circled the block and headed for Passages. She removed the photographs and studied them as though viewing vermin through a microscope. She put them back in the envelope without a word, her expression impossible to read.

I found what was possibly the last space in the underground parking garage, which stretched like a low-ceilinged gray cavern that ran the length of the mall. We hiked to the escalator and went up to level one, where all the shops were located. Manila envelope in hand, Reba walked two paces ahead of me, forcing me to trot to keep up with her. She didn't seem as hyper as she had been, and for that I was glad. "Where are we going?"

"Dale's."

"Why Dale's? That's a dive."

"Not true. It's a Santa Teresa landmark."

"So's the dump," I said.

Dale's was strictly a no-frills bar. People went there to drink, pure and simple. I could feel the now familiar conflict arise: should I be protective and suggest we go somewhere else, òr keep my mouth shut and let her take responsibility for the choices she made? In this instance, self-interest prevailed. I wanted to meet Marty Blumberg.

We entered the place, pausing in the open doorway to get our bearings. I hadn't been in Dale's for years, but it looked much the same—narrow room with a bar running along the left and a jukebox in back. There were six or eight small tables jammed up against the wall on the right. The lighting was primarily of the neon beer-sign variety, blue and red. There were numerous patrons on hand, occupying half of the bar stools and most of the tables. Eighty-seven percent of those present were smoking, the air as gray as morning fog. The overhead fixture made the light seem flat, very close to the quality of waning daylight outside. The jukebox, I remembered, was stocked with old 45-rpm records. At that very moment, the Hilltoppers were crooning "P.S. I Love You" while a couple danced on a narrow expanse of floor by the unisex bathroom. The sawdust underfoot and the acoustical ceiling tiles muffled the noise level so that both music and conversation seemed to be taking place in another room.

The walls were lined with black-and-white photographs, taken in the forties, to judge by the ladies' hairstyles and clothing. Each photo featured the same balding middle-aged man, perhaps the eponymous Dale. He had his arm slung around various minor sports figures— baseball players, professional wrestlers, and Roller Derby queens—their signatures scrawled across the bottoms of the pictures.

At the far end of the room, a concession-sized machine produced a steady spill of popcorn that the bartender scooped into paper cups and set out for general consumption. At intervals along the bar, there were collections of assorted popcorn seasonings: garlic salt, lemon pepper, Cajun spices, curry powder, and Parmesan cheese in a green cardboard container. The popcorn wasn't sufficient to keep patrons sober, but it gave them something to fiddle with between the downing of drinks. As we were taking our seats, a peevish argument flared up, the topic being politics, about which no one present seemed to have the faintest clue.

"So where is he?" I said, looking around the room.

"What's your hurry? He'll be here in a bit."

"I thought we were having dinner. I didn't know they served food in here."

"Well, they do. Seven-way chili." She started ticking off the choices on her fingers. "Macaroni, chopped onions, cheese, oyster crackers, sour cream, or cilantro in any combination."

"That's only six."

"You can have it *plain*."

"Oh."

The next 45 selection came into play and Jerry Vale launched into his version of "It's All in the Game": *"Many a tear has to fall . . ."* I refused to think about Cheney lest I jinx the relationship.

A waitress appeared. Reba asked for iced tea and I ordered a beer. I'd have ordered iced tea myself, but only to demonstrate a virtue I didn't actually possess. In the face of her sobriety, I was acutely conscious of every sip I took. I was also worried the minute I turned my head, she'd snatch up my beer and suck half of it down.

As there was nothing else on the menu, we ordered seven-way chili, electing all six options. The chili arrived hot, spicy, and rich. The recipe, I noticed, was printed on our paper place mats. I was tempted to snitch mine, but the note at the bottom said "Serves 40," which seemed excessive for someone who usually eats alone standing over the sink. "You never finished telling me about Passages and Beck's participation," I said.

"Glad you asked. I didn't think you'd pursue the subject."

"Here I am," I said. "Care to fill me in?"

She paused to light a cigarette. "It's simple enough. A developer in Dallas bought the land in 1969 and submitted all the plans. He thought it'd be a cakewalk. The guy was so optimistic, he was already putting up signs: 'Passages Shopping Plaza. Coming in the fall of 1973.' The city planners had a ball, running him ragged with all the codes and requirements. He revised the plans sixteen times, but nothing ever seemed to suit. Twelve years later, when the developer still hadn't managed to get approval, he put the word out on the street and someone introduced him to Beck. That was 1981. The project was finished in '85, a speedy three years after construction began."

I waited for the rest.

"I can tell by the look on your face you're not getting it," she said.

"Just tell me, okay? Guessing slows us down and makes me cranky."

"Well, think about it. How do you think Beck got all those approvals and permits? Because he's nice?"

I stared, feeling dense.

Reba rubbed her thumb against her fingers in the universal gesture denoting money changing hands.

"Payoffs?"

"Exactly. That's where the money went—the three hundred and fifty thou I was accused of snitching. I delivered most of it myself, though I didn't realize what it was until later. All I knew was he had me driving to hell and gone with these bulky manila envelopes. Granted, some of it was earmarked for the boys in Sacramento— Beck is forever greasing palms on behalf of pending legislation—but most was for local guys who had the power to say no. Once they pocketed the dough, they were more than happy to be of help."

"But that's political money laundering."

"Wow, you are *quick*," she said, rolling her eyes. "Isn't that why you're setting up this meeting with the feds, to get the goods on him?"

"I wasn't sure how far you meant to go."

"Right to the bitter end."

"But when we first talked, didn't you say he was depositing the money offshore so he could hide it from his wife?"

"That's the story he gave me. I didn't figure out what he was really doing until the audit came up. I'm sure he's still funneling cash out of the country as fast as he can, but at least I get it now; his efforts were never meant to benefit me."

"I'm sorry. I know that's tough on you."

"Tough, but true," she said, her tone matter-of-fact.

At 9:00, just about on the dot, Marty Blumberg appeared.

Reba had been watching for him, and she gave him a big wave and motioned him over the minute he walked in. He paused at the bar to light a cigarette. The bartender was already setting up his usual drink, whiskey so dark it looked like Coke. Glass in hand, he ambled over to our table. He was probably in his fifties, a good-looking guy once upon a time. Now he was overweight by a good hundred pounds, his wardrobe lagging one size behind. His trouser pockets bulged open like a set of ears and the buttons on his shirt were straining against his bulk. He was baby-faced and florid, with sorrowful-looking blue eyes, a pug nose, and a full head of dark frizzy hair. He seemed genuinely glad to see her. Reba invited him to join us, hooking a thumb in my direction by way of introduction. "This is Kinsey Millhone. Marty Blumberg," she said.

I said, "Hi, Marty. Nice to meet you," and the two of us shook hands.

Marty gave Reba a quick visual appraisal. "You're none the worse for wear. When'd you get back?"

"Monday. Kinsey drove down and brought me back. The whole experience was an education . . . in what, I don't know."

"I'll bet."

"I hear you're in the new offices. Nice to be so close. Dale's was always your favorite."

Marty smiled. "I've only been coming in the past fourteen years. I could be part owner with all the money I've spent."

Reba took out a cigarette and Marty picked up her Dunhill and extended a light. Reba tucked a strand of hair behind one ear as she bent to the flame, her hand resting casually on his. She inhaled, her eyes closing briefly. Smoking was like prayer, something you approached with reverence. "Beck says the offices are awesome."

"Pretty slick," he said.

"Coming from you, that's high praise. How about a tour? Beck said he'd show me around, but he's in Panama."

"A tour? Sure, why not? Give me a call and we'll set it up."

"How about tonight? As long as we're down here, it would be a hoot."

He hesitated. "I could do that, I guess. I need to pick up my briefcase anyway and clean off my desk."

"You're cleaning your desk on a Friday night? That's devotion."

"Beck's new dictum—no files or papers on any of the surfaces overnight. Place looks like a showroom. I'm mostly playing catch-up, taking care of stuff I've let slide. I'll probably work tomorrow, too."

"The guy's a workaholic," she said to me as an aside and then turned back to him. "Kinsey's a PI . . . a pri-vate de-tec-tive," she said, separating each syllable for emphasis. She turned to me. "You have a business card on you?"

"Let me look," I said. I fumbled in my shoulder bag until I found my wallet, where I kept a stash of cards. Reba had her hand out so I passed one to her and she handed it on to Marty, who studied it, pretending it mattered when he couldn't have cared less.

He tucked it in his shirt pocket. "Guess I better watch my backside."

Reba smiled. "That is so so true. You have no idea."

He shook a cigarette from the pack, placing it directly

between his lips. Smoking didn't seem like a good idea as he was already wheezing.

Reba said, "Allow me," as she picked up her Dunhill, flicked it, and offered him a light.

"Such service."

"You bet. Tit for tat," she said. She propped her chin on one hand. "Aren't you curious what she's doing here?"

Marty looked from Reba to me. "A drug bust?"

"Don't be dumb," she said, giving him a smack on the arm. She leaned forward flirtatiously and murmured, "She's part of a task force—federal and local dicks—looking into Beck's finances. All very hush-hush. Promise you won't tell." She put a finger to her lips and I could feel myself blanch. I couldn't believe she'd laid it out like that, without a word to me. Not that I'd have agreed. I checked his reaction.

His smile was tentative as he waited for the punch line. "No, seriously."

"Seriously," she said. I could see she enjoyed doling it out to him bit by bit.

"I don't get it."

"What's to get? I'm telling you the truth."

"Why tell me?"

"Fair warning. I like you. You're right in the line of fire."

He must have been one of those men who operated with his body thermostat cranked up into the red zone because his face now bore a sheen of perspiration. Without seeming to be aware of it, he took the flap of his tie and blotted the beads of sweat from his cheek. "What do you mean, I'm right in the line of fire? How do you figure that?"

"Well, A: You know what he's been up to, and B: Beck

won't go down for this any more than he'd accept blame for the missing three hundred and fifty thou."

"I thought you volunteered."

"Stupnagel that I am, I made it easy for him. I'd like to think you're smarter than me, but maybe not."

"He can't do anything to me. I'm covered."

"You really think so? All he has to do is point. You've got your fingerprints on everything. You're the one who set up the accounts. Same with the offshore banks and the IBC."

"Exactly. I've got leverage on him. I'm the last guy on earth he ought to fuck with."

"I don't know," she said, with skepticism. "You've been with him a long time . . ."

"Ten years."

"Right. Which means you know a lot more than I do."

"So?"

"So if he stuck it to me, he can stick it to you as well. Believe me, the trap's there. You just can't see it at this point any more than I saw what he was doing to me until it was too late."

"I got no beef with Beck. The guy takes good care of me. Ten years, you know how much money I've managed to sock away? I could retire anytime I want, walk out tomorrow and still be living like a king."

"It may feel cushy, but it's a trap all the same."

Marty was shaking his head. "No. Uhn-uhn. I'm not buying it."

"What if they lean on you?"

"They, who?"

"The feds. What do you think I just got done telling

you. The FBI, IRS, what's the other one?" she asked me, snapping her fingers impatiently.

"Department of Justice," I said.

She turned to me and frowned. "I thought you mentioned a couple more."

I cleared my throat. "Customs and Treasury. And the DEA."

"See?" she said to him as though that explained that.

"Why lean on me? Based on what?"

"Based on all the shit they've picked up so far."

"From who?"

"You think they don't have agents in place?"

He laughed, albeit uneasily. "What 'agents'? That's bull."

"Sorry. I misspoke myself. I said 'agents' in the plural. There's really only one."

"Who?"

"See if you can guess. Here, I'll give you a hint. Who in the company has gotten close to Beck in the last umpty-many months? Hmmm." She put a finger against her cheek, deep in mock thought. "Starts with O."

"Onni?"

"There you go," she said. "Talk about a break. I get sent to prison and that gives her the chance to slide right in."

"She works for the feds?"

Reba nodded. "Oh yeah, for *years*, and trust me, Little Miss Onni wants his ass on a plate."

"I don't believe it."

"Marty, this is her golden opportunity. You know how it is with women in these shit government jobs. Sure, they get hired. The guys let 'em do all the grunt work, but forget about promotion. There's no upward mobility without a coup of some kind. She doesn't pull this off, she'll be stuck where she is."

"Doesn't sound right. Are you sure? This makes no sense at all. The girl's dumb as a post."

"That's the *impression* she gives, but she's wily as they come. I'm telling you, she's good. You watch. This lady can write her own ticket, provided she nails Beck first. I mean, look at it this way. Does anybody in the company suspect? You sure as shit didn't and Beck doesn't have a clue. If he knew what was going on, he'd be out the door like a shot. Wouldn't he?"

"Well, yeah."

"You better believe it," she said. "Meanwhile, there she is with a finger in every pie, access to everything. What a sweet deal for her."

Marty seemed to be getting annoyed, though I noticed two blotches on the front of his shirt where the sweat was soaking through. "Look, Reb. I know you're pissed at him and I don't blame you—"

"Sure, I'm pissed at him, but I'm not pissed at you, which is why I'm here. I'm trusting you to keep your mouth shut. I haven't breathed a word of this to anyone else. She's after his balls. She's so gung-ho she's willing to screw the guy to get the drop on him."

Marty was silent. I could hear him breathing as though he'd just finished running six blocks. "You can't just make claims—"

"I know. You're a man of common sense and you're hard to convince, which is why I brought these." She slid the black-and-white photos from the envelope and passed them over to him.

Marty leafed through them. "Jesus."

"See what I mean?"

"What's he *thinking?*"

"He's not thinking. He's got his brain between his legs. Really, you hadn't guessed he was screwing her? You knew he was doing me."

"Yeah, but you made no secret you had the hots for him. This, I don't know. Shouldn't somebody tell him what's going on?"

Reba raised her brows and gave him the big eyes. "You want to do that? Because I sure as hell don't."

"Poor guy."

"'Poor guy,' my butt. Are you kidding? If he was willing to work me over, why not you? Thing is, the stakes are bigger this time. You tell him about Onni, the only effect is giving him more time to cover his tracks."

Marty held up his glass and rattled the ice. The bartender caught the gesture and began to make him another drink. "Onni. I can't believe it. Beck must have walked right into it."

"Of course. Minute she makes her move, he'll turn right around and lay it off on you. He'll claim you acted on your own. He never authorized you to do anything. You took it on yourself."

"But it's his signature. Loan aps, incorporation papers—"

"Marty, get *serious.* He'll say he's never had a head for the financial end of things. That's how I was able to get away with the money I stole. Gosh. Guess he should have wised up, but some guys never learn. You told him to sign so he signed. He trusted you and this is what he gets for it. Shamey-shame on him. Meanwhile, you're under federal indictment."

Marty shook his head. "I don't know. This is freaking me out." The bartender brought his drink. Marty took out his wallet and extracted two twenties. "Keep that," he said. As the bartender left, he was well on his way to draining his glass.

During the brief interchange between the two, Reba shot me a look. It's your show, I thought, before she glanced away.

She patted Marty's arm, her tone brisk. "Anyway, ponder the implications. That's really all I ask. Even if you decide I'm making it up, it wouldn't hurt to cover your ass. Once the subpoenas are issued and all the warrants are in place, you'll be shit out of luck. In the meantime, if you're on your way upstairs, how about the two of us tagging along?"

19

I'd passed the entrance to Beck's office building half a dozen times without ever taking in the sight. The façade was thickly overgrown with ivy, integrated seamlessly into the architectural conceit of an ancient Spanish town. Flowering trees had been planted along the front. To the left of the entrance were side-by-side stairs and escalators, giving access to the additional parking structure at the corner of the mall. A high-end luggage shop occupied a portion of the ground floor, presumably paying Beck a big whack of high-end rent.

We pushed through glass doors that swung closed soundlessly as we entered. Windows stretched upward the full four stories to a slanting glass roof. The interior atrium was oblong, done in a mottled rosy granite, floors and walls forming a hard canvas on which natural and artificial light played according to the time of day. High on the wall, there was a clock with long brass minute and hour hands and six-inch-diameter brass dots representing the hours. A curtain of dark green ivy and philodendron hung from a miniature oasis above the clock.

There were two elevators on the wall dead ahead. To the right of these, in an alcove, there were two more elevators, facing each other, one with a much wider door, which I assumed was designed to accommodate freight. A digital readout next to each elevator showed that all were at lobby level.

In the center of the lobby, a perfect circle of granite was sunk in the floor, sloping sides washed with a constant Niagara of water spilling from a six-inch channel around its rim. The sound was soothing, but the look, I fear, was closer to toiletlike than the restful pool it was meant to suggest.

A uniformed guard sat at a high polished-onyx desk. A lean man in his sixties, he had salt-and-pepper hair and a blank handsome face. Briefly I wondered what curious set of circumstances had landed him here. Surely there was little to guard and less to secure. Did he simply sit for the whole of his eight-hour shift? I saw no indication he had a book in his lap discreetly shielded from view. No radio or pint-size television set. No sketch pad or crossword puzzle book. His eyes tracked us, his face turning slowly as we clattered across the cold expanse of polished granite floor.

Marty lifted his hand and received an unblinking stare in response. Reba smiled at the guy, giving him the full benefit of those big dark eyes of hers. She was rewarded with a tentative smile. She caught up with Marty outside the elevator doors. "What's *his* name? He's cute."

"Willard. He's on nights and weekends. Can't remember who's been covering days."

We entered the elevator and Marty pushed the button for four. "You made a conquest. First time I've ever seen him smile," he said.

"Getting along with guards turns out to be a specialty of mine," she said. "Although, in my case, 'correctional officer' is the appropriate term."

Since Beck's offices took up the entire fourth floor, the elevator doors opened directly into the reception area, hushed with thick pale green carpet. Lights blazed everywhere, but it was clear there was no one on the premises but us. Modern furniture and contemporary art were mixed with antiques. Etched-glass partitions separated the reception area from an airy conference room beyond. From our perspective, corridors opened on four sides like the spokes of a wheel. The hallways appeared to stretch on at length with wide bands of color forming sweeping loops along the wall.

"Oh, Marty. This is gorgeous. Beck said it was spectacular, but this is really over the top. Mind if we look around?"

"Just don't take long. I want to get home."

"I promise we'll make it quick. Think of it this way, if it weren't for that stint in prison, I'd be working here myself. Isn't there a roof garden?"

"The stairs are back that way. You can't miss 'em. I'll be in my office down that hall."

"You could get lost in this place," Reba said.

"Well, don't. Beck's not going to like it if he hears you've been here."

"Mum's the word," she said, producing her dimples for him.

Reba circled the reception area with me following in

her wake. As long as Marty was present, she was almost childlike in her hand-clapping enthusiasm, popping her head into offices here and there along the way, oohing and aahing. He watched us briefly and then went off in the opposite direction.

The minute he was out of sight, Reba dropped all pretense of touring and got down to business. I kept pace with her as she checked the names posted on the wall outside each office. When she reached Onni's, she shot a look down the hall to make sure Marty wasn't there. She moved to Onni's desk, grabbed a tissue from the box, and used it as she started opening drawers. "Keep a lookout, okay?"

I checked the corridor behind me. Searching is my all-time favorite sport (except for time spent with Cheney Phillips of late). The edgy thrill of invading someone's private space is heightened by the possibility of getting caught in the act. I wasn't sure what she was looking for or I'd have joined her in the game. As it was, somebody had to stand guard.

Still opening and shutting drawers, Reba said, "God, I can't believe Marty's so paranoid. Must be off his meds. Ah." She held up a chunky ring of keys that she jingled midair.

"You can't take those."

"Poo. Onni won't be in until Monday. I can put 'em back by then."

"Reba, don't. You're going to ruin everything."

"No, I won't. This is scientific research. I'm testing my hypothesis."

"What hypothesis?"

"I'll tell you later. Quit worrying."

She left Onni's office, trailing a hand along the wall as she returned to the reception area, scanning the lines of the ceiling. When she reached the elevators, she circled the central core, measuring with her eyes. Large abstract paintings dominated the walls and the lighting was such that one's attention was irresistibly drawn from one artwork to the next.

"It would help if I knew what you were looking for," I said.

"I know how his mind works. There's something here he doesn't want us to see. Let's try his office."

I wanted to protest but knew she wasn't listening.

Beck's corner location was prime—spacious, with clear cherry paneling and the same footstep-muffling green carpeting. The room was furnished with low-slung chrome-and-leather chairs of the sort that require winch and pulley action to remove yourself once you've been foolish enough to sit. His desktop was black slate, a curious surface unless he favored doing his long division in chalk along the length. Reba used the same tissue to avoid leaving latent prints on his desk drawers. I loitered uneasily in the doorway.

Dissatisfied, she pivoted. She studied every aspect of the room and finally crossed to the paneled wall, where she tapped her way across, listening for evidence of a hollow space behind. At one point, she activated a touch latch and a door sprang open, but the only treasure revealed was his liquor supply, complete with cut glass decanters and assorted glasses. She said, "Shit." She pushed the door shut and returned to his desk. She sat in his swivel chair and did a second survey from that vantage point.

"Would you hurry up?" I hissed. "Marty could show up any minute, wondering where we went."

She pushed the chair back and leaned down so she could examine the underside of his desk. She extended her hand, almost to the length of her arm. I wasn't sure what she'd discovered and I didn't care to be a witness. I stepped out into the hall and looked toward the reception area. So far no Marty. Idly I noted the fact that the paintings were graduated in size with the largest near the elevators and the smaller ones, in diminishing proportions back here. From the viewpoint of a visitor, the effect would be to create the illusion of corridors much longer than they were—an amusing trompe l'oeil effect.

Reba emerged from Beck's office and grabbed me by the elbow, steering me toward the wide stairs that led up to the roof.

"What's up there besides the roof garden?"

"That's why we're going up—because we don't know," she said. She took the steps two at a time and I kept pace with her. A glass door at the top opened into a fully landscaped garden: trees, shrubs, and flower beds separated by gravel paths that meandered out of sight. Landscape lighting made the whole of it glow. Chairs and umbrella-shaded tables were placed in assorted patios that were dotted throughout. A four-foot wall encircled the perimeter with dazzling city views in all directions.

Central to the garden was what looked like a gardener's cottage, the exterior encompassed by trellises on which gaudy passionflower vines wound up and across, thick with purple blossoms. There was a sign half-concealed in the profusion of greenery. Curious, I pulled the foliage aside.

"What is it?" she asked.

"'Danger. High Voltage.' There's a phone number for the building supervisor if work needs to be done. Must be a transformer or maybe part of the electrical service. Who knows? I guess it could be housing for the elevators, along with central heating and air conditioning. You have to put stuff like that somewhere." The little building seemed to hum in a way that suggested you'd be fried to a crisp if you made one wrong move.

From the stairway, Marty called up to us. "Hey, Reba?"

"Up here."

"I don't mean to rush you, but we ought to get going. Beck doesn't like strangers on the premises."

"I'm hardly a stranger, Marty. I'm his favorite screw."

"Yeah, well, he'll be pissed anyway and take it out on me."

"No problem. We're ready anytime you are," she said, and then to me: "Take your car keys and wallet out of your shoulder bag and leave it behind that thing."

"My bag? I'm not going to leave my shoulder bag. Are you nuts?"

"Do it."

Marty appeared at the top of the stairs, apparently not trusting us to come down the stairs on our own. He leaned against the stair rail, his breathing stertorous from the climb. Reba crossed to the landing and linked her arm into his, turning to admire the mountains visible in the distance. "What a view! Perfect setting for an office party."

Marty took out a handkerchief and wiped his face, which was glistening with perspiration. "We haven't done that so far. Good weather, the gals eat their lunch out here and grab a little sun. Bad days, they use the break room like they did at the old place, only this one's fancier."

"The break room? I didn't see that."

"I can show you on the way out."

Reba turned to me. "Everything okay?"

"Right behind you," I said.

The two started down the stairs. Grousing to myself, I'd done as she'd instructed, removing my keys and wallet from my bag, which I shoved behind a big potted ficus tree. I hoped she knew what she was doing because I sure as shit didn't. Looking back wistfully, I moved toward the stairs.

I caught up with them in what looked like a midsize kitchen. Sink, dishwasher, two microwaves, a side-by-side refrigerator-freezer, and two vending machines, one with soft drinks, the other with candy bars, potato chips, peanut butter crackers, cookies, packages of nuts, and other fatty snacks. There was a large table in the center of the room surrounded by chairs.

"Is this great?" she said.

I said, "Swell."

"You ready?" Marty asked me.

"Sure. I'm fine. It's been fun."

"Good. Let me get my briefcase and I can lock up."

The three of us proceeded down the hall toward the elevators. As Marty passed his office, he ducked out of sight and reappeared with his briefcase. Reba leaned around the door frame. "Nice office. Did you do this yourself?"

"Oh god, no. Beck hired a design firm to handle everything, except the plants. We have another company for those."

"Pretty highfalutin," she remarked.

We watched as Marty pushed the elevator button,

calling the car from down below. While we waited, Reba pointed to a third elevator on the far side of the reception desk. "What's that one for?"

"Service elevator. It's mostly for hauling cartons up and down, file cabinets, furniture, stuff like that. We have fifteen, twenty firms on these three upper floors. That's a lot of office supplies and copy machines. Plus, the cleaning crew uses it when they come in."

"Bart and his brother still work weekends?"

"Fridays, same as ever. They'll be coming in at midnight," he said.

"Nice to know some things don't change. The rest is a major upgrade. Might know Beck would do that as soon as I'm out the door."

The elevator arrived and the doors slid open. Marty reached around and pressed the Door Open button while he entered the alarm system code on the keypad to the right. Reba displayed only cursory interest. Once the three of us got on, Marty released the button and pressed 1 for the first floor. We descended without saying much, all three of us watching the digital floor numbers flash from 4 to 3 to 2 to 1.

As we emerged, the doors to one of the two elevators in the alcove opened and a two-man cleaning crew emerged with their cart and loaded a vacuum cleaner, assorted brooms and mops, industrial-size bottles of cleaning solutions, and packets of paper toweling to resupply the restrooms. Both wore coveralls with a company logo stitched across the back. One gave Willard a nod and he returned a one-finger salute. Reba watched the two men cross the alcove and enter the service elevator.

"What are they up to?"

Marty shrugged. "Beats me. I think they work on two."

The doors closed behind them and the three of us continued to the entrance while Willard made a note of our departure time with the same blank stare he'd given us before. Marty didn't bother to nod his good-byes, but Reba gave Willard a merry finger wave. "Thanks, Willie. Nighty-night."

He hesitated and then lifted a hand.

"Did you see that? True love," she said.

We went down to the lower-level parking garage. At the foot of the stairs, Marty said, "I'm parked over here. Where're you guys?"

"That way," I said, pointing in the opposite direction.

Reba shoved her hands in her jacket pockets and watched him walk toward his car. "Hey, Marty?"

He paused and looked back.

"Think about what I said. You don't act soon, Beck's gonna have your nuts in a vise."

Marty nearly spoke, and then seemed to change his mind. He shook his head, his expression withdrawn, and turned on his heel.

She watched until he was out of sight and then the two of us walked the length of the garage.

"I didn't like the look of those cleaning guys," she said.

"Would you give it a rest?"

"I'm going on record. There's something bogus about them."

"Thanks for telling me. I'll put a note in the file."

When we reached the VW, I unlocked the door on my side, slid behind the wheel, and then leaned over and unlocked the passenger-side door for her. She got in and pulled the door shut, but when I went to insert the key in the ignition, she put her hand out. "Hang on a minute."

"Why?"

"Because we're not done yet. Soon as Marty pulls out, we can have another go."

"You can't go back up there. How're you going to pull that off?"

"We can tell Willie you left your shoulder bag upstairs and you have to have it back."

"Reba! You gotta quit this. You're going to screw up the government's case."

"It's the government that screws up. Look at the state we're in. The country's a mess."

"That's not the point. You can't violate the law."

"Listen to you, Miss Prissy Ass. What law?"

"Shall we start with breaking and entering?"

"That wasn't breaking and entering. We went up with Marty. He let us in of his own free will."

"And then you stole the keys."

"I didn't *steal* them. I borrowed them. I intend to put 'em back."

"It doesn't matter. I'm telling you, I'm through with this," I said. I turned the key in the ignition, shifted gears, and backed out of the space.

"Don't you want your bag?"

"Not now. I'm taking you home."

"Tomorrow morning, then, and I swear that'll be the end of it, okay? I'll pick you up at eight."

"Why so early? It's Saturday. The mall doesn't open until ten."

"We'll be long gone by then."

"Having done what?"

"You'll see."

"Uhn-uhn. No way. You can count me out."

"You don't come with me, I'll do it on my own. No telling what kind of trouble I'll get into."

I would have closed my eyes in despair, but I was already pulling up the exit ramp and didn't want to crash in my haste to get us out of there.

I turned right on Chapel. Out of the corner of my eye, I saw Reba pull something from her jacket pocket, saying, "Well, this is cool."

"What."

"Looks like I stole something after all. Naughty me."

"You didn't."

"Yes, I did. These are Beck's. I found 'em in his desk in that Mickey Mouse secret drawer. Must be planning to skip town, the little so-and-so." She was holding up a passport, a driver's license, and assorted documents.

Abruptly I pulled over to the curb, greatly annoying the driver of the car behind me, who leaned on his horn and made a rude hand gesture. "Give me those," I said, grabbing for them.

She held the documents out of my reach. "Hang on. This is the real deal here. A passport, birth certificate, driver's license, credit cards. 'Garrison Randell' with Beck's photograph. Must have cost a mint."

"Reba, what do you think's going to happen when he realizes that stuff's gone?"

"How's he going to know?"

"How about he looks in his drawer the minute he gets back? That's his means of escape. He probably checks the docs twice a day."

"You're right," she said. "On the other hand, why would he suspect me?"

"He doesn't have to suspect you. All he has to do is figure out who's been in. Once he gets a bead on Marty, it's over. Marty's not going to risk his neck on your account. You'll end up back in the clink."

She thought about that. "Well, okay. I'll put 'em back in his desk when I return Onni's keys."

"Thank you," I said, but I knew I couldn't take her at her word.

I dropped her at her place and rolled into my apartment at 11:15. The red message light was blinking on my answering machine. Cheney, I thought. There was something erotic in the very idea, and like one of Pavlov's dogs, I nearly whimpered in response. I pressed the button and heard his voice. Eight words. "Hey, babe. Call me when you get in."

I punched in his number and when he picked up, I said, "Hey yourself. Did I wake you?"

"I don't mind. Where you been?"

"Out with Reba. I have tons to report."

"Good. Come on over and spend the night," he said. "I'll make you French toast in the morning if you're good."

"Can't. She's picking me up here at eight."

"How come?"

"Long story. I'll tell you when I see you."

"So how about I come get you and take you home in the morning in time to meet her?"

"Cheney, I can handle the drive. You're only two miles away."

"I know, but I don't want you rattling around the streets at this hour. The world's a dangerous place."

I laughed. "Is that how it's going to be? You're all protective and I'm docile as a lamb."

"You have a better idea?"

"No."

"Great. I'll pick you up in ten," he said.

20

I waited for him outside, sitting on the curb, wearing a
black turtleneck T-shirt and one of my new skirts. This
was the third night in a row I'd be seeing him. Like a
winning streak at the craps table, the roll was bound to
come to an end. I couldn't decide if I was being cynical or
sensible in acknowledging the fact. I knew how the night
was going to go. In the first moments of seeing him, I'd
feel neutral—glad to be in his company, but not irresistibly
drawn to him. We'd chat about nothing in particular and
gradually, I'd become aware of him: the smell of his skin,
his face in profile, the shape of his hands as he gripped
the steering wheel. He'd sense my attention and turn to
look at me. The minute we made eye contact, that low
distant humming would start up again, vibrating through
my body like the first rumbles of an earthquake.

Curiously, I didn't feel I was in danger with him. Having
blundered so often in relationships with men, I tended to
be cautious, remote, keeping my options open in case
things didn't work out. Inevitably, things turned sour,

which only served to reinforce my wariness. In retrospect, I could see that Dietz played the game exactly the way I did, which meant I was also safe with him, but for all the wrong reasons: safe because he was always off somewhere, safe because he probably wasn't capable of coming through for me, and safe, most of all, because his detachment was a mirror of my own.

I heard Cheney's car long before he turned the corner from Bay onto Albanil. His headlights flashed into view and I got to my feet, silently cursing the loss of my shoulder bag. I'd been forced to pack—if you want to call it that—a few things in a paper sack, like a kid's brown-bag lunch: clean underwear, a toothbrush, my wallet, and keys. Cheney was driving with the top down again, but when I got in the car I realized the heater was turned on full blast, which meant that half of me would be warm.

He spotted the sack. "That your overnight case?"

I held up the brown bag. "It's part of a matching set. I have another forty-nine just like it in my kitchen drawer."

"Nice skirt."

"Thanks to Reba. I wasn't going to buy it, but she insisted."

"Good deal." He waited until I'd fastened my seat belt and then he pulled away.

I said, "I can't believe we're doing this. Don't you ever sleep?"

"I promised you a house tour. Last time, all you saw was the bedroom ceiling."

I held up a finger. "I have a question."

"What's that?"

"Is this how you ended up married so fast? You meet old What's-Her-Face and spend every night with her for the first three weeks. Week four, she moves in. Week five, you're engaged, and by week six, you're married and off on your honeymoon. Is that the way it went?"

"Not quite, but close. Why, does that bother you?"

"Well, no. I just wondered how much time I had to get the invitations out."

Cheney conducted a tour, starting with the downstairs rooms. The house was more than a hundred years old and reflected a way of life long past. Most of the original mahogany fireplaces, doors, window trim, and baseboards were still intact. Tall, narrow windows, high ceilings, transoms above the doors to aid the circulation of air. There were five working fireplaces on the first floor and four more in the bedrooms upstairs. The parlor (a concept that has since gone the way of the dodo bird) continued into the morning room, which in turn opened onto a gracious screened-in porch. In the adjacent laundry room, the old double tubs existed side-by-side with a wood-fueled stove for heating water.

Cheney was in the process of redoing the living room, where the hardwood floor was covered in canvas drop cloths. Wallpaper had been steamed off and lay in discouraged-looking clumps. The plaster had been patched and the windowpanes had been taped in preparation for painting. He'd taken off one of the doors, which he'd laid across two sawhorses and covered with canvas to provide a surface for any tools not in use. The brass hardware—doorknobs, lock plates, window latches, and pulls—were jumbled into cardboard boxes in one corner of the room.

"How long have you had the house?"

"Little over a year."

Additional drop cloths extended through a set of glass-paned pocket doors into the dining room, which was in marginally better shape. Here the ladder, paint cans, brushes, rollers, paint trays, and liners—not to mention the smell—attested to his having primed and painted, though he hadn't yet replaced the fixtures or the incidental hardware, which littered every sill.

"This the dining room?"

"Right, though the couple who owned the place were using it as a bedroom for her aged mother. They converted the butler's pantry into a makeshift bathroom, so the first thing I did was tear out the toilet, shower, and sink and restore the built-in china cupboards and silverware drawers."

Through the bay of dining room windows, I found myself looking into Neil and Vera's kitchen next door. Cheney's driveway and theirs ran parallel with a modest strip of grass separating the two. I could see Vera standing at the sink, rinsing dishes before she put them in the machine. Neil was perched on a stool at the counter with his back to me, the two chatting as she worked. No sign of the children so they must have been in bed. I seldom witnessed even the briefest moments of a marriage in progress. Occasionally I'd be struck by the sight of one of those couples in restaurants who spend the meal not looking at each other and not exchanging a word. Now that's a scary proposition: all the minor day-to-day frictions with none of the companionship.

Cheney put his arms around me from behind and laid

his face against my hair, following my gaze. "One of the few happy couples I know."

"Or so it would appear."

He kissed my ear. "Don't be a cynic."

"I *am* a cynic. So are you."

"Yes, but we both have a streak of optimism way down deep."

"Speak for yourself," I said. "Where's the kitchen?"

"Through here."

The previous owners had done extensive remodeling in the kitchen, which was now a streamlined vision of granite counters, stainless-steel appliances, and high-tech lighting. Far from detracting from the overall Victorian feel of the house, there was a wonderful sense of hope and efficiency at work. I was exploring a walk-in pantry the size of my loft when the telephone rang. Cheney caught the call and his end of it was brief. He replaced the handset on the wall-mounted phone. "That was Jonah. There's been a shoot-out in a parking garage on Floresta. One of my hookers got caught in the crossfire. I said I'd drop you at your place and meet him at the scene."

"Sure thing," I said, thinking, *Great . . . now that Jonah knows we're an item, the entire STPD will be informed by midday tomorrow.* Men are worse gossips than women when it comes right down to it.

_____

I crawled into bed at midnight and found myself tossing and turning, possibly because of the lengthy nap I'd taken in the afternoon. I don't remember the moment when I sank into a leaden sleep, but vaguely, I became aware of a pounding on my door. I opened my eyes and checked the clock. 8:02. Who the heck was it? Oh, shit. Reba was down there.

I pushed the covers back and swung my feet out on the floor, yelling, "Just a minute!" . . . like she could actually hear me. I dry-washed my face, pressing my fingers into my eyes until light sparks appeared on the insides of my lids. I went downstairs and let her in, saying, "Sorry, sorry, sorry. I overslept. I'll be with you in a sec."

I left her to make herself at home while I went upstairs, though in the interest of good manners, I leaned over the loft rail and called down to her. "You can put on a pot of coffee if you can figure out how."

"Don't worry about it. We can stop off at McDonald's."

"You got a deal."

I did an abbreviated bathroom tour and then pulled on jeans, a T-shirt, and tennis shoes. I retrieved my wallet and car keys from the brown-paper bag and in six minutes flat, I was ready to go out the door.

We ordered from the take-out window and then sat in the parking lot with two enormous coffees and four Egg Mc-Muffins with extra packets of salt. Like me, Reba ate like she was competing for the land speed record. "They don't call this fast food for nuttin'," she remarked, her mouth full. There were a scant few minutes when we sank into quiet, focused on our food.

Having finished, we bundled up our trash and shoved it

in the bag, which Reba pitched into the container on the sidewalk nearby. She said, "Two points. Hot damn."

While I sipped my coffee, she reached over to the rear seat and picked up three rolled cylinders of architectural plans, bound with a rubber band. She slipped the band on her wrist for safekeeping, then unfurled the first oversize sheet, which she spread across the dashboard. The paper itself was a whitish blue, with the two-dimensional rooms laid out in blue ink. The legend along the bottom read: THE BECKWITH BUILDING, 3-25-81.

Reba said, "These are the old blue-line drawings. I'm hoping they'll tell us what Beck's hiding and where he's hiding it."

"Where'd you get these?"

"We had multiples at the office—everything from framing plans to plumbing plans, heating and air conditioning, fixture requirements, you name it. Every time the architect made changes, he'd print out a new set of drawings for all the principals. Beck told me to toss 'em."

"And you had the foresight to hang on to them? I'm impressed."

"I wouldn't call it foresight. I just love the information. It's like looking at X-rays—all those cracks and bone spurs where you least expect them. Here, take a look at these and we'll compare notes. I realized last night we were going about this all wrong."

She passed me the second batch of drawings on sheets of paper that must have measured eighteen inches by twenty-four. I wrestled the first sheet into a reasonably flat position and studied the particulars. As nearly as I could tell, this had something to do with the service entrance and electrical rooms, showing the location of the meter, the transformer vault, the switchgear, electrical closets, and individual circuits. The wiring diagrams were made up of circles and wavy lines, showing the relationship of outlets to controls.

The next sheet was more interesting. It looked like a cutaway of one corner of the building from the rooftop down. According to the legend at the bottom of the page, every eighth of an inch represented one linear foot. The architect had labeled every aspect of the drawing in that freehand block lettering students must be taught the very first day at architectural school. Reba glanced over, saying, "What they're using there for stablization is a rigid core that runs down the center of the building—a structural tower that contains the restrooms, stairs, and elevators. I remember them talking about diagonal bracing and shear panels, whatever that means."

I could see the concrete columns, the location of precast concrete spandrel panels, the slab on grade and concrete pile foundation, which was backed up by a steel-stud and drywall assembly. I was hoping to spot the correlation between the lines on the page and the spaces I'd seen. The detailed drawing of the rooftop, for instance, did show the mechanicals of the elevator equipment in roughly the same position as the fakey-looking gardener's cottage. Reba put a finger on the page. "I don't like it. That other drawing shows the elevators on the far side, not this. So which is it?"

"Maybe we should take another look," I said. "I don't get how anybody figures this shit out. I wouldn't know where to begin."

Reba unfurled another floor plan, this one dated August of '81. We studied a couple of the drawings next to one another. Having seen the offices firsthand, I had a fair idea what I was looking at, with certain notable exceptions. Where the employee break room was located in reality, the floor plan indicated a conference room, which had been moved closer to reception. "How many sets do you have?"

"Tons, but these seemed the most relevant. From March to August, there's not that much difference. It's the changes that show up in October that looked interesting to me." She wrestled a fourth sheet open and placed it atop the third. Much crackling of paper as the two of us examined the specifics of employee restrooms, wheelchair clearances, metal decks, and rigid insulation—the whole of Beck's fifteen-office suite visible in one sweep.

"Are we looking for anything in particular?" I asked.

She pointed to an oblong area on my sheet adjacent to fire stairs and the elevator envelopes. "See that? The location of the elevators shifted from there to there," she said, moving her finger from my drawing to hers.

"Break room moved, too, but so what?"

"Well, look at it. I mean, I understand they made changes, but there's space unaccounted for. Here it's called storage, but in this drawing, the space is still there with no reference to it at all."

"I still don't see the significance."

"I just think it's odd. I'm telling you, there was a room there on one of the early floor plans. I asked Beck what it was and he blew me off, like I didn't need to know. On the initial blue-line drawings, the architect labeled it a gun vault, which is totally ridiculous. Beck's a pussy about firearms. He doesn't even own one gun, let alone a collection of the damn things. At the time, I figured maybe it was a panic room or whatever you call them . . ."

"A safe room?"

"Like that. Something he didn't want anyone else to know about. Later I wondered if he intended to use it as a love nest, a hidey-hole where he could take his lady friends. I mean, what could be better? In the same building but out of the public eye. Think how easy it'd be to get a little ass on the side."

"Maybe the architect vetoed the idea."

"Nobody vetoes him. He knows exactly what he wants and he gets it." She laid a finger on an unmarked area just off reception. "Couldn't there be space behind this wall?"

I went back in my mind and pictured the gallery of paintings and the trompe l'oeil effect created by the diminishing sizes of objects as the eye traced them down the hall. I looked back at the floor plan. "I don't think so. If there's a room there, how the heck do you get in? There aren't any doors in that wall that I remember."

"My recollection, too. Because I counted off five offices and Onni's was in the middle. After Jude's office—you know the one with all the black-and-white photographs?"

"Right, right."

"Yeah, well, the gallery picked up from there and that wall had to be a good twenty-five feet long."

"What about that room where they kept office supplies?"

"That's right there. I went around this part twice and there weren't any doors there either, so if it's a room, it's been sealed."

"Maybe it's something to do with the building infrastructure. All the nuts-and-bolts stuff. Don't you have plans any later than this?"

Reba shook her head. "I was in prison by then."

We were both silent for a moment. Then I said, "Too bad we don't have plans for the offices below his. You're just assuming that's a room, but it could be a mechanical chase or something that goes all the way down."

She curled the plans together and made a cylinder of them, replacing the rubber band. She tossed them into the backseat and turned the key in the ignition. "Only one way to find out."

Reba drove around the block, slowly circling Passages Shopping Plaza, peering across me through the passenger-side window as she scanned the exterior. On the south side of the mall she pulled over to the curb, her attention taken up by an entrance marked "Deliveries." A steep ramp led down into the shadows and out of sight.

"Hang on. I gotta see this," she said. She killed the engine and got out on her side of the car while I got out on mine. We walked down the ramp, which descended two levels to what must have been a subbasement. At the foot of the ramp was a portcullis secured with a big handsome padlock. Through the grillwork, we could see ten parking spaces, a blank double door at the end of a cul-de-sac, and a single metal door to the right. I said, "You think this is the only way in?"

"Can't be. When merchandise is delivered, there has to be some way to distribute goods to the individual stores."

We retraced our steps, huffing and puffing slightly as

we made the climb. When we reached the sidewalk, she backed up a few steps, her gaze tracking the length of the building. At street level, along this aspect of the fortress-like structure, there were no shop windows and no access to retail establishments. "Second ramp just like this down the block," she remarked. "Oh, wait a minute. I got it. Let's just see if I'm correct."

I looked at her. "Are you going to tell me or not?"

"If I'm right, of course. If I'm wrong, you don't need to know."

"You're very tedious."

She smiled, unfazed.

We returned to the car. She started the engine and glanced over her left shoulder to check for oncoming cars. She pulled out and continued her circuit of the mall, passing the twin of the entrance we'd just seen. She turned right at the corner and headed north on Chapel.

At Passages there was no charge for parking on week-ends, probably to encourage spending. The gate to the underground parking lot was up. Reba turned in and eased her car down the ramp. At the bottom she hung a right and drove the length of the garage, parking in a space near the darkened glass doors that marked the lower-level entrance to Macy's. The store at this hour was still closed and wouldn't open until 10:00.

Reba pointed. Ten car lengths to our right there was a nondescript door marked "Service. No Admittance." Beyond that, the ramp for second-, third-, and fourth-level parking spiraled up and out of sight.

"Won't that be locked?" I asked, feeling that queasy sense of excitement at the notion of going where we weren't supposed to be.

"For sure. I told you I did some reconnoitering before, but I couldn't get in. Now I have these." She held up the chunky ring of keys she'd snitched from Onni's desk. She sorted through the keys one by one, smiling at the sight. "My, oh my. I'm sorry for every mean thing I ever said about the girl. Catch this."

Onni, Little Miss Compulsive, had labeled every key with a strip of neatly embossed tape: OFFICE, BECK'S, CNFRCE ROOM, SRVICE COR, WRHSE, S.ELE., S.DEPOSIT MID-CITY, S. DEPOSIT, ST SV'GS & LO. Reba pinched the two safe-deposit keys together and jangled the rest. "Bet these contain a shitload of information. Safe-deposit box is where Beck keeps his second set of books."

"A second set? That's not smart."

"Not real books. The information's all on disks. He's over there every couple of days, dropping off the updates. What's he going to do? He's a businessman. Even if what he's doing is illegal, he still has to keep records. You think he doesn't have to provide a full accounting to Salustio?"

"Sure, but it still seems risky."

"Beck adores taking risks. He's addicted to the rush."

"I can relate to that."

Reba continued to finger the safe-deposit keys. "Wonder if there's any way to get into these boxes . . ."

"Reba . . ."

"I didn't say I'd *do* it. He changed banks the minute I went to prison, so I wouldn't be a signatory in any event. It's probably Marty now."

"Swear you're going to put those back."

"I told you I would. As soon as I've made dupes."

"Goddamn it, Reba. Are you totally out of your mind?"

"Pretty much." She glanced back over her shoulder at

the vast empty garage. "We better get going before some-one else shows up."

We got out of the car and walked to the service door, our footsteps echoing against the bare concrete walls. Reba tried the knob, locked as anticipated, and then used the key Onni had so thoughtfully designated. The door opened into a stairwell. We walked down a flight and discovered two additional doors about ten feet apart. Reba said, "The lady or the tiger? You pick."

I pointed to the left. She shrugged and handed me the keys. I had to do a bit of experimenting to find the right one. Onni's paucity of imagination had resulted in her labeling some of the keys numerically. I tried three before I came to the one that worked. I unlocked the door and opened it. We found ourselves in the same ten-parking-space cul-de-sac we'd seen from the street.

Reba said, "Aha!"

We closed the first door and moved to the second. "Your turn," I said. "I'd go for the key marked number four."

"No sweat. I already know what's behind this one." She eased the key into the lock, turned it, and pushed the door open. We stood looking into a long windowless corridor. Flats of fluorescent lights affixed to the ceiling lent a bluish cast to the air. At regular intervals, oversize metal doors on either side of the hall opened into the shipping and receiving departments of the various shops along the mall, some of which fronted on Chapel Street and some on the mall's interior esplanade. Signs above the doors indicated the respective retailers: the luggage shop, a children's clothing store, an Italian pottery outlet, the jewelry store, and so on down the line.

I studied the layout. There was no sign of the two elevators I'd seen in the lobby above, but a solid wall of concrete suggested the bottom of the shaft that housed them. A short distance away, a mirror located in the upper right-hand corner was tilted to reveal the alcove, reflecting an image of the service elevator and the second elevator I'd noticed on the lobby level. I started to move forward, but Reba extended her arm, effectively blocking me like the gate at a railroad crossing. She put a finger to her lips and pointed up and to the right.

I spotted a corner-mounted security camera, its aperture focused squarely on the far end of the hall. There was a telephone attached to the wall, presumably to facilitate communication between the front desk and deliverymen. We backed up and eased the door shut. Even so, she dropped her voice to an almost inaudible murmur. "After you dropped me off last night, I picked up my car and came back so I could chat with Willie. He's nice, not as tight-assed as you'd think. Big chess buff. Plays duplicate bridge, and I swear to god, he bakes sourdough bread. Says he's had the same starter for nine years. Whole time we're yakking, I'm checking out the monitors—all ten of 'em—so I'll know what he sees. I was catching flashes of this view, but I didn't know where it was until we opened the door down here. Upstairs, he's got line of sight in both directions on all the hallways, but nothing in the elevators and nothing on the roof."

"What about Beck's offices?"

"Oh, please. Beck wouldn't put up with that Big Brother shit. He doesn't mind Willie spying on his tenants, but not on him."

"Seems like heavy security for a building this size."

"Interesting, isn't it? I thought so myself."

"So where'd the elevators disappear to?"

"The public elevators stop at lobby level. Clearly, Beck doesn't want anyone to have access to his offices from down here," she said. "One elevator does a short loop between the parking garage and the lobby. Anybody who needs to reach floors two, three, or four has to exit into the lobby and cross to the public elevators. That way, Willie can intercept them and quiz them. You better have a pretty good reason for being in the building or you're out of luck. If you need to take an elevator down this far, you have to have a key. There isn't any button you can push."

"But if the service elevator originates down here, can't someone hop on down here and bypass Willard altogether?" I asked. "I mean, even with the cameras rolling he can't be watching all ten monitors at once."

"In theory, you're right, but it'd be tricky. For one thing, all these passageways are kept locked—"

"Which didn't keep us out."

"And for another," she said, plowing right on, "there's a security code for every floor. You *could* risk the service elevator—assuming Willie didn't spot you in the corridor down here—but you couldn't get off unless you knew the code for the alarm panel on any given floor. Mess up the numbers and all hell breaks loose."

"Which means what to us, exactly?"

"Which means we better impose on Willie's good nature and retrieve your purse before the end of his shift."

21

We retraced our steps, emerging from the service corridor in the parking garage near Macy's. We crossed to the escalator and went up one level to the esplanade. When we reached the front entrance to the Beckwith Building, Reba pushed the door and discovered that it was locked. She cupped her hands to the plate glass. "Hey, Willie. Over here."

She tapped on the glass to get the security guard's attention. The minute he looked up, she gave him an enthusiastic wave and pantomimed his unlocking of the door. Willard shook her off, like a pitcher shaking off a sign. Reba motioned him over with an exaggerated rolling of her arm. He stared at her, unmoved, and she clasped her hands together earnestly as though in prayer. Reluctantly he left his perch at the desk and crossed to the door, where he said, "Building's closed!" from his side of the glass.

"Come onnn. Open up," she said.

SUE GRAFTON

He considered the request, his ambivalence clearly evident.

She put her mouth against the glass and made a big sucky kiss. She gave him the big eyes and produced the dimples for effect. "Please, please, please?"

He wasn't happy, but he did pick up the keys attached to the chain on his belt. He unlocked the door and opened it a cautious three inches. "What do you want? I can't be doing this unless you're one of the tenants."

"I know, but Kinsey left her bag upstairs and she needs her car keys and wallet."

Unimpressed, Willard flicked a look at me. "She can come back on Monday. Building opens at seven."

"How's she going to do that? Without her car keys, she can't even drive. I had to pick her up at her house and bring her over here myself. This is her *handbag*, Will. Do you know what it's like when a woman's separated from her purse? She's going berserk. She's a private detective. She has her *license* in there. Plus her address book, makeup, credit cards, checkbook, every nickel she owns. Even her birth control pills. She gets pregnant, the burden's on you, so get ready to raise a kid."

"Okay, okay. Tell me where it is and I'll bring it down to her."

"She doesn't *know* where it is. That's the *point*. All she knows is she had it when we went up with Marty last night. Now it's gone and that's the only place she went. It has to be there somewhere. Come on. Be a peach. It won't take five minutes and we'll be out of your hair."

"Can't. The alarm system's on."

"Marty gave me the code. Honest. He said it's fine with him as long as we cleared it with you first."

The long-suffering Willard opened the door and allowed us in. I thought he'd insist on coming upstairs with us, but he was serious about his monitoring duties and didn't want to leave his post. Reba and I took one of the two public elevators, which made the four-floor journey at an agonizingly slow pace.

"You sure you know the code?" I asked.

"I watched Marty do it. Same code we had before when I was working for Beck."

"How come he's such a nut about security and so careless about his codes? Sounds like anybody who ever worked for him could get in."

Reba waved the observation away. "We used to change 'em all the time—once a month—but with twenty-five employees, somebody was always messing up. The alarm would go off three and four times a week. The cops came out so many times, they started charging fifty bucks a pop."

The doors slid open and Reba hit the Stop Run button while she stepped out of the elevator. I leaned around and watched as she punched in the seven-digit code: 4-19-1949. "Beck's birthday," she said. "For a while he used Tracy's, but he was the one who kept forgetting that date so he switched to his own."

The status light on the keypad shifted from red to green. She left the elevator on Stop Run, awaiting our return. I followed her into the reception area.

The offices were dead quiet. There were numerous lights on, which oddly contributed to the overall feeling of abandonment. "Bart and Bret, the cleaning twins, were in last night. Check the vacuum cleaner tracks. We better hope whoever comes in here first thing Monday morning doesn't wonder about our footprints running up and down the halls."

"How do you know the vacuuming was done by Bart and Bret and not the guys with the cleaning cart?"

"I'm so glad you asked. Because I'll tell you why. They weren't real cleaning guys, which is something I figured out in the dead of night. Know what bugged me about them?" She paused for effect. "Wrong shoes. What guy mops the floors wearing four-hundred-dollar shiny Italian loafers?"

"You are Sherlock Holmes."

"You're damn straight. You grab your shoulder bag while I satisfy my curiosity. This shouldn't take long."

I made a beeline for the roof, heading down the corridor closest to the stairs. Given Beck's edict about clean surfaces, every desk I spotted en route looked as barren and untouched as an ad for office furniture. I took the steps two at a time and pushed through the big glass door that opened onto the roof. The morning sky was immense, the perfect shade of blue. I slowed and crossed to the parapet, drawn by a desire to see downtown Santa Teresa from this vantage point. The sun had warmed the air in the rooftop garden, coaxing fragrance from the flowering shrubs while a light breeze rustled through the foliage. In the distance, light spilled like pancake syrup across the mountain peaks. I leaned over and looked at the street, which was largely empty at this hour. I tilted my face to the light and took a deep breath before I righted myself and turned back to the task at hand. I retrieved my bag from behind the big potted ficus tree and went downstairs. Reba had been right about my birth control pills. I pulled out my packet and popped two like after-dinner mints.

When I got downstairs, she'd taken out a tape measure and was busy checking the length and breadth of the corridor, one foot on the metal ribbon while she extended the tape to the full. She released the button and I could hear the metal tape sing as she brought it zinging back to her hand. The tip-end whipped against her finger and dealt her a nasty blow. "Shit. Son of a bitch!" She sucked on her knuckle.

"You need a medic?"

"Look at that. I'm bleeding to death."

The nick on her index finger was a quarter of an inch long and she studied it with a frown. "Anyway, bet you dollars to donuts the friggin' room is right there. Press your ear to the wall and see if you can hear anything. Minute ago I heard a humming. Like machinery."

"Reba, that's the elevator shaft. You probably caught the sound of the service elevator going down."

"Not from this floor. We're the only ones up here."

"But we can't be the only people in the building. The elevator equipment is right above us. Of course you'd hear it."

"You think?"

"Let's try the obvious and check it out," I said.

She followed me around the corner where the service elevator was located. From the digital readout on the wall, we could track the car going down, the number changing from 1 to G.

"Told you," I said, and then glanced at my watch. "Shit. We better get out of here before Willard gets anxious and comes looking for us. I can't believe the nonsense you laid on him. Talk about maneuvering."

"I thought I did great . . . though that begging and

pleading shit is only good for limited use. The next time we want in, I'll have to screw the guy for sure."

"You're making a joke, right?"

"Don't be such a prude. Screw one guy, you've screwed 'em all. You're only a virgin once, and after that, you might as well reap the benefits. Besides, I wouldn't mind. I think he's cute." Her gaze was raking the wall again and I could tell she was still speculating about the missing space. She said, "Maybe you get in by way of the roof. Through that little building that looks like a gardener's shack."

"Skip it. We don't have time. Let's get out of here."

"You're such a worrywart," she said, taking out Onni's key ring. "Just give me a second to return these, okay? I'm trying to be a good citizen."

"What about Beck's phony docs."

"Right. I got 'em right here," she said, patting her jacket pocket. She took the hem of her shirt and began cleaning fingerprints from the keys. "Wiping off the prints," she said. "In case they ever dust."

"Just get on with it."

She walked down the hall to Onni's office—not nearly fast enough for my taste—and disappeared from sight. I checked my watch again. We'd been up here twelve minutes. How long was it supposed to take us to find my shoulder bag? By now Willard would be out from behind his desk and on his way up. Reba took her time returning and when she finally appeared, hands shoved in her jacket pockets, instead of getting in the elevator as anticipated, she returned to the alcove where the service elevator was located and stood there staring at it.

"What are you *doing?*"

"I just figured it out. Hot damn." She reached out and

pressed the button, calling the service elevator to the fourth floor. As we watched the digital readout, the elevator began its slow and dutiful climb. Eventually the doors opened. She reached in and pressed Stop Run, then entered the service elevator with me close behind her. The space was twice the width and half again as long as an ordinary elevator, apparently to accommodate moving boxes, file cabinets, and oversize office equipment. The walls were hung with quilted gray fabric like the blankets movers use to protect furniture.

Reba moved to the wall opposite the elevator doors and pulled the padding aside to reveal a second set of elevator doors. On a wall-mounted panel to the right of them, there was a nine-digit keypad. She studied it for a moment and then raised a tentative hand.

"You know the code?"

"Maybe. I'll tell you in a minute."

"Guess wrong and won't you set off the alarm?"

"Oh, come on. It's like a fairy tale—you get three tries before the thing goes berserk. If I blow it, we'll tell Willie we made a wee mistake."

"Just leave it for now. You're really pushing your luck."

She ignored me, of course. "I know it's not going to be his birth date—even Beck wouldn't be dumb enough to use that again. But it might be a variation. He's a narcissist. Everything he does relates to him."

"Reba . . ."

She flashed a look at me. "If you'd quit whining and help me out we can get on with it and be on our way. I can't pass this up. It may be the only chance we have."

I rolled my eyes, trying to control my panic, which was already accelerating. She wasn't going to budge until we figured it out or got caught. I said, "Shit. Try the same date backwards."

"Not bad. I like it. That'd be what?"

"9-4-9-1-9-1-4."

She thought about it briefly and then made a face. "Don't think so. Too tough for him to rattle the number off the top of his head. Let's try this . . ."

She punched in 1949-19-4.

No deal.

She punched in 19-4-1949.

I could feel my heart thud. "That's two."

"Would you get off it? I know it's two. I'm the one punching in numbers. Let's just think about it for a second. What's another possibility?"

"What about Onni's birthday?"

"Let's hope not. I know it's November 11, but I'm not sure what year. Anyway, Beck hasn't been boffing her long so he probably doesn't have a clue himself."

I said, "11-11 any year would be eight digits, not seven."

She pointed at me, apparently impressed with my ability to count.

"What's his wife's birthday?" I asked.

"3-17-1952. But he's blown that one so many times he's probably spooked by now. Besides, he prefers numbers with internal connections or sequences. Know what I mean? Repeats or patterns."

"I thought you said he used your birthday at one point."

"True. That'd be 5-15-1955."

"Hey, mine's 5-5-1950," I chirped, sounding like a lunatic.

"Great. We'll do a joint celebration when the dates roll

around next year. So what should I try? His birth date backwards or mine straight ahead?"

"Well, his birth date backwards has an internal logic if you group the numbers. 949-191-4. Would he break it down that way?"

"Might."

"Just do one or the other before I have a heart attack."

She punched in 5-15-1955. A moment of silence and then the doors slid open. "My birthday. Sweet. You think he still cares?"

I pushed the Stop Run button and watched her wipe her prints off the keypad, taking care not to trigger the alarm. "Wouldn't want anyone to know we were here," she said, happily.

Meanwhile, I was staring straight ahead. The room was probably six feet by eight—not much bigger than a closet. The cleaning cart we'd seen was shoved up against the left wall. A U-shaped counter took up much of the remaining floor space. I looked up. The room seemed to be well ventilated, the walls heavily padded. A smoke detector and a heat detector had been installed in the shadowy upper reaches of the ceiling, where I could see sprinkler heads as well. Rungs embedded in the wall formed a ladder that went straight up. Around the perimeter of the ceiling, I could see rectangles of daylight roughly corresponding to the vents in the fake gardener's cottage on the roof. Reba was right. In a pinch, you could probably gain entry to the room from the roof. Or escape that way.

There were three currency-counting machines on one arm of the counter and four currency-bundling machines on the adjacent counter. Open suitcases were lined up on the third section, packed with tightly wrapped bundles of hundred-dollar bills. Under the counter, ten cardboard cartons were lined up, their top flaps open, packed with additional bundles of hundreds, fifties, and twenties in U.S. currency. Each bundle was shrink-wrapped, with paper adding-machine tape circling packets of five. There were two styrofoam coffee cups visible and a pile of empty cups in a wastebasket, which also contained wads of discarded plastic wrappers. Several silver-dollar-size plastic disks with small blades were being used to slit the wrappers.

Reba said, "Geez. I've never seen so much money."

"Me neither. It looks like they're pulling bundles from these boxes, removing the wrappers, running the bills through the currency counter, and then rewrapping them for transport."

She advanced a few steps and checked the total on one of the currency counters. "Take a peek at this puppy. They've run a million bucks through this." She picked up a bundle and weighed it in her hand. "Wonder how much this is. Wouldn't you love to know?" She sniffed it. "You'd think it would smell good, but it doesn't smell like anything."

"Would you keep your hands to yourself?"

"I'm just looking. I'm not *doing* anything. How much do you figure is in one of these, twenty grand? Fifty?"

"I have no idea. Don't mess with that. I'm serious."

"Aren't you curious what it feels like? It doesn't weigh all that much," she said. She wiped her prints from the wrapper and put the bundle back, surveying the space. "How many guys you think work here besides the two we saw?"

"There's not room for three. They probably come in

weekends when the activity's less conspicuous," I said. I reached out and put my hand on one of the styrofoam cups and nearly moaned in fear. "This is still warm. Suppose they come back?"

"No one can get to us. The elevator's on hold."

"But if they find the elevator on hold, won't they know something's wrong? We have to get out of here. I'm begging you."

"Okay, okay. But I knew I was right about the room. This is incredible, isn't it?"

"Absolutely. Who gives a shit? Let's go."

I backed out of the room and into the service elevator. The other set of doors was still open and I stuck my head out into the corridor to assure myself that no one had entered the premises while we were in the room. Reba was having trouble dragging herself away. I said, "Reba, come on!" sounding every bit as tense and impatient as I felt.

She moved into the elevator as though mesmerized and entered the seven-digit code. The doors on that side of the elevator slid closed. She replaced the wall padding and adjusted the quilted matting to conceal the second set of doors.

"What took you so long?"

"It's all so beautiful. Can you imagine having even half the bundles in there? You'd never have to lift another finger as long as you lived."

"No problem. Your life wouldn't last that long."

We exited through the elevator doors that opened into Beck's offices and Reba released the Stop Run button. We waited until the service elevator doors closed, and then went around the corner and got back on the public elevator.

She released the hold button, the doors closed, and we began our leisurely descent. I was nearly sick with anxiety, but she didn't seem affected. The woman had nerves of steel.

When we reached the lobby level and stepped off, Willard looked up from his desk with a smile. "You find it?"

I held up my shoulder bag to show our mission had been accomplished. My hands were shaking so badly I thought he'd spot the trembling from across the lobby. I was doing what I could to maintain a semblance of normality until we could ease out the front door and be on our way.

Reba, true to form, made a point of crossing to his desk, where she stretched up on tiptoe and rested her arms on the counter, holding her injured finger close to his face. "You got a first-aid kit? Look at this. I about crippled myself."

Willard peered at her knuckle, inspecting the wound that was no bigger than a hyphen. "How'd you do that?"

"I must have snagged it on something. Sucker hurts. You can kiss it and make it better if you want."

He shook his head, smiling indulgently, and started opening his desk drawers. While he rummaged around in search of a Band-Aid, I noticed Reba's gaze flicking across the monitors, taking in all ten views.

Willard held up a bandage. "Think you can manage this yourself?"

"Don't be mean. After all I've done for you?" She held out her finger and he pulled the red thread that opened the paper packaging. He removed the Band-Aid and applied it.

She said, "Thanks. You're a doll. I'll recommend a raise." She made a kissing noise at him as we headed for the door.

Behind us, Willard left his perch and followed, taking out his jumble of keys so he could unlock the front door. "Don't you be coming back. This is the last of it."

"I won't, but you'll miss me," she said as we scooted through the door.

"I doubt that," he said, and Reba blew him another kiss. I thought she was laying it on a bit thick, but Willard didn't seem to mind. He turned the keys in the lock and we were safe.

22

Reba slowed her BMW to a stop in front of my apartment. As I got out and shut the car door behind me, I saw that Cheney's little red Mercedes was parked at the curb. I felt a surge of anxiety. I'd intended to fill him in on my adventures with Reba over the past couple of days, but Jonah's call had intervened and he'd gone off to the shooting scene without my having spoken a word. The omission made me uneasy, as though I were deliberately holding out on him. Even referring to our activities as "adventures" sounded like an attempt to minimize the fact that what we'd done could jeopardize the investigation. Last night's incursion into Beck's offices had been risky enough. In a pinch, an argument could be made that Marty had invited us to tour the premises, but his offer hadn't extended to our rifling through desk drawers and stealing Onni's keys. He'd certainly never given us permission to return in his absence and enjoy the run of the place. I wanted to tell Cheney about the bundles of cash being counted, repackaged, and packed into suitcases, but I knew the discovery encompassed a little matter of criminal trespass, which tainted the knowledge. Nonetheless, I needed to unload before my withholding the information became an issue in itself.

I went through the gate and around the side of my studio, as burdened with guilt as though I'd slept with another man. I could make excuses for my conduct, but I was accountable all the same. Cheney was sitting on my front step, still in the clothes he'd been wearing the night before. He smiled when he saw me, looking exhausted, but good. Confessing was bound to impact our relationship. I dreaded the consequences, but I had to speak up.

I sat down on the step and slipped my hand into his. "How'd it go? You look beat."

"Big mess. Two gangbangers dead. Hooker got caught in the crossfire and she's dead, too. Jonah sent me home to shower and change clothes. I'm due back at one. How's by you?"

"Not that good. We need to talk."

He focused on my face, his eyes searching. "Can it wait?"

"I don't think so. This is about Reba. We've got a problem."

"Meaning what?"

"You're not going to like this."

"Just spit it out," he said.

"She and I connected up for dinner last night. She wanted to introduce me to Marty Blumberg, Beck's company comptroller, and I couldn't see the harm. He has dinner at Dale's every Friday night so that's where we went. He comes in and the three of us are schmoozing away. Next thing I know, she tells him how the feds are

SUE GRAFTON

mounting a case against Beck and he—Marty—is going to
end up taking the blame if he doesn't do something quick.
I had no idea what she thought she was doing, but there it
was."

Cheney closed his eyes and hung his head. "Geez. I
don't believe it. What the hell's wrong with her?"

"It gets worse. She tells him Onni's a federal agent and
she's screwing Beck's brains out as a way of getting the
goods on him. At first, Marty resists. He really doesn't
want to believe it, but Reba shows him the photos and
reels him in. Then she gets us invited up to the offices—
ostensibly for a tour—but she uses the opportunity to
scour the place for anything she can lay her hands on,
which turns out to be Onni's keys."

I continued the rundown, giving him an unvarnished
account of what had happened over the course of the past
two days. I could tell he was getting annoyed before I was
even halfway through. He was tired. He'd had a long night
and this was the last thing he needed. At the same time, I
felt compelled to tell him the truth. Either I revealed the
whole of it—of myself—or what was the point?

I moved on to events of the morning and when I'd
finished, Cheney blew. "You gotta be out of your head!
Aside from the issue of unlawful entry, if Beck gets wind
of it, he'll know something's off and that's the end of it for
us."

"How's he going to find out?"

"Suppose Marty spills the beans or the security guy has
second thoughts about letting you in. He knows both of
you by name. All it'd take is one offhand remark from
either of those guys. Doesn't matter how solid the government's case is, defense attorney puts you on the stand and

268

he'll take you apart. Not that he'll have the chance. Long before it comes to that, the feds will slap you with charges of obstruction of justice, tampering with evidence, and god knows what else. Perjury for sure the minute you try to cover your ass. Reba's got no credibility. Convicted felon, woman scorned. Anything she says is automatically suspect."

"Then why'd you bring her into it? If she's so useless, why recruit her in the first place?"

"Because we needed a confidential informant, not a friggin' one-man posse. You're a pro. You know better—or I assumed you did. The feds play for keeps. Compromise an operation like this and you're the one who pays. What's it to her? She's got nothing to lose."

"Cheney, I hear you. I know I should have stopped her, but I couldn't see a way to do it. Once she told Marty what was going down, events just started to escalate—"

"Bullshit. You were a willing participant. What you did was illegal—"

"Got it. I know. I'm aware of it," I said. "On the other hand, how could I walk away? She's in this because of us—because of me to be specific. I feel *some* responsibility for what's happening to her."

"Well, you better start taking responsibility for your own behavior. If this sting goes down the shitter, you'll be in more trouble than you can shake a stick at."

"Wait a minute. Wait. I don't mean to sound defensive, but I got backed into this. When the deal first came up, I told you I didn't want to do it, but you talked me into it, smutty photographs and all. Fade out, fade in. I'm sitting there at Dale's and she opens her mouth and blows the deal wide open. What was I supposed to do? If I'd gotten up and left, there was no way of guessing what the hell she'd do next. Believe it or not, I was trying for damage control. I'll admit the situation snowballed—"

"Just do me a favor and stay the hell away from her, okay? She calls you, hang up and leave the rest of it to us. I'll get Vince on the horn and bring him up to speed. We'll see what he can salvage, if anything."

"I'm sorry. I didn't mean to screw things up."

"Well, you can't do anything about it now. What's done is done. Just keep your distance from Reba. Promise."

I held a hand up like I was taking an oath.

"I'll call you later," he said brusquely. He got up and headed around the corner to his car. I heard him fire up his engine and peel away from the curb with a chirp of rubber on pavement. I could feel my face burning for an hour afterward.

I locked myself in my apartment and tidied my underwear drawer. I needed to do something small and useful. I had to get a handle on life in a risk-free arena where I could feel competent again. Maybe folding underpants didn't amount to much, but it was the best I could do. I moved on to the chest of drawers and refolded my shirts. Then I tackled the junk drawer downstairs. I hated the idea of being prosecuted. Obstruction of justice was serious damn shit. I pictured myself in jail garb, legs shackled, hands manacled in front, doing the traditional inmate two-step while shuffling to and from court. That began to seem a bit melodramatic and I decided there was no point in going overboard on the self-flagellation. So I'd goofed. Big deal. I hadn't *killed* anyone.

After an hour, I became aware of voices outside my door, one being Henry's. I glanced out the kitchen window, but the angle was too extreme for me to see who else was there. I went to the front door, popped the locks, and opened it a crack. Henry, Lewis, and William were standing together in the driveway. Lewis and William were both in three-piece suits while Henry wore his usual shorts, T-shirt, and flip-flops. He'd backed the station wagon out of the garage and Lewis was loading his bags in the rear. As I looked on, I heard a soft ping, and William removed his pocket watch from his vest and checked the time. He took out a small packet of trail mix and made a production of opening the sealed cellophane, which generated copious crackling noises. Henry flicked him a look of annoyance but continued the conversation with Lewis, which seemed to be about nothing in particular. I eased the door shut, gratified that one conflict had been peacefully resolved, or so I hoped. The truth about strong emotion is that it's difficult to sustain. Despite how victimized we feel, it's hard work hanging on to anger, even when it's tinged with righteousness. Holding a grudge against someone is (sometimes) more trouble than it's worth.

Reba called at 2:00. As I'm constitutionally unable to resist a ringing phone, I was on the verge of snatching up the handset. I hesitated, curbing the impulse, and let the machine pick up. She said, "Oh, poo. I was hoping you'd be there. I just had this big ol' stinkin' fight with Lucinda and I'm dying to tell you about it. I practically threw her out on her ass only not really, but you know, figuratively speaking. Anyway, call me when you can and I'll fill you in. Also, there's something else we need to talk about. Bye-bye."

She called again at 3:36. "Hey, Kinsey, me again. Don't you check messages these days? I'm going stir-crazy up here. We really need to talk so give me a buzz when you get in, okay? Otherwise, I can't be responsible for what I do. Ha ha ha. That's a joke . . . sort of."

At 5:30, she left only her name with a request that I call.

I went into the office Monday morning and buried myself in the work I'd neglected the previous week. I'd read about the parking-lot shootout in the morning paper, and I knew the STPD vice and homicide detectives were working with the gang detail, interviewing witnesses and running down leads. The Santa Teresa gang population tends to be stable, its activities carefully monitored. Periodically, however, gang members from Olvidado, Perdido, and Los Angeles will swing through town, especially on holiday weekends when the homeboys, like everyone else, are hoping for a change of scene. Happily police officers from those communities make the same swing through town so that unbeknownst to the gangbangers, they're still under the watchful eye of the law.

I didn't hear from Reba again until late Monday afternoon, after I arrived home from work. Mercifully she hadn't called the office, where good business practice dictates that I answer the phone. She'd called my apartment twice, leaving a message at noon and then another one at 2:00.

She sounded cheerful at the outset but increasingly plaintive as the day wore on. "Kinsey? Yoo hoo! Did you tell
me you were going out of town or something? Don't think
so, but I really can't remember for sure. I'm sorry to be
such a pest, but Beck's back in town and I'm antsy as hell.
I really don't know how much longer I can hold out. I'm
on my way to Holloway's to pee in a jar and shoot the shit
with her. Then I'm supposed to go to an AA meeting, but
I'm thinking I might skip. Too depressing, you know?
Anyway, call me when you get this. Hope everything's
okay. Bye."

It was hard to leave her hanging when I'd been so
available to her the week before. I felt like a mother cow
separated from her calf—I could hear Reba's bleating
cries, but I wasn't free to respond. I'd been serious when I
promised Cheney I'd keep my distance, at least until the
situation was under control. Once she'd talked to Vince
and his pals, I could reassess. By then, of course, she
might well have severed our relationship.

In the meantime, I heard nothing from Cheney, a
silence I ascribed to his being up to his ears in work. To
avoid the silence, I left the apartment and headed over to
see Henry. I tapped on the frame and he motioned me in.
He had his heavy-duty mixer on the counter, a ten-pound
sack of bread flour, yeast packets, sugar, salt, and water at
the ready.

"Can you put up with company?"

He smiled. "If you can put up with the racket my mixer
makes. I'm about to throw together a batch of bread, which
I'll let rise overnight and bake first thing tomorrow morning. Grab a stool."

I watched him measure ingredients, which he dumped

in the big stainless-steel mixing bowl. Once he turned on the machine, we put our conversation on hold until he was done. We chatted while I watched him remove the sticky mass of dough, kneading and adding flour until the whole of it was smooth and elastic. He oiled a big wash pan, turned the dough in it until its surface glistened, and then covered it with a towel. He put the pan in the oven where the pilot light would generate the warmth necessary for the bread to rise.

"How much are you making?" I asked, looking at the quantity of dough.

"Four big loaves and two batches of dinner rolls, all for Rosie," he said. "I may do up a pan of sticky buns if you're interested."

"Always. I take it Lewis went home?"

"I dropped him at the airport Saturday. And speaking of him, he did apologize for butting in, which may be a first. I guess it never occurred to him that his flying out would have that effect. I told him there was no point worrying. What's done is done."

"Someone said the same thing to me yesterday under different circumstances," I said. "At any rate, I'm glad the two of you are back on solid ground."

"Never any doubt of that," he said. "What about you? I didn't see much of you this weekend. How's your new fellow?"

"Good question," I said. I told Henry the sorry saga of my bad behavior, risks taken, laws broken, gains, losses, and tension-filled escapes. He enjoyed the tale a lot more than Cheney had and for that I was grateful.

A little after six, I returned to my place and fixed myself a hot hard-boiled-egg sandwich, with more mayo and salt than your internist would recommend. I was wadding up my paper towel when the phone rang. I tossed the wad and waited until the caller began to speak. Marty Blumberg identified himself and I picked up. "Hey, Marty. It's me. I just now walked in."

"I hope you don't mind me calling you at home. Something weird's come up and I'd be curious what you think."

"Sure." I picked up traffic noises in the background and pictured him calling from a pay phone.

"You want the long version or the short?"

"Long stories are always better."

"Right," he said. "So here's how this goes." I could hear that momentary lull as he inhaled and released a mouthful of smoke. "I get home from work today and my housekeeper's wringing her hands. She's upset about something, but won't say what. I press because I can tell she needs to unburden herself. She says, don't get mad. I say, fine. She tells me she arrived at the house at nine, like always, and she sees this phone company truck parked in the drive and a couple of guys on the porch. She goes ahead and lets herself in the back and then answers the front door. This one guy says the phone company's received a number of calls complaining the service is out and they're going through the neighborhood checking all the lines. They want to know is my phone working, so she asks 'em to wait, tries the line, and sure enough it's dead. Well, she's paranoid—comes from watching way too many cop shows on TV—so she asks 'em to show some ID. Both have these pinch-on plastic picture dealies that say California Bell. Huerta writes down their names and employee numbers. Second guy has a clipboard and he shows her the work order, typed up as neat as you please. She figures it's legit so she lets 'em in. You with me so far?"

"Yes, but I don't like the sound of it."

"Me neither," he said. "She's telling me this shit and I can feel the rocks piling up in my gut. The guys are in my study fifteen, twenty minutes, and then they come out and tell her everything's hunky-dory. She asks what it was and they say the roof rats must've chewed through the outside wires, but now all's well. Afterwards, she's thinking none of this makes sense and she's worried she did wrong. I act like no big deal and tell her I'll handle it from here. So what I'm thinking is somebody's either bugged my house or put a tap on my phone."

"Or both," I supplied.

"Shit, yes. Why else would I be calling from a fuckin' minimart parking lot? I feel like an idiot, but I can't take the chance. My phone's tapped; I don't want whoever's doing it to realize I figured it out. That way I can feed 'em any bullshit I want. You think it's the feds?" I could hear him take another puff on his cigarette.

"I have no clue, but I think you're right to worry."

"How can they do that? I mean, assuming they planted a bug, or, like, a listening device, wouldn't that be illegal?"

"Without a court order, sure."

"Trouble is, if it's not them, it might be someone a whole lot worse."

"Like who?" I was thinking Salustio Castillo, but wanted to hear him say it.

"Never mind who. Either way, I don't like it. Friday night, when Reba laid out that shit about Beck, I figured she was yanking my chain. More I think about it, the more I'm thinkin' maybe she was telling the truth. Beck always made a point of keeping me in the thick of it. Like she says, could be he's setting me up."

"Who else is in on it?"

"On what?"

"The money laundering."

"Who says anyone? I never said that."

"Oh come on, Marty. You can't launder that much money without help."

"I'm not a snitch," he said, his tone indignant.

"But other people are involved, right?"

"I don't know, maybe. A few, but you're never going to get me to name names."

"Fair enough. So what's in it for you?"

"Same as everyone else. We're paid to keep our mouths shut. We help Beck now and he'll see that we're set up for life."

"Life in a federal pen. That'll be a treat," I said.

Marty ignored that, saying, "Truth is, I got plenty and I'd skedaddle right now if I could figure out how. If Customs is in on the deal, I can't leave the country without getting my ass nailed. They flag my name in the computer, minute I check in for my flight, boom, I'm done for."

"I'm telling you, you better throw in your lot with the guys who count. Beck isn't looking after you. He's got himself to protect."

"Yeah, I'm getting that. I mean, sure he may need us, but how far is he willing to go? Beck's about Beck. Comes right down to it, he'd throw us to the wolves."

"Probably so." I nearly confided the rumor I'd heard, that Beck was on the move and likely to disappear within the next few days, but the likelihood hadn't been confirmed and the information wasn't mine to pass on. "Of course, it's always possible the phone company story is on the up and up . . ."

"Nuh-uhn. Don't think so."

"Well, I'm sorry I can't help."

"What about Reba? I've been trying to reach her all day."

"Probably at the house. She had a meeting with her parole officer earlier so you might try her again."

"You talk to her, tell her to give me a call. This is making my stomach hurt. I'm anxious as hell."

"Look, let me talk to a friend of mine and see what I can find out."

"I'd appreciate that. You call back, you be careful what you say. Meantime, you hear from Reba, tell her the two of us gotta talk. I don't like workin' with a noose around my neck."

"Hang in there," I said, and then winced at my choice of words.

Once he disconnected, I dialed both Cheney's home and work numbers and left messages. I tried his pager, punching in my home number in hopes he'd call back. Marty was moving into panic mode, which made him as unpredictable as Reba, though more vulnerable.

I spent the evening stretched out on the couch, book propped in front of me pretending to read while I waited for Cheney's call. I wondered where he was and whether he was still pissed off at me. I needed to talk to him about Marty, but more than that, I craved the physical contact. My body was remembering his with a low-level yearning disruptive to concentration. Before he arrived on the scene, I'd lived in a dead zone—not exactly buzzing with joy, but certainly not discontent. Now I felt like a pup just coming into heat.

One of the problems with being celibate is that once sexual feelings resurface, they're almost impossible to repress. I found myself remembering what had happened between us and fantasizing about what might come next. Cheney had a laziness about him, a natural tempo half the speed of mine. I was beginning to see that operating in high gear was a means of protecting myself. Living at an accelerated pace allowed me to feel only half as much because there wasn't time to feel more. I made love the same way I ate—eager to satisfy the immediate hunger without acknowledging the deeper desire, which was to feel connected at the core. Avoiding the truth was easier if I was on the run. With quick sex, as with fast food, there was no savoring the moment. There was only the headlong rush to be done with it and move on.

At 10:00, when the phone rang, I knew it was him. I turned my head, listening until the machine began recording the sound of his voice. I reached over and picked up, saying, "Hey."

"Hey, yourself. You called."

"Hours ago. I thought you were ignoring me. Are you still mad?"

"About what?"

"Good."

"How about you? Are you pissed off?"

"Not my nature," I said. "Not with you at any rate. Listen, we need to talk about Marty. Where are you?"

"Rosie's. Come join me."

"You trust me to walk half a block by myself? It's pitchy dark outside."

"I was going to meet you halfway."

"Why don't you go the whole distance and meet me here."

"We can do that later. For now, I think we should sit and stare into each other's eyes while I put a hand up your skirt."

"Give me five minutes. I'll step out of my underwear."

"Make it three. I've missed you."

"I've missed you, too."

By the time I locked the door behind me and reached the front gate, he was waiting on the other side of Henry's wrought-iron fence. The sidewalk on his side was one step lower than the walk on mine, which made me feel tall. The night air was chill and the dark settled over us like a veil. I slid my arms around his neck. He tilted his head and ran his mouth down along my throat and across my collarbone. The fence pales were cold, blunt-tipped spears that pressed against my ribs. He rubbed his hands up and down my arms. "You're cold. You should have a jacket on."

"Don't need one. I have you."

"That you do," he said, smiling. He eased a hand between the fence pales, ran his fingers under my skirt and up between my legs. I heard him catch his breath and then he made a sound low in his throat.

"Told you."

"I thought it was a metaphor."

"What do either of us know about metaphors?" I said, laying my face against his hair.

"I know this."

My turn to hum. "We should go to Rosie's," I whispered.

"We should go in and lie down before impaling ourselves on this fence."

At midnight we made grilled cheese sandwiches—the only instance in life when Velveeta isn't such a terrible idea. I found myself sidetracked by the crust, which was crisp, fully saturated with butter. Still munching, I said, "Hate to ask, but what'd Vince say when you told him about Reba and me?"

"He stuck his fingers in his ears and hummed. Actually, he loved the information about the counting room. Said he'd put a note in the file and attribute the tip to an anonymous call. He's scheduling the meeting with Reba for Thursday."

"Can't he make it any sooner than that? He's the one telling us Beck's about to take off. Reba's worried she'll run into him."

"I can mention it to Vince, but I wouldn't hold out much hope. That's the downside of an operation like this, it's unwieldy as hell. All she has to do is lay low."

"You give her the news. I'm not allowed to talk to her."

"That's right. Because I'm looking after you."

"What about Marty? He's the one you ought to be worried about. He's really feeling the squeeze, convinced his phone's tapped or he's got a bug planted in his house."

"Could well be. Tell him to give us a call and we can talk about a deal."

"He's not ready for that. He's still looking for a way out of the bind he's in."

"What do these guys think? They're so smart they're never going to get caught?"

"They haven't been caught so far."

23

Tuesday morning passed in a great big boring blur. Given the egocentric nature of the world, I imagined that since nothing in particular was happening to me, there was nothing in particular happening to anyone else. In truth, events were transpiring that I would hear about only when it was too late to alter either cause or effect. My phone rang at 11:00—Cheney asking me to sit tight for the next half-hour as there was something he wanted me to hear. "You have a tape recorder?" he asked.

"An old one, but it takes a regular-size cassette."

"That'll do."

Fifteen minutes later he walked in the door. While I was waiting for him, I searched through my closet until I found the tape recorder. I opened a fresh package of AA batteries and by the time Cheney arrived, the tape recorder was set up and ready to go. "What is it?"

He slipped the cassette in the machine. "Something the FBI picked up this morning. Some of it sounds garbled, but the techs have taken it as far as they can." He pressed the Play button, triggering a generalized hissing and the ringing of a phone. A man on the other end picked up without identifying himself. "Yes?"

The calling party said, "Problem."

The minute I heard the voice, I shot a look at Cheney. "Beck?"

He pressed the Pause button. "The guy he's talking to is Salustio Castillo. This was the first call he placed when he got to the office." He pressed Play again.

On the tape, Castillo was saying, "What?"

"When I took delivery on that shipment, the inventory was off."

Silence. Hissing. "Impossible. 'Off' meaning what?"

"Short."

"By how much?"

"A pack."

"Large or small?"

"Large. We're talking twenty-five."

Salustio was silent. "I supervised the count myself. What about the invoices?"

"Not a match. I checked three times and the numbers don't tally."

Salustio said, "I told you I wanted someone supervising your end—"

"This wasn't on my end."

"Or so you say."

Silence from Beck. "You know I wouldn't do this."

"Do I? You've argued for a bigger cut of the action, which I can't . . . there's no way I can justify from my end. Now you say . . . missing, all I have is your word."

"You think I'd lie?"

"Let's call it inventory shrinkage. It's been known to

happen. From my perspective, you're adequately compensated . . . don't see it that way. So maybe you siphon off a percentage of the goods and that satisfies your need for a pay increase. What better cover than claiming I shorted you?"

"I never said that."

"Then what?"

"I said the total's off. Might be the . . . mistake . . ."

"Yours. Not mine."

". . ."

"Fix it."

Silence. There was a stretch of pure hissing on the tape. Tightly Beck said, "Tell me what you want me to do and I'll do it."

"Make up the shortfall out of your end, which is where the loss occurred. My total's correct and I want full payment deposited to my account. In the meantime, not to worry. I know you're good for it. Pleasure doing business," Salustio said, and clicked off.

Beck said, "Fuck!" as he banged down the phone.

Cheney turned off the tape.

I thought the conversation was interesting, but I wasn't clear why he wanted me to hear it. I was on the verge of making a comment when Cheney said, "A tightly packed bundle of hundred-dollar bills is one inch thick," he said. "That's twenty-five thousand dollars. I know because I asked the Treasury boys. Beck's been back a day. If a currency delivery came in while he was gone, it makes sense he'd double-check the totals first thing."

"Okay," I said. And then I shut my mouth because I could hear the penny drop. He knew Reba and I had ventured into the counting room on Saturday when the currency was being unwrapped and run through the machines. All either of us had to do was clip a pack of hundreds and who'd be the wiser? Beck didn't know we'd been there and all Salustio cared about was having the right total credited to his account. "You think she took it?"

"Sure. Vince was apoplectic. I thought he'd pop a vein. Beck doesn't know she was up there, but he'll rip the place apart looking for that dough. Once he pulls the security tapes, he's got her. You, too, for that matter."

"She has to be nuts. Why take the risk?"

"Because Beck can't report the loss. He calls the cops and he'll generate the kind of scrutiny he can't afford. Not when he's on the verge of skipping out."

I could feel myself flush, overtaken by alternating surges of denial and guilt. I suddenly understood what she'd been doing in the counting room for those few beats after I'd entered the elevator. I'd felt anxious, impatient to be gone while she'd been smitten with the sight of all that cash. Meanwhile, I was preoccupied, intent on checking the corridor to make sure we were in the clear. It wouldn't have taken any time—two seconds?—to stuff a packet of cash down her shirt or in her jacket pocket. I'd been thinking "nerves of steel," amazed at her nonchalance while I was wetting my drawers. Then, of course, there was her exuberance with Willard once we got downstairs. She'd flirted and I'd assumed she was hyper because we'd discovered Beck's counting room. Must have been the feel of all that money next to her skin. Crazy. Reba wiping down her fingerprints. Cheney verbally boxing my ears when I'd confessed our misdeeds. And I'd defended her. Shit! My palms were damp and I rubbed them against my jeans. "What now?"

"Vince wants her in as soon as possible. The meeting with the IRS and Customs has been moved up to tomorrow afternoon at four in the FBI offices. Vince wants to talk to her first, like at one o'clock, and see if he can iron this out. Otherwise, the shit's really going to hit the fan."

"Can't he help her?"

"Sure, if she's willing to put herself in his hands."

"Fat chance. She's never even met the man."

"Why don't you talk to her?"

"If you think it'd do any good. I've been ducking her for days, but I can give it a try."

"Do that. Worst-case scenario, he'll put her in a safe house until he can figure out what's what."

Cheney checked his watch, popped the Eject button on the tape recorder, and removed the tape. "I gotta get this back. You have Vince's number?"

"You better give it to me again."

He snagged a pen and a scratch pad and made a note, tearing off the top sheet, which he handed to me. "Let me know what she says. If you can't reach me, you can talk directly to him."

"Will do."

After he left, I sat at my desk, trying to figure out what to say to Reba. There was really no point in pussyfooting around. She'd dug herself a hole and the sooner she climbed out of it, the better off she'd be. As long as Beck got the money back, he might not inquire too closely how it had disappeared. I picked up the handset and punched in the number for the Lafferty estate. I went through a preliminary round of conversation with the housekeeper, Freddy, who told me Reba was still in bed. "Shall I wake her?"

"I think you better."

"One moment. I'll put you on hold and have her take the call in her room."

"Great. Thanks."

I pictured Freddy in her crepe-soled shoes, padding down the hall and up the stairs, holding on to the rail. The silence went on for a bit, but I imagined her knocking on Reba's door and then a groggy interval before she picked up, which was sure enough how she sounded when she came on the line. "'Lo?"

"Hi, Reeb. It's Kinsey. I'm sorry to wake you."

"That's okay. I should probably be getting up anyway. What d'you want?"

"I need to ask you about something and you have to swear to tell the truth."

"Sure." She was already sounding more alert, so I thought she had a fair idea what was coming.

"Remember when we were together Saturday morning on that little voyage of discovery?"

Silence.

"Did you lift a packet of hundred-dollar bills?"

Silence.

"Never mind admitting it. The point is, Beck knows."

"So what? Serves him right. It's like I told him at Bubbles, he owes me, big time."

"Only one tiny problem. The money wasn't his. It was Salustio's."

"No."

"Yes."

"Shit. Are you sure? I thought it was Beck's, like he was packing it to take with him when he left."

"Nuhn-uhn. He was verifying Salustio's total before

making a deposit to his account. Now he's twenty-five grand short."

I could hear her lighting a cigarette. I said, "What made you think you could get away with it?"

"It was a *whim*, like an impulse. Haven't you ever done anything like that? Spur of the moment. I just did it, that's all."

"Well, you better put it back before Beck figures it out."

"How'm I supposed to do that?"

"How would I know? Stick it in an envelope and leave it at Willard's desk. He can pass it on to Marty or take it up himself—"

"But why do I have to do anything? Beck can't prove it, can he? I mean, how can he prove it when I didn't leave fingerprints?"

"For one thing, he's got security tapes that show you going in and out of the building. Beyond that, he doesn't have to prove a thing. All he has to do is tell Salustio and you're screwed."

"He wouldn't do that to me, would he? I mean, I know he's a shit, but he wouldn't tell Salustio. You think?"

"Of course he would! Salustio expects him to cough up the missing twenty-five grand."

"Shit. Shit, shit, shit."

"Look, Reeb. I'll say this again. Vince Turner can probably help if you'll turn around and help him."

"What good does that do me with Salustio?"

"Maybe Vince can put you somewhere safe until it's all ironed out."

"Oh, man. This is bad. You think I should call Beck?"

"You'd be smarter to keep away from him and talk to

Vince instead. He wants to see you anyway before you meet with the feds."

"What feds? I don't have a meeting with the feds. The guy dropped the ball."

"He did not. The meeting's been changed to tomorrow afternoon at four. I'll pick you up at twelve-thirty and you can spend a couple of hours with him first."

"About bloody time."

"I told you it would take time."

"Yeah, well, it's too late *now*."

"Meaning what?"

"Meaning, I gotta think how to handle this. I'll call you back." The line went dead.

So much for my powers of persuasion.

That night, Cheney was busy with softball practice, so I was on my own. I had dinner at Rosie's, after which I retired to my apartment and spent the evening with a book.

Twelve fifteen on Wednesday, I headed south on the 101, relieved to be in motion again. Once I delivered Reba to Vince's office, he could take charge of her and I'd be off the hook. The drive up Bella Sera was exactly as it had been on prior occasions, right down to the scent of bay laurel and the smell of dry grass. It had been thirteen days since I'd taken this route on my way to meet Nord Lafferty, wondering what he could possibly want with me. Escort his daughter home from prison. How complicated was that? In the days since we'd returned, her life had slowly come unraveled. The crazy part was that I liked her. Despite the differences between us, I responded to her out of the outrageous elements in my own nature. Watching her operate was like seeing a distorted version of myself, only larger than life and much more dangerous.

When I reached the property, the gates were standing open. As I rounded the bend in the drive, I saw the same Lincoln Continental and Mercedes sedan. Now a third vehicle sat beside the other two—this one a Jaguar convertible, a handsome dark green with a caramel interior that looked good enough to eat. I parked, leaving my car unlocked as I moved up the walk to the house. Reba's massive long-haired orange cat, Rags, sauntered out to greet me, looking at me with startling blue eyes. I extended my hand and he sniffed at my fingers. He allowed me to scratch his head, nudging me repeatedly to keep the action afloat.

I rang the bell and waited while he circled my legs, leaving long orange hairs on the legs of my jeans. From inside, I heard the muffled tap of high heels on hard marble tile. The door was opened by a woman I immediately pegged as the legendary Lucinda. She appeared to be in her midforties, thanks to the work of a first-rate plastic surgeon. I knew this because her neck and hands were fifteen years older than her face. Her hair was short, streaked with varying shades of blond as though bleached by the sun. She was slim and beautifully dressed in a designer outfit I recognized, though I'd forgotten the name. The two-piece black knit was banded in white and the jacket had brass buttons running down the front. The knee-length skirt revealed a knotty set of calves. "Yes?"

"I'm Kinsey Millhone. Could you tell Reba I'm here?"

She studied me carefully with eyes as dark as tar. "She's not home. Is this something I can help you with?"

"Ah, no. Don't think so. I'll just wait for her."

"You must be the private investigator Nord's spoken of.

I'm Lucinda Cunningham. I'm a friend of the family," she said, extending her hand.

"Nice meeting you," I said, shaking hands with her. "Did Reba say when she'd be home?"

"I'm afraid not. It might help if you told me what this was about."

Pushy woman, I thought. "She has a meeting this afternoon. I told her I'd give her a lift."

Her smile was not entirely warm, but she stepped out onto the porch and pulled the door shut behind her. "I don't mean to pry, but this . . . um . . . appointment, is it important?"

"Very. I called her myself to let her know."

"Well, this may present a problem. We haven't seen Reba since dinnertime last evening."

"She was gone all night?"

"And this morning as well. There's been no note and no call. Her father hasn't said as much, but I know he's concerned. When I saw you at the door, I assumed you had news of her, though I was almost afraid to ask."

"That's weird. I wonder where she went?"

"We have no idea. As I understand it she was out late the night before. She slept until noon and then she had a phone call—"

"That was probably me."

"Oh. Well, we wondered about that. She seemed upset afterwards. I believe she had a visitor. She was gone much of the afternoon and finally put in an appearance while her father was in the midst of his evening meal. He eats early most days, but this was closer to normal—shortly after six, I'd say. The cook had prepared chicken soup and his appetite seemed good. Reba wanted to chat with him and I decided to leave so the two could be alone."

"And she didn't mention anything to him?"

"He says not."

"I better talk to him myself. This is worrisome."

"I understand your concern, but he's resting right now. He's been working with his respiratory therapist and he's exhausted. I'd prefer not to disturb him. Why don't you come back later this afternoon? He should be up and about by four."

"I can't do that. This meeting is urgent, and if she's not going to make it, I need to know right now."

Her gaze dropped from mine and I could almost see her calculate the extent of her authority. "I'll see if he's awake and if he's up to it. You'd have to keep it brief."

"Fine."

She reached behind and opened the door, gesturing me inside. I noticed she put a foot out to prevent the cat from coming in. Rags was offended, shooting her a look. I stepped into the foyer, waiting for directions.

"This way."

She crossed toward the stairs and I followed in her wake. As she climbed the stairs, one hand trailing along the bannister, she delivered a comment over her shoulder to me. "I'm not sure what Reba's told you, but the two of us have never really gotten along."

"I wasn't aware of that. I'm sorry to hear."

"I'm afraid there's been a misunderstanding. She was under the impression I had designs on her father, which couldn't be further from the truth. I don't deny I'm protect-ive. I'm also outspoken when it comes to her behavior. Nord seems to think if he's 'supportive' and gives her everything she wants, eventually she'll straighten out. He's never understood what good parenting is about. Children have to take responsibility for what they've done. Only my opinion . . . not that anybody's asked."

I let that one slide. I knew little of their history and didn't feel a response would be appropriate.

We traversed the wide landing, moving down a carpeted corridor with bedrooms on both sides. The door to the master bedroom was closed. Lucinda tapped softly, then opened the door and looked in on him. "Kinsey's here about Reba. May I show her in?"

I didn't hear his response, but she stepped aside, allowing me to enter. "Five minutes," she said firmly.

24

Nord Lafferty lay propped up against a pile of pillows, his oxygen tank close by. His frail white hands trembled on the crocheted coverlet. I knew his fingers would be icy to the touch, as though his energy and warmth were retreating from his extremities to his core. It wouldn't be long until the last bright spark would be snuffed out. I moved to the side of his bed. He turned to look at me and a smile brought color to his face. "Just the person I was thinking of."

"And here I am. Are you feeling up to this? Lucinda says you had a session with the respiratory therapist. She doesn't want me wearing you out."

"No, no. I've rested a bit and I'm fine. I'm sorry to have to waste so much time in bed, but some days I'm not capable of anything else. I trust you received my check."

"I did. The bonus wasn't necessary, but I appreciate the thought."

"You deserve every penny. Reba enjoys her time with you and I'm grateful for that."

"Lucinda tells me she's been gone since dinnertime last night. Do you happen to know where?"

He shook his head. "She sat with me through supper and helped me into the library afterwards. I heard her making a call. A cab arrived thirty minutes later. She said not to worry, gave me a kiss, and that was the last time we spoke."

"She has a meeting at one o'clock today and then a second meeting at four. I can't imagine her a no-show. She knows how critical this is."

"She made no mention of it. I take it she hasn't been in touch with you."

"We talked briefly yesterday. She said she'd get back to me, but then she never called."

"She did have a visitor. Fellow she used to work with."

"Marty Blumberg?"

"That's him. He came up to the house and the two had their heads together for quite some time. She went out afterwards."

"Lucinda mentioned she was out late the night before."

"She didn't arrive home until two-thirty in the morning. I was still awake when she finally pulled in the drive. I saw the headlights flash across the ceiling and I knew she was safe. Old habits die hard. The months she was in prison—those were the only nights I didn't lie awake waiting for her. I imagine I'll die with an eye on the clock, frightened something's happened."

"Why'd she call a cab? Is something wrong with her car?"

He hesitated. "My guess is she was leaving town and didn't want her car sitting in a parking lot somewhere."

"But where would she go?"

Helplessly, Nord shook his head.

"Did she take any luggage?"

"I asked Freddy myself and she says she did. Mercifully, Lucinda'd left by then, or I'd never hear the end of it. She knows something's happened, but so far I've kept her in the dark. Lucinda's relentless, so do be careful or she'll wheedle it out of you."

"I gathered as much. Which cab company?"

"Freddy might remember if you want to talk to her."

"I'll do that."

A soft tap at the door and Lucinda appeared, holding up two fingers. "Two more minutes," she said, with a smile to indicate her good intent.

Nord said, "Fine," but I saw a flash of irritation cross his face. As soon as she closed the door, he said, "Lock that. And lock the door to the connecting bath while you're about it."

I gave him a momentary look and then crossed to the door and turned the thumb lock. A large white-tiled bathroom opened off to the right, apparently joining his bedroom with the one next to it. I locked the far bathroom door, leaving the near one ajar, and then returned to my seat.

He pulled himself up against the pillows. "Thank you. I suppose she means well, but there are times when she takes too much on herself. To date, I haven't appointed her my guardian. As for Reba, what do you propose?"

"I'm not really sure. I need to find her as soon as possible."

"Is she in trouble?"

"I'd say so. Shall I fill you in?"

"It's best I don't know. Whatever it is, I trust you to take care of it and bill me afterwards."

"I'll do what I can. Couple of government agencies are interested in talking to her about Beck's financial dealings. This is going to get sticky and my position's precarious as it is. When it comes to the feds, I don't want to end up on the wrong side of the fence. If I'm working for you, no privilege attaches to our relationship in any event, so hiring me won't serve as protection for either one of us."

"I understand completely. I wouldn't ask you to compromise yourself in the eyes of the law. That said, I'd be grateful for any help you can give her."

"Is her car still here?"

He nodded. "It's parked in the garage, which is unlocked as far as I know. You're welcome to take a look."

There was a tapping at the door and the handle turned. Lucinda rattled the knob impatiently, her voice muffled. "Nord, what's wrong? Are you in there?"

He gestured toward the door. I crossed and unlocked it. Lucinda turned the knob abruptly and pushed her way in, almost banging me in the face. She stared at me, apparently assuming I'd locked the door on my own. "What's this about?"

Nord strained to raise his voice. "I told her to lock it. I didn't want any further interruptions."

Her body language shifted from suspicion to injury. "You might have mentioned it. If you and Miss Millhone have private business to discuss, I wouldn't dream of interfering."

"Thank you, Lucinda. We appreciate that."

"Perhaps I've overstepped my bounds." Her tone was

frosty, the content designed to generate apologies or reassurances.

Nord offered neither. He lifted a hand, almost a gesture of dismissal. "She'd like to see Reba's room."

"What for?"

Nord turned to me. "Down the hall to your right—"

Lucinda cut in. "I'll be happy to show her. We don't want her wandering around on her own."

I glanced at Nord. "I'll get back to you," I said.

I followed Lucinda down the hall, noting her stiff posture and her refusal to look at me. When we reached Reba's room, she opened the door and then stood in my path forcing me to squeeze by her. Her eyes trailed after me. "I hope you're satisfied. You think you're so helpful, but you're killing him," she said.

I locked eyes with her, but she was far more practiced than I at delivering the withering glance. I waited. Her smile was set, and I knew she was the sort who'd find ways to get even. Lucinda, the bitch indeed. She stepped into the hall. I shut the door and locked it, knowing she'd get the point.

I turned and leaned against the door, making a visual survey, taking in the whole of the room before starting my search. The bed was made, a few personal mementos neatly arranged on the bedside table: a framed photo of her father, a book, a scratch pad, and a pen. No clutter. No clothing on the floor. Nothing under the bed. A phone, but no personal address book. I went through the desk drawers, uncovering items that must have been there for years: school papers, exam books, unopened boxes of stationery, which were probably gifts—certainly not her taste, unless she favored kitty-cat cards with cute sayings on the front. No personal correspondence. Dresser drawers were neat.

I checked the closet, where several empty hangers suggested the number of garments missing—six by my count. Among the articles she'd left behind were a navy blue blazer and a leather bomber jacket, askew on its hanger. I had no way of knowing what she'd packed. I wasn't even sure the size or the number of suitcases she owned. I sorted through idly, thinking back to the clothes I'd seen her in. I didn't spot her boots or either of the sweaters I remembered—the one red cotton, the other dark blue with a cowl neck. She'd worn both within the first few days of being home, which meant they might well be her favorites, garments she'd want with her on the road.

I went into the bathroom, which was close to barren: tawny marble floor tiles and countertop, spotless mirrors, and the smell of soap. The medicine cabinet had been emptied of items. No deodorant, cologne, or toothpaste. No prescription drugs. I could see a whitish spot on the marble counter where her toothbrush had lain. The hamper had been stuffed with blue jeans, T-shirts, and underwear; a bath towel, still faintly damp, crowded in on top. The shower pan was dry. Nothing in the trash.

I went back to the closet and studied the clothes. I took the bomber jacket off its hanger and checked the pockets. I found some loose change and a slip from a generic order pad that showed she'd paid for a cheeseburger, chili fries, and a Coke. No date and the restaurant wasn't mentioned by name. I slipped the receipt into my jeans pocket and returned the jacket to its hanger. I let myself out of the room and retraced my steps. As I passed Nord's room, I paused and leaned my head close to the door. I could hear the murmur of voices, primarily Lucinda's, and she sounded aggrieved. Any further conversation with him would have to wait. I went downstairs and found my way to the back part of the house.

The housekeeper was sitting at the kitchen table. She'd spread newspapers across the surface, on which she'd laid twelve place settings of sterling silver, two silver water pitchers, and a series of silver beakers. Some of the more ornate pieces had been sprayed with an aerosol polish that was drying to a strange shade of pink. The cloth she used on the flatware was black from the tarnish she'd removed. Her gray hair was wispy, curled and back-combed into a dandelion-like aureole with patches of scalp showing through.

I said, "Hi, Freddy. I've been chatting with Mr. Lafferty. He says you saw Reba last night before she left."

"Going out the door," she said, addressing her remark to the spoon.

"She took a suitcase?"

"Two—a black canvas overnight case and a hard-sided gray suitcase on wheels. She was wearing jeans and boots and a leather hat, but no jacket."

"Did you have a conversation?"

"She put a finger to her lips, like this was our little secret. I was having none of that. I've worked for Mr. Lafferty forty-six years. We don't keep secrets from one another. I went straight into the library and spoke to him, but before I managed to get him up from his chair, she was gone."

"Did she say anything about her intentions? Any talk of a trip?"

Freddy shook her head. "There were calls going back and forth, but she was quick to catch the phone so I never heard who it was. I couldn't even tell if the caller was a man or woman."

"You know it's a parole violation if she leaves the state," I said. "She could be sent back to prison."

"Miss Millhone, as fond as I am of her, I wouldn't withhold information or cover for her in any way. She's breaking her father's heart and the shame's on her."

"Well, if it makes any difference, I know she adores him, which doesn't change anything, of course." I took out a card with my home number scribbled on the back. "If you should hear from her, would you call me?"

She took my card and slipped it into her apron pocket. "I hope you find her. He doesn't have much time."

"I know," I said. "He told me her car's still parked in the garage."

"Use this back door. It's closer than going out the front. There's a set of keys on the hook," she said, indicating the service porch and mud room visible through the open doorway behind her.

"Thanks."

I snagged the keys and then took a diagonal path across a large brick apron, approaching what must have been the original carriage house, converted now to a four-car garage. Rags appeared from around the corner of the house. Clearly, his job was to oversee arrivals, departures, and all activities involving the property. Above the garage, I could see a stretch of dormer windows with curtains drawn across the glass, which suggested servants' quarters or an apartment, possibly Freddy's. One garage was empty, the retractable door standing open. I used it as ingress and

quickly spotted Reba's BMW parked against the far wall.
I felt obliged to explain myself to Rags as he followed in
my tracks. I got in on the driver's side and slid under the
wheel. I put the key in the ignition and checked the gas
gauge. The arrow jumped to the top, indicating a full tank
of gas.

I leaned over and popped the door to the glove compartment and then spent a few minutes sorting through the
accumulation of gasoline receipts, outdated registration
slips, and an owner's manual. In the side pocket to my
left, I found another handful of gasoline receipts. Most
were dated three to four months before Reba went to
prison. The single exception was a receipt dated July 27,
1987—Monday. She'd bought gas at a Chevron station on
Main Street in Perdido, twenty miles to the south. I added
the receipt to the other one in my pocket. I checked under
the front seats, the backseat, the floorboards, and the
trunk, but found nothing else of interest. I left the garage
and returned the keys to the hook in the mud room, then
collected my car. Last I saw of Rags, he was sitting on the
porch, calmly grooming himself.

I returned to the 101 and made a speedy round-trip to
my apartment, stopping off long enough to pick up the
photograph of Reba her father had given me. I folded it
and eased it into my shoulder bag before I headed for
Perdido. The four-lane highway follows the coastal contours with the foothills on one side and the Pacific Ocean
on the other. The concrete seawall all but disappears in
places, and waves crack up along the rocks in an impressive display of power. Surfers park their cars on the berm
and tote their surfboards down to the beach, looking as
sleek as seals in their form-fitting black wetsuits. I counted

eight of them in the water, straddling their boards, faces turned toward the waves as they waited for the surf to mount the next assault on the shore.

To my left, the steeply rising foothills were bare of trees and thick with chaparral. Paddle-shaped cactus had taken over large patches of eroding soil. The lush green, encouraged by the winter rains, had given way to spring wildflowers, and then died back to this tinderbox of vegetation, ripe for the autumn fires. The railroad tracks ran sometimes on the mountain side of the road and sometimes crossed under the highway and tracked the surf.

On the outskirts of Perdido, I took the first off-ramp and proceeded toward town on Main, checking addresses along the way. I spotted the Chevron station on a narrow spit of land that bordered the Perdido Avenue off-ramp. I pulled in and parked on the side of the station nearest the restrooms. A uniformed attendant was standing at the rear of a station wagon, topping off the tank. He spotted me, eyes lingering briefly before returning to his task. I waited until the customer had signed the credit card slip and the wagon had pulled away before I crossed to the pumps. I pulled out the photograph of Reba, intending to inquire if he'd worked on Monday and if so, if he remembered her. As I approached, however, something else occurred to me. I said, "Hi. I need directions. I'm looking for a poker parlor called the Double Down."

He turned and pointed. "Two blocks down on the right. If you get to the stoplight, you've gone too far."

It was close to two in the afternoon when I pulled into the one remaining space in the parking lot behind a low cinder-block building painted an unprepossessing beige. The sign in front flashed a red neon spade, a heart, a diamond, and a club in succession. The Double Down was written out in blue neon script across the face of the building. In lieu of stairs, a wheelchair ramp angled up to a windowless entrance, approximately four feet above ground. I climbed the ramp to the heavy wooden door with its rustic wrought iron hinges. A sign indicated that the hours ran from 10:00 A.M. until 2:00 A.M. I pushed my way in.

There were four large tables, covered in green felt, each with eight to ten poker players seated in wooden captain's chairs. Many turned and looked at me, though no one questioned my presence. Along the rear wall there was a galley-style kitchen with a menu posted above the service window. The selections were listed in removable black letters mounted in white slots: breakfast dishes, sandwiches, and a few dinner items. I was already partial to the scrambled egg and sausage breakfast burrito. I checked the receipt I'd found in Reba's jacket pocket—cheeseburger, chili fries, and Coke. The same items were listed on the board and all the prices matched.

The walls were paneled in pine. Along the acoustical-tile ceiling, a picture rail was festooned with strands of fake ivy and hung with framed reproductions of sports art, football dominant. The lighting was flat. All the players were men except for a woman at the back who was probably in her sixties. A chalkboard mounted on the side wall bore a list of names, presumably guys waiting for an open seat. To my surprise, there was no cigarette smoke and no alcohol in sight. Two color television sets mounted in opposing corners flickered silently with two different baseball games. There was scarcely any conversation, only the sound of plastic chips clicking together softly as the dealer paid off the winners and pulled in the losing bets. As I looked on, the dealers changed tables and three guys took advantage of the break to order something to eat.

There was a counter to my left and behind it, in a cubbyhole, a fellow was sitting on a stool. "I'm looking for the manager," I said. I was wondering, of course, if poker parlors had managers, but it seemed like a safe bet, so to speak. The guy said, "Yo," raising his hand without lifting his gaze from his book.

"What's the book?"

He held it up, turning the cover into view as though wondering himself. "This? Poetry. Kenneth Rexroth. You know his work?"

"I don't."

"The guy's awesome. I'd lend you this, but it's the only copy I have." He put his finger between the pages, marking his place. "You want chips?"

"Sorry, but I'm not here to play." I took Reba's picture from my bag, unfolded it, and held it out to him. "Look familiar?"

"Reba Lafferty," he said, as though the answer was self-evident.

"You remember when you saw her last?"

"Sure. Monday. Night before last. She sat at that table. Came in about five and stayed until we closed the place at two. Played Hold 'Em most of the night and then switched to Omaha, for which she has no feel whatever. Had a roll of bills about like this," he said, making a circle of his thumb and middle finger. "Chick's been out of prison a week, or that's the scuttlebutt. You her parole officer?"

I shook my head. "A personal friend. I was the one who went down to Corona and drove her home."

"Should have saved yourself the trip. Before you know it, she'll be on the sheriff's bus, heading the other way. Too bad. She's cute. About the way a raccoon's cute before it bites the shit out of you."

I said, "Yeah, well, there you have it. She took off last night and we're trying to track her down. I don't suppose you know where she went."

"Off the top of my head? I'd say Vegas. She dropped a bundle in here, but you could tell she was on a roll. She had that look in her eye. Bad luck or good, she's the kind who keeps going till all the money's gone."

"I don't get it."

"You don't gamble?"

"Not at all."

"My theory? Chick runs on empty. She gambles for the hype, thinking she can use that to fill herself up. Ain't never gonna happen. She needs help."

"Don't we all," I said. "By the way, why the Double Down? I thought the term was blackjack."

"We used to have blackjack until the owner phased it out. The locals prefer poker—skill over luck, I guess."

As soon as I reached my office, I grabbed a pencil and notepad, hauled out the phone book, and chose a travel agent at random. I dialed and when she answered, I told her I needed information about a trip to Las Vegas.

"What day?"

"Don't know yet. I work until five and I'm not sure what day I want to go. What flights do you show for weekdays after six P.M.?"

"I can check," she said. I heard *tappity-tap-tap* in the background and after a silence, "I see two. USAir at 7:55 P.M. by way of San Francisco, arriving Las Vegas at 11:16, or United Airlines 8:30 through Los Angeles, arriving LV at 11:17 P.M."

"Where else would I find poker parlors?"

"Say again?"

"Card parlors. Poker."

"I thought you wanted to go to Las Vegas."

"I'm looking at all the options. Anything closer to home?"

"Gardena or Garden Grove. You'd have to fly to LAX and find ground transport."

"That sounds doable. What flights do you have to Los Angeles after six P.M.? I know about the United flight at 8:30. Is there anything else?"

"I show a United at 6:57, arriving in Los Angeles at 7:45."

I was taking notes as she spoke. "Oh wow, thanks. This is great."

Somewhat testily, the travel agent said, "You want to book one of these or not?"

"I'm not sure. Let's try this. Say I had a few bucks in my hot little hand. Where else could I go?"

"After six P.M. weekdays?" she said, drily.

"Exactly."

"You could try Laughlin, Nevada, though there aren't any flights into Laughlin-Bullhead unless you want to fly charter."

"Don't think so," I said.

"There's always Reno-Lake Tahoe. The same airport services both."

"Could you . . ."

"I'm doing it," she sang, and again I could hear her tapping her computer keys. "United Airlines departing Santa Teresa at 7:55, arrives San Fran 9:07 P.M., departs 10:20, arriving in Reno at 11:16. That's all there is."

"I'll call you back," I said, and hung up. I circled the word "Reno," thinking about Reba's former cellmate, Misty Raine, allegedly living up there. If Reba were on the run, it might make sense to try connecting with a friend. Of course, consorting with a known felon was a parole violation, but she was already racking them up, so what was one more to her?

I dialed directory assistance in Reno, the 702 area code, and asked the operator for a listing under the last name Raine. There was one: first initial M, but with no address listed. I thanked her and hung up. I drew a second circle around the word "Raine," wondering if Reba had been in touch with Misty since her release. I picked up the phone again and dialed the number I'd been given for M. Raine. After four rings, a mechanical male voice said, "No one is home. Please leave a number." So uninformative. I really hate that guy.

At 4:30, I drove back to the Lafferty estate. As I pulled into the parking pad, I was happy to note Lucinda's car was gone. Rags was asleep in a wicker chair, but he roused himself to greet me, sitting at my feet politely while I rang the bell. When Freddy let me in, Rags took the opportunity to slip inside. He followed as Freddy led me to the library where Nord was entrenched on the sofa, propped up against a mass of bed pillows and covered with a throw. He said, "I had Freddy bring me down. I couldn't stand another minute upstairs." Rags jumped up on the sofa, walked the length of Nord's body, and sniffed at his breath.

I said, "You look better. You have some color in your cheeks."

"It's temporary, but I'll take what I can get. I'm assuming you've learned something or you wouldn't be back so soon."

I told him about the gasoline receipt and my drive to Perdido, where I'd been directed to the card parlor. I related the report I'd had about her poker losses Monday night. I couldn't see any point in plaguing him with the suspicion that she'd stolen twenty-five thousand dollars so I left that part out. "Reba mentioned a stripper named Misty Raine, a former cellmate of hers. Apparently, Misty moved to Reno after she got off parole. I'm thinking if Reba's caught up in gambling, it'd be smart to scout out a place where she could also lie low—"

"In which case she might try hooking up with this friend," Nord said, idly stroking the cat.

"Right. That way, instead of laying out money for a room, she could drop it all at the tables and hope for some return. According to directory assistance, there is an 'M. Raine' in Reno, with no published address."

"But wouldn't traveling to Reno be a violation of her parole?"

"So's the gambling," I said. "There's always the possibility she'll come back before she's missed, but I hate to see her take the chance. Has she been to Reno before?"

"Often," Nord said. "But how can you be sure she's there? Her friend isn't likely to admit to it."

"That's my thought, too. Reba didn't mention Reno?"

"She never said a word."

"What about the phone company? I've been wondering if you could ask about any long-distance calls in the past seven days. A match on Misty's number would at least suggest the two have been in touch."

"I can try."

I rounded up the phone book and dialed the number for him, taking him as far as the billing department before I handed him the phone. He identified himself by name and phone number and explained what he wanted. In the most glib and convincing manner imaginable, he spun a tale of an out-of-town visitor who'd made some long-distance calls but neglected to ask for time and charges. After chatting with the woman, he jotted a number in the 702 area code to which three calls had been made. He thanked her for her help, hung up, and handed me the slip. "I'm afraid this still doesn't give you an address."

"I have a police pal and I'm hoping he can help."

25

By the time I left Nord's it was close to 5:00. There was no point returning to the office so I headed for home. I let myself into my place and tossed my bag on a chair. Cheney had left two cranky messages wanting to know where the hell Reba was as she'd missed her 1:00 appointment with Vince and her 4:00 meeting with the FBI. I called Cheney's pager, punched in my number, and waited for the phone to ring, which it did ten minutes later.

"You called?"

"I need a favor. Can you check a phone number in Reno and get me an address?"

"Who for?"

"A friend of a friend."

"Is this about Reba?"

"Who else?"

He thought about it briefly. "She's already in more trouble than she knows. If she's up there, the best thing for all of us is to have Reno PD pick her up."

"That's one approach," I said. "On the other hand, you

still need her cooperation. I'm thinking about driving up to Reno and talking her into coming back—assuming I can find her."

"Does Holloway know she's gone?"

"I doubt it, but Reba doesn't see her until Monday, which means we have five days before she'll be missed. I'd hate to do anything behind Priscilla's back so you can tell her if you like. Or . . ."

"Or what?"

"You can run it by your IRS buddies and see what they have to say. Maybe her value to them takes precedence and they can square it with her PO. There's plenty of time to tell Priscilla once Reba's been debriefed."

"Give me the number in Reno and I'll get back to you."

"Why don't you talk to Vince first and then I'll give you the number. We can work it out from there."

"You don't trust me?"

"Of course I trust *you*. He's the one I'm worried about."

"What about tonight? You want to meet me at Rosie's? I've got a couple of reports to write, but it shouldn't take me long."

"Sounds good."

"I'll be there in a bit."

———

I left my front door ajar and crossed the patio to Henry's. His kitchen door was open and I knocked on the frame. "Henry? It's me."

"Come on in. I'll be right there," he said.

He had a pot of homemade soup simmering on a back

burner and I took that as a good sign. Henry seldom cooks
or bakes when he's feeling down. His glass of Black Jack
over ice was sitting on the kitchen table, the newspaper
neatly folded and waiting in his rocking chair. A newly
opened bottle of Chardonnay was sitting in a cooler on the
counter. He appeared from the hallway with a stack of
clean towels. "You should have poured yourself some wine.
I opened that for you. Something I want to talk to you
about. You have a few minutes?" He put the towels in a
kitchen drawer and took a wineglass out of the kitchen
cabinet and filled it halfway.

"Thanks. I have all the time you need. I've been feeling
out of touch. How are you?"

"I'm fine, thanks. What about you?" He resumed his
seat in the rocking chair and took a sip of his drink.

"I'm good," I said. "Now that we've cleared that pithy
matter, you want to tell me what's on your mind?"

He smiled. "Here's what I've been considering. I don't
think there's any remedy for my relationship with Mattie.
At the moment, she's calling the shots and I don't feel I
can impose if she's not interested. That's the way of the
world. We didn't know each other long and there are all
kinds of reasons it couldn't work—age, geography—the
particulars aren't relevant. What I realize is I enjoyed
having someone in my life. It put a spring in my step, even
at the age of eighty-seven. So I've been thinking it wouldn't
be such a terrible idea to make a phone call or two. There
were several women on the cruise who seemed lively and
nice. Mattie may be one of a kind, but that's beside the
point." He paused. "That's as far as I got, but I'd be
interested in your thoughts on the matter."

"I think it sounds great. I remember after you got home, you had all kinds of women leaving messages on your machine."

"Embarrassed me."

"Why?"

"I'm old-fashioned. I was taught men should be the pursuers, not the other way around."

"Times have changed."

"For the better?"

"Perhaps. You meet someone you like, why not make an effort? There's nothing wrong with that. If it works, it works, and if it doesn't, oh well."

"That's what I've been thinking. There's a woman named Isabelle, who lives here in town. She's eighty, which is a little closer to my age. She loves to dance, which I haven't done for ages. And another woman, Charlotte. She's seventy-eight and still active in real estate. She lives in Olvidado, close enough," he said. "You think one at a time might be good?"

"Nothing wrong with both. Get your feet wet. The more the merrier."

"Good. Then that's what I'll do." He clicked his glass against mine. "Wish me luck."

"All the luck in the world." I leaned forward and gave him a quick kiss on the cheek.

I sat in my favorite booth in Rosie's, the one in the rear where I can sip a glass of wine while I keep a close eye on the place. I've been a regular at the tavern for seven years and I still can't tell you the names of the day-drinkers or the other steady customers like me. Rosie's the only common thread, and I suspect if the other patrons and I compared notes, we all have the same complaint. We'd grouse at how she bullies us, but we'd all feel smug, seeing her mistreatment as a sign of just how special we are to her. William was working behind the bar. I'd stopped off on the way in and picked up the wine he poured when he saw me enter. He was busy, otherwise, I was certain, he'd have given me the latest in his medical reports.

Once settled, I took a sip of white wine so close to vinegar it was almost enough to make me swear off the stuff. Cheney had called back within minutes to tell me Vince was favoring the personal approach. He offered his blessings as long as he was given the contact number as well. I gave Cheney the number I'd picked up from Nord's telephone bill. I assumed Vince Turner would keep the information to himself, but I worried the FBI would get wind of what was going on and make trouble.

I put in another call to Nord to tell him I'd be taking off in the morning. He'd offered to underwrite the trip and I'd accepted, any charitable impulse quickly overridden by the need to pay my bills. I'd brought along a pocket atlas and I was flipping back and forth between Southern California and the western border of Nevada, considering my route. The obvious choice was to take Highway 101 to the 126, travel east as far as Highway 5, and then north to Sacramento, where I'd connect to the 80 on a north-to-east trajectory that would take me straight into Reno. If Cheney couldn't manage to get me Misty's address, I'd revert to the old-fashioned method—check the public library for the criss-cross directory where phone numbers are listed in numerical order and matched with the corresponding address.

Before I hit the road, I'd make a stop at the auto club and get a proper series of strip maps. I really didn't need them, but I like the white spiral binding and that arrow penned in orange that marches up the page. Makes me feel like I'm getting my money's worth for the cost of my annual membership. I moved on, making a mental list of clothing and toiletries I'd need to pack. I felt a hand on my shoulder and looked up with a smile, anticipating Cheney.

Beck slid into the booth across from me. "You seem happy to see me."

"I thought you were someone else." I took in the sight of him: chinos, dress shirt, with a windbreaker over it.

He laughed, thinking I was making a joke. Casually I closed the atlas and laid it on the seat beside me, then leaned to the right as though scanning the entrance. "Reba's not with you?"

"Not at all. That's why I stopped in. I'm trying to track her down." His eyes strayed to the atlas. "Are you taking a trip?"

"Just indulging in fantasy. I've got too much work piled up to go anywhere."

"Oh, that's right. You're a private detective. What are you working on?"

I knew he couldn't care less about my caseload unless it involved him. I figured he was fishing, wondering if I was part of the government conspiracy to reel him in. I said, "The usual. A skip-trace, a couple of employee background checks for the Bank of Santa Teresa. Stuff like that." I droned on for a bit, making it up as I went along. I could see his eyes glaze over and I hoped sincerely that I was boring him to death.

I looked up in time to see Rosie appear through the swinging kitchen doors. Her eyes lighted on Beck like a terrier spotting a rat. She made a beeline for the booth, barely able to suppress her happiness. Beck collected himself and rose to his feet. He extended a hand to her, then leaned forward and bussed her on the cheek. "Rosie, you look beautiful. You've had your hair done."

"I did myself. Is home permanent," she said.

As far as I could see, her hair looked the way it always did—badly dyed, badly cut.

She dropped her gaze modestly. "I'm remember what you want. Scotch. Double wit ice and water back. The twenty-fours year, not the twelve."

"Very good. No wonder your customers are loyal."

I thought she'd see through the flattery, but she lapped it up, nearly dropping a little curtsy before she scurried off to get his drink. He sat down again, watching her departure with a fond smile as though he really gave a shit. His gaze drifted back to mine. He was a cold, cold man. The missing twenty-five thousand had put him on red alert. He was out hunting to see who his enemies were.

I crossed my arms and leaned forward, resting my elbows on the table. There was something restful about being in the company of someone I disliked so much. I didn't have to worry about impressing him, which allowed me to focus on the game at hand. "How was Panama City?"

"Fine. Good. The problems started as soon as I came home. A little birdie tells me you and Reba got into trouble while I was gone."

"Me? Well, dang. What'd I do now?"

"You don't know what I'm referring to?"

"We went shopping at the mall if that counts for anything."

"The pow-wow with Marty. What was that about?"

I blinked at him twice as though drawing a blank and then allowed the light to dawn. "Friday night? We ran into him at the mall. Once the stores closed down, we stopped in at Dale's and ordered a couple of bowls of that chili guaranteed to give you the runs. Geez, Louise. Have you ever eaten that crap? Completely gross—"

"Enough already. Just get on with it."

"Sorry. So anyway, about that time Marty came in. He was happy to see Reba. She introduced us and we chatted for a bit. End of story."

He seemed to watch me from a distance, not yet satisfied. "What'd you chat about?"

"Nothing in particular. I meet the guy. I'm nice. That's all it amounted to. Why do you care?"

"You didn't talk about me?"

"You? Not at all. Your name never came up."

"Then what?"

"What do you mean, 'Then what'?"

"Where'd you go from there?"

I shrugged. "The office. Marty was bragging about the new digs and said he'd show us around, so we ended up doing a quick tour. He said you'd be pissed if you heard. Is that what this is about?"

"I don't believe you've finished. Isn't there something else?"

"Well, let's see now. Oh. Now this is earth shattering. I left my purse on the roof and we had to pop back the next day and go in search of it. What a pain in the ass *that* was."

Rosie approached with Beck's Scotch on a tray. We dropped the topic of conversation and smiled at her blandly while she set down a ceremonial doily and put his drink on it. Beck murmured his thanks without engaging her in further conversation.

She hesitated, hoping for another round of fawning and compliments, but he was intent on me. I was wishing she'd sit down and talk to us the rest of the night. Instead she flicked me a look, suspicious that this was romance a-brewing. Little did she know I was sitting there frantically assessing the situation, trying to guess how much Beck knew and how he'd acquired the information. If he'd seen security tapes, I had to make sure I accounted for all our comings and goings. I was aware my being a wiseass was getting on his nerves, but I couldn't help myself. Rosie manufactured a bit of small talk and then departed. I looked at Beck, waiting for his next move.

He picked up his Scotch and took a sip, watching me over the rim of his glass. "Clever. You explain it all so nicely, but somehow I'd swear you're lying through your pearly whites."

"My reputation must precede me. I'm good at lying," I said.

He set his drink on the table, making a circular pattern with the moisture from the bottom of the glass. "So where is she?"

"Reba? Beats me. We're not joined at the hip."

"Really. You've been with her constantly and now suddenly you have no idea? She must have said something."

"Beck, I think you've gotten the wrong impression. We're not friends. Her father paid me to go get her. That's the kind of pal I am. I took her to the parole office and the DMV. She was lonesome. We had dinner—"

"Don't forget Bubbles."

"Big deal. We went to Bubbles. I was feeling sorry for her. She doesn't have any friends, except Onni, who treats her like a piece of shit."

He thought about that briefly and shifted gears. "What's she told you about me?"

I tried to make the big eyes like Reba did when she was feigning innocence. "About *you*? Well, gosh now. She told me you screwed her brains out in the car the other night. She was going to give me all the nitty-gritty details about the size of your dick, but I begged off. No offense, but I don't find you nearly as fascinating as she does. Except for the current conversation. What are you fishing for?"

"Nothing. Maybe I misjudged you."

"Well, I doubt that, but so what? Sounds like you're the one in trouble and projecting it on us." I might have pushed the line too far because I wasn't that crazy about the look he turned on me.

"Why do you say that?"

"Because you're laying out all this bullshit and I don't have a clue what you want. You've peppered me with questions from the minute you sat down."

He was dead silent for about fifteen seconds—a long time in the middle of a conversation of this type. Then he said, "I believe she stole money from me when she was in the office that night."

"Ah. Got it. That's a serious accusation."

"Yes, it is."

"Why not turn the matter over to the cops?"

"I can't prove she did it."

I shook my head. "Doesn't sound right to me. I was with her when we toured the office and she never touched a thing. Me neither, for that matter. I hope you don't think I'm involved, because I swear I'm not."

"It's not you I'm worried about. It's her."

"You're worried?"

"I think she's in trouble. I'd hate to see her hurt."

"Why didn't you just say so up front?"

"You're right. I'm sorry. I went about this all wrong and I apologize. Truce?"

"We don't need a truce. I'm worried about her, too. She's back to smoking a pack a day and god knows what else. This morning, she was talking about booze and poker parlors. Scared the crap out of me."

"I didn't realize you'd seen her."

"Oh sure. I thought I mentioned that."

"You didn't, but that's good. I haven't heard a word from her since I got back. She's usually on the phone first thing, tugging at my sleeve. You know Reeb. She tends to cling."

"I'll say. Look, she talked about us having lunch tomorrow. Why don't I tell her to give you a call?"

He smiled tentatively, wanting to believe me. At the same time, I could sense his scrutiny, testing my comments for any false notes. Happily, since I'm a thoroughly accomplished liar, I could pass a polygraph, disavowing murder with blood still dripping from my fingers. He reached out and tapped my hand, something I'd seen him do with her. I wondered what the gesture meant, a sort of tag . . . you're it. "I hope I wasn't out of line. You're a good egg," he said.

"Thanks. You are, too." I reached out and tapped his hand in return.

He pushed up from the booth. "Better to let you go. I've taken up enough of your time as it is. Sorry if I was rude. I didn't mean to grill you."

"Hey, I understand. Stay and have another drink if you like."

"Nah, I gotta hit the road. Just tell Reba I'm looking for her."

"What's your schedule like tomorrow? Are you at the office all day?"

"You bet. I'll be waiting for her call."

Good luck, I thought. I watched him crossing the room, trying to see him as I had at first. I'd thought he was sexy and good-looking, but those qualities had vanished. Now I saw him for what he was, a guy accustomed to having his own way. The world centered on him and others were simply there to service his whims. I wondered if he were capable of killing. Possibly, I thought. Maybe not with his own hands, but he could have it done. Belatedly, a warm drop of sweat trickled down the middle of my back. I allowed myself a deep breath, and by the time Cheney showed up, I was feeling calm again and slightly bemused.

He slid in next to me and pushed a folded slip of paper in my direction. "Don't say I never did you one. Address is a rental. Misty's been in residence the past thirteen months."

"Thanks." I glanced at the address and put the paper into my pocket.

He said, "What's the smile about? You're looking pleased with yourself."

"How long have I known you? A couple of years, right?"

"More or less. You haven't *really* known me until this past week."

"Know what I realized? I've never lied to you."

"I should hope not."

"I'm serious. I'm a natural-born liar, but so far I haven't lied to you. That puts you in a category all by yourself . . . well, except for Henry. I can't remember ever lying to him. About anything important."

"Good news. I love the part where you say 'so far.' You're the only person I know who could say something like that and think it was a compliment."

Rosie reappeared and when she caught sight of Cheney, she shot me a quizzical look. She seldom saw me with one man, let alone two on the same night. Cheney ordered a beer. Once she was gone, I rested my chin on my fist so I could look at him. His face was smooth and there was the faintest web of lines at the outer corners of his eyes. Dark suede sport coat the color of coffee grounds. Beige shirt, brown silk tie hanging slightly askew. I reached out and straightened it. He caught my hand and kissed my index finger.

I smiled. "Have you ever dated an older woman?"

"Talking about yourself? I got news for you, kiddo. I'm older than you."

"You are *not*."

"I'm thirty-nine. April 1948." He took out his wallet, flipped it open, removed his driver's license, and held it up.

"Get serious. You were born in 1948?"

"How old did you think I was?"

"Somebody told me you were thirty-four."

"Lies. All lies. You can't believe a word you hear on the street." He put his license in his wallet, which he flipped shut and returned to his hip pocket.

"In that case, your body's even better than I thought. Tell me the day and month again. I wasn't paying attention."

"April 28. I'm a Taurus, like you. That's why we get along so well."

"Is that true?"

"Sure. Look at us. We're Earth signs, the Bull. We're the Boy Scouts of the Zodiac. Determined, practical, reliable, fair-minded, stable—in other words, boring as hell. On the downside, we're jealous, possessive, opinionated, and self-righteous—so what's not to like? We hate change. We hate interruptions. We hate being rushed."

"You really believe all that stuff?"

"No, but you have to admit there's a certain ring of truth to it."

Rosie returned to the table with Cheney's beer. I could tell she was tempted to loiter, hoping to catch a snippet of conversation. Both of us sank into silence until she left again.

Then I said, "Beck was here."

"You're changing the subject. I'd rather talk about us."

"Premature."

"Then why don't we talk about you?"

"Absolutely not."

"For instance, I like it that you don't wear makeup."

"I've worn it twice. That first day at lunch and then again the other night."

"I know. That's how I figured I could get you between the sheets."

"Cheney, we need to talk about Reba. I leave for Reno first thing tomorrow morning. We have to be operating off the same page."

His expression sobered to some extent, and I could see him shift into business mode. "Okay, but don't be dragging it out. We have better things to do."

"Business first."

"Yes, ma'am."

We spent the next ten minutes talking about Reba and Beck—what he'd said, what I'd said, and what, if anything, it meant. Cheney intended to call Priscilla Holloway in the morning and bring her up to speed. He thought the straightforward approach was preferable to taking the risk that she'd find out anyway. He'd refer her to Vince Turner and let the two of them work out their arrangements. If Holloway wanted Reba picked up, then all the better for him. Vince would be thrilled to have her under lock and key.

Finally, Cheney said, "Can we go now? All this talk about criminals is turning me on."

26

The drive from Santa Teresa to Reno took nine hours, including two potty stops and a fifteen-minute lunch break. The first seven hours got me as far as Sacramento, where Highway 80 intersects the 5 and begins its slow climb toward the Donner Summit, 7,240 feet above sea level. Smoke from a series of brush fires in the Tahoe National Forest had saturated the air with a pale brown haze that followed me across the Nevada state line. I reached the Reno city limits at suppertime and cruised through town just to get a feel for the place.

Most of the buildings were two and three stories tall, dwarfed by the occasional chunky hotel. Aside from the casinos, businesses seemed to be devoted to making cash readily available. The working theme was cheap food and pawnshops, with the word "GUNS" writ large on two out of every seven signs.

I chose an unprepossessing two-story motel in the heart of town, its prime attraction being that it sat on a lot adjacent to a McDonald's. I checked in, found my second-floor room, and put my duffel bag on the bed. Before I left again, I picked up the Reno phone book I found in my bed-table drawer. I went downstairs, left the phone book in my car, and then proceeded to McDonald's, where I sat in a window seat and treated myself to a couple of QPs with Cheese.

According to the strip maps I'd picked up at the auto club, Carson City—the last known domicile of the erstwhile Robert Dietz—was only thirty miles away. Because of Cheney, I thought about Dietz without bitterness, but without much interest. While I munched fries doused in ketchup, I opened the Reno city map and looked for the street where Misty Raine was supposedly living these days. Wasn't far away and I thought my next order of business was to pay a visit to the place.

I dumped my trash and returned to my car. With the map propped against the steering wheel, I sketched out my course. The route took me through spartan neighborhoods of pines, chain-link fences, and ranch houses faced in stucco or brick. Even at seven in the evening, the light was good. The air was hot and dry and smelled of pine pitch and charred oak from the California fires. I knew the temperatures would drop as soon as the sun went down. The lawns I passed were parched, the grasses scorched to a soft yellow-brown. The trees, on the other hand, were surprisingly green, dense healthy foliage a relief in the relentless washed-out beige of the surrounding landscape. Maybe the whole of it was designed to keep all the gamblers indoors where gaudy colors dazzled the eye, the air temperature was constant, and lights were ablaze twenty-four hours a day.

I spotted the house I was looking for—a one-story

yellow wood-frame bungalow with three stingy windows across the front. The trim was brown and the door to the single-car garage was decorated with three vertical rows of triangles, yellow paint on brown. Shaggy evergreens marked the corners of the house, and the flower beds along the drive were filled with desiccated plant stalks. I parked on the far side of the street about four houses down with a clear view of the drive. When sitting surveillance, there's always a concern that a neighbor will call the cops to complain about a suspicious vehicle parked out front. To create a diversion, I removed two orange plastic construction cones from the well of my car and then went around to the rear, where I opened the engine compartment. I set up the cones nearby, signaling engine trouble in case anyone got curious.

I stood near the car and scanned the surrounding houses. I saw no one. I crossed the street to Misty's front door and rang the bell. Three minutes passed and then I knocked. No response. I leaned my head against the door. Silence. I walked down the drive and scrutinized the padlocked garage, which was connected to the house by a short enclosed breezeway. Both garage windows were locked and the glass had been painted over. I headed around the front of the house. A wooden fence on the far side opened into a backyard that was depressingly bare. No sign of pets, no children's toys, no lawn furniture, and no barbecue. The windows that overlooked the patio were dark. I cupped my hands to the glass and found myself staring at a home office equipped with the usual desk and swivel chair, a computer, phone, and copier. No sign of Misty or Reba. I was disappointed, having persuaded myself that Reba was staying with her. Now what?

I returned to the car and settled in to wait, amusing myself by browsing the yellow pages of the borrowed phone book. Bored with that, I picked up the first one of three paperbacks I'd brought for this purpose. It was comforting that most of the nearby houses remained dark, suggestive of occupants at work. At 8:10, I saw a Ford Fairlane slow on approach and ease into Misty's drive. In the fading daylight, primer paint on the driver's side of the car glowed as though luminescent. A woman emerged, wearing a white halter, tight jeans, and high heels without hose. She reached into the backseat for two cumbersome plastic grocery bags, crossed to the front door, and let herself in. I could see interior lights go on as she moved through the house. This had to be the very Misty Raine that I was looking for.

So far no one had questioned my presence on the block. I got out, retrieved the orange plastic cones, and returned them to my car—this by way of being prepared for whatever might come next. I resumed my reading with the help of a penlight I dug out of my bag. At intervals I glanced up, but the house remained quiet and nobody entered or left. At 9:40, prison-strength exterior spots came on, flooding the driveway with harsh white light. Misty emerged from the house, leaving lights on behind her as she got in her tank-size Ford and backed out of the drive. I waited fifteen seconds, fired up the VW, and followed.

Once we reached the first intersection, there was sufficient traffic to provide cover, though I didn't think she had any reason to suspect she was being tailed. She drove sedately, refraining from any abrupt or tricky moves that would indicate a concern about the thirteen-year-old pale blue VW traveling three car lengths behind.

We proceeded into town. She took a right on East 4th and after half a block turned into a small city parking lot that sat between an Asian restaurant and a minimarket with a marquee that read: GROCERIES * BEER * SLOTS. I slowed and pulled over to the curb. I left the engine running while I spread out my Reno map and studied the layout. I don't know why I went to such trouble to disguise my purposes. Misty didn't seem to be aware of me and certainly no one else in Reno cared if I was lost. I watched her enter the minimarket and took advantage of her absence to pull into the same lot. I parked as close to the entrance as I could manage. Each space was numbered in paint, and a board posted on the brick wall of the market indicated that fees were paid on the honor system. Dutifully, I searched out the requisite window and inserted the number of dollar bills I thought would cover my stay. I was so engrossed in this display of municipal virtue that I didn't spot Misty until she was halfway across the street, munching a candy bar. She had a carton of cigarettes under one arm.

Her destination lay dead ahead, an adult-entertainment establishment called the Flesh Emporium. Under the double row of lightbulbs spelling out the name of the place, a blinking neon sign flashed: GIRLS, GIRLS, GIRLS ... NUDE, LEWD, AND CRUDE. And in smaller letters: TATTOOS AND PIERCING DONE WHILE YOU WAIT. And smaller still: BOOKS, VIDEOS, LIVE REVUES. The bouncer waved her in. I waited a decent interval and then crossed the street. There was a twenty-dollar cover charge that it grieved me to pay, but I ponied up the cash. I made a note to myself to add it to my expense account in a manner that didn't suggest play-for-pay sex.

Inside the entrance, a modest-size casino was hazy with

cigarette smoke, the air aglow with the ambient light from a hundred slot machines lined up back-to-back. In passing, I picked up the soft, goofy flute-and-bell music that accompanies play. The acoustical-tile ceiling was low, dotted with can lights, cameras, smoke alarms, and sprinkler heads. Scarcely anyone was seated at the slots, but farther in, beyond the blackjack tables, I could see a darkened bar with a wide apron built along one side. On three hotly lighted platforms nude dancers undulated, strutted, and otherwise exhibited body parts. Nothing they did seemed particularly lewd or crude. I found a table toward the rear, feeling ill at ease. Most of the customers were men. All were drinking and most paid little or no attention to the breasts and buttocks on parade in front of them.

There was no sign of Misty, but a waitress named Joy arrived at my table and placed a cocktail napkin in front of me. Sequined pasties the size of dinner mints chastely shielded her nipples from public scrutiny, and she wore a glittering fig leaf over what my aunt Gin would call her "privates." I ordered a bottle of Bass ale, theorizing there was no way the management could water it down. When Joy returned with my beer and a basket of tinted yellow popcorn, I paid the fifteen-dollar tab and tipped her an extra five bucks. "I'm looking for Misty. Is she here?"

"She just went to change. She'll be out in a bit. You're a friend of hers?"

"Not quite, but close enough," I said.

"Give me your name and I'll tell her you're here."

"She won't know me by name. A friend of a friend said I should look her up if I was ever passing through."

"What's the friend's name?"

"Reba Lafferty."

"Lafferty. I'll tell her."

I sipped my beer and picked at the cold, chewy popcorn, glad for the distraction as I didn't really favor watching nude women shaking their booties at me even from a distance. I'd imagined voluptuous, showgirl-style bodies, but only one of the three had the requisite football-size knockers. I figured the other two were saving up.

As it turned out, Misty hadn't gone to change clothes so much as to strip off the garments she was wearing when she got to work. Her legs were bare and only a thong and her high heels remained. She was tall and lanky, with pitch-black hair, a prominent collarbone, and long, thin arms. By way of contrast, she had breasts of burdensome dimensions, the kind that give you back problems and require a bra with straps so fierce they create permanent tracks across your shoulder blades like ruts worn in rock. Not that I've ever suffered from such a fate, but I've heard women complain. I couldn't imagine *choosing* to haul those things around. Her eyes were large and green with dark circles underneath that even heavy makeup couldn't hide. I placed her in her forties though I wasn't sure quite where.

"Joy says you're a friend of Reba's."

I didn't know stripper-greeting etiquette, but I stood and shook her hand. "Kinsey Millhone. I'm from Santa Teresa."

"Same as Reba," she remarked. "How's she doing these days?"

"I was hoping you'd tell me."

"Can't help you there. I haven't seen her in years. Are you in town on vacation or what's the deal?"

"I'm here looking for her."

One of Misty's shoulders went up in what passed for a shrug. "Last I heard she's in prison. California Institution for Women."

"Not anymore. She was released on the twentieth of this month."

"No fooling. Well, good for her! I'll have to drop her a line. The real world's a shock when you're not used to it," she said. "Hope she makes it."

"The prospects of that are dim. She did well at first, but lately things haven't been so hot."

"Sorry to hear that, but why come to me?"

"Just a long shot," I said.

"Must have been awful long. I've worked here a week. I don't get how you managed to track me down."

"Process of elimination. Reba told me you worked as an exotic dancer. With a name like yours, it wasn't difficult."

"Get off it. You know how many strip joints there are in this town?"

"Thirty-five. This is the thirteenth I've tried. Must be my lucky number. Can we chat?"

"About what? I start work in two minutes. I need time to get centered. Gig like this is tough unless you have your head on straight."

"I won't keep you long."

Gingerly she perched and I wondered if the wooden chair seat felt cold on her bare butt. The sensation couldn't be that keen, but she didn't yelp or otherwise vocalize dismay. She said, "Is this a fishing expedition or did you want something in particular?"

"Why do you ask?"

"I just thought if I heard from her, I could pass the message along—provided it's not obscene."

"I've heard she's in town. I'm hoping to talk her into coming back to California before she blows the terms of her parole."

"It's no skin off my nose what she blows. Or who, for that matter."

"I understand you were cellmates."

"Six months or so. I got out before she did—obviously."

"She told me you kept in touch."

"Why not? She's a nice kid and she's fun to be around."

"When was the last time you heard from her?"

Mock thought. "Must have been last Christmas. I sent her a card and she sent one back." She glanced over her shoulder. "Sorry to cut this short, but that music is my cue."

"If she happens to get in touch, tell her I'm in Reno. We really need to talk." I'd written the name of the motel, the telephone number, and my room number on a slip of paper that I handed her as she stood.

She took the note, though she had no place to put it unless she stuck it up her bum. "So who's paying you?"

"Her dad."

"Nice job. Like a bounty hunter, huh."

"It's more than a job. I'm a friend and I'm concerned about her welfare."

"I wouldn't lose any sleep over it. One thing about Reba, she can take care of herself."

I watched her head for the bar. The matching moons of her ass scarcely wobbled as she walked, and I could see the muscles in her thighs flex and relax with every step she took. Bumping and grinding must be better than Jazzercise, plus she didn't have to pay the weekly freight. I made a stop in the ladies' room, where I availed myself of the facilities before returning to my car.

Once there, I fired up the engine and sat with the windows rolled down, listening to the radio to pass the time. An hour later I began to worry about (1) running out of gas, or (2) asphyxiating myself with my own exhaust fumes. I cut the radio, killed the engine, and stared at the brick wall in front of me. This was the perfect screen on which to project recent memories of Cheney Phillips, probably not such a hot idea as he was many miles away.

Unwittingly, I dozed. Lights from a passing car flashed across my windshield and I woke with a start. I looked to my right as Misty's car passed behind me and slowed. She exited the parking lot and turned right. I started my car, backed out of the space with a quick chirp of tires, and pulled out shortly after she did. A glance at my watch showed it was 4:00 A.M. Apparently she did a six-hour shift instead of the usual eight put in by the ordinary working bloke. Then again, it was hard to imagine prancing around in high heels for more than a couple of hours at a stretch.

I kept the Ford Fairlane in view, allowing as big a lead as I could give her without losing sight of her altogether. There were fewer cars on the road now and many of the storefronts were dark. The big casinos were still doing a lively business. Misty pulled up to the front entrance to the Silverado Hotel. The wide overhang that stretched across the eight-lane drive was so densely studded with lightbulbs that the air seemed to shimmer with artificial heat. Misty got out of the car and handed the keys to a valet. The big glass doors opened and closed automatically as she approached and disappeared inside.

There were two vehicles in line between her car and mine. I leaped out and tossed my keys to an irritated-looking valet who'd been chatting with a pal. "Could you keep the car close? There's a twenty in it for you. I shouldn't be long."

Without waiting for a reply I trotted toward the front doors and entered the vast lobby, which was sparsely populated at that hour. I did a quick survey. There was no sign of Misty. She could have slipped into a waiting elevator, into the ladies' room to my right, or into the casino dead ahead. Pick one, I thought. As I moved into the casino, smoke settled around me like a delicate man-tilla. The silvery pings and grace notes from the slots were like a series of falling coins, the chirping of money as it trickled down the drain. Aisles ran in grids between the slot machines, the faces of which glowed bright red, green, yellow, and a saturated blue. I was struck by the patience of the few late-night players—like ants tending aphids on the underside of a leaf.

As I walked, I was glancing right and left, looking for Misty, whose height and black hair would surely set her apart. Toward the rear there were restaurants. I could see a coffee shop, a sushi bar, a pizza parlor, and an "authen-tic" Italian bistro offering six kinds of pasta and a variety of sauces, complete with Caesar salad, for $2.99. I spotted Misty in the lounge, though my gaze slid right past her at first and touched on the man who sat across the table from her. He was red-haired and gaunt, his complexion ruddy and pitted with acne scars. Neither saw me. I eased into

the lounge, which was open on two sides. I sat at the bar
some distance away, watching as the two conferred. The
bartender ambled over and I ordered a glass of Chardonnay. There were not many patrons present at that hour,
and I worried I'd be conspicuous sitting alone.

Out on the casino floor a great whooping and hollering
went up, and shortly thereafter a party of five women came
in, drunk and triumphant. One flourished a bucket of
quarters, having won a five-hundred-dollar jackpot. My
line of vision was obscured by their boisterous presence,
but they provided me cover. I watched Misty engaged in a
lengthy discussion with the man, leaning forward intently
as the two examined something on the table in front of
them. Finally, satisfied, she passed him a fat white number
10 envelope that I was betting contained a wad of cash. In
exchange, he returned the item to a manila mailing pouch
and handed it to her. I watched as she shoved it in her
oversize purse. I tossed a five-dollar bill next to my empty
glass and got up, leaving the bar in anticipation of her
departure. I paused near the elevators, sliding a glance in
her direction as she passed me and hurried toward the
door. I followed in her wake.

She gave the valet parker her ticket, and while she
waited for her car, I angled left, keeping my head turned
and my back to her. My car was parked near the entrance.
I reclaimed my keys, tipped the valet, and slid under the
wheel. Two minutes later, her car rolled into view and the
valet hopped out. She handed him a tip and took his place
under the wheel. I watched her exit the lot. I eased in
behind her, this time with only one car between. Once I
was convinced she was on her way home, I took a left and
sped along a parallel course. I arrived moments before she

did. I killed my lights and slouched in my seat, eyes barely clearing the steering wheel. She turned into her drive as she had before, parked, crossed to her front door, and went in.

The front light went out. I sat there for a minute, sorely tempted to return to my motel and crawl into bed. Surely she was in for the night, or what little was left of it. I was tired, I was bored, and I was hungry again. I pictured breakfast in a twenty-four-hour coffee shop: orange juice, bacon and scrambled eggs, buttered rye toast covered with strawberry jam. Then sleep. There had never been any guarantee that Reba was in Reno. I'd taken the chance because it made sense, given what I knew of her. The two of them had certainly been in touch—why else would her number show up on Nord Lafferty's telephone bill? But that hardly spoke to the issue of her present whereabouts. I sat up, staring at Misty's half-darkened house and the narrow line of light running along the bottom of her garage door.

Why park in the driveway when she had a garage right there in front of her? In one of those unexpected jolts, I was clunked in the noggin by the obvious. If Misty were alone, she probably wouldn't need two bulging bags of groceries or a carton of smokes. The groceries might have represented her weekly run, but the woman didn't smoke. In the time we'd spent chatting, most smokers would have found an excuse to light up. It was actually that thin line of light at the bottom of the garage door that made me curious. I got out of the car and crossed the street.

27

I checked the garage windows first. Nicks in the brown paint that covered the glass revealed a makeshift guest room: a chair, a chest of drawers, a double bed, and a lamp sitting on an end table fashioned from a cardboard box. The disheveled linens suggested current occupancy, as did the red cotton sweater flung at the bottom of the bed, which I recognized as Reba's. A hard-sided gray suitcase lay open on the floor near the chest of drawers. The duffel was unzipped on the chair, clothes spilling out.

I circled the house as I had before. The pull latch on the wooden gate made scarcely a sound as I moved into the backyard and approached the lighted window. I ducked and came up at an angle, peering over the sill. Reba and Misty sat together at the desk with their backs to me. I couldn't see what they were doing and their voices were too muffled to discern the topic of conversation, but it was sufficient for the moment to know that Reba was in range.

Here was the question I asked myself: did I dare go back to my motel without confronting them? I was desperate for sleep, but I worried if I waited until morning, one or both of the women would be gone. Of course, I'd be facing the same dilemma anytime I let Reba out of my sight. For the moment, I was reluctant to give up the only advantage I had, which was that I knew where she was, but she didn't know that I knew.

Blessedly, as I watched, Misty gathered up the items they'd been inspecting and tucked them into the mailing pouch I'd seen earlier. Reba left the room and Misty followed, flicking the light switch as she passed. I made my way to the front of the house and hovered in the shadow of the evergreens. Ten minutes later, the living room light went out. I eased across the front of the house to the drive. Another fifteen minutes passed and then the line of light under the garage door was extinguished as well. I figured my little chickadees were in for the night.

I drove back to my motel through a city that was wide awake but quiet. The sun wouldn't be up for another hour or so, but the sky had already lightened to a pearly gray. I parked, took the stairs to the second floor, and unlocked my door. The room was drab but clean enough, as long as you didn't use a black light or get down on your hands and knees with a magnifying glass. I peeled off my clothes and took a good hot shower, then did what I could to secure the drapes across the window. The fabric was a heavyweight plastic, dark red, and very tastefully flocked. Add to that vinyl wallpaper with its lightning bolts of silver and black, and you had a most amazing decor. I pulled back the pink chenille spread and settled between the sheets, turned off the lights, and slept like the dead.

At some point, my subconscious gave me a nudge. I remembered Reba telling me what a whiz Misty was at reproducing fake passports and other phony documents. Was that why Misty was meeting the fellow at the Silverado? Even in my sleep, I felt a whisper of fear. Maybe Reba was planning to make a run for it.

At 10:00 the next morning the phone rang. I lifted the handset and laid it against my ear without moving my head. "What."

"Kinsey, this is Reba. Did I wake you?"

I rolled over on my back. "Don't worry about it. I appreciate the call. How're you doing?"

"Pretty much okay until I heard you were here. How'd you find me?"

"I didn't find you, I found Misty," I said.

"So how'd you do that? I'm just curious."

"Detective work, dear. That's what I do for a living."

"Huh. That surprises me."

"What does?"

"I figured Pop was able to hire you because you weren't any good. Clearly you weren't busy, or why would you agree to such a dumb-ass job? Drive his daughter back from prison? You can't be serious."

"Thanks, Reeb. That's nice."

"I'm saying I was wrong. Truth is, it shocked the hell out of me when Misty said you showed. I still don't get how you did it."

"I have my little ways. I hope you called for something more important than congratulating me for being less incompetent than you thought."

"We need to talk."

"Tell me when and where and I'll be there with bells on."

"We'll be at Misty's until noon."

"Great. Give me the address and I'll be over in a bit."

"I thought you'd already have the address."

"Guess I'm not perfect," I said, though as a matter of fact I was. She recited the address and I pretended to make a note.

Once she hung up, I got out of bed and crossed to the window. I pushed open the drapes and winced at the harsh desert sun. My room looked out over the backside of another dingy two-story motel, so there wasn't much to see. By resting my forehead against the glass, I could see the flashing neon sign on the casino down the street still winking its invitation. How could anyone drink or gamble at this hour?

I brushed my teeth and showered again, trying to jump-start myself. I dressed and then sat down on the edge of the bed and put a call through to Reba's father. Freddy told him I was on the line and he took the call in his room, sounding frail. "Yes, Kinsey. Where are you?"

"At the Paradise. It's a motel in downtown Reno. I thought I'd give you an update. Reba called a while ago. I'm on my way over to Misty's to talk to her."

"You found her, then. I'm glad. That didn't take long."

"I cheated. Someone gave me Misty's home address before I left Santa Teresa. I kept an eye on the place for hours, but I didn't think Reeb was there. Misty has a very promising career as a nude dancer at a strip joint called the Flesh Emporium. I followed her to work and chatted with her before she went on. When I asked about Reba, she never batted an eye. Swore up and down the two of 'em hadn't been in touch since Christmas. I gave her the number of my motel and lo and behold, Reba called."

"I hope you'll be able to persuade her to come home."

"Hey, me too. Wish me luck."

"Ring me anytime you like. I appreciate your efforts on her behalf."

"Happy to be of help."

We exchanged a few more remarks and I was preparing to disconnect, when I heard a small click. I said, "Hello?"

"I'm still here."

I hesitated. "Is Lucinda there?"

"Yes. She's downstairs. Did you want to speak with her?"

"No, no. I was just curious. I'll call you as soon as I know where we stand."

After I hung up, I sat for a moment and stared at the phone. I was almost certain Lucinda had been listening in. Freddy would never be guilty of such an offense. Lucinda, on the other hand, was clearly someone who needed to insert herself in the thick of every situation, someone who needed to be informed so she could exercise control. I thought about how she'd pumped me for information, how much she'd resented being locked out of Nord's room when he and I conferred. Under the guise of being oh-so-concerned, she'd wreaked havoc in Reba's life, and she'd do so again if she had the chance. She was the kind of woman you didn't want to turn your back on when leaving a room.

I crossed the motel parking lot to McDonald's, where I ordered three large coffees, three OJs, three hash browns, and three Egg McMuffins to go. According to my calculations, Misty, Reba, and I—assuming we cleaned our plates—would each be supplied with 680 calories, 85 grams of carbohydrate, and 20 grams of fat. I amended my order, adding three cinnamon buns just to round things out.

I drove back to Misty's, this time parking in the driveway. Reba was waiting when I knocked on the door. She was barefoot, in a pair of red shorts and a white tank top without benefit of a brassiere. I held the bag out. "Peace offering."

"What for?"

"Invading your turf. I'm sure I'm the last person in the world you wanted to see."

"Second to last, just ahead of Beck. You might as well come in," she said. She took the bag and moved down the hall toward the kitchen, leaving me to close the door. I did a quick check of the living room in passing. The interior was sparsely furnished: bare linoleum flooring, wood-laminate coffee table, one of those brown tweed couches that can flatten to a bed. Brown tweed chair, end table, lamp with a flouncy shade. The next room on the right was the office I'd seen. There was a modest-size bedroom across the hall.

"Getting an eyeful?" Misty asked. She sat at the kitchen table in a black satin robe that was tied at the waist, boobs close to bulging out of her lapels. I was surprised the weight didn't cause her to lose her balance and flop over in her plate.

Reba had a lighted cigarette on the ashtray in front of her. She was drinking a Bloody Mary.

Oh, perfect, I thought.

"You want one?"

"Why not? It's after ten," I said. I reached into the McDonald's bag and unloaded the goodies while Reba made me a drink and set it at my place. I looked at Misty. "You're not having a drink?"

"I got bourbon in here," she said, pointing to her coffee with a red-lacquered nail.

I sat down and doled out hash browns and Egg Mc-
Muffins, leaving the cinnamon buns, orange juice, and
coffee in the center of the table. "Sorry if I seem rude, but
I'm starving to death." Neither seemed to object as I
unwrapped my Egg McMuffin.

There was a blissful few minutes while the three of us
munched. I figured business could wait. I didn't have a
clue what we were doing anyway.

Reba finished first. She wiped her mouth on a paper
napkin she kept wadded in her fist. "How's Pop?"

"Not that well. I'm hoping to talk you into going home."

She took a drag of her cigarette. The house felt chilly
and I marveled at her bare arms and legs. I tried a sip of
Bloody Mary—largely vodka with a thin mist of Bloody
Mary mix on top, like blood in a toilet bowl. I could feel
my eyes cross as the burning liquor went down. She said,
"Does Holloway know?"

"What? That you left the state? That'd be my guess.
Chency told me he'd be getting in touch with her."

"Lucky I'm having fun."

"Mind if I ask why you left?"

"I got bored being good."

"Must be a record. You lasted ten days."

She smiled. "Actually, I wasn't all that good, but I got
bored anyway."

"Is Misty in on this?"

"Meaning, can we talk in front of her? She's my best
friend. You can say anything you like."

"You blew all the money, didn't you? Salustio's twenty-
five grand."

"Not *all* of it," she said.

"How much?"

She shrugged. "Little over twenty. Well, maybe more like twenty-two. I have a couple of thousand left. I figure there's no point talking to him if I don't have the rest. What am I supposed to do, offer him small monthly payments until I've satisfied the debt?"

"You have to do something. How long do you think you can duck a guy like that?"

"Don't worry about it. I'm working on it. I'll figure it out. Anyway, maybe I'll be back in prison before he catches me."

"That's a happy thought," I said. "I don't understand why you can't go back to Santa Teresa and talk to Vince. There's still a chance the feds can cut you a deal."

"I don't need to make a deal with the feds. I got something in the works."

I turned to Misty. "She's nuts, right? I mean, how nuts is she?"

"Might as well leave her alone. Truth is, you can't save anybody but yourself."

"I'm afraid I'd have to agree with you there," I said, then to Reba, "Look, all I want is to get you back to Santa Teresa before shit comes raining down on your head."

"I get that."

"So why don't we leave it at this? You know where I'm staying. I'll hang out until seven tomorrow morning. If I don't hear from you by then, I'll drive back alone. But I gotta warn you—at that point, I'm calling the Reno PD and telling 'em where you are. Fair enough?"

"Oh, thanks. You think that's fair? Calling the Reno cops?"

"As fair as you're going to get. You'd be wise to spend time with your dad while you can."

"That's the only reason I'd go back, assuming I do."

"I don't care about your motive—just getting you there."

I went back to the motel, where I spent one of the most wickedly enjoyable days I've experienced in some time. I finished one paperback novel and started the next. I napped. At 2:30 I bypassed McDonald's and ate at a rival fast-food place. Afterward, I would have taken a walk, but I really didn't care what was out there. Reno is probably a very keen town, but the day was hotter than blue blazes, and my room, while glum, was at least habitable. I slipped my shoes off and read some more. At supper time, I called Cheney and brought him up to speed.

I went to bed at 10:00 and got up at 6:00 the next morning, showered, dressed, and packed my bag. When I got down to my car, I found Reba perched on her suitcase with her duffel at her feet. She had on the same red shorts and tank top she'd been wearing the morning before. Bare legs. Flip-flops.

I said, "This is a surprise. I didn't think I'd see you."

"Yeah, well, I surprised myself. I'll go with you on one condition."

"There aren't any conditions, Reba. You go or you don't. I'm not going to bargain with you."

"Oh, come on. Hear me out. It's no big deal."

"Okay, what."

"I need to make a stop in Beverly Hills."

"I don't want to make a detour. Why Beverly Hills?"

"I have to drop something off at the Neptune Hotel."

"The one on Sunset?"

"That's right. I swear it won't take any time at all. Will you just do me this one tiny thing. Please, please, please?"

I swallowed my irritation, thankful she'd agreed to come at all. I unlocked the car door on the passenger side, flipped the seat forward, and tossed my duffel in the rear. As Reba added her two bags, I noted that the duffel bore a United Airlines tag and a small green sticker showing the bag had cleared security. I'd been right about the fact she'd flown to Reno.

"We might as well have a decent breakfast before we take off. My treat," she said.

We had the McDonald's to ourselves. We gorged on the usual, though even as I ate, I swore off junk food for life, or at least until lunch. A couple of guys came in after us and then the place began to fill up with people on their way to work. By the time we visited the ladies' room and got into the car, it was 7:05. I gassed up at the nearest Chevron station and we headed out of town. "If you smoke in my car, I will kill you," I said.

"Blow it out your butt."

Reba was in charge of the map, directing me to the 395, which cut straight south to Los Angeles. Somehow I knew the detour would be a pain in the ass, but I was so relieved to have her with me, I decided not to make a fuss. Maybe she'd experienced a change of heart and she was ready to take responsibility for herself. Skittish as she was, I figured the best thing I could do was to keep my observations and opinions to myself.

Conversation was in short supply. The problem in dealing with people who are out of control is that the choices are so few—two being the actual number if you want to know the truth: (1) You can play counselor, thinking that perhaps no one (save yourself) has ever offered the rare tidbit of wisdom that will finally cause the light to dawn. Or (2) You can play persecutor, thinking that a strong dose of reality (also delivered by you) will shame or cajole the person into turning her life around. In both instances, you'll be wrong, but the temptation is so strong to take one role or the other that you'll have to bite your tongue bloody to keep from jumping in with all the lectures and the finger wagging. I kept my mouth shut, though it required an effort on my part. She was mercifully quiet, perhaps sensing my struggle to mind my own business.

28

On the road, Reba fiddled with the radio until she found a station that didn't sound like it was broadcasting from Mars. We listened to country-western tunes while I played bumper tag with the same three cars: a pickup with a camper shell, an RV, and a couple of college students in a U-Haul truck. One would pass me and then the next and then I'd pass one of them, a form of vehicular leapfrog that had us hopping over one another at irregular intervals. At the back of my mind, I wondered if we were being followed, but I couldn't imagine how Beck or Salustio could manage to get a bead on us.

Where the 395 and Highway 14 intersected, the kids in the U-Haul went straight while we stayed on Highway 14, angling south and west. Eventually we connected to the San Diego Freeway and drove south. By then the RV had disappeared and I saw no sign of the pickup with the camper shell. Nervous-making nonetheless.

It was close to 3:00 when I got off the freeway at Sunset Boulevard, took a left, and followed the road east again through Bel Air and into Beverly Hills. Reba played navigator, tracking street addresses though it really wasn't necessary. A few blocks beyond Doheny, the Hotel Neptune loomed into view, an Art Deco wonder that vaguely mimicked the Empire State Building, its shoulders narrowing to a point. I'd read an article about the place in a copy of *Los Angeles Magazine*. The property had recently been expanded to encompass a large parcel of land on each side, which allowed the creation of a sweeping entrance and additional guest parking. A name change and the multimillion-dollar renovation had propelled the old hotel into prominence again. Now it was the hot new destination for rock stars, actors, and wide-eyed tourists hoping to be considered hip.

I pulled into the sweeping semicircular drive, taking my place sixth in line behind two stretch limousines, a Rolls, a Mercedes, and a Bentley. This was clearly check-in time. A car-park valet and two to three uniformed bellhops hovered around each vehicle, assisting the guests as they emerged, unloading bag after bag from open trunks onto rolling brass luggage carts. A doorman in livery and white gloves whistled up a taxicab that cut around me on the left and pulled up in front. Two hotel guests dressed like tramps ducked into the cab and I watched it pull away.

Reba said, "This is nuts. Why don't I just run in?"

"Forget it. I don't want you out of my sight."

"Oh, for heaven's sake," she said. "What do you think, I'm going to duck out the back and leave you here by yourself?"

As that was exactly what I thought, I didn't bother to reply. When our turn came, I handed the keys to the

SUE GRAFTON

parking valet while Reba dazzled him with a smile and pressed a folded bill against his palm. "Hey, how're you? We'll be back in two minutes."

"We'll have it ready for you."

"Thanks." She moved on into the hotel, boobs jiggling, her slim legs flashing in her red shorts. The guy was so busy ogling her, he nearly dropped the car keys.

The interior of the hotel was a pastiche of dark green marble and mirrors, wall sconces, torchères, and potted palms. The carpet was done in shades of green and blue, stylized waves, which were part of the nautical motif. Not surprisingly, the Roman god Neptune was depicted in a series of massive gilt-and-stucco bas-relief panels, driving his chariot across the waters, shaking his trident to bring down floods, saving a damsel from a satyr. Artificial light glowed from a five-tiered fountain of glass. The chairs were blond wood, the occasional tables lacquered in black. A wide marble staircase curved up to the mezzanine, where I could see black pedestals set in green fluted niches, each bearing an urn filled with fresh flowers.

The lobby walls were curved, with banquettes covered in a fabric that mimicked undulating sea grasses. Swing tunes playing at almost subliminal levels. Two lines had formed in front of the marble-sheathed reception desk— guests checking in, picking up messages, conversing with the staff.

Reba paused to get her bearings and then said, "Wait here."

I took a seat in a curved-back chair, one of four arranged around an etched-glass coffee table. In the center was a crystal bowl in which gardenias floated. I watched as she crossed to the concierge, a middle-aged man in a tuxedo. His desk was a sinuous curve of inlaid woods, banded in chrome and topped with a green glass counter, subtly lighted from below. She removed a manila mailing pouch from her purse, wrote something on the front, and handed it to him. After a brief conversation, he placed the manila envelope on a credenza against the wall behind his desk. She asked him a question. He consulted his files and extracted a white envelope, which he handed to her. She put it in her purse and then crossed to the house phone and picked up the handset. She had a conversation with someone and then returned. "We're meeting in the cocktail lounge."

"Oh, happy day. Can I join you?"

"Don't be a smartass. Of course."

The cocktail lounge was located on the far side of the lobby, across from the elevators. The bar itself was a streamlined curve, sheathed in glass panels that were etched with coral reefs, sea creatures, and goddesses in various states of undress. The space was large and dark, the indirect lighting augmented by a votive candle in the center of each table. The place was almost empty, but I was guessing that within the hour the bar would start filling up with hotel guests, starlets, hookers, and local business types.

Reba snagged a table close to the door. It was only 3:10, but knowing Reba, she'd be ready for a drink. A cocktail waitress wearing a snug gold satin vest, matching shorts, and gold mesh hose, delivered an order of drinks to a nearby table and then approached ours.

Reba said, "We're expecting someone else."

"You want to order now or wait?"

"Now is fine."

The waitress looked to me.

"I'll have coffee," I said, already focused on the drive ahead. This was Saturday so at least we wouldn't have to deal with rush-hour traffic, but it would still be a hard couple of hours, given the seven and a half we'd done.

"And for you?"

"Vodka martini with three olives and a double whiskey for my friend."

The waitress moved toward the bar.

"I don't get it," I said. "You know drinking's a parole violation. If Holloway finds out, she'll come down on you like a ton of bricks."

"Oh, please. It's not like I'm doing *drugs*."

"But you're doing everything else. Don't you want to hang on to your freedom?"

"Hey, you know what? I was free when I was in. I didn't drink or smoke or do drugs or screw around with any dumb-ass guys. You know what I did? I picked up computer skills. I learned to upholster a chair, which I'll bet you sure as shit can't do. I read books and made the kind of friends who'd give their lives for me. I didn't know how happy I was till I got out in this kiss-ass world. I don't give a shit about Holloway. She can do anything she wants."

"Okay by me. It's your lookout," I said.

Reba's sullen gaze was fixed on the bank of elevators directly across from us. Above each elevator there was an old-fashioned half-moon of brass, with a moving brass arrow indicating the progress of the elevators going up or coming down. I watched as the last elevator in line paused at the eighth floor and then worked its way down. The doors slid open and Marty Blumberg emerged. Reba waved and he headed in our direction. When he reached our table, she tilted her head so he could kiss her cheek. "You're lookin' good," he said.

"Thanks. So are you."

Marty pulled out a chair with a glance at me. "Nice seeing you again," he said. His attention shifted back to her. "Everything okay?"

"We're cool. I left something for you at the desk. Thanks for this," she said, patting her bag.

He reached into the pocket of his sport coat and took out a claim check that he slid across the table.

"What's this for?"

"Surprise. A little something extra," he said.

Reba glanced at the claim check and slipped it in her purse. "I hope it's something good."

"I think you'll like it," he said. "What's your timetable? Can you hang out long enough to have dinner with me?"

I opened my mouth to protest, but Reba surprised me by wrinkling her nose, saying, "Nah, better not. Kinsey's anxious to get home. Maybe some other time."

"God willing and the creek don't rise."

Marty took out a cigarette pack and placed it on the table. Without asking, Reba helped herself to one, which she stuck between her teeth, giving it a waggle to request a light. Marty picked up a packet of hotel matches, struck one, held the flame to her cigarette, and then fired up one for himself.

The waitress returned with our order, placing the bill at Marty's elbow. Reba took a sip of her martini and closed her eyes, savoring the vodka with such reverence that I could almost taste it myself. The two of them launched into an inconsequential conversation. I was peripherally included, but it was all low-key chat, a series of drifting subjects that didn't signify much of anything as far as I could tell. I drank two cups of coffee while they tossed down their drinks and ordered a second round. Neither showed the slightest sign of inebriation. Marty's face was more flushed than I'd seen it, but he was in control of himself. Eventually their cigarette smoke began to get on my nerves. I excused myself and retired to the ladies' room, where I wasted as much time as I dared before returning to the table. I sat down again and sneaked a look at my watch. We'd been in the hotel bar forty-five minutes and I was ready to hit the road.

Reba leaned forward and put a hand on Marty's arm. "We probably ought to get going. I'll make a quick trip to the loo and meet the two of you out there." She tipped her glass and sucked down the rest of her drink, chomping on the olive as she moved toward the ladies' room.

I watched Marty calculate a tip and sign the drinks off to Room 817. "How long have you been here?" I asked.

"Couple of days."

"I take it you won't be driving back with us."

"Don't think so," he said, amused.

I didn't see the humor myself, but whatever he and Reba'd cooked up between them had left him feeling smug.

"What happened with your phone? Was the line tapped or not?"

"Don't know. I decided not to hang around and find out."

He pocketed his copy of the receipt and then got up, holding my chair politely. The two of us moved toward the elevators and stood together saying nothing while we waited for Reba. Across the lobby, I saw her emerge from the ladies' room. Marty's gaze followed mine. I saw his focus shift to the left. Two men in chinos and sport coats were crossing the lobby with purposeful strides. I thought they were heading for the cocktail lounge. I turned and looked behind me, half-expecting to see what was generating such urgency. Marty took a step to one side to get out of their path. One man caught the doors to the nearest elevator before they slid shut. He stepped in and extended his hand again as though to hold the door for his friend. The second man bumped up against Marty, who said, "Hey, watch it!"

The man gripped Marty's arm, his forward motion forcing Marty to walk in lockstep into the waiting elevator. Marty flailed and struggled to free himself. He might have succeeded, but one of the two men knocked his feet out from under him. Marty went down on his back, flinging his arms across his face to ward off the savage kick he could see coming at him. The shoe made contact with a wet, thick sound that opened a split in his cheek. The other man pressed the button. In that moment before the doors slid shut, Marty's gaze caught mine.

I said, "Marty?"

The doors closed and the floor indicator moved up.

Two other people in the lobby turned to see what was wrong, but by then everything appeared to be normal. The entire sequence took no more than fifteen seconds.

Reba reached my side, her eyes enormous, the color draining out of her cheeks. "We gotta get out of here."

I banged on the Up button, transfixed by the sight of the arrow as it inched toward the eighth floor and came to a halt. Fear was bathing my internal organs with sufficient acid to eat through my chest wall. Two elevators down, the doors slid open. I grabbed her arm and turned her toward the lobby. "Go get hotel security and tell 'em we need help."

She pulled at my fingers and then lifted her elbow and swung upward to break my grip. "Bullshit. Get off me. Marty's on his own."

I didn't have time to argue. I pushed her as though I could propel her all the way to the front desk, and then I got on the waiting elevator and pushed the button for 8. I had no faith whatever that she'd do as I said. My heart thumped as adrenaline pushed through my system like a drug rush. I needed a game plan, but I didn't know what I was facing. As the elevator climbed, I searched my shoulder bag, though I already knew there was nothing in it in the way of weapons. No gun, no penknife, no pepper spray.

The elevator doors slid open on 8. I stepped into the hall and trotted to the T intersection where the long and short corridors met. I spotted the sign indicating which grouping of room numbers was located on the left and which was on the right, but I could barely make sense of it. I was talking to myself, a litany of cuss words and instructions. I heard a muffled shout of pain, someone banging into a wall somewhere to my left. I race-walked in that direction, scanning room numbers as I went. The hall had a claustrophobic feel to it, Nile green paint, a low ceiling that consisted of four thick cutaway layers stair-stepped back from a central panel of dull artificial light. Every twenty feet there were fluted niches of the sort I'd seen when looking up from the lobby toward the mezzanine. In each niche, there were two black lacquered wooden chairs arranged on each side of a round, glass-topped table set with an urn of fresh flowers. I picked up a chair and held it in front of me, searching for 817 at a pace that reminded me of dreams I'd had: I couldn't make my body move. I walked but I didn't seem to get anywhere.

The door to Marty's room was ajar. I kicked it inward, but the two guys were already on their way out, dragging Marty between them. I was saying *Pick-one-pick-one-pick-one* to myself, so I chose the guy on my right and thrust hard, hitting him bang-on in the face with the legs of the chair. I made contact, jamming hard. The sound he made was savage but the blow didn't seem to do any harm. He grabbed the chair, wrenching it out of my hands. I saw his fist coming at me, low and fast, smacking into my solar plexus with a paralyzing punch that put me down on my butt. The sour taste of regurgitated coffee rose in my throat in a blinding burst of nausea. I couldn't catch my breath and for a terrifying few minutes I thought I'd suffocate where I sat. I looked up in time to see the chair coming down at me. I felt the bang and registered the jolt, but no pain. I was gone.

29

I was lying on a bed, caught up in a confusion of conversations, which seemed to be about me. It reminded me of car trips as a kid, listening to the low, lazy buzz of adults talking in the front seat while I snoozed in the rear. I experienced the same sweet certainty that if I could just remain still, feigning sleep, others would take responsibility for the journey. Something flat and icy cold was pressed against the side of my head, causing a stinging sensation so sharp that I hissed. Someone put the towel-wrapped ice pack in my hand and encouraged me to hold it myself at a pressure I could tolerate.

The hotel doctor arrived and spent an inordinate amount of time checking my vital signs, making sure I still knew my name, the date, and how many fingers he was holding up—a number he varied in an attempt to trick and deceive. There was talk of paramedics, whose services I declined. Next thing I knew, there were two more guys in the room. One I gathered was the head of hotel security, a hefty gentleman in a business suit with a gaping lapel. I caught a glimpse of leather that I hoped was a shoulder holster and not a back brace. The notion of a man with a gun was comforting. He was in his sixties, balding and beefy-faced with a thick gray mustache. The man with him, I was guessing, was part of the hotel-management team. I turned my head slightly. A third man appeared in the doorway with a walkie-talkie in his hand. He was slim, in his forties, sporting what was surely a toupee. He entered and conferred with the other two.

The beefy-faced guy with the mustache introduced himself, saying, "I'm Mr. Fitzgerald, hotel security. This is my associate, Mr. Preston, and the manager, Mr. Shearson. How do you feel?"

I said, "Fine," which was ridiculous, as I was flat on my back with a very tender lump on my head. Someone had removed my shoes and put a blanket over me that really wasn't warm enough.

The manager leaned close to Fitzgerald and spoke to him as though I wasn't there. "I notified corporate. The attorney suggested we have her sign a waiver, releasing us from any liability . . ." He glanced at me and then lowered his voice.

There was a squawk from the walkie-talkie. Mr. Preston retired to the corridor and conducted his conversation beyond my hearing. When he returned moments later, he chatted with Fitzgerald, but in a tone so subdued I couldn't pick up the content. The manager excused himself and after a brief conference Mr. Preston left as well.

I struggled to get my bearings. They had apparently settled me in an empty guest room, though I didn't remember how I'd arrived. For all I knew, they'd dragged me through the halls by my heels. I could see a desk, sofa, two upholstered chairs, and the Art Deco armoire that housed the minibar and TV. I'd never stayed in such an upscale hotel so it was all a revelation to me. The management at the Paradise in Reno could take a lesson from the Neptune when it came to interior design. I adjusted my ice pack and said, "What happened to Marty?"

Fitzgerald said, "We don't know. They managed to get him out of the building without being seen. I had the parking lot attendant check for his car, but someone had already claimed it and had driven it away. No one remembered the driver so we're not sure if Mr. Blumberg left on his own or in the company of the men who abducted him."

"Poor guy."

"The police are here talking to the woman with you. They'd like to ask you a few questions when you're up to it."

"I don't remember much, but sure," I said. In truth, I didn't feel like conversation. I was cold. The knot on the side of my head throbbed sharply with every beat of my pulse. My midsection was sore. I had no idea what Reba was telling them, but I suspected she'd be less than candid. The whole situation was too complicated to explain, especially since I didn't know how much the feds considered confidential. I was sick about Marty. My last glimpse of him—cheek split, blood running down the side of his face—he'd seemed resigned to his fate, like a man being hauled off to the gas chamber, priest at his side. It was the dread in his eyes I found haunting, as though he knew that something far worse was in store for him. I wanted to rewind the reel of film, let events unfold again so I could find a way to help him.

Fitzgerald said something else, but I wasn't taking it in. I removed the ice pack and checked the soggy terry cloth with its blush of blood in the loops. I rearranged the fold and laid the fresh cold of a new spot against my poor banged-up head. I was shivering, but I couldn't bring myself to ask for another blanket. "Sorry. Could you repeat that?"

"Had you ever seen these men before?"

"Not to my recollection. I thought they were on their way to meet someone else. They were coming right at us, but it's like a stranger waving in your direction. You turn around and look back, assuming it isn't you they mean. Reba might remember more than I do. Can I talk to her?"

He debated, wanting to press for information, trying at the same time to appear compassionate and concerned, hotel liability being what it was. "As soon as the police are finished, I'll have her come in."

"Thanks."

I closed my eyes again. I was tired and I didn't think I'd ever want to get out of this bed. I felt a touch on my arm. Reba now sat in a chair she'd pulled over close to the bed. Fitzgerald wasn't in the room.

"Where'd Fitzgerald disappear to?"

"Who knows. I told the cops to call Cheney and he'd fill 'em in. I didn't want to put my foot in my mouth with the FBI involved. How's your head?"

"Hurts. Help me up and let's see if I can sit up without passing out or puking." She held my outstretched hand and eased me into an upright position. I pushed the blanket aside and placed my other hand on the bed table for stability. It really wasn't as bad as I'd thought.

"You're not planning to go anywhere, I hope."

"Not until I know what kind of shape I'm in. You ever see those guys before?"

She hesitated. "I think so. In the pickup truck on the way down from Reno. They're probably Salustio's goons. Beck must have told him I took his twenty-five grand."

"But why snatch Marty? He had nothing to do with it."

"I don't know what's going on. Shit, I wish I'd never told Marty the feds were closing in. All that did was scare him into running. He'd have been better off if he were under arrest. At least he'd be safe."

"What about the claim check he gave you? What was that about?"

She blinked. "I don't know. I'd forgotten about that." She rooted through her bag, pulled it out, and turned it over in her hand. "Hotel luggage claim. I should talk to the bell captain and see what this is. Will you be okay? It shouldn't take me long."

"Sure. Why don't you wait for me downstairs? As soon as I've talked to the cops, I'll meet you in the lobby."

She said, "Great."

I waited until she was gone and then made my way into the bathroom, where I washed my face and ran my head under the faucet to wash away the dried blood that was matted in my hair. I took a bath towel and blotted gingerly until the strands were dry enough to comb. Really, I was doing better than I'd expected, now that I was on my feet.

By the time the uniformed beat officer arrived, I was sitting in a chair, feeling somewhat restored. He was a clean-cut fellow in his twenties with a serious demeanor and a slight, disarming lisp. I repeated what I knew, watching him scribble in his notebook. We went over the sequence of events until he seemed satisfied that he'd wrung as much from me as I was able to remember. I gave him my Santa Teresa address and my phone number, as well as Cheney's. He gave me a card and said I could request a copy of the crime report if I wrote to the Records Section, though it would take about ten days for processing.

Once the door closed behind him, I slipped on my shoes. Bending down to tie the laces was not a happy occasion, but I managed it. I found my shoulder bag and let myself out into the hall, then located the bank of elevators and went down.

In the lobby, I looked across to the bell captain's desk, expecting to catch sight of Reba. No bell captain and no Reba. I'd been talking to the officer for a good ten minutes, so it didn't surprise me to think she'd already retrieved whatever Marty had left for her. I circled the area, peering into the cocktail lounge, the ladies' room, and the corridor near the public phones. I tried the gift boutique and the newsstand next door. Where the hell had she gone? I kept expecting to spot her, and it annoyed me no end that she'd wandered off without leaving me some word. I sat in the lobby for six or seven minutes and then stepped outside. The bell captain was tagging a set of suitcases. When he finished, I said, "I'm looking for a friend . . . petite, dark hair. She came down a little while ago with a claim check for—"

"Of course. She picked up the rolling bag and then she left."

"Do you know where she went?"

He shook his head. "Sorry. I wish I could help." He excused himself to tend to an incoming guest and left me standing there perplexed. Now what?

A car pulled up, the parking valet delivering the vehicle to a waiting guest. The driver got out and as the valet closed the door, he caught my eye. I realized he was the same kid we'd seen when we first arrived. "You looking for your friend?"

"Yes."

"You just missed her," he said.

"What do you mean, 'missed her'?"

"The doorman whistled her up a cab a few minutes ago."

"You mean she left the hotel? Going where?"

"I didn't hear. She gave the driver instructions and then the taxi pulled away."

"Was she alone?"

"Looked like it. She had her suitcase with her so maybe she was headed for the airport."

"Thanks."

Now what?

I couldn't figure out what she was up to. I was anxious to hit the road, but how could I leave the hotel when I had no idea where she was or if she meant to return? Had she left on an impulse or had she intended to ditch me from the moment we left Reno? Whatever the reality, I felt I had to hang around for a while, at least until I was convinced she was gone for good.

In the meantime, there must be something I could do. I returned to the lobby, where I took a seat in the same chair I'd occupied when we first arrived. I closed my eyes and went back over the entire sequence of events. I pictured Reba crossing to the desk. She'd removed a mailing pouch from her purse, printed something on the face of it, and left it with the concierge. She'd then asked for and received an envelope. Which suggested what?

I got up and approached the concierge's desk. There was only one man on duty—Carl, according to his name tag—and he was in the process of setting up dinner reservations for a well-dressed older gentleman. I waited. Once the gentleman left, Carl turned a blank look on me, his eyes straying to the side of my head, where I suddenly imagined a bump the size of the Palmdale Bulge. "May I be of assistance?"

"Is the manager available?"

"I can certainly check. Are you a guest of the hotel?"

"Well, no, but I seem to have a little problem and I could use his help."

"I see. And will he know what this is in reference to?"

"Probably not. You can tell him the name is Millhone."

He picked up his desk phone and punched in a number, gaze fixed on me. When the line was picked up on the other end, he turned away from me and conducted his conversation with a hand across his mouth like someone trying to be polite while picking his teeth in public. "He'll be with you in just one moment."

"Thanks."

He smiled and his gaze slid past me as he busied himself. For some minutes he was occupied with a ledger and the phone. I started to speak, but he held up a finger—denoting, *One minute, please*—and then went on with his task. Was I being stonewalled? I remembered the comment the manager had made about the hotel's liability in light of Marty's (alleged) abduction and the assault on me. Perhaps he'd put a call through to corporate and his boss, or his boss's boss, had warned him to avoid any further contact with me. Anything said might be used against the hotel in a court of law. I might as well have had a flashing sign on my forehead: LAWSUIT * LAWSUIT * LAWSUIT. "Excuse me. Sir?"

"If you'd care to have a seat, the manager will be with you." His tone was pleasant, but this time he didn't look at me at all. He picked up a sheaf of papers, rapped them against the counter to align the edges, and moved into the inner office as though on a mission related to national security.

Irritated, I noticed that my bad angel was now perched on my shoulder, pointing mutely. I could see the manila mailing pouch Reba'd left earlier. It was still lying on the credenza less than five feet away. From where I stood, Marty's name was visible, printed in bold black ink. *Here we go* ... I moved down the counter and caught the attention of an idle desk clerk, a kid about twenty, probably still in training for the job. He said, "Yes, ma'am. May I help you?"

"I hope so. My name is Mrs. Blumberg. My husband and I are guests of the hotel. He said he was leaving a package for me and I believe that's it." I pointed at the pouch.

The clerk picked it up. "You're Marty?"

"Yes, I am."

He handed it over, happy to be of service.

I was happy, too. "Thank you."

I made my way to the ladies' room, where I shut myself in a stall. I perched on the toilet seat despite the fact that it had no lid. In correctional facilities, lids are removed to prevent suicide attempts, though offhand it's hard to imagine the procedure whereby one would hang oneself with a toilet seat, especially with that cunning gap in the middle separating the two halves. In some institutions, there's no toilet seat at all, just a tankless one-piece commode, fashioned out of stainless steel. I propped my feet on the door, worried the clerk would burst in and raise a hue and cry about unlawful possession. The pouch had the bulk and heft of a couple of paperbacks. The flap was self-sealed, but I picked at it until the two lines of adhesive loosened their grip. I peered in.

Now this was the perfect example of why it's so impossible to cure me of the naughty lies I tell. Fibs and related forms of deception often have the most remarkable rewards. Inside I found the following:

A United States passport, issued to one Garrisen Randolph, with a two-by-two photograph of Martin Blumberg.

A California driver's license issued to Garrisen Randolph, with a slightly shrunken version of the same photograph. His residence address was listed in Los Angeles, 90024 zip code, which was actually Westwood. Sex: M   HAIR: Brn   EYES: Brn   HT: 5-11   WT: 272 DOB: 08-25-42, this latter printed in red. Above the picture, also in red, was the license expiration date: 08-25-90.

In addition, there was an American Express card, a Visa credit card, and a MasterCard issued to the same Garrisen Randolph, plus a birth certificate from Inyo County, California, detailing the particulars of Garrisen Randolph's birth.

These were, of course, versions of the phony documents Reba'd stolen from the hidden drawer in Alan Beckwith's desk. The name on these documents was a variation on the name Garrison Randell, probably to ensure that a computer search wouldn't pick up a match. Technically, Marty could leave the country anytime he liked and no one would be the wiser. There was no doubt in my mind that Misty Raine had done the work. I remembered Reba's telling me Misty's newly discovered forging talents had netted her the bucks to pay for that bodacious set of tits. The fellow she'd met in the lounge at the Silverado was probably supplying counterfeit paper, seals, or credit card blanks.

But what did it mean?

Phony documents of this caliber cost plenty. Reba was the one who'd made all the arrangements, but in exchange for what? Clearly she and Marty had a deal. I could see what he was getting out of it, but what was the benefit to her? I thought about the envelope she'd received at the desk. Maybe he'd given her the twenty-five thousand dollars she needed to pay Salustio. Which left the issue of the suitcase, which contained god knows what. I glanced at my watch. It was now close to 6:00. I shoved the manila pouch in my shoulder bag and left the ladies' room.

I took the elevator up to 8. As I'd hoped, there were maid's carts parked at intervals along the corridor. Many guests had departed for the evening, on their way to dinner. The maids were now going room by room, emptying the trash, replacing towels, replenishing amenities, and turning down the beds. I waited until the maid had entered Marty's room and then I scurried down the hall. I paused near her cart, where I spotted a box of disposable latex gloves. I slipped a pair in my shoulder bag and rapped on the open door. I wondered if the cop had been through Marty's room. Perhaps not, as there wasn't any crime scene tape.

The maid looked up from the bed where she was folding the heavy quilted spread into something the size and shape of a giant Tootsie Roll.

I said, "Sorry to interrupt, but is there any way you can come back and finish this later? I have a dinner date in twenty minutes and I have to get dressed."

She murmured her apologies, picked up her plastic carrier of supplies, and exited.

I hung the Privacy Please sign on the outside knob, pulled on my gloves, and did a thorough search. Marty must have had his wallet, room key, and other items on his person when his assailants hurried him away. I went through the hard-sided suitcase he'd left open on the luggage rack. Underwear, shirts, socks, a few toiletries he hadn't transferred to the bathroom counter. I opened the closet door and ran a hand into the pockets of the pants he'd left. Empty. I made a systematic search of the hanging garment bag, but there was just what you'd expect: suits, trousers, belts, shoes. Aside from the hotel robe, there was no other clothing in the closet and no sign of the usual hotel safe with its four-digit combination lock.

I searched the bathroom, including the underside of the toilet tank lid, and found nothing. I opened the dresser drawers and ran a hand around the interiors. Empty. I pulled each drawer all the way out, wondering if there was something secured under or behind. When I reached the bed table, I went through the same routine. I removed the Gideon Bible. Inside the cover there was a Delta Air Lines ticket, first class to Zurich, issued in Garrisen Randolph's name. The booking was one-way and the flight was scheduled to depart at 9:30 the next morning.

I replaced the ticket between the pages, returned the

Bible to the drawer, and closed it. I didn't believe Marty was coming back, but on the off-chance he made it, the ticket would be waiting. I removed my gloves, plucked the Privacy Please sign from the outside knob, and hung it on the inside. I took the elevator down. I went into the newsstand and bought three dollars' worth of stamps, which I pasted on the front of the mailing pouch. I penned my home address under Marty's name and then pinched the adhesive to secure the opening. I took a seat within sight of the concierge's desk, watching to see if Carl was still on duty. Ten minutes passed and there was no sign of him. A smartly dressed woman, with a name tag pinned to her lapel, had stepped into the job.

I approached the desk. She appeared to be capable, her smile properly cool and professional. "Yes, ma'am."

I put the mailing pouch on the counter. "I'd like to leave this for Mr. Blumberg in Room 817, but I wonder if you could attach a note. If he hasn't picked it up by tomorrow afternoon, I'd appreciate someone's dropping it in the mail to him."

"Of course."

She wrote the appropriate note and clipped it to the top edge of the pouch. I said, "Oh, and do you happen to have a stapler? This has popped open."

"Not a problem." She reached behind the counter and took out a stapler. I watched while she crunched a succession of staples into the upper edge of the pouch, tightly sealing it. She placed it back on the credenza where it had sat earlier. I thanked her, silently sending up a prayer for Marty's survival.

At 7:15 I shelled out twenty-five bucks to the bell captain and retrieved my VW. I drove west on Sunset as far as the on-ramp to the northbound 405, traveling up the long hill toward the valley and down the other side. Once I connected to the 101, I pointed the car toward home.

30

I reached Santa Teresa at 9:00 that night. The summer temperatures had cooled rapidly as the sun inched its way down toward the horizon. Along Cabana Boulevard, the streetlights had flicked on and the wide stretch of ocean had turned all silvery and white. I stopped by my apartment, where I dropped my bags and wrote a quick note to Henry letting him know I was home. I left a message to the same effect on Cheney's answering machine, saying I'd catch up with him when I could.

By 9:20 I was back in the car, heading south toward Montebello and the Lafferty estate. Gingerly I put a hand to the knot on my head—still sore, and still undiminished in size. Happily the headache was gone and I thought it safe to assume that I was on the mend. I didn't think I'd jog for a day or two, but at least my thinking seemed clear.

The drive up from Los Angeles had given me a chance to reflect. I still had no clue how the two goons had found us in Reno. As odious as Beck was, I didn't picture him with thugs on his payroll, which meant they were sent by

Salustio Castillo. I was baffled by their snatching Marty. Reba's theft of Salustio's twenty-five grand made her the logical target. Unless Marty had done something even more foolish than she. Such as what? I wondered if he'd packed the remainder of Salustio's money in the rolling bag. But to what end? From what he'd said that night at Dale's, he'd set aside sufficient funds to take care of himself. So why steal more and why pass it on to Reba when all that would do was place her in greater jeopardy than she was in? Meanwhile, where was she?

I thought it was entirely possible she'd commissioned Misty to dummy up a passport and other phony documents for herself as well as for Marty. If that were the case, she might be on her way out of the country, though I couldn't believe she'd go without saying good-bye to her dad. She might not confide her destination, but surely she'd find a way to let him know that she was okay. Not for the first time, I was thinking my relationship with Reba was at an end. She'd blow off her parole and take her chances as a fugitive.

When I reached the entrance to the Lafferty estate, the gates were closed. I pulled up to the keypad, rolled down my window, and pressed the call button. I could hear the line ring inside. Once. Twice. Freddy picked up, her voice sounding scratchy over the intercom system.

I stuck my head out the window and raised my voice. "Freddy? It's Kinsey. Can you let me in, please?"

I heard a series of peeps and then a low humming noise as the gates swung open to the full. I flipped on my brights and eased my way down the drive. I could see house lights twinkling through the trees. As I rounded the last curve, I saw that the second story was dark but the lights were on in many of the first-floor rooms along the front. Lucinda's car was parked in its usual spot and I could feel my eyes cross at the notion of encountering her. As I got out of the car, I caught motion to my right. Rags sauntered along the drive at a pace perfectly calculated to intercept my path. When he reached me, I leaned down and scratched between his ears. His long pumpkin-colored fur was silky, his purr becoming more pronounced as he arched his big head and pushed against my hand. "Listen, Rags. I'd be happy to take you in, but if Lucinda answers the door we got no shot at it."

He trailed up the walk with me, sometimes running around in front to inspire additional stroking and conversation. I could see where owning a cat would render a grownup completely goofy in time. I reached for the bell, but the front door swung open in advance of my ring. Lucinda was framed in the porch light, wearing a crisp-looking yellow coatdress, with pale hose and matching yellow heels. She looked tanned and fit, her streaky blond hair arranged as though permanently swept by wind. She said, "Oh! Freddy said someone rang at the gate, but I didn't realize it was you. I thought you were out of town."

"I was. I just got back and I need to talk to Mr. Lafferty."

She let that sink in. "I suppose you might as well come in." She stepped aside to let me enter, frowning with annoyance when she caught sight of Rags. She barred him with a quick foot and pushed him out of the way. That's the kind of person she was, a cat-kicker. What a bitch. As I stepped into the foyer, I spotted a small overnight case sitting near the door. She'd set her purse on the console table and she paused to check her reflection in the mirror, adjusting an earring and an errant strand of hair. She opened her purse, apparently searching for her keys. "Nord's not here. He collapsed this morning and I had to call the paramedics. He's been admitted to Saint Terry's. I'm on my way over to take him his toiletries and robe."

"What happened?"

"Well, he's desperately ill," she said, as though I'd been stupid to inquire. "All this upset over Reba has taken its toll."

"Is she here?"

"Of course not. She's never here when he needs her. That's a job that falls to Freddy or me." Her smile was self-satisfied and brittle, her manner brisk. "Well now. What can we do for you?"

"Is he allowed to have visitors?"

"You must not have heard me. He's ill. He shouldn't be disturbed."

"That wasn't what I asked. What floor is he on?"

"He's on the cardiac ward. If you insist, I suppose you could speak to his private-duty nurse. What is it you want?"

"He asked me to do a job. I'd like to give him my report."

"I'd prefer you didn't."

"But I don't work for you. I work for him," I said.

"She's in trouble again, isn't she?"

"I guess you could say that."

"You don't understand what this has done to him. He's had to rescue her all his life. Reba keeps putting him in the same position. She sets it up so that if he doesn't step in, she'll be doomed, or so she'd like him to think. I'm sure she'd deny this, but she's really still a child, doing anything she can to get her father's attention. If anything happened to her, he'd forever blame himself."

"He's her father. He gets to help her if he wants."

"Well, I may have put an end to *that*."

"How so?"

"I called Priscilla Holloway, Reba's parole officer. I thought she should be aware of what's been going on. I'm sure Reba's been drinking and probably gambling as well. I told Ms. Holloway Reba left the state, and she was furious."

"You'll get her sent back to prison."

"That's my hope. We'd all be better off, including her."

"Great. That's perfect. Who else did you tattle to?" I meant the question as a piece of sarcasm, but the silence that followed suggested I'd scored an unexpected bull's-eye. I stared at her. "Is that how Beck found out where she was?"

She dropped her gaze. "We had a conversation on the subject."

"You *told* him?"

"That's right. And I'd do it again."

"When was this?"

"Thursday. He came to the house. Nord was sleeping so I spoke to him myself. He'd been looking for her and he was very concerned. He said he didn't want to cause a problem, but he thought she'd taken something. He was quite uncomfortable and I had to work very hard persuading him to tell me what it was. He finally admitted she stole twenty-five thousand dollars. He said he didn't want to make trouble, but I thought that was nonsense and told him where she was."

"How'd you get Misty's address?"

"I didn't have her address, I had yours. Nord scribbled a note to himself the night you called. The Paradise Motel. I saw it written on the pad beside his bed."

"Lucinda, Beck *manipulated* you. Don't you see that?"

"Hardly. He's a lovely man. After what she did to him, I'd have told him even if he hadn't asked."

"Do you have any idea what you've done? A man was kidnapped because of you."

She laughed, tucking her purse under one arm as she picked up the overnight case. "No one was *kidnapped*," she said, as though the notion were absurd. "Really. You're just like her, creating drama where there is none. Everything's a crisis. Everything's the end of the world. It's never anything she's done. She's always the victim, always expecting someone else to pick up after her. Well, this time she'll have to take responsibility. Now, if you'll excuse me, I'd like to get over to the hospital and leave these items for Nord."

She opened the door and snapped it shut behind her. In the face of her conviction, I hadn't managed to challenge her view or express even the first shred of protest. There was an element of truth in what she'd said, but it wasn't the whole truth.

"Miss Millhone?"

I turned to find Freddy standing in the hall behind me. "Did you hear her? The woman's horrible," I said.

"Now that she's gone, I wanted to let you know. Reba was here. She arrived shortly before Miss Cunningham stopped by to pick up Mr. Lafferty's things."

"Where'd she go?"

"I don't know. She came by cab and she was only home long enough to pick up her car and a change of clothes.

She said she'd go over to the hospital to see her father, but she'd time it to avoid crossing paths with Miss Cunning-ham. She's going to call Mr. Lafferty's doctor and have his visitors restricted to family only, including me, of course." Freddy permitted herself a sly smile. "That was my idea."

"Serves Lucinda right. How serious is his condition?"

"The doctor says he'll be fine. He was dehydrated and his electrolytes were out of balance. I believe he's suffering from anemia as well. The doctor intends to keep him for a couple of days."

"Well, good. That's one less thing to worry about, especially if the staff can keep Lucinda at bay. Did Reba say anything at all about where she'd be?"

"Staying with a friend."

"She doesn't have a friend. Here in town?"

"I believe so. This was a fellow, someone she met after she got home."

I thought about that briefly. "Maybe someone from AA . . . though now that I say that, it seems unlikely. I can't see her at a meeting this late in the game. What about reaching her? Did she leave a number?"

Freddy shook her head. "She said she'd call by the house at nine, but she was concerned Mr. Beckwith would find her again."

"I'll bet. Lucinda's been dishing out the information right and left," I said. "Look, if you hear from her, tell her it's important we talk. Did she leave a suitcase by any chance?"

"No, but she did have one with her. She put it in the trunk of her car before she left."

"Well, let's hope she calls in." I glanced at my watch.

"I'll be at my office for the next couple of hours and then I'll head home."

My office always feels odd at night, its flaws and shabbiness exaggerated by the artificial light. As I sat at my desk, all I saw through the window was dinginess reflected back at me, the dust and ancient rain streaks barring any view of the street. On weekends this part of downtown Santa Teresa is dead after 6:00 P.M., city buildings closed for the night, the courthouse and public library dark. The bungalow I occupied was the middle unit of three; identical stucco structures that, at some point, represented modest housing. Since I'd moved in, the bungalows on both sides of mine had remained vacant, which afforded me the quiet I preferred, at the same time creating an unsettling sense of isolation.

I sorted through the mound of mail the carrier had shoved through my slot. Much junk, a few bills, which I sat down and paid. I was restless, eager to get home, but felt I should stay, in the hopes that Reba would call. I did some filing. I straightened out my pencil drawer. It was make-work but gave me something useful to do. I kept glancing at the phone, willing it to ring, so when someone rapped on my side window, I nearly leaped out of my skin.

Reba was outside, concealed in the shadowy space between my bungalow and its twin next door. She'd traded her shorts for jeans and her white T-shirt looked like the one she'd been wearing when she left CIW. I unlocked the window and raised the sash. "What are you *doing?*"

"You have access to those garages out back?"

"Sure, the one for this unit. I've never used it, but the landlord did give me the keys."

"Grab 'em and let's go. I gotta get my car off the street. I've had those goons on my tail ever since I left the house."

"The ones we saw in L.A.?"

"Yeah, only one of 'em now has a black eye, like he walked into a door."

"Oh, dear. Wonder if I did that with my widdle chair," I said. "How'd you get away?"

"Fortunately, I know this town a lot better than they do. I led 'em around for a while, then sped up, doused my lights, turned down a little side road, and then behind a hedge. The minute I saw their car pass, I doubled back and came here."

"Where have you been all this time?"

She seemed agitated. "Don't ask. I've been busy as a little bee. Get a move on. I'm cold."

"I'll meet you out back."

I closed the window and locked it. In my bottom desk drawer I lifted aside the phone book and picked up two silver keys hooked together on a paper clip. I picked up my bag and found my trusty penlight, checking the strength of the batteries as I moved down the hallway and out the rear door. A short patch of stubby grass separated the bungalows from the row of three garages along the alley. Reba'd parked her car in the shadow of a pyracantha bush that had probably scratched the shit out of the paint on the right-hand side. I could see her at the wheel, smoking a cigarette while she waited for me.

There was a light fixture with a forty-watt bulb attached to the wood beam above the middle garage, which was the one assigned to me. The bulb yielded just enough light to see by if your eyes were good. I fumbled with the padlock and finally popped it open. I unhooked it from the hasp and hauled up the overhead door with a labored groaning of wood and rusty hinges. I flashed my penlight across the walls and floor, which were bare, smelling of motor oil and soot. There were cobwebs everywhere.

Reba flipped her cigarette out the window and started her car. I stood back as she pulled into the garage. She got out, locked her car door, and came around to the rear. She popped the trunk lid and hauled out a suitcase of a size appropriate for an airplane carry-on, though you'd have to maneuver it to get it in the overhead bin. The bag had an extendable handle and a set of wheels. She seemed preoccupied, caught up in a mood I couldn't read.

"You okay?" I asked.

"Fine."

"Just for the yucks, are you going to tell me what's in there?"

"Want to see?"

"I do."

She collapsed the handle and laid the suitcase flat, unzipped the top portion and flipped it open.

I found myself looking at a metal box, maybe fifteen inches high, eighteen inches long, and eight inches deep. "What the hell is that?"

"You're joking. You don't know?"

"If I knew, I wouldn't ask, Reeb. I'd exclaim with joy and surprise."

"It's a computer. Marty took his with him when he left. He also stopped by the bank and picked up all the floppy disks from the safe-deposit box. You're looking at Beck's business records—the second set of books. Hook it up to a keyboard and monitor, you've got access to everything: bank accounts, deposits, shell companies, payoffs, every dime he laundered for Salustio."

"You're turning it over to the feds, right?"

"Probably. As soon as I'm done . . . though you know how cranky they get about stolen property."

"But you can't even think about keeping this. That's why those guys went after Marty, to get it back. Isn't it?"

"Exactly. So let's put a call through to Beck and offer him a trade. We get Marty, he gets this."

"I thought you just said you'd turn it over to the feds?"

"You weren't listening. I said 'probably.' I'm not sure their crappy investigation is worth Marty's life."

"You can't handle this yourself. Negotiate with Beck? Are you out of your mind? You have to tell Vince. Bring in the cops or the FBI."

"No way. This is my only chance to get even with that son of a bitch."

"Oh, I get it. This isn't about Marty. It's about you and Beck."

"Of course it's about *Marty*, but it's also about settling the score. It's like a test. Let's see what Beck's made of. I don't think it's such a bad deal—Marty in exchange for this. The fact the feds want it is what makes it so valuable."

"There are more important things in life than revenge," I said.

"Well, that's bullshit. Name one," she said. "Besides, I'm not talking about revenge. I'm talking about getting even. Those are two different things."

"No, they're not."

"Yes, they are. Revenge is you hurt me and I grind you

underfoot until you wish you were dead. Getting even restores the balance in the Universe. You kill him, I kill you. Now we're even. What else is capital punishment about? Getting even is just what it sounds like. Tit for tat. You hurt me, I hurt you back. We're square again and all's right with the world."

"Why not get even by turning him over to the IRS?"

"That's business. This is personal, between him and me."

"I don't get what you want."

"I want him to say he's sorry for what he did to me. I gave up two years of my life for him. Now I have something he wants so let him beg for it."

"That's asinine. So he pulls a long face and says sorry. What difference will that make? You know what he's like. You can't ever do business with a guy like him. You'll get screwed."

"You don't know that."

"I do. Reba, would you listen to me? He'll work you over the first chance he gets."

Her face was set. "Why don't you go get your car and bring it around? I'll wait for you here."

I shut my mouth and closed my eyes. Why argue the point when her mind was made up? "You want help with this garage door?"

"I can handle it."

I returned to the office. I locked the back door behind me, then moved down the hall turning off lights as I went. I grabbed my shoulder bag and went out the front door, pausing long enough to lock up. I stood for a moment, scanning the darkened street. All the cars in range belonged to neighbors, vehicles I'd seen before and could identify on sight. I let myself into my car and fired up the engine. I drove around the corner and nosed my VW into the alleyway.

Reba had closed and padlocked the garage. She opened the passenger-side door, put the suitcase in the backseat, and got in. I reached over into the rear and grabbed my denim jacket. "Here. Put this on before you catch cold."

"Thanks." She shrugged into the jacket and locked her seat belt in place.

"Where to?"

"The nearest public phone."

"Why not my office, as long as we're here?"

"I don't want you tied into this in any way."

"Tied into what?"

"Just find a phone," she said.

31

Reba wanted me to make the call to Beck. We found a phone booth outside a supermarket. The store was a bright island, icy fluorescent lights reflected in the shiny paint finish of the dozen or so cars in the parking lot out front. This was the store where I did my weekly shopping, and I longed for nothing so much as to buy milk and eggs and then wend my way home.

Reba put a handful of coins and a slip of paper with Beck's home and office numbers on the metal shelf under the phone. "Try his home phone first. If Tracy answers, maybe she'll think he has a girlfriend," she said.

"He does. Her name is Onni."

"She probably knows about her. I'm talking someone new. Might as well bug the shit out of her while we can."

"That's not nice. I thought women were supposed to be nice."

"I wouldn't bet on it if I were you."

I picked up the handset. "So what am I supposed to say to him?"

"Tell him to meet us at the East Beach parking lot in fifteen minutes. As soon as he hands Marty over, he gets his computer."

I held the handset against my chest. "Please don't do this. I'm begging you. What's to prevent him from snatching the damn thing? You don't even have a gun."

"Of course I don't have a *gun*. I'm a convicted felon. I can't carry," she said, as though offended by the very idea.

"What if Beck has one?"

"He doesn't even own a gun. Besides, we'll be right out in plain sight. Anyone driving along Cabana Boulevard can see us. Here, give me that."

She grabbed the handset and put it against my ear, picked up some coins, and dropped them in the slot. In addition to the dial tone, I could have sworn I heard the buzz of electricity running through my frame. My heart rate was picking up and my insides felt like a fuse box with all the lines shorting out. She punched in Beck's home number just to hurry things along. At the first ring, Reba leaned her head against mine and tilted the handset so she could listen in. I said, "This feels like high school. I hate this."

"Would you shut up?" she hissed.

After three rings, he picked up. "Yes."

My mouth was dry. "Beck, this is Kinsey."

"God damn you! Where's Reba? The fuckin' bitch. I want what's mine and she better make it quick."

Reba grabbed the handset, all sweetness and light now that she had him by the balls. "Hey, baby. How's by you? I'm right here."

Whatever Beck's reply, it must have been tart because she laughed with delight. "Oh my, now. You don't have to

388

be crude. I was thinking we should get together and have a chat."

I waited, staring off across the parking lot, while she spelled out the proposal and the nature of the trade. Then they argued about the rendezvous, tussling to see which of them was going to come out on top. The East Beach bathhouse, at the corner of Cabana and Milagro, was where I did the turnaround on my morning runs. Even at night, the area is exposed and well lit from the Santa Teresa Inn just across the street from the entrance to the parking lot. There's a small separate lot at the far end of the building, but she'd opted for the more public of the two. This showed a grain of common sense unusual for her. She insisted on meeting in fifteen minutes while he swore he couldn't be there any sooner than half an hour. To this, she finally agreed. Score one for him. I was uneasy. I figured the more time she gave him, the more likely he was to round up some help. This must have occurred to her as well. "And Beck, one more thing. You bring anyone but Marty and you'll eat it, big time. Yeah, well, same to you, you little shit!" She slammed down the phone and then shoved her hands in her jacket pockets. "God, I hate him. What a hairball."

I picked up the handset and reached for some coins. "I'm calling Cheney."

She took the handset and returned it to the cradle. "I don't want Cheney. I don't want anyone but us."

"I can't do this. You and Beck can play all the games you want, but I'm out of it," I said.

"Okay. Fine. Take a hike. Drop me at my car and you're off the hook," she said. She turned and walked off.

I'd hoped to jolt her into getting help, but she was

having none of it. I blinked, staring at the pavement. What were my choices? Do it her way or risk . . . what? That she'd die or get hurt? Because Marty'd stolen the computer, she'd assumed Beck was the one who'd ordered the snatch, but what if he hadn't? It might have been Salustio Castillo, who had just as much to lose. Beck might be bluffing. He might not have a clue where Marty was being held, and then what? All he had to do was grab the suitcase and what could she do? If it came right down to it, what could I do? Nothing. At the same time, she knew I wouldn't leave her. There was too much at stake.

Reluctantly, I followed. The car doors were locked and she waited, gaze averted, while I let myself in and tossed my bag on the backseat. I slid under the wheel, leaned over, and opened the door on her side. Reba got in and we sat there. I had my hands on the steering wheel, stalling while I racked my brain for some alternative. "There has to be a better way to do this."

"Great. Spell it out. I'm all yours," she said.

I didn't have an answer. The meeting was scheduled for 11:00 P.M., in roughly twenty-five minutes. Technically we had time enough to drive to my place, where I could pick up my gun. I nearly banged my head on the steering wheel. What was I thinking? A gun was out of the question. I wasn't going to *shoot* anyone. Over a *computer?* How absurd.

On the other hand . . . shit . . . on the *other* hand . . . if Marty's home phone was tapped, the FBI must have a tap on Beck's telephone lines as well. One of their agents must have heard Beck and Reba wrangling, so maybe they'd taken note and the cavalry was already on the way.

Out of the corner of my eye, I saw Reba check her watch, saying, "Tick-tock. Tick-tock. Time's a-wasting."

"So where's Marty all this time?"

"He didn't say. I'm assuming somewhere close."

I shook my head in frustration. "I don't believe I'm doing this." I turned the key in the ignition and backed out of the space. "Let's at least take a minute to scope out the area, or have you done that?"

"Not really. Why bother? I figure you're the expert."

The drive seemed to take forever. I cut over to the freeway, thinking to speed our progress. Big mistake. Traffic was heavy, taillights stacked up, as two lanes of cars amassed in the wake of an accident in one of the northbound lanes. I could see lights flashing where the CHP and the emergency vehicles had converged on the scene. There wasn't actually an obstruction on our side of the road, but we were at a dead stop, anyway, while people paused to gawk.

By the time we reached the off-ramp at Cabana, we had less than a minute to spare. I confess I sped the final mile and a half, hoping a cop would spot us and make a traffic stop. No such luck. The ocean was to our right, separated from the road by the beach, a bike path, and a wide strip of grass that was dotted with palm trees. On our left, we passed a string of motels and restaurants. The sidewalk was populated with tourists, which was oddly comforting somehow.

At Milagro, I turned into the designated parking lot. There were no cars in evidence, which meant (perhaps) that if Beck was bringing goons, at least they hadn't arrived before us. Reba told me to make a U-turn at the far end of the lot and circle back to the entrance. I did as instructed and then backed into a parking space, my car facing the street in case we needed to make a hasty retreat. We got out of the car. She flipped her seat forward and removed the suitcase. She popped the handle, extending it, and then rolled the case to the front of the car. "Might as well let him know we mean business," she said.

Behind us, the waves were drumming on the sand, gathering momentum before they battered the shore and then rolled back again. The water was intensely black with a fine sheen of white where moonlight caught the peaks of each wave. A damp breeze buffeted my hair and pushed against the legs of my jeans. I turned and scanned the beach behind us, hopping from foot to foot to keep warm. So far, to all appearances, we were alone.

Reba leaned on the front fender, lit a cigarette, and smoked. Ten minutes passed. She checked her watch. "What's this about? Does he want the friggin' thing or not?"

Across the street, hotel guests pulled in at the entrance to the Santa Teresa Inn. There were two valet parkers and a smattering of pedestrians. In the restaurant on the second floor, tables were arranged along the big curved front window. Diners were visible, though as dark as it was now, I doubted they could see us. A black-and-white patrol car approached and turned right, speeding up Milagro. I could feel my hopes flare and fade.

"I think we should get out of here. I don't like this," I said.

She looked at her watch again. "Not yet. If he doesn't show by 11:30, we'll bail."

At 11:19 two cars crawled into view and turned into the lot. Reba dropped her cigarette and stepped on it. "That's Marty's car in front. The second one's Beck."

"Is that Marty at the wheel?"

"I can't tell. It looks like him."

"Well, great then. No sweat. Get it over with," I said.

Reba crossed her arms, whether from cold or tension, I couldn't be sure. Once in the lot, Marty's car turned left, circled as we had, and made a slow return. He stopped his car thirty feet away and sat, engine idling, while Beck pulled up fifteen feet closer to us. The two sets of headlights formed a line of harsh spots. I raised a hand and shaded my eyes. I could see Beck at the wheel of his car, but I wasn't at all convinced the second driver was Marty.

A minute passed.

Reba shifted restlessly. "What's he doing?"

"Reba, let's go. There's something off about this."

Beck got out of the car. He stood by the open door, his attention fixed on the rolling bag. He wore a dark raincoat, open along its length, sides flapping in the wind. "Is that it?"

"No, Beck, it's not. I've decided to leave town."

"Bring it over here and let's have a look."

"Tell Marty to get out so we can see it's him."

Beck called over his shoulder. "Hey, Marty? Give Reeb a wave. She thinks you're someone else."

The driver in Marty's car waved to us and blinked his headlights, then revved his engine like a stock car driver at the start of a race. I touched Reba's arm, warbling, "Run . . ."

I took off, breaking left, as Marty's car pitched forward, tires chirping, the vehicle gathering speed as it bore down on us. Reba grabbed the handle of the rolling bag and scrambled after me. The suitcase teetered on the uneven surface of the parking lot and then toppled to one side. She headed for the street, dragging it after her. I could hear it scraping along the pavement, as awkward as an anchor if she hoped to escape. I yelled, "Dump that!"

The driver in Marty's car slammed on his brakes and turned the wheel so his rear end swung around, missing my car by inches. Two men jumped out, the driver and a second man who suddenly appeared from the back where he'd been concealed.

Beck stood with his hands in his coat pockets, watching with detachment as Reba abandoned the suitcase and took off at a dead run. The two men were fast. She'd gone no distance at all when one tackled her from behind and the two of them went down.

I reversed myself and headed in her direction. I had no plan. I didn't give a shit about the suitcase, but I wasn't going to leave Reba on her own. She was struggling, kicking at the guy who'd tackled her. He punched her in the face. Her head jerked and banged against the ground. I reached him as he raised his fist to punch her again. I hooked my arms around his right arm and hung on for dear life. Someone grabbed me from behind. He pinned my arms against my sides, lifted me off the ground, and then swung me away from his pal. I craned my neck for sight of Reba, who'd rolled over on her side. I watched as she pulled herself up on her hands and knees. She seemed dazed, blood pouring out of her mouth and nose. The guy who'd punched her turned to me. He lifted my feet and the two hauled me over to Marty's car. I arched my back, trying to free myself, but the guy simply tightened his grip and there was nothing I could do.

Beck crossed to Marty's car and opened one of the rear doors. The guy in whose arms I was locked fell into the backseat and dragged me in on top of him. He flipped me so that I was pinned under him, my face mashed against the upholstery. His weight was so crushing, I couldn't draw a breath. I thought my ribs would collapse, crushing my lungs in the process. I tried a groan, but all I could manage was a huffing sound, barely audible.

"Get the fuck off her," someone snapped.

The guy dug an elbow in my back as he lifted himself off me. At the same time, he took my right wrist and wrenched my arm up behind me while he shoved my head toward the floor. I was staring at the floor mats, my nose six inches away. Someone folded my legs in and slammed the door. Half a second later, I heard Beck's car door slam. He started his engine while the driver of Marty's car slid under the wheel, shut the door, and started the car. He pulled away sedately. We slowed at the exit to the parking lot. No squealing of brakes. No calling attention to ourselves in any way. As far as I knew, Reba was still out there on the asphalt, trying to stanch the blood gushing from her nose. I'd caught a glimpse of my backseat companion, who had a white gauze patch taped across his left eye. Two harsh red and purple bruises ran along his cheek like streaks of paint. The chair leg must have come close to taking that eye out, which is probably why he'd so relished mauling me. I focused on the drive. I assumed we were forming a two-car motorcade. I thought about the kidnappings I'd seen in movies, how the heroine later identified the final destination by the sound of the tires crossing railroad tracks or the bleat of a foghorn in the distance. Most of what I heard was my companion's labored breathing. Neither of the two guys was in as good a shape as they appeared. Or perhaps, more flattering to us, Reba and I had put up more of a fight than they'd expected.

We turned left onto Cabana Boulevard and proceeded at an easy pace for less than a minute before we slowed to a stop. I was guessing this was the light at the intersection of State and Cabana. The driver turned on the radio and music filled the car, a male vocalist singing, *"I want your sex . . ."*

My new best friend said, "Turn that shit off."

The driver said, "I like George Michael." But the radio did go off.

"Roll your window down and see what Beck wants."

I could picture Beck's car in the lane next to ours, him making that rolling gesture, leaning across the front seat of his car to converse. Annoyed, our driver said, "Okay, okay. Got it. I'm doing that!" And to the fellow in the backseat, "He has the key card, so we're supposed to follow. How many times he tell us that?"

Faintly, in the distance, I heard sirens approaching. The wailing grew louder, the sound splitting in two. Two cop cars, oh please.

I tried turning my head, hoping for a glimpse of something out the window, but all that netted me was a searing jerk to my arm. The sirens were almost on top of us. I caught the strobe of lights from two patrol cars that passed in rapid succession. The sirens trailed down Cabana Boulevard, volume diminishing until it faded altogether. So much for help being on the way.

We turned right on what I was guessing was Castle. When we slowed to a second stop, I imagined the light at Montebello Street. We started up again, proceeding at maybe ten miles an hour. I caught the hollow sound of the road as it went under the freeway. We came up the incline on the other side, which would put us on Granizo.

Left on Chapel. We had to be going to Beck's office, which was only a couple of blocks away. I knew the stores along the mall would be closed and the office buildings locked. The "card" the driver had referred to probably triggered the mechanical barrier to the underground garage. Sure enough, I felt us slow and then turn right, easing down a ramp. At this hour, the garage would be empty. We drove the length of the cavernous space and pulled into a spot. Beck must have parked just ahead of us because I heard his car door slam before our driver had a chance to shut his engine down.

I was hauled unceremoniously from the backseat and set on my feet. I'd hoped to catch Beck's eye, establish a connection, thinking I had a better chance of charming him than the goons on each side of me. He avoided my eyes, his face set. We waited while he opened his trunk and extracted the rolling bag. The sides were scraped gray, embedded with the beach sand accumulated from its being dragged across the pavement. The handle had snapped. Beck flipped the suitcase and knelt beside it. He unzipped the compartment and pulled open the flap.

Empty.

I stared as though trying to catch the mechanics of a magic trick. Reba had *showed* me the computer. It had been in there less than an hour ago, but where had it gone? The only time we'd been separated was when I'd left her in the alley while I went to fetch my car. She must have taken advantage of my absence to remove the computer and lock it in the trunk of her car. Which meant she'd anticipated Beck's betrayal and she'd beaten him to the punch. By the same token, he must have known she was going to pull a fast one, or why snatch me?

Beck stood up and pushed the bag with his toe, his expression thoughtful. I was expecting fury, but he seemed bemused instead. Maybe he liked Reba's taking the conflict to such extremes, imagining his ultimate victory the sweeter for it. He turned and walked toward the elevators.

The three of us followed, our footsteps clattering like a herd of beasts in the vast empty space. The guy with the injured eye kept a steady pressure on the arm he'd wrenched up behind me. There was no way I could move without ripping my arm out like a cooked chicken wing. The elevator doors opened and the four of us trooped in. Beck pressed the button. The doors closed and the elevator began its ascent.

"Why here?" I asked.

"So Reba will know how to reach me. In case you haven't noticed, we're engaged in a little battle of wits."

"That'd be hard to miss."

Beck sent me a fleeting smile.

The doors opened at shop level. We emerged inside the Beckwith Building and trooped across the marble lobby to the public elevators that would take us to the fourth floor. I turned to look at Willard, who was sitting at his desk. He watched us pass without comment, his face the same handsome blank. I sent him what I hoped was a pleading look, but I got nothing in return. How could such a good-looking guy have so little life in his eyes? Couldn't he see what was going on? Beck was his boss. Maybe he was paid the big bucks to look the other way.

We went up to the fourth floor. The elevator doors opened to reveal offices filled with artificial light, the colors as dazzling as a Disney cartoon. Long sweeps of green carpeting, bright abstract paintings in a line down the hall.

Healthy plants, modern furniture. I expected to be marched off to Beck's office, but he steered me around the corner to the freight elevator. He pressed the call button and the doors opened. He moved to the back wall of the elevator and pushed aside the gray quilted padding. He punched the code into the keyboard mounted on the elevator wall. The door to his counting room slid open. Beck pressed the Stop Run button and stepped aside, turning to look at me. He had his hands in his raincoat pockets.

Nobody said a word.

Peripherally, I saw the counting and bundling machines. In the same flash, I saw that all the cardboard boxes had been emptied of loose bills, which were now packaged and stacked on the countertop.

What I had no way to avoid was the sight of Marty. He'd been tied to a chair, beaten almost beyond recognition. His head was slumped on his chest. Even without a full view of his face, I knew he was dead. The curve of his cheek was puffy and dented, dried blood turning black at his hairline. Blood had oozed from his ears and coagulated along the collar of his shirt. I made a sound and jerked my head, blocking out the sight. Pain shot through me as though I'd been tapped with a taser gun. My palms were instantly damp and a flash of heat swept over me. I felt the blood drain out of my head. My legs buckled. The guy with the eye patch caught me and supported me briefly. Beck pressed a button and the doors to the counting room eased shut.

I was walked, rubber-legged, to Beck's office, where I sank onto the couch and covered my face with my hands. The image of Marty was like a photograph that I saw now in negative, light and dark reversed. There was conversation going on above my head—Beck instructing the two guys to get the body out of there and dispose of it. I knew they'd take him down in the service elevator to the ground floor, where they could drag him through the service corridor and out to the garage. They'd stick him in the trunk of his car and dump his body by the side of the road. Odd, so odd. I'd seen it in his eyes—this ending, this death—but I'd been unable to intervene.

My vision condensed, threatening to shut down. Dark closed in from the periphery and I had that curious sensation in my ears—white noise—that told me how close I was to fainting. I put my head down between my knees. I remembered to breathe. Within a minute, the air seemed to cool and I could feel the darkness recede. When I looked up, the two guys were gone and Beck was sitting at his desk. "Sorry about that. It's not what you think. He had a heart attack."

"He's dead all the same and it's your fault," I said.

"Reba had her share in it."

"How do you figure that?"

"Take a look at what she did. We're supposed to have a deal and she shows up with an empty suitcase? What's she think, she can fuck with me and get away with it?"

"She didn't steal the computer. Marty took it with him when he left."

"I don't give a shit who *took* it. All she had to do was give it back and he might be alive. The stress was what killed him. Couple of harmless punches and he was gone."

I couldn't argue with the man. He was so sure of himself and his thinking was so bent. Where was this going to end? The contest between them had spiraled out of control and matters could only escalate. Beck had the upper hand. It was as simple as that. He had me.

He smiled slightly. "You're hoping she'll call the police, but she won't. You know why? Because it wouldn't be any fun. She's a gambler. She likes betting against the house. Poor girl's not nearly as smart as she thinks she is."

"I don't want to talk about this shit. The two of you can hash it out."

"I'm sure we will."

We sat, the two of us, waiting for the phone to ring. I'd given up trying to predict what either would do. My job was taking care of me. The problem was, I was tired and feeling panicky. The jitters were causing my hands to shake and I was having trouble marshaling my thoughts. Beck rocked back in his swivel chair, fiddling with a paperweight, tossing it from hand to hand.

I noticed a row of cardboard boxes, lined up along the wall, all of them neatly taped and ready to be shipped. His office was a mess—shelves half empty, numerous bulging files on his desk. It looked as if Beck was all packed and ready to go. No wonder he was hell-bent on reclaiming his computer and his floppy disks. The disks and his hard drive contained his entire enterprise, every nickel he owned, all the money he'd salted away, shell corporations, Panamanian bank accounts. He wasn't a man who remembered numbers or dates. He had to have it written down or it was lost to him. He knew as well as I did the data would be his undoing if it fell into the wrong hands.

I said, "I have to go to the ladies' room."

"No."

"Come on, Beck. You can tag along with me and listen at the door while I tinkle."

He shook his head. "Can't do it. I want to be by the phone when she calls."

"What if it takes an hour?"

"Tough."

We waited in silence. I checked my watch. The crystal was smashed, the hands permanently frozen at 11:22. I couldn't see a clock from where I sat. Time dragged on and on. If and when Reba called, I had one more chance to signal the agents recording Beck's calls. I wasn't sure how I'd manage it or what I'd say, but the possibility was there.

The silence went on for so long that when the phone finally rang, I jumped. Beck picked up the handset and held it loosely against his ear. He smiled and leaned forward, resting his elbows on his desk. "Hey, Reeb, good girl. I knew you'd touch base. Are you ready to do business? Oh wait. Hang on a second. I have a friend of yours here and wondered if you wanted a chance to speak to her."

He pressed the speaker function on the phone and the office was filled with the hollow sound of Reba's voice. "Kinsey? Oh, geez . . . are you okay?"

I said, "I could use some help here. Why don't you call Cheney and tell him what's going on?"

"Forget him. Let me talk to Beck," she said, irritated.

Now that his hands were free, Beck opened his desk drawer and took out a gun. He slipped the safety off and pointed it at me. "Hey, Reeb? Sorry to interrupt, but let's cut to the chase. Listen to this."

He pointed at the wall above my head and fired. A sound came out of my throat, half scream and half moan. Tears sprang into my eyes. He said, "Oops. I missed."

She said, "Beck, don't."

"I'm not very good with this thing. Willard tried to show me, but I can't seem to get the hang of it. Should I try again?"

"Ohmygod, ohmygod. Oh, please, Beck, don't hurt her."

"I didn't hear your answer. You ready to do business?"

"Don't fire again. Don't shoot. Don't do that. I'll bring the thing. I got it. It's in the trunk of my car. I put it in a duffel."

"You said that before. I believed you then, but look what you went and did. You pulled the big switcheroo."

"I swear. I'll do it right this time. I'm not far. Give me two minutes. Just hang on. Please."

His tone was skeptical. "Gee, I don't know, Reeb. I trusted you. I thought you'd play fair. What you did was bad. I'd say very bad indeed."

"This time I'll bring it for sure. No tricks. I swear."

Beck was watching me while she spoke. He winked and smiled, having a wonderful time. "How do I know you won't pull the same old gag? Give me a duffel and there's nothing inside."

I stood up and pointed at the door, mouthing, "I have to pee."

He motioned me to sit again while Reba, sounding desperate, was saying, "I know what we can do. I'll come in through the service corridor. You can go to Willard's desk and watch on the monitor. I'll unzip the bag and show you the computer. You can see it with your own eyes."

I clutched the crotch of my jeans and then clasped my hands, mouthing, *Please* . . . I pointed at the hall again.

Distracted, he waved the gun at me, motioning me to sit

down. I was edging out of the room. I held up a finger, whispering, "I'll be right back."

I left the room and walked rapidly down the hall, footsteps soundless on the carpeting. I pulled office doors shut as I passed, letting them *bang, bang, bang.* I could hear him yell, "Hey!" He didn't sound angry so much as annoyed at my disobedience.

I doubled my pace. I reached the vestibule. Mercifully, the service elevator doors stood open. I moved to the back wall and punched in the code for the counting room. 5-15-1955. Reba's birthday. The doors slid open.

Out in the corridor, I could hear Beck shout my name, banging into offices in search of me. He fired a shot that made me jump even at this remove. While I'd known I wouldn't shoot him, I wasn't at all convinced he wouldn't shoot me, accidentally if nothing else. I yanked off one shoe and set it in the path of the open elevator door. The door slid shut, encountered the shoe, and popped open again, a process that repeated like a tic. I turned and pressed the G button on the opposite panel, dispatching the freight elevator to the garage level. The doors were slow to respond, which gave me time enough to cross to the second set of doors. I yanked my shoe from the track and slipped into the counting room as the corridor doors slid shut. The doors to the counting room slid shut half a beat later, and I was safe. Temporarily, at any rate.

Marty's body was still there.

I went on disconnect and blocked any and all emotional responses. Now was the wrong time. I tossed the shoe aside, not daring to take time to slip it on again. I looked at the ladder affixed to the wall, following the sight of it, rung by rung, all the way to the top. I started climbing, one shoe off and one shoe on, diddle-diddle-dumpling, my son John. I knew the trap door at the top opened onto the roof. Once there, I'd hide or hang over the parapet screaming until the cops showed up. Maybe officers were already scrambling—regular Santa Teresa cops, the SWAT team, hostage negotiators—all of them decked out in bulletproof vests.

I flicked a look at Marty, still bound to his chair. Why hadn't the guys done as Beck instructed? They were supposed to get him out of there, but they'd left him where he was. My hands were perspiring, but I ventured a second quick look down, noting what I'd failed to spot earlier. The counting and bundling machines were still sitting on the counter. The currency was gone. Instead of disposing of the body, the goons must have packed up the cash and removed that instead.

I reached the top rung of the ladder and reached for the door directly above my head. I couldn't find a lock or a knob or any means to open it. I ran my hand across the surface, looking for a hook or a handle, any kind of lever that might cause it to spring open. Nothing. I clung to the top rung, hanging on for dear life while I tried to get my fingertips in the crack. I banged on it with the flat of my hand, then pushed as hard as I could.

Below, I heard the elevator door slide open. I laid my head against the ladder and held my breath.

In a conversational tone, Beck said, "That door's locked so you might as well come down. Reba's on her way. Soon as we've settled up, you're free to go."

I looked down at him. He was wearing his raincoat, apparently in preparation for his departure. He had the gun in one hand and it was pointed right at me. He probably didn't have a clue how much pressure it took to pull the trigger. If he inadvertently blew my head off, I'd be dead all the same. He leaned down and picked up my shoe.

He waggled the gun. "Come on. I don't want to hurt you. This is almost over. Wrong time to cut and run when we're down to the wire."

I eased my way down, feeling for each rung with my foot, suddenly fearful of heights. I considered letting go, plunging down on top of him, but I'd only hurt myself and there was no guarantee I'd do him any harm at all. He watched me patiently until I reached the bottom. He probably preferred keeping his eyes on me to looking at Marty. He hadn't seemed to register the fact that the body hadn't been removed.

He smiled slightly. "Good try. You had me goin' there. I thought you ran the other way . . ." He handed me my shoe. I paused, leaning against the wall while I pulled the shoe on.

He took my elbow and urged me through the service elevator to the corridor. He was right. It was almost over so what was the point of risking my neck. In the end, this had nothing to do with me. I hunkered, taking my time while I tied my shoelaces. Beck was getting short on patience, but I didn't like to walk with laces flapping loose. He took me by the elbow again and steered me around the corner to the public elevators. He'd left his briefcase in the hall. He picked it up and used the knuckle of his index finger to push the call button. The elevator must have been sitting right there because the doors opened instantly. The two of us got in. Beck pressed the button for the lobby. Like strangers, we stood silently against the back wall, eyes on the digital readout while the floor numbers dropped from 4 to 3 to 2 to the lobby. I had one brief hope that when the doors opened, I'd see cops, guns drawn, ready to arrest him and put an end to this.

The lobby was empty except for Willard, sitting at his desk. The fountain in the center of the lobby was gushing like a toilet. My bladder was so full I could have drawn a diagram of its shape and size. Outside the plate-glass windows, the walkway was dark, not a soul in sight. The stores across the way were shut down tight. Willard was on his feet, his attention focused on his bank of ten monitors. He held an arm out and snapped his fingers rapidly. Beck and I crossed the lobby and rounded the end of Willard's desk. He pointed. The image on one of the black-and-white screens showed the underground parking lot. Reba, driving my VW, nosed down the ramp and turned right. The car passed from our view. Three minutes later, we saw her enter the service corridor, one floor below. She was using two hands to haul the duffel, which was clearly heavy. She eased it down on the floor and looked up at the corner-mounted security camera. "Hey, Beck?" Her cheek was swollen from the blow she'd taken, lips puffy, one eye black. Her nose looked as though it had been flattened across the bridge.

She waited, looking up at us.

Willard handed Beck the handset from the phone on his desk. He pressed a button and we could hear the wall phone ring in the service corridor. Reba picked up, her gaze fixed on the camera.

Beck said, "Hey, baby. How's by you?" Mocking her earlier greeting.

"Knock it off, Beck. You want this or not?"

"Show me first."

She dropped the handset and it banged against the wall, bouncing on its spiral cord. Beck jerked his head back, murmuring "Shit." Below, Reba leaned over and opened the duffel bag. The computer was clearly visible.

"And the floppy disks?"

She opened a side pocket and extracted a handful of disks, probably twenty by the look. She held them toward the camera, holding them face forward so he could read the sequence of dates he'd probably written himself. "Okay. Good enough," he said.

She slipped them back inside and zipped the duffel shut. "Happy now, you asshole?"

"I am. Thanks for asking. Come on up to the lobby and behave yourself. I've got Kinsey right here in case you want to get cute about this."

Reba flipped him the bird. Attagirl, I thought. That would show him.

I glanced at Willard. "You just going to stand there?"

No response. Maybe Willard had died and no one had remembered to mention it. I wanted to wave a hand in front of his eyes to see if he would blink.

The service elevator reached the lobby level and the doors slid open. Reba stepped forward, struggling with the weight of the duffel. Beck, gun in hand, watched her for any hint of rebellion or treachery. She set the duffel on the floor in front of him.

He motioned with the gun. "Open it."

"Oh, geez. You think it's booby-trapped?"

"I wouldn't put it past you."

She leaned down and unzipped the duffel, exposing the

computer for the second time. Without his having to ask, she took out the floppy disks and handed them to him.

"Now step back."

She backed up about ten feet, her hands in the air. "So worried," she remarked.

Beck passed the gun to Willard. "Keep an eye on both."

He knelt and freed the computer case from the duffel. He reached in his coat pocket and took out a small Phillips-head screwdriver, which he used to loosen the screws that held the housing in place. He tossed the screws aside and then took off the back panel. I couldn't figure out what he was up to.

The inner workings of the computer were now exposed. I don't own a computer and I'd never seen the inside of one. What a complex assortment of multicolored connectors, wires, circuits, transistors, or whatever they were called, lots of weensy things at any rate. Willard held the gun steady, barrel pointing first at Reba and then at me, but almost idly I thought. Beck opened his briefcase and took out a glass beaker with a glass stopper wedged in the top. He opened it and dolloped a clear liquid across the circuits like salad dressing. It must have been acid because a hissing went up and the smell of chemical burning filled the air. Insulated wires dissolved, small parts curling as though alive, shriveling and shrinking as the caustic liquid made contact. He took out a second beaker and poured acid over the floppy disks, spreading them out so as not to miss any. Holes appeared instantly, and a sizzling smoke developed as the disks disintegrated.

Reba said, "You won't remember all that stuff."

"Don't worry about it. I have dupes in Panama."

"Well, goody for you." Her voice sounded odd.

I glanced at her. Her mouth had begun to tremble and tears glistened in her eyes as she watched. Hoarsely, she said, "I really loved you. I did. You were everything to me."

I found myself staring at her with interest. Why did I think she was faking?

"Geez, Reeb, you never learn, do you. What's it going to take to get it through that thick head of yours? You're just like a kid. Someone tells you there's a Santa Claus and you believe."

"But you said I could trust you. You said you loved me and you'd take care of me. You said that."

"I know, but I lied."

"About everything?"

"Pretty much," he said, ruefully.

I caught a glimpse of motion on one of the monitors. In the underground garage, two Santa Teresa black-and-whites were coming down the ramp. Two unmarked cars followed.

Meanwhile, Beck was intent on his task. He took the screwdriver and jammed it into the workings of the computer, twisting metal parts, snapping wires, careful to avoid any direct contact between the acid and his hands. He had his back to the big plate-glass windows so he didn't see Cheney step out of the shadows with his gun drawn. Vince Turner appeared along with four agents in FBI vests.

Too late to salvage the data, but I was grateful nonetheless.

Reba caught sight of them. I saw her gaze flick to the window and back to Beck. "Oh, poor Beck. You are *so* screwed," she said.

He stood up and reached for his briefcase. He looked at her, his expression pleasant. "Really? How do you figure that?"

Reba was silent for a beat, a slow smile lighting her battered face. "The minute I got back to town, I put in a call to a man who works for the IRS. I spilled the beans, spelled it all out—names, numbers, dates—everything he needed to get his warrants. He had to call the judge at home, but he was happy to be of help."

Facetiously, Beck said, "Oh, Jesus, Reba, get a grip. I've known for months they were on to me. This is the only thing I was really worried about and now it's taken care of. How much incriminating data do you think they'll salvage from this mess?"

"Probably none."

"That's right. Thank you very much."

Beck saw Reba's attention shift. He looked over his shoulder and spotted Cheney, Vince Turner, and assorted cops and federal agents lined up on the walk. His smile might have faltered, but he didn't seem concerned. He signaled to Willard to let them in. Willard set the gun on the floor, raised his hands to show he had no weapons, and used his jumble of keys to unlock the doors.

Reba wasn't finished. "Only one problem."

Beck turned back to her. "Which is?"

"That's not Marty's."

Beck laughed. "You're full of crap."

Reba shook her head. "Nope. Not so. The feds didn't like the fact the computer had been stolen so I swapped it back."

"How'd you get into the building?"

"He let me in," she said, indicating Willard.

"Give it up, baby. The man works for me."

"Maybe so but I'm the one who's been screwing his brains out. We're just like this." She raised her left hand and made a circle with the thumb and index finger. She stuck her right index finger in the hole and pumped it like a piston. Beck winced at the crudity, but Reba laughed.

I shot a quick look at Willard, who dropped his gaze with appropriate modesty. Cops and FBI agents were crowding into the lobby. Cheney picked up Beck's gun and flicked the safety before he handed it to Vince.

Reba was saying, "After Willie let me in, I took Marty's computer up to your office. I disconnected your computer, pulled it out, and put Marty's in its place. Then I put your computer under Marty's desk. That one's Onni's. Nothing much on it but personal correspondence and a bunch of stupid computer games. I can't believe you paid her so well when all she did was waste time."

Beck still wasn't buying it. He shook his head, sliding his tongue across his front teeth while trying to suppress a smile. She might as well have been telling him she'd been abducted by aliens for use in sexual experiments.

She said, "Want to know what else I did? I'm tellin' you, Beck, I've been a busy little girl. After I swapped computers, I drove over to Salustio's and paid him the twenty-five grand I stole. Marty gave me the cash in exchange for documents he never got to use. Truth is, Salustio didn't give a damn where the money came from. Problem is, I pay him and he's still pissed at me. So I figure to compensate him for the inconvenience, I'd warn him about the raid. That gave him *just* enough time to get his money out of here. So now all's forgiven. He and I are square. You're the one who's left standing out in the cold."

Beck's expression was opaque. He was never going to give her the satisfaction of ceding the win, but she knew it was hers.

Epilogue

That wasn't the end of it, of course.

Beck was indicted on charges of murder, assault with a deadly weapon, kidnapping, money laundering, income tax evasion, conspiracy to defraud the United States government, tampering with evidence, obstruction of justice, failure to report currency transactions, and corruption of public officials. At first, Beck was undismayed. After all, he knew he had enough money stashed away to support an army of attorneys for as long as it took. There was just that one small matter Reba had neglected to mention. This was something I guessed at, but couldn't persuade her to confirm. Before she swapped the two computers, she'd tapped into Beck's accounts, consolidated all his funds, and moved the money out of the country, probably to another of Salustio's numbered accounts. I'm sure she'd thought of some way to repay him for holding the money until she could lay claim to it.

The feds suspected this as well because the cranky little shits refused to cut her a deal. Reba was returned to

Acknowledgments

The author wishes to acknowledge the invaluable assistance of the following people: Steven Humphrey; Boris Romanowski, California State Parole Agent; Alice Sprague, Deputy District Attorney, Alameda County, California; Pat Callahan, Public Relations Officer, Valley State Prison for Women; at the California Institution for Women, Warden John Dovey, Lieutenant Larry J. Aaron, Public Information Officer, and Pam Clark, Community and Parole Relations; Bruce Correll, Chief Deputy (retired), Santa Barbara Sheriff's Department; Lorrinda Lepore, Investigator II, Ventura County District Attorney's Office; Bill Kracht, General Manager, The Players Club; Joan Francis, Francis Pacific Investigations; Julianna Flynn and Kurt Albershardt; and Gail and Harry Gelles.

And for the generous offers of support and expertise for the subplot that ended up on the cutting-room floor, thanks go to Detective Sergeant Bill Turner (retired), Santa Barbara County Sheriff's Department; Dona Cohn, Cohn Law Firm; attorneys Joseph M. Devine, Lawrence Kern, and Philip Segal of Kern Noda Devine & Segal; Daniel Trudell, President, Accident Reconstruction Specialists; James F. Lafferty, P.E., Ph.D., biomechanics and mechanical engineering; Dr. Anthony Sances, Jr., President, Biomechanics Institute; and Nancy Degger, President, Rudy Degger & Associates. Maybe next book.

CIW on the first sheriff's bus. I don't worry about her. In prison, she has good friends, she's fond of the staff, and she knows her only choice is to behave herself. In the meantime, her father's doing fine. He's not going to die as long as Reba needs him.

As for Cheney and me, that's still up in the air, but I'm feeling the teeny-tiniest bit optimistic. I'm about due, don't you think?

So here's what I've learned. In the passing drama of life, I'm usually the heroine, but occasionally I'm simply a minor character in someone else's play.

Respectfully submitted,
Kinsey Millhone